HELLENISTIC
COLLECTION

LCL 508

HELLENISTIC COLLECTION

PHILITAS · ALEXANDER OF
AETOLIA · HERMESIANAX ·
EUPHORION · PARTHENIUS

EDITED AND TRANSLATED BY

J. L. LIGHTFOOT

HARVARD UNIVERSITY PRESS
CAMBRIDGE, MASSACHUSETTS
LONDON, ENGLAND
2009

Library of Congress Control Number 2009933436

ISBN 978-0-674-99636-6

*Composed in ZephGreek and ZephText by
Technologies 'N Typography, Merrimac, Massachusetts.
Printed on acid-free paper and bound by
The Maple-Vail Book Manufacturing Group*

CONTENTS

CONTENTS

INTRODUCTION

This volume contains a selection of Hellenistic literature.
It was built around a revision of the old Loeb of Parthenius
of Nicaea, where the *Sufferings in Love* and the poetic
fragments were combined with Longus' pastoral novel
Daphnis and Chloe. In other words, the old volume was
themed on "love", but in the revision we took the opportu-
nity of combining Parthenius with some other significant
Hellenistic figures who are not covered elsewhere in the
Loeb series.

The result ranges chronologically from the proto-Hel-
lenistic (Philitas of Cos), through some first-generation
Hellenistic poets (Alexander of Aetolia, Hermesianax of
Colophon), then extends across Euphorion of Chalcis in
the next generation after Callimachus to Parthenius, in
some respects (not all) the "last Hellenistic poet". Their
prose works are included alongside their poetry—the
glosses of Philitas, the prose fragments of Euphorion, and
the *Sufferings in Love* of Parthenius, all philological and
grammatical labours that both derived from and generated
further literary production. Much of this material has not
appeared in English translation before, and in some cases
a new edition is overdue. This is particularly true of
Euphorion, of whom our picture has been significantly al-

tered by papyrological discoveries in the last century. The present edition has benefited greatly from the meticulous preliminary work carried out by Enrico Magnelli (2002), but will be naturally be replaced by his promised edition and commentary. The edition of Parthenius is a lightly-corrected version of my earlier text (Oxford, 1999).

In editing these texts, I have had two main provisions in mind: first, readable translations, and second, a reasonable amount of annotation, in order to guide the reader through what can sometimes seem like a slew of minor mythography. Rather than reproducing the order of earlier editions, I have arranged the fragments according to my own judgement, and within the inevitable constraints of the Loeb series, I have also tried to provide some basic scholarly guidance. The reader of papyri needs some indication as to what is restoration and what is conjecture; so too the reader of a fragment preserved in a very corrupt manuscript, such as the long fragment of Hermesianax's *Leontion*. Manuscript sigla are used in the apparatus; for their meaning, one must consult the standard edition of the text in question. The bibliographies are certainly not comprehensive, but do aim at basic coverage, as well as listing works cited in the course of a discussion. There are author-specific bibliographies, but also a general bibliography at the beginning which includes a few works of general orientation on the period. A certain amount of cross-referencing is inevitable: so, where Parthenius is cited à propos of Philitas, the reader will find Parthenian bibliography *chez* the former. Fragment numbers are cited in bold (**15**), while testimonia are prefixed with "Test." (Test. **15**); again, cross-referencing sometimes occurs between poets, but it should always be clear from the context where this happens.

The volume has a wide geographical coverage. The poets represented here came from throughout the Mediterranean, both from places with high-profile poetic traditions (Colophon) and from apparent backwaters (Pleuron!), but there is a strong tendency for them to gravitate to the major intellectual centres. Not that this volume is particularly Alexandria-centric. True, it seems likely that it was in Alexandria that Philitas acted as tutor to the young Ptolemy Philadelphus (Philitas, Test. **1**), who later summoned Alexander of Aetolia there to edit the texts of tragedy and comedy. But before (or after) his time in the capital of the Ptolemies Alexander worked in Pella, the court of Antigonus, together with a fairly enviable collection of other litterati and philosophers (Alexander, Test. **5a–b**, **10**). Euphorion was first patronised by the royal family in Euboea, and then by Antiochus in Antioch (Test. **1**): his case illustrates the reception of the first wave of Alexandrian poets in a different, and rival, cultural centre a generation later. It was war, not royal patronage, that took Parthenius from his native Bithynia to Rome, but it was the patronage of Roman aristocrats to which Parthenius owed his freedom and subsequent career (Test. **1**).

The chronological arrangement of the volume might encourage diachronic comparisons between poets. One could also arrange it around an obvious, if absent, focus—from the pre-Callimachean Philitas, who seems already to be developing a poetic self-consciousness that involves refinement, *labor*, and knowledge (**8**); to his contemporaries

Hermesianax and Alexander (well characterised as a Hellenistic, but only superficially Callimachean, poet[1]); to the post-Callimachean Euphorion, who rewrites the first-generation Hellenistic poets with a highly personal stamp; to Parthenius, Callimachus' vicar on earth in late Republican Rome. But instead I should like to mention four important themes that concern the authors in their own right (as, of course, they are central to Callimachus' work too): elegy, catalogue poetry, the sense of literary history, and finally scholarship.

First, there are many examples of the expansion of the domain of elegy, a process that was already underway before the third century and then increasingly so within it. There are hymns (Philitas **1–5**) and other kinds of narrative experiment (Alexander of Aetolia **5**); catalogue poetry (Hermesianax **3**, **13**; Alexander **6**, **8**?); and other works now difficult to assess (Philitas **6–7**). When Parthenius takes up elegy again, after an apparent lapse of a couple of centuries, he applies it—as well as to his famous multi-book *Arete* (**1–5**)—to epicedia (**6**, **27**?), mythographical narrative (**28**) and other works whose genre is not easy to determine (**8–9**, **13**, **14**).

Second, many kinds of poem—consolatory, mythographical, amatory, literary, imprecatory—were born of the Hellenistic fascination with Hesiodic catalogue poetry (Hermesianax **3**, **13**; Euphorion **11**, **24–26**, **37–40** and **49–54** with Test. **1**, **108**?).[2] None has survived in anything other than fragments, but even these seem to suggest the

[1] Magnelli 2000, 123–124.

[2] Cameron 1995, 380–386 (and passim); Fantuzzi and Hunter 2004, 160; Asquith 2005.

richness and complexity of the form. Our longest continuous fragment, from book 3 of Hermesianax's *Leontion*, may not be to all tastes[3] but well illustrates some of the literary currents of its age. To begin with, it seems to hark back to several different antecedents. The fragment consists of a list of poets and philosophers who have all succumbed to love. The connectives *hoios, hoiē* ("such", "such as") are a hallmark or "generic signature" of Hesiodic catalogue poetry, which is also adapted to erotic subject-matter elsewhere (Phanocles fr. 1 P.). The persuasive use of exempla—since all the instances of enamoured poets and intellectuals are directed to a female addressee—is in keeping with elegy's traditional character; and the naming of a long elegiac poem after a wife or mistress seems to stand in the tradition that goes back to a work by Hermesianax's fellow-countryman, the *Lyde* of Antimachus of Colophon (and, at least in literary-historical representations, to the *Nanno* of Mimnermus), possibly Philitas' *Bittis* (though there is no trace of a poem of this name), and will continue to Parthenius' *Arete*.

Above all, the fragment revolves around the two favourite subjects of Hellenistic poetry: love and literary history. The former seems already to have its place in Philitas (**9**); the latter is not yet explicit, though we do find close engagement with, and implicit scholarly commentary upon, works of the literary canon. But in the works of the next generation we find not only implicit engagement with earlier poetry through allusion, intertextuality, and "midrashic" commentary, but also explicit and express discussions of matters of literary history and criticism.

[3] Cameron 1995, 318–319, 383.

Several versions of this engagement can be seen in the present volume. Hermesianax offers a literary-historical survey based partly on genre and partly on chronology; the interest in genre, and in the series of different genres, recalls Callimachus' taxonomy of Greek literature in the *Pinakes*, while the information about each poet and philosopher seems to have been a tongue-in-cheek application of the classic Peripatetic technique of inferring biography and ethical character from the contents of an author's work. The *Leontion* was certainly not the only literary-historical catalogue, and though we can no longer discern the structure or organising principles of other works extant only in fragments, we can compare a review of the poets of Halicarnassus in a famous inscription in elegiac couplets from that city.[4] One, possibly two, fragments of Alexander of Aetolia's *Musae* review a given poet's life and times, and/or offer a critical evaluation of his works (**6**, **8**; **19** is in the same vein, but the authorship is uncertain and the metre differs). We do not know at what stage of his career Alexander wrote this work (in Alexandria or elsewhere?), but we may compare a fragment from Callimachus' *Against Praxiphanes* (fr. 460 Pf.), where Aratus is described as a "learned and excellent poet", or another fragment from the *Grapheion* (*Archive*?) which contains a brief and pithy description of Archilochus' style of writing (fr. 380 Pf.)—as in Alexander, in elegiac metre. Yet another type of literary history is represented by Euphorion's *Hesiod*, from which

---

[4] Text in Merkelbach and Stauber 1998, 39–45 (01/12/02); for the literary catalogue, see lines 43–54 (and cf. also no. 01/12/01); d'Alessio, in Isager and Pedersen 2004, 48–50.

only tatters survive but which it is reasonable to see as a verse account of the life—or death—of a poet in whom the Hellenistic period was keenly interested.

It is worth reflecting on the kinds of textual scholarship that are produced in a period whose poetry is so informed by literary-historical and literary-critical concerns. There are monographs aplenty. The treatise "about" something was the Peripatetic form *par excellence*; Euphorion's *On Lyric Poets* (**203**) stands in this tradition, and his *On the Isthmian Games* (**201–202**) goes right back, across Callimachus' *On Games* (fr. 403 Pf.), to Aristotle and before.[5] The curious, miscellaneous, and diverting information in his *Historical Commentaries* (**193–195**) also thoroughly recalls the Peripatetic taste (shared by Callimachus) for the curious anecdote. On the other hand, we do not find literary commentary, in the sense of extracts or lemmata from a text followed by explanatory or interpretative comment on it. Perhaps surprisingly, this form of scholarship was not really developed until the end of the Hellenistic, or beginning of the Roman, period.

In Pfeiffer's famous construction, it was Philitas, the combined "poet and critic", who set the tone for the philological character of early Hellenistic poetry. Even so, editions of texts seems to have been a fairly specialised activity. Of the poets represented here, only Alexander of Aetolia is credited with the "correction" of texts of tragedy and satyr-drama (Test. **7**); the word (διόρθωσις) at least implies the exercise of a critical faculty, but it is very con-

[5] Pfeiffer 1968, 134.

troversial just what that involves at this date.[6] Philitas was the tutor of Zenodotus (Test. **11**), Homeric scholar and Ptolemy's first librarian. He himself is never credited with an "edition" (ἔκδοσις) or a "corrected text" (διόρθωσις) of Homer, but five fragments (**56–60**) consist of textual remarks on the *Iliad*, in whatever form these were presented. It is difficult to get a feel for the whole: while some defend readings known elsewhere, one or two others are decidedly eccentric. A century later, Aristarchus still felt obliged to write a treatise against him.

What Philitas *did* do was glossography. Collections of rare words sprang from the need to explicate ancient or dialectally difficult texts, and there was a long scholarly and schoolmasterly tradition of this in the case of Homer. Euphorion's comprehensive six-book Hippocratic glossary (**196–197**) also belongs to a tradition that goes back to Xenocritus of Cos, the home of the famous medical school. Philitas was famous for his glossary, which is one of the earliest, if not the earliest, of which we have certain knowledge. But though a contemporary witness (Test. **13**) sees it, in the time-honoured tradition of Greek glossography, as a dictionary of difficult poetic words, it seems in fact to have been more interested in the living language. Philitas is particularly interested in dialectal forms, and/or in the minutiae of local practice. Rarely does he seem to be de-

---

[6] Fantuzzi and Hunter 2004, 434. For different kinds of διόρθωσις, see West 2001, 25, 38, 50, 62. That of Zenodotus, who worked on the text of Homer at the same time as Alexander and Lycophron's work on tragedy and comedy, was concerned with the identification of spurious lines and passages rather than with choices between textual variants.

pendent on literary texts, or to quote them to support his meanings. An anonymous couplet is quoted in **42**, part of a trimeter in **52**, and a poetic citation again appears in **30**, from a work called *Hermeneia*, apparently *Interpretation*—though whether by Philitas, or an anonymous author quoting Philitas, is impossible to say for sure.

Finally, and at the end of the period covered by this volume, we have Parthenius' *Sufferings in Love*, a prose collection of love-stories taken from earlier poets and prose-writers. Modest as it is, it is still an important, slightly idiosyncratic, witness to a vast genre of writing which, in this case, predates Hellenistic scholarship. Just what sort of a work of mythography is it? Since the fourth, if not the fifth, century BC, there was an industry for the production of helpful prose reductions or summaries of longer works (Homer, Herodotus, tragedies); but the *Sufferings in Love* is not an epitome. On the contrary, so far from setting out to contract, it sets out to expand and amplify. In the preface, Parthenius seems to be undertaking to provide a full account of certain myths that are only alluded to glancingly (μὴ αὐτοτελῶς) in the poets, so his purpose is more akin to the suppletive function that mythographical works also fulfilled, providing helpful ancillary details (background, sources, variants): we see the expansion and amplification in action in stories XIII and XXVI *vis-à-vis* the Euphorionic original. But where other works of mythography are geared to a single text, or closely related groups of texts, the *Sufferings in Love* is not so confined, and in fact is our earliest extant example of a subgenre of mythography—the collection of miscellaneous narratives (usually themed, occasionally not) served up not as a secondary aid to something else but for the information and diversion of the reader *per se*.[7]

Above all, Parthenius sets up the *Sufferings in Love* not (or not only, depending on whether the source-citations go back to him) as explicative of earlier texts, but as generative of new ones. He tells Cornelius Gallus in the preface that he hopes his protégé will be able to draw on them as subject-matter for his own epic or elegiac verse. We do not know whether he did. There is barely a trace of the *Sufferings in Love* in any extant Latin poetry. But that may be an accident of survival. Roman poets could draw on mythography for a multitude of purposes—for details, lists, names and family relationships; to guide them through a labyrinth of variants; and for certain kinds of raw material.[8] If Ovid garnered metamorphosis myths from prose sources, then another poet could have culled erotic ones. Poets had drawn subject-matter from prose sources since Callimachus trawled local historians for various stories in the *Aitia*. Whether or not his pupil made use of his treatise, Parthenius was expecting his poetic protégé to behave in a rather Callimachean way.

[7] Examples: Conon's *Diegeses* (not themed); Antoninus Liberalis' *Metamorphoses*; ps.-Plutarch's *Amatoriae Narrationes* and the *Parallela Minora*.

[8] Cameron 2004, 253–303.

BIBLIOGRAPHY

H. Asquith, "From genealogy to *Catalogue*: the Hellenistic adaptation of the Hesiodic catalogue form", in R. L. Hunter, *The Hesiodic Catalogue of Women: Constructions and Reconstructions* (Cambridge, 2005), 266–286.

G. Cambiano, L. Canfora, D. Lanza (edd.), *Lo spazio letterario della Grecia antica*, i. *La produzione e la circulazione del testo*, 2. *L'ellenismo* (Rome, 1993).

A. Cameron, *Callimachus and his Critics* (Princeton, 1995).

——*Greek Mythography in the Roman World* (New York, 2004).

M. Fantuzzi and R. Hunter, *Tradition and Innovation in Hellenistic Poetry* (Cambridge, 2004).

K. J. Gutzwiller, *A guide to Hellenistic literature* (Oxford, 2007).

G. O. Hutchinson, *Hellenistic Poetry* (Oxford, 1988).

S. Isager and P. Pedersen, *The Salmakis inscription and Hellenistic Halikarnassos* (Odense, 2004).

R. Merkelbach and J. Stauber, *Steinepigramme aus dem griechischen Osten*, i. *Die Westküste Kleinasiens von Knidos bis Ilion* (Stuttgart, 1998).

R. Pfeiffer, *History of Classical Scholarship: from the beginnings to the end of the Hellenistic age* (Oxford, 1968).

M. L. West, *Studies in the Text and Transmission of the Iliad* (Munich, 2001).

U. von Wilamowitz-Moellendorff, *Hellenistische Dichtung in der Zeit des Kallimachos* (Berlin, 1924).

A very full Hellenistic bibliography, currently maintained by Martin Cuypers at the University of Leiden, is available online; it covers all authors reprsesented in this volume.

ABBREVIATIONS

EtGen	Etymologicum Genuinum. For a–β, see L.–L.
EtGud	Etymologicum Gudianum. For a–$\zeta\epsilon\iota\alpha\acute{\iota}$, see E. L. de Stefani, *Etymologicum Gudianum*, 2 vols. (Leipzig, 1909–1920, repr. Amsterdam, 1965). Otherwise, F. W. Sturz, *Etymologicum Graecae linguae Gudianum et alia grammaticorum scripta* (Leipzig, 1818, repr. Hildesheim, 1973).
EtMag	Etymologicum Magnum. For a–β, see L.–L. Otherwise, T. Gaisford, *Etymologicon magnum: seu verius lexicon . . .* (Oxford, 1848).
EtParv	Etymologicum Parvum. See R. Pintaudi, *Etymologicum Parvum quod vocatur* (Milan, 1973).
EtSym	Etymologicum Symeonis. For a–β, see L.–L.
FGE	*Further Greek Epigrams,* ed. D. L. Page (Cambridge, 1981).
FGrH	*Die Fragmente der griechischen Historiker*, ed. F. Jacoby (Leiden, 1923–1958).
FHG	*Fragmenta Historicorum Graecorum*, ed. K. Müller (Paris, 1878–1885).

BIBLIOGRAPHY

Garland *The Garland of Philip*, edd. A. S. F. Gow and D. L. Page (Cambridge, 1968).

GG *Grammatici Graeci*, edd. var.

GGM *Geographi graeci minores* (Paris, 1855–1882), ed. C. F. W. Müller.

HE *Hellenistic Epigrams*, edd. A. S. F. Gow and D. L. Page (Cambridge, 1965).

L.–L. F. Lasserre and N. Livadaras (edd.), *Etymologicum magnum genuinum: Symeonis etymologicum una cum Magna grammatica ; Etymologicum magnum auctum* (Rome, 1976–).

Ll.-J.–P. H. Lloyd-Jones and P. J. Parsons (edd.), *Supplementum Hellenisticum* (Berlin, 1983).

M.–W. R. Merkelbach and M. L. West (edd.), *Fragmenta Hesiodea* (Oxford, 1967).

RE *Paulys Real-Encyclopaedie der classischen Altertumswissenschaft*, ed. A. F. von Pauly, rev. G. Wissowa, *et al.* (Stuttgart, 1893–1972).

SH see Ll.-J.–P.

TrGF *Tragicorum Graecorum Fragmenta*, i. (Göttingen, 1986), ed. B. Snell, rev. R. Kannicht.

PHILITAS OF COS

INTRODUCTION

Philitas[1] of Cos is one of the least well preserved and most tantalising of the Hellenistic poets. His reputation is based on several well-known facts: that he was chosen by Ptolemy I, the man who founded the Alexandrian Library and Museum, as tutor to his son and successor; that Callimachus critically evaluates his elegies in the *Aitia* prologue, and that he is praised in one of Theocritus' best-known *Idylls*;[2] and that he is mentioned several times in Propertius and Ovid, suggesting that for the former, in particular, he, or his image, had taken on a programmatic, poetological significance. It is frustrating that there is no surviving fragment of Philitas longer than four lines, and that papyri, so far, have served us very ill.

His reputation must have been established by the time he was asked to tutor Ptolemy II, who was born on Cos in 308. Strabo calls him, famously, a "poet and critic" (Test. **3**), and we have fragments both of hexameter and elegiac poems and of his work of glossography. His hexameter *Hermes* told, or contained, the story of Odysseus and Aeolus' daughter summarised in Parthenius, *Sufferings in*

---

[1] His name appears in a bewildering number of variants, but the modern consensus favours Philitas, and in editing him I have preferred the manuscripts that support this spelling.

[2] Test. **1**, **17**, **8**.

Love, III (**9**), though we cannot yet tell how the title related to the work's content or its form; was it a narrative hymn? What emerges from Parthenius' summary is that the poem closely engaged with Homeric geography and narrative sequence, offering a sort of midrashic revision of the older poem.[3] The *Demeter* was in elegiacs, the metre for which Philitas was most famous. It is very likely that this is the work Callimachus refers to in the *Aitia* prologue (Test. **17**) as the "bounteous Thesmophoros". Approaches of both extreme maximalism and extreme minimalism have been taken towards it, though at least we can say that Cos had a well-attested cult of Demeter, which contained a version of the myth of Demeter's search for her daughter; the cult underlies Theocritus' seventh *Idyll*, and so may Philitas' treatment of it.[4] Other than these two works, two fragments are cited from Philitas' *Epigrams*, two from his *Paignia* ("Light Verse"), and one mythological datum from a *Telephus*—unless this is simply a garbled allusion to Philitas' father. Although most of the non-assigned fragments have been conjecturally ascribed to one poem or another in the course of time, I have preferred to steer clear of all but what seems to me well-founded conjecture.

Philitas has also been credited with poetry which finds no obvious correspondence among the known fragments. An excerpt from an elegy by Hermesianax, detailing the loves of poets and philosophers, speaks of the poet's love for Bittis (Test. **4**). Ovid associates him with erotic themes (Test. **25b**), and on a couple of occasions refers to Bittis in a way that suggests she was Philitas' wife (Test. **25c, d**). Beyond this all is obscure—the length of such poems (epi-

---

[3] Sbardella 2000, 16–28.
[4] Σ Theocr. *Id*. 7.5–9f and *k*, citing **21**.

grams or more extended elegies?), their degree of sub-
jectivity; potentially, though, this is a matter of literary-
historical importance. So too the question of Philitas' role
in the development of bucolic, which is raised by the
figure of Philitas the cowherd, rustic singer, and "love-
counsellor" in Longus' novel *Daphnis and Chloe*, com-
bined with the hints of the importance of (the original)
Philitas in Theocritus' seventh *Idyll*. Some of the glosses
(**31**, **36**, **46**, **48**) in fact are on bucolic subjects. But without
any indication of an interest in rustic themes among the
miserable remnants of Philitas' verse (unless **20** is pressed
into service), we must for the moment be content either to
speculate or to wait until new evidence turns up.

The other half of Philitas' activity is represented by
a glossary, a compilation of more or less obscure terms
whose meanings were discussed. Its full title, the *Ataktoi
Glossai*, is usually rendered *Miscellaneous Glosses*, on the
understanding that the entries were not drawn up in any
order (hardly conducive to ready-reference), but has also
been suggested to denote words that somehow stand out-
side the rank and file, irregular, unusual, or heterogeneous
words.[5] A well-known fragment of the comic poet Strato
(Test. **13**) imagines a cook who speaks in nothing but Ho-
meric vocables, much to the consternation of his master,
who feels the need of Philitas' reference-work to explain
what it all means. For the joke to work, all we need is for
Philitas' work to have a reputation as a repository of arcane
terms. It was not a specifically Homeric glossary, and al-
though several words do occur in Homer, none is directly
referable to the Homeric context (and some have com-

5 Sbardella 2000, 65–66; Dettori 2000, 27; Bing 2003.

pletely different senses).[6] Almost all (save **54**) are nouns, mostly (save **52**) common nouns, on the subjects of drinking vessels, sympotic practice, food. Several are noted as dialectal peculiarites,[7] and sometimes the definition is expanded into a little disquisition on local customs and practices (**39**, cf. **41**). Rarely is a literary source identifiable (though, given the subject-matter, several words are paralleled in comedy); several will have a subsequent career in Hellenistic poets, although it is hard to prove that it was Philitas who gave them that impetus.[8] They do not suggest that Philitas legislated for correct and incorrect usage, although this is apparently the point of a joke in Athenaeus' *Deipnosophistae* (Test. **22**); has the Atticistic purism of Athenaeus' own day crept into the interpretation of an early Hellenistic work of glossography?

There are several sources that make a joke of Philitas' supposed thinness, apparently seeking to explain real, physiological thinness or slightness of build with reference to Philitas' tireless questing after glosses: the absent-minded professor who forgets to eat. Two of the sources (Test. **23a**, **b**) use the word *leptos*, and allusion is possible (though not necessary) to the literary-critical aesthetic of *leptotēs* (refinement), so important for Callimachus and Aratus. One would like to be better informed about the relation of Philitas' linguistic interests to his literary-critical values and practice.

[6] **35** (*Il*. 16.642), **39** (*Il*. 9.206), **43** (*Od*. 18.300), **48** (*Il*. 18.553–554), **50** (*Od*. 17.295), **51** (Σ T *Il*. 23.332–333). **56–60** are quite different from the glossographic fragments and presumably referable to a different work.   [7] **32**(?), **34**, **35**, **37**, **39**, **40**, **42**, **44**.   [8] **32**, **35**, **39**, **45**, **46**, **48**, **50**.

EDITIONS

For a complete list of the editions of Philitas, see L. Sbardella (as below), 185–186.

Among the most important, see:

N. Bach, *Philetae Coi, Hermesianactis Colophonii atque Phanoclis reliquiae* (Halle, 1829).

T. Bergk, *Anthologia Lyrica* (Leipzig, ²1868), 131–133.

J. U. Powell, *Collectanea Alexandrina* (Oxford, 1925), 90–96.

A. Nowacki, "Philitae Coi fragmenta poetica" (Diss. Münster, 1927).

W. Kuchenmüller, "Philetae Coi Reliquiae" (Diss. Berlin, 1928).

E. Diehl, *Anthologia Lyrica Graeca*, vol. ii. 6 (Leipzig, ²1942), 49–55.

H. Lloyd-Jones, and P. J. Parsons, *Supplementum Hellenisticum* (Berlin & New York, 1983), 318–320.

E. Dettori, *Filita grammatico. Testimonianze e frammenti. Introduzione, edizione e commento* (Rome, 2000).

L. Sbardella, *Filita. Testimonianze e frammenti poetici. Introduzione, edizione, traduzione e commento* (Rome, 2000).

C. Spanoudakis, *Philitas of Cos* (Leiden, 2002).

CRITICISM

P. Bing, "The unruly tongue. Philitas of Cos as scholar and poet", *CPh* 98 (2003), 330–348.

E. L. Bowie, "Theocritus' seventh *Idyll*, Philetas and Longus", *CQ* 35 (1985), 67–91.

E. Dettori, "La 'filologia' di Filita di Cos (con qualche osservazione sulla filologia del III sec. a. C.)", in R. Pretagostini (ed.), *La letteratura ellenistica: problemi e prospettive di ricerca* (Rome, 2000), 183–198.

A. Hardie, "Philetas and the Plane Tree", *ZPE* 119 (1997), 21–36.

———"The statue(s) of Philitas (P. Mil. Vogl. VIII 309 Col. X 16–25 and Hermesianax fr. 7.75–78 P.)", *ZPE* 143 (2003), 27–36.

A. S. Hollis, "Callimachus, Aetia fr. 1.9–12", *CQ* 28 (1978), 402–406.

———"Heroic honours for Philetas?", *ZPE* 110 (1996), 56–62.

R. Hunter, *Theocritus and the archaeology of Greek Poetry* (Cambridge, 1996), 17–19.

P. E. Knox, "Philetas and Roman Poetry", *PLILS* 7 (1993), 61–83.

H. Lloyd-Jones, *Supplementum Supplementi Hellenistici* (Berlin and New York, 2005), 80–84.

E. Maass, *De tribus Philetae carminibus* (Marburg, 1895).

R. Pfeiffer, *History of Classical Scholarship*, i. (Oxford, 1968), 88–93.

L. Sbardella, "L'opera 'sinora ignota' di Filita di Cos", *QUCC* 52 (1996), 93–119.

———"Βιττίδα . . . θοήν: il problema dell' elegia erotica in Filita", in R. Pretagostini (ed.), *La letteratura ellenistica: problemi e prospettive di ricerca* (Rome, 2000), 79–89.

TESTIMONIA

1 *Suda* s.v. Φιλήτας, φ 332

Φιλήτας, Κῷος, υἱὸς Τηλέφου, ὧν ἐπί τε Φιλίππου καὶ
Ἀλεξάνδρου, γραμματικὸς κριτικός· ὃς ἰσχνωθεὶς ἐκ
τοῦ ζητεῖν τὸν καλούμενον Ψευδόμενον λόγον ἀπέθα-
νεν. ἐγένετο δὲ καὶ διδάσκαλος τοῦ δευτέρου Πτολε-
μαίου. ἔγραψεν ἐπιγράμματα, καὶ ἐλεγείας καὶ ἄλλα.

⟨καὶ⟩ κριτικός Toup   ἰσχνωθεὶς . . . λόγον] ἰσχνωθεὶς
ἐκ τοῦ ζητεῖν καὶ διώκειν ἀκίχητα M^mgV

2

(a) Σ Theocr. *Id.* 7.40(?), ap. P. Oxy. 2064, col. xii, mg. inf.
(ed. A. S. Hunt and J. Johnson, *Two Theocritus Papyri*
(London, 1930), 8)

Φιλίτας π]ǫιητὴς ἐγέν[ετο
    μητρὸ]ς δ(ὲ) Εὐκτιόνης [
    θανο]ῦσαν ἔθαψεν [

πατρὸς μὲν Τηλέφου, μητρὸ]ς κτλ. conj. Hunt

8

TESTIMONIA

1 *Suda* s.v. Philitas

Philitas, of Cos, son of Telephus, lived at the time of Philip and Alexander, a grammarian and critic. He died of a consumption, caused by pursuing the so-called "lying word".[1] He was tutor to the second Ptolemy. He wrote epigrams, elegies, and other works.

2

(a) Scholiast on Theocritus, *Idylls*

> Philitas was a poet
>> his mother Euctione
>>> when she died, he buried her

---

[1] The Liar Paradox: statements that are true only if false ("This sentence is false"). This is a philosophical problem, of interest e.g. to Chrysippus the Stoic. Philitas was a grammarian; perhaps the joke is that he was interested in "false words" in the sense of those incorrectly used (see Test. **22**).

PHILITAS

(b) Σ KU ibid. *f*, p. 89.21 Wendel

Φιλητᾶς Κῷος τὸ γένος, ὡς δέ τινες Ῥόδιος, υἱὸς
Τηλέφου. ἐγένετο δὲ καὶ αὐτὸς ποιητής.

καὶ αὐτὸς ποιητὴς K: ποιητὴς ἄριστος U

(c) Σ GPT ibid. *g*, p. 90.1 Wendel

οὐδὲ Φιλητᾶν] ὁ Φιλητᾶς Κῷος ἦν ἢ ὡς ἔνιοι Ῥόδιος
ποιητής, υἱὸς Τηλέφου.

Φιλητής codd., corr. Wendel

3 Strab. 14.2.19

οὗτός τε [sc. Hippocrates] δή ἐστι τῶν ἐνδόξων Κῷος
ἀνὴρ καὶ Σῖμος ὁ ἰατρός, Φιλίτας τε ποιητὴς ἅμα καὶ
κριτικός, καὶ καθ᾽ ἡμᾶς Νικίας ὁ καὶ τυραννήσας
Κῴων . . .

4 Hermesianax, *Leontion* **3**.75–78, ap. Athen. *Deipn.*
13.598 E–F

75   οἶσθα δὲ καὶ τὸν ἀοιδόν, ὃν Εὐρυπύλου πολιῆται
        Κῷοι χάλκειον στῆσαν ὑπὸ πλατάνῳ
     Βιττίδα μολπάζοντα θοήν, περὶ πάντα Φιλίταν
        ῥήματα καὶ πᾶσαν τρυόμενον λαλιήν.

75 τὸν A, corr. Casaubon   76 θῆκαν A, corr. Hecker,
Meineke   77 Βαττίδα Scaliger   78 ῥυόμενον A, corr.
Hermann

10

(b) Scholia KU ibid.

Philitas, a Coan by nationality, but according to others a
Rhodian, son of Telephus. He too was a poet.

(c) Scholia GPT ibid.

"Nor Philitas"] Philitas was a Coan, or, according to some,
a Rhodian poet, son of Telephus.

3 Strabo

He (Hippocrates) is among the famous men of Cos; so too
Simus the physician, Philitas the poet and critic, and in our
times Nicias who also reigned as tyrant over the Coans . . .

4 Hermesianax, *Leontion*

And you know that even the bard set up in bronze   [75]
By Eurypylus' folk in Cos, beneath a plane,
Sings of the flighty Bittis: Philitas, well-worn
In every utterance and all the forms of speech.

5 Posidippus, *Ep.* 63 Austin–Bastianini

τόνδε Φιλίται χ[αλ]κὸν [ἴ]σον κατὰ πάνθ'
  Ἑκ[α]ταῖος
ἀ]κ[ρ]ιβὴς ἄκρους [ἔπλ]ασεν εἰς ὄνυχας,
καὶ με]γέθει κα[ὶ σα]ρκὶ τὸν ἀνθρωπιστὶ διώξας
  γνώμο]ν', ἀφ' ἡρώων δ' οὐδὲν ἔμειξ' ἰδέης,

5 ἀλλὰ τὸν ἀκρομέριμνον ὅλ[ηι κ]ατεμάξατο
  τέχνηι
πρ]έσβυν, ἀληθείης ὀρθὸν [ἔχων] κανόνα·
αὐδήσ]οντι δ' ἔοικεν, ὅσωι ποικίλλεται ἤθει,
ἔμψυχ]ος, καίπερ χάλκεος ἐὼν ὁ γέρων·
ἐκ Πτολε]μαίου δ' ὧδε θεοῦ θ' ἅμα καὶ βασιλῆος

10 ἄγκειτ]αι Μουσέων εἵνεκα Κῷος ἀνήρ.

9 ἐκ suppl. J. Gascou

6 Vita Arati (Vita 2), p. 11.5 Martin = Alexander Aetolus
Test. **4**

[ἐν] τοῖς χρόνοις δὲ ἐγένετο κατὰ Φιλάδελφον τὸν
βασιλέα, συνήκμαζε δὲ Ἀλεξάνδρῳ τῷ Αἰτωλῷ καὶ
Φιλητᾷ καὶ Διονυσίῳ τῷ φιλοσόφῳ ⟨τῷ⟩ εἰς ἡδονὰς
μεταθεμένῳ.

[ἐν] Westermann   ⟨τῷ⟩ Maass

5 Posidippus, *Epigram* 63

> This bronze, matching Philitas in each detail,
> Was Hecataeus' work,[2] authentic to the toe-nails.
> In height and substance he strove for humanity's
> True standard, mixing nothing of heroic form,
> But rendered that punctilious old man   [5]
> With his whole art, maintaining truth's strict canon.
> It seems he'll speak, such character is in the likeness,
> A living soul, although the old man's bronze.
> At Ptolemy's behest, both god and king,
> The Coan stands, the Muses' acolyte.[3]   [10]

6 *Life of Aratus* 2

As to his date, he (sc. Aratus) lived at the time of Philadelphus the king, and he flourished at the same time as Alexander of Aetolia, Philitas, and Dionysius the philosopher who converted to hedonism.[4]

---

[2] Mentioned as a silversmith by Pliny, *NH* 33.156, 34.85.

[3] Literally "for the sake of the Muses". The phrase may indicate that the statue was set up in a shrine of the Muses.

[4] These lives date Philitas too late. They may have inferred that he belonged to the same generation as Aratus and Alexander of Aetolia on poetological grounds, or may have been misled by the reference to Ptolemy Philadelphus. For Dionysius, see Alexander of Aetolia, Test. **4** n. 3.

cf. Vita Arati (Vita 4), p. 19.4 Martin = Alexander Aetolus
Test. **6**

ἦν δὲ ἐπὶ Πτολεμαίου τοῦ Φιλαδέλφου, καὶ ἐσχόλασε
Διονυσίῳ τῷ Ἡρακλεώτῃ, συνῆν δὲ Ἀντιγόνῳ τῷ
Μακεδονίας βασιλεῖ καὶ Φίλᾳ τῇ τούτου γαμετῇ,
συνήκμασε δὲ Ἀλεξάνδρῳ τῷ Αἰτωλῷ καὶ Καλλιμάχῳ
καὶ †Μελάνδριῳ καὶ Φιλιτᾷ.

Μενάνδρῳ, μελανχρίῳ, μελανδρίῳ codd. (om. SV): Νικάνδρῳ
Ritschl: Μαιανδρίῳ Meineke: Λεανδρίῳ Wendel, *Hermes* 70
(1935), 360

7 Σ Nic. *Ther.* 3, p. 35.13 Crugnola = Hermesianax
Test. **1**

φίλ' Ἑρμησιάναξ] ὁ Ἑρμησιάναξ οὗτος φίλος τῷ
Φιλιτᾷ [*vll* Φιλητᾷ, Φιλητῇ] καὶ γνώριμος ἦν . . . οὐ
δύναται δὲ Νίκανδρος μνημονεύειν τούτου διὰ τῆς
προσφωνήσεως, διὰ τὸ τὸν Φιλιτᾶν [*vl* Φιλητὴν]
πρεσβύτερον εἶναι Νικάνδρου.

8 Theoc. *Id.* 7.39–41

. . . οὐ γάρ πω κατ' ἐμὸν νόον οὔτε τὸν ἐσθλόν
40 Σικελίδαν νίκημι τὸν ἐκ Σάμω οὔτε Φιλίταν
ἀείδων, βάτραχος δὲ ποτ' ἀκρίδας ὥς τις ἐρίσδω.

40 Φιλῆταν vario accentu codd., corr. Croenert

cf. *Life of Aratus* 4

He lived in the time of Ptolemy Philadelphus, and studied with Dionysius of Heraclea. He lived at the court of Antigonus the king of Macedon and Phila his wife, and was in his prime at the same time as Alexander of Aetolia, Callimachus, †Melandrius, and Philitas.

7 Scholiast on Nicander, *Theriaca* = Hermesianax Test. **1**

"Dear Hermesianax"] This Hermesianax was a friend and associate of Philitas . . . It is impossible for Nicander to have addressed himself directly to him, since Philitas was older than Nicander.[5]

8 Theocritus, *Idylls*

> . . . Not yet, I think, do I surpass the excellent
> Sicelidas of Samos,[6] nor Philitas, in my songs, [40]
> Contending like a frog against cicadas.

[5] See Hermesianax, Test. **1**, n. 1.
[6] Identified by the scholiast as Asclepiades the epigrammatist.

9 Choeroboscus, in Theodos. *Canon.*, *GG* IV.1, p. 333.10 Hilgard

Φιλητᾶς ὁ διδάσκαλος Θεοκρίτου

Φιλητᾶς Bernhardy: Φιλίππας, Φιλητὸς codd.

10 Vit. Theocr., p. 1.9 Wendel

ἀκουστὴς δὲ γέγονε [sc. Theocritus] Φιλιτᾶ καὶ Ἀσκληπιάδου, ὧν μνημονεύει [7.40]. ἤκμασε δὲ κατὰ Πτολεμαῖον τὸν ἐπικληθέντα ‹Φιλάδελφον τὸν Πτολεμαίου τοῦ› Λάγου.

‹Φιλάδελφον . . . τοῦ› suppl. Wendel post Ahrens: ἤκμασε . . . Λαγ. delendum voluit Wilamowitz   Λάγων, Λαγωόν, Λάγον codd., corr. Dindorf

cf. Anecd. Estense, p. 9.10 Wendel

ἐγένετο δὲ ἀκουστὴς Φιλητᾶ καὶ Ἀσκληπιάδου, ὧν καὶ μνημονεύει. ἤκμασε δὲ ἐν τοῖς χρόνοις Πτολεμαίου τοῦ ἐπικληθέντος Λαγωοῦ.

11 *Suda* s.v. Ζηνόδοτος, ζ 74 (cf. ps.-Zonaras, col. 956 Tittmann)

Ζηνόδοτος, Ἐφέσιος, ἐποποιὸς καὶ γραμματικός, μαθητὴς Φιλητᾶ, ἐπὶ Πτολεμαίου γεγονὼς τοῦ πρώτου, ὃς καὶ πρῶτος τῶν Ὁμήρου διορθωτὴς ἐγένετο καὶ τῶν ἐν Ἀλεξανδρείᾳ βιβλιοθηκῶν προΰστη καὶ τοὺς παῖδας Πτολεμαίου ἐπαίδευσεν.

Φιλητοῦ ps.-Zonaras

9 Choeroboscus, scholia on Theodosius' *Canones*

Philitas, teacher of Theocritus.

10 *Life of Theocritus*

He was a pupil of Philitas and Asclepiades, both of whom he mentions. He flourished in the time of Ptolemy surnamed ⟨Philadelphus, son of Ptolemy son⟩ of Lagus.

cf. Anecdoton Estense

He was a pupil of Philitas and Asclepiades, both of whom he also mentions. He flourished in the time of Ptolemy surnamed Lagous.

11 *Suda* s.v. Zenodotus

Zenodotus, of Ephesus, a hexameter poet and grammarian, a pupil of Philitas, lived in the time of the first Ptolemy. He was the first corrector of Homer, head of the libraries in Alexandria, and educated the children of Ptolemy.

12 Σ A *Il.* 1.524*c*, i. p. 142.82 Erbse

οὕτως κατανεύσομαι, οὐχὶ "ἐπινεύσομαι" Ἀρίσταρχος
ἐν τοῖς Πρὸς Φιλίταν προφέρεται.

cf. Σ A *Il.* 2.111*b*, i. p. 202.76 Erbse
ἐν γοῦν τῷ Πρὸς Φιλίταν συγγράμματι . . .

Φιλιτᾶν A, corr. Erbse (sed cf. ii. p. 548)

13 Strato, *Phoenicides, PCG* vi. fr. 1.40–46, ap. Athen.
Deipn. 9.383 A–B + P. Cair. 65445

40   . . . ἔθυεν, ἔλεγεν ἕτερα μυρία
        τ͵ο͵ι͵αῦ͵θ᾽ ἅ, μὰ τὴν Γῆν, οὐδὲ εἷς συνῆκεν ἄν,
        μίστυλλα, μοίρας, δίπτυχ᾽, ὀβελούς· ὥστ᾽ ἔδει
        τὰ τοῦ Φιλίτα λαμβάνοντα βυβλία
        σκοπεῖν ἕκαστον τί δύναται τῶν ῥημάτων.
45   ἀλλ᾽ ἱκέτευον αὐτὸν ἤδη μεταβαλὼν
        ἀνθρωπίνως λαλεῖν τι.

40 ετερα μυρια pap.: ἄλλα ῥήματα A   41 συηκεν αν pap.:
ἤκουσεν ἄν A   42 ὥστε με A   43 τῶν τοῦ Φιλτα . . .
βιβλίων A   44 ἕκαστα A   τωμβυβλιων pap.
45 πλὴν ἱκέτευω γ᾽ . . . μεταβαλεῖν A   46 τε A

14 Tzetzes, *Exegesis in Homeri Iliadem*, p. 126.9 Hermann

Πολλοὶ τῆς Ὁμηρικῆς ἐτυμολογίας ἐπεμελήθησαν . . .
Ζηνόδοτος, Φιλητᾶς, Σαπφώ, καὶ ἕτεροι.

18

12 Scholiast on Homer, *Iliad*

Aristarchus adduces the form thus, *kataneusomai* (nod in assent), not *epineusomai*, in his *Against Philitas*.

cf. Scholiast on Homer, *Iliad*

In his treatise *Against Philitas* . . .

13 Strato, *Phoenicides*

. . . He sacrificed, he said dozens of other things [40]
Of the same sort which, by Earth, not a single person
    could understand,
Cuttings-up, apportionments, double folds, spits; so
    you needed
To fetch Philitas' books,
And look to see what each of the words meant.
Well, changing my tack, at long last I begged him [45]
To say something intelligible to human beings.

14 Tzetzes, *Exegesis on Homer's Iliad*

Many took an interest in Homeric etymology . . . Zenodotus, Philitas, Sappho, and others.

PHILITAS

15 *HE* 1371 = *AP* 11.218 (Crates) = Euphorion Test. **8**

3   καὶ κατάγλωσσ᾽ ἐπόει τὰ ποήματα καὶ τὰ Φιλίτα
    ἀτρεκέως ᾔδει· καὶ γὰρ Ὁμηρικὸς ἦν

3 φίλιτρα cod., corr. Müller: Φιλητᾶ Dobree

16 EtGen AB = EtGud = EtMag (Call. fr. 532 Pf.)

Κῷος· . . . Καλλίμαχος·

    τῷ ἴκελον τὸ γράμμα τὸ Κώϊον

17 Call. fr. 1.9–12 Pf. (P. Oxy. 2079)

    ......]..ρεην [ὀλ]ιγόστιχος· ἀλλὰ καθέλ.κει
10   ....πο.λὺ τὴν μακρὴν ὄμπνια Θεσμοφόρο[ς·
    τοῖν δὲ] δυοῖν Μίμνερμος ὅτι γλυκύς, α.ί α[
    ......] ἡ μεγάλη δ᾽ οὐκ ἐδίδαξε γυνή.

9] γὰρ ἔην Lobel   init. ἦ μὲν δὴ] Pfeiffer: Κώιος οὐ]κ ἄρ᾽
ἔην Wimmel: Κῷος δὴ] γὰρ ἔην Matthews: Κώιος -ῆ] γὰρ ἔην
Müller: χὼ Κῷος] γὰρ ἔην Luppe   10 δρῦν Housman:
θεῦν Hollis, Matthews: γραῦν Gallavotti, Milne: Κῶν Vitelli
11 init. suppl. Housman   de fine, cf. Σ Lond. 11: α.ί κατὰ
λεπτόν Milne: α.ί μεγάλαι dub. Lehnus   11–12 α.ί κατὰ
λεπτόν | ῥήσιες] Rostagni: α.ί κ. λ. | Κώιαι] Puelma: α.ί γ᾽
ἀπαλαί τοι (vel μὲν) | νήνιες] Luppe: α.ί μὲν ἀραιαί | Κώϊαι]
Sier   12 κῶραι γ᾽] Allen

---

[7] See Euphorion Test. **8**, n. 14.
[8] Presumably one of Philitas' poems, but it is unclear what it is
being compared to (fine Coan cloth, as in Propertius, Test. **24a**?),
and indeed whether the comparison is intended to flatter.

15 = Euphorion Test. **8**

> And he made poems full of glosses; as for Philitas'
> works,[7]
> He knew them all; a true Homerist was he.

16 Etymologicum Genuinum

Coan . . . Callimachus:

> Like that ⟨is⟩ the Coan writing[8]

17 Callimachus, *Aitia*

> . . . had few lines. But bounteous
> Thesmophoros[9] far outweighs the tall [[10]
> Of the two, that Mimnermus is sweet was
> demonstrated by the [
>], but not by the large woman.[10]

[9] Demeter: very likely a reference to Philitas' poem of this name.

[10] A complex interpretative problem: either Mimnermus' and Philitas' short poems are being compared favourably with their long ones (in Philitas' case, respectively *Demeter* and perhaps another poem bearing the name of a goddess), or short poems (again including Philitas' *Demeter*) are compared favourably with longer poems by a *different* author or authors, Antimachus' *Lyde* ("the large woman") being a likely target.

PHILITAS

cf. Σ Flor., ap. PSI 1219 i. 12–15

παρα]τίθεταί τε ἐν σ(υγ)κρίσει τὰ ὀλίγων στί-
χ(ων) ὄν]τ̣(α) ποιήματα Μιμνέρμου τοῦ Κο-
λοφω]νίου καὶ Φιλ{ε}ίτα τοῦ Κῴου βελτ{ε}ίονα
15 τ(ῶν) πολ]υστίχων αὐτ(ῶν) φάσκων εἶναι [....

cf. Σ Lond., ap. P. Lit. Lond. 181 ii. 9–13

⁹ἤτοι πολὺ καθέλ|¹⁰κει ἢ τ(ὴν) πολὺ μακ(ρήν) |
¹¹ἐδίδαξαν αἱ α̣..., | ¹²οὐκ ἐδίδ(αξεν) ἡ
μεγάλ(η)· | ¹³λέγει ὅτι γλυκ(ὺς) ὁ Μίμ(νερμος)

11 α̣ τ̣α̣ Bell (ed. princ., qui prius αἱ μεγά(λαι) dispicere sibi
visus est), Hunt (P. Oxy. XVII, p. 55), sscr. ̣.τα̣ Bell, μ̣..α̣ Hunt
(qui prius μεγ̣α̣ legerat): αἱ κ̣[α]τὰ (λεπτόν), sscr. μ[ικρ]ά
Rostagni, unde αἱ κ̣[α]τὰ, sscr. λεπτ(όν) Milne: αἱ ʿμετὰ ʾ
μεγάλ(ην) Bastianini: αἱ ἀ[π]α̣λ̣(αί), sscr. μ̣ε̣τα[φ(ορά)] Luppe

18 Quintilian, *Inst. Or.* 10.1.58

tunc et elegiam vacabit in manus sumere, cuius princeps
habetur Callimachus, secundas confessione plurimorum
Philetas occupavit.

Philetas, Philatas, Phileta *codd.*

19

(a) Proclus, ap. Photius, *Bibl.* 239, p. 319 ʙ 11

λέγει δὲ καὶ ἀριστεῦσαι τῷ μέτρῳ [sc. ἐλεγείᾳ] Καλ-

22

cf. Florentine Scholia ad loc.

He juxtaposes by way of comparison the short
poems of Mimnermus of Colophon
and Philitas of Cos, saying that they are better
than their long poems.

cf. London Scholia ad loc.

Either "immensely weighs down" or "immensely
 large"
The . . . demonstrated, the large ( )
did not. He says that Mimnermus is sweet

18 Quintilian, *The Orator's Education*

Then we will have leisure to study the elegiac poets as well.
Of these, Callimachus is regarded as the best, the second
place, according to the verdict of most critics, being occu-
pied by Philitas.

19

(a) Proclus, ap. Photius, *Library*

He [Proclus] says that the masters in that metre (sc. elegy)

λῖνόν τε τὸν Ἐφέσιον καὶ Μίμνερμον τὸν Κολοφώ-
νιον, ἀλλὰ καὶ τὸν τοῦ Τηλέφου Φιλίταν τὸν Κῷον καὶ
Καλλίμαχον τὸν Βάττου· Κυρηναῖος οὗτος δ᾽ ἦν.

Φιλῆταν, Φιλῆτα codd.: Φιλίταν, Φιλήταν edd.

cf. Photius, *Bibl.* 115 A 20, qui Philitam inter poetas libro
iv Stobaei *Anthologiae* excerptos nominat.

(b) Canones Byzantini, tab. M, ap. O. Kroehnert, "Cano-
nesne poetarum scriptorum artificum per antiquitatem
fuerunt?" (Diss. Königsberg, 1897), 6

ἐλεγειοποιηταὶ δ᾽· Καλλῖνος, Μίμνερμος, Φιλήτας,
Καλλίμαχος.

cf. tab. C, ap. Rabe, *RhM* 65 (1910), 342

ἐλεγείων ποιηταί. Καλλῖνος, Μίμνερμος, Φιλίτας,
Καλλίμαχος.

(c) Tzetzes, *Praef. Schol. Lyc. Al.*, p. 3.15 Scheer

ἐλεγείων δὲ ποιηταὶ Καλλίμαχος, Μίμνερμος, Φιλη-
τᾶς.

20 Antig. Caryst. *Hist. Mirab.* 19, ed. A. Giannini, *Para-
doxographorum Graecorum Reliquiae* (Milan, 1966),
42.126

ᾧ καὶ φαίνεται Φιλίτας προσέχειν, ἱκανῶς ὢν περί-
εργος [dein **20**]

24

were Callinus of Ephesus and Mimnermus of Colophon, but also Philitas of Cos, son of Telephus, and Callimachus son of Battus; the latter came from Cyrene.[11]

(b) Byzantine Canons, tab. M

Four elegiac poets: Callinus, Mimnermus, Philitas, Callimachus.

cf. tab. C

Elegiac poets: Callinus, Mimnermus, Philitas, Callimachus.

(c) Isaac Tzetzes, Preface to the Scholia on Lycophron's *Alexandra*

Elegiac poets: Callimachus, Mimnermus, Philitas.

20 Antigonus of Carystos, *Collection of Wonderful Tales*

This [*bugonia*] is a subject that seems to have interested Philitas, who was of a particularly enquiring cast of mind.

---

[11] For the date of the formation of these canons, see Lightfoot 1999, 89–91. The *terminus ante quem* for elegy is Quintilian, but the *Aitia* prologue already seeks to commend and discommend particular elegists.

21 Plut. *Mor.* 791 E

ὥσπερ οὖν ὁ Πρόδικον τὸν σοφιστὴν ἢ Φιλήταν τὸν
ποιητὴν ἀξιῶν πολιτεύεσθαι, νέους μὲν ἰσχνοὺς δὲ καὶ
νοσώδεις καὶ τὰ πολλὰ κλινοπετεῖς δι' ἀρρωστίαν
ὄντας, ἀβέλτερός ἐστιν· οὕτως ὁ κωλύων ἄρχειν καὶ
στρατηγεῖν τοιούτους γέροντας, οἷος ἦν Φωκίων . . .

22 Athen. *Deipn.* 9.401 D–E

ἀεί ποτε σύ, ὦ Οὐλπιανέ, οὐδενὸς μεταλαμβάνειν εἴωθας
τῶν παρασκευαζομένων πρὶν μαθεῖν εἰ ἡ χρῆσις μὴ εἴη
τῶν ὀνομάτων παλαιά. κινδυνεύεις οὖν ποτε διὰ ταύτας
τὰς φροντίδας ὥσπερ ὁ Κῷος Φιλίτας [Φιλιτᾶς A: Φιλη-
τᾶς C] ζητῶν τὸν καλούμενον ψευδολόγον [ψευδόμενον
Herwerden] τῶν λόγων ὁμοίως ἐκείνῳ διαλυθῆναι [ἀφαυ-
ανθῆναι Kaibel]. ἰσχνὸς γὰρ πάνυ τὸ σῶμα διὰ τὰς
ζητήσεις γενόμενος ἀπέθανεν, ὡς τὸ πρὸ τοῦ μνημείου
αὐτοῦ ἐπίγραμμα δηλοῖ·

> ξεῖνε, Φιλίτας εἰμί. λόγων ὁ ψευδόμενός με
> ὤλεσε καὶ νυκτῶν φροντίδες ἑσπέριοι.

2 νυκτῶν] καὶ νικτῶν Kaibel

23

(a) Athen. *Deipn.* 12.552 B

λεπτότερος δ' ἦν καὶ Φιλίτας ὁ Κῷος ποιητής, ὃς καὶ
διὰ τὴν τοῦ σώματος ἰσχνότητα σφαίρας ἐκ μολύβου
πεποιημένας εἶχε περὶ τὼ πόδε, ὡς μὴ ὑπὸ ἀνέμου
ἀνατραπείη.

21 Plutarch, *On whether public affairs should be managed by the elderly*

The man who would require Prodicus the sophist or Philitas the poet to be involved in public affairs—young men, admittedly, but frail, prone to disease, and often bed-ridden through illness—shows his foolishness, in just the same way as the one who would debar from public office and military command such elderly men as Phocion . . .

22 Athenaeus, *Deipnosophistae*

Ulpian, you never take a share in any dish that is put in front of you until you have found out whether or not the use of its name is ancient. Like Philitas of Cos, who was constantly searching for the so-called "lying word", through these worries of yours you run the risk of perishing in the same way as he did. Through his researches he became extremely emaciated in body, and died, as indicated by the epigram on his monument:

> Stranger, I am Philitas. The "lying word"
> Proved my undoing, and nocturnal cogitations.

23

(a) Athenaeus, *Deipnosophistae*

The poet Philitas of Cos was also rather thin, and on account of his slender build he used to have leaden balls attached to his feet so that he would not be overturned by the wind.

(b) Aelian, *VH* 9.14

Φιλίταν [Φιλητᾶν codd., corr. Dilts] λέγουσι τὸν Κῷον λεπτότατον γενέσθαι τὸ σῶμα. ἐπεὶ τοίνυν ἀνατραπῆναι ῥᾴδιος ἦν ἐκ πάσης προφάσεως, μολίβου φασὶ πεποιημένα εἶχεν ἐν τοῖς ὑποδήμασι πέλματα, ἵνα μὴ ἀνατρέπηται ὑπὸ τῶν ἀνέμων, εἴ ποτε σκληροὶ κατέπνεον.

(c) Aelian, *VH* 10.6

Ἐκωμῳδοῦντο ἐς λεπτότητα Σαννυρίων ὁ κωμῳδίας ποιητὴς καὶ Μέλητος ὁ τραγῳδίας ποιητὴς καὶ Κινησίας κυκλίων χορῶν καὶ Φιλίτας [Φιλητᾶς codd., corr. Dilts] ποιητὴς ἑξαμέτρων [πενταμέτρων Ruhnken].

24

(a) Prop. 2.1.4–6

> ingenium nobis ipsa puella facit.
> sive illam Cois fulgentem incedere cerno,
> totum de Coa veste volumen erit.

5 cogis *vel* togis *codd., corr. Leo*   6 totum de ς: hoc totum e *codd.*

cf. id. 4.5.57–58

> qui versus Coae dederit nec munera vestis,
> istius tibi sit surda sine aere lyra.

58 arte *codd. plerique*

(b) Aelian, *Historical Miscellany*

They say that Philitas of Cos was very slightly built. Since the slightest cause would throw him off his feet, it is reported that he wore shoes with lead soles, to prevent his being overturned by the wind whenever it blew hard.

(c) Aelian, *Historical Miscellany*

Sannyrion the comic poet, Meletus the tragic poet, Cinesias the poet of circular choruses, and Philitas the hexameter poet, were all ridiculed on the comic stage on account of their thinness.

24

(a) Propertius, 2.1.4–6

> The girl herself provides our inspiration.
> If I see her walking radiant in a Coan garment,
>   The result will be an entire volume woven from
>   Coan cloth.

cf. 4.5.57–58

> The one who gives you verses, not gifts of Coan
>   cloth,[12]
> May his penniless lyre be dumb as far as you're
>   concerned.

[12] In both passages there seems to be a play on "Coan": Coan cloth was famously fine, but the island's name also recalls its famous poet and the finesse of his literary productions.

(b) id. 2.34.29–32

aut quid Cretaei tibi prosunt carmina plectri?
30   nil iuvat in magno vester amore senex.
tu potius †memorem Musis imitere Philitan
et non inflati somnia Callimachi.

29 erechtei, erichtei, erechti *vll*: Smyrnaei *Heinsius*: Dircaei
Palmer: Aratei *Nairn*: Lucreti *Turnebus*   plectri] lecta
codd., corr. Palmer   31 satius *codd., corr. Schrader*
memorem musis *vel* musis memorem *codicum maior pars*: musis
meropem *codd. Lusaticus, ex quo* Meropem Mus. *Jacob*, Mus.
Meropen imit. Philitae *G. Luck*: mollem Mus. *Schottus*: tenuem
Mus. *Camps*: Musam leviorem (Cererem Musis *Stroh*) . . .
Philitae *Santen*

(c) id. 3.1.1–2

Callimachi Manes et Coi sacra Philitae,
in vestrum quaeso me sinite ire nemus.

(d) id. 3.3.51–52

talia Calliope, lymphisque a fonte petitis
ora Philitea nostra rigavit aqua.

(e) id. 3.9.43–46

inter Callimachi sat erit placuisse libellos
et cecinisse modis, Coe poeta, tuis.
45   haec urant pueros, haec urant scripta puellas,
meque deum clament et mihi sacra ferant!

30

(b) 2.34.29–32

> What is the good of songs from the Cretan[13] lyre?
>> That old man of yours is no good where a grand   [30]
>>> passion is concerned.
> Better to imitate Philitas . . .
>> And the dreams of lean Callimachus.

(c) 3.1.1–2

> Shades of Callimachus and rites of Coan Philitas,
>> Permit me, pray, to enter your sacred grove.

(d) 3.3.51–52

> With that, Calliope drew water from a spring
>> And wet my lips with Philitean draughts.

(e) 3.9.43–46

> Among Callimachus' books it will suffice me to have
>> given pleasure
> And, Coan poet, to have chanted in your strains.
> May boys, may girls, be kindled by my writings,   [45]
>> Acknowledge me a god, and bring me rites![14]

[13] If correct, a reference to the semi-legendary poet and seer Epimenides.

[14] For the possible echoes here of a wish by Philitas for heroic honours, see Hollis 1996.

---

44 Coe ⟨: dure *codd.*: Dore *Scriverius*: docte *Foster*: clare *Ayrmann*

(f) id. 4.6.1–4

> Sacra facit vates: sint ora faventia sacris;
>> et cadat ante meos icta iuvenca focos.
> serta Philiteis certet Romana corymbis,
>> et Cyrenaeas urna ministret aquas.

3 serta *Scaliger*: cera *codd.*   certent *Scaliger*: niteat *Giardina*

25

(a) Ov. *Ars Am.* 3.329–330

> sit tibi Callimachi, sit Coi nota poetae,
330 >> sit quoque vinosi Teia Musa senis.

(b) Ov. *Rem. Am.* 759–760

> Callimachum fugito, non est inimicus amori;
760 >> et cum Callimacho tu quoque, Coe, noces.

759 Amori *Heinsius*

(c) Ov. *Tristia* 1.6.1–4

> Nec tantum Clario Lyde dilecta poetae
>> nec tantum Coo Bittis amata suo est,
> pectoribus quantum tu nostris, uxor, inhaeres,
>> digna minus misero, non meliore viro.

1 Clario est Lyde, Clario est idem, Lyde Clario *vll*: Clario Lyde est *ed. Bonon. (1471)*   poetae est *vl*   2 Battis, baccis, vel sim. *codd., corr. Merkel*   Coo] Clario *vl*   amica *vl* suo *vl*   3 pectoribus nostris quantum tu *vl*

32

(f) 4.6.1–4

> The priest performs the rites; for them may pious
>> silence reign;
>> And, stricken, may a heifer fall before my altar-fire.
> May Roman garlands vie with Philitean ivy clusters,
>> And Cyrenaean waters be provided from an urn.

25

(a) Ovid, *The Art of Love*

> Acquaint yourself with Callimachus' muse, the Coan
>> poet's,
>> And the Teian inspiration of the bibulous old
>> man.[15]

(b) Ovid, *Remedies for Love*

> Avoid Callimachus, who is not indisposed to love;
>> Along with Callimachus, you too, Coan, inflict
>> harm.

(c) Ovid, *Tristia*

> Not so adored was Lyde by the Clarian bard,
>> Nor so beloved was Bittis by her Coan swain,
> As much as you, my wife, inhere within my breast,
>> Deserving of a man, not better, but more
>> fortunate.

[15] Anacreon.

(d) Ov. *Ex Pont.* 3.1.57–58

> nec te nesciri patitur mea pagina, qua non
> inferius Coa Bittide nomen habes.

58 coa battide *s*: coabit tibi de, coa pithyde, coa batide, choa bachide *vel sim. cett., corr. Merkel*

26 Statius, *Silvae* 1.2.252–255

> . . . hunc ipse Coo plaudente Philitas
> Callimachusque senex Umbroque Propertius antro
> ambissent laudare diem, nec tristis in ipsis
> Naso Tomis divesque foco lucente Tibullus.

(d) Ovid, *Ex Ponto*

> My writings will not suffer you to be unknown; in
>   them
>   No less than Coan Bittis' is your name.

26 Statius, *Silvae*

> . . . This day, to Coan plaudits, Philitas
> And old Callimachus, Propertius in his Umbrian
>   cave,
> Would all have thronged to praise; even in Tomi
> Ovid himself would not have wanted cheer,
> Nor yet Tibullus, rich while his hearth burned.[16]

[16] This is a wedding-poem; Statius evokes five past masters of elegy who would have been glad to celebrate the day (Hollis 1996, 58–59). "Coan plaudits" should parallel the allusions to specific works by other poets, and may be another sign that Philitas aspired to heroic honours from his countrymen.

FRAGMENTA POETICA

1–13 FRAGMENTA CERTIS CARMINIBUS TRIBUTA

1–8 Elegiaca

Δημήτηρ

Test.: Call. fr. 1.9–10 Pf. [= Test. **17**]

1 Stobaeus, *Flor.* 4.40.11 (Περὶ κακοδαιμονίας), v. p. 922 Hense

Φιλήτα Δήμητρος·

    νῦν δ' αἰεὶ πέσσω· τὸ δ' ἀέξεται ἄλλο νεωρὲς
    πῆμα, κακοῦ δ' οὔπω γίνεται ἡσυχίη.

1 αἰεὶ] ἄλγος Jacobs   πτήσσω Bergk

2 Stobaeus, *Flor.* 4.40.15 (Περὶ κακοδαιμονίας), v. p. 923 Hense

Φιλήτου·

    τῷ οἴμοι πολέω γαίης ὕπερ ἠδὲ θαλάσσης
    ἐκ Διὸς ὡραίων ἐρχομένων ἐτέων.

POETIC FRAGMENTS

1–13 FRAGMENTS OF KNOWN LOCATION

1–8 Elegiac Fragments

Demeter

Testimonium: cf. Test. **17**.

1 Stobaeus

Philitas' *Demeter*:

> As it is,[1] I always suffer; some new sorrow
> Always arises, and from grief there is no rest.

2 Stobaeus

Philitas:

> And so, alas, I traverse land and sea
> As the annual cycle of seasons comes from Zeus.

[1] With Demeter as speaker, the sense is perhaps: "Had I been mortal, there would have been a limit to my sufferings, but as it is . . .".

οὐδ' ἀπὸ μοῖρα κακῶν μελέῳ φέρει, ἀλλὰ
    μένουσιν
ἔμπεδ' ἀεί, καὶ τοῖς ἄλλα προσαυξάνεται.

1 τῷ οὔ μοι S, corr. Kuchenmüller: τῷ αἰεὶ Gesner: πτοιοῦμαι
Bach   πολέων S, corr. Grotius   οὐδὲ S, corr. Gesner
2 ἔσχομεν ὧν S, corr. Jacobs   inter 2–3 lacunam suspicatus
est Spanoudakis   3 μελέω κακῶν S, corr. Passow
φέρουσιν S, corr. Grotius   4 ἔμπεδα καὶ S, corr. Meineke

Δήμητρι attrib. Bergk; Ἑρμῇ Nowacki

3 Stobaeus, *Flor.* 4.56.26 (Παρηγορικά), v. p. 1129
Hense

Φιλήτα Δήμητρος·

ἀλλ' ὅτ' ἐπὶ χρόνος ἔλθῃ, ὃς ἐκ Διὸς ἄλγεα
    πέσσειν
ἔλλαχε, καὶ πενθέων φάρμακα μοῦνος ἔχει.

4 Stobaeus, *Flor.* 4.56.26a (Παρηγορικά), v. p. 1129
Hense

Φιλήτα Δήμητρος·

καὶ γάρ τις μελέοιο κορεσσάμενος κλαυθμοῖο
    κήδεα δειλαίων εἷλεν ἀπὸ πραπίδων.

Nor—wretched me—does fate remit my evils; fixed
They stay, and still by others are increased.[2]

3 Stobaeus

Philitas' *Demeter*:

But when the time should come for nursing grief
From Zeus—time which alone has remedies for hurt

4 Stobaeus

Philitas' *Demeter*:

For when one has one's fill of tears and lamentation,
One lifts the sorrows from one's wretched heart.[3]

[2] The emendation of the masculine participle in the first line
facilitates the conjecture that the speaker is again Demeter.

[3] It is likely that both this and the previous fragment come
from a consolatory speech addressed to Demeter by one of her
Coan hosts.

5 P. Oxy. 2258 A fr. 2 Back (*c*), marg. ad v. 33 (Call. *Hymn* 2.33)

1   ].. /

       ] τ[ὸ] τόξον κ(αὶ) Φιλί

τας ἐν] Δήμητρι αυτα εγε

       ].[.].. γυμνὸν ἄεμμα

5   ].

2–3 Suppl. Lobel: de Φίλι[κος] etiam cogitavit   3 αυτα . ο γε Ll.-J.-P.

Unde sic restituerunt Ll.-J.-P.:

$$αὐτὰρ \ ὅ \ γε \ \cup\cup- \ γυμνὸν \ ἄεμμα \ \cup-$$

αὐτὰρ ὅ γ᾽ ἐ[ἵλκυσε] Hollis

Ἐπιγράμματα

6 Stobaeus, *Flor.* 4.17.5 (Περὶ ναυτιλίας καὶ ναυαγίου), iv. p. 401 Hense

Φιλήτα Ἐπιγραμμάτων·

    γαῖαν μὲν φανέουσι θεοί ποτε· νῦν δὲ πάρεστιν
      αἰψηρῶν ἀνέμων μοῦνον ὁρᾶν τέμενος.

2 λαιψηρὸν, αἰψηλῶν *vll*   τέμενος] τὸ μένος Valckenaer

5 P. Oxy. 2258

> . . . the bow is also (mentioned?) by Phili-   2
> tas(?) in the] *Demeter*: "but he(?) . . .   3
> . . . the naked bow . . . "⁴   4

Epigrams

6 Stobaeus

Philitas' *Epigrams*:

> Some day the gods will bring to light a land, though
>   now
> The eye sees only the domain of the swift winds.⁵

---

⁴ Ll.-J.–P. compare *Od.* 11.607 γυμνὸν τόξον ἔχων, of Heracles.

⁵ Though this fragment is cited by Stobaeus in a series of excerpts about seafaring, in which case the speaker could be a sailor anticipating the appearance of land, the lines have also been interpreted as part of an allegory, or as a reference to the emergence of the island of Rhodes from the waves.

7 Stobaeus, *Flor.* 4.56.10–11 (Παρηγορικά), v. p. 1125
Hense

"ἐκ θυμοῦ κλαῦσαί με τὰ μέτρια, καί τι
προσηνὲς
εἰπεῖν, μεμνῆσθαί τ' οὐκέτ' ἐόντος ὁμῶς."
οὐ κλαίω ξείνων σε φιλαίτατε· πολλὰ γὰρ ἔγνως
καλά, κακῶν δ' αὖ σοι μοῖραν ἔνειμε θεός.

1–2 citantur a Stob. cum lemmate Φιλήτα Παιγνίων (Παιγνίων
om. S); 3–4 cum lemmate Φιλέα Ἐπιγραμμάτων [om. Ἐπι-
γραμμάτων S]. Fragmenta coniunxit Schneidewin

1 με τὰ] μέγα codd., corr. Jacobs: μάλα Brunck   2 ὁμῶς
Bergk   4 καλά, καλῶν Kuchenmüller: κάλ' ἄκακον Maas
νέμει codd., corr. Gesner

Παίγνια

8 Stobaeus, *Flor.* 2.4.5 (Περὶ λόγου καὶ γραμμάτων), ii.
p. 27 Wachsmuth

Φιλήτα Παιγνίων·

οὐ μέ τις ἐξ ὀρέων ἀποφώλιος ἀγροιώτης
αἱρήσει κλήθρην, αἱρόμενος μακέλην·
ἀλλ' ἐπέων εἰδὼς κόσμον καὶ πολλὰ μογήσας,
μύθων παντοίων οἶμον ἐπιστάμενος.

7 Stobaeus

> "Mourn me sincerely, but in reason; speak
> A kind word; and remember one who is no more."
> I do not mourn you, dearest stranger; you enjoyed
> Much blessing, though god gave you, too, a share of
>   pain.

Light Verse

8 Stobaeus

Philitas' *Light Verse*:

> No lumbering rustic snatching up a hoe
> Shall bear me from the mountains—me, an alder
>   tree;
> But one who knows the marshalling of words, who
>   toils,
> Who knows the pathways of all forms of speech.[6]

[6] If the second line is to be taken literally, the speaker may be the tree itself, or, derived from it, a poet's staff (cf. Hes. *Th.* 30) (so Maass), or writing-tablet (so Kuchenmüller). Other scholars have suggested that a Philitan poem, or collection of poems, or poetry itself is speaking. Alternatively, the speaker could be a girl who prefers to marry a poet rather than a rustic (so Reitzenstein). On any reading, the lines contain an image, perhaps self-image, of the refined, learned, and dedicated poet.

PHILITAS

9–12 Hexametrica

Ἑρμῆς

9 = Parthenius, Ἐρωτικὰ Παθήματα, ιι Περὶ Πολυμήλης

Ἱστορεῖ Φιλίτας Ἑρμῇ . . .

10 Stobaeus, *Flor.* 4.51.3 (Περὶ θανάτου), v. p. 1066 Hense

Φιλήτα Ἑρμοῦ [A: Ἑρμοῦ om. S]·

    . . . ἀτραπὸν εἰς Ἀίδαο
ἤνυσα, τὴν οὔπω τις ἐναντίον ἦλθεν ὁδίτης.

1 Ἀίδαο recc. (‹καὶ› . . . Ἀίδαο Magnelli): ἄδεω SA: ἄδεα ed. princ.: Ἀίδεω Scaliger   ἀτραπὸν Ἄιδεω Meineke

11 Stobaeus, *Flor.* 1.4.4 (Περὶ ἀνάγκης), i. p. 71 Wachsmuth

Φιλήτα Ἑρμοῦ·

  ‹–∪∪› ἰσχυρὰ γὰρ ἐπικρατεῖ ἀνδρὸς Ἀνάγκη,
  ἥ ῥ᾽ οὐδ᾽ ἀθανάτους ὑποδείδιεν, οἵ τ᾽ ἐν Ὀλύμπῳ
  ἔκτοσθεν χαλεπῶν ἀχέων οἴκους ἐκάμοντο.

1 ‹τλήσομαι› Meineke: ‹ἄνσχεο› Scheibner

44

POETIC FRAGMENTS

9–12 Hexameter Fragments

Hermes

9 = Parthenius, *Sufferings in Love*, "About Polymela"
The story is told by Philitas in the *Hermes* . . .

10 Stobaeus
Philitas' *Hermes*:

> . . . the path to Hades' house
> I mastered, whence no traveller has yet returned.[7]

11 Stobaeus
Philitas' *Hermes*:

> . . . for mankind is in thrall to strong Necessity,
> Who fears not even gods, who on Olympus' peak
> Away from pain and anguish built their homes.[8]

[7] It is likely that Odysseus is speaking to Aeolus.
[8] The gnomic content suggests direct speech, though the speaker is uncertain (Odysseus again?).

12 Stobaeus, *Flor.* 4.40.12 (Περὶ κακοδαιμονίας), v. p. 922 Hense

τοῦ αὐτοῦ (sc. Philitae)·

ἦ μὲν δὴ πολέεσσι πεφύρησαι χαλεποῖσι,
θυμέ, γαληναίη δ' ἐπιμίσγεαι οὐδ' ὅσον ὅσσον,
ἀμφὶ δέ τοι νέαι αἰὲν ἀνῖαι τετρήχασιν.

1 πολέεσι S: πολέεσσι Spc, ed. princ.: πελάγεσσι Wilamowitz

Ἑρμῇ attrib. Bach

13 Incerta Elegiaca an Hexametrica

Τήλεφος [dub.]

13 Σ Ap. Rhod. 4.1141, p. 307.17 Wendel

ἐν τῷ ἄντρῳ ‹τῷ› Μάκριδός φησι τὸν γάμον γεγενῆσθαι Μηδείας καὶ Ἰάσονος, Φιλητᾶς δὲ ἐν Τηλέφῳ ἐν τῇ Ἀλκινόου οἰκίᾳ.

ὁ Τηλέφου Bach: ἐν τῇ Λητοῖ Sbardella

12 Stobaeus

By the same:

> You have indeed been tossed on many woes,
> My soul, and not enjoyed the slightest calm;
> By evils ever fresh are you beset.[9]

13 Elegiac or Hexametric

Telephus(?)

13 Scholiast on Apollonius of Rhodes, *Argonautica*

It was in the cave of Macris that he [sc. Apollonius] says that the wedding of Jason and Medea took place, whereas Philitus in the *Telephus*[10] said it was in the palace of Alcinous.

---

[9] Probably the much-enduring Odysseus who speaks.

[10] A poem on the subject of the mythological hero, or named after Philitas' father (Test. **1**, **2**), or perhaps corrupt for "Philitas son of Telephus".

14–27 FRAGMENTA INCERTAE SEDIS

14–19 Elegiaca

14 Steph. Byz., p. 668.2 Mein.

Φιλήτας δέ φησι·

> Φλιοῦς γὰρ πόλις ἐστί, Διωνύσου φίλος υἱός
> Φλιοῦς ἦν αὐτὸς δείματο λευκολόφος.

1 γὰρ om. A   τοῦ Διονύσου codd., corr. Salmasius
2 λευκολόφον Heinrich

Δήμητρι attrib. Maass; Τηλέφῳ Campbell

15 Athen. Deipn. 2.71 A

καὶ Φιλητᾶς ὁ Κῷος·

> γηρύσαιτο δὲ νεβρὸς ἀπὸ ψυχὴν ὀλέσασα,
> ὀξείης κάκτου τύμμα φυλαξαμένη.

cf. Antig. Caryst. Hist. Mir. 8 οὐχ ἧττον δὲ τούτου
θαυμαστόν, καθωμιλημένον δὲ μᾶλλον τὸ περὶ τὴν ἐν
τῇ Σικελίᾳ ἄκανθαν τὴν καλουμένην κάκτον· εἰς ἣν
ὅταν ἔλαφος ἐμβῇ καὶ τραυματισθῇ, τὰ ὀστᾶ ἄφωνα
καὶ ἄχρηστα πρὸς αὐλοὺς ἴσχει. (2.) ὅθεν καὶ ὁ
Φιλητᾶς ἐξηγήσατο περὶ αὐτῆς εἴπας· γηρύσαιτο,
κτλ.; Hesychius κ 363.

1 νεκρὸς Athen.   ζωὴν Antig.   ὤλεσσα, ὤλεσα Athen.

Παιγνίοις attrib. Reitzenstein; Δήμητρι Maass

14–27 FRAGMENTS OF UNCERTAIN LOCATION

14–19 Elegiac Fragments

14 Stephanus of Byzantium

Philitas says:

> For Phlius is a town which Dionysus' dear son,
> Phlius, established, town of the white crest.[11]

15 Athenaeus, *Deipnosophistae*

And Philitas of Cos:

> Let the voice be heard of the fawn that has lost its
> life,
> One that has fled the cactus' sharp sting.[12]

cf. Hesychius s.v. *cactus*; Antigonus of Carystus, *Collection of Wonderful Tales*, 8: No less astonishing than this, but better-known, is the species of thorn in Sicily known as "cactus". When a deer steps on this and is wounded, its bones are rendered unmusical and useless for the manufacture of *auloi*. Philitas gives some information about this, when he says: "Let the voice", etc.

[11] Town in the Argolid, famous for its wine. Demeter had a mystery-cult at nearby Celeae, whence the conjectural attribution to the *Demeter*.

[12] Perhaps a riddling call for music on an *aulos*, hence from a poem presuppoosing a sympotic context?

16 P. Oxy. 2260, col. i, ll. 1–3

⌞καί κεν Ἀθηναίης δολιχαόρου⌟ ἱερὸν ἄστυ
καί κε[ν Ἐλευ]σῖνος θεῖον ἴδοι[̣ ̣ λό]φον

1 Suppl. e Σ T *Il.* 21.179*b*, v. p. 163.24 Erbse, ἄορι· τῷ δόρατι·
Φιλήτας· "καί κεν Ἀθ. δολ." ἀντὶ τοῦ "μέγα δόρυ ἐχούσης" +
Σ T *Il.* 14.385, iii. p. 656.64 Erbse, ἄορ· τινὲς τὴν τρίαιναν, ἐπεὶ
καὶ Ἀρκάδες καὶ Αἰτωλοὶ πᾶν ὅπλον ἄορ καλοῦσιν· ὅθεν καὶ
. . . " Ἀθ. δολ. ἱερ. ἄστ."   2 Suppl. Lobel, qui et ἴδοι[μι
temptavit: ἴδοι[τε] Snell

Δήμητρι attrib. Alfonsi, ob Eleusinis mentionem

17 Σ Theocr. *Id.* 2.120*b*

μᾶλα μὲν ἐν κόλποισι ⟨Διωνύσοιο⟩] τὰ ἐράσμια καὶ
ἔρωτος ποιητικά, καθὸ ⟨τὰ⟩ ὑπὸ Ἀφροδίτης διδόμενα τῷ
Ἱππομένει μῆλα ἐκ τῶν Διονύσου, ταῦτα δὲ εἰς ἔρωτα τὴν
Ἀταλάντην ἐκίνησεν, ὥς φησιν ὁ Φιλητᾶς·

        . . . τά οἵ ποτε Κύπρις ἑλοῦσα
μῆλα Διωνύσου δῶκεν ἀπὸ κροτάφων.

1 ἑλοῦσα K: ἐλοῖσα cett.   2 μῆλα K: μᾶλα cett.
Διωνύσοιο K, corr. Casaubon: Διόνυσον cett.

16 P. Oxy. 2260

And perhaps long-speared Athena's holy city
And Eleusis' sacred summit I(?) might see[13]

17 Scholiast on Theocritus, *Idylls*

"Apples of Dionysus in my bosom"] Apples that are seductive and engender erotic desire, like the apples from Dionysus' fruits given by Aphrodite to Hippomenes, which stirred up desire in Atalanta, as Philitas says:

... apples which once the Cyprian took
And gave to him from Dionysus' temples.[14]

[13] The passage is quoted to show that the word ἄορ, normally "sword", may mean "spear".

[14] The Atalanta story goes back to Hesiod, but Philitas' version most recalls Theocr. *Id*. 3.40–42, where the apples cause Atalanta to fall in love, and Call. fr. 412 Pf., where they come from Dionysus' garland. Some manuscripts attribute Doric dialectal forms to Philitas, though they may have crept in from Theocritus.

18 Strab. 8.5.3

παρὰ Φιλίτᾳ δέ·

δμωΐδες εἰς ταλάρους λευκὸν ἄγουσιν ἔρι
⟨τὸ ἔριον⟩.

Φιλε[ι]ται Π: φιλήτᾳ cett.   δμωΐδες Π: δ . . . δες Α: δμῶες,
δμῶτες cett.   ἐς Π   ⟨τὸ ἔριον⟩ Corais

Δήμητρι attrib. Spanoudakis

19 Athen. *Deipn.* 7.327 c

Ἕρμιππος δὲ ὁ Σμυρναῖος ἐν τοῖς περὶ Ἱππώνακτος [fr.
93 Wehrli] ὕκην ἀκούει τὴν ἰουλίδα· εἶναι δ᾽ αὐτὴν δυσθή-
ρατον. διὸ καὶ Φιλίταν φάναι·

οὐδ᾽ ὕκης ἰχθὺς ἔσχατος ἐξέφυγε.

ὕκη AC, corr. Dindorf

Δήμητρι attrib. Spanoudakis; Ἐπιγράμμασι Kuchen-
müller

20–27 Incerta Elegiaca an Hexametrica

20 Antig. Caryst. *Hist. Mirab.* 19

ἴδια δὲ καὶ περὶ τὰς συγκρίσεις καὶ ἀλλοιώσεις τῶν
ζῴων, ἔτι δὲ γενέσεις, οἷον ἐν Αἰγύπτῳ τὸν βοῦν ἐὰν
κατορύξῃς ἐν τόποις τισίν, ὥστε αὐτὰ τὰ κέρατα τῆς γῆς
ὑπερέχειν, εἶθ᾽ ὕστερον ἀποπρίσῃς, λέγουσιν μελίττας

18 Strabo

And in Philitas:

> Serving maidens place white wool in baskets.

19 Athenaeus, *Deipnosophistae*

Hermippus of Smyrna in his book *On Hipponax* understands the rainbow-wrasse by the term *hŷkēs*, and says that it is hard to catch; which is the reason why Philitas also says:

> Not even the farthest *hŷkēs*-fish escaped.

20–27 Elegiac or Hexametric

20 Antigonus of Carystus, *Collection of Wonderful Tales*

There are also peculiarities concerning the similarities and differences in animal species, and in the manner of their births, such as the fact that in Egypt if you bury an ox in certain places, so that their horns emerge above the surface, and then later saw them off, they say that bees will fly

ἐκπέτεσθαι· σαπέντα γὰρ αὐτὸν εἰς τοῦτο διαλύεσθαι τὸ ζῷον. (2) ᾧ καὶ φαίνεται Φιλίτας προσέχειν, ἱκανῶς ὢν περίεργος· προσαγορεύει οὖν αὐτὰς βουγενεῖς λέγων·

βουγενέας φ⟨θ⟩άμενος προσεβήσαο μακρὰ
μελίσσας.

φάμενος codd., corr. J. Barnes: Φαμενός Bergk (scil. filium Teiresiae)   προσεβήσατο Bach: προσεβώσατο Hartung

Δήμητρι attrib. Pfeiffer

21 Σ Theocr. *Id.* 7.5–9k, p. 79.20 Wendel

Βούριναν] κρήνην λέγει τῆς Κῶ. Φιλίτας [Φιλίτας Κ: Φιλιτᾶς vel Φιλητᾶς cett.]·

νάσσατο δ' ἐν προχοῇσι μελαμπέτροιο Βυρίνης.

δάσαντο codd., corr. Heinsius: δάσσατο Kayser: δέξατο Bergk: δύσατο Lobeck   σελαμπέτροιο Βουρίννης vel Βουρρίνης codd.: μελαμπ. Βορίνης vel Βυρίνης Heinsius: μελαμπέτρου Βουρίνης Hartung: μελαμπέτροις Βουρίνης Nowacki: μελαμπέτροιο ⟨∪– –⟩ | Βουρίνης Ahrens

De Δήμητρι cogitaverunt Knaack, alii.

22 Athen. *Deipn.* 5.192 E (cf. Eustath. ad *Od.* 4.51, i. p. 145.35–38 Stallbaum)

ὁ γὰρ θρόνος αὐτὸ μόνον ἐλευθέριός ἐστιν καθέδρα σὺν ὑποποδίῳ, ὅπερ θρῆνυν καλοῦντες ἐντεῦθεν αὐτὸν ὠνό-

forth. For these creatures are the result of the ox's decomposition. And this is a subject that seems to have interested Philitas, who was of a particularly enquiring cast of mind, since he calls them "born of an ox" when he says:

> With long strides first you reached the ox-born
>   bees.[15]

21 Scholiast on Theocritus, *Idylls*

Bourina] He means a spring in Cos. Philitas:

> S/he lived at the sources of the black-rocked
>   spring Burina.[16]

22 Athenaeus, *Deipnosophistae*

The *thronos*, taken by itself, is a seat for a man of free birth, together with a footstool, which they call a *thrēnys*. Hence

---

[15] The sense is uncertain. It may or may not be relevant that the bee is sacred to Demeter.

[16] There is a good chance that this fragment belongs to the *Demeter*, since the same stream is mentioned in Theocr. *Id*. 7.6, in a poem about a Demeter festival on Cos, and Philitas' poem seems to have told a story about the goddess on that island.

μασαν θρόνον τοῦ θρήσασθαι χάριν, ὅπερ ἐπὶ τοῦ καθέ-
ζεσθαι τάσσουσιν, ὡς Φιλίτας·

  θρήσασθαι πλατάνῳ γραίῃ ὕπο

θρήσασθαι δὲ AC: δὲ del. Musurus: ‹τὸ› θρ. δὲ Sbardella
γαίῃ AC, corr. Schneider

Δήμητρι attrib. Spanoudakis

23 Choeroboscus, in Theodos. *Canon.*, *GG* IV.1, p.
333.10 Hilgard

ἰστέον δὲ ὅτι τὸ αἰδὼς Φιλητᾶς [Φιλίππας, Φιλητὸς
codd.] ὁ διδάσκαλος Θεοκρίτου χωρὶς τοῦ ς̄ προηνέγκατο,
εἰπών·

  ἀγαθὴ δ' ἐπὶ ἤθεσιν αἰδώ.

δὲ ἐπὶ codd.: δ' ἔπι Bergk

cf. Photius, *Lexicon*, α 552

αἰδώ· χωρὶς τοῦ ς̄· "ἀγαθὴ δὲ ἐπὶ ἤθεσιν αἰδώ." ἡ λέξις
Ἡρωδιανοῦ.

Ἑρμῇ attrib. Powell

the word *thronos* itself, derived from the verb *thrēsasthai*, which they use of sitting down. Philitas:

> to sit beneath an aged plane-tree.[17]

23 Choeroboscus, scholia on Theodosius' *Canones*

Philitas, the teacher of Theocritus, employed the word *aidōs* (shame) without an *s*, when he said:

> and goodly shame in one's ways

cf. Photius, *Lexicon*

aidō: without an *s*: "and goodly shame in one's ways". The word comes from Herodian.

---

[17] Often compared with Test. **4**: the Coans set up a statue for Philitas himself beneath a plane-tree.

24 EtMag 602.40

νή· στερητικόν ἐστιν ἐπίρρημα· ὁρᾶται δὲ καὶ ἐπιτατικὸν,
ὡς ἐν τῷ νηλὴς, νήνεμος,

νήχυτον ὕδωρ,

Φιλήτας.

cf. *Suda* ν 295, sine auctoris nomine; Hesychius ν 552.

Τηλέφῳ attrib. Knaack; Δήμητρι Cessi

25 EtGen AB, α 1131, ii. p. 176.6 L.–L. = EtMag 135.26,
α 1726

Ἀργανθώνειον . . . τινὲς δ᾽ Ἀργανθώνην αὐτό φασίν.
Εὐφορίων [**180**] καὶ Φιλί<τ>ας [Φιλίας AB, EtMag: Φιλή-
τας EtMag Vb, suprascr. γρ. Φιλίας: Φιλέας Toup]

Ἀργανθώνιον

λέγουσι διὰ τοῦ ῑ, οἷον· "χθιζόν μοι κνώσσοντι παρ᾽
Ἀργανθώνιον αἶπος."

"χθίζον . . . αἶπος" Philitae attrib. Bach, al. Ἀργανθώνιον αἶπος
Philitae dubitanter tribuit Kuchenmüller

Τηλέφῳ attrib. Cessi

24 Etymologicum Magnum

Nē is a privative prefix, also found in an intensive sense, as in *nēlēs* (pitiless), *nēnemos* (windless),

> full-flowing water,

Philitas.

25 Etymologicum Genuinum

Arganthoneion . . . Some call it *Arganthōnē*. Euphorion and Philitas say:

> Arganthonion

with an *i*, as in: "To me as yesterday I slept beside the Arganthonian height."[18]

---

[18] See Euphorion **180** and n. 203. Philitas could have used the word in the context of the Argonauts, Telephus, or Arganthone herself (Parthenius, *Sufferings in Love*, XXXVI).

PHILITAS

26 Steph. Byz. p. 342.17 Mein.

Ἴχναι, πόλις Μακεδονίας. Ἡρόδοτος ἑβδόμῃ [7.123.3]. Ἐρατοσθένης δὲ Ἄχνας αὐτήν φησι. Φιλίτας δ' ἄλλην [Ἄχνην Xylander] φησὶ [<τὴν> Meineke] διὰ τοῦ ᾱ.

27 Σ Ap. Rhod. 1.1297, p. 117.13 Wendel

ὄστλιγγες] αἱ λαμπηδόνες. ἐν ἄλλοις δὲ σημαίνει ἡ λέξις τοὺς βόστρυχας . . . τοῦτο δέ φησιν Ἡρωδιανὸς ἐν τῷ β′ τῆς Καθόλου [GG III.1, p. 44.4 Lentz]· "παρὰ μὲν Ἀπολλωνίῳ καὶ Φιλητᾷ διὰ τοῦ ᾱ."

cf. EtMag 159.38, a 1979 †ἀττίαγας· τὰς ὑποφυλλίδας τῶν βοτρύων· οἱ δὲ, ἀκτῖνος αὐγάς; Hesychius a 7862 ἄστλιγγας· αὐγάς. ἢ ἄστριγγας.

Δήμητρι attrib. Spanoudakis (cf. HHom. Dem. 278–280)

28–29 DUBIE TRIBUTA

28 Athen. *Deipn*. 14.639 D

Κῷοι δὲ τοὐναντίον δρῶσιν, ὡς ἱστορεῖ Μακαρεὺς ἐν τρίτῳ Κωακῶν [FGrH 456 F 1b]· ὅταν γὰρ τῇ Ἥρᾳ θύωσιν, δοῦλοι οὐ παραγίνονται ἐπὶ τὴν εὐωχίαν. διὸ καὶ Φύλαρχον [FGrH 81 F 84; Εὐφορίωνα Meineke: Φιλητᾶν conj. Kaibel] εἰρηκέναι·

26 Stephanus of Byzantium

Ichnae, a city of Macedonia. Herodotus in book seven. Eratosthenes calls it *Achnae*. Philitas says that the one with an *a* is different.[19]

27 Scholiast on Apollonius of Rhodes, *Argonautica*

ostlinges] Curling flames. In other writers the word signifies "hair" . . . This is what Herodian says in the second book of his *General Prosody*: "in Apollonius and Philitas the word has an ā."

cf. Etymologicum Magnum, s.v. †*attiagas*: among grapes, the small ones left for the gleaners; according to others, rays of light. Hesychius s.v. *astlingas*: rays; or *astringas*.

28–29 DUBIOUSLY ATTRIBUTED

28 Athenaeus, *Deipnosophistae*

The Coans do the opposite of this, as recounted by Macareus in the third book of his *Coan affairs*; for when they sacrifice to Hera, slaves are not present at the festivities. And for that reason Phylarchus[20] said:

[19] Perhaps meaning the Thessalian city of Ichnae. It is not certain that this is a poetic fragment.

[20] The historian Phylarchus is not otherwise said to have written poetry. Kaibel and Bergk attributed these lines to Philitas, Meineke to Euphorion. Jacoby suggested that Phylarchus may have cited a poet whose name is missing.

Νισύριοι μοῦνοι μὲν ἐλεύθεροι ἱεροεργοὶ
ἀνδράσι πὰρ Κῴοισιν, ἐλεύ‹θε›ρον ἆμαρ
   ἔχοντες,
δούλων δ᾽ οὔτις πάμπαν ἐσέρχεται οὐδ᾽ ἠβαιόν.

1 σουριηι A, corr. Dalecamp: Ῥειώνη Meineke: Ἡραίοις Bergk:
Οὐρανίη Herzog   2 πρὸς A: πὰρ Meineke   κείνοι-
σιν A, corr. Villebrune   ἔλευρον A, corr. Musurus
ἔχοντες] ἄγουσιν conj. Meineke, ἄγοντες Kuchenmüller

cf. Athen. *Deipn.* 6.262 c, sine "Phylarchi" testimonio

29 [Dub.] Nicetas Choniates, *Historia* 491.9 van Dieten

ὅθεν ὅπερ ἐπὶ τῶν σωματικῶν ἕξεων ὁ Κῷός φησι
ποιητής, ὡς εἰς τὸ ἄκρον προελθοῦσαι φιλοῦσι πρὸς
τὸ κάταντες ὡς φιλυπόστροφοι μεταφέρεσθαι, μὴ
ἀτρέμας ἔχουσαι μένειν τῷ συνεχεῖ ἀεὶ τῆς κινήσεως,
τοῦτο καὶ . . .

Nisyrian[21] free men alone perform the rites
Among the Coans, those enjoying freedom;
Whereas no slave may gain the least admittance.

29 Nicetas Choniates

Just as the Coan poet[22] says of physical conditions, that
once they have reached their uttermost they tend to de-
cline again, as if apt to return to their starting point, being
unable to remain in the same state by reason of the contin-
uousness of motion, so too . . .

[21] The Greek is corrupt. Nisyros is an island near Cos (cf. *Il.*
2.676), but there may alternatively be a reference to Hera ("the
Ouranian goddess"?) or her festival.

[22] The Coan doctor, Hippocrates, would be a more obvious
reference; the passage has been explained in various ways.

FRAGMENTA GRAMMATICA

30 ΕΡΜΗΝΕΙΑ(?)

30 Strab. 3.5.1

σφενδόνας δὲ περὶ τῇ κεφαλῇ τρεῖς ⟦μελαγκρα‹ν›ίνας
[suppl. Coray:—κρανίας Salmasius]· σχοίνου εἶδος, ἐξ οὗ
πλέκεται τὰ σχοινία· καὶ Φιλήτας γε [τε vel δὲ codd., corr.
Kramer] ἐν Ἑρμηνείᾳ [Α: ἑρμενείᾳ cett.: Ἑρμῇ vel ἑρμῇ
ἐλεγείᾳ Tyrwhitt: Ἑρμείᾳ vel ἐλεγεῖ α′ dub. Meineke]·

> λευγαλέος δὲ χιτὼν πεπινωμένος, ἀμφὶ δ' ἀραιὴ
> ἰξὺς εἰλεῖται κόμμα μελαγκράνινον

ὡς σχοίνῳ ἐζωσμένου⟧ μελαγκρα‹ν›ίνας [suppl.
Coray] ἢ τριχίνας ἢ νευρίνας.

μελαγκρανίνας . . . ἐζωσμένου del. Tyrwhitt, scil. ut lemma cum
scholio in textum illatum: μελαγκρανίνας (μελάγκρανις σχοί-
νου εἶδος . . . ἐζωσμένου) ἢ τριχίνας Radt, qui scholium
Straboni ipsi tribuit

1–2 ἀραιῇ | ἰξυῖ Bach: ἀραιὴν | ἰξύν Scaliger: ἀραιὰς | ἰξῦς
Xylander   2 ἰλεῖται, εἰλεῖται, εἰλεῖται codd.: εἴλυται
Meineke   ἄμμα Salmasius: ζῶμα Toup: ῥάμμα Clack
μελάγκραινον, μελαγκραῖνον codd., corr. Meineke: μελαγκρά-
νιον Xylander: μελαγκραῖνον Casaubon

64

GRAMMATICAL FRAGMENTS

30 INTERPRETATION(?)

30 Strabo

. . . and three slings worn round the head, ‹of black-tufted rush, which is a sort of reed from which ropes are woven; and Philitas, too, in the *Interpretation*,[1] says:

> A wretched tunic, all befouled with dirt;
> And round his slender waist is girt a strip
> Of blackly-tufted rush

of a man girdled with a rope of rushes;› of black-tufted rush, or of hair, or of sinews.

---

[1] An unsolved problem: a reference to an otherwise-unattested grammatical work, in which case Philitas would be citing lines not by himself; or is an anonymous glossographer adducing Philitas in an otherwise-unknown poem? The fragment, on account of its metre, cannot be assigned to the *Hermes*. Strabo is describing the inhabitants of the Balearics, but Meineke suggested that Philitas has in mind an abandoned wretch like Virgil's Achaemenides (*Aen.* 3.613–614) or Philoctetes.

31–55 ΑΤΑΚΤΟΙ ΓΛΩΣΣΑΙ

31 Athen. *Deipn.* 11.783 D

ἄμφωτις ξύλινον ποτήριον, ᾧ χρῆσθαι τοὺς ἀγροί-
κους Φιλίτας φησι [τοὺς] ἀμέλγοντας εἰς αὐτὸ καὶ
οὕτως πίνοντας.

ἄμφωξις Kaibel ex Hesych., Et Mag.   [τοὺς] Kaibel

cf. Eustath. ad *Od.* 9.209, i. p. 335.7 Stallbaum

ἡ ἄμφωτις· ξύλινόν φασιν αὕτη ποτήριον, ᾧ χρῆσθαι
τοὺς ⟨ἀγροίκους⟩ ἀμέλγοντας εἰς αὐτὸ καὶ οὕτω πί-
νοντας.

⟨ἀγροίκους⟩ Kuchenmüller

Hesych. α 4166 (cf. EtMag α 1218, 94.7)

ἄμφωξις· ὑδρεῖον ξύλινον ἀγροικικόν, εἰς ὃ καὶ ἀμέλ-
γουσιν.

ἀμφωτίς Salmasius

32 Athen. *Deipn.* 11.783 A

ἄωτον παρὰ Κυπρίοις τὸ ἔκπωμα, ὡς Πάμφιλος. Φιλί-
τας δὲ ποτήριον οὓς οὐκ ἔχον.

cf. *Suda* α 2860

ἄωτον· . . . ἄωτον δὲ ἀγγεῖον, τὸ μὴ ἔχον ὦτα.

31–55 MISCELLANEOUS GLOSSES

31 Athenaeus, *Deipnosophistae*

An *amphōtis* is a wooden drinking-vessel, which according to Philitas is used by rustics, who milk into it and drink from it.

cf. Eustathius on Homer, *Odyssey*

. . . *amphōtis*: this, they say, is a wooden drinking-vessel, used by ⟨rustics⟩ who milk into it and drink from it.

Hesychius

amphōxis: a wooden container for liquids, used by rustics, also used as a milk-pail.

32 Athenaeus, *Deipnosophistae*

aōton is a cup among the Cypriotes; so Pamphilus. Philitas says it is a drinking-vessel without ears.[2]

cf. *Suda*

aōton: . . . and a vessel that is *aōton* is one without ears.

---

[2] cf. Call. fr. 399.2 Pf.

Hesych. α 8997

ἄωτοι· ὦτα μὴ ἔχοντες.

33 Athen. *Deipn*. 11.467 c

γνάλα· Φιλίτας ἐν Ἀτάκτοις Μεγαρέας οὕτω φησὶ
καλεῖν τὰ ποτήρια, γνάλας. Παρθένιος δ' ὁ τοῦ Διονυ-
σίου ἐν α΄ περὶ τῶν παρὰ τοῖς ἱστορικοῖς Λέξεων
ζητουμένων φησί· "γνάλας ποτηρίου εἶδος, ὡς Μαρ-
σύας γράφει . . . οὕτως [FGrH 135–136 F 21]· 'ὅταν
εἰσίῃ ὁ βασιλεὺς εἰς τὴν πόλιν, ὑπαντᾶν οἴνου πλήρη
γνάλαν ἔχοντά τινα, τὸν δὲ λάβοντα σπένδειν'."

γνάλα A, περὶ γύλης mg.: γνάλα ποτήριον Μεγαρικόν C:
γνάλα ποτήρια Μεγαρικά E: γνάλαι Casaubon: γνάλας
Schweighäuser

34 Athen. *Deipn*. 11.467 d–f

δῖνος [δεῖνος codd.]· ὅτι καὶ τοῦτο ποτηρίου ὄνομα . . .
ἐστὶ καὶ γένος ὀρχήσεως . . . Τελέσιλλα δὲ ἡ Ἀργεία
[PMG 723] καὶ τὴν ἅλω καλεῖ δῖνον [δεῖνον A, δῖνον
sscr. εἶ E]. Κυρηναῖοι δὲ τὸν ποδονιπτῆρα δῖνον ὀνο-
μάζουσιν, ὡς Φιλίτας φησιν ἐν Ἀτάκτοις [Ἀττικοῖς
A].

35 Athen. *Deipn*. 11.495 c–e

πέλλα. ἀγγεῖον σκυφοειδές, πυθμένα ἔχον πλατύ-
τερον, εἰς ὃ ἤμελγον τὸ γάλα . . . Κλείταρχος δὲ ἐν

Hesychius

aōtoi: without ears.

33 Athenaeus, *Deipnosophistae*

gyala: Philitas in his *Miscellany* says that this is the name given by the Megarians to drinking-vessels, *gyalas*. Parthenius, son (or pupil) of Dionysius, in the first book of his *On words discussed in the historians*, says: "*Gyalas* is a sort of cup, as Marsyas . . . writes: 'When the king enters the city, he is met by someone holding a *gyalas* full of wine, which he takes, and pours a libation.'."

34 Athenaeus, *Deipnosophistae*

dīnos: this, too, is the name of a cup . . . it is also a sort of dance . . . Telesilla the Argive even calls the threshing-floor *dīnos*. The people of Cyrene call the footbasin *dīnos*, as Philitas says in his *Miscellany*.

35 Athenaeus, *Deipnosophistae*

pella. A vessel in the shape of a skyphos, with a rather broad base, into which they did their milking . . .

ταῖς Γλώσσαις πελλητῆρα μὲν καλεῖν Θεσσαλοὺς καὶ
Αἰολεῖς τὸν ἀμολγέα, πέλλαν δὲ τὸ ποτήριον. Φιλίτας
δ' ἐν Ἀτάκτοις τὴν κύλικα Βοιωτούς.

36 Athen. *Deipn*. 11.496 c

προχύτης· εἶδος ἐκπώματος, ὡς Σιμάριστος ἐν τετάρτῳ
Συνωνύμων. Ἴων δ' ὁ Χῖος ἐν Ἐλεγείοις [fr. 27.2–3 West]·

    ἡμῖν δὲ κρητῆρ' οἰνοχόοι θέραπες
    κιρνάντων προχύταισιν ἐν ἀργυρέοις.

Φιλίτας δ' ἐν Ἀτάκτοις ἀγγεῖον ξύλινον, ἀφ' οὗ τοὺς
ἀγροίκους πίνειν. μνημονεύει αὐτοῦ καὶ Ἀλέξανδρος
†ἐν τιγονι [**24**].

37 Athen. *Deipn*. 11.498 a

σκάλλιον· κυλίκιον μικρόν, ᾧ σπένδουσιν Αἰολεῖς, ὡς
Φιλίτας φησιν ἐν Ἀτάκτοις.

κάλλιον A: σκάλλιον Schweighäuser: σκαλλίον Casaubon ex
Hesych.

cf. Hesych. σ 817

σκαλλίον· κυλίκιον μικρόν. οἱ δὲ σκαλλόν.

Cleitarchus in his *Glosses* says that *pellētēr* is the Thessalian and Aeolian word for a milk-pail, whereas *pella* is the cup. Philitas in his *Miscellany* says that it is the Boeotian word for a wine-cup.[3]

36 Athenaeus, *Deipnosophistae*

prochytēs is a sort of cup, as reported by Simaristus in the fourth book of his *Synonyms*. Ion of Chios in the *Elegies*:

> Let the wine stewards mix a bowl for us
> With silver *prochytai*.

Philitas in the *Miscellany* says it is a wooden vessel from which country-people drink. Alexander also mentions it in the . . .

37 Athenaeus, *Deipnosophistae*

skallion: a miniature wine-cup, with which the Aeolians pour libations, as Philitas says in the *Miscellany*.

cf. Hesychius

skallion: a miniature wine-cup. Others say *skallon*.

---

[3] Philitas stands out from other sources that use the word to mean a milk-pail (first in *Il.* 16.642), but see Phoenix fr. 4.4 P., Lyc. *Al.* 708.

38 Athen. *Deipn.* 14.646 D

ἀμόραι· τὰ μελιτώματα Φιλίτας ἐν Ἀτάκτοις ἀμόρας
φησὶν καλεῖσθαι. μελιτώματα δ' ἐστὶν πεπεμμένα.

πεπεμμένα ‹σὺν μέλιτι› Kayser: ‹μέλιτι› πεπεμμένα conj.
Kaibel

39 Athen. *Deipn.* 14.645 D

κρήϊον· πλακοῦς, ἄρτος, ὃν Ἀργεῖοι παρὰ τῆς νύμφης
πρὸς τὸν νυμφίον φέρουσιν. ὀπτᾶται δ' ἐν ἄνθραξιν,
καὶ καλοῦνται ἐπ' αὐτὸν οἱ φίλοι, παρατίθεται δὲ μετὰ
μέλιτος, ὥς φησιν Φιλίτας ἐν Ἀτάκτοις.

κρήϊον A: κηρίον Kaibel ex Hesych. κ 2546 κηρίον· ... καὶ εἶδος
πλακοῦντος.

40 Athen. *Deipn.* 11.482 E–483 A

κύπελλον· τοῦτο πότερόν ἐστιν ταὐτὸν τῷ ἀλείσῳ καὶ
τῷ δέπαι ‹καὶ μόνον› ὀνόματι διαλλάσσει ... Φιλίτας
δὲ Συρακοσίους κύπελλα καλεῖν τὰ τῆς μάζης καὶ τῶν
ἄρτων ἐπὶ τῆς τραπέζης καταλείμματα.

‹καὶ μόνον› Kaibel: ‹καὶ› ὀνόματι ‹μόνον› Casaubon: ἢ A

38 Athenaeus, *Deipnosophistae*

amorai: in his *Miscellany* Philitas says that honey-cakes are
called *amorai*. Honey-cakes are baked ‹with honey?›.

39 Athenaeus, *Deipnosophistae*

krēion: a cake or loaf, among the Argives carried from the
bride to the bridegroom. It is baked on coals, and friends
are invited to a meal at which it is served with honey, as
Philitas reports in his *Miscellany*.[4]

40 Athenaeus, *Deipnosophistae*

kypellon (cup): is this the same as the *aleison* and the
depas, differing from them only in name ... ? ... Philitas
says that *kypella* is the name given by the Syracusans to
crumbs of barley-cake and bread left behind on the table.

---

[4] A different sense in Euphorion **149** (*Il.* 9.206).

41 Athen. *Deipn*. 3.114 E

Φιλητᾶς δ᾽ ἐν τοῖς Ἀτάκτοις σποδέα καλεῖσθαί τινα
ἄρτον, ὃν ὑπὸ τῶν συγγενῶν μόνον καταναλίσκεσθαι.

σποδέα Schweighäuser: σπολέα codd.   ἐγγενῶν conj.
Kaibel: εὐγενῶν Coray

42 Athen. *Deipn*. 15.678 A

ἀλλὰ μὴν καὶ ἰάκχαν τινὰ καλούμενον οἶδα στέφανον
ὑπὸ Σικυωνίων, ὥς φησι Τιμαχίδας ἐν ταῖς Γλώσσαις.
Φιλίτας δ᾽ οὕτως γράφει· "Ἴακχα, ἐν τῇ Σικυωνίᾳ στε-
φάνωμα εὐῶδες [Φιλίτας . . . εὐῶδες post στέφανον
transt. Hartung]·
    ἕστηκ᾽ ἀμφὶ κόμας εὐώδεας ἀγχόθι πατρὸς
    καλὸν Ἰακχαῖον θηκαμένη στέφανον."

1 ἀμφίκομα A, corr. Villebrune   εὐώδεα Villebrune

cf. Hesych. ι 21 ἰάκχα· στεφάνωμα εὐῶδες ἐν Σικυῶνι;
ibid. θ 567 θιάκχα· ἄνθη ἐν Συκιῶνι; ibid. ι 5 ἰάγχετον·
στεφάνωμα.

43 Athen. *Deipn*. 15.677 B-C

ἰσθμιακόν . . . Φιλίτας δέ φησι· "⟨Ἴσθμιον·⟩ στέφα-
νος ἤγουν ὁμωνυμία ἀμφοτέρωθι οἷον τῆς κεφαλῆς
καὶ τοῦ †πρώτου κόσμου. λέγω δὲ τὸ ἐπὶ τοῦ φρέατος
καὶ τοῦ ἐγχειριδίου ἴσθμιον."

41 Athenaeus, *Deipnosophistae*

Philitas in his *Miscellany* says that *spodeus* is the name of a type of bread which is consumed only by kinsmen.

42 Athenaeus, *Deipnosophistae*

I know, moreover, of a certain kind of garland called *iakcha* by the Sicyonians, as reported by Timachidas in his Glossary. Philitas writes thus: "*Iakcha*, in the Sicyonian region, is a fragrant garland:

> She stands beside her father, having placed
> A fair Iacchus-wreath upon her fragrant locks."[5]

cf. Hesychius ss.vv. *iakcha*: a fragrant garland in Sicyon; *thiakcha*: flowers in Sykion; *iagchetos*: a garland.

43 Athenaeus, *Deipnosophistae*

Isthmiakon . . . and Philitas says: "An Isthmian: a wreath, or rather, a case of homonymity, i.e. as an ‹adornment› for the head ‹and for the neck?›.[6] I note also the *isthmion* of a well, and of a dagger."

---

[5] This is a quotation by, not of, Philitas: it is a rare instance where he can be shown to have cited a poetic text in his *Miscellaneous Glosses* (cf also **52**). The word suggests a connection with Bacchus, Eleusis, or both.

[6] Various solutions have been proposed for the textual corruption; my translation merely supplies one possible sense, founded on the basic meaning "something circular bounding the perimeter of an object". Certainly not all of Philitas' meanings are relevant to *Od.* 18.300, where ancient lexicographers take ἴσθμιον to mean a necklace.

<Ἴσθμιον·> Fränkel: <Ἴσθμιος> Kaibel   πρώτου: τραχή-
λου dub. Dettori post Kuchenmüller: περὶ αὐτῷ Fränkel
κόσμος Lumb   λέγεται δὲ <καὶ> Fränkel   <στόμι-
ον> ἴσθμιον conj. Kaibel: <περιστόμιον> ἴσθ. Fränkel

44 Athen. *Deipn.* 15.678 D

ὑποθυμὶς δὲ καὶ ὑποθυμίδες στέφανοι παρ᾽ Αἰολεῦσιν
καὶ Ἴωσιν, οὓς περὶ τοὺς τραχήλους περιετίθεντο, ὡς
σαφῶς ἔστιν μαθεῖν ἐκ τῆς Ἀλκαίου καὶ Ἀνακρέοντος
ποιήσεως. Φιλίτας δ᾽ ἐν τοῖς Ἀτάκτοις ὑποθυμίδα
[ὑποθυμίδας A, corr. Kaibel] Λεσβίους φησὶν καλεῖν
μυρσίνης κλῶνα, περὶ ὃν πλέκειν ἴα καὶ ἄλλα ἄνθη.

cf. Athen. 15.674 C–D

ἐκάλουν δὲ καὶ οἷς περιεδέοντο τὸν τράχηλον στε-
φάνους ὑποθυμίδας [ὑποθυμιάδας AE], ὡς Ἀλκαῖος ἐν
τούτοις [fr. 362] . . . καὶ Σαπφώ [fr. 94.15–17] καὶ
Ἀνακρέων [PMG 397].

Athen. 15.688 B–C (cf. Plut. *Mor.* 647 E–F)

ἀλλὰ μὴν καὶ τοὺς στεφάνους τοὺς περικειμένους τῷ
στήθει ὑποθυμίδας [ὑποθυμιάδας AE] οἱ ποιηταὶ κε-
κλήκασιν ἀπὸ τῆς τῶν ἀνθῶν ἀναθυμιάσεως, οὐκ ἀπὸ
τοῦ τὴν ψυχὴν θυμὸν καλεῖσθαι, ὥς τινες ἀξιοῦσιν.

Hesych. υ 642

ὑποθυμίς· στέφανος ὑποτράχηλος.

44 Athenaeus, *Deipnosophistae*

Hypothȳmis and *hypothȳmides* are wreaths, in use among the Aeolians and Ionians, which are worn around the neck, as one can learn plainly enough from the poetry of Alcaeus and Anacreon. In his *Miscellany* Philitas says that the Lesbians use the word *hypothȳmis* for a spray of myrtle, around which they twine violets and other flowers.

cf. Athenaeus

They used to call garlands bound around the neck *hypothȳmidas*, as witness Alcaeus in the following verses . . . and Sappho . . . and Anacreon . . .

Athenaeus

However, it is from the exhalations of the flowers that poets have called the garlands laid on the breast *hypothȳmidas*, and not, as some people think, from the fact that the soul is called *thȳmos*.

Hesychius

hypothȳmis: a wreath worn round the neck.

45 EtGen AB, ε 384 L. = EtMag 330.40, ε 402 L.

ἐλινός· ἡ ἄμπελος, ὡς Ἀπολλόδωρος [FGrH 244 F 247]. Φιλήτας δ᾽ ἐν Γλώσσαις τὸν κλάδον τῆς ἀμπέλου.

cf. Σ Nic. *Al.* 181*f*, p. 88 Geymonat

καὶ ἐλίνοιο] τοῦ κλάδου τῆς ἀμπέλου

Hesych. ε 1998

ἐλινοί· κλήματα [τὰ] τῶν ἀμπέλων.

ἐλενοι H, corr. Latte   τὰ del. Latte

46 Σ Ap. Rhod. 4.989*i*, p. 302.7 Wendel

στάχυν ὄμπνιον] πολύν, δαψιλῆ. Φιλητᾶς ἐν Ἀτάκτοις γλώσσαις ἀπέδωκεν ὄμπνιον στάχυν τὸν εὔχυλον καὶ τρόφιμον. Κυρηναίων δέ τινες τὸν πλούσιον καὶ εὐδαίμονα ὄμπνιον καλοῦσιν. ἄμεινον δὲ τὸν φερέσβιον εἰπεῖν, οἱονεὶ ἔμπνοόν τινα ὄντα καὶ ὄμπνιον.

47 Orion, *Etymologicon*, p. 185.32 Sturz (cf. EtGud p. 248.13 de Stefani)

Ἀχαιά· ἡ Δημήτηρ παρὰ Ἀττικοῖς. εἴρηται παρὰ τὸ ἄχος τῆς λύπης [τῆς Κόρης EtGen AB, α 1501, ii. p. 352.4 L.–L.; EtGud; EtMag 180.37, α 2204]. οὕτω Δί-

45 Etymologicum Genuinum

elinos: the vine. Thus Apollodorus. Philitas in his *Glosses* says it is the branch of the vine.

cf. Scholiast on Nicander, *Alexipharmaca*

kai helinoio] The branch of the vine

Hesychius

helinoi: branches of vines.

46 Scholiast on Apollonius of Rhodes, *Argonautica*

"An *ompnios* ear of corn"] Plenteous, abundant. Philitas in the *Miscellaneous Glosses* renders "an *ompnios* ear of corn" as one that is succulent and nourishing. Some of the Cyreneans call one who is rich and prosperous *ompnios*, but it is better to define it as life-giving, as it were animate (*empnoon*) and *ompnion*.[7]

47 Orion, *Etymologicon*

Achaia: Demeter's epithet in Attic writers. It comes from the ache of her grief. Thus Didymus. Also because she

---

[7] A popular word in the Hellenistic poets: see Call. *Hecale* fr. 111 Hollis = 287 Pf., and both editors ad loc. "The demand on Callimachus' readers would be considerably lightened if Philetas had used the words ὄμπνια Θεσμοφόρος together at some important place in the *Demeter*" (Hollis 1978, 402 n. 3).

δυμος. καὶ ὅτι μετὰ κυμβάλων ἠχοῦσα τὴν Κόρην ἐζήτει· ἢ, ὡς Φιλήτας, τὰς ἐρίθους ἀχαιὰς ἐκάλουν.

cf. Hesych. α 8806 Ἀχαία· ἐπίθετον Δήμητρος ... οἱ δὲ ἔρια μαλακά; ibid. α 8877 ἀχιά· ἔρια μαλακά.

48 Hesych. α 3417

ἄμαλλα [ἄμαλλα‹ι› Alberti]· δράγματα, δέσμη τῶν ἀσταχύων. Σοφοκλῆς Τριπτολέμῳ [fr. 607]. ἀγκάλη, δράγματα ρ΄, ὥς φησι Ἴστρος [FGrH 334 F 62], Φιλίτας δὲ ἱστορεῖ ἐκ σ΄. καὶ Ὅμηρος χρῆται τῇ λέξει [Il. 18.553].

cf. Σ Theocr. Id. 10.44a, p. 235.22 Wendel

ἀμαλοδέται δὲ οἱ τὰς ἀμάλας συνδέοντες. ἀμάλη δὲ συνέστηκεν ἐκ δραγμάτων ρ΄ ἢ καὶ ϛ΄.

EtGen AB, α 581, i. p. 370.14 L.–L. = EtSym α 723; EtMag 76.45, α 1007

Ἀμαλλοδετῆρες· οἱ τὰς ἀμάλλας δεσμοῦντες· ἄμαλλα δὲ ἡ ἐκ πολλῶν δραγμάτων συναγωγή.

made an echoing noise with her cymbals when she was searching for Kore. Or, according to Philitas, hired labourers [*or*, weavers] were called *achaiai*.

cf. Hesychius s.v. *Achaia*: an epithet of Demeter . . . according to others, soft wool; *achia*: soft wool.

48 Hesychius

amalla: trusses of corn-stalks, bundles of ears of corn. Sophocles in the *Triptolemus*. Sheaves, consisting of a hundred trusses, according to Istros, but of two hundred according to Philitas. Homer, too, uses the word.[8]

cf. Scholiast on Theocritus, *Idylls*

Amalodetai are those who bind together the *amalai* (sheaves). A sheaf consists of a hundred or two hundred trusses.

Etymologicum Genuinum

amallodetēres: those who bind the sheaves. A sheaf is a gathering of many trusses.

---

[8] While Hesychius does not preserve the context in which Philitas discussed the word, it elsewhere occurs in cultic contexts, connected with the culture-hero Triptolemus (Sophocles fr. 607 Radt) or with Delian Apollo and his retinue (Call. 186.27 Pf.; Euphorion **66**).

49 Hesych. β 71

βαίβυκος· πελεκᾶνος Φιλίτας, Ἀμερίας ⟨δὲ⟩ βαυβυ-
κᾶνας.

βαβυκως πελεκαν ως H, corr. Dindorf e Choerob.   αμερι-
ασας H, corr. Musurus   ⟨δὲ⟩ Dobree   βαυκαλας H,
corr. O. Hoffmann ex Hesych. β 355 βαυβυκᾶνες· πελεκᾶνες

cf. Choeroboscus, Εἰς τὸ ὀνοματικόν, i. p. 80.19 Gaisford

βαῖβυξ βαίβυκος (βαίβυχες δὲ λέγονται οἱ πελε-
κᾶνες)

50 Σ Ap. Rhod. 2.279a, p. 148.7 Wendel (cf. EtGen AB
s.v. πρόκας; EtMag 689.15; ps.-Zon., col. 1579 Tittmann)

ἠὲ πρόκας ἰχνεύοντες] ζῷόν τι ὅμοιον ἐλάφῳ, ὁ
λεγόμενος νεβρός. Διονύσιος δέ φησιν ὁ Ἀθηναῖος ἐν
ταῖς Κτίσεσι [FHG iv. p. 395, fr. 12] τὰς ἐλάφους οὕτω
λέγεσθαι, πρόκας . . . Φιλητᾶς δέ φησι πρόκας
λέγεσθαι ἐλάφους τὰς πρώτως τικτομένας, οἷον πρω-
τοτόκους.

κυήσεσι codd. Ap. Rhod.: corr. Sylburg

51 Hesych. σ 893

σκεῖρος· ῥύπος. καὶ ὁ δριμὺς τυρός. καὶ ἄλσος καὶ
δρυμός. Φιλητᾶς δὲ τὴν ῥυπώδη γῆν.

σκῖρος M. Schmidt   πυρρώδη H, corr. Meineke: γνψώδη

GRAMMATICAL FRAGMENTS

49 Hesychius

baibykos: "of a pelican", Philitas; *baubykanas,* Amerias.

cf. Choeroboscus, *On the substantive*
baibyx–baibykos (*baibyches* means "pelicans").

50 Scholiast on Apollonius of Rhodes, *Argonautica*

"Or hunting *prokas*"] An animal like a deer; what is known
as a fawn. Dionysius of Athens in his *Foundations* say that
female deer are named thus, *prokas* . . . Philitas says that
prokas is the name given to female deer when they bear
young for the first time: does with their first offspring.[9]

51 Hesychius

skeiros: filth. Also, tangy cheese. Also, a grove, a copse.
Philitas defines it as filthy earth.[10]

---

[9] The word occurs in *Od.* 17.295; Philitas may have taken it
thence. So too the later Hellenistic poets who use it (Call. *Hymn*
3.154, 5.92, *al.*): it is not clear that it was mediated through
Philitas.

[10] Aristarchus read σκῖρος in an uncertain sense (thicket?
chalky soil?) at *Il.* 23.332–333.

PHILITAS

conj. Dettori ex Eustath. ad *Il*. 23.332–333, iv. 742.13 van der Valk
. . . ὁ σκῖρος καὶ γύψον ἢ γῆν γυψώδη δηλοῖ.

52 Hesych. σ 1148

σκύζης· παρὰ Φιλίτᾳ· "παύσω σε τῆς σκύζης" [Adesp.
Com. fr. 740 K.], ἀντὶ τοῦ τῆς κάπρας [cf. Hesych. κ
738].

σχύζης H, corr. Musurus

53 Hesych. υ 262

†ὑπ' αὐνήν· παρ' Ἑκαταίῳ [*FGrH* 1 F 365]. Φιλίτας.

ὑπ' Ἄχνην (cf. **26**) LSJ: ὑπ' αὐλήν· ⟨ὑπ' οἶκον⟩ (cf. υ 260)
Kuchenmüller

54 Hesych. υ 274

ὑπεζῶσθαι· τὸ εἰς ἄνδρας ἐλθεῖν. Φιλήτας.

ἀλίδρας cod., corr. Salmasius: ἀλινδήθρας Junius (id est, aream
sive palaestram)

55 Hesych. θ 405

Θεσσαλαί· αἱ Κῷαι παρὰ Φιλήτᾳ καὶ αἱ φαρμακίδες.

θεσπάλαι H, corr. Salmasius

de Δήμητρι cogitavit Kuchenmüller, attrib. Spanoudakis

52 Hesychius

skyzēs: in Philitas: "I'll put a stop to your *skyzēs*", that is, lewdness.[11]

53 Hesychius

"under the *aunēn*": in Hecataeus. Philitas.[12]

54 Hesychius

"to gird oneself up": come to man's estate. Philitas.

55 Hesychius

Thessalai: Coan women in Philitas,[13] and witches.

[11] The words scan as an iambus. Another anonymous literary citation (cf **42**), presumably from comedy; or did Philitas write iambic verse?

[12] The presence of an author's name, but absence of any gloss, is quite out of character with the rest of the fragments, and very likely indicates corruption.

[13] Genealogical connections were traced between Thessaly and Cos. Although this has been ranked among the poetic fragments, it is as a glossographer that Hesychius cites Philitas elsewhere.

85

56–58 INCERTI LOCI

56 Σ A *Il.* 2.269c, i. p. 242.24 Erbse

ἀλγήσας δ᾽ ἀχρεῖον ἰδών] ὅτι Φιλίτας [Φιλιτᾶς cod.]
τὸ ἰδών περισπᾷ, οἷον τῶν ὀφθαλμῶν, ἰδεῶν. οὐδέποτε
δὲ Ὅμηρος ἰδέας τοὺς ὀφθαλμοὺς εἶπεν. ἔστιν οὖν τὸ
ἀχρεῖον ἰδών εὐτελῶς σχηματίσας.

cf. gloss. interl. cod. A ad loc., ii. 312.33 Dindorf: ἰδών·
ὀξύνεται· μετοχὴ γάρ ἐστι.

57

(a) Σ A *Il.* 21.126–127a, v. p. 148.59 Erbse

θρώσκων τις κατὰ κῦμα μέλαιναν φρῖχ᾽ ὑπαΐξει ⟨|
ἰχθύς, ὅς κε φάγῃσι- -δημόν⟩] πρὸς τὸ σημαινό-
μενον· Φιλήτας γὰρ καὶ Καλλίστρατος γράφουσι·
"φρῖχ᾽ ὑπαλύξει", λέγοντες ὅτι οἱ πίονες τῶν ἰχθύων
καὶ εὔτροφοι τὸ ψῦχος ὑπομένουσι καὶ οὐ φθείρονται.
ὁ δὲ ποιητὴς οὐδέποτε φρίκην τὸ ψῦχος εἴρηκεν, ἀλλὰ
τὸ ἐκ γαλήνης πρῶτον ἐξορθούμενον κῦμα.

lemma suppl. Friedländer   Diple ante utrumque versum in
A, unde ⟨ἡ διπλῆ⟩ πρὸς τὸ σημαινόμενον Villoison: ⟨αἱ δι-
πλαὶ⟩ πρὸς τὸ σ. Erbse

56–58 FRAGMENTS OF UNCERTAIN
LOCATION[14]

56 Scholiast on Homer, *Iliad*

"In pain, with an impotent look"] Philitas places a circumflex accent on *idōn* ("looking"), making it refer to eyes, *ideōn*. But Homer never calls eyes *ideas*; instead he has used "with an impotent look" in an ordinary construction.

cf. interlinear gloss ad loc.: *idōn*: is oxytone. It is a participle.

57

(a) Scholiast on Homer, *Iliad*

"Leaping through the waves a fish will dart up to the dark ripple, to eat the fat . . ."] With regard to what is meant: Philitas and Callistratus adopt the reading "will escape the chill", explaining that the rich and well-fed fish endure the cold and do not die of it. But the poet never uses *phrīkē* to mean cold, but the first ripples that stir on the surface after a calm.

[14] The following fragments concern the text and interpretation of Homer. Their provenance is uncertain (perhaps the *Hermeneia*, **30**?).

(b) Σ bT ibid., v. p. 152.94 Erbse

Φιλίτας δὲ ἀρεσκόμενος τῇ "ὑπαλύξει" γραφῇ φησιν
ὡς ἐκεῖνος ὁ λιπανθεὶς ἰχθὺς ὑπὸ τοῦ δημοῦ τὴν
ψυχρασίαν ὑπαλύξει.

(c) P. Oxy. 221, col. iv. ll. 26–32, Σ ibid.

[Φιλίτας καὶ Καλλίστρατος]
δὲ "ὑ[παλύξει" γράφουσι, λέγοντες ὅτι ὁ]
ἰχθ[ὺς ὁ Λυκάονος τὸν δημὸν φαγὼν]
π{ε}ιμ[ελώδης γενόμενος τὸ κρύ-]
30   ος φε[ύξεται. ἀγνοεῖ δὲ ὅτι τὸ δια-]
νεστ[ηκὸς τῆς θαλάσσης ἐπιπολῆς,]
οὐ τὸ κ[ρύος φησὶν Ὅμηρος φρῖκα·]

Suppl. Grenfell–Hunt, Erbse (v. pp. 86–87)

(d) Σ A *Il.* 6.459, ii. p. 209.30 Erbse

εἴπῃσιν] ὅτι τὸ "εἴπῃσιν" ἀντὶ τοῦ "εἴποι ἄν". ἡ δὲ
ἀναφορὰ πρὸς Φιλίταν [Φιλητὰ cod.] γράφοντα
"θρῴσκων τις κατὰ κῦμα μέλαιναν φρῖχ᾽ ὑπαλύξει".
οὗτος γὰρ μὴ νοήσας ὅτι τὸ "ὑπαΐξει" ἐστὶ τὸ ἐφορ-
μῆσαι ὑπὸ τὴν φρῖκα, τουτέστι τὸ τοῦ ὕδατος ἐπα-
νάστημα, ὃς φάγοι ἂν Λυκάονος τοῦ δημοῦ, τὴν φρῖ-
κα ἐδέξατο τὴν ὑπὸ τοῦ ψύχους γινομένην φρίκην καὶ
φησι τοὺς πιμελώδεις τῶν ἰχθύων ὑπομένειν τὸ ψῦχος,
ὥστε ὃς ἂν τὸ τοῦ Λυκάονος λίπος φάγῃ, ἐκκλινεῖ τὴν
φρίκην.

(b) Scholiast ibid.

Favouring the reading "will escape", Philitas says that the fish glutted on human fat will escape the cold.

(c) P. Oxy. 221

        Philitas and Callistratus
adopt the reading "will escape", explaining that the
fish that has eaten Lycaon's fat
will be fattened itself and escape
the cold. He is unaware that it is the   [30]
ruffling of the surface of the sea,
not the cold, that Homer calls *phrīx*.

(d) Scholiast on Homer, *Iliad*

eipēsin] "May say" instead of "might say". See Philitas, where he adopts the reading "Leaping through the waves (a fish) will dart up to the dark ripple". For, as he did not know that "dart up" means to rush up to the ripple, that is, to the disquieted surface of the water, in order to eat Lycaon's fat, he understood *phrīx* to mean shivering due to cold, and says that the fattened fish endure the cold, so that the fish that eats the fat of Lycaon will avoid the shivering cold.[15]

---

[15] Philitas is cited here and in the next fragment for his interpretation of *Il.* 21.127 ὅς κε φάγῃσι, not as a relative clause with a final sense ("that it might eat"), but as an indefinite relative ("whichever fish eats").

ὑπαίξει] ὑπαῖξαι conj. Erbse   πημελώδεις A, corr. Villoison
φάγῃ] φάγοι A, corr. Friedländer

(e) Σ A *Il.* 7.171*a*, ii. p. 258.41 Erbse

⟨ὅς κε λάχῃσιν⟩] ὅτι τηρεῖ τὴν διαφορὰν τοῦ κλη-
ρώσασθαι καὶ λαχεῖν. καὶ πρὸς τὸ "λάχῃσιν", ὅτι ὃς
ἂν λάχοι. ἡ δὲ ἀναφορὰ πρὸς τὸ "ἰχθύς, ὅς κε φάγῃσι"
πρὸς Φιλίταν.

λάχοι] λάχῃ A, corr. Friedländer

(f) Porphyrius, *Quaest. Hom.* lib. 1, Rec. χ, p. 45.13
Sodano

Φιλητᾶς δὲ τῇ "ὑπαλύξει" γραφῇ συντιθέμενός φησιν,
ὅτι ὁ φαγὼν ἰχθῦς τὸν Λυκάονος δημὸν πιμελώδης
γενόμενος τὸ κρύος ἐκφεύξεται. ἀγνοεῖ δὲ καὶ τοῦτο,
ὅτι τὸ διανεστηκὸς τῆς θαλάσσης ἐπιπολῆς, οὐ τὸ
κρύος φησὶν Ὅμηρος φρῖκα.

58

(a) Eustath. ad *Il.* 21.252, iv. p. 496.26 van der Valk

Τὸ δὲ "αἰετοῦ οἴματ᾽ ἔχων" Φιλήτας, φασί, γράφει
"αἰετοῦ ὄμματ᾽ ἔχων". κρεῖττον δὲ τὸ οἴματα, ᾧ ἀκό-
λουθον καὶ τὸ "οἴμησε δ᾽ ἀλείς" [*Il.* 22.308].

GRAMMATICAL FRAGMENTS

(e) Scholiast on Homer, *Iliad*

"To whomsoever the lot falls"] He observes the distinction between "to cast lots" and "to obtain by lot". As for "the lot falls", it stands for "the lot might fall" [i.e., the optative]. See Philitas, the note on "the fish, which eats".

(f) Porphyry, *Homeric Questions*

Adopting the reading "will escape", Philitas says that the fish that eats the fat of Lycaon will become fattened and not suffer the cold. He is also unaware of this, that Homer calls the ruffled surface of the water, not the cold, *phrīx*.

58

(a) Eustathius on Homer, *Iliad*

For "with the swoop of an eagle" Philitas is reported to prefer the reading "with the eyes of an eagle". But "swoop" is better, and is in keeping with "he collected himself together and swooped".

(b) Σ A *Il.* 22.308*a*, v. p. 324.73 Erbse (cf. Σ T ibid.)

οἴμησεν δὲ ἀλεὶς ‹ὥς τ᾽ αἰετὸς ὑψιπετήεις›] ὅτι κἀκεῖ
[sc. *Il.* 21.252] γραπτέον "αἰετοῦ οἴματ᾽ ἔχων", οὐχ ὡς
Φιλήτας "ὄμματα".

59–60 INCERTA

59 Σ A *Il.* 1.524*c*, i. p. 142.78 Erbse

κεφαλῇ κατανεύσομαι] οὕτως "κατανεύσομαι", οὐχὶ
"ἐπινεύσομαι" Ἀρίσταρχος ἐν τοῖς Πρὸς Φιλίταν προ-
φέρεται.

60 Σ A *Il.* 2.111*b*, i. p. 202.69 Erbse

Ζεύς με μέγα Κρονίδης] . . . ἐν γοῦν τῷ Πρὸς Φιλίταν
συγγράμματι τῇ γραφῇ [sc. μέγας] κέχρηται [sc.
Ἀρίσταρχος], δύο λέγων τὸ μέγας σημαίνειν, τοτὲ μὲν
τὸ καθ᾽ αὑτό, καθάπερ νῦν "Ζεύς με μέγα‹ς› Κρονί-
δης" καὶ "κεῖτο μέγας μεγαλωστί, λελασμένος ἱππο-
συνάων" [*Il.* 16.776], τοτὲ δὲ αὖ τὸ πρὸς τὴν κατὰ τὸν
Αἴαντα τὸν ἕτερον διάκρισιν "Αἴας δ᾽ ὁ μέγας" [*Il.*
16.358].

μέγα‹ς› suppl. Villoison

(b) Scholiast on Homer, *Iliad*

"He collected himself together and swooped, like a high-flying eagle"] There, too, one should adopt the reading "with the swoop of an eagle", not, with Philitas, "eyes".

59–60 UNCERTAIN

In the following two cases, it is uncertain whether the readings challenged by Aristarchus go back to Philitas or not:

59 Scholiast on Homer, *Iliad*

"I shall nod with my head": Aristarchus in his *Against Philitas* cites it thus, *kataneusomai* ("nod"), not *epineusomai*.[16]

60 Scholiast on Homer, *Iliad*

"Zeus the son of Cronos has greatly . . ."] In the treatise *Against Philitas*, he (Aristarchus) adopts the reading "mighty" (i.e., the adjective), explaining that *megas* has two significations: one in and of itself, as here, "Zeus the mighty son of Cronos", and "he lay, a mighty man mightily fallen, forgetful of his horsemanship", and the other in order to distinguish one Ajax from the other, "Ajax the great(er)".[17]

[16] From which we infer that Aristarchus' target preferred the latter form.
[17] From which we infer that Aristarchus' target preferred the better-attested adverbial form.

COMPARATIVE NUMERATION

I. CONVERSION OF OTHER EDITIONS TO THIS EDITION
Table to be read as follows: fr. 1 Diehl = fr. 3 Lightfoot;
fr. 1 Kuchenmüller = fr. 9 Lightfoot, etc.

	Diehl	Powell	Kuchenmüller	Spanoudakis	Sbardella	Dett
1	3	1	9	9	9	31
2	4	3	12	11	10	32
3	1	2	10	10	11	33
4	30	14	11	12	12	34
5	10	9	1	23	1	35
6	11	10	2	21	2	36
7	12	12	3	24	3	37
8	8	11	4	22	4	38
9	7.1–2	23	13	1	5	39
10	6	8	8	2	16	40
11	7.3–4	7.1–2	15	27	21	41
12	2	7.3–4	7	4	8	42
13	14	6	6	3	7	43
14	17	22	17	20	6	44
15	15	13	21	55	13	45
16	20	15	55	5	14	46
17	16	30	14	18	20	47
18	21	17	20	19	15	48
19	18	18	19	14	17	49
20	19	19	22	15	18	50

21	23	24	18	16	19	51
22	22	20	23	13	22	52
23		16	24	7	23	53
24		21	27	6	24	54
25		28	26	8	55	55
26		—	25	25	25	56
27		42	16	17	26	57
28			28	26	27	58
29			31	31	28	30
30			32	32	29	59
31			33	33	30	60
32			34	34		
33			35	35		
34			36	36		
35			37	37		
36			38	38		
37			39	39		
38			40	40		
39			41	41		
40			42	42		
41			43	43		
42			44	44		
43			45	45		
44			46	46		
45			47	47		
46			48	48		
47			49	49		
48			50	50		
49			51	51		
50			52	52		
51			53	53		
52			54	54		
53			30	30		

54	59	59
55	60	60
56	56	56
57	57	57
58	58	58

II. Conversion of This Edition to Other Editions

1	3	1	5	9	5	
2	12	3	6	10	6	
3	1	2	7	13	7	
4	2	2.3–4	8	12	8	
5	—	—	—	16	9	
6	10	13	13	24	14	
7	9 + 11	11–12	12	23	13	
8	8	10	10	25	12	
9	—	5	1	1	1	
10	5	6	3	3	2	
11	6	8	4	2	3	
12	7	7	2	4	4	
13	—	15	9	22	15	
14	13	4	17	19	16	
15	15	16	11	20	18	
16	cf. 17	23	27	21	10	fr. mai trib. 3
17	14	18	14	27	19	
18	19	19	21	17	20	
19	20	20	19	18	21	
20	16	22	18	14	17	
21	18	24	15	6	11	
22	22	14	20	8	22	
23	21	9	22	5	23	
24	—	21	23	7	24	
25	—	—	26	26	26	

26	—	—	25	28	27	fr. male trib. 38
27	—	—	24	11	28	fr. male trib. 37
28		25	28	fr. fals. 3	29	
29	—	—	—	cf. pp. 17–18	30	
30	4	17	53	53	31	fr. dub. 29
31			29	29		1
32			30	30		2
33			31	31		3
34			32	32		4
35			33	33		5
36			34	34		6
37			35	35		7
38			36	36		8
39			37	37		9
40			38	38		10
41			39	39		11
42			40	40		12
43			41	41		13
44			42	42		14
45			43	43		15
46			44	44		16
47			45	45		17
48			46	46		18
49			47	47		19
50			48	48		20
51			49	49		21
52			50	50		22
53			51	51		23
54			52	52		24
55			16	15		25

ALEXANDER OF AETOLIA

INTRODUCTION

We know more about the life of Alexander of Aetolia than about many other early Hellenistic figures, partly because he is mentioned in the *Lives of Aratus*. The first one gives his *floruit* as 280–276, and another names Callimachus, as well as Aratus, as a contemporary. He came from Pleuron (Test. **1**), but was one of many who forsook their provincial origins for greater cultural centres:[1] in Alexander's case, Pella, where Antigonus Gonatas was also patron of poets and philosophers such as Aratus, Antagoras, Timon of Phlius, and Bion of Borysthenes (Test. **2**, **3**, **5**, **6**); and Alexandria, where Ptolemy Philadelphus hired him to "correct" the texts of tragedy (Test. **6**, **7**; Test. **7e** adds satyr drama). He stands in the broad tradition of scholar-poets, a γραμματικός (Test. **1**) like Antimachus, Philitas, Simmias of Rhodes, Callimachus, Nicander, Lycophron and others. The word used in the Greek sources for his work on the texts of tragedy at the court of Ptolemy is ὀρθοῦν or διορθοῦν (Test. **7**)—whatever that means exactly.[2] He was

---

[1] Like his fellow-Aetolian Arcesilaus of Pitane, head of the Academy in Athens (Diog. Laert. 4.28). *Suda ν* 374 and the *Vita Nicandri* also record a tradition of Aetolian origin for the, or *a*, poet Nicander, who is credited with an Αἰτωλικά.

[2] See General Introduction and n. 6 there.

also active as a tragic poet (Test. **8**, **10**) and was included in a group of seven tragedians called the *Pleias* (Test. **1**, **9**).

Generic diversity and range of interests are among the most obvious features of the surviving evidence about his poetry. Apart from tragedy, and possibly satyr drama, we know of elegiac and hexameter poetry and epigrams, and Ionic or "cinaedological" (scurrilous) verse which witnesses (**18**) mention in the same breath as that of Sotades, although it is not clear whether Alexander used the same, Sotadean, metre. This diversity invites comparison with that of Callimachus himself (Test. 1 Pf.). Some fragments reveal an interest in mythological subjects (Glaucus the sea-god, **3**; Circe, **4**; cf. also **9**, **11**, **12**, **14**, fr. dub. **21**, **22**), in some cases perhaps in the form of epyllia; the mythico-historical story of Antheus, **5**, from the *Apollo*, seems to be a playful, Hellenistic experiment with narrative in the form of prophecy. The *Phaenomena* (**7**) obviously makes one think of Aratus, Alexander's contemporary at the court of Antigonus Gonatas, although nothing else is known about the work (not even its metre—or even whether it was in metre).

The other quality is its literariness, which is to say that it evinces an interest in literary history, in evaluations and assessments of literary figures, and perhaps even a recreative interest in classical metres (see on **19** below). The *Musae* was an elegiac poem from which one certain fragment (**6**) deals with Timotheus' hymn for the temple of Artemis at Ephesus, and another possible or likely fragment (**8**) with two epic parodists active in Sicily. The first discusses the circumstances of a certain work's composition; the second surveys an *oeuvre*; both deal with relatively recent literary history, within the last century at least. The title *Musae* suggests a poem about poetry, perhaps a literary review. If so, this would be an early, perhaps the earliest, example of Hellenistic catalogue poetry on a literary subject, with other examples including Callimachus' Γραφεῖον (fr. 380 Pf.) and even the catalogue from Hermesianax's *Leontion* (Hermesianax **3**).[3] A mock epitaph for Alcman (**2**) is also literary-historical in emphasis: the poet himself reviews his achievement, entering the discussion about his place of origin (Sardis or Sparta), and seeming to allude to a famous passage from Archilochus concerning the Lydian tyrant Gyges (fr. 19.1–3 West).[4] A fragment from an unknown work discusses Euripides (**19**), but there are frustrating alternative attributions to Alexander and to Aristophanes. The metre is particularly associated with Old Comedy, and if the attribution to Alexander is correct (he may have discussed Euripides' biography elsewhere: **23**), it is possible that he was trying to capture the effect of a genre where Euripides was often held up for criticism. Here, though, the tone is not hostile: the speaker—unfortunately unknown—does not make the assumption, standard in Aristophanes and in ancient biography in general, that the man's works reflect his character, but instead contrasts his personal demeanour with the character of his literary works.[5]

The fragments of Alexander do not suggest much of Callimachus' *avant garde* quality; but in his polyeideia, use of elegy, perhaps specifically catalogue elegy, interest in literary history, and scholarly activites, Alexander is a true Hellenistic, and indeed Alexandrian, poet.[6]

---

[3] Cameron 1995, 383; d'Alessio 2000, 427–428.

[4] For Alexander and Stesichorus, see **11**, **12**.

[5] d'Alessio 2000, 428–429.

[6] Magnelli 2000, 123–124.

EDITIONS

For a complete list of the editions of Alexander of Aetolia, see E. Magnelli (as below), 57–58.

Among the most important, see:

A. Meineke, *Analecta Alexandrina* (Berlin, 1843; repr. Hildesheim, 1964), 215–251.

T. Bergk, *Anthologia Lyrica* (Leipzig, ²1868), 139–141.

J. U. Powell, *Collectanea Alexandrina* (Oxford, 1925), 121–130.

E. Diehl, *Anthologia Lyrica Graeca*, vol. ii. 6 (Leipzig, ²1942), 74–80.

J. Defradas, *Les élegiaques grecs. Édition, introduction et commentaire* (Paris, 1962), 106–108 [**5** only].

B. Snell (ed.), *Tragicorum Graecorum Fragmenta*, i. (Göttingen, 1986), no. 101 [**14**, **17** only].

E. Magnelli, *Alexandri Aetoli: Testimonia et Fragmenta* (Florence, 1999).

CRITICISM

G. B. d'Alessio, rev. of Magnelli, *Eikasmos* 11 (2000), 425–430.

M. Di Marco, "Euripides in Alessandro Etolo (fr. 7 Magnelli). Una nuova ipotesi", *SemRom* 6 (2003), 65–70.

H. Lloyd-Jones, "Alexander Aetolus, Aristophanes and the Life of Euripides", in *Storia poesia e pensiero nel mondo antico: Studi in onore di M. Gigante* (Naples, 1994), 371–379.

——*Supplementum Supplementi Hellenistici* (Berlin and New York, 2005), 2–3.

E. Magnelli, "Alessandro Etole poeta 'di provincia' (o i limiti del callimachismo)", in R. Pretagostini (ed.), *La letteratura ellenistica. Problemi e prospettive di ricerca. Atti del colloquio internazionale* (Rome, 2000), 113–126.

D. Ricci, "Alessandro Etolo e l'origine novellistica dell'elegia su Anteo e la moglie di Fobio (fr. 3 Pow.)", *QUCC* 56 (1997), 125–139.

C. M. Schroeder, "Hesiod and the fragments of Alexander Aetolus", in M. A. Harder, R. F. Regtuit & G. C. Wakker (edd.), *Beyond the Canon* (Leuven, 2006), 287–302.

K. Spanoudakis, "Alexander Aetolus' *Astragalistai*", *Eikasmos* 16 (2005), 149–154.

TESTIMONIA

1 *Suda* α 1127

Ἀλέξανδρος Αἰτωλός· ἐκ πόλεως Πλευρῶνος, υἱὸς Σατύρου καὶ Στρατοκλείας, γραμματικός. οὗτος καὶ τραγῳδίας ἔγραψεν, ὡς καὶ τῶν ἑπτὰ τραγικῶν ἕνα κριθῆναι, οἵπερ ἐπεκλήθησαν ἡ Πλειάς.

2 *Suda* α 3745

γεγονὼς [sc. Ἄρατος] ἐν τῇ ρκδ′ Ὀλυμπιάδι [284–280], ὅτε ἦν Ἀντίγονος βασιλεὺς Μακεδονίας, υἱὸς Δημητρίου τοῦ Πολιορκητοῦ, ὁ Γονατᾶς κληθείς· καὶ συνῴκει τε αὐτῷ καὶ παρ' αὐτῷ ἐτελεύτησε, σύγχρονος Ἀνταγόρᾳ τῷ Ῥοδίῳ καὶ Ἀλεξάνδρῳ τῷ Αἰτωλῷ.

3 Vita Arati (Vita 1), p. 8.12 Martin

γέγονε δὲ Ἀντίγονος κατὰ τὴν ρκε′ Ὀλυμπιάδα [280–276], καθ' ὃν χρόνον ἤκμασεν ὁ Ἄρατος καὶ Ἀλέξανδρος ὁ Αἰτωλός. μέμνηται δὲ τοῦ Κατόπτρου Εὐδόξου [fr. 6 Lasserre] καὶ Ἀντιγόνου ‹καὶ› Ἀλεξάνδρου τοῦ

TESTIMONIA

1 *Suda*

Alexander of Aetolia. From the city Pleuron, son of Satyrus and Stratocleia, grammarian. He also wrote tragedies, so that he was included among the seven tragedians who were known as the *Pleias*.

2 *Suda* s.v. Aratus

Lived[1] in the 124th Olympiad, when the king of Macedon was Antigonus son of Demetrius Poliorcetes, known as Gonatas. He spent time at his court and died there, a contemporary of Antagoras of Rhodes and Alexander of Aetolia.

3 *Life of Aratus* 1

Antigonus became ⟨king⟩[2] in the 125th Olympiad, at the time when Aratus and Alexander of Aetolia were at the height of their powers. Aratus in his own letters mentions the *Mirror* of Eudoxus and Antigonus and Alexander

---

[1] Both the *Suda* and *Life of Aratus* 1 seems to have confused or over-simplified a notice that Antigonus Gonatas came to the throne in the 125th or 124th Olympiad, and that Aratus (and other poets including Alexander) spent time at his court.

[2] See n. above.

Αἰτωλοῦ καὶ ὡς ἠξιώθη ὑπὸ τοῦ βασιλέως γράψαι ἐν ταῖς ἰδίαις ἐπιστολαῖς Ἄρατος [SH 119].

4 Vita Arati (Vita 2), p. 11.5 Martin = Philitas Test. **6**

[ἐν] τοῖς χρόνοις δὲ ἐγένετο κατὰ Φιλάδελφον τὸν βασιλέα, συνήκμαζε δὲ Ἀλεξάνδρῳ τῷ Αἰτωλῷ καὶ Φιλητᾷ καὶ Διονυσίῳ τῷ φιλοσόφῳ ⟨τῷ⟩ εἰς ἡδονὰς μεταθεμένῳ.

[ἐν] Westermann

5 Vita Arati (Vita 3) / Aratus Latinus, p. 15.17–26 Martin

(a) . . . Δημητρίου δὲ Ἀντίγονος ὁ Γονατᾶς, παρ' ᾧ διέτριβεν αὐτός, καὶ σὺν αὐτῷ Περσεὺς ὁ Στωικὸς καὶ Ἀνταγόρας ὁ Ῥόδιος ὁ τὴν Θηβαΐδα ποιήσας καὶ Ἀλέξανδρος ὁ Αἰτωλός, ὡς αὐτός φησιν ὁ Ἀντίγονος ἐν τοῖς πρὸς Ἱερώνυμον.

(b) . . . Demetrii autem Antigonus Geniculosus, apud quem frequentabat ut Perseus Stoicus et Antagoras Rodius qui Thebaida fecit et Alexander Aetolus, ut ipse ait Antigonus apud quem Hieronimus.

6 Vita Arati (Vita 4), p. 19.4–8 Martin = Philitas Test. **6**

ἦν δὲ ἐπὶ Πτολεμαίου τοῦ Φιλαδέλφου, καὶ ἐσχόλασε Διονυσίῳ τῷ Ἡρακλεώτῃ, συνῆν δὲ Ἀντιγόνῳ τῷ

of Aetolia, and how he was asked by the king to write (*sc.* the *Phaenomena*).

4 *Life of Aratus* 2

As to his date, he (sc. Aratus) lived at the time of Philadelphus the king, and he flourished at the same time as Alexander of Aetolia, Philitas, and Dionysius the philosopher who converted to hedonism.[3]

5 *Life of Aratus* 3 / Latin *Life of Aratus*

Demetrius' son was Antigonus Gonatas, at whose court he (Aratus) was resident, and with him Perseus the Stoic, Antagoras of Rhodes the author of the *Thebais*, and Alexander of Aetolia, as Antigonus says in his *Against Hieronymus*.

6 *Life of Aratus* 4

He lived in the time of Ptolemy Philadelphus, and studied with Dionysius of Heraclea. He lived at the court of

---

[3] For Philitas, see Philitas, Test. **6** and n. 4 ad loc.; for Dionysius, *RE* v (1905), s.v. Dionysius (no. 119), 973–974.

ALEXANDER OF AETOLIA

Μακεδονίας βασιλεῖ καὶ Φίλᾳ τῇ τούτου γαμετῇ,
συνήκμασε δὲ Ἀλεξάνδρῳ τῷ Αἰτωλῷ καὶ Καλλιμάχῳ
καὶ †Μελάνδριῳ καὶ Φιλιτᾷ.

Μενάνδρῳ, μελανχρίῳ, μελανδρίῳ codd. (om. SV): Νικάνδρῳ
Ritschl: Μαιανδρίῳ Meineke: Λεανδρίῳ Wendel, *Hermes* 70
(1935), 360

7 Tzetzes, *Prolegomena de comoedia Aristophanis*

(a) Proemium I, 1–7, p. 22 Koster

Ἀλέξανδρος ὁ Αἰτωλὸς καὶ Λυκόφρων ὁ Χαλκιδεὺς
μεγαλοδωρίαις βασιλικαῖς προτραπέντες Πτολεμαίῳ
τῷ Φιλαδέλφῳ τὰς σκηνικὰς διωρθώσαντο βίβλους,
τὰς τῆς κωμῳδίας καὶ τραγῳδίας καὶ τὰς τῶν σατύ-
ρων φημί, συμπαρόντος αὐτοῖς καὶ συνανορθοῦντος
καὶ τοῦ τοιούτου βιβλιοφύλακος τῆς τοσαύτης βιβλι-
οθήκης Ἐρατοσθένους· ὧν βίβλων τοὺς πίνακας Καλ-
λίμαχος ἀπεγράψατο [Test. 14b Pf.]. Ἀλέξανδρος ὤρ-
θου τὰ τραγικά, Λυκόφρων τὰ κωμικά· νεανίαι ἦσαν
Καλλίμαχος καὶ Ἐρατοσθένης.

(b) Proemium II, 1–4, pp. 31–32 Koster

Ἀλέξανδρος ὁ Αἰτωλὸς καὶ Λυκόφρων ὁ Χαλκιδεύς,
ἀλλὰ καὶ Ζηνόδοτος ὁ Ἐφέσιος τῷ Φιλαδέλφῳ Πτολε-
μαίῳ συνωθηθέντες βασιλικῶς ὁ μὲν τὰς τῆς τραγῳ-
δίας, Λυκόφρων δὲ τὰς τῆς κωμῳδίας βίβλους διώρ-
θωσαν, Ζηνόδοτος δὲ τὰς ὁμηρείους καὶ τῶν λοιπῶν
ποιητῶν.

110

Antigonus the king of Macedon and Phila his wife, and was in his prime at the same time as Alexander of Aetolia, Callimachus, †Melandrius, and Philitas.

7 Tzetzes, *Prolegomena on Aristophanic comedy*

(a) Proem I

Alexander of Aetolia and Lycophron of Chalchis were induced by generous royal subsidies from Ptolemy Philadelphus to correct the texts of drama, that is to say, of comedy, tragedy, and satyr-drama; with no less a figure to join them and aid them in their task of correction than Eratosthenes, the library's librarian. Of these texts, Callimachus wrote the catalogues. Alexander corrected the tragedies, Lycophron the comedies; Callimachus and Eratosthenes were youths.[4]

(b) Proem II

Alexander of Aetolia, Lycophron of Chalchis, and also Zenodotus of Ephesus, under royal compulsion from Ptolemy Philadelphus, corrected texts—the first, those of tragedy; Lycophron, those of comedy, and Zenodotus, those of Homer and the other poets.

---

[4] They were not contemporaries, as Tzetzes seems to imply. In fact, Tzetzes may have misunderstood an official title, "court youth" (Cameron 1995, 4–5).

ALEXANDER OF AETOLIA

(c) Scholion Plautinum 1–6, p. 48 Koster

Alexander Aetolus et Lycophron Chalcidensis et Zeno-
dotus Ephesius impulsu regis Ptolemaei Philadelphi cog-
nomento, qui mirum in modum favebat ingeniis et famae
doctorum hominum, Graecos artis poeticae libros in
unum collegerunt et in ordinem redegerunt, Alexander
tragoedias, Lycophron comoedias, Zenodotus vero Home-
ri poemata et reliquorum illustrium poetarum.

(d) Proemium II, 22–25, p. 33 Koster

τῶν Ἑλληνίδων δὲ βίβλων, ὡς καὶ προλαβὼν ἔφην,
τὰς τραγικὰς μὲν διώρθωσε [sc. Πτολεμαῖος] δι᾽ Ἀλεξ-
άνδρου τοῦ Αἰτωλοῦ, τὰς τῆς κωμῳδίας δὲ διὰ τοῦ
Λυκόφρονος, διὰ δὲ Ζηνοδότου τοῦ Ἐφεσίου τὰς τῶν
λοιπῶν ποιητῶν, τὰς ὁμηρείους δὲ κατ᾽ ἐξαίρετον . . .

(e) Anonymus Crameri II, 1–4, p. 43 Koster = *TrGF* 100
T 6

ἰστέον, ὅτι Ἀλέξανδρος ὁ Αἰτωλὸς καὶ Λυκόφρων ὁ
Χαλκιδεὺς ὑπὸ Πτολεμαίου τοῦ Φιλαδέλφου προτρα-
πέντες τὰς σκηνικὰς διώρθωσαν βίβλους, Λυκόφρων
μὲν τὰς τῆς κωμῳδίας, Ἀλέξανδρος δὲ τὰς τῆς τραγῳ-
δίας, ἀλλὰ δὴ καὶ τὰς σατυρικάς.

(c) Scholion on Plautus

At the behest of king Ptolemy, surnamed Philadelphus, who promoted the talents and fame of learned men with remarkable zeal, Alexander of Aetolia, Lycophron of Chalchis, and Zenodotus of Ephesus gathered together Greek poetic texts and set them in order, Alexander the tragedies, Lycophron the comedies, Zenodotus the poems of Homer and the other illustrious poets.

(d) Proem II

Of the works of Greek literature, as I said in my introduction, he (Ptolemy) had the tragedies corrected by Alexander of Aetolia, the comedies by Lycophron, and those of the other poets by Zenodotus of Ephesus, the Homeric poems in a special category . . .

(e) Anonymus Crameri

Encouraged by Ptolemy Philadelphus, Alexander of Aetolia and Lycophron of Chalchis corrected the dramatic texts, Lycophron the comedies, Alexander the tragedies and also the satyr-plays.

ALEXANDER OF AETOLIA

(f) ibid. 17–19, p. 43 Koster

τὰς δέ γε σκηνικὰς Ἀλέξανδρός τε, ὡς ἔφθην εἰπών, καὶ Λυκόφρων διωρθώσαντο. τὰς δέ γε ποιητικὰς Ζηνόδοτος πρῶτον καὶ ὕστερον Ἀρίσταρχος διωρθώσαντο.

8 Polemon, ap. Athen. *Deipn.* 15.699 B = fr. 45 Preller

Ἀλέξανδρος ὁ Αἰτωλὸς ὁ τραγῳδοδιδάσκαλος . . .

9

(a) Choeroboscus, in Hephaestionem, p. 236.5 Consbruch (cf. Σ B, p. 279.5 Consbruch) = *TrGF* pp. 54–55, CAT A 5

ἰστέον ὅτι ἐπὶ τῶν χρόνων Πτολεμαίου τοῦ Φιλαδέλφου ἑπτὰ ἄριστοι γεγόνασι τραγικοί, οὓς Πλειάδα ἐκάλεσαν διὰ τὸ λαμπροὺς εἶναι ἐν τῇ τραγικῇ ὡς τὰ ἄστρα τῆς Πλειάδος. εἰσὶ δὲ οὗτοι· Ὅμηρος, οὐχ ὁ ποιητής (περὶ τραγικῶν γὰρ ὁ λόγος), ἀλλ᾽ ὁ Μυροῦς τῆς ποιητρίας υἱὸς τῆς Βυζαντίας, καὶ Σωσίθεος καὶ Λυκόφρων καὶ Ἀλέξανδρος, Αἰαντιάδης, Σωσιφάνης καὶ οὗτος ὁ Φίλικος [Φίλισκος Σ Β].

περὶ τραγικῶν γὰρ ὁ λόγος add. Choeroboscus: om. Σ B

114

(f) ibid.

The dramatic texts were corrected, as I said before, by Alexander and Lycophron. The poets were corrected first by Zenodotus, and later by Aristarchus.

8 Polemon, quoted by Athenaeus, *Deipnosophistae*

Alexander of Aetolia, the tragic poet . . .

9

(a) Choeroboscus, scholia on Hephaestion

In the days of Ptolemy Philadelphus there were seven outstanding tragedians who were known as the *Pleias* because they were illustrious in the art of tragedy like the stars of the Pleiades. Their names are as follows: Homer—not the poet (since we are dealing with tragedians), but the son of Myro the poetess from Byzantium; Sositheus; Lycophron; Alexander; Aiantiades; Sosiphanes; and this Philicus.

(b) Σ A in Hephaestionem, p. 140.8–12 Consbruch

ἑπτὰ γὰρ ἐλέγοντο εἶναι τραγῳδοί· διὸ καὶ πλειὰς
ὠνομάσθησαν, ὧν εἷς ἐστιν οὗτος ὁ Φίλικος· ἐπὶ
Πτολεμαίου δὲ γεγόνασιν οὗτοι ἄριστοι τραγικοί· εἰσὶ
δὲ οὗτοι· Ὅμηρος νεώτερος, Σωσίθεος, Λυκόφρων,
Ἀλέξανδρος, Φίλικος, Διονυσιάδης.

10 Diog. Laert. 9.113 = *TrGF* 112 T 1; cf. *SH* 848

φιλογράμματός [sc. Τίμων] τε καὶ τοῖς ποιηταῖς μύ-
θους γράψαι ἱκανὸς καὶ δράματα συνδιατιθέναι. μετ-
εδίδου δὲ τῶν τραγῳδιῶν Ἀλεξάνδρῳ καὶ Ὁμήρῳ
[*TrGF* 98 T 8].

11 *HE* 3964 = *AP* 4.1.39 (Meleager)

τοῖς δ᾽ ἅμ᾽ Ἀλεξάνδροιο νέους ὄρπηκας ἐλαίης.

(b) Scholiast on Hephaestion

There were said to be seven tragedians, who were for that reason known as the *Pleias*, and this Philicus was one of them. They were the best tragedians in the time of Ptolemy, and their names are as follows: Homer the younger, Sositheus, Lycophron, Alexander, Philicus, and Dionysiades.

10 Diogenes Laertius

He (Timon) loved literature, and was capable of writing plots for poets and collaborating in the writing of plays. He gave a share of his tragedies to Alexander and Homer.

11 Palatine Anthology 4.1.39 (Meleager)

With these, young shoots of Alexander's olive

FRAGMENTA

1–2 ΕΠΙΓΡΑΜΜΑΤΑ

1 *HE* 156–157 = A. Plan. 4.172

εἰς τὸ αὐτὸ (sc. Ἀφροδίτην ὡπλισμένην) Ἀλεξάνδρου
Αἰτωλοῦ·

> αὐτά που τὰν Κύπριν ἀπηκριβώσατο Παλλὰς
> τᾶς ἐπ' Ἀλεξάνδρου λαθομένα κρίσιος.

2 *HE* 150–155 = *AP* 7.709

Ἀλεξάνδρου· ζήτει, ὅτι ἔσφαλται καὶ ἔστιν ἀδιανόητον
[C]·

> Σάρδιες ἀρχαῖαι, πατέρων νομός, εἰ μὲν ἐν ὑμῖν
> ἐτρεφόμαν, κερνᾶς ἦν τις ἂν ἢ βακέλας
> χρυσοφόρος, ῥήσσων λάλα τύμπανα· νῦν δέ μοι
> Ἀλκμὰν
> οὔνομα, καὶ Σπάρτας εἰμὶ πολυτρίποδος,

---

1 Praise of the artistry of a statue of Aphrodite, Pallas being
the patronness of artistic skill; there is nothing in the lines, how-
ever, to suggest that the statue represented Aphrodite armed.

2 In antiquity it was controversial whether Alcman had been
born in Sparta or Sardis. Alexander's mock funerary epigram al-

FRAGMENTS

1–2 EPIGRAMS

1 Planudean Appendix 4.172

On the same subject (sc. Aphrodite in arms), by Alexander of Aetolia:

> Pallas herself has brought the Cyprian to perfection,
> Forgetting the contest that Alexander judged.[1]

2 Palatine Anthology 7.709

By Alexander. Note that he has made a mistake and the epigram is incomprehensible.

> Ancient Sardis, my fathers' home, had I been reared
> In you,[2] I would have been a kernos-bearer or a
>   eunuch[3]
> Wearing gold, beating the vocal drums; but now, my
>   name
> Is Alcman, and I come from Sparta of the many
>   tripods,

lows that his ancestors came from Sardis, but is ambiguous about whether Alcman was born in Sardis and raised elsewhere, or not born there at all.

[3] A *kernos* is a tray with cups attached for individual offerings, used in mystery cults.

5   καὶ Μούσας ἐδάην Ἑλικωνίδας, αἵ με τυράννων
      θῆκαν Κανδαύλεω μείζονα καὶ Γύγεω.

cf. Plut. *Mor.* 599 E, ὡς ὁ γράψας τὸ ἐπιγραμμάτιον
πεποίηκε· "Σάρδιες", κτλ.

1 Σάρδιες C, Plut.: -ιαι P   ἀρχαῖος Plut.   2 κέλσας
Plut.   ἥστισαν ἢ P, corr. Salmasius: ἤ τις ἀνὴρ Plut.
μακέλας P, Plut., corr. Ursinus: μακελᾶς Reiske   3 καλὰ P,
Plut., corr. Meineke   Ἀλκμάν Plut.: ἄλλο P   4 οὔ-
νομ' ἐκ P: οὔνομ', ἐπεὶ dub. Stadtmüller   πολίτης Plut.
5 Ἑλληνίδας Plut.   τύραννον Plut. cod. n, Meineke: -ω
Hecker: -ου Waltz   6 Δασκύλεω C, Plut., corr. Bentley:
Δυσκυλέω P, *vl* ap. Plut.: Δασκυλίδεω Hecker

3–7 FRAGMENTA CERTIS
CARMINIBUS TRIBUTA

3–4 Hexametrica

Ἁλιεύς

3 Athen. *Deipn.* 7.296 E

ἱστορεῖ δὲ περὶ αὐτοῦ καὶ ὁ Αἰτωλὸς Ἀλέξανδρος ἐν τῷ
ἐπιγραφομένῳ Ἁλιεῖ, ὡς ὅτι

    γευσάμενος βοτάνης

κατεποντώθη,

                ἣν Ἡελίῳ φαέθοντι
ἐν μακάρων νήσοισι λιτὴ φύει εἴαρι γαῖα,

And know the Heliconian Muses, who have made me   [5]
Greater than the tyrants Candaules and Gyges.

3–7 FRAGMENTS OF KNOWN LOCATION

3–4 Hexametric Fragments

Fisherman

3 Athenaeus, *Deipnosophistae*

Alexander of Aetolia also writes of him in the poem entitled *Fisherman*, that he jumped into the sea

Having tasted the plant which, for the shining Sun,
The sacred earth grows in the Blessed Isles in spring,

'Ήέλιος δ' ἵπποις θυμήρεα δόρπον ὀπάζει,
ὕλην αἰενάουσαν, ἵνα δρόμον ἐκτελέσωσιν
5   ἄτρυτοι, καὶ μή τιν' ἕλοι μεσσηγὺς ἀνίη.

2 γαίη A, corr. Hermann   4 ὕλη Musurus   ναιετάου-
σαν A, corr. Diels: -σιν Hartung   5 μή νιν Valckenaer: μή
τις Meineke   ἕλῃ Meineke

Κίρκα

4 Athen. *Deipn.* 7.283 A

'Αλέξανδρος δ' ὁ Αἰτωλὸς ἐν Κίρκᾳ [Κρίκᾳ A, corr.
Schweighäuser], εἰ γνήσιον τὸ ποιημάτιον·

πηδαλίῳ ἄκρῳ ἔπι πομπίλος ἀνιοχεύων
ἧστ' ἀκάτω κατόπισθε, θεᾶς ὕπο πόμπιμος ἰχθύς.

1–2 ἀνιοχευ|νησ τὰ κατω A, corr. Meineke   2 θεοῖς A, corr.
Meineke: θεῆς Wilamowitz   πομπίλος A, corr. Meineke

5–6 *Elegiaca*

Ἀπόλλων

5 Parthenius, Ἐρωτικὰ Παθήματα, XIV Περὶ Ἀνθέως

(5) . . . ἔφασαν δέ τινες οὐ πέρδικα, σκεῦος δὲ χρυσοῦν
εἰς τὸ φρέαρ βεβλῆσθαι· ὡς καὶ Ἀλέξανδρος ὁ Αἰτω-
λὸς μέμνηται ἐν τοῖσδε ἐν Ἀπόλλωνι, κτλ.

And the Sun feeds as a nourishing meal to his steeds
An immortal herb, that they may run their course
Unwearied, and not tired out midway.[4]

[5]

Circe

4 Athenaeus, *Deipnosophistae*

Alexander of Aetolia in the *Circe*, if the poem is genuine:

Like a charioteer upon the rudder's tip, a pilot-fish
Sat behind the ship, an escort sent by the goddess.[5]

5–6 Elegiac Fragments

Apollo

5 Parthenius, *Sufferings in Love*, "About Antheus"

Some said that it was not a partridge but a gold vessel that
was thrown into the well, as Alexander of Aetolia mentions
in the following verses from his *Apollo*, etc.

---

[4] The subject is Glaucus, originally a mortal fisherman, who
became a sea-god after he ate a magic herb.
[5] The pilot fish was believed to act as an escort for mariners;
Meineke suggested that Circe sent one to guide Odysseus.

ALEXANDER OF AETOLIA

Μοῦσαι

6 Macrobius, *Sat.* 5.22.4–5

Alexander Aetolus, poeta egregius, in libro qui inscribitur Musae refert quanto studio populus Ephesius dedicato templo Dianae curaverit, praemiis propositis, ut qui tunc erant poetae ingeniosissimi in deam carmina diversa componerent. in his versibus Opis non comes Dianae, sed Diana ipsa vocitata est. loquitur autem, uti dixi, de populo Ephesio:

> ἀλλ᾽ ὄγε πευθόμενος πάγχυ Γραικοῖσι μέλεσθαι
> Τιμόθεον, κιθάρης ἴδμονα καὶ μελέων,
> υἱὸν Θερσάνδρου †τὸν ἤνεσεν ἀνέρα σίγλων
> χρυσείων ἱερὴν δὴ τότε χιλιάδα
> 5 ὑμνῆσαι ταχέων τ᾽ Ὦπιν βλήτειραν ὀϊστῶν,
> ἥ τ᾽ ἐπὶ Κεγχρείῳ τίμιον οἶκον ἔχει,

et mox:

> μηδὲ θεῆς προλίπῃ Λητωίδος ἀκλέα ἔργα.

1 μενλεσθαι P   3 τον vel θον codd.: κλυτόν Schneidewin ἤννσεν "impetravit" Brunck: ποτήνεσεν Salmasius   4 ερην ... χιωλαιαλα vel χειλιαδα codd.: ἱερη ... χιλιάδι Gronovium secutus Meineke, qui postea ἱερὴν ... χιλιάδα maluit   pro ερην αἴρων Wilamowitz, ἱερῶν "consacrans" Diels: alii alia   5 ταχειων codd.: ταχέων ⟨τ᾽⟩ Meineke, Bergk   6 η δ επι κεγεχριον (vel κεγχριων) τυμιον (vel τιμιων) οκον codd., unde Κεγκρείῳ Meineke   7 ἀγλαά Bergk: εὐκλέα Meineke "si quid mutandum"

124

Muses

6 Macrobius, *Saturnalia*

Alexander of Aetolia, an excellent poet, recounts in the book entitled *Muses* how seriously the Ephesian populace took the (re)dedication of the temple of Diana, even offering awards so that the most gifted poets of the time would compose various poems for the goddess. In these verses, Opis is not a companion of Diana, but Diana herself. For she speaks, as I have said, about the Ephesian people:

> But learning that Timotheus was most famed
> Among the Greeks, for skill in harp and song,
> Thersander's son, it pleased them he should sing,
> For a fee of golden shekels, of the holy
> Thousand-year feast,[6] Opis darter of swift arrows,   [5]
> And her who dwells in honour at Cenchrius.[7]

And shortly after:

> Nor leave the works of Leto's divine child unsung.

[6] A very corrupt sentence: the translation follows Meineke's interpretation, where *chilias* refers, not to a specific sum of money, but to a festival celebrating the thousandth anniversary of the temple. But the occasion remains unclear. The temple was burned down in 356 and rebuilt, but Timotheus was dead by then, so the temple in question must be the one begun in the middle of the 6th c. Did some piece of spurious reckoning produce the notion of a thousand-year festival? The hymn in question was presumably the *Artemis* (*PMG* 778 *a–b*).

[7] River in Ephesus, where Leto washed after giving birth to Apollo and Artemis.

ALEXANDER OF AETOLIA

7 Incerti Metri

Φαινόμενα

7

(a) Sextus Empiricus, *Adv. Math.* 8.204

ὡσαύτως δὲ καὶ παρὰ τοῖς τὰ οὐράνια πραγμα-
τευσαμένοις, καθάπερ Ἀράτῳ καὶ Ἀλεξάνδρῳ τῷ Αἰ-
τωλῷ . . .

(b) Vit. Arati (Vita II), p. 12.18–13.3 Martin

πολλοὶ μὲν γὰρ καὶ ἄλλοι Φαινόμενα ἔγραψαν, καὶ
Κλεόπατρος καὶ Σμίνθης καὶ Ἀλέξανδρος ὁ Αἰτωλὸς
καὶ Ἀλέξανδρος ὁ Ἐφέσιος καὶ Ἀλέξανδρος ὁ Λυ-
καῖτης καὶ Ἀνακρέων καὶ Ἀρτεμίδωρος καὶ Ἵππαρχος
καὶ ἄλλοι πολλοί.

Κλεοπάτρης MaMa[2]: Κλεόστρατος Bergk, Meineke

(c) Scriptorum Astronomicorum Index Vaticanus, Vat. gr.
191, fo. 209[v] (ed. E. Maass, *Aratea*, 121)

οἱ περὶ τοῦ ποιητοῦ συνταξάμενοι·
Α* . . . Ἀλέξανδρος Αἰτωλός, Ἀλέξανδρος Ἐφέσιος . . .

οἱ περὶ τοῦ πόλου συντάξαντες Vat. gr. 381, fo. 163[v] sine
Alexandri Aetoli nomine

7 Uncertain Metre

Phaenomena

7

(a) Sextus Empiricus, *Against the Professors*

So too with those who study the heavens, such as Aratus and Alexander of Aetolia . . .

(b) *Life of Aratus* 2

Many others wrote *Phaenomena*, including Cleopatrus, Sminthes, Alexander of Aetolia, Alexander of Ephesus, Alexander of Lycaea, Anacreon, Artemidorus, Hipparchus, and many others.

(c) Vatican Index of Astronomical Writers

Those who have written on the poet [i.e. Aratus; another manuscript reads "on the heavens"]:
. . . Alexander of Aetolia, Alexander of Ephesus . . .

8–16 FRAGMENTA INCERTAE SEDIS

8 Polemon, ap. Athen. *Deipn.* 15.699 B–C = fr. 45 Preller

ὅτι δὲ ἦν τις περὶ αὐτοὺς δόξα παρὰ τοῖς Σικελιώταις
Ἀλέξανδρος ὁ Αἰτωλὸς ὁ τραγῳδοδιδάσκαλος ποιήσας
ἐλεγεῖον τρόπον τοῦτον δηλοῖ·

> . . . ὡς Ἀγαθοκλεῖος λάσιαι φρένες ἤλασαν ἔξω
> πατρίδος. ἀρχαίων ἦν ὅδ᾽ ἀνὴρ προγόνων,
> εἰδὼς ἐκ νεότητος ἀεὶ ξείνοισιν ὁμιλεῖν
> ξεῖνος, Μιμνέρμου δ᾽ †εἰς ἔπος ἄκρον ἰὼν
> 5 παιδομανεῖ σὺν ἔρωτι ποτὴν ἴσον†· ἔγραφε δ᾽
> ὡνὴρ
> εὖ παρ᾽ Ὁμηρείην ἀγλαΐην ἐπέων
> πισσύγγους ἢ φῶρας ἀναιδέας ἤ τινα χλούνην
> φλύοντ᾽ ἀνθηρῇ σὺν κακοδαιμονίῃ,
> οἷα Συρηκόσιος, καὶ ἔχων χάριν· ὃς δὲ Βοιωτοῦ
> 10 ἔκλυεν, Εὐβοίῳ τέρπεται οὐδ᾽ ὀλίγον.

1 ὡς] οὖς Schweighäuser: ὅν γ᾽ Capellmann   Ἀγα-
θοκλῆος Jacobs   4 δεισεποσακρονιων A, dist. Casaubon
5 πότην A: ποτ᾽ ἦν Schweighäuser: πόθημ᾽ Meineke, qui etiam
ἔρῳ πτοίημ᾽, ἔρῳ πόθον (vel πότον) ἤνεσεν temptavit: ποτὴν
Headlam, qui inter ἔρωτι et ποτὴν lacunam unius distichi statuit
7 πισσυγγασ A, corr. Weston   8 φλοιων A, corr. Powell post
φλύων Schweighäuser   ἀτηρῇ Meineke   9 τοῖα Συ-
ρηκοσίοις A, corr. Hecker   τῷ ῥα (Hermann) Συρηκόσιοι
οἱ ἔχον χάριν Kaibel, alia possis   ὡς δὲ A, corr. Jacobs
Βοιωτους A, corr. Casaubon

Μούσαις hoc pertinere verisimile est.

8–16 FRAGMENTS OF UNCERTAIN LOCATION

8 Polemon, quoted by Athenaeus, *Deipnosophistae*

That they[8] enjoyed a certain repute among the Sicilians is shown by Alexander of Aetolia, the tragic poet, in an elegiac passage that runs as follows:

> . . . When Agathocles' savage heart expelled them
> From home. The man came from an ancient stock,
> From youth accustomed as a guest to mix
> With guests; and, borrowing Mimnermus' axiom,
> For love of boys . . . the man composed   [5]
> Good parodies of Homer's glorious works—
> Cobblers, or brazen thieves; or some eunuch[9]
> Babbling a lot of crazy, florid words—
> Just like a Syracusan, and admired: who's heard
> Boeotus, relishes Euboeus not at all.   [10]

[8] The epic parodists Boeotus and Euboeus. Euboeus lived in the time of Philip (Athen. *Deipn.* 15.698 A) and wrote four books of parodies; Boeotus is being discussed here.

[9] Adopting the interpretation of Magnelli 1999, 214–216.

ALEXANDER OF AETOLIA

9 Strab. 12.4.8

ὅτι δ' ἦν κατοικία Μυσῶν ἡ Βιθυνία πρῶτον μαρτυρήσει
Σκύλαξ ὁ Καρυανδεὺς [*FGrH* 709 F 11] φήσας περιοικεῖν
τὴν Ἀσκανίαν λίμνην Φρύγας καὶ Μυσούς, ἔπειτα Διονύ-
σιος ὁ τὰς κτίσεις συγγράψας [*FHG* iv. 395 fr. 7], ὃς τὰ
κατὰ Χαλκηδόνα καὶ Βυζάντιον στενά, ἃ νῦν Θράκιος
Βόσπορος καλεῖται, πρότερόν φησι Μύσιον Βόσπορον
προσαγορεύεσθαι· τοῦτο δ' ἄν τις καὶ τοῦ Θρᾷκας εἶναι
τοὺς Μυσοὺς μαρτύριον θείη· ὅ τε Εὐφορίων "Μυσοῖο
παρ' ὕδασιν Ἀσκανίοιο" [**73**] λέγων, καὶ ὁ Αἰτωλὸς Ἀλέξ-
ανδρος·

> οἳ καὶ ἐπ' Ἀσκανίων δώματ' ἔχουσι ῥοῶν
> λίμνης Ἀσκανίης ἐπὶ χείλεσιν, ἔνθα Δολίων
> υἱὸς Σιληνοῦ νάσσατο καὶ Μελίης

τὸ αὐτὸ ἐκμαρτυροῦσιν, οὐδαμοῦ τῆς Ἀσκανίας λίμνης
εὑρισκομένης ἀλλ' ἐνταῦθα μόνον.

cf. Strab. 14.5.29, ubi 1 Ἀσκανίῳ . . . ῥόῳ et 3 Σειληνοῦ
(*vl*) leguntur

10 Athen. *Deipn.* 10.412 F

Τίτορμός τε ὁ Αἰτωλὸς διηριστήσατο αὐτῷ [sc. Miloni
Crotoniatae] βοῦν, ὡς ἱστορεῖ ὁ Αἰτωλὸς Ἀλέξανδρος.

9 Strabo

Scylax of Caryanda will be our first witness that Bithynia
was a settlement of the Mysians, when he says that
Phrygians and Mysians live around the Ascanian Lake;
next, Dionysius author of the *Foundations*, who reports
that the straits at Chalcedon and Byzantium, now known
as the Thracian Bosporus, were formerly called the Mysian
Bosporus. One might also adduce this as evidence that the
Mysians were Thracians. Euphorion's "By the waters of
the Mysian Ascanius" and Alexander of Aetolia's

> Those with homes beside the Ascanius' streams
> On the edge of lake Ascania, where Dolion
> Settled, son of Silenus and of Melia

are witnesses to the same thing, since the Ascanian Lake is
to be found nowhere else but here alone.

10 Athenaeus, *Deipnosophistae*

Titormus of Aetolia ate an ox at breakfast in competition
with him (sc. Milon of Croton), as recorded by Alexander
of Aetolia.[10]

[10] Strictly anachronistic (given Herodotus' dating of Titor-
mus), but the encounter has taken on the quality of legend. An-
other version in Aelian, *VH* 12.22, and for the subject see also
Posidippus 120 Austin–Bastianini.

11 Paus. 2.22.7

καὶ ἐπὶ τῷδε Εὐφορίων Χαλκιδεὺς [cf. **86**] καὶ Πλευ
ρώνιος Ἀλέξανδρος ἔπη ποιήσαντες, πρότερον δὲ ἔτι
Στησίχορος ὁ Ἱμεραῖος [PMG 191], κατὰ ταὐτά φασιν
Ἀργείοις Θησέως εἶναι θυγατέρα Ἰφιγένειαν.

12 Σ, Tzetzes ad Lyc. Al. 265, p. 115ᵃ28, ᵇ21 Scheer (cf. Σ
AD Il. 3.314) = Euphorion **80**

Στησίχορος [PMG 224] δὲ καὶ Εὐφορίων τὸν Ἕκτορά
φασιν εἶναι υἱὸν τοῦ Ἀπόλλωνος καὶ Ἀλέξανδρος ὁ
Αἰτωλῶν ποιητής.

Ἀπόλλωνι attrib. Düntzer; eidem carmini ac **11** Capellmann

13 Σ AD ad Il. 16.235

Ἀλέξανδρός φησιν ὁ Πλευρώνιος ἔθνος εἶναι τῶν
Ἑλλῶν ἀπόγονον Τυρρηνῶν, καὶ διὰ πατρῷον ἔθος
οὕτω τὸν Δία θρησκεύειν.

τὸν Ἑλλὸν A: τοὺς Ἑλλούς Lascaris   Τυρρηνόν ZS

14 Σ Theocr. Id. 8, Argumentum b, p. 204.2 Wendel

Ἀλέξανδρος δέ φησιν ὁ Αἰτωλὸς ὑπὸ Δάφνιδος μα
θεῖν Μαρσύαν τὴν αὐλητικήν.

ἁλιευτικήν K, corr. Meineke: λυρικήν cett.

tragoediae vel satyro cuidam attrib. Snell

11 Pausanias

And on this matter, the hexameter poets Euphorion of Chalcis and Alexander of Pleuron, and still earlier Stesichorus of Himera, agree with the Argives that Iphigenia was the daughter of Theseus.

12 Scholiast, Tzetzes on Lycophron, *Alexandra*

Stesichorus and Euphorion say that Hector was son of Apollo.[11]

13 Scholiast on Homer, *Iliad*

Alexander of Pleuron says that the race of the Helloi are descended from the Etruscans, and that it is an ancestral custom of theirs to worship Zeus.[12]

14 Scholiast on Theocritus, *Idylls*

Alexander of Aetolia says that Marsyas was taught to play the *auloi* by Daphnis.[13]

[11] See Euphorion **80** n. 108.

[12] The Helloi, or Selloi, were priests of Dodona. The area around Dodona was associated with the Pelasgians, who were connected with the Etruscans. For the idea of an Etruscan migration into Greece, see Myrsilus of Lesbos, *FGrH* 477 F 8–9.

[13] Implying a Phrygian setting for Daphnis, as also in a drama by Sositheus, *TrGF* 99 F 1a–3. Hermesianax **8** sets Daphnis in Euboea.

15 EtMag 288.3 = Parthenius **49**

δροίτη . . . ὁ δὲ Αἰτωλός φησι τὴν σκάφην ἐν ᾗ τιθηνεῖται τὰ βρέφη.

16 P. Oxy. 2085 col. ii.35–36 = Euphorion **109**

35   μήποτε δ[ὲ τῶι
     Α[ἰ]τωλῶι πεπίστευκεν [

17–18 DIVERSA

Tragoediae

cf. Test. **1**, **7**, **8**, **9**, **10**

Ἀστραγαλισταί

17 Σ Τ *Il.* 23.86 *a*, v. p. 382.21 Erbse

ἀνδροκτασίης] καταχρηστικῶς· παῖδα γὰρ ἀνεῖλεν, ὃν ⟨οἱ⟩ μὲν Κλεισώννυμον, οἱ δὲ Αἰανῆ, οἱ δὲ Λύσανδρον καλεῖσθαι. ἀπέκτεινε δὲ αὐτὸν παρὰ Ὀθρυονεῖ τῷ γραμματιστῇ, ὥς φησιν Ἀλέξανδρος ὁ Αἰτωλὸς ἐν Ἀστραγαλισταῖς.

ἑανῆ T, corr. Bekker   Ἀστρολογισταῖς T, corr. Meineke

cf. Σ b *Il.* 23.86 *a*², v. p. 382.26 Erbse

15 Etymologicum Magnum

droitē . . . the Aetolian says it is the cradle in which babies are nursed.

16 P. Oxy. 2085

. . . Perhaps he relied on the Aetolian[14]

17–18 OTHER WORKS AND GENRES

Tragedies

Astragalus-Players

17 Scholiast on Homer, *Iliad*

"Manslaughter"] A catachresis, since it was a child that he killed, whose name according to some was Cleisonymus, according to others Aeanes or Lysander. He killed him at the house of Othryoneus his teacher, according to Alexander of Aetolia in the *Astragalus-players*.[15]

[14] i.e. Alexander; see Euphorion **109** and nn. ad loc.

[15] Usually considered a drama, and perhaps a satyr drama with the satyrs as Patroclus' fellow-pupils (so Schenkl); Wilamowitz, however, suggested the work was an idyll or epyllion. The story is also told in Σ AD *Il*. 12.1, where it is attributed to Hellanicus (*FGrH* 4 F 145).

ALEXANDER OF AETOLIA

Ionica

18

(a) Strab. 14.1.41

ἦρξε δὲ Σωτάδης μὲν πρῶτος τοῦ κιναιδολογεῖν, ἔπει-
τα Ἀλέξανδρος ὁ Αἰτωλός· ἀλλ' οὗτοι μὲν ἐν ψιλῷ
λόγῳ, μετὰ μέλους δὲ Λῦσις, καὶ ἔτι πρότερος τούτου
ὁ Σῖμος.

(b) Athen. *Deipn.* 14.620 E

ὁ δὲ ἰωνικολόγος τὰ Σωτάδου καὶ τῶν πρὸ τούτου
ἰωνικὰ καλούμενα ποιήματα Ἀλεξάνδρου τε τοῦ Αἰ-
τωλοῦ καὶ Πύρητος τοῦ Μιλησίου [*SH* 714(*b*)] καὶ
Ἀλέξου [*SH* 41] καὶ ἄλλων τοιούτων ποιητῶν προ-
φέρεται. καλεῖται δ' οὗτος καὶ κιναιδολόγος.

Ἰωνικὸς λόγος AE, corr. Dobree

(c) *Suda* σ 871 (cf. φ 547)

Σωτάδης . . . ἰαμβογράφος. ἔγραψε Φλύακας ἤτοι
Κιναίδους διαλέκτῳ Ἰωνικῇ· καὶ γὰρ Ἰωνικοὶ λόγοι
ἐκαλοῦντο οὗτοι. ἐχρήσατο δὲ τῷ εἴδει τούτῳ καὶ
Ἀλέξανδρος ὁ Αἰτωλὸς καὶ Πύρης ὁ Μιλήσιος καὶ
Θεόδωρος [*SH* 748 = 756] καὶ Τιμοχαρίδας καὶ Ξέναρ-
χος.

Πύρης Μ*γρ*: Πύρρος cett.

136

FRAGMENTS

Ionic Poems

18

(a) Strabo

Sotades was first to write obscene verse, then Alexander of Aetolia.[16] But they did so without musical accompaniment, whereas Lysis did so to the accompaniment of song, and before him Simus.

(b) Athenaeus, *Deipnosophistae*

The *Iōnikologos* recites the so-called Ionic poems of Sotades and his predecessors, of Alexander of Aetolia and Pyres the Milesian and Alexus and other such poets. He is also known as a *kinaidologos* ("writer on obscene subjects").

(c) *Suda*

Sotades . . . writer of iambi. He wrote *Phlyākes* (tragic burlesques) or *Kinaidoi* (obscene poems) in the Ionic dialect; for these were known as Ionic poems. This form was also used by Alexander of Aetolia, Pyres the Milesian, Theodorus, Timocharidas, and Xenarchus.

16 We do not know whether he adopted the metre, and/or manner, of Sotades. The two were approximately contemporaries, and (since Strabo and Athenaeus contradict one another) we do not know which wrote first.

19–26 DUBIE TRIBUTA

19 Aulus Gellius, *NA* 15.20

Alexander autem Aetolus hos de Euripide versus composuit:

> ὁ δ' Ἀναξαγόρου τρόφις ἀρχαίου στρυφνὸς μὲν
>   ἐμοί γε προσειπεῖν,
> καὶ μισογέλως, καὶ τωθάζειν οὐδὲ παρ' οἶνον
>   μεμαθηκώς,
> ἀλλ' ὅ τι γράψαι τοῦτ' ἂν μέλιτος καὶ Σειρήνων
>   ἐπεπνεύκει.

cf. Vit. Eur. I, p. 5.2–4 Schwartz = I, p. 3.65–68 Méridier
σκυθρωπὸς δὲ καὶ σύννους καὶ αὐστηρὸς ἐφαίνετο καὶ
μισογέλως, καθὰ καὶ Ἀριστοφάνης [fr. 676b Kock]
αὐτὸν αἰτιᾶται "στρυφνὸς ἔμοιγε προσειπεῖν"; ibid.
19–22 = 87–90 ὑπὸ γὰρ Ἀθηναίων ἐφθονεῖτο. μει-
ρακίου δέ τινος ἀπαιδευτοτέρου στόμα δυσῶδες ἔχειν
ὑπὸ φθόνου αὐτὸν εἰπόντος "εὐφήμει" ἔφη "μέλιτος
καὶ Σειρήνων γλυκύτερον στόμα".

1 τρόφιμος codd., corr. Bergk   ΑΡΧΙΔΟΤ cod. X Gell.:
χαοῦ Valckenaer   στρυφνὸς Vit. Eur.: στρ(ε)ιφνὸς Gell.
ἐμοί γε codd. Gell. et Vit. Eur.: ἐμοί γε ἔοικε edd. vett. Gell.:
ἔοικε Meineke   2 παρ' οἴνῳ Wilamowitz   3 ἐτετεύχει
codd., corr. Nauck

19–26 DUBIOUSLY ATTRIBUTED

19 Aulus Gellius, *Attic Nights*

But Alexander of Aetolia composed the following verses about Euripides:

> Old Anaxagoras' nursling was gruff, I found, in
>   speech,
> A foe of mirth, unschooled in jesting even over wine,
> Yet whatever he wrote breathed of honey and the
>   Sirens.

cf. the *Life of Euripides*: He presented a sullen, gloomy, and severe appearance, and was not fond of laughter, an accusation Aristophanes[17] makes against him: "gruff, I found, in speech" . . . The Athenians were not well disposed towards him. When an uncouth boy maliciously told him he had foul-smelling breath, he said, "Speak respectfully of a mouth sweeter than honey and the Sirens."[18]

[17] For the alternative attributions, see Lloyd-Jones 1994, Magnelli 1999, 223–227, d'Alessio 2000, 428–429.

[18] The anecdote is more fully and better told in Satyrus, Vit. Eur. 39 xx. 1–15, p. 76 Arrighetti, though without so clear an echo of the verse in question.

20 *FGE* p. 4 = *AP* 7.507 *a*

ἄνθρωπ᾽, οὐ Κροίσου λεύσσεις τάφον, ἀλλὰ γὰρ
  ἀνδρὸς
χερνήτεω· μικρὸς τύμβος, ἐμοὶ δ᾽ ἱκανός.

507 *a* et *b* conjunctum lemma exhibent, quod ad 507 *a* scriptum,
ad 507 *b* pertinet; unde et titulum C Σιμωνίδου pertinere ad 507
b iure conicias: Ἀλεξάνδρου Planudes

1 ἀλλά γ᾽ ἄρ᾽ Scaliger   2 χερνήτεω· CPl: interpunctionem
del. Bergk   ἔμοιγ᾽ Edmonds

21 [Prob.] ad Virg. *Ecl.* 2.23 (p. 329.18 Hagen)

Amphionem et Zethum Euripides [*Antiope* Test. iv b
Kannicht] *et apud nos Pacuvius* [*Ant.* fr. I Ribbeck] *Iovis
ex Antiopa Nyctei ait natos.* <*Amphionem autem*> *cantan-
do potuisse armenta vocare testantur Thebae, quas Apol-
lonius in Argonautis* [1.735–741] *a fratribus ante dictis
muro esse clausas ait, sed Zethus humeris saxa contulit
operi, Amphion cantu evocavit* [*cantu armenta convocavit*
dub. Hagen], *si quidem sensus animalium facilius quam
saxa vincuntur.* †*Panocus* [*Panyassis* ed. princ.: *Phanocles*
Schneidewin: *Phanodicus* Dübner: *Pacuvius* K. Wernicke]
*et Alexander lyram a Mercurio muneri datam dicunt, quod
primus* †*Euianaram liberavit* [*Cynaram* ed. princ.: *Io
Inachiam* Lloyd-Jones: *ei aram dedicaverit* vel *ei in ara
libaverit* Meineke: *exta e. i. a. libaverit* Schneidewin: *e. e.
i. a. litaverit* Powell].

20 Palatine Anthology 7.507

> This is not Croesus' tomb you see, bypasser, but a
> > poor man's;
> > Small is the tomb, yet adequate for me.

21 ps.-Probus on Virgil's *Eclogues*

Euripides and, among our own writers, Pacuvius say that
Amphion and Zethus were sons of Jupiter by Antiope,
daughter of Nycteus. Amphion's power to summon the
herds by song is witnessed by Thebes, which Apollonius
says in the *Argonautica* was enclosed with a wall by the
brothers under discussion, though Zethus brought the
stones to the work on his shoulders, while Amphion made
them follow him by singing—inasmuch as it is easier to
prevail on the senses of animals than on stones. †Panocus
and Alexander[19] says that (Amphion) was given the lyre by
Mercury, because he was the first to [dedicate an altar to
him, make offerings to him on an altar, etc.[20]].

---

[19] Not at all clear which one.

[20] The passage is corrupt, but Moero fr. 6 P. says that Amphion
was given the lyre because he first established an altar for Hermes.

22 Σ Eur. *Andr.* 32, ii. p. 254.3–5 Schwartz

Σωσιφάνης [*TrGF* 92 F 7] δὲ καὶ Ἀσκληπιάδης [*FGrH* 12 F 23, *SH* 220] φασὶν ἐξ αὐτῆς [sc. Ἑρμιόνης] Νεοπτολέμῳ Ἀγχίαλον γενέσθαι, Δεξιὸς δὲ Φθῖον, Ἀλέξανδρος δὲ Πηλέα.

23 Σ Ar. *Ran.* 840 *d*, p. 112 Holwerda

ὅτι λαχανοπώλιδος υἱὸς ἦν Κλειτοῦς ὁ Εὐριπίδης, Ἀλέξανδρός φησιν.

Κλειτοῦς add., Ἀλέξανδρός φησιν om. R

24 Athen. *Deipn.* 11.496 c

προχύτης· εἶδος ἐκπώματος, ὡς Σιμάριστος ἐν τετάρτῳ Συνωνύμων. Ἴων δ᾽ ὁ Χῖος ἐν Ἐλεγείοις [fr. 27.2–3 West] . . . Φιλίτας δ᾽ ἐν Ἀτάκτοις [**36**] ἀγγεῖον ξύλινον, ἀφ᾽ οὗ τοὺς ἀγροίκους πίνειν. μνημονεύει αὐτοῦ καὶ Ἀλέξανδρος †ἐν τιγονι.

ἐν Τρυγόνι aut Ἀντιγόνῃ Dalechamp: ἐν γ´ Ἰωνικῶν Friebel: ἐν Τιγονίῳ Meineke: ἐν Τιτιγονίῳ Kock

25 *Garland of Philip* 1581–1586 = *AP* 7.534

ἄνθρωπε ζωῆς περιφείδεο, μηδὲ παρ᾽ ὥρην
ναυτίλος ἴσθι· καὶ ὡς οὐ πολὺς ἀνδρὶ βίος·

22 Scholiast on Euripides, *Andromache*

Sosiphanes and Asclepiades say that Neoptolemus' son by Hermione was called Anchialos, Dexius that he was called Phthius, Alexander that he was called Peleus.[21]

23 Scholiast on Aristophanes, *Frogs*

That Euripides was the son of the vegetable-seller Cleito is asserted by Alexander.[22]

24 Athenaeus, *Deipnosophistae*

Prochytēs is a sort of cup, as reported by Simaristus in the fourth book of his *Synonyms*. Ion of Chios in the *Elegies* ... Philitas in the *Miscellany* says it is a wooden vessel from which country-people drink. Alexander also mentions it in the ... [23]

25 Palatine Anthology 7.534[24]

Mortal, be careful of your life; be not a sailor
Out of season; even so, a man's life is not long.

[21] Again unclear which Alexander is meant, but among a list of authors who deny the childlessness imputed to Hermione and Neoptolemus by Euripides.

[22] The legend goes back to Aristophanes. Again the Alexander is unclear, but perhaps it came from the same work as **19**.

[23] Given the subject-matter, the work is perhaps a comedy.

[24] Attributed to "Aetolus Automedon", which *may* (but need not) conceal a reference to Alexander of Aetolia.

δείλαιε Κλεόνικε, σὺ δ' εἰς λιπαρὴν Θάσον
  ἐλθεῖν
ἠπείγευ, Κοίλης ἔμπορος ἐκ Συρίης,
5 ἔμπορος, ὦ Κλεόνικε· δύσιν δ' ὑπὸ Πλειάδος
  αὐτὴν
ποντοπορῶν αὐτῇ Πλειάδι συγκατέδυς.

Titulus: Αἰτωλοῦ Αὐτομέδοντος C: ‹Ἀλεξάνδρου› Αἰτ. ‹ἢ›
‹οἱ δὲ› Gow) Αὐτ. Jacobs: Θεοκρίτου Planudes

3–6 om. Pl   5 ὑποπληάδων P, corr. Graevius   6 πον-
τοπόρῳ ναύτῃ P, corr. Pierson: -πόρος ναύτης Graevius

26 FGE pp. 4–5 = AP 6.182

Πίγρης ὀρνίθων ἄπο δίκτυα, Δᾶμις ὀρείων,
  Κλείτωρ δ' ἐκ βυθίων σοὶ τάδε, Πάν, ἔθεσαν,
ξυνὸν ἀδελφειοὶ θήρης γέρας, ἄλλος ἀπ' ἄλλης,
  ἴδρι τὰ καὶ γαίης, ἴδρι τὰ καὶ πελάγευς.
5 ἀνθ' ὧν τῷ μὲν ἁλός, τῷ δ' ἠέρος, ᾧ δ' ἀπὸ
  δρυμῶν
πέμπε κράτος ταύτῃ, δαῖμον, ἐπ' εὐσεβίῃ.

Titulus: εἰς τὸ αὐτὸ Ἀλεξάνδρου Μαγνήτου P, Pl (Μαγνήτου
om. Pl: Μάγνητος Meineke)

4 ap. Suda ι 131   ἰδρίτα bis P, Suda, corr. Hecker: ἰδρυτὰ
Pl   καὶ prius om. Pl   5 ᾧ] τῷ P

Poor Cleonicus, you were making haste to wealthy
Thasos, as a trader bound from Hollow Syria:
A trader, Cleonicus, sailing when the Pleiades set;[25] [5]
And as they set your star went down with them.

26 Palatine Anthology 6.182[26]

Pigres these nets from fowling, Damis from the hills,
Cleitor from fishing—Pan, to you, the brothers,
Each from his own domain, devote a common gift,
To you, who know the earth, who know the sea.
In turn, lord, grant dominion over each man's [5]
  realm—
Sea, air, and woodlands—for this piety.

[25] End of October / beginning of November: not the sailing
season.
[26] Attributed to Alexander of Magnesia, who is unknown; the
Aetolian is merely a possibility here. There are numerous varia-
tions on this theme.

HERMESIANAX OF COLOPHON

INTRODUCTION

Hermesianax came from Colophon, a city with a rich poetic tradition. His dates are nebulous. We learn that he was a friend of Philitas (cf. Test. **1**), who was born *c*. 340. Pausanias thought that he was no longer alive when Colophon was sacked (Test. **2**), but the argument from silence is not strong (cf. n. 2 ad loc.). Nothing connects him with Alexandria.

He is always referred to as an elegist, and the one work for which we have uncontrovertible testimony is the *Leontion* in three books, named after his lover. That suggests a place somewhere in the tradition that reaches back to Mimnermus' *Nanno* and Antimachus' *Lyde*, and forwards to Parthenius' *Arete*. What we can see of its content was erotic. The love-lorn Cyclops made famous by Philoxenus' fourth-century dithyramb figured in book 1, and perhaps also the bucolic folk-hero Daphnis, though in a version different from Theocritus'. The second book contained a love-story whose aetiological point, as Antoninus Liberalis tells it, is submerged in its historical, Hellenistic setting. Two more stories are shared with Parthenius, one from the colonisation period, the other a novelistic variant of the fall of Sardis. But the one extended excerpt is not in the epyllion style that some of the testimonia might have suggested. It is a list of exempla, addressed to Leontion, in order to prove that even the poets and philosophers of old were all susceptible to love. To demonstrate this it marshalls a list of twelve poets from the mythological period to the poet's friend and contemporary Philitas, and three philosophers, also in chronological order, all equipped with little anecdotes about their *affaires de coeur*.

It is frustrating that the fragment is corrupt, sometimes to the point of incomprehensibility, but its literary-historical interest is considerable. It seems to be an early example of the influence of Hesiodic catalogue poetry. As a stylistic signature of the genre, Hermesianax borrows the initial *hoiē* ("such a woman as . . . "); the erotic subject-matter, the formal signature (or its clever reapplication), and the elegiac metre, all find ready parallels in third-century poetry.[1] But it stands out for its engagement with the literary-critical methods of Peripatetic scholars—not necessarily solemnly, but certainly with erudition. It ranks its poets in chronological order, in pairs, observing chronological order (or what was believed to be so) within each pair. Thus, Hesiod precedes Homer, and Sophocles Euripides. The poets are chosen because they represent certain genres, presented in an order that can be paralleled fairly closely in other literary-historical reviews such as Quintilian's *Institutio Oratorica* and Proclus' *Chrestomathy*: epic comes first, followed by elegy, lyric, then tragedy; this only goes awry in the pairing of the most recent poets, Philoxenus (dithyramb) and Philitas (elegy). Finally, biography is derived by inference from a poet's *oeuvre*. These are tall sto-

---

[1] Phanocles' elegiac Ἔρωτες ἢ καλοί (fr. 1 P., beginning ἢ ὡς); Nicaenetus' *Catalogue of Women* (fr. 2 P.) and Sosicrates or Sostratus of Phanagoreia's *Ēoioi* (*SH* 732).

ries, though their methodology is in fact well-etablished in Peripatetic scholarship. Hermesianax makes Alcaeus and Anacreon rivals for the love of Sappho. The chronology is obviously nonsense (as Athenaeus himself points out); yet the Peripatetic scholar Chamaeleon of Heraclea, in one of a series of monographs on classical poets, reports an identification of Sappho as the Lesbian girl in Anacreon *PMG* 358, and cites some spurious lines in which Sappho addresses the Teian. The story about Philoxenus and Galatea seems also to be connected with existing biographical interpretation of the *Cyclops* poem (see n. 15). Other stories are patently absurd, and presumably meant to seem so. Many of the love affairs involve travels, or wandering; Homer is brought to Ithaca by love of Penelope, Hesiod to Ascra by a girl called Eoie, the very signature device of his catalogue poetry.

The Hellenistic genre of curse poetry is, of course, another affiliate of catalogue literature, and a recently-recovered fragment of an elegiac curse poem has been attributed to Hermesianax on the grounds that it mentions the centaur Eurytion, as Hermesianax is also said to have done (**6**).[2] What distinguishes this piece is the speaker's threat to tattoo his victim with images of the punishments he will inflict. The repeated στίξω is the formula that links the minatory stories together, though they are told at greater length and in a more leisurely style than in, say, Euphorion: the story of Eurytion himself occupies over twenty lines. But the direct apostrophe of the malefactor,

[2] For the attribution, see Huys 1991, 77–98, criticised by Slings 1993; see further Cameron 1995, 384–386; Lloyd-Jones 2005.

and the Hesiodic appeal to personified justice and the ineluctability of punishment, can both be paralleled in the *Thrax*. The style is rather epic / Homeric—not unexpected, given the subject-matter, but not, according to the editor, incompatible with the long fragment of the *Leontion* either. But the attribution remains uncertain, resting, as it does, on the presence of Eurytion in both fragments. Pausanias says that Hermesianax also gave information about the city Olenus (**6**), which is not mentioned in the papyrus. Perhaps it has been lost in a lacuna; alternatively, Huys suggests that Pausanias is drawing on a mythographical summary that filled out details, such as geographical names, not present in the original. Yet Pausanias is citing Hermesianax, not just for an incidental detail, but for a specific fact; there hardly seems room for a large enough lacuna, and the recourse to an intermediary source looks correspondingly more like special pleading.

EDITIONS

Among the most important, see:

N. Bach, *Philetae Coi, Hermesianactis Colophonii atque Phanoclis reliquiae* (Halle, 1829), 115–180.

C. Giarratano, *Hermesianactis fragmenta* (Milan, 1905).

J. U. Powell, *Collectanea Alexandrina* (Oxford, 1925), 96–106.

E. Diehl, *Anthologia Lyrica Graeca*, vol. ii. 6 (Leipzig, ²1942), 56–64.

Editions of **3**:

J. Schweighäuser, *Athenaei Naucratitae Deipnosophistarum Libri Quindecim* (Straßburg, 1801–1807), v. 159–167 + xii. 224–255.

J. G. J. Hermann *Hermesianactis Elegi* (Leipzig, 1828) = *Opuscula*, iv. (Leipzig, 1831), 239–252.

C. Schubart, "De Hermesianactis elegis", *Jahresbericht über das Gymnasium und die mit demselben verbundene Realschule zu Plauen* (1857–1858), 1–22 [textual comment].

A. Meineke, *Athenaei Deipnosophistae*, iii. (Leipzig, 1859), 75–78; iv. (Leipzig, 1867), 282–285.

T. Bergk, *Anthologia Lyrica* (Leipzig, ²1868), 134–137 [+ 1]; textual discussion in *Commentatio de Hermesianactis elegia* (Progr. Marburg, 1844) = *Kleine philologische Schriften*, ed. R. Peppmüller, ii. (Halle, 1886), 158–182 + 182–184.

G. Kaibel, *Athenaei Naucratitae Deipnosophistarum Libri XV*, iii. (Leipzig, 1890), 316–320.

J. Defradas, *Les élégiaques grecs: édition, introduction et commentaire* (Paris, 1962), 92–102.

CRITICISM

P. Bing, "The Bios-tradition and poets' lives in Hellenistic poetry", in R. M. Rosen, J. Farrell (edd.), *Nomodeiktes: Greek Studies in Honor of M. Ostwald* (1993), 619–631.

C. L. Caspers, "Hermesianax fr. 7.75–78 Powell. Philitas, Bittis . . . and a parrot?", *Mnemosyne* 58 (2005), 575–581.

————"The loves of the poets. Allusions in Hermesianax fr. 7 Powell", in M. A. Harder, R. F. Regtuit and G. C. Wakker (edd.)., *Beyond the Canon* (Leuven, 2006) (Hellenistica Groningana 11), 21–42.

O. Ellenberger, "Quaestiones Hermesianacteae" (Diss. Gießen, 1907).

M. Huys, *Le poème élégiaque hellénistique P. Brux. Inv. E. 8934 et P. Sorb. Inv. 2254: édition, commentaire et analyse stylistique* (Brussels, 1991).

J. Latacz , "Das Plappermäulchen aus dem Katalog", in C. Schäublin (ed.), *Catalepton: Festschrift für Bernhard Wyss* (Basel, 1985), 77–95 = *Erschließung der Antike* (Stuttgart, 1994), 427–446.

H. Lloyd-Jones, "Again the Tattoo Elegy", *ZPE* 101 (1994), 4–7 = *The Further Academic Papers of Sir Hugh Lloyd-Jones* (Oxford, 2005), 253–256.

————*Supplementum Supplementi Hellenistici* (Berlin and New York, 2005), 62–63.

V. J. Matthews, "Interpreting the Euripides Narrative of Hermesianax", in D. Accorinti & P. Chuvin (edd.)., *Des Géants à Dionysos. Mélanges de mythologie et de poésie grecques offerts à Francis Vian* (Alessandria, 2003), 281–286.

E. Rohde, *Der griechische Roman und seine Vorläufer*[4] (Hildesheim, 1960), 80–88.

S. Slings, "Hermesianax and the Tattoo Elegy (P. Brux. inv. E 8934 and P. Sorb. inv. 2254)", *ZPE* 98 (1993), 29–37.

TESTIMONIA

1 Σ Nic. *Ther.* 3, p. 35.13 Crugnola = Philitas Test. **7**

φίλ᾽ Ἑρμησιάναξ] ὁ Ἑρμησιάναξ οὗτος φίλος τῷ Φιλιτᾷ καὶ γνώριμος ἦν. τούτῳ τὰ Περσικὰ γέγραπται, καὶ τὰ εἰς Λεόντιον τὴν ἐρωμένην. οὐ δύναται δὲ Νίκανδρος μνημονεύειν τούτου διὰ τῆς προσφωνήσεως, διὰ τὸ τὸν Φιλιτᾶν πρεσβύτερον εἶναι Νικάνδρου, καὶ αὐτὸς δὲ ὁ Νίκανδρος μέμνηται τοῦ Ἑρμησιάνακτος ὡς πρεσβυτέρου ἐν τῷ περὶ τῶν ἐκ Κολοφῶνος ποιητῶν [*FGrH* 271/2 F 10]. ἔστιν οὖν οὗτος ἑταῖρος Νικάνδρου, ὁμώνυμος τῷ προτέρῳ. δῆλον δὲ ὅτι συγγενὴς αὐτοῦ ἦν.

2 Paus. 1.9.7

συνῴκισε [sc. Λυσίμαχος] δὲ καὶ Ἐφεσίων ἄχρι θαλάσσης τὴν νῦν πόλιν, ἐπαγαγόμενος ἐς αὐτὴν Λεβεδίους τε οἰκήτορας καὶ Κολοφωνίους, τὰς δὲ ἐκείνων ἀνελὼν πόλεις, ὡς Φοίνικα ἰάμβων ποιητὴν Κολοφωνίων θρηνῆσαι τὴν ἅλωσιν. Ἑρμησιάναξ δὲ ὁ τὰ

TESTIMONIA

1 Scholiast on Nicander, *Theriaca*

"Dear Hermesianax"] This Hermesianax was a friend and associate of Philitas. He is the author of the *Persica*, and the verses dedicated to Leontion his beloved. It is impossible for Nicander to have addressed himself directly to him, since Philitas was older than Nicander, and Nicander himself mentions Hermesianax as being older in his work *On the Poets of Colophon*.[1] This Hermesianax, then, is a friend of Nicander, having the same name as the earlier one. Obviously, the two were related.

2 Pausanias

He (sc. Lysimachus) also founded the modern city of Ephesus near the sea, introducing into it as settlers the inhabitants of Lebedos and the Colophonians, whose cities he had destroyed, so that Phoenix the iambic poet was moved to write a lament for the capture of Colophon. In

[1] The scholium begins by identifying Hermesianax as the addressee of Nicander's didactic poem. Then a second writer disputes this on the grounds of chronology, making Hermesianax a contemporary of Philitas and both older than Nicander.

ἐλεγεῖα γράψας οὐκέτι ἐμοὶ δοκεῖν περιῆν· πάντως
γάρ που καὶ αὐτὸς ἂν ἐπὶ ἁλούσῃ Κολοφῶνι ὠδύρατο.

3 Athen. *Deipn.* 13.597 A

παρέλιπον δὲ καὶ τὴν Μιμνέρμου αὐλητρίδα Ναννὼ
καὶ τὴν Ἑρμησιάνακτος τοῦ Κολοφωνίου Λεόντιον·
ἀπὸ γὰρ ταύτης ἐρωμένης αὐτῷ γενομένης ἔγραψεν
ἐλεγειακὰ τρία βιβλία.

my opinion, Hermesianax the elegiac poet was no longer
alive, for otherwise he too would have lamented the fall of
his city.[2]

3 Athenaeus, *Deipnosophistae*

I also omitted to mention Mimnermus' *aulos*-playing girl-
friend Nanno, and Hermesianax of Colophon's Leontion,
who was his lover, and in whose name he wrote three books
of elegies.

[2] The fall of Colophon has been dated to 302 or at least to be-
fore 289/8, but Pausanias' argument from silence is not necessar-
ily correct. In any case, by the time *Leontion* was written, Philitas
(born *c.* 340) must have attained sufficient celebrity to have been
honoured publicly (though not necessarily posthumously) by his
fellow-citizens.

FRAGMENTA

1–7 FRAGMENTA CERTIS CARMINIBUS TRIBUTA

Λεόντιον

cf. Test. **1**, **3**.

Lib. 1

1 Herodian, περὶ μον. λεξ., GG III.2, p. 922.20 Lentz

. . . τῷ Ἑρμησιάνακτι ἐν Λεοντίου αʹ·

δερκόμενος πρὸς κῦμα, μόνη δὲ οἱ ἐφλέγετο
γλήν.

οὐ γὰρ ἐντελές, ἀποκεκομμένον δὲ ἐκ τοῦ γλήνη.

Lib. 2

2 Antoninus Liberalis, *Met.* 39

Ἀρκεοφῶν. Ἱστορεῖ Ἑρμησιάναξ Λεοντίῳ βʹ.

(1) Ἀρκεοφῶν ὁ Μιννυρίδου πόλεως μὲν ἦν Σαλαμῖνος
τῆς ἐν Κύπρῳ, γονέων δὲ οὐκ ἐπιφανῶν (ἦσαν γὰρ

FRAGMENTS

1–7 FRAGMENTS OF KNOWN LOCATION

Leontion

Book 1

1 Herodian, *On unique word-formation*

. . . in the first book of Hermesianax's *Leontion*:

> Looking towards the waves, and his one pupil was
>   aflame.[1]

For the word (*glēn*) is not complete, but an apocopated form of *glēnē*.

Book 2

2 Antoninus Liberalis, *Metamorphoses*

Arceophon. Hermesianax relates the story in the second book of the *Leontion*.[2]

(1) Arceophon son of Minnyris came from Salamis in Cyprus. His parents were undistinguished (they were Phoe-

---

[1] Presumably referring to the Cyclops and his love for the sea-nymph Galatea.   [2] So does Ovid in the *Metamorphoses* (14.698–761), but he changes the names to Iphis and Anaxarete.

ἐκ Φοινίκης), χρήμασι δὲ καὶ τῇ ἄλλῃ εὐδαιμονίᾳ
πλεῖστον ὑπερήνεγκεν. οὗτος ἰδὼν τὴν θυγατέρα τὴν
Νικοκρέοντος τοῦ Σαλαμινίων βασιλέως ἠράσθη. (2)
γένος δ' ἦν τοῦ Νικοκρέοντος ἀπὸ Τεύκρου τοῦ ξυν-
ελόντος Ἴλιον Ἀγαμέμνονι, παρ' ὃ καὶ μᾶλλον ὁ
Ἀρκεοφῶν ἐφίετο τοῦ γάμου τῆς παιδός, καὶ ὑπέσχετο
πλεῖστα παρὰ τοὺς ἄλλους μνηστῆρας ἀποίσειν ἕδνα.
Νικοκρέων δ' οὐχ ὑποδέχεται τὸν γάμον κατ' αἰσχύ-
νην γένους τοῦ Ἀρκεοφῶντος, ὅτι αὐτῷ πατέρες ἦσαν
Φοίνικες. (3) Ἀρκεοφῶντι δ' ἀποτυγχανομένῳ πρὸς
τὸν γάμον πολὺ χαλεπώτερος ἦν ὁ ἔρως καὶ νυκτὸς
ἐπὶ τὰ οἰκία τῆς Ἀρσινόης ἐφοίτα καὶ διενυκτέρευσε
μετὰ τῶν ἡλικιωτῶν. ἐπεὶ δὲ αὐτῷ πρὸς τὸ ἔργον οὐδὲν
ἐτυγχάνετο, πείθει τροφὸν αὐτῆς καὶ πλεῖστα δῶρα
πέμψας ἐπειράθη τῆς παιδός, εἴ πως αὐτῷ δύναιτο
κρύφα μιχθῆναι τῶν γονέων. (4) ἡ δὲ παῖς, ἐπεὶ τὸν
λόγον ἡ τροφὸς αὐτῇ προσήνεγκε, κατεμήνυσε πρὸς
τοὺς γονέας· οἱ δὲ γλῶσσαν ἄκραν καὶ ῥῖνα καὶ
δακτύλους ἀποτεμόντες τῆς τροφοῦ καὶ λωβησάμενοι
ἀνοίκτως ἐξήλασαν ἐκ τῶν οἰκίων. καὶ πρὸς τὸ ἔργον
ἐνεμέσησεν ἡ θεός. (5) Ἀρκεοφῶν μὲν οὖν καθ' ὑπερ-
βολὴν πάθους καὶ ἀπορίαν [Martini: ὑπόψιαν P: ὑπερ-
οψίαν Muncker: ἀποτυχίαν Jacobs] τὴν πρὸς τὸν γάμον
ἑκὼν ἀποθνήσκει κατὰ τροφῆς ἔνδειαν· οἱ δὲ πολῖται
τὸν θάνατον οἰκτείραντες ἐπένθησαν, ἡμέρᾳ δὲ τρίτῃ
τὸ σῶμα προήνεγκαν εἰς ἐμφανὲς οἱ προσήκοντες. (6)
καὶ οἱ μὲν ἔμελλον κηδεύσειν, Ἀρσινόη δὲ πρὸς ὕβριν
ἐπεθύμησεν ἐκ τῶν οἴκων ἐκκύψασα τὸ σῶμα τὸ τοῦ

nicians), but in money and every other form of prosperity he was absolutely pre-eminent. Now this man happened to see the daughter of Nicocreon, king of Salamis,[3] and fell in love with her. (2) Nicocreon traced his lineage back to Teucer, who had helped Agamemnon capture Troy, and for this reason Arceophon was all the more desirous of marrying the girl. He promised gifts for the bride that were vastly in excess of those of her other suitors, but Nicocreon did not agree to the marriage because he was ashamed of Arceophon's lineage, his parents being Phoenicians. (3) When Arceophon's hopes of marrying the girl were dashed, his love became much harder to bear; he would go to the house of Arsinoe by night and spend the night there with his companions. When he still got no further forward in his suit, he suborned the nurse and sent the girl a great deal of gifts to try to tempt her to sleep with him in secret from her parents. (4) But when the girl's nurse brought the proposition to her, she denounced Arceophon to her parents, who cut off the tip of the nurse's tongue and her nose and her fingers and treated her with pitiless cruelty before throwing her out of the house. This deed aroused the goddess' anger. (5) In excess of passion and through disappointment of his marriage, Arceophon willingly embraced suicide by starvation. The citizens pitied his death and went into mourning for him. On the third day his relatives brought his body out into the open, (6) on their way to bury it. Now Arsinoe in her pride conceived the wish to peer out of the house in order to see Arceophon's body being cre-

3 Succeeded 332.

Ἀρκεοφῶντος κατακαιόμενον ἰδεῖν. καὶ ἡ μὲν ἐθεᾶτο,
μισήσασα δὲ τὸ ἦθος Ἀφροδίτη μετέβαλεν αὐτὴν καὶ
ἐποίησεν ἐξ ἀνθρώπου λίθον καὶ τοὺς πόδας ἐρρίζω-
σεν ἐπὶ τὴν γῆν.

Lib. 3

3 Athen. *Deipn.* 13.597 в

. . . ὧν ἐν τῷ τρίτῳ κατάλογον ποιεῖται ἐρωτικῶν, οὑτωσί
πως λέγων·

οἵην μὲν φίλος υἱὸς ἀνήγαγεν Οἰάγροιο
Ἀγριόπην Θρῆσσαν στειλάμενος κιθάρην
Ἁιδόθεν· ἔπλευσεν δὲ κακὸν καὶ ἀπειθέα χῶρον,
ἔνθα Χάρων κοινὴν ἕλκεται εἰς ἄκατον
5 ψυχὰς οἰχομένων, λίμνης δ' ἐπὶ μακρὸν ἀυτεῖ
ῥεῦμα διὲκ μεγάλων χευομένης δονάκων.
πόλλ' ἔτλη παρὰ κῦμα μονόζωστος κιθαρίζων
Ὀρφεύς, παντοίους δ' ἐξανέπεισε θεούς·
Κωκυτόν τ' ἀθέμιστον ὑπ' ὀφρύσι μηνίσαντα
10 ἠδὲ καὶ αἰνοτάτου βλέμμ' ὑπέμεινε κυνός,
ἐν πυρὶ μὲν φωνὴν τεθοωμένου, ἐν πυρὶ δ' ὄμμα
σκληρὸν, τριστοίχοις δεῖμα φέρον κεφαλαῖς.

2 Ἀργιόπην Zoega   4 κοινὴν] ἀκοὴν A, corr. Lennep:
κοίλην Toup: κυανὴν Meineke   5–6 λίμνηι . . . ῥυομένη
A, corr. Ruhnken (λίμνης), Bailey (χευομένης)   7 ἀλλ' A,
corr. Kaibel   μονόζωστον A, corr. Ruhnken   9 ἐπ'
ὀφρύσι μηδείσαντα A: corr. Ruhnken (ὑπ') et Kaibel (μηνί-
σαντα)   10 εἶδε Hermann   12 φέρων A, corr. Ruhnken

mated. But as she was watching, Aphrodite, loathing the
girl's disposition, transformed her and made her a stone in-
stead of a human being, and rooted her feet to the ground.[4]

Book 3

3 Athenaeus, *Deipnosophistae*

. . . in the third book of which he made a catalogue of love-
affairs, writing as follows:

> Such as Oeagrus' dear son summoned back
> From Hades, furnished with his lyre: Agriope
> Of Thrace.[5] He sailed to that implacable, harsh place
> Where Charon draws into his public craft
> Departed souls, and cries across the lake   [5]
> That pours its stream through beds of lofty reed.
> That lone musician Orpheus suffered much
> Beside the wave, but won the various gods;
> Lawless Cocytus with his menacing scowl
> And the dread regard of Cerberus he withstood,   [10]
> His voice sharpened in fire, in fire his cruel eye,
> On triple rank of heads freighted with fear.

[4] An aetiology underlies this; it may have been clearer in the
original. Ovid connects the petrified Anaxarete with the cult
statue of Venus Prospiciens ("Venus Looking Forth") in Salamis
(cf. Plut. *Mor.* 766 C–D).

[5] Oeagrus' son is Orpheus. This is the earliest source in which
his wife is named; Eurydice appears for the first time in Moschus'
Epitaphion Bionis.

ἔνθεν ἀοιδιάων μεγάλους ἀνέπεισεν ἄνακτας
Ἀγριόπην μαλακοῦ πνεῦμα λαβεῖν βιότου.

15 οὐ μὴν οὐδ᾽ υἱὸς Μήνης ἀγέραστον ἔθηκεν
Μουσαῖος, Χαρίτων ἤρανος, Ἀντιόπην·
ἥ τε πολὺν μύστησιν Ἐλευσῖνος παρὰ πέζαν
εὐασμὸν κρυφίων ἐξεφόρει λογίων,
Ῥάριον ὀργειῶνα νόμῳ διαπομπεύουσα
20 Δημήτρᾳ· γνωστὴ δ᾽ ἐστὶ καὶ εἰν Ἀΐδῃ.

φημὶ δὲ καὶ Βοιωτὸν ἀποπρολιπόντα μέλαθρα
Ἡσίοδον, πάσης ἤρανον ἱστορίης,
Ἀσκραίων ἐσικέσθαι ἐρῶνθ᾽ Ἑλικωνίδα κώμην·
ἔνθεν ὅ γ᾽ Ἠοίην μνώμενος Ἀσκραϊκὴν
25 πόλλ᾽ ἔπαθεν, πάσας δὲ λόγων ἀνεγράψατο
βίβλους
ὑμνῶν, ἐκ πρώτης παιδὸς ἀνερχόμενος.

αὐτὸς δ᾽ οὗτος ἀοιδός, ὃν ἐκ Διὸς αἶσα φυλάσσει
ἥδιστον πάντων δαίμονα μουσοπόλων,
λεπτὴν ἧς Ἰθάκην ἐνετείνατο θεῖος Ὅμηρος
30 ᾠδῇσιν πινυτῆς εἵνεκα Πηνελόπης·

13 λυδιάων A, corr. Musurus   16 ηραν· ὃς A, corr. Musaeus
17 πολυμνηστησιν A, corr. Blomfield   19 ὀργιωνανεμωι
A, corr. Blomfield   διαποιπνωιουσα A, corr. Powell: δια-
ποιπνύουσα Musurus   20 Δήμητρα A, corr. Hermann
21 μελαθραν A, corr. Schweighäuser: μέλαθρον Musurus
23 ἐρῶνθ᾽] ἔχων A, corr. Riegler   25 γόων Meineke:
ἐλέγων Anon. Lond.: λόγων = καταλόγων Kaibel
26 ὕμνων A, corr. Casaubon

With song he won the underworld's great lords,
For Agriope to regain the gentle breath of life.

Nor did the Graces' master, Mene's son,   [15]
Musaeus, leave Antiope unsung,[6]
Who, to the adepts by Eleusis' strand,
Expressed glad cries from secret oracles,
Leading Demeter's Rarian celebrant[7]
With ordered step; in Hades still she's known.   [20]

And I say that even Boeotian Hesiod
Lord of all knowledge, left his home and came,
In love, to Ascra, Heliconian town;
And, wooing Eoie, Ascraean maid,[8]
He suffered much, composed whole catalogues   [25]
In homage, with the girl heading the list.

The very bard, whom Zeus' fate upholds
Sweetest divinity of all versed in song,
The godlike Homer set mean Ithaca
To verse for love of wise Penelope.   [30]

---

[6] Antiope, elsewhere called Deiope, is a figure of Eleusinian myth, mother (or daughter) of Triptolemus.

[7] Connected with the Rarian plain in Eleusis, which claimed to be the birthplace of agriculture.

[8] The joke is that the formula with which the genealogies begin in the *Catalogue of Women* is turned into the name of a woman with whom Hesiod was in love.

---

28 μουσοπόλον A, corr. Musurus   29 λεπτὴν δ' εἰς A, corr.
Kaibel ([δ'] iam Diels): λεπτυνθεὶς Couat   ἀνετείνετο A,
corr. Bergk

ἦν διὰ πολλὰ παθὼν ὀλίγην ἐσενάσσατο νῆσον,
πολλὸν ἀπ' εὐρείης λειπόμενος πατρίδος·
ἔκλεε δ' Ἰκαρίου τε γένος καὶ δῆμον Ἀμύκλου
καὶ Σπάρτην, ἰδίων ἁπτόμενος παθέων.

35 Μίμνερμος δὲ, τὸν ἡδὺν ὃς εὕρετο πολλὸν
          ἀνατλὰς
     ἦχον καὶ μαλακοῦ πνεῦμ' ἀπὸ πενταμέτρου,
καίετο μὲν Ναννοῦς· πολιῷ δ' ἐπὶ πολλάκι λωτῷ
κημωθεὶς κώμους εἶχε σὺν Ἐξαμύῃ.
ἤχθεε δ' Ἑρμόβιον τὸν αἰεὶ βαρὺν ἠδὲ Φερεκλῆν
40   ἐχθρὸν μισήσας οἷ' ἀνέπεμψεν ἔπη.

Λύδης δ' Ἀντίμαχος Λυδηΐδος ἐκ μὲν ἔρωτος
πληγεὶς Πακτωλοῦ ῥεῦμ' ἐπέβη ποταμοῦ·
†δαρδάνη δὲ θανοῦσαν ὑπὸ ξηρὴν θέτο γαῖαν
κλαίων, †αἰζαον δ' ἦλθεν ἀποπρολιπὼν
45   ἄκρην ἐς Κολοφῶνα· γόων δ' ἐνεπλήσατο
          βίβλους
     ἱράς, ἐκ παντὸς παυσάμενος καμάτου.

31–32 εἰσενάσσατο, λιπόμενος A, corr. Musurus
33 ἔκλαιε A, corr. Bergk   36 πνεῦμα τὸ Dalecamp
37 πολλιωι A, corr. Hermann   ἔτι Caspers
38 κνημωθεὶς A, corr. Hermann   σιχεσυνεξαμύη A, corr.
Schweighäuser (εἶχε), Dindorf (reliqua)   39 ἠδήχθεε A,
corr. Musurus: ἤχθετο Schubart   οὐδὲ A, corr. Casaubon
40 μισ. τ' οιαν ἔπεμψεν A, corr. Hermann   41 Λυδῆς A,
corr. Bach   λυσηΐδος A, corr. Ruhnken (cf. AP 9.63)
43 Δαρδανίη Dalecamp: λάρνακί νιν Ruhnken: alii alia

Smarting for her, he settled in a tiny isle,
Leaving his own broad homeland far behind;
And hymned Icarius' race, Amyclas' town
And Sparta,[9] touching on his own distress.

Long-suffering Mimnermus, who found out   [35]
Sweet song and the pentamenter's soft breath,
For Nanno burned; and binding on his ancient flute
Held many a revel with Examyes.[10]
He warred with ever-cruel Hermobius, and loathed
His enemy, Pherecles, for his jibes.[11]   [40]

Antimachus, for Lydian Lyde struck
With passion, trod beside Pactolus' stream;
. . . and when she died, laid her beneath dry earth
Lamenting, and departing (from . . . ?) came
To Colophon's hill; and holy books with tears   [45]
He filled, when he had ceased from all his grief.[12]

[9] Icarius was father of Penelope, and Amyclas ancestor of
Helen. Sparta was the home of Menelaus and / or Agamemnon,
the latter post-homerically. So reference to both *Odyssey* and
Iliad seems to be intended.   [10] The reference is unclear,
but the name was also that of Thales' father.

[11] Perhaps rivals for the love of Nanno?

[12] For the story of Antimachus' consolatory poetry on the
death of his wife, see also Plut. *Mor.* 106 B–C. Pactolus is the river
that runs through Sardis: did Lyde drown there?

---

44 καλλίων αϊζαον διῆλθεν A: κλαίων αἰάζων τ᾽ ἦλθεν Ilgen (δ᾽
ἦλθεν iam Casaubon): nomen loci fors. latet   45 ἄκρον ἐς
A, corr. Hermann: ἄκρον ἔσω Meineke   46 ἱερὰς A, corr.
Musurus: γηράς Meineke   παυσόμενος Villebrune

Λέσβιος Ἀλκαῖος δὲ πόσους ἀνεδέξατο κώμους,
　Σαπφοῦς φορμίζων ἱμερόεντα πόθον,
γινώσκεις. ὁ δ᾽ ἀοιδὸς ἀηδόνος ἠράσαθ᾽ ὕμνων
50　Τήιον ἀλγύνων ἄνδρα πολυφραδίῃ.
καὶ γὰρ τὴν ὁ μελιχρὸς ἐφημίλλητ᾽ Ἀνακρείων
　στελλομένην πολλαῖς ἄμμιγα Λεσβιάσιν·
φοίτα δ᾽ ἄλλοτε μὲν λείπων Σάμον, ἄλλοτε δ᾽
　　αὐτὴν
　οἰνηρῇ δείρῃ κεκλιμένην πατρίδα,
55　Λέσβον ἐς εὔοινον· τὸ δὲ Μύσιον εἴσιδε Λέκτον
　πολλάκις Αἰολικοῦ κύματος ἀντιπέρας.

Ἀτθὶς δ᾽ οἷα μέλισσα πολυπρήωνα Κολώνην
　λείπουσ᾽ ἐν τραγικαῖς ᾖδε χοροστασίαις
Βάκχον καὶ τὸν ἔρωτα Θεωρίδος ‹–∪∪––
60　ἥν ποτε γηραιῷ› Ζεὺς ἔπορεν Σοφοκλεῖ.

φημὶ δὲ κἀκεῖνον τὸν αἰεὶ πεφυλαγμένον ἄνδρα
　καὶ πάντων μῖσος κτώμενον ἐκ †συνοχῶν
πάσας ἀμφὶ γυναῖκας ὑπὸ σκολιοῖο τυπέντα
　τόξου νυκτερινὰς οὐκ ἀποθέσθ᾽ ὀδύνας·

47 πόσοις ἀνεδήσατο κώμοις conj. Powell　49 ὑμνῶν A,
corr. Musurus　51 ἐφωμίλησ᾽ Ἀνακρέων A, corr. Powell
(ἐφημιλλήσατ᾽ Ἀνακρέων iam Bergk): ἐφωμίλησ᾽ Ἀνακρείων
Musurus: Ἀνακρείων ἐφίλησεν dub. Hermann　52 τελλο-
μένην Hartung　54 οἰνηρὴν δοῦριν A, corr. Kaibel
55 μυριον A, corr. Wensch　λέκτρον A, corr. Hermann
57 αὖθις . . . πολυπριωνα κοδώνην A, corr. Ruhnken

How many revels, singing his desire
For Sappho, Lesbian Alcaeus held
You know. The bard who loved the nightingale gave
    pain
To the Teian through the eloquence of his songs.   [50]
For honey-tongued Anacreon contended
For her, arrayed among the many Lesbians.
Sometimes he went from Samos, else his own
Home nestling on a hillside clad with vines,
To Lesbos rich in wine. He often gazed   [55]
At Mysian Lektos over the Aeolian sea;

And how the Attic bee, leaving Colone's
Many hills, in tragic choral dances sang
Of Bacchus and his passion for Theoris . . .
Which Zeus inspired in aged (?) Sophocles.[13]   [60]

And I say that even that man so well-defended,
Whose reprobations(?) of the female sex
Won him the hate of all, was struck by the curved
Bow, and never quit his nightly pains;

[13] For Theoris, see the *Life of Sophocles* and Athen. 13.592 B.
Sophocles came from Colonus, and "bee" (a frequent image for
bards and poets) was his nickname (Dunbar on Ar. *Av.* 748–751).

59–60 ἔρωτ' ἀγειραιθειαρειδος Ζεὺς A: Θεωρίδος agnovit
Lennep   60 suppl. Kaibel   62 αἰσχρολογῶν vel ἠδ'
ἁπαλῶν μῖσ. κτ. ἐξ ὀνύχων Jacobs: ἐξ ὑλακῶν Headlam

65   ἀλλὰ Μακηδονίης πάσας κατενίσατο λαύρας
       Αἰγάων, μέθεπεν δ᾽ Ἀρχέλεω ταμίην·
       εἰσόκε <σοι> δαίμων, Εὐριπίδη, εὗρετ᾽ ὄλεθρον,
       Ἀρριβίου στυγνῶν ἀντιάσαντι κυνῶν.

       ἄνδρα δὲ τὸν Κυθέρηθεν, ὃν ἐθρέψαντο τιθῆναι
70   Βάκχου καὶ λωτοῦ πιστότατον ταμίην
       Μοῦσαι παιδευθέντα Φιλόξενον, οἷα τιναχθεὶς
       Ὀρτυγίῃ ταύτης ἦλθε διὰ πτόλιος,
       γινώσκεις, ἀίουσα μέγαν πόθον ὃν Γαλατείη
       αὐτοῖς μηλείοις θήκαθ᾽ ὑπὸ προγόνοις.

75   οἶσθα δὲ καὶ τὸν ἀοιδόν, ὃν Εὐρυπύλου πολιῆται
       Κῷοι χάλκειον στῆσαν ὑπὸ πλατάνῳ
       Βιττίδα μολπάζοντα θοήν, περὶ πάντα Φιλίταν
       ῥήματα καὶ πᾶσαν τρυόμενον λαλιήν.

66 αἰγείων A, corr. Bergk: ἀγρεύων Headlam   μεθεπε δ᾽
ἀρχελάωι A, corr. Musurus   67 <σοι> Bergk: <δὴ>
Schweighäuser   68 ἀμφὶ βίου A: Ἀρριδίου vel Ἀρριβίου
Headlam (cf. *Suda* ε 3695)   ἀντιάσαντα A, corr Musurus
69 ἀνεθρέψαντο A, corr. Hermann   71 Μούσαις Emperius
παίδευσάν τε vel παιδεύσαντο Kaibel (qui Βάκχου cum τιθῆ-
ναι construit)   72 ὠρυγῇ A, corr. Couat: Ὀρτυγίην Bergk
(id est, Ephesum, cf. *Suda* φ 393)   πτόλεως A, corr.
Meineke   73 γιγνώσκει καὶ οὖσαν A, corr. Dalecamp
(γιγνώσεις), Ruhnken (ἀίουσα)   Γαλατείης A, corr.
Weston   74 μηλίοις A, corr. Heringa   75 τὸν A, corr.
Casaubon   76 θῆκαν A, corr. Hecker, Meineke
77 Βαττίδα Scaliger   78 ῥυόμενον A, corr. Hermann
79 ἐκτήσαντο Porson

But roamed all the alleyways of Macedonian [65]
Aegae, pursuing Archelaus' housekeeper;
Until the god, Euripides, worked your doom,
Meeting the grim hounds of Arribius.[14]

And him of Cythera, most faithful squire
Of Bacchus and the flute, nurtured and reared [70]
By Muses for his nurses—how, distressed
In Ortygia he travelled through this city,
You know, and that great love which Galatea
Inspired into the very first-born lambs.[15]

And you know that even the bard set up in bronze [75]
By Eurypylus' folk in Cos, beneath a plane,
Sings of the flighty Bittis: Philitas, well-worn
In every utterance and all the forms of speech.

[14] There are many versions of the story that Euripides was killed by dogs. Headlam's conjecture in 68 rests on *Suda* ε 3695, which names Arribaeus as a Macedonian poet who, jealous of Euripides, persuaded one of the royal slaves to let the king's dogs loose on him. The story about the housekeeper is otherwise unknown (and the gender unclear). The *Suda* also alludes to Euripides' visits to Craterus, boyfriend (not housekeeper) of Archelaus, but in this latter version, he was torn apart by women. For a textually conservative discussion of this section, see Matthews 2003.

[15] Philoxenus of Cythera, who spent time at the court of Dionysius I in Syracuse, and composed a dithyramb *Cyclops, or Galatea*. The story was that Galatea was the name of Dionysius' mistress, with whom Philoxenus was in love, and the Cyclops a cipher for Dionysius himself (Athen. 1.6 F–7 A). The places in 72 are unclear. The name Ortygia attached, *inter al.*, to both Syracuse and Ephesus (where, according to the *Suda*, Philoxenus died). "This city" could be Colophon, near to Ephesus, but may well be corrupt.

οὐδὲ μὲν οὐδ' ὁπόσοι σκληρὸν βίον ἐστήσαντο
80   ἀνθρώπων, σκοτίην μαιόμενοι σοφίην,
οὓς αὐτὴ περὶ πυκνὰ λόγοις ἐσφίγξατο μῆτις
καὶ δεινὴ μύθων κῆδος ἔχουσ' ἀρετή,
οὐδ' οἵδ' αἰνὸν ἔρωτος ἀπεστρέψαντο κυδοιμὸν
μαινόμενου, δεινὸν δ' ἦλθον ὑφ' ἡνίοχον.

85   οἵη μὲν Σάμιον μανίη κατέδησε Θεανοῦς
Πυθαγόρην, ἑλίκων κομψὰ γεωμετρίης
εὑρόμενον, καὶ κύκλον ὅσον περιβάλλεται αἰθὴρ
βαιῇ ἐνὶ σφαίρῃ πάντ' ἀποπλασσόμενον.

οἵῳ δ' ἐχλίηνεν ὃν ἔξοχον ἔχρη Ἀπόλλων
90   ἀνθρώπων εἶναι Σωκράτη ἐν σοφίῃ
Κύπρις μηνίουσα πυρὸς μένει. ἐκ δὲ βαθείης
ψυχῆς κουφοτέρας ἐξεπόνησ' ἀνίας,
οἰκί' ἐς Ἀσπασίης πωλεύμενος· οὐδέ τι τέκμαρ
εὗρε, λόγων πολλὰς εὑρόμενος διόδους.

80 σκολιὴν A, corr. Heinrich   81 αὐτὴ] λιτὴ, λεπτὴ
Meineke   πικρὰ A, corr. Porson   λόγοις Bergk
82 κῆδος edd. ante Schweighäuser: κῦρος Hecker   83 οὐδ'
οἶδεν ὃν A, corr. Weston   84 φαινόμενον A, corr. Anon.
Londin.   86 γεωμετρίη conj. Kaibel   87 εὐράμενον
A, corr. Musurus   88 βίης ἐν A, corr. Musurus (βαιῇ),
Dindorf (ἐνὶ)   ἀποτασσόμενον A, corr. Powell, Harberton:
-μασσ- Hemsterhuys   89 οιωιδεχλειημενον A, corr.
Heringa   89–90 ἐχρὴν πολλων δ' ἀνθρώπων A, corr.
Porson   90 σοφῆι A, corr. Musurus   91 μηνιόωσα
Cuypers   92 ἐξεπόνησαν ἀνίας A, corr. Musurus
94 λόγῳ A, corr. Heringa   εὐράμενος A, corr. Dindorf

Not even those who chose a toilsome path
In life in quest of dark Sagacity, [80]
Whose very skill hedged them about with words
And formidable gifts regarding speech(?)—
Not even they could shun the maddening force
Of Love, but underwent the dreaded charioteer.[16]

Such madness for Theano[17] bound the Samian [85]
Pythagoras, of elegant geometric whorls
Discoverer, who figured in a little sphere
The whole circuit encompassed by the ether.

And Socrates, whom Apollo called pre-eminent
In wisdom among men: with what strong flames [90]
The angry Cyprian burned him; and his soul,
So deep, withstood a lighter kind of trial,
When visiting Aspasia's;[18] remedy
He found none, though he found mazes of words.

[16] These lines refer to philosophers. The charioteer image occurs in Anacreon *PMG* 360.

[17] Elsewhere named as Pythagoras' wife (Diog. Laert. 8.42; *Suda* π 3120).

[18] There is a tradition that Socrates was her pupil in various fields (politics, rhetoric, love); Hermesianax has transformed this into the story that he was in love with her.

95   ἄνδρα <δὲ> Κυρηναῖον ἔσω πόθος ἔσπασεν
       Ἰσθμοῦ
       δεινὸς, ὅτ᾽ Ἀπιδανῆς Λαΐδος ἠράσατο
       ὀξὺς Ἀρίστιππος, πάσας δ᾽ ἠνήνατο λέσχας
       φεύγων, †ουδαμενον ἐξεφόρησε βίῳ.

95 ἄνδρα Κυρ. εἴσω A, corr. Hermann   96 δεινὸν A, corr.
Ruhnken   98 οὐδὲ μένων Dobree: οὐδαμινὴν Schweig-
häuser   ἐξ Ἐφύρης ἐβίω Porson   εὐλιμένων ἐξ
Ἐφύρης ὁρίων Hermann: οὐδαμινόν τ᾽ ἐξεφόρησε βίον Har-
berton

Incerti Libri

4 = Parthenius, Ἐρωτικὰ Παθήματα v

5 = Parthenius, Ἐρωτικὰ Παθήματα xxii

In Eurytionem (?)

6 Paus. 7.18.1

ὁπόσοι δὲ ἐς Ἡρακλέα καὶ τὰ ἔργα αὐτοῦ πεποιή-
κασιν, ἔστιν οὐκ ἐλάχιστά σφισι δείγματα τοῦ λόγου
Δεξαμενὸς ὁ ἐν Ὠλένῳ βασιλεὺς καὶ ὁποίων Ἡρα-
κλῆς παρ᾽ αὐτῷ ξενίων ἔτυχε. καὶ ὅτι μὲν ἦν πόλισμα
ἐξ ἀρχῆς μικρὸν ἡ Ὤλενος, μαρτυρεῖ τῷ λόγῳ μου
καὶ ἐλεγεῖον ἐς Εὐρυτίωνα Κένταυρον ὑπὸ Ἑρμησι-
άνακτος πεποιημένον.

174

And dreadful longing drew within the Isthmus [95]
The Cyrenean, smitten with Apidanian Lais,
Keen Aristippus, who renounced all conversation
In his flight, and . . . [19]

From Uncertain Books

4 = Parthenius, *Sufferings in Love*, "About Leucippus"

5 = Parthenius, *Sufferings in Love*, "About Pisidice"

On Eurytion (?)

6 Pausanias

Poets who have written on Heracles and his deeds have
found a favourite theme in Dexamenus, king of Olenus,
and the entertainment Heracles received at his court.
There is support for my claim that Olenus was a small town
from its inception in an elegiac passage on Eurytion the
Centaur by Hermesianax.[20]

[19] For Aristippus and the courtesan Lais, see Athen. 13.588 E–
F. "Apidane" is an antiquarian name for the Peloponnese; Lais
lived in Corinth.

[20] Eurytion the Centaur is a disruptive force in all houses
he enters; in this myth, he tries to marry the daughter of Dexame-
nus, but is killed by Heracles (ps.-Apoll. 2.5.5; Diod. Sic. 4.33.1;
Hygin. 31, 33). It is unclear whether Pausanias means that Her-
mesianax wrote an entire poem on the subject; *elegeion* may mean
either "an elegiac couplet" (or shorter passage) or "an elegiac
poem".

HERMESIANAX

Περσικά (??)

7 Σ Nic. *Ther*. 3, p. 35.14 Crugnola

τούτῳ δὲ τὰ Περσικὰ γέγραπται . . .

8–12 FRAGMENTA INCERTAE SEDIS

8 Σ Theocr. *Id*. 8.53–56*d*, p. 210.9 Wendel

οὐκ ἀνιστορήτως δὲ τοῦτο ὁ Θεόκριτός φησι· καὶ
Ἑρμησιάναξ γὰρ λέγει τὸν Δάφνιν ἐρωτικῶς ἔχειν
τοῦ Μενάλκα. ἀλλ᾽ ὁ μὲν ἐπ᾽ Εὐβοίας τὰ περὶ αὐτοῦ
διατίθεται, οὗτος δὲ ἐπὶ Σικελίας.

Fortasse e primo Leontii libro.

9 Arg. ad Theocr. *Id*. 9, p. 215.2 Wendel

τὰ μὲν πράγματα ἐπὶ Σικελίας ὑφίστανται. παρα-
καλοῦνται δὲ ὑπὸ συννομέως Δάφνις καὶ Μενάλκας,
ὅπως ἀλλήλοις ἀντᾴσωσιν. οὐδὲν δὲ ἔχει πρὸς τὸν
Μενάλκαν τοῦτον ὄντα Σικελὸν <τὰ> ὑπὲρ Μενάλκου
Χαλκιδέως, ὅν φησιν Ἑρμησιάναξ ἐρασθῆναι τῆς
Κηναίας Εὐίππης καὶ διὰ τὸ μὴ τυγχάνειν αὐτῆς
κατακρημνισθῆναι.

Κρηναίας K, defendit Rohde: Κυρηναίας cett.: Κηναίας
Wilamowitz (sc. nomen Euboici montis)

Fortasse e primo Leontii libro.

176

Persica (??)

7 Scholiast on Nicander, *Theriaca*

He is the author of the *Persica* . . . [21]

8–12 FRAGMENTS OF UNCERTAIN LOCATION

8 Scholiast on Theocritus, *Idylls*

It is not without grounds that Theocritus says this, for Hermesianax says that Daphnis was in love with Menalcas. But he sets the story on Euboea, whereas Theocritus sets it on Sicily.

9 *Argument* to Theocritus, *Idyll* 9

The action takes place in Sicily. Daphnis and Menalcas are summoned by a fellow herdsman for a singing competition. This Menalcas, who is a Sicilian, has nothing to do with Menalcas of Chalcis, who according to Hermesianax was in love with Euippe of Kenaion and, because he failed to win her, jumped off the cliff.[22]

---

[21] No other mention of this work, nor trace of anything that could conceivably belong to it, save for the story of Nanis, which is ascribed to the *Leontion* (**5**); the pun on Cyrus' name (**14**) is not certainly by Hermesianax.

[22] Kenaion is a rocky promontory at the north-west tip of Euboea. The love affair with the nymph sits puzzlingly beside the affair with Daphnis. Rohde 1960, 83–84 n. 1, suspected that the scholiast of **8** was confused, and that Hermesianax only mentioned the nymph.

10 Paus. 7.17.9–10

Δυμαίοις δὲ ἔστι μὲν Ἀθηνᾶς ναὸς καὶ ἄγαλμα ἐς τὰ μάλιστα ἀρχαῖον· ἔστι δὲ καὶ ἄλλο ἱερόν σφισι Διν-δυμήνῃ μητρὶ καὶ Ἄττῃ πεποιημένον. Ἄττης δὲ ὅστις ἦν, οὐδὲν οἷός τε ἦν ἀπόρρητον ἐς αὐτὸν ἐξευρεῖν, ἀλλὰ Ἑρμησιάνακτι μὲν τῷ τὰ ἐλεγεῖα γράψαντι πεποιημένα ἐστὶν ὡς υἱός τε ἦν Καλαοῦ Φρυγὸς καὶ ὡς οὐ τεκνοποιὸς ὑπὸ τῆς μητρὸς τεχθείη· ἐπεὶ δὲ ηὔξητο, μετῴκησεν ἐς Λυδίαν τῷ Ἑρμησιάνακτος λόγῳ καὶ Λυδοῖς ὄργια ἐτέλει Μητρός, ἐς τοσοῦτο ἥκων παρ᾽ αὐτῇ τιμῆς ὡς Δία αὐτῇ [Ἄττῃ Schubart–Walz] νεμεσήσαντα ὗν ἐπὶ τὰ ἔργα ἐπιπέμψαι τῶν Λυδῶν. ἐνταῦθα ἄλλοι τε τῶν Λυδῶν καὶ αὐτὸς Ἄττης ἀπέθανεν ὑπὸ τοῦ ὑός· καί τι ἑπόμενον τούτοις Γαλα-τῶν δρῶσιν οἱ Πεσσινοῦντα ἔχοντες, ὑῶν οὐχ ἁπτό-μενοι.

11 Paus. 8.12.1

Ἀρκάδων δὲ ἐν τοῖς δρυμοῖς εἰσιν αἱ δρῦς διάφοροι . . . αἱ τρίται δὲ ἀραιὸν τὸν φλοιὸν . . . ταύτης τῆς δρυὸς τὸν φλοιὸν ἄλλοι τε Ἰώνων καὶ Ἑρμησιάναξ ὁ τὰ ἐλεγεῖα ποιήσας φελλὸν ὀνομάζουσιν.

Fragmentum elegiae in Eurytionem tribuit Powell (ad suum fr. 10).

10 Pausanias

The people of Dyme have a temple of Athena and an extremely ancient image; they also have another temple built in honour of the Dindymenean mother and Attes. I could not find out any secret about the identity of Attes; but Hermesianax, the elegiac poet, says in a poem that he was son of Calaus the Phrygian, and that he was born incapable of reproducing himself. When he grew up, still according to Hermesianax's account, he moved to Lydia and celebrated the rites of the Mother for the Lydians, attaining such honour with her that Zeus grew angry with her and sent a boar to ravage the crops of the Lydians. The boar brought about the deaths of several Lydians, including Attes; and as a consequence of this, the Galatians who inhabit Pessinous abstain from pork.

11 Pausanias

In the groves of the Arcadians are various species of oak . . . the third have light bark . . . The bark of this oak is called "cork" by several Ionians, including Hermesianax, the elegiac poet.

12 Paus. 9.35.5

Ἑρμησιάνακτι δὲ τῷ τὰ ἐλεγεῖα γράψαντι τοσόνδε οὐ κατὰ τὴν τῶν πρότερον δόξαν ἐστὶν αὐτῷ πεποιημένον, ὡς ἡ Πειθὼ Χαρίτων εἴη καὶ αὐτὴ μία.

13 DUBIE TRIBUTA

13 P. Brux. Inv. E. 8934 + P. Sorb. Inv. 2254

col. i

```
                    ].[
            ].[.......]...[.].[
        ].π.[..].μνήσονται ἀοιδαὶ
        ]..[.].[.]. ὥς τε πυρὶ φλέγομαι
5       ]νῶτον στίξω μέγαν Εὐρυτί[ω]να
        Ν]εφέλης υἱὸν ἀτρεστοβίην
    Ἀμφιτρυωνι]άδαο δαϊζόμενον ὑπὸ χερσίν
        ]κ..τος τε μνηστεύετο κούρην
    ἀνθ]ρώπων ἀζόμενος ν.μεσιν
10      ]ας δεινὸν χόλον, ὅς τ' ἐπὶ δειλ[.].
        ].ον δριμὺν [ἀεὶ] τίθεται
        ]τίσις τω.σ..ο.οι· ἦ γὰρ ὅ γ' οὐδὲν
        ]π[.]..... κακῆς ὕβριος
        ]...ε [τ]ρίποδα μμέγαν ......
15      ].φο..[.] ις κρατὸς ὕπε[ρ] λασίου
        ].ει μέσσον δ' εἰς στῆθ[ο]ς ἔρεισεν
```

12 Pausanias

When Hermesianax the elegiac poet says that Peitho (Persuasion) is herself one of the Graces, he parts company with earlier writers.

13 DUBIOUSLY ATTRIBUTED

13 P. Brux. Inv. E. 8934 + P. Sorb. Inv. 2254[23]

col. i

. . . songs shall mention	[3]
. . . how I burn with fire	
. . . I shall tattoo on (your) back a great Eurytion	[5]
. . . son of a Cloud, fearless in might,	
Being cloven by the hands of the son of Amphitryon	
. . . he was wooing the maiden	
. . . with (no) regard for the anger of mankind	
. . . (or) the dread wrath (of the gods) which against	[10]
wretched	
. . . always makes bitter	
. . . vengeance . . . for truly nothing . . .	
. . . of wicked insolence	
. . . a large tripod	
. . . above its shaggy head	[15]
. . . and pressed against the middle of his chest	

23 These fragments from a curse poem, in which the speaking subject threatens to tattoo his enemy with representations of terrific punishments, has been conjecturally assigned to Hermesianax on the grounds of the overlap between col. i and **6** (Eurytion the Centaur). The other myths are the punishment of Tantalus, and the Calydonian boar-hunt.

]ν ἀνέρος οὐδεμίαν
]έθηκε βέλος Τριτωνὶς Ἀθήνη
]του φειδομένη μεγάλως
20   ἐτ]έρηι μὲν ὑπ' ἀσφάραγον λάβε χειρί,
τῇ δ' ἑτέρηι ῥ]όπαλον σκληρὸν ἀνασχόμενος
] κρόταφον σύν [τ' ὀ]στέα πάντα
ἄραξεν
]νων ἔκπεσεν [ἐγ]κέφαλος
] πλήγην ψυχὴ [δ'] ἀνὰ ἠέρα δῦνε

5 πρῶτά σ' ἐπὶ ν]νῶτον (aut νώτοις) Huys   7 -μενου pap.,
corr. Huys   8 ὅς τε vel ἀέ]κοντός τε Huys
10 οὔτε θεῶν δείσ]ας Parsons   10–11 δειλ[ῶ]ι | ὑβριστῆι
πόλε]μον vel δειλ[οῖ]ς | ὑβρισταῖς πότ]μον Huys: δειλ[ὸν |
ὑβρισταῖς πόλε]μον δριμὺς Parsons   16 Ἡρακ]λεῖ
Parsons   17 καί κεν ἴδοις φυλακὴ]ν Parsons
18 ἀλλ' ἐν χερσὶν] ἔθηκε Huys: εἰ τότε μὴ παρ]έθηκε Parsons
19 αὐ]τοῦ vel βιό]του Huys: ἀνδρὸς τηλυγέ]του Ll.-J.
20 init. Ἡρακλέης Parsons   22 Κενταύρου] Parsons
23 ῥι]νῶν Parsons

col. ii

μείδησεν [δ]ὲ Δίκη παρθένος ἀθάνα[τος],
ἥτε ἀναπεπ|ταμένοις ἀτενὲς βλέπε[ι
ὀφθαλμοῖσιν],
ἐν δὲ Διὸς Κρ[ο]νίδεω στήθεσιν ἑδριά[ει.
στίξω δ' ἐν κ|ορυφῆι σε μέγαν καὶ ἀναιδέα λᾶαν,
5   ὅς τε καὶ εἰν Ἀΐ|δ[εω κρατὸς ὑπερκρέμαται
Ταντάλωι ἀ|ξυνέτου γλώσσης χάριν· ἦ μέγ'
ἐκείνωι
πῆμα καὶ εἰν | Ἀΐδεω δώμασιν ἐστρέφετο.

. . . of the man . . . no . . .
. . . Tritonian goddess Athena placed a weapon
. . . sparing in her might
. . . with one hand he seized him by the throat,   [20]
With the other he held up his stiff club,
. . . he shattered the temple with all its bones
. . . and the brains came tumbling out
. . . and with the blow his soul dispersed through the
    air.

col. ii

Justice, immortal maiden, gave a smile,
Who watches fixedly with open eyes,
And lodges in the breast of Cronian Zeus.
I'll tattoo on your head the great and shameless stone
Which even in Hades hangs above the head   [5]
Of Tantalus for his foolish tongue; in truth, a great
Woe overhung him even in Hades' halls.

ἢ μὲν δὴ καὶ | θεοῖσιν ὁμέστιος ἀθανάτοισιν,
  ἦεν καὶ Ζηνὶ‌ος παῖς νεφεληγερέος,
10 καὶ πλούτωι | καὶ παισὶ μέγας καὶ τίμιος αὔτως.
  ἀλλ᾽ οὐδ᾽ ὣς γλώ‌σσηι δοὺς χάριν ἀξυνέτωι
  ποινὴν ἐξή‌λυξε· σὺ δ᾽ ἔλπεαι ἐκφεύξεσθαι;
  μήπω τοῦτο [θ]εοῖς ἀνδάνοι ἀθανάτοι[ς].
  αὐτὰρ ὑπέρθ᾽ ὀ‌φρύων στίξω σὺν ἀργιόδοντα,
15 ὅς ποτ᾽ ἀν᾽ Αἰτ[ω]λῶν ἐρχόμενος καμάτ[ους]
  Ἀρτέμιδος βο‌υ‌λῆισι—τὸ γὰρ φίλον ἔπλετ[ο]
    κούρηι—
  σίνετο μὲν [σῖτ]ον, σίνετο δὲ σταφυλάς,
  πολλοὺς δὲ σκ[ύλ]ακας θηρήτορας ἐξενά[ρι]ξεν,
  πρίν γ᾽ ὅτε οἱ μ‌ελίην πῆξεν ὑπὸ λλαπά[ρ]ην
20 Οἰ‌νεΐδης | Μ‌ελέαγρος· ὁ γὰρ θηρέστατος ἦεν
  πολλῶν ἡρώων σὺν τότ᾽ ἀθροισαμένων.
  ἤλυθε μὲν Θησεὺς Πιτθηΐδος, ἤλυθε δ᾽ Αἴθων,
  ἤλυθε δ᾽ Ἀγκ‌αῖος σὺμ μεγάλωι πελέκει,
  ἦλθον δὲ Λή‌δης κοῦροι καὶ Ζηνὸς ἄνακτος

2 suppl. Barns   6 -νωι vel –νος   11 αλλουσδ pap.,
corr. Huys   ἀξυνέτως Papathomopoulos
12 ἐχφεν‌.‌σθαι pap., corr. Papathomopoulos   14 ὕπερθ᾽
(vel ὑπέρ σ᾽) Huys   15 καμάτ[ους] vel –[ον]   19 οἱ
Luppe: δὴ Huys   20 ειεν pap., corr. Papathomopoulos

Indeed, he feasted with the immortal gods,
And was the son of cloud-gathering Zeus,
Both rich in wealth, and sons, and honoured too.   [10]
Yet, giving licence to his foolish tongue, even so
He could not sidestep punishment; and you hope to
    flee?
May this never be pleasing to the immortal gods.
I'll tattoo above your brows a white-tusked boar,
Which once, falling upon the Aetolians' toils,   [15]
At Artemis' command—it was her will—
Ravaged their standing crops, ravaged their vines,
Slew many hunting dogs, until there fixed
His ashen spear beneath the monster's jowls
Oeneus' son, Meleager, best of those   [20]
Many heroes then assembled for the hunt.
There came Theseus from Pittheus, came Aithon,
Came Ancaeus with a colossal axe,
Came the sons of Leda and of sovereign Zeus.

14 FRAGMENTUM PROSAE ORATIONIS

Ἐγκώμιον Ἀθηνᾶς (?)

14 Agatharchides, *De mari Erythraeo* 21 (Phot. *Bibl.* 250 p. 446 B 33)

διὸ καὶ ψυχρότητα ἐσχάτην ἐμφαίνει [Hegesias, *FGrH* 142 T 3], ὥσπερ καὶ Ἑρμησιάναξ ὁ τὴν Ἀθηνᾶν ἐγκωμιάσας οὕτως· "ἐκ γὰρ τῆς τοῦ Διὸς γεγενημένη κεφαλῆς εἰκότως ἔχει τῆς εὐδαιμονίας τὸ κεφάλαιον." τοιοῦτον καὶ τὸ "τίς δ᾽ ἂν δύναιτο ποιῆσαι τὴν Κύρου δόσιν ἄκυρον;" καὶ τόδε δὲ ὅμοιον· "τόπος δὲ πῶς γένοιτ᾽ ἄβατος, βάτου περικειμένου;"

FRAGMENTS

14 PROSE FRAGMENT

Encomium of Athena (?)

14 Agatharchides, *On the Red Sea*

So he [Hegesias] displays the utmost frigidity, like Hermesianax who sang the praises of Athena in the following way: "For it is reasonable that one born from the head of Zeus should have attained the height of blessedness." "Who could make Cyrus' gift invalid (*akȳron*)?" and "How could a place be inaccessible (*abatos*) if brambles (*batos*) surround it?" are similar kinds of saying.[24]

---

[24] The last two quotations could come from Hegesias, whose style Agatharchides has been criticising at length, rather than from Hermesianax (see *FGrH* 142 F 25–26).

EUPHORION OF CHALCIS

INTRODUCTION

The *Suda* is our main source for Euphorion's life. He came
from the Euboean city of Chalcis, and was born in the
126th Olympiad, 276–272. He studied in Athens, though
the date of Lacydes, one of his philosophical teachers,
would seem to put this period puzzlingly late. He first en-
joyed the patronage of Alexander, ruler of Euboea, and his
wife, Nicaea, and then, having presumably made a name
for himself as a scholar and a poet, was invited by
Antiochus the Great (succeeded 222) to be head of the
library established by the Seleucids in Antioch. He thus
offers us a precious insight into literary culture under a
rival centre to Alexandria; we should like to be better
informed about this library, which the *Suda* describes as
"public", although the king evidently had the right of
appointment of its librarian.[1] Our sources disagree over
whether Euphorion died in Syria (so Test. **1**) or in Athens
(so Test. **7**), where he is said to have enjoyed honorary citi-
zenship (Test. **3**).

Euphorion wrote in hexameters. The *Suda* lists only
hexameter poems, and Athenaeus calls him an *epopoios*

[1] The *Lives of Aratus* claim, perhaps problematically, that
Antiochus I (d. 262) had already invited Aratus to Syria in order
to work on the text of Homer (*Vita* 1 p. 8.21–24 Martin; cf. *Vita* 3
p. 16.18–23 Martin).

(hexameter poet) even where he is citing his prose works.[2] Other than this, we know he wrote epigrams, but there is currently no evidence that he wrote elegies. That seems to be a mistaken inference by Roman scholars, misled by his connection with the Latin elegist Cornelius Gallus (Test. **15**).

As for his hexameter poems, the *Suda* gives just three titles (*Hesiod*, *Mopsopia*, *Chiliades* in five books). Wilamowitz suggested that the book-number applies to the whole corpus, not just to the *Chiliades* (which are never cited by book number), and that, rather than *Atakta* being an alternative title for the *Mopsopia*, this was the title of the whole corpus. This helps to reduce the difficulties about the *Chiliades*—for it is hard to see how five whole books could have been filled with material about long-delayed prophecies, and as the text stands there is a puzzling reduplication in what is said of the poem as a whole, and what is said of the fifth book in particular. In practice, when later sources cite Euphorion, they use many other titles in addition to the three named by the *Suda*, and the relationship of these additional works to the *Suda*'s three (parts of a whole? or different works altogether?) remains an unsolved problem.

Many of the titles not mentioned in the *Suda*, but cited by later authorities, are personal names. In most cases the citations themselves are unhelpful. Some names are divine (*Dionysus*, *Gaping Dionysus*); these suggest hymns or aetiological narrative poems. Others are mythological (*Anius*, *Hyacinthus*, *Philoctetes*) or the names of historical individuals (*Apollodorus*, *Artemidorus*, *Demosthenes*, *Polychares*, *Responses to Theodoridas*); in several cases it

---

[2] **201a**, **202**, **203**, cf. also, for citations of poetry, **52**, **76**.

is hard to tell (*Alexander, Cle(i)tor, Hippomedon*). Poems named after gods and mythological characters—implying hymns, epyllia, and other types of narrative verse—can readily be found among the works of the earlier Hellenistic poets. But for poems named after historical individuals—if this is what they are—we must look forward: to Parthenius' poems for Arete, Archelais, Auxithemis, Bias, and Crinagoras. In Parthenius' case, the titles often have a further specification of genre (encomium; epicedium), which in Euphorion's case they usually lack. But we do hear of a funerary lament for Protagoras (**22**), while the *Hippomedon Meizon* (**34**) begins apparently with an instruction to the Muses to sing a ὕμνο[ν for the honorand: that sounds like a praise poem. There is little sign of *ad hominem* poems among the works of Philitas, or Apollonius, or Eratosthenes.[3] Callimachus, of course, wrote several pieces celebrating the royal family and governing classes (*Victory of Berenice, Lock of Berenice, Deification of Arsinoe, Victory of Sosibius*), and it is possible that some of the bare personal names among Euphorion's poems are concealing occasional, commemorative, poetry of this sort. Such connections have been suggested for the *Hippomedon* and the *Alexander* (the Euboean ruler whose patronage Euphorion enjoyed?), and although it is unplaced, **119** demonstrates an interest in Seleucid dynastic myth.

The fragmentary state of Euphorion's poetry, where all too often title cannot even be related to content, might have been expected to throw serious obstacles in the way

---

[3] A faint possibility that Philitas wrote a *Telephus* (**13**) in honour of his father. Eratosthenes wrote an Epithalamium (fr. 28 P.); we do not know whether its subject was contemporary or mythological.

193

of trying to assess it. But even before papyrus discoveries began to fill out the picture, it was obvious that Euphorion had cultivated a style of poetry with marked idiosyncrasies. Then in 1907, Wilamowitz published two sides of a parchment fragment which made continuous sense, one side of which seemed to come from a curse poem (**11**), the other side a description of Cerberus when Heracles fetched him up from Hades (**71**). This was further supplemented by papyrus discoveries at Oxyrhyncus and elsewhere, and what is now our longest fragment comes from the *Thrax*, previously known only through a handful of fragments and a couple of stories in Parthenius (XIII, XXVI). We are fortunate that this not only gives some sense of Euphorion in a genre—curse poetry—that he seems to have favoured (cf. also *Curses, or the Cup-Thief*; *Chiliades*), but has also provided an opportunity in a couple of cases to assess the "source" ascriptions in the manuscript of Parthenius' Ἐρωτικὰ Παθήματα (XIII ~ 24 and XXVI ~ 26).

Further discoveries will be very welcome, but the general outlines are by now clear. Euphorion was one of the *avant garde*. He regarded Homer as "unattainable" (**120**), and, like several other Hellenistic poets, shows considerable interest in Hesiod, who furnishes both matter and manner, myths and a suitable theodicy for curse poetry, with its calls for Justice and Retribution.[4] There are also signs of interest in Stesichorus.[5] Euphorion took a very Hellenistic approach to mythography: old myths were told in startlingly new ways (**31?, 56, 58, 97**), or given new set-

[4] See above all **26** col. ii; the *Hesiod* (**23**); mythography in **25** (scholia), **26** col. i. 7–8, **32, 61, 191 A fr. 3**.11, B fr. 3.6 (with nn. ad loc.); further lexical parallels in Magnelli 2002, 37–38.

[5] **80, 86, 87**, cf. **72, 83** n. 111.

tings (**85**, **102**); local aetiologies (**20–21**); the careful registration of variants (**44**). There are technical *jeux d'esprit*—not as obvious as other Hellenistic experiments, such as the pattern-poems, but illustrated by the division of a metrically intractable name Apollo-dorus across two hexameters (**7**). A very Hellenistic feature is the high proportion of spondeiazontes (three in a row in **37**).[6] They add a certain ponderousness to Euphorion's poetry, which is reinforced by his penchant for four-word lines. As for glosses (Test. **8**), we find not only the inevitable Homerisms (cf. Test. **8**.4), interpretations and variations thereof,[7] but also dialect words (**24**.12, **151**, cf. **59**, **63**, **125**); heteroclites, new terminations, and various kinds of morphological oddity (**4**, **84**, **133**, **147**, cf. the proper names in **15c**, **170**, **174**); and etymological *jeux-d'esprit* (**123**, **152**, cf. **81**, **158** and perhaps **191** B fr. 2.8).

Lucian mentions that Callimachus, Euphorion, and Parthenius all had reputations for wordiness and/or excruciating detail (Test. **9** = Parthenius Test. **6**). It is an interesting genealogy. Evidence suggests that Euphorion is indeed influenced by the language of his Hellenistic predecessors—especially Callimachus, but also Apollonius, and to a lesser extent Aratus, Alexander of Aetolia, and Theocritus. From these poets Euphorion gleans, or adapts, rarities, both lexical and mythographical, and, where one can tell, may allude to the context from which a word is drawn. But the chill and lugubrious tone, the obscurity, the determination to throw dust in the eyes of the reader, could never be mistaken for Callimachus; better comparisons for Euphorion are Lycophron—with whom

---

[6] A. S. Hollis, *Callimachus* Hecale (Oxford, 1990), 18.

[7] Magnelli 2002, 5–21.

contact is certain, though it is not yet clear who depends on whom[8]—and Nicander. This is mannerism built on mannerism, an imitator who goes further than his models.

Ultimately, though, what makes Euphorion a Hellenistic poet is more than allusiveness. It is the heavy representation among his works of poems that accumulate related material of one sort or another, especially narratives. Euphorion belongs with the Hellenistic catalogues and curses, prophecies and aetiologies, experiments in various methods of combination and arrangement. Our fragments of the *Curses or Cup-Thief*, and of the *Thrax*, seem to contain a succession of mythological stories whose kinship with catalogue poetry emerges not least through the repeated use of "or" as a connective. The segments are uneven in length—especially in the *Thrax*—but relatively short. There is a wry contrast between their gloomy, minatory tone and the possibly frivolous, even fictitious, events that occasioned the poems (was it really a human being who was murdered—or was it a dog?). The *Mopsopia* may have worked in a not dissimilar way: the *Suda* describes it as containing "various stories", and suggests a connection with Attica. So too the *Chiliades* (whether one book or five), which the *Suda* says had a *hypothesis*, or underlying theme: again it consisted of mythological stories with a notional point of departure in a real situation. And the bewildering succession of mythographical details in **108** may suggest a poem of a similar kind. Although we cannot work it out in detail, it is tempting to see in these tesselated narratives the general influence of Callimachus' *Aitia*, with its baffling diversity of material held together by an apparently simple idea.

[8] Magnelli 2002, 22–37.

Euphorion's poetry famously influenced the neoteric or "modernist" movement in Rome in the middle of the first century BC. Cicero's disparaging reference to the *cantores Euphorionis* (Test. **13**) belongs in 45 BC; scholars have sometimes suspected that Cinna is the main, if not the only, culprit,[9] but the young Gallus was coming on the scene, and Virgil's homage to Gallus and his "Chalcidian verse" dates to the years after 39 BC (Test. **14–15**). Euphorion's influence has been detected in the linguistic texture of Cinna's fragments,[10] and indirectly, too, in his epyllion on the incestuous heroine *Zmyrna*, in which we can certainly trace the influence of Parthenius (**29**). For Gallus, we have not only the express testimony of Virgil, but also an infuriatingly imprecise reference by Servius to Gallus' "adaptations" of Euphorion's poetry (Test. **14**). At the moment, at least, we can see parallels in Euphorion's curse poetry for the stories about deviant behaviour (especially sexual behaviour) beloved of the neoterics. We can certainly adduce him for the craze of spondeiazontes that seems to have afflicted this generation. We cannot, however, parallel the affective tone—the pathos, the emotionalism, the apostrophe,[11] the heroines' monologues. Nor, although Euphorion has been cited as an influence on Catullus 64,[12] do we find any analogy for the boxed narratives here. Part of the problem is assuredly that our most substantial fragments of Euphorion at the moment are

9 Watson 1982; Hollis 2007, 19.

10 Watson 1982.

11 Apostrophe is certainly to be found in Euphorion, but addresses in a curse-poem are very different from the narrator's address in an epyllion.

12 Latte 1935, 154–155.

from curse-poems, not epyllia. But we must also keep in mind is that literary movements and poetological creeds in Republican Rome cannot simply be transposed back into the Hellenistic period; what Euphorion *represents* for the Roman poets is not necessarily the same thing as what he *was*.

Of Euphorion's prose works, the titles and fragments reveal little more than the antiquarian and paradoxographical interests that are the stock-in-trade of Hellenistic prose: *Historical Commentaries*, *On the Aleuadae*, *On the Isthmian Games* (the one surviving *datum* from which is musicological), *On Lyric Poets*. There was also a *Hippocratic Lexicon* in six books, and a further fragment that indicates glossographic interests but is not medical (**206**). In **109**, apparently from a Euphorion commentary, ll. 28–30 contain a cross-reference to the *Chiliades*, and the restoration of a first-person verb here would open the possibility that Euphorion himself was the subject: author of the *Chiliades*, and of a commentary on another of his own poems. It is an intriguing possibility, but for caution see n. 150 ad loc.

The modern numeration of Euphorion's fragments goes back to Scheidweiler, and has lasted for a century. From at least two separate points of view it has ceased to be satisfactory. It was based on various criteria, beginning with the secure attribution of fragments to known works, and continuing with conjectural attributions; but many of these latter are very conjectural indeed, no more than possibilities. Second, we have so many new papyrus fragments of Euphorion that any new edition is bound to spring apart the original sequences, disturbing the original numeration beyond recall. My own edition notes conjectural attributions, but, after the fragments of known location, simply adopts the principle of one of Scheidweiler's sections by ranking the fragments in mythographical–historical sequence.

EDITIONS

A. Meineke, *De Euphorionis Chalcidensis vita et scriptis* (Danzig, 1823).

H. D. Düntzer, *Die Fragmente der epischen Poesie der Griechen von Alexander dem Grossen bis zum Ende des fünften Jahrhunderts nach Christus* (Cologne, 1842), 40–65.

A. Meineke, *Analecta Alexandrina* (Berlin, 1843; repr. Hildesheim, 1964), 3–168.

F. Scheidweiler, "Euphorionis fragmenta" (Diss. Bonn, 1908).

J. U. Powell, *Collectanea Alexandrina. Reliquiae minores poetarum Graecorum aetatis Ptolemaicae 323–146 A.C.* (Oxford, 1925).

L. A. de Cuenca, *Euforión de Calcis, fragmentos y epigramas* (Madrid, 1976).

B. A. van Groningen, *Euphorion* (Amsterdam, 1977).

H. Lloyd-Jones, and P. J. Parsons, *Supplementum Hellenisticum* (Berlin & New York, 1983), 196–233.

J. A. Martín García, *Poesía helenística menor (Poesía fragmentaria). Introducción, traducción y notas* (Madrid, 1994).

CRITICISM

A. Barigazzi, "Il Dionysos di Euforione", in *Miscellanea di studi alessandrini in memoria di Augusto Rostagni* (Torino, 1963), 416–454.

T. Bergk, *Analectorum Alexandrinorum particula prima* (Marburg, 1846), 26–31 = *Kleine Philologische Schriften*, ed. R. Peppmüller, ii. (Halle, 1886), 218–221.

J. A. Clúa Serena, *Estudios sobre la poesía de Euforión de Calcis* (Cáceres, 2005).

M. W. Dickie, "Poets as initiates in the mysteries: Euphorion, Philicus and Posidippus", *A&A* 44 (1998), 49–77.

R. L. Fowler, "P. Oxy. XXVI 2442 fr. 29: a citation of Euphorion?", *ZPE* 96 (1993), 15–16.

M. Giangiulio, "Una presunta citazione di Euforione in Tzetze", *Hermes* 121 (1993), 238–242.

A. Henrichs, "Philodems 'De Pietate' als mythographische Quelle", *CErc* 5 (1975), 5–38.

A. S. Hollis, "« Apuleius » de Orthographia, Callimachus fr. [815] Pf. and Euphorion 166 Meineke", *ZPE* 92 (1992), 109–114 [= 1992 *a*].

———"Attica in Hellenistic poetry", *ZPE* 93 (1992), 1–15 [= 1992 *b*].

———"Suppl. Hell. 1044: Euphorion?", *ZPE* 95 (1993), 48–49.

———"Traces of ancient commentaries on Ovid's *Metamorphoses*", *PLILS* 9 (1996), 159–174.

———*Fragments of Roman Poetry, c. 60 BC–AD 20* (Oxford, 2007).

A. Kolde, "Euphorion de Chalcis, poète hellénistique", in M. A. Harder, R. F. Regtuit & G. C. Wakker (edd.),

Beyond the Canon (Leuven, 2006) (Hellenistica Groningana 11), 144–165.

K. Latte, "Der Thrax des Euphorion", *Philologus* 44 (1935), 129–155.

J. L. Lightfoot, "An early reference to perfect numbers? Some notes on Euphorion, *SH* 417", *CQ* 48 (1998), 187–194.

E. Livrea, "Euphor. fr. 73 v. Gr.", *RhM* 123 (1980), 235–237.

———*Studia Hellenistica* (Florence, 1991), 293–294.

———"Sul Dioniso di Euforione, Nonno e Dionisio", *ZPE* 108 (1995), 55–57.

H. Lloyd-Jones, rev. of van Groningen, *CR* 29 (1979), 14–17 = *The Academic Papers of Sir Hugh Lloyd-Jones: Greek Comedy, Hellenistic Literature, Greek Religion, and Miscellanea* (Oxford, 1990), 153–157.

———*Supplementum Supplementi Hellenistici* (Berlin and New York, 2005), 52–59.

E. Magnelli, *Studi su Euforione* (Rome, 2002).

F. Nietzsche, "Der Florentinische Tractat über Homer und Hesiod, ihr Geschlecht und ihren Wettkampf, III-V", *RhM* 28 (1873), 211–249.

J. Sitzler, Review of Scheidweiler, *Wochenschrift für Klassische Philologie*, 26 (1909), 679–682.

L. Watson, "Cinna and Euphorion", *SIFC* 54 (1982), 93–110.

———*Arae: The Curse Poetry of Antiquity* (Leeds, 1991).

U. von Wilamowitz-Moellendorff, "Lesefrüchte 183", *Hermes* 59 (1924), 262–263 = *Kleine Schriften* IV. (Berlin, 1962), 356–357.

TESTIMONIA

1 *Suda* s.v. Εὐφορίων, ε 3801

Εὐφορίων, Πολυμνήστου, Χαλκιδεύς, ἀπὸ Εὐβοίας, μαθητὴς ἐν τοῖς φιλοσόφοις Λακύδου καὶ Πρυτάνιδος καὶ ἐν τοῖς ποιητικοῖς Ἀρχεβούλου τοῦ Θηραίου ποιητοῦ, οὗ καὶ ἐρώμενος λέγεται γενέσθαι. ἐγεννήθη δὲ ἐν τῇ ρκϛ΄ Ὀλυμπιάδι, ὅτε καὶ Πύρρος ἡττήθη ὑπὸ Ῥωμαίων· καὶ ἐγένετο τὴν ἰδέαν μελίχρους, πολύσαρκος, κακοσκελής. τῆς Ἀλεξάνδρου, τοῦ βασιλεύσαντος Εὐβοίας, υἱοῦ δὲ Κρατεροῦ, γυναικὸς Νικ‹α›ίας [suppl. Bernhardy] στερξάσης αὐτόν, εὔπορος σφόδρα γεγονὼς ἦλθε πρὸς Ἀντίοχον τὸν μέγαν ἐν Συρίᾳ βασιλεύοντα καὶ προέστη ὑπ' αὐτοῦ τῆς ἐκεῖσε δημοσίας βιβλιοθήκης· καὶ τελευτήσας ἐκεῖσε τέθαπται ἐν Ἀπαμείᾳ, ὡς δέ τινες ἐν Ἀντιοχείᾳ. βιβλία δὲ αὐτοῦ ἐπικὰ ταῦτα· Ἡσίοδος· Μοψοπία ἢ Ἄτακτα [Ἀττικά Scheidweiler]· ἔχει γὰρ συμμιγεῖς ἱστορίας, Μοψοπία δέ, ὅτι ἡ Ἀττικὴ τὸ πρὶν Μοψοπία ἐκαλεῖτο ἀπὸ τῆς Ὠκεανοῦ θυγατρὸς Μοψοπίας, καὶ ὁ λόγος τοῦ ποιήματος ἀποτείνεται εἰς τὴν Ἀττικήν· Χιλιάδες· ἔχει δὲ

TESTIMONIA

1 *Suda* s.v. Euphorion

Euphorion, son of Polymnestus, from Chalcis in Euboea, in philosophy a pupil of Lacydes and Prytanis[1] and in poetry of Archebulus the poet of Thera, whose boy-friend he is said to have been. He was born in the 126th Olympiad, when Pyrrhus was defeated by the Romans.[2] In appearance he was olive-skinned, very fleshy, and had bad legs. He was a favourite of Nic‹a›ea, whose husband, Alexander son of Craterus, was ruler of Euboea,[3] and as a result became exceedingly well off. He then went to Antiochus the Great,[4] ruler of Syria, by whom he was put in charge of the public library there. That is where he died, and was buried in Apamea, or, according to others, in Antioch. His books of hexameter poems are as follows: *Hesiod*; *Mopsopia*, or *Miscellanies*, because it contains various stories, and *Mopsopia* because Attica was formerly called Mopsopia after the daughter of Ocean, and the subject-matter of the poem extends to Attica; the *Chiliades*, which are di-

---

[1] Lacydes: head of Plato's Academy 241/240–224/223 or 216/215. Prytanis: Peripatetic philosopher whose dates are uncertain, though he was involved in the refoundation of Megalopolis in 222.

[2] Battle of Beneventum, 275 BC.

[3] *c*. 290–245 BC.   [4] Reigned 222–187 BC.

ὑπόθεσιν εἰς τοὺς ἀποστερήσαντας αὐτὸν χρήματα, ἃ
παρέθετο, ὡς δίκην δοῖεν κἂν εἰς μακράν· εἶτα συν-
άγει διὰ χιλίων ἐτῶν χρησμοὺς ἀποτελεσθέντας· εἰσὶ
δὲ βιβλία ε΄, ἐπιγράφεται δὲ ἡ πέμπτη χιλιάς. περὶ
χρησμῶν, ὡς διὰ χιλίων ἐτῶν ἀποτελοῦνται.

περὶ χρησμῶν ... ἀποτελοῦνται om. vel in mg. codd. plerique

2 *Suda* s.v. Ἀπολλώνιος Ἀλεξανδρεύς, α 3419

Ἀπολλώνιος, Ἀλεξανδρεὺς, ἐπῶν ποιητὴς . . . μαθη-
τὴς Καλλιμάχου, σύγχρονος Ἐρατοσθένους καὶ Εὐ-
φορίωνος καὶ Τιμάρχου, ἐπὶ Πτολεμαίου τοῦ Εὐερ-
γέτου ἐπικληθέντος.

3 Helladius, ap. Photius, *Bibl.* 279, p. 532 в 18

ὅτι παρὰ Εὐφορίωνι τῷ φύσει μὲν Χαλκιδεῖ, θέσει δὲ
Ἀθηναίῳ, κακοζήλους ἐστὶν εὑρεῖν λέξεις . . . [cf. **152,
148**] . . . παρεζήλωσε δὲ τὸν πρῶτον Διονύσιον τὸν
Σικελίας τύραννον, ὃς ὑπὸ τῆς ἐξουσίας καὶ τῶν
κολάκων καὶ τῆς τρυφῆς διαφθειρόμενος ἐπεχείρησε
καὶ τραγῳδίας γράφειν, ἐν αἷς καὶ τοιαῦτα συνεφό-

---

5 Confusion in the manuscripts seems to have concealed the
real name of the fifth book. But it was the view of Wilamowitz that
Euphorion's whole *oeuvre* was divided into five books, and known
as *Miscellanies*. The *Chiliades* would have been the name of just
one of these books.

6 Aside from the titles mentioned by the *Suda*, Euphorion is
credited with sixteen poems whose fragments prove them to have

rected against people who deprived him of money he had deposited with them, and whose premise is that they will eventually be punished, no matter how long in the future; then he assembles a collection of oracles that were fulfilled after [*or* in the course of] a thousand years. There are five books, and the fifth is entitled *chilias* ("thousand").[5] On oracles, how they are fulfilled after [*or* in the course of] a thousand years.[6]

2 *Suda* s.v. Apollonius of Alexandria

Apollonius of Alexandria, hexameter poet . . . pupil of Callimachus, contemporary of Eratosthenes, Euphorion, and Timarchus, in the time of Ptolemy surnamed Euergetes.[7]

3 Helladius, ap. Photius, *Library*

In Euphorion, a native of Chalcis though an adopted citizen of Athens,[8] one can find affected vocabulary . . . He emulated Dionysius the first, tyrant of Sicily who, ruined by power, flatterers, and luxury, set his hand at writing tragedies, in which he also collected such vocables as the

---

been hexametric, and three more that possibly or probably were. It may be that at least some of these were part of larger collections mentioned in the *Suda*, such as the *Miscellanies* or *Chiliades*. The *Suda* entry takes no notice of Euphorion's prose works, and recognises no non-hexametric poetry.

[7] This notice does not help to establish a firm chronology. Ptolemy Euergetes reigned 246–221.

[8] Perhaps in his student days, or between his residence in the courts of Alexander in Euboea and Antiochus.

ρησε ῥήματα, τὸ μὲν ἀκόντιον καλῶν βαλάντιον, τὸν
δὲ κάδον ἑλκύδριον, σκέπαρνον δὲ τὸ ἔριον, τὴν δὲ
χλαῖναν ἐριόλην οἷον ὄλεθρον οὖσαν τῶν ἐρίων, καὶ
πολλὰ τοιαῦτα καταγελαστά.

4 Academicorum Philosophorum Index Herculanensis,
p. 78.20 Mekler

διαδόχους [δ]ὲ τούτους κατ̣[α]λιπὼν θν[ῄσκ]ει [sc. La-
cydes]· . . . [Τ]ηλ[εκλέα καὶ Εὐφορί]|ωνα . . .

5 Athen. *Deipn.* 11.477 E

Ἡγήσανδρος ὁ Δελφὸς Εὐφορίωνά φησι [*FHG* IV
417] τὸν ποιητὴν παρὰ Πρυτάνιδι δειπνοῦντα καὶ
ἐπιδεικνυμένου τοῦ Πρυτάνιδος κιβώριά τινα δοκοῦν-
τα πεποιῆσθαι πολυτελῶς, τοῦ κώθωνος εὖ μάλα προ-
βεβηκότος, λαβὼν ἓν τῶν κιβωρίων ὡς ἐξοινῶν [καὶ
μεθύων] ἐνεούρησε.

6 Plutarch, *Mor.* 472 D

τούτου δ' οὐδέν τι βελτίων ὁ βουλόμενος ἅμα μὲν
Ἐμπεδοκλῆς ἢ Πλάτων ἢ Δημόκριτος εἶναι περὶ
κόσμου γράφων καὶ τῆς τῶν ὄντων ἀληθείας, ἅμα δὲ
πλουσίᾳ γραῒ συγκαθεύδειν ὡς Εὐφορίων.

following, calling a javelin a *balantion* [a "throwing device"], a jar a "water-drawer", wool "lamb-coverer", a cloak "wool-perisher", inasmuch as it is the ruination of wool, and many other such absurdities.

4 Herculanean Index of Philosophers of the Academy

He [Lacydes] died, leaving the following successors: . . . [T]el[ecles and Euphori]on . . .

5 Athenaeus, *Deipnosophistae*

Hegesander of Delphi records that once, when Euphorion the poet was dining with Prytanis[9] and Prytanis was showing off some cups that gave every appearance of expensive workmanship, the diners being by then well advanced in their cups, Euphorion took one of the cups and, tipsy as he was, urinated into it.

6 Plutarch, *On Tranquility of Mind*

No better than him is the man who wants, at the same time, to be Empedocles or Plato or Democritus writing about the universe and the true nature of reality, and at the same time to sleep with a rich old woman like Euphorion.

[9] Head of the Lyceum, mentioned in Test. **1**; the anecdote is set in Athens.

EUPHORION

7 *HE* 3558 = *AP* 7.406 (Theodoridas)

εἰς τὸν Εὐφορίωνος τάφον τοῦ μύστου τῶν Ἑλληνικῶν
μυθολογημάτων ἢ τελεσιουργημάτων [J]·

Εὐφορίων, ὁ περισσὸν ἐπιστάμενός τι ποῆσαι,
Πειραϊκοῖς κεῖται τοῖσδε παρὰ σκέλεσιν.
ἀλλὰ σὺ τῷ μύστῃ ῥοιὴν ἢ μῆλον ἄπαρξαι
ἢ μύρτον· καὶ γὰρ ζωὸς ἐὼν ἐφίλει.

8 *HE* 1371 = *AP* 11.218 (Crates) = Philitas Test. **15**

Χοιρίλος Ἀντιμάχου πολὺ λείπεται· ἀλλ᾽ ἐπὶ
πᾶσιν
Χοιρίλον Εὐφορίων εἶχε διὰ στόματος
καὶ κατάγλωσσ᾽ ἐπόει τὰ ποήματα καὶ τὰ Φιλίτα
ἀτρεκέως ᾔδει· καὶ γὰρ Ὁμηρικὸς ἦν.

3 φίλιτρα cod., corr. Müller: Φιλητᾶ Dobree

9 Lucian, *De hist. conscr.* 56–57 = Parthenius Test. **6**

---

10 According to the *Suda*, Euphorion died in Syria. Either it is
wrong (for Euphorion's connection with Athens see Test. **3**), or
the epigram is facetious. Several *doubles entendres* have been
read into it, in which case the last line would read "for in life he
was a lover"; but for a defence of the face-value reading, see
Dickie 1998, 54–58.

11 Symbols of the mysteries (Dickie ibid.).

12 Uncertain whether the Stoic grammarian from Mallus,

7 Palatine Anthology 7.406 (Theodoridas)

On the tomb of Euphorion,[10] the initiate into Hellenic mythology or ritual practices:

> Euphorion, who well understood the special turn of
>   phrase,
> Reposes beside these, Piraeus' walls.
> For the initiate offer up a pomegranate or an apple,
>   Or myrtle,[11] for in life he used to love (them).

8 Palatine Anthology 11.218 (Crates[12]) = Philitas Test. **15**

> Choerilus falls far short of Antimachus.[13] Yet, above
>   all else,
> Euphorion had Choerilus upon his lips
> And he made poems full of glosses; as for Philitas'
>   works,[14]
> He knew them all; a true Homerist was he.

9 Lucian, *On writing history* = Parthenius Test. **6**

head of the Pergamene library, or an epigrammatist mentioned by Diog. Laert. 4.23.

[13] A poet in the entourage of Alexander the Great, Choerilus had a reputation for the low quality of his verses. Crates complains that Euphorion prefered a bad poet to a good one (though Callimachus famously objected to Antimachus' *Lyde*).

[14] If φίλητρα is right, an allusion to Euphorion's erotic reputation, as also found in Test. **1**(?), **6**, **7**(?), **12**. With "Philitas", a combined allusion to Philitas' book of glosses and a punning allusion to this same reputation.

10 Cic. *de Div.* 2.132–133

quid? poeta nemo, nemo physicus obscurus? illi vero.
nimis etiam obscurus Euphorio. at non Homerus. uter
igitur melior?

11 Clem. Al. *Strom.* 5.8.50.3

Εὐφορίων γὰρ ὁ ποιητὴς καὶ τὰ Καλλιμάχου Αἴτια
καὶ ἡ Λυκόφρονος Ἀλεξάνδρα καὶ τὰ τούτοις παρα-
πλήσια γυμνάσιον εἰς ἐξήγησιν γραμματικῶν ἔκκει-
ται παισίν.

12 *HE* 3948 = *AP* 4.1.23 (Meleager)

λυχνίδα τ᾽ Εὐφορίωνος . . .

13 Cic. *Tusc.* 3.45

o poetam egregium! quamquam ab his cantoribus Eu-
phorionis contemnitur.

14 Servius ad Virg. *Ecl.* 6.72

. . . hoc autem Euphorionis continent carmina, quae Gal-
lus transtulit in sermonem Latinum: unde est illud in fine,
ubi Gallus loquitur "ibo et Chalcidico quae sunt mihi con-
dita versu carmina" [*Ecl.* 10.50–51]; nam Chalcis civitas
est Euboeae, de qua fuerat Euphorion.

10 Cicero, *On divination*

What, is no poet, no natural philosopher obscure? They most certainly are. Euphorion is excessively obscure, but not Homer. Which is better?

11 Clement of Alexandria, *Stromateis*

Euphorion the poet and the *Aitia* of Callimachus and the *Alexandra* of Lycophron and similar works constitute a veritable playground for grammatical exegesis.

12 Palatine Anthology 4.1.23 (Meleager)

And the rose-campion of Euphorion . . .[15]

13 Cicero, *Tusculan Disputations*

O noble poet![16] Despite the fact that he is despised by these chanters of Euphorion.

14 Servius on Virgil, *Eclogues*

. . . This subject is to be found in the poetry of Euphorion, which Gallus adapted into the Latin language. Hence that line at the end, where Gallus says: "I'll go, and the songs I composed in Chalcidian verse." For Chalcis is a city of Euboea, from which Euphorion came.

---

[15] The flower is associated with Aphrodite and with love in Nonn. *D.* 32.19–20, Athen. *Deipn.* 15.681 F.

[16] Ennius.

15 Quintilian, *Inst. Or.* 10.1.56

quid? Euphorionem transibimus? quem nisi probasset
Vergilius, idem numquam certe "conditorum Chalcidico
versu carminum" fecisset in *Bucolicis* mentionem.

cf. Virg. *Ecl*. 10.50–51

> ibo et Chalcidico quae sunt mihi condita versu
> carmina pastoris Siculi modulabor avena.

Probus ad loc.: Euphorion elegiarum scriptor Chalcidensis fuit,
cuius in scribendo secutus colorem videtur Cornelius Gallus.

Philargyrius I ibid.: Chalcis civitas in Euboea, in qua fuit Eu-
phorion, qui Euphorion distichico versu usus est.

Philargyrius II ibid.: civitas enim in Euboea Chalcis dicitur, in qua
fuit Euphorion, quem transtulit Gallus.

Servius ibid.: Euphorion, quem transtulit Gallus.

Servius ad Virg. *Ecl*. 10.1: Gallus . . . fuit poeta eximius; nam et
Euphorionem, ut supra diximus, transtulit in Latinum sermonem
et amorum suorum de Cytheride scripsit libros quattuor.

16 Diomedes, *GL* 1.484.21

quod genus carminis praecipue scripserunt apud Roma-
nos Propertius et Tibullus et Gallus, imitati Graecos Cal-
limachum et Euphoriona.

17 Suetonius, *Tib*. 70 = Parthenius Test. **3**

15 Quintilian, *The Orator's Education*

What—are we to pass over Euphorion? If Virgil had not approved of him, he would certainly never have mentioned "songs composed in Chalcidian verse" in the *Eclogues*.

cf. Virgil, *Eclogue* 10.50

I'll go and, what I wrote in Chalcidian verse,
I'll play those songs on a Sicilian shepherd's pipe.

Probus ad loc.: Euphorion was a writer of elegies from Chalcis, whose style of writing Cornelius Gallus can be seen to have followed.

Philargyrius I ibid.: Chalcis is a city in Euboea, home of Euphorion, who made use of elegiac couplets.

Philargyrius II ibid.: Chalcis is said to be a city in Euboea, home of Euphorion, whom Gallus adapted.

Servius ibid.: Euphorion, whom Gallus adapted.

Servius on Virgil, *Eclogue* 10.1: Gallus . . . was an excellent poet; for, as we said above, he adapted Euphorion into the Latin language and wrote four books about his love for Cytheris.

16 Diomedes

A genre of poetry [sc. elegy] whose principal representatives among the Romans are Propertius, Tibullus, and Galllus, who imitated the Greeks Callimachus and Euphorion.

17 Suetonius, *Tiberius* = Parthenius Test. **3**

FRAGMENTA POETICA

1-2 ΕΠΙΓΡΑΜΜΑΤΑ

1 *HE* 1801–1804 = *AP* 6.279

πρώτας ὁππότ᾽ ἔπεξε καλὰς Εὔδοξος ἐθείρας,
Φοίβῳ παιδείην ὤπασεν ἀγλαΐην.
ἀντὶ δέ οἱ πλοκαμῖδος, Ἑκηβόλε, κάλλος ἐπείη
ὠχαρνῆθεν ἀεὶ κισσὸς ἀεξομένῳ.

1 ap. *Sud.* ε 319   ἔπεξε *Suda*: ἔπλεξε P   3 ap. *Sud.* π
1784   δέτοι P, corr. Toup: δέ σοι *Suda*   κάλος *vl* ap.
Sud.   4 χὠ Meineke   ἀεξόμενος C: ἀεξομένῳ Toup,
Hecker

2 *HE* 1805–1810 = *AP* 7.651

Εὐφορίωνος εἰς ναυηγὸν ὁμοίως ἀνώνυμον ἐν τῷ Ἰκαρίῳ
πελάγει ναυαγήσαντα [J]·

οὐχ ὁ τρηχὺς ἔλαιος ἐπ᾽ ὀστέα κεῖνα καλύπτει
οὐδ᾽ ἡ κυάνεον γράμμα λαχοῦσα πέτρη·
ἀλλὰ τὰ μὲν Δολίχης τε καὶ αἰπεινῆς Δρακάνοιο
Ἰκάριον ῥήσσει κῦμα περὶ κροκάλαις·

POETIC FRAGMENTS

1–2 EPIGRAMS

1 Palatine Anthology 6.279

> When first Eudoxus shore his lovely locks,
> To Phoebus he devoted the beauty of his youth.
> In that lock's place, Far-Shooter, as he grows
> May Acharnian ivy beautify his head.[1]

2 Palatine Anthology 7.651

Euphorion, for a likewise unknown man who was ship-
wrecked in the Icarian sea:

> The jagged olive does not hide those bones,
> Nor rock inscribed with sombre lettering;
> No: the Icarian sea breaks them upon the pebbly
>   shore
> Of Doliche and lofty Dracanon;[2]

[1] Presumably as a token of success as a poet. But Eudoxus' age
is unclear (the first ever hair-cutting, or the first on coming of
age?), and so too the time-lapse between the dedication and the
hoped-for dramatic victories.

[2] Doliche is the older name for the island of Icarus, west of
Samos, and Dracanon is a hill in the north east of the island.

5   ἀντὶ δ᾽ ἐγὼ ξενίης Πολυμήδεος ἡ κενεὴ χθὼν
     ὠγκώθην Δρυόπων διψάσιν ἐν βοτάναις.

1 σελι θαῖος P, corr. Meineke: Ἐλαιὸς Kaibel   οὐ Τρηχίς
σε λίθειος Graefe   2 Κυανέη Mähly: κυανέη van
Groningen   λαβοῦσα P, corr. Hecker   5 πολυκηδέος
Salmasius   κεινὴ P, corr. Reiske

3–54 FRAGMENTA CERTIS
CARMINIBUS TRIBUTA

Ἀλέξανδρος

3 Steph. Byz., p. 581.12 Mein.

Σόλοι, Κιλικίας πόλις, ἡ νῦν Πομπηιούπολις. Ἑκα-
ταῖος Ἀσίᾳ. κέκληται δὲ ἀπὸ Σόλωνος, ὡς Εὐφορίων
ἐν Ἀλεξάνδρῳ.

Huic carmini attrib. 116, et fort. 115, 172 Scheidweiler

Ἄνιος

4 Steph. Byz., p. 248.5 Mein.

Δωδώνη . . . καὶ τὴν αἰτιατικήν φησιν Εὐφορίων Δωδῶνα
ἐν Ἀνίῳ·

ἷκτο μὲν ἐς Δωδῶνα Διὸς φηγοῖο προφῆτιν

cf. 190.

While for guest-friendship's sake with Polymedes, I,   [5]
   the hollow earth,
Am heaped up in the thirsty pastures of the
   Dryopes.[3]

3–54 FRAGMENTS OF KNOWN LOCATION

Alexander

3 Stephanus of Byzantium

Soloi, a city of Cilicia, now called Pompeioupolis. Hecataeus in *Asia*. It is named after Solon: so Euphorion in *Alexander*.

Anius

4 Stephanus of Byzantium

Dodona . . . and the accusative *Dōdōna*[4] is used by Euphorion in the *Anius*[5]:

He came to Dodon, interpreter of Zeus' oracular oak.

---

[3] Perhaps Trachis, though there were settlements of the Dryopes throughout Greece.

[4] Of the variant form of the name, Dodon.

[5] Anius was a hero of Delos, son of Apollo. He and his three daughters, who had the miraculous ability to produce corn, wine, and olive oil, were visited by the Greeks on the outward voyage to Troy.

EUPHORION

Ἀντιγραφαὶ Πρὸς Θεοδωρίδαν

5 Clem. Al. *Strom.* 5.8.47.2

ζὰψ δὲ τὸ πῦρ οἱ μὲν παρὰ τὴν ζέσιν ἀμαθῶς ἐδέξαντο·
καλεῖται δ' οὕτως ἡ θάλασσα, ὡς Εὐφορίων ἐν ταῖς πρὸς
Θεοδωρίδαν [Θεωρίδαν L, corr. Meursius] ἀντιγραφαῖς·

ζὰψ δὲ ποτὶ σπιλάδεσσι νεῶν ὀλέτειρα κυκαίνει.

κακύνει L, corr. van Groningen: καχλάζει Meineke: κυκᾶται
Ziemann

Ἀπολλόδωρος

6 Σ, Tzetzes ad Lyc. *Al.* 513

κρὲξ δὲ ὄρνεόν ἐστι θαλάσσιον ποικίλον ἴβιδι ἐοικὸς ὡς
Ἡρόδοτος [2.76.1]. ἔστι δὲ ἶβις ὄρνεον περὶ τὴν Αἴ-
γυπτον ῥυπαροφάγον. Καλλίμαχος δὲ ἐν τοῖς Περὶ ὀρ-
νέων φησὶ τοῖς γαμοῦσι δυσοιώνιστον εἶναι [fr. 428 Pf.].
καὶ Εὐφορίων ἐν Ἀπολλοδώρῳ·

ποικίλον οὐδὲ μέλαθρον ‹   › ὀρχίλος ἔπτη
Κυζίκῳ, ὃν δ' ἤεισε κακὸν γάμον ἐχθομένη κρέξ.

1 ὧδε s   ποικιλόνους δὲ Scheidweiler (cf. Ant. Lib. 14)
π. οὐδὲ μ. ‹ἐναίσιμος› van Groningen   2 Κύζικος ss⁴,
corr. van Groningen: Κυζίκου Thryllitzsch

7 Choeroboscus, in Hephaestionem, p. 226.22 Cons-
bruch

ἰστέον δ' ὅτι διὰ τὸ ἀδύνατον ὁ Εὐφορίων τὸ Ἀπολλό-
δωρος διέλυσε φάσκων

Responses to Theodoridas

5 Clement of Alexandria, *Stromateis*

Some have explained *zaps* as "fire", with reference to effervescence (*zesis*); but this is ignorant. It is a word for the sea, as Euphorion says in his *Responses to Theodoridas*:

> The surf, wrecker of ships, seethes against the rocks.

Apollodorus

6 Scholiast, Tzetzes on Lycophron, *Alexandra*

Krex is a seabird with variegated plumage, like the ibis as described by Herodotus. The ibis is an Egyptian bird that eats filth. Callimachus in his work *On Birds* says that it is a bird of ill-omen to those getting married. And Euphorion in the *Apollodorus*:

> Nor did a (well-omened?) wren alight on the
>   patterned timbers
> Of Cyzicus' roof; no, the hated *krex* sang his blighted
>   union.[6]

7 Choeroboscus, scholia on Hephaestion

On account of its intractability, Euphorion split apart the name Apollodorus, saying:

[6] For the story of Cyzicus, see **9**. Call. fr. 428 Pf. has the same legend about the *krex* (corncrake).

EUPHORION

καί τις Ἀπολλό-
δωρος ‹   › ἐφ᾽ υἱέα Λειοφόωντος.

1–2 Ἀπολλό-δωρον Sitzler   2 Κλειοφόωντος Scheidweiler

8 Didymus, ap. Harpocration, *Lex.* i. p. 220.10 Dindorf

ὅτι γάρ, φησι (sc. Δίδυμος), βουστροφηδὸν ἦσαν οἱ
ἄξονες καὶ οἱ κύρβεις γεγραμμένοι δεδήλωκεν Εὐφο-
ρίων ἐν τῷ Ἀπολλοδώρῳ.

9 Parthenius, Ἐρωτικὰ Παθήματα, XXVIII Περὶ Κλεί-
της

Ἱστορεῖ Εὐφορίων Ἀπολλοδώρῳ, τὰ ἑξῆς Ἀπολλώ-
νιος Ἀργοναυτικῶν αʹ [1012–1077] . . .

cf. Σ Ap. Rhod. 1.1063, p. 93.21 Wendel

ὁ μὲν Ἀπολλώνιος νεόγαμον τὸν Κύζικον καὶ ἄπαιδα
ἱστορεῖ, Εὐφορίων δὲ ἐν Ἀπολλοδώρῳ μελλόγαμον.
τὴν δὲ ‹γαμετὴν› οὐ Κλείτην ‹τὴν› Μέροπος λέγει
θυγατέρα, Λάρισαν δὲ τὴν Πιάσου· οὐδὲ παθεῖν τι,
ἀπαχθῆναι δὲ αὐτὴν ὑπὸ τοῦ πατρός.

τὴν δὲ Κλείτην οὐ Μέροπος codd., corr. Keil: τὴν δὲ γαμετὴν
οὐ Μέροπος Meineke   Θρῆσσαν codd.

And a certain Apollo-
Dorus ‹   › to the son of Leiophoon.

8 Didymus, cited by Harpocration

That the inscribed wooden tablets and the triangular tablets of the Athenian law were written *boustrophēdon*[7] is shown by Euphorion in the *Apollodorus*.

9 Parthenius, *Sufferings in Love*, "About Cleite"

The story is told by Euphorion in the *Apollodorus*; thereafter, by Apollonius in the first book of the *Argonautica* . . .

cf. Scholiast on Apollonius of Rhodes, *Argonautica*

Apollonius relates that Cyzicus was recently married and childless; Euphorion in the *Apollodorus* that he was engaged to be married. He makes his wife, not Cleite daughter of Merops, but Larisa daughter of Piasus. Nor did anything happen to her; she was taken back by her father.

---

[7] Usually left-to-right then right-to-left, but in this case, top-to-bottom followed by bottom-to-top (as indicated by Harpocration's heading, ὁ κάτωθεν νόμος, "law going downwards").

Ἀραὶ ἢ Ποτηριοκλέπτης

Partem Χιλιάδων esse suspicati sunt Powell (cf. ad eius fr. 46), van Groningen (cf. ad eius fr. 11).

10 Steph. Byz., α 233 Billerbeck

Ἀλύβη . . . Εὐφορίων ἐν Ἀραῖς ἢ Ποτηριοκλέπτῃ·

ὅστις μευ κελέβην Ἀλυβηΐδα μοῦνος ἀπηύρα

μευ κελέβην Casaubon: μὲν κέλβην vel κέλκην codd.; cf. Σ Theocr. *Id.* 2.2a, p. 270.11 Wendel: Εὐφορίων ἐν Ποτηριοκλέπτῃ· "ὅστις ἐμὴν κελέβην", κτλ., ubi ἐμὴν K: ἐμεῦ cett. μοῦνον codd. Theocr.

11 *Berliner Klassikertexte*, V. i, ed. W. Schubart and U. von Wilamowitz–Moellendorff (Berlin, 1907) p. 58, col. ii

. . .] ὄπισθε
. . .]α φέροιτο
. . .]θι κάππεσε λύχνου
]α κατὰ Γλαυκώπιον Ἔρσῃ,
5   [οὕνεκ᾽ Ἀθ]ηναίης ἱερὴν ἀνελύσατο κίστην
[. . . . .]ης. ἢ ὅσσον ὁδοιπόροι ἐρρήσσοντο,
[Σκε]ίρων ἔνθα πόδεσσιν ἀεικέα μήδετο χύτλα

---

8 i.e. silver.

9 A fragment of a curse poem, attributed by Powell and others to the *Curses, or Cup-Thief*. This is entirely possible, though Euphorion wrote other curse poems, including the *Chiliades*. The fragment is unlikely to belong to the *Thrax*, which had a second-person addressee.

Curses, or the Cup-Thief

10 Stephanus of Byzantium

Alybe . . . Euphorion in *Curses, or the Cup-Thief*:

The one and only man who stole my Alybeian[8] cup.

11 *Berliner Klassikertexte*[9]

behind
may (s/he) be carried
fell . . . of the lamp[10]
on the Glaucopion . . . for Herse,
[because] she opened up the sacred casket of   [5]
Athena[11]
. . . Or as travellers were rent
Where Sciron's cunning planned unseemly foot-
baths—

10 Perhaps the lamp in Athena's temple on the acropolis. Nonnus connects it with the story of how Athena suckled the infant Erichthonius, born of the earth when Hephaestus tried and failed to rape her (*D.* 27.115, cf. 319–20).

11 Athena placed the infant Erichthonius in a casket and entrusted it to the three daughters of Cecrops, commanding them not to open it. Euphorion makes Herse guilty of disobeying her orders, but other versions differ (Callimachus' *Hecale* seems to have made all sisters equally guilty: fr. 70.12–13 Hollis). The Glaucopion may refer to Mount Lycabettos, the Acropolis (from which all three sisters throw themselves in Eur. *Ion* 274), or the Parthenon (see Hollis on Call. *Hecale* fr. 17.11).

[ο]ὐκ ἐπὶ δήν· Αἴθρης γὰρ ἀλοιηθεὶς ὑπὸ παιδὶ
†νωιτέρης χέλυος πύματος ‹ἐ›λιπήνατο λαιμόν.
10   ἢ καί νιν σφεδανοῖο τανυσσαμένη ἀπὸ τόξου
Ταιναρίη λοχίῃσι γυναικῶν ἐμπελάτειρα
Ἄρτεμις ὠδίνεσσιν ἑῷ ταλάωρι μετάσποι.
ὀκχοίη δ' Ἀχέροντι βαρὺν λίθον Ἀσκαλάφοιο,
τόν οἱ χωσαμένη γυίοις ἐπιήραρε Δηώ,
15   μαρτυρίην ὅτι μοῦνος ἐθήκατο Φερσεφονείῃ.

4 Ἔρσῃ Schubart–Wilamowitz: Ἔρσῃ van Groningen
5 suppl. Schubart–Wilamowitz: [ἡνίκ' Ἀ.] van Groningen
6 [δεσποίν]ης K. F. W. Schmidt, spatio longius   7 [Σκ]ίρων
Hollis (cf. Call. *Hecale* fr. 60)   9 σφωϊτέρης Morel
‹ἐ›λιπήνατο Schubart–Wilamowitz: λειήνατο Sitzler

Ἀραῖς attrib. Körte, al.; negant Wilamowitz, Skutsch;
dub. Scheidweiler

Huic carmini attrib. **117–118** Scheidweiler

Ἀρτεμίδωρος

12 Steph. Byz., α 494 Billerbeck

Ἄσσωρον, ὄρος Σάμου, ὅθεν ῥεῖ ὁ Ἀμφίλυσος. Εὐφορίων
Ἀρτεμιδώρῳ·

    δαῖμον ὃς Ἀμφιλύσοιο ῥόον

δαίμονος codd., corr. Meineke   ‹νέμεις› ῥόον ‹Ἀσσω-
ρίνου› id.   ῥόον ‹λάχες Ἀσσωρίνου› Scheidweiler

Yet not for long. For, felled by Aethra's son,
At last he made a rich meal down our(?) tortoise's
    throat.[12]
Or, taking aim from her death-dealing bow,   [10]
May the Taenarian,[13] visitor of child-birth pangs,
Artemis, hunt him down with her arched weapon.[14]
In Acheron may he bear Ascalaphus' heavy stone,
Which Deo fixed in wrath upon his limbs,
Since he against Persephone alone bore witness.[15]   [15]

Artemidorus

12 Stephanus of Byzantium

Assōron, a mountain in Samos, source of the river Amphilysus. Euphorion in the *Artemidorus*:

God, who the stream of Amphilysus . . .

---

[12] Sciron lived on a cliff in the Megarid. He forced passers-by to wash his feet, and as they were doing so kicked them into the sea, where they were eaten by a giant turtle. Theseus threw him into the sea, where he suffered the same fate. Euphorion may be alluding to Callimachus' *Hecale* (frr. 59–60 Hollis). "Our" tortoise would seem to indicate that the speaker was from the Megarid or at least had ties with it. Euphorion was an honorary citizen of Athens [Test. **3**], which laid claim to the Megarid; but the word may be corrupt.   [13] Cape Taenarum is the southernmost point of the Peloponnese, but it was also the site of an entrance to the underworld.   [14] Although Artemis is patroness of women in childbirth, and although she is specially responsible for the death of women, it need not follow that the object of the curses is female.   [15] For the story, see ps.-Apoll. 1.5.3: Ascalaphus bore witness to the pomegranate seed which Hades tricked Persephone into eating, and Demeter laid a heavy rock on him in Hades. According to Ov. *Met.* 5.538–550 (cf. ps.-Apoll. 2.5.12), he was turned into an owl.

225

EUPHORION

Δημοσθένης

13 Choeroboscus, in Theodos. *Canon.*, *GG* IV.1, p. 252.26 Hilgard

ὅτι γὰρ ἐκτείνει (sc. ἵλαος) τὸ ᾱ, ἐδήλωσε Παρθένιος [8]
... καὶ ἐν τῷ Εὐφορίωνος Δημοσθένει ὁμοίως ἐκτεταμένον
εὑρίσκεται, οἷον·

δαίμονος ἱλάοιο.

Διόνυσος

14 Tzetzes ad Lyc. *Al.* 207, p. 98.5 Scheer

ἐτιμᾶτο δὲ καὶ Διόνυσος ἐν Δελφοῖς σὺν Ἀπόλλωνι οὕτω-
σί· οἱ Τιτᾶνες τὰ Διονύσου μέλη σπαράξαντες Ἀπόλλωνι
ἀδελφῷ ὄντι αὐτοῦ παρέθεντο ἐμβαλόντες λέβητι, ὁ δὲ
παρὰ τῷ τρίποδι ἀπέθετο, ὥς φησι Καλλίμαχος [fr. 643
Pf.] καὶ Εὐφορίων λέγων·

ἐν πυρὶ Βάκχον δῖον ὑπερφίαλοι ἐβάλοντο.

Βάκχαν, Βάκχοις vel Βάκχας codd., corr. Meineke   post
βάκχον finem versus statuit Meineke 1823, van Groningen; cf.
Magnelli 2002, 149–150   δῖον, δῖαν, δίαν codd.
ὑπὲρ φιάλην codd., corr. O. Müller: φιάλης Lobeck
ἐβάλοντο, ἐβάλλοντο, ἐμβάλλοντες codd.

cf. EtMag 255.14–16, sine poetarum testimoniis

226

Demosthenes

13 Choeroboscus, scholia on Theodosius' *Canones*

That it (ἵλαος) does lengthen the *a* is demonstrated by Parthenius [**8**] . . . It is also found in Euphorion's *Demosthenes* likewise lengthened, as in:

> Of a propitious deity

Dionysus

14 Tzetzes on Lycophron, *Alexandra*

Dionysus, too, was honoured in Delphi together with Apollo, in the following way. The Titans tore asunder Dionysus' limbs, threw them into a cauldron, and set it before his brother Apollo. Apollo stowed it away beside his tripod, as we learn from Callimachus and Euphorion, who says:

> In(to) the fire those arrogant beings cast divine
>   Bacchus.[16]

---

[16] See also **40**. This story was told of Dionysus' third incarnation as Zagreus, son of Zeus and Persephone. It figured in the Orphic poems (59 F Bernabé), in which Dionysus seems to have been boiled, then reassembled by Rhea.

EUPHORION

15

(a) Σ Arat. *Phaen*. 172, p. 165.9 Martin

ἡ δὲ προσωνυμία (sc. Ὑάδες) ὅτι τὸν Διόνυσον ἀνεθρέψαντο, Ὕης δὲ ὁ Διόνυσος. Εὐφορίων·

Ὕῃ ταυροκέρωτι Διωνύσῳ κοτέσσασα

ταυροκέρῳ τε conj. van Groningen

(b) EtGen AB = EtSym = EtMag 703.10

Ῥειώνην· τὴν Ἥραν φησὶν Εὐφορίων.

Ῥειώνη EtGen B, EtMag

(c) Σ HQ *Od*. 4.228, i. p. 195.9 Dindorf

εἴτε κύριόν ἐστιν ὄνομα ἡ Πολύδαμνα ὡς Μήθυμνα, εἴτε ἐπιθετικὸν τῶν φαρμάκων, τρίτη ἀπὸ τέλους ἡ ὀξεῖα. βέλτιον δὲ ὄνομα κύριον αὐτὸ δέχεσθαι, ἐπεὶ καὶ Εὐφορίων ἐν Διονύσῳ φησὶ·

βλαψίφρονα φάρμακα χεῦεν,
ὅσσ᾽ ἐδάη Πολύδαμνα, Κυτηϊὰς ἢ ὅσα Μήδη.

2 κυταῖς, κυταῦς codd., corr. Meineke: Κυταϊκὴ Kaibel, cf. Lyc. *Al*. 174 cum Σ, Tzetz.

Fragmenta primus coniunxit Meineke (sed cf. *contra* Sitzler 1909, 680–681). Sic supplevit Livrea 1995, 56:

Ὕῃ ταυροκέρωτι Διωνύσῳ κοτέσσασα

15

(a) Scholiast on Aratus, *Phaenomena*

The name (Hyades) arises from the fact that they nurtured Dionysus, and Hyes is Dionysus. Euphorion:

> Wroth with Hyes, bull-horned Dionysus

(b) Etymologicum Genuinum

Rheione: a name used of Hera by Euphorion.

(c) Scholiast on Homer, *Odyssey*

Whether Polydamna is a proper name like Methyma, or an epithet of *pharmaka*, the acute accent is on the antepenultimate syllable. It is preferable to take it as a proper name, since Euphorion in the *Dionysus* also says:

> . . . she cast mind-destroying drugs,
> All those in which Polydamna or Cytaean Mede were
>   skilled.

First combined by Meineke, and supplemented by Livrea:

> Wroth with Hyes, bull-horned Dionysus,

⟨Φηρσὶν⟩ ‛Ρείωνη βλαψίφρονα φάρμακα χεῦεν
ὅσσ᾽ ἐδάη Πολύδαμνα, Κυτηϊὰς ἢ ὅσα Μήδη.

2 ‛Ρείωνη ⟨ἄμυδις⟩ Meineke: ⟨τοσσάδε⟩ ‛Ρείωνη conj. van
Groningen

16 Steph. Byz., p. 421.6 Mein.

Λυκαψός, κώμη πλησίον Λυδίας. Εὐφορίων Διονύσῳ.

17 Steph. Byz., α 176 Billerbeck

Ἀκτή . . . ἔστι καὶ

  Ἄκτιος Αἰγεύς

ὡς Εὐφορίων Διονύσῳ.

18 Steph. Byz., p. 710.14 Mein.

Ὠρύχιον, τόπος τῆς Ἀττικῆς. τὸ τοπικὸν Ὠρύχιος. Εὐφο-
ρίων Διονύσῳ·

  ἴχνος ἂν Ὠρυχίοισιν ἐν ἔρκεσιν ὀκλάσσαιντο.

ἐν codd., corr. Salmasius   ὀκλάσαιντο codd., corr.
Meineke: ὀκλάξαιντο Powell(?)

⟨Upon the Pheres⟩ Rheione cast mind-destroying
　drugs—
All those in which Polydamna or Cytaean Mede were
　skilled.[17]

16　Stephanus of Byzantium

Lycapsus, a village in the vicinity of Lydia. Mentioned in
Euphorion's *Dionysus*.

17　Stephanus of Byzantium

Acte . . . there is also a form

　Actian Aegeus

used by Euphorion in the *Dionysus*.

18　Stephanus of Byzantium

Orychion, a place in Attica. The adjectival form of the
place-name is Orychios. Euphorion in the *Dionysus*:

　They might stumble over their footsteps in Orychian
　　nets.

[17] Livrea's supplement produces a reference to the myth in
Nonn. *D.* 14.143–185: angry because they had nursed the infant
Dionysus, Hera poisoned the Pheres, turning them into a breed of
Centaurs with cow's horns.

19

(a) P. Oxy. 2219 frr. 1–3 + P. Oxy. 2220 frr. 1–4

.ας

.η

. νύμφη

.ωροις

].κ[αεσσαι

].ν ἥβην

.τ̣]η

].̣ιησ[ι

]οοικο.ν

].ορ.ειην

].[   ].ατο .μή[λων

].ολε[...]ες ἀλ.οί[τ]ην

Ἐ]ρεχθέος, ὅς μιν ἔμελλε

] ἄπο πενθ.ερίοιο

αἰ]πήεσσ[α]ν Ἀφ.ιδναν

]ενος Ἡράκλει.ος

]έσσυτο βουφό.ντης λίς

].λλομένας . ἀνὰ κώμας

]α[...]ανδ.ρείης

ὀ].μοκλή

].υν Ἀχερδοῦς

5
10
15
20

13 γαμβρὸς vel γαμβρὸν Ἐ]ρεχθέος Lobel   16 ξ]ένος
Lobel   18 ἀσχ]α̣λλομένας van Groningen: ἀγ]α̣λλομένας
Livrea

19

(a) P. Oxy. 2219 frr. 1–3 + P. Oxy. 2220 frr. 1–4[18]

> of flocks
> avenger
> (Son-in-law?) of E]rechtheus, who was to (abduct?)
> her
>
> from his father-in-law's . . . [19]
> lofty Aphidna[20]   [15]
> (host?) of Heracles
> cattle-slaying lion[21]
> throughout the (stricken?) villages
> courage(?)
> onslaught   [20]
> Acherdous[22]   [21]

[18] Fragments of two separate papyrus rolls which overlap. They were attributed *in toto* to the *Chiliades* by Lloyd-Jones and Parsons, on the strength of one certain overlap with that poem (**51**.3). But the overlapping sections seem to derive from a poem with Dionysian subject-matter, and were attributed to the *Dionysus* by Barigazzi and van Groningen, and I have followed them.

[19] A reference to Boreas, who abducted Erechtheus' daughter Oreithyia?

[20] Attic deme, sited on a hill.

[21] The Nemean lion, with a reference in 1.16 to Molorchus, who hosted Heracles on his way to slay it (as told in Callimachus' *Victoria Berenices*)? Or the lion of Cithaeron, when Heracles' host was Thespius, king of Thespiae (ps.-Apoll. 2.4.9–10)?

[22] Another Attic deme.

                                    ͺτε]ς
                                 κολώ]νην
                                 ]ͅεντο
25   ἀλλὰ Διωνύσου Ἀπατήνοροͺς, ὅͺς ῥα Μελ]αινὰς
        ὤπασ]ε Κε[κροπίδαις, ἱεͺρῆς δείκͺηλ]α σισύρνης
        ]λλο[ͺ.... ενεπͺ   ]σαιο θυηλάς
        ]μοͺ[ͺγεγωνήσωͺσι] τόμουροι
                          ͺ.ͺρηͺροͺ[..]ͺͺ
30   ͺͺκερͺωͺονοͺ
                          ͺ.[.]ͺͺ[.]ͺͺ
                            ͺ.[.]πομͺ[.]ͺͺ
                            ͺυνͺ
        ]ͺν[ͺͺͺͺ
35   ]ͺͺν βου[
        ἧχι π]οͺλυκρο[κάλοιο παρ᾽ ἀνδͺήροισι Νεμείης
        ...]άπιαι νͺͺͺέβρεια Μιμαλλόνͺ
           ͺͺ ἵν[α] τύμ[β]οͺς ἐδέξαͺτͺ
             ͺνͺ[ͺͺ]παιδακατͺͺͺ
40   ͺͺαρͺ[ͺͺ] δͺεκάσσι γυναͺ

25–26 ap. EtGen AB, α 1576, ii. p. 377.4 L.–L., sine auctoris
nomine   28 μή τί] μοι [ἐκ φηγοῖο] Lobel   36 ap.
EtGen ABJ s.v. κρόκαλα [ἧχι A] = EtGud p. 348.21 Sturz =
EtMag 539.57, sine auctoris nomine   37 Ἄπιαι, ἐνδ]άπιαι
Lobel   ἐνδ]άπιαι νέβρεια Μιμαλλόν[ες ἐστείλαντο
Hollis   40–41 cf. EtGen AB = EtSym = EtMag 687.33–37
πρηνίξαι· . . . ὁ δὲ Εὐφορίων οὐκ ὀρθῶς λέγει περὶ τοῦ Διο-
νύσου, ὅτι ταῖς γυναικείαις τάξεσιν ἐγκελευσάμενος ἐπρήνι-
ξε τὴν Εὐρυμέδοντος πόλιν, τουτέστι τὸ Ἄργος. Εὐρυμέδων
δὲ ὁ Περσεὺς ἐλέγετο.

hill (*or*, Colone?[23])   [23]

But of Dionysus Apatenor, who gained Melaenae   [25]
For the sons of Cecrops through the display of his
    sacred goatskin[24]

sacrifices
the seers[25] should cry aloud

.   .   .

Where, beside the banks of the pebbly Nemea,   [36]
The (native?) Mimallones[26] . . . their fawn-skins
    where a tomb received
        child[27]
        to his companies of women   [40]

23 κολώνην could be an alternative form of the deme-name
Colonae (cf. Hollis on Call. *Hecale* fr. 51).

24 According to the legend (EtGen 1576, *Suda* α 2940, al.),
there was a single combat between an Athenian and Boeotian war-
rior in which Dionysus appeared clad in a goatskin, standing be-
hind the latter; when he turned round to look, the Athenian struck
and killed him. The story was the *aition* of the Athenian festival
the Apaturia. δείκηλον should mean "display", "manifestation"; I
take it to mean by extension "the results of displaying".

25 Euphorion's word τόμουρος means strictly a priest of
Dodona, but Lycophron uses it to mean simply "seer" (*Al.* 223).
Euphorion may be using it in the stricter or looser sense.

26 i.e. Bacchants.

27 Given the setting at Nemea, a reference to Archemorus /
Opheltes, in whose memory the Nemean games were re-estab-
lished?

..]εξ[άμ‿ε‿ν‿ος πρή‿νιξε δορυσσόο‿ν Εὐρυμέδοντος
ὃ]ν Δι[ὶ ‿χρυσ‿.... ‿αιηι τέκεν Ἀκρι‿σιώνη
ἤ] ῥά μ[ιν ἀ]‿μφο[τέρως ἔτυμον ε‿.
ὁ]θνεί[ω]‿ν Π[ερσῆ῎‿ ἐ‿τέων γε μὲ‿ν
‿Εὐ‿ρυμέδοντα
45   ]νθυ[
       ]‿῎[

41 κλ]εξ[άμ‿ε‿ν‿ος Ll.-J.–P.: πλ]εξ[άμ‿ε‿ν‿ος Livrea, de thyrso
δορυσσόο[ν Εὐρυμέδοντος Lobel   42 ὅ]ν Δι[ὶ] χρυσ[είῳ]
Lobel   Ἀπίη Lobel: γ]αίη Livrea   43 ἤ] Lobel: ἦ]
Barigazzi   ἐπ[εφήμισε μήτηρ Barigazzi   44 ap. Σ Τ
Il. 14.319, iii. p. 641.62 Erbse, sic: ὀθνεῖον πέρσης λέων γε μὲν
εὐρυμέδοντα.

(b) P. Oxy. 2219 fr. 8

— — — —

                ]‿[
       ]‿   [
]ωρηι   [
]   [
5   ]δη   [
]ΘΕΣΣΑΛΙΚΩΝ [

6]ΘΕΣΣΑΛΙΚΩΝ adnot. manus secunda

Huic carmini attrib. **107**, **161** Scheidweiler

Calling(?), he brought down (the city of) the spear-
  shaking Eurymedon,
Whom Acrisius' daughter bore to Zeus the golden (in
  the Apian land?);[28]
And she(?) called him by two names, both truly
  given:
"Destroyer" of aliens, "wide ruler" of his kinsmen.[29]

(b) P. Oxy 2219 fr. 8

Of the Thessalians. [6]

---

[28] Danae, to whom Zeus came in the form of a shower of gold.
"Apia" would be a reference to Argos.

[29] "Destroyer" renders Greek "Perseus" (cf. **184**), and "wide
ruler" "Eurymedon". For the double name, see Ap. Rhod.
4.1513–1514.

EUPHORION

Διόνυσος Κεχηνώς

Test.: EtGen AB, α 1308, ii. p. 262.5 L.–L. (**121**).

20 Aelian, *NA* 7.48

καὶ συνῳδὸν τοῖς προειρημένοις καὶ ἐς τὸ αὐτὸ δέ ἐστι
νεῦον τὸ [ἐστιν εὔδοντος codd., corr. Sitzler] ἐν τῇ Σάμῳ
ἐπὶ τοῦ κεχηνότος Διονύσου· †νομίζοιτο ἂν καὶ τὸ
φώλιον εἶναι†. καὶ τοῦτο ἀκουέτω Ἐρατοσθένους τε
καὶ Εὐφορίωνος καὶ ἄλλων περιηγουμένων αὐτό.

De fabula, cf. Plin. *NH* 8.57–58: Elpis Samius natione in
Africam delatus nave, iuxta litus conspecto leone hiatu
minaci arborem fuga petit Libero patre invocato, quoniam
tum praecipuus votorum locus est, cum spei nullus est.
Sed neque profugienti, cum potuisset, fera institerat, et
procumbens ad arborem, hiatu, quo terruerat, miserati-
onem quarebat; os morsu avidiore inhaeserat dentibus,
cruciabatque inedia, non tantum poena in ipsis eius telis,
suspectantem, ac velut mutis precibus orantem. Diu for-
tuitis fidens non est contra feram, multoque diutius mira-
culo quam metu cessatum est. Degressus tandem evellit
praebenti, et qua maxime opus esset accommodanti; tra-
duntque, quamdiu navis ea in litore steterit, retulisse
gratiam venatus adgerendo. Qua de causa Libero patri

Gaping Dionysus

Testimonium: Etymologicum Genuinum (see **121**).

20 Aelian, *On the Nature of Animals*

In agreement with, and to the same effect as, the afore-
mentioned story [i.e. that of Androcles and the lion] is one
set in Samos concerning(?) the gaping Dionysus . . . For
this let him consult Eratosthenes, Euphorion, and other
authors who narrate it.

For the story, see Pliny, *Natural History*: Elpis, a Samian
by origin, having been brought by ship to the coast of Af-
rica, caught sight of a lion near the shore with its jaws open
threateningly wide. He made straight for a tree, calling
on father Liber, because the time for prayers is precisely
when there is none for hope. But although the beast could
have chased him when he fled, it did not, and instead, lying
down before the tree, it tried to elicit pity with the very
same jaws that had been the case of so much fright. As the
creature had been gaping too greedily, a bone had stuck in
its teeth, and the creature was perishing, not only of the
pain naturally caused by the bone's shaft, but of starvation,
as it looked up at him and seemed with silent entreaty to
plead with him. For some time he did not trust to luck in
his dealings with the beast, and remained stationary longer
through amazement than through fear. But at last he de-
scended and pulled out the bone from the lion, who of-
fered himself for the operation and aided it insofar as it was
in its power to do so. They even say that, as long as the ship
stood on the shore, the lion showed its gratitude by bring-
ing its prey. It was for this reason that Elpis consecrated a

EUPHORION

templum in Samo Elpis sacravit, quod ab eo facto Graeci
Κεχηνότος Διονύσου appellavere.

21 EtGen AB (cf. EtSym, EtMag 701.9–12 sine carminis
titulo)

ῥαιβός· ὃν καλοῦσιν οἱ πολλοὶ σκελλόν, ὁ διεστραμ-
μένος . . . καὶ ῥαιβηδὸν ἐν Διονύσῳ Κεχηνότι.

Ἐπικήδειον εἰς Πρωταγόραν

Test.: Diog. Laert. 9.56

γέγονε δὲ καὶ ἄλλος Πρωταγόρας ἀστρολόγος, εἰς ὃν
καὶ Εὐφορίων ἐπικήδειον ἔγραψε.

22 Stobaeus, *Flor.* 4.56.12, v. p. 1126 Hense

Εὐφορίωνος·

> τῷ καὶ μέτρια μέν τις ἐπὶ φθιμένῳ ἀκάχοιτο,
> μέτρια καὶ κλαύσειεν· ἐπεὶ καὶ πάμπαν ἄδακρυν
> Μοῖραι ἐσικχήναντο.

1 τῷ καὶ Par. gr. 1985: τόκα cett.: καὶ τόκα Gesner
3 ἐσημήναντο, ἐσκμήναντο vel sim. codd., corr. Meineke: ἐπη-
μήναντο Gesner: ἐλυμήναντο Sitzler: μοῖραν ἀπηνήναντο (sc.
θεοί) Gaisford

Ἡσίοδος

Test.: *Suda* ε 3801

βιβλία δὲ αὐτοῦ ἐπικὰ ταῦτα· Ἡσίοδος . . .

temple in Samos to father Liber which the Greeks called the temple of "Gaping Dionysus" in commemoration of that deed.

21 Etymologicum Genuinum

rhaibos: what is commonly known as "bandy-legged", crooked . . . and "crookedly" in the *Gaping Dionysus*.

Funerary Lament for Protagoras

Testimonium: Diogenes Laertius
There was another Protagoras, an astrologer, for whom Euphorion also wrote a funerary lament.

22 Stobaeus

Euphorion:

> For him, now he is dead, let grief be measured
> And measured, too, the wailing; for the Fates
> Disdain one who is wholly free of tears.

Hesiod

Testimonium: *Suda*, s.v. Euphorion [= Test. **1**]
His books of hexameter poems are as follows: *Hesiod* . . .

EUPHORION

23 Steph. Byz., p. 455.12 Mein.

Μολυκρία, πόλις Αἰτωλίας . . . Εὐφορίων δὲ Μολυ-
κρίαν αὐτήν φησι.

Μολύκρειαν Bergk

Ἡσιόδῳ attrib. Bergk 1846, 28 [= 1886, 219]. Huic car-
mini etiam **163** attrib. Bergk; **114** (dubitanter; cf. Paus.
9.38.3), **130** Nietzsche 1873, 236.

Θρᾷξ

24–26 PSI 1390, frr. A–C

24 (fr. A)

```
        ]τῆρσι[
    ].ης γα[
  ].με.ε..[
 ]παιδος ἀγάσ..[..]οσ.[
5 ]δειπνα λυγρῆι ἐπ[
θ]αρσες, ἀπὸ κλυτονω[..].[
 ].ν τε καὶ ἔρχματα κ[α]λλυν.[
 ]..δομόνδε διὲκ θαλάμοιο.[
 ].θύρετρα καὶ ὑψόθ[ι] δωμηθέν[τ
10 ]ος ἐπ᾽ [ε]ὐρυρόηι Αἴαντι
 ].ν ὑ[π]ειρέχει ἀκρεμόνεσ[σι
ἔ]κητι θεοὶ καὶ ἀεικέος αἴκλου
 ]ν Ἀθηναίης θεράπαιναν
 ].ροισιν ἀπεχθομένην ὄρνισιν
```

242

23 Stephanus of Byzantium

Molycria, a city of Aetolia . . . Euphorion names it as
Molykria.

Thrax

24–26 PSI 1390

24

  . . . of the child[30]
  . . . the dinner on the cheerless (table?)   [5]
  . . . dreadful in your daring(?)[31]
  . . . putting a fair face on her plot(?) and deeds(?)
  . . . through the chamber to the porch(?)
  . . . the doorway, though its lintel was built high(?)
  . . . on the banks of the broad-flowing Aias[32]   [10]
  . . . towers over with its branches
  . . . because of . . . and the ghastly banquet, the gods
  . . . hand-maiden of Athena
  . . . (the chalcis?), hated by (the other?) birds

[30] This fragment alludes to the story of Harpalyce (Parthenius, *Sufferings in Love*, XIII; see ad loc.), certainly from l. 12, and quite possibly earlier; the child in this line could be Harpalyce's brother. The connection of ll. 10–11, however, with the Harpalyce story is not yet clear.

[31] The punctuation in the papyrus suggests an apostrophe (to Harpalyce?).

[32] Alternative name of Aous, a river of northern Epirus.

243

15   ἀ]πόθεστος ἑῶι θάνεν ἀμφὶ σιδήρω[ι
       ]ενου Κλυμένου ἐπεὶ αινος ἔρωτο[ς
       ἐ]πιμίσγεται Ὠκεανοῖο
       ]ͅκορέσσομεν ἧι ποτε Μῆδος
       ]σσεναν [...].ͅα[...]ρͅ.υ...ν
20   ].φωεσ[   ]..[
       ]κερασ.[
       ]..αιͅ..[

1 λωβη]τῆρσι Livrea   4 ἀγάστρ[ιος] ὅς ῥ'[Ll.-J.–P.
5 ἐπ[έθηκε τραπέζῃ Cazzaniga   6 κυνοθ]αρσές Ll.-J.–P.
7 βουλ]ήν Bartoletti   ad fin. κ[α]λλύνο[υσα, κ[α]λλύ-
νε[σθαι etc.   8 π]ροδομόνδε Latte   9 δώματος
ἀμφ]ὶ̣ θύρετρα, ἀμφ]ι̣θύρετρα Ll.-J.–P.   12 μαργοσύνης
(Latte) γὰρ (Bartoletti) ἕ]κητι   αἴκλου: cf. Athen. 4.139
B–C, 140 C   13 οἰόβιόν μιν ἔθηκα]ν Latte
14 χαλκίδα, τοῖς ἑτ]έροισιν Latte   μι]κροῖσιν Lobel
16 ἐπί̣ pap.   αἶνος, Αἶνος, Αἶμος Ll.-J.–P.

25 (fr. B)

    .[
    λ[
    του[
    ἀμφοτερα[
5   ἀτρεκὲς ι[
    τοὔνεκαπ[
    ἀλλά ἑ καὶ φθιμ[
    σ]φύρηισιν κεκ[
    ὡς ἂν μὴ ληθοι[

. . . the loathed (father) died by his own steel [15]
. . . for the story(?) of Clymenus' love
. . . mingles with (the stream of) Ocean
. . . I shall give you your fill as once the Mede[33]

25

Both
Accurately [5]
And for that reason
But him even when dead(?)
Striking with hammers
Lest . . . should fail to recognise(?)

[33] Given the content of the previous story, a reference to the story of Astyages and Harpagus (Hdt. 1.117–119, Ov. *Ib*. 545–6)?

10   τῶι σε παρακλινα[
      πατροκασιγνη[τ
      Πελλιάδες κουρ[
      Θρηικίου Τηρῆος ἐφ[
      .].ρομεν ἀδμωλη[
15   θ]ηγαλέηι αἱ δὲ δρεπ[
      ...]φας οἰωνο[..].[
      ....].παρ[

7 φθίμ[ενον Ll.-J.–P.   8 κεκ[όφασι, κεκ[οπόντες Ll.-J.–P.
9 λήθοι, λήθοι[ο, λήθοι[το   10 παρακλῖνα[ι
15 θ]ηγαλέηι αἱ δὲ δρεπ[ανηι Vitelli–Norsa

Scholia in mg. sin., quae ad col. praecedentem respicere
videntur

    ].ἅμα γ(ὰρ) αὐτὸν εἰς ὄρνιθ[α
    ].....ται κ(αὶ) τοῖς ἄλλο[ις
    ]....νεω[.] ἐστιν ὀρνέοις
    ]ενονγηοισι
5   ]σα..ται ἔνθεν κ(αὶ)
    ]ξετάζει.
    ]..
    ] τὴν Κρῖσαν· κ(αὶ) αὐτὴ δὲ
    ] κ(αὶ) ὁ Πανοπεὺς ἐκλήθ(ησαν)
10   ] ἀπὸ Κρίσου κ(αὶ) Πανοπέως

6 ἐ]ξετάζειν vel sim.

Lay you down beside him(?)   [10]
Uncle[34]
The maiden daughters of Pelias[35]
Of Thracian Tereus
. . . ignorance
And they, with a sharpened sickle(?),[36]   [15]
. . . bird

Scholia in the left margin, apparently referring to the previous column

for at the same time ‹ › him into a bird[37]   [1]
. . . and for the others
. . . for the birds   [3]
. . . whence also   [5]
Crisa. And it (i.e. the town)   [8]
and Panopeus were named
after Crisus and Panopeus[38]   [10]

[34] Pelias, uncle of Jason.

[35] Medea persuaded them that if they cut up their father and boiled his body, he would be rejuvenated (see Frazer's note on ps.-Apoll. 1.9.27; Ov. *Ib*. 441–442).

[36] Given the reference to Tereus in l. 13, Procne and Philomela? They dismembered Procne's son Itys, as an act of revenge on her husband, Tereus, for raping Philomela.

[37] The masculine pronoun rules out a reference to Harpalyce's metamorphosis into the chalcis-bird (**24**.12–14). But the story of Tereus, who was transformed into a hoopoe, does not seem to begin until **25**.13.

[38] For these brothers and their famous enmity, see Hesiod, fr. 58.10 ff. M.–W. Crisa and Panopeus were towns near Delphi.

26 (fr. C)

col. i

```
....].οι.[....]αιον..ε.[.........].μ..ο
...]... ἀφυ[σ]σάμενος βορ[.......]....θωι
..]....κουσσης φορέοις α[......]ν ὕδωρ
...].ου ὅτ᾽ ἄεθλα Διὸς στελλ[....]σηι
```
5
```
....].νεκ.α.ης κενεὸν μ[ε]τὰ λέκτρον ἵκοιο.
ἀ]λλὰ σύ γ᾽ ακ[ ].δ[ ]ων δαίσα[ι]ς γάμον
   ηεφ.[..].ρος
ἢ Ἰφικλείδαο δαϊθρασέος Ἰολάου
Ἄκτωρ Λειπεφίλην θ[α]λ[ε]ρὴν μνήσαιο
   θύγατρα,
καὶ δέ σ᾽ ἐράσμιο[ν] ἄνδρα Σεμείραμις
   ἀγκάσσαιτο
```
10
```
ὄφρα [σ]οι εὐόδμοιο [π]αρὰ πρόδομον θα[λάμοι]ο
παρθενίωι [χ]αρίεντα ποδὶ κροτέοιτο [ ].ε.[
ἤ νύ τ[ο]ι Ἀπριάτης [τ]εύξω γάμον ὧκ[ ]..α[ ]..ς
ἦν ὅτ[ε] Τραμβήλοιο λέχ[ος] Τελαμ[ω]νιάδα[ο
εἰς ἅλα δειμήνασα κατ᾽ [α]ἰγίλιπος θόρε πέτρ[ης
```
15
```
.].....[. ]τι πνειο.[.....]....ιηι..[
```

1 ποτ]αμοῖο Livrea   2 Βορ[έη Ll.-J.–P.
3 Ἀ[χερούσιο]ν ὕδωρ Ll.-J.–P.   6 Αἰολιδ[έ]ων conj. P. von
der Mühll: Ἀκ[τ]ιδίων, sc. Ἀθηναίων van Groningen
11 κρα[ἃ]] pap.   μέλ[αθρα Livrea   12 ὦ κυνanαιδές
Latte: ὦ κυνάπαιδες Page (prob. spatio longius nisi corruptela
latet)   15 [ἔ]τι πνείον[σαν Latte

26

col. i

. . . drawing off   [2]

. . . may you carry . . . water

. . . when contests   of Zeus[39]

. . . may you (not?) approach a bed that is empty.   [5]

And may you celebrate the marriage of (the sons of
    Aeolus?[40]),

Or may you woo Leipephile, the comely daughter

Of brave Iolaus, son of Iphiclus: a second Actor(?)[41]

And may Semiramis embrace you as her lover

So that, beside the porch of your perfumed chamber,   [10]

Lovely . . . should be rattled by a maiden foot.[42]

Or I'll devise for you the marriage of Apriate[43]—

Whom, when she feared the bed of Telamon's son
    Trambelus

And leaped from a goat-abandoned rock into the sea,

. . . still breathing . . .   [15]

---

[39] Lloyd-Jones and Parsons suggest a reference to the labours
of Heracles.

[40] i.e., an incestuous one: *Od.* 10.7; Parthenius, *Sufferings in
Love*, II. 3; Ov. *Ib*. 562.

[41] The story is unknown. Hes. fr. 252 M.–W. mentions the
marriage of Leipephile and Phylas, and in fr. 17a.12 that of Actor
and (?)Molione (which resulted in a monstrous pair of Siamese
twins). Alternatively, Euphorion may be using ἄκτωρ as a com-
mon noun meaning "fiancé", "bridegroom".

[42] For Semiramis' ill-fated lovers, see Diod. Sic. 2.13.4. I take
this as a grim parody of a bridal song and dance; for another
interpetation, see Watson 1990, 119.

[43] See Parthenius, *Sufferings in Love*, XXVI.

δελφῖνες πηγοῖο δ[ι' ὕδ]ατος ἐγκονέεσκον,
αὖθις ἵν' ἀείσωμεν ἀ[μ]όρδιον ἰχθύσ[ι] κυρ[
αὖθι δὲ Τραμβήλοι[ο] μόρον Ἀχιλῆι δ[
ξειν φονε[ ]..[.....]νδε κρύος ει.[

20   ].ταδ' ἀμφί σ[ε τ]ετρήχοιεν
         ]ε περὶ πλά[ζ]οντα Μάλειαν
         ].χάορος ω[..].[..].[
         ]ς ὅτε Λίβες αἰθύσσωνται
         ἐ]νιχρίμπτοιο χελείοις

25   ].νήχοιο θάλασ[σα]ν
            ].ισαλ.ισι
            ].νακρα.ιμα.[
            ]ονα.....τας
            ]ρ..[.....]...[

30   ]ολι...τ' α[
            ]νδη[ ]ασενου[
         ] πτόλιν αιμον[
                  ]..[
                  ]..[

17 ἀ[μ]όρδιον Bartoletti: ἀ[φ]όρδιον Page   κύρ[μα Latte:
κύρ[σαι Ll.-J.–P.   18 δ[αμέντος Maas   19 ξεινοφόν',
ε[ἰ]δῶ[μεν Bartoletti   ε[ἰ]δει[ης vel ε[ἰ] δ(έ) Ll.-J.–P.:
ἔξωρον vel sim. van Groningen   βαθ]ὺ δὲ Ll.-J.–P.
22 ἀ]γχάορος Ὠ[ρί]ῳ[νο]ς Ll.-J.–P.   24 δυνομένοισιν
ἐ]νιχρίμπτοιο Χελείοις Latte   25 δια]ι̣νήχοιο Ll.-J.–P.
32 Αἵμον[ίδαο Maas: Αἵμον[ιῆες Ll.-J.–P.

Dolphins hastened through the white (black?
    swelling?[44]) water,
So that we should sing once more of the fish
    despoiled of their booty(??).[45]
And then the fate of Trambelus, who (fell victim) to
    Achilles,
Host-slayer . . . and (may) a deep chill
. . . may this (the sea) be in uproar around you   [20]
. . . as you rove around Cape Malea[46]
. . . of O(rion, with his sword near the horizon??)[47]
. . . when the winds from Africa are all astir[48]
. . . may you encounter the Crab's claws
. . . may you swim (through?) the sea   [25]

[44] Several meanings were attributed to this controversial Homeric epithet (Σ bT *Il.* 9.124*a*). Euphorion might well be thought to have chosen one that is unexpected, but the passage as it stands provides no clues.

[45] In Parthenius, the maiden drowns and there is nothing about dolphins. In Euphorion her fate is unclear, but death would sort better with Trambelus' punishment. For stories of dolphins escorting both living and dead, see Plut. *Mor.* 162 E–163 C, 984 A–985 C; Euphorion fr. 22 P.

[46] South-eastern tip of the Peloponnese, notorious for mariners.

[47] That is, when Orion is setting (in November), season of storms and peril for sailors.

[48] For their stormy reputation see Gow on Theocr. *Id.* 9.11.

EUPHORION

Scholium in mg. dextra ad ll. 1–2

[. . .] αι τόπος τῆς Φ. . . . .
[?παρ'] ὃν ῥεῖ ποταμὸς καλούμ(ενος) Ψυχρός

[Πάγ]ραι conj. Ll.-J.–P., cf. *RE* s.v. Ψυχρὸς ποταμός, 3).

col. ii

(desunt c. 8 versus)

Πανδ]ώρη κακόδ[ωρ]ος, ἑκούσι[ον] ἀνδράσιν
    ἄλγ[ος
.]ρ[. .]νωμήσειεν ἑῶι ἐπίχειρα ταλάντωι,
αὖτις δὲ κρυόεντος ἐρωήσας πολέμοιο
εἰρήνην πολύβοιαν ἐπ' ἀνέρας εἰθύσειεν,
5   ἐν δ' ἀγορῆι στή[σ]αιτο Θέμιν, τιμωρὸν ἑάων,
σὺν δὲ Δίκην, ἥτ' ὦκα τὸ γρήιον ἴχνος ἀεί[ρ]ει
σκυζομένη μετὰ ἔργα, τέων τ' επι.ρ.τ.[. . . .]νδρ.[
οἵ ῥα θεοὺς ἐρέθωσι, παρὰ ῥήτρας τ'
    ἀγάγωντ[αι,
ἠ]πεδανοὺς ἢ ο[ἵ] κεν ἀγηνορέωσι τοκῆας
10 στύξαντες ζωῶν τε παρα‹ι›φασίας τε καμόν[των,

4 πολυβοιὰν pap. Cf. **185**.2   7 ἐπιδέκτορες ἄ.-ες conj.
Maas: ἐπιέρκτορες ἄ.-ες Ll.-J.–P.: ἐπιίστορες ἄ.-ες Bartoletti
ἄ]νδρε[ς, ἀ]νδρῶ[ν   9 ἀγηνορέωσι Drachmann
10 θᾶν̇ pap.

─────────────

49 First of a series of Hesiodic reminiscences.
50 If this line refers to Ares, compare Aesch. *Ag.* 439, where
Ares is described as "holder of scales". But Zeus would be a better

Scholium in the right margin on l. 1

[Pagr]ai is a place in Ph. . . . .
[beside?] which flows a river called Psychros
("Chilly")

col. ii

(about eight lines missing)
Pandora of the evil gifts,[49] a willing bane for men
Let (Zeus? Ares?) pay the wages with the scales (of
    war),[50]
But then desist from war that chills the blood
And make straight among men the peace that
    multiplies oxen
And in the market-place establish Themis,[51] defender   [5]
    of goods,
And with her Justice, who lifts her aged foot in swift
    pursuit,[52]
When she is angry, after deeds (of which men are
    culpable?)
Who provoke the gods, renege on covenants,
Or show their pride by spurning feeble parents,
And precepts of the living and the dead—   [10]

subject for the verbs in ll. 4 and 5, in which case his name must
have been mentioned in a previous line. Zeus' scales are a familiar
Iliadic motif.

[51] For Themis' association with the market-place, see *Il.* 20.4,
Od. 2.68–69, Hesych. *a* 708.

[52] Justice *leaves* the earth in disgust at human wickedness in
Arat. *Phaen.* 133–134, where she is a maiden. "Aged" here pre-
sumably because she sustains an ancient set of values (so too Aes-
chylus' Eumenides: see next note).

ἢ οἳ ξείνια δόρπα Διός τ᾽ ἀλίτωσι τραπέζας.
ο[ὔ] κεν ὁ κουφότατος ἀνέμων ἄλληκτον ἀέν[των
ῥε[ῖα φ]ύγοι, λαιψηρὰ Δίκης ὅτε γούνατ᾽ ὄρηται.
οὐ γάρ κεν νήσοισιν Ἐχινά[σ]ιν ἐσκίμψαντο
15   οἳ [ ]νεον Κεφάλοιο καὶ Ἀμφιτρύωνος αμο[
ἐκ [δὲ τ]ρίχα χρυσέην κόρσης ὤλοψε Κομ[αιθὼ
πα[τρ]ὸς ἑοῦ—ὡς δή ῥ᾽ ἄταφος τάφος εἷο
        πέλοιτο—
εἰ μὴ ληϊδίῃσι γύας ἐτάμοντο βόεσσι
Τηλεβόαι διὰ πόντον ἀπ᾽ Ἀρσίνοιο μο[λόντες·
20   οὐ [ ]λα ρω ς ἐπεφράσσαντο νε[
τ. . . .εν βοτάνῃσιν Ἀχαιίδος ἰχ[
εἰ. . . .[ ] α[ ] [ ] εν ἐκείρατο δουρα[
οὕνεκ[α] τὸν μὲν ἔολπα κακώτερα γῃ[
ὅς σεο λ[αυ]κανίην ἡμάξατο καμμορ[
25   σοὶ δ᾽ ὀλί[ί]γη μὲν γαῖα, πολὺς δ᾽ ἐπικείσε[τ
χα[ί]ρο[ις, εἰ ἐτεόν τι πέλει καὶ ἐν Ἄϊδι χ[άρμα.

14 κεν vel κ᾽ ἐν   15 οἳ κ[ό]νεον (π[ό]νεον) Ll.-J.–P.: οἶκ[ο]ν
ἑόν Maas: οἶμ[ο]ν ἑόν West   ἀμο[ρβοί Maas (cf. Hollis ad
Call. Hec. fr. 76): ἀμο[ιβήν (ἀμο[ρβήν) Ll.-J.–P.
20 οὐδέ Ll.-J.–P.   Τρῶες Ll.-J.–P.   νέ]εσθαι Latte
21 Τευκρῶν Ll.-J.–P.   22 εἰ μὴ Bartoletti   δούρα[τι
Ll.-J.–P.   23 γῃ[ράσεσθαι Maas   24 λ[ευ]κανίην van
Groningen   κάμμορ[ε χαλκῶι Latte, Pfister
25 ἐπικείσε[ται οἶκτος vel αἶνος Latte   26 suppl. Maas

---

53 Three staples of traditional Greek ethics were reverence for
gods, parents, and guests (e.g. Aesch. *Eum.* 270–271).

54 Amphitryon and his Athenian ally Cephalus went to the
Echinades (off the coast of Acarnania) to take revenge on the

Or sin against the table of a host, Zeus' common
    board.[53]
The lightest of the winds that blow without respite
Could barely flee when Justice's swift knees are set in
    motion.
For never would have fallen on the Echinades
The forces of Amphitryon and Cephalus;[54]   [15]
Never Comaetho hewn the golden lock of hair
From her father's temples[55]—may her burial be no
    burial!—
Had not the Teleboeans, setting forth across the sea
    from Arsinus,
Husbanded their fields with plundered kine.[56]
Nor would . . . have contrived (to come?)   [20]
    in the pastures . . . of the Achaean
Had not . . . ravaged by the spear(?)
So, as for *him*, I hope that he . . . worse
Who bloodied your throat (with bronze?), ill-fated
    wretch(?);
And for *you*, a little burden of earth, but a great one   [25]
    (of praise?).
Fare well, if anything be well in Hades.

Teleboeans, who had plundered the cattle of Amphitryon's father-
in-law and killed his sons. The story is again Hesiodic (fr. 193.16–
18 M.–W., cf. *Scut.* 11–19, ps.-Apoll. 2.4.6–7).

    [55] Comaetho was daughter of Pterelaus, king of the Taphians
(an alternative name for the Teleboeans). The Taphian forces fell
to the attackers when she fell in love with Amphitryon and for his
sake cut off a talismanic golden lock from her father's head. Am-
phitryon killed her.   [56] According to ps.-Apollodorus, the
plundered cattle were deposited in Elis, but Euphorion seems to
know a different version. The Arsinus, also called Erasinus, is a
river of the Argolid, Amphitryon's home.

EUPHORION

27 Steph. Byz., α 471 Billerbeck

Ἄσβωτος, πόλις Θεσσαλίας. τὸ ἐθνικὸν Ἀσβώτιος. Εὐφορίων Θρᾳκί·

> τὸν μὲν ἄρ᾽ ἐκ φλοίσβου Ἀσβώτιοι ὦκα
>   φέροντες
> ὑστάτιον ῥώσαντο κονισαλέῃσιν ἐθείραις
> ἵπποι καλὰ νάουσαν ἐπορνύμενοι Φυσάδειαν.

περὶ τῶν ἵππων Ἀμφιαράου.

2 ῥύσαντο Pflugk   3 Φυγάδειαν PN

28 EtGen AB, α 1229, ii. p. 224.19 L.–L.

ἄρρατος· Εὐφορίων ἐν Θρᾴκι [ἐν Θρᾴκῃ A, om. B]·

> ἀνέρος ἀρράτοι<ο> φόωσδ᾽ ἀνὰ Κέρβερον ἄξων.

καὶ Πλάτων [*Rep.* 535 c] . . . οἷον ἄφθαρτος, ὁ μὴ ῥαιόμενος, ἵν᾽ ᾖ ὁ ἀκαταγώνιστος· ἢ ὁ ἀνέκφραστος, ἄρρητός τις ὤν· ἢ ἰσχυρός, ἢ δυσνίκητος.

ἄρρατοι codd.: ἀρράτοι<σι> Knaack, cum <ἐννεσίῃσιν> (Meineke) versu praecedenti

cf. Plat. *Crat.* 407 D

τὸ σκληρόν τε καὶ ἀμετάστροφον, ὃ δὴ ἄρρατον καλεῖται; *Axioch.* 365 A.

27 Stephanus of Byzantium

Asbotos, a city of Thessaly. The ethnic adjective is Asbotios. Euphorion in the *Thrax*:

> Carrying him swiftly from the melée one last time
> The Asbotian horses sped with dusty manes
> Making for Physadeia of the lovely springs.[57]

28 Etymologicum Genuinum

arrātos: Euphorion in the *Thrax*:

> (at the command of?)
> An unconquerable man, bringing Cerberus up to the
> light.[58]

And Plato . . . meaning "imperishable", "one who is not beaten", or "invincible"; or "indescribable", "unspeakable"; or "mighty", "hard to conquer".

cf. Plato, *Cratylus*

. . . tough and unbending, which is also called *arrāton*.

---

[57] The reference is to Amphiaraus, whose Thessalian horses (Σ Pind. *Ol.* 6.21*d*) carry him from the combat in Thebes back in the direction of Argos (for the Argive spring Physadeia see Call. fr. 66.7 Pf., *Hymn* 5.47). "One last time" because Amphiaraus will be swallowed by the earth.

[58] Heracles, who fetched up the hound of hell as one of his labours for Eurystheus.

EUPHORION

29 Σ Genev. *Il.* 21.319*d*, v. p. 199.87 Erbse

χεράδος] . . . τινὲς γράφουσι ⟨διὰ⟩ δύο σσ "ἅλις σχεράδος", ἐπεὶ Εὐφορίων ἐν Θρᾳκί·

τύμβος ὑπὸ κνημοῖσι πολυσχεράδος Μυκόνοιο.

Ἀπολλόδωρος δέ φησι περισσὸν τὸ σ παρ᾽ αὐτῷ εἶναι, ὡς παρ᾽ Ὁμήρῳ τὴν φερέσβιον [HHom. Ap. 341].

Μυκήνοιο cod., corr. Nicole   αὐτὸ cod., corr. Nicole
γῆν φερέσβιον Nicole: γαῖα φερέσβιος HHom. loc. cit.: τὸ
φερέσβιον Erbse

30 Steph. Byz., p. 482.20 Mein.

Ὀγκαῖαι, πύλαι Θηβῶν. Εὐφορίων Θρᾳκί. Ὄγκα γὰρ ἡ Ἀθηνᾶ κατὰ Φοίνικας.

31 Σ Clem. Al. *Protr.* 27.11, p. 308.3 Stählin

Ἱπποκόων τις ἐγένετο Λακεδαιμόνιος, οὗ ⟨οἱ⟩ υἱοὶ ἀπὸ τοῦ πατρὸς λεγόμενοι Ἱπποκοωντίδαι ἐφόνευσαν τὸν Λικυμνίου υἱόν, Οἴωνον ὀνόματι, συνόντα τῷ Ἡρακλεῖ, ἀγανακτήσαντες ἐπὶ τῷ πεφονεῦσθαι ὑπ᾽ αὐτοῦ κύνα αὐτῶν. καὶ δὴ ἀγανακτήσας ἐπὶ τούτοις ὁ Ἡρακλῆς πόλεμον συγκροτεῖ κατ᾽ αὐτῶν καὶ πολλοὺς ἀναιρεῖ, ὅτε καὶ αὐτὸς τὴν χεῖρα ἐπλήγη. μέμνηται καὶ Ἀλκμὰν ἐν α΄ [cf. *PMG* 1.1 ff.]. μέμνηται καὶ Εὐφορίων ἐν Θρᾳκὶ τῶν Ἱπποκόωντος παίδων τῶν [ὡς Kroll] ἀντιμνηστήρων τῶν Διοσκούρων.

29 Scholiast on Homer, *Iliad*

cherados (gravel)] . . . Some write it with two *s*'s, "sufficient *scherados*", since Euphorion in the *Thrax* writes:

> A tomb under the hills of gravelly Mykonos.[59]

Apollodorus says the *s* in Euphorion is superfluous, as it is in Homeric *pheresbios*.

30 Stephanus of Byzantium

Onkaiai, gates of Thebes. Euphorion in the *Thrax*. For *Onka* is the name of Athena among the Phoenicians.[60]

31 Scholiast on Clement of Alexandria, *Protrepticus*

Hippocoon was a Spartan whose sons, called the Hippocoontids after their father, slew Licymnius' son Oionos, the companion of Heracles, in anger because he had killed their dog. Outraged at this, Heracles opened hostilities against them and slew many of them, in the course of which he himself received a wound to his hand. Alcman mentions it in his first book. Euphorion in the *Thrax* also mentions the sons of Hippocoon as rival suitors to the Dioscuri.[61]

or to Oilean Ajax slain by Poseidon and buried by Thetis (ps.-Apoll. *Epit.* 6.6; Aristotle fr. 640.16 Rose; Lyc. *Al.* 387–402 and Σ, Tzetz. ad 401).   [60] See Aesch. *Sept.* 164 (where the scholia reveal that Antimachus and Rhianus also used the name), 487, 501. Perhaps connected with the mention of Amphiaraus (although, according to Aeschylus, he did not attack the Oncaean gate) in **27**?   [61] The rivals of the Dioscuri in their wooing of the Leucippides are usually named as Idas and Lynceus, the Apharetidae. Perhaps Euphorion introduced a variant version of the story.

EUPHORION

'Ιππομέδων

32 Σ, Tzetzes ad Lyc. *Al.* 451, p. 166.8 Scheer

Κυχρεὺς Σαλαμῖνος καὶ Ποσειδῶνος υἱός. ἐβασίλευσε δὲ
οὗτος Σαλαμινίων, ὥς φησιν Εὐφορίων ἐν Ἱππομέδοντι·

τοῖος γὰρ Κυχρεῖος ἐνὶ ψαφαρῇ Σαλαμῖνι.

τοῦτον δέ τινες τὸν διφυῆ Κέκροπά φασιν. ἄλλοι δέ, ὅτι
ὄφις ποτὲ ἐλυμαίνετο τὴν Σαλαμῖνα καὶ ἀοίκητον ἐποίη-
σεν, ἕως ὁ Κυχρεὺς αὐτὸν ἀπώλεσε, καὶ διὰ τοῦτο ἐκλήθη
Ἀνάξιφος.

Κυχρῆος ss[4]

cf. Tzetzes ad 110, p. 56.27 Scheer

Κυχρεὺς δὲ ὁ Ποσειδῶνος καὶ Σαλαμῖνος υἱός, ὥς
φησιν Εὐφορίων, ἀνεῖλε τὸν δράκοντα καὶ τὴν Σαλα-
μῖνος βασιλείαν κατέσχε.

33 Steph. Byz., p. 422.12 Mein.

Λυκώνη, Θρᾴκης ὄρος. Εὐφορίων Ἱππομέδοντι.

ὄρος R: πόλις V

260

Hippomedon

32 Scholiast, Tzetzes on Lycophron, *Alexandra*

Cychreus, son of Salamis and Poseidon. He was king of the Salaminians, as reported by Euphorion in the *Hippomedon*:

> For such was the Cychreian (*or* of Cychreus)[62] in sandy Salamis

Some say he is the bi-form Cecrops. Others, that a serpent once ravaged Salamis and made it uninhabitable until Cychreus killed it, and for this reason was called *Anaxiphos*.

cf. Tzetzes

Cychreus, son of Poseidon and Salamis, as Euphorion says, slew the dragon and became king of Salamis.[63]

33 Stephanus of Byzantium

Lycone, a mountain in Thrace. Euphorion in the *Hippomedon*.

---

[62] The manuscripts essentially offer a choice between the genitive and the adjectival form of the name; in either case, the noun from which the form depends is not revealed by the quotation.

[63] Again related to a story in Hesiod (fr. 226 M.–W.), although according to the earlier poet Cychreus reared the serpent, and it was Eurylochus who drove it out. It became Demeter's attendant at Eleusis. Others identify the serpent with Cychreus *tout court* (Steph. Byz. p. 400.1 Mein.; Eustathius on Dion. Per. 506, 507).

[Ἱππ]ομέδων Μείζων

34 PSI 1390 (post **26** col. ii)

ὕμνο[ν....]φ[..].[..]ο μεγακλέος Ἱπ[πομέδοντ
γαίης παρθενικαὶ Λ[ι]βηθρίδος ἐντυ[ν
Πόλ]τυος ὡς Αἶν[ο]υ τε ˌερˌˌιάδαο π[
]ρ.[...]δησιν ἀνάρσ[ι]ον [
5]ν˙ · πρὸ δέ μιν Θρηϊ[κ
]ˌησδε θανὼνˌˌ[
]ενταπιˌν Περραιβ[
]ε μετὰ πρυλέεσσιν [
]ποδας ἐπάλυνε κο[νίη
10]ˌν ἔθεν μέτα λεξα[

Titulum dat pap. post *Thracem*　　　1 ὑπερ]φ[ιά]λ[οι]ο
Bartoletti: nomen celebrandi heroos latere suspicatus est Latte
Ἱπ[πομέδοντος Vitelli–Norsa: Ἱπ[πομέδοντι Latte
2 Λ[ι]βηθρίδος Maas: -δες pap.　　　ἐντύ[νοιτε Latte:
ἐντύ[νεσθε Vitelli–Norsa　　3 ὡς Vitelli–Norsa: εἰς Barigazzi
ˌερω · τ · ιαδαο (ᵒᵛ sscr. supra ω · τ ·) pap.: Γερωνιάδαο Barto-
letti: Γεροντιάδαο Latte　　π[ολίχνην Latte
4 Δα]ρδ[ανί]δησιν Latte　　7 πίον Ll.-J.–P. "dubitanter"
Περραιβ[οί, -β[όν, –β[ίδα etc.　　9 κο[νίη Latte

Scholium in mg. inf. ad l. 3

] πρότερον μ(ὲν) Πολτυμβρίαν κ[α]λου-
μ(ένην) ˌ[.]ˌαι αὖθι[ς

Hippomedon Meizon

34 PSI 1390

A song of praise . . . . for famous
    Hippomedon(?)[64]
Maidens of the Libethrian land,[65] now prepare(?),
How (the city?) of Poltys and Ainos, son of . . . [66]
. . . (to the Dardanians?) hostile
. . . him Thracians(?)   [5]
. . . having died
. . . the Perrhaiboi (drank?)
. . . among the foot-soldiers
. . . dust covered

Scholium in the lower margin on l. 3

] previously called Poltymbria . . . thereafter

[64] Given the Thracian interest in the poem, Wilamowitz suggested this was the Hippomedon who was regent of Thrace under Ptolemy III (*RE* VIII.2 (1913), 1884–1887).

[65] Nymphs sometimes credited with the power to inspire poetry and hence equated with the Muses (Virg. *Ecl.* 7.21; see Coleman ad loc.). There was a town Libethron near Olympus (Strab. 10.3.17, Paus. 9.30.9), and a mount Libethrion in Boeotia (Strab. 9.2.25, Paus. 9.34.4) where the nymphs were linked with the Muses.

[66] The Thracian city of Ainos was once named Poltyobria (Strab. 7.6.1) or Poltymbria (Steph. Byz. α 135 Billerbeck, p. 446.17 Mein.) after its mythological ruler Poltys. Livrea suggests further an etymological play on the common noun *poltos*, "porridge". Euphorion explained the later name in **88**, which perhaps also belongs in this poem.

EUPHORION

ἐ]καλεῖτο δ(ὲ) Πολτυμβρία ἀπὸ Πόλτυος τ[οῦ]
β[α]σ[ι]λ(έως) [
] Ἑλλάνικος [FGrH 4 F 197 bis]

[αὐτῆς | ὡς] Ἑλλάνικος Vitelli–Norsa

Huic carmini attrib. **88** Bartoletti (ad PSI 1390, p. 43)

Ἱστία· Ἴναχος

35 Σ Clem. Al. *Protr.* 11, 8, p. 300.12 Stählin

αἶγες] Καρανῷ τῷ Ποιάνθους υἱῷ ἐξ Ἄργους μέλλοντι
ἀποικίαν στέλλειν ἐπὶ Μακεδονίαν εἰς Δελφοὺς ἐλθόντι
ἔχρησεν ὁ Ἀπόλλων·

φράζεο, δῖε Καρανέ, νόῳ δ᾽ ἐμὸν ἔνθεο μῦθον·
ἐκπρολιπὼν Ἄργος τε καὶ Ἑλλάδα καλλιγύναικα
χώρει πρὸς πηγὰς Ἀλιάκμονος· ἔνθα δ᾽ ἂν αἶγας
βοσκομένας ἐσίδῃς πρῶτον, τότε τοι χρεών ἐστιν
5   ζηλωτὸν ναίειν αὐτὸν γενεάν τε πρόπασαν.

ἐκ δὴ τοῦ χρησμοῦ προθυμότερος γενόμενος ⟨ὁ⟩ Καρα-
νός, σύν τισιν Ἕλλησιν ἀποικίαν στειλάμενος, ἐλθὼν εἰς
Μακεδονίαν ἔκτισεν πόλιν καὶ Μακεδόνων ἐβασίλευσεν
καὶ τὴν πρότερον καλουμένην Ἔδεσσαν πόλιν Αἰγὰς
μετωνόμασεν ἀπὸ τῶν αἰγῶν. ᾠκεῖτο δὲ τὸ παλαιὸν ἡ
Ἔδεσσα ὑπὸ Φρυγῶν καὶ Λυδῶν καὶ τῶν μετὰ Μίδου
διακομισθέντων εἰς τὴν Εὐρώπην. ταῦτα Εὐφορίων ἱστο-
ρεῖ ἐν τῇ Ἱστίᾳ καὶ τῷ Ἰνάχῳ.

Ἱστίᾳ] Ἱστιαίᾳ Meineke   Ἱστιαίᾳ ἢ Ἰνάχῳ Bergk, cf.
Theocr. *Id.* 16 Χάριτες ἢ Ἱέρων

It was named Poltymbria after Poltys the king [
] Hellanicus.

Istia. Inachus

35 Scholiast on Clement of Alexandria, *Protrepticus*

"Goats"] When Caranus son of Poanthes was about to
send a colony from Argos to Macedonia and went to con-
sult the oracle at Delphi, Apollo prophesied to him:

> Reflect, god-like Caranus, and take my words to
>   heart:
> Leaving Argos and Hellas, the land of beautiful
>   women,
> Go to the sources of the Haliacmon; and where you
>   first
> Set eyes on grazing goats, then it is fated for you
> To settle there, the envy of others, and all your   [5]
>   descendants.

Encouraged by the oracle, and accompanied by certain
Greeks, Caranus sent out his colony and, arriving in Mace-
donia, founded a city. He ruled over the Macedonians
and re-named the city formerly known as Edessa "Aegae"
after the goats (*aiges*). Edessa was formerly inhabited by
Phrygians and Lydians and those who crossed over into
Europe along with Midas. These things are mentioned by
Euphorion in the *Histia* and *Inachus*.[67]

---

[67] It is unclear how much or little of the foregoing story was in
Euphorion, and similarly whether the scholiast refers to one work
or two. It is easy to see the connection of a work entitled *Inachus*
with the subject-matter, but not so easy with *Histia*. Meineke's
emendation *Histiaia* refers to a female grammarian of Alexandria
(*RE* VIII.2 (1913), Hestiaia, 4).

EUPHORION

Κλήτωρ / Κλείτωρ

36 Steph. Byz., p. 710.17 Mein.

Ὠρωπός . . . καὶ ἄλλη Βοιωτίας, περὶ ἧς Εὐφορίων Κλείτορι [Κλιτορίς codd., corr. Meineke (cf. Paus. 8.4.4–7): Κλήτορι Scheidweiler (cf. Clem. Al. *Protr.* 2.39.6)]·

Αὐλίς τ᾽ Ὠρωπός τε καὶ Ἀμφιάρεια λοετρά.

Αὐλίς τ᾽ Holsten: Αὐλὶς ἴδ᾽ Salmasius: αὐλίστης vel αὐλιστής vel αὐλητής vel αὐλητής codd.

cf. **178**?

Μοψοπία ἢ Ἄτακτα

Test.: *Suda* ε 3801

Μοψοπία ἢ Ἄτακτα· ἔχει γὰρ συμμιγεῖς ἱστορίας, Μοψοπία δέ, ὅτι ἡ Ἀττικὴ τὸ πρὶν Μοψοπία ἐκαλεῖτο ἀπὸ τῆς Ὠκεανοῦ θυγατρὸς Μοψοπίας, καὶ ὁ λόγος τοῦ ποιήματος ἀποτείνεται εἰς τὴν Ἀττικήν.

Ἄτακτα] Ἀττικά conj. Scheidweiler (quod iam corruptum aut Hesychius aut fons eius invenisse putandus est)

37 Σ Dion. Perieg. 620, *GGM* ii. p. 452[b]10 Müller

καὶ ἡ Ἀττικὴ δὲ Ἀσία πρώην ἐκαλεῖτο, ὡς ἱστορεῖ ὁ Διονύσιος ὁ Κυζικηνός. οὐ μὴν ἀλλὰ καὶ Ποσειδωνία ἐκαλεῖτο, ὡς Εὐφορίων φησίν·

. . . Ἀκτῆς δὲ παροίτερα φωνηθείσης,

Cletor / Cleitor

36 Stephanus of Byzantium

Oropos . . . and another in Boeotia, concerning which Euphorion says in the *Cle(i)tor*:

> Aulis and Oropus and the baths of Amphiaraus.[68]

Mopsopia or *Miscellanies*

Testimonium: *Suda*, s.v. Euphorion [= Test. **1**]

. . . *Mopsopia*, or *Miscellanies*, because it contains various stories, and *Mopsopia* because Attica was formerly called Mopsopia after the daughter of Ocean,[69] and the subject-matter of the poem extends to Attica.

37 Scholiast on Dionysius the Periegete

Attica, too, was formerly called Asia, as is related by Dionysius of Cyzicus. It was also called Posidonia, as Euphorion says:

> . . . previously spoken of as Acte,

---

[68] Places on the Boeotian side of the Gulf of Euboea. The cult of Amphiaraus at Oropus employed baths in its therapeutic regime (A. Schachter, *Cults of Boiotia*, i. (London, 1981), 23 n. 7).

[69] Apparently in competition with Call. fr. 709 Pf. and Lyc. *Al.* 733, who speak of an ancient king Mopsops. Strab. 9.1.18 has an alternative form, Mopsopos.

οἱ μὲν δὴ ἐνέπουσι καὶ Ἀσίδα κικλήσκεσθαι,
οἱ δὲ Ποσειδάωνος ἐπώνυμον αὐδηθῆναι.

1 Ἀσίης codd., corr. Bernhardy   παροίτερα Par. gr. 2771,
Bernhardy: παυρότερα cett.

Versus Μοψοπίᾳ attrib. Bernhardy; Μοψοπίας initio
Scheidweiler

38(a–b) Choeroboscus, in Theodos. *Canon.*, *GG* IV.1, p.
191.25 Hilgard

εἰ γὰρ καὶ εὕρηται τὸ λίς συνεσταλμένον ἔχον τὸ ῑ, ὡς
ἐπὶ τοῦ "ὥστε λὶς ἠυγένειος" [*Il.* 17.109, al.] ποιητικῶς, ὡς
παρ᾽ Εὐφορίωνι ἐν Μοψοπίᾳ, ὡς ἐπὶ τοῦ

οἶ<οι> ἐπιθύουσι βοῶν λίες,

καὶ πάλιν

κάπροι τε λίες τε

ἀλλ᾽ οὖν καὶ ἐκτεταμένον ἔχει αὐτό, ὡς ἐπὶ τοῦ "λῖες μέν
τοι λίεσσι" [Antim. fr. 65 Matthews].

οἶ<οι> Haupt, Schneider   βῶν codd., corr. Schneider

39

(a) Ps.-Elias (ps.-David), *In Porphyrii isagogen commen-
tarium*, 8.21

τούτοις δὲ τοῖς τελείοις ἀριθμοῖς μαρτυρεῖ καὶ ὁ Εὐφο-
ρίων ἐν τῇ Μοψοπίᾳ λέγων οὕτω·

Some declare that it was entitled Asis
Others that it was styled after the name of
    Poseidon.[70]

38(a–b) Choeroboscus, scholia on Theodosius' *Canones*

If "lion" is found with a short *i* in poetry—as in "like a noble lion", and as in Euphorion's *Mopsopia*, in

    As lions pounce on cattle

and again

    wild boars and lions

—it also has the longer form, as in "lions with lions".

39

(a) Pseudo-Elias (pseudo-David), Commentary on Porphyry's *Isagoge*

Euphorion in his *Mopsopia* also bears witness to these perfect numbers, when he says:

[70] Since the poem's title is an ancient name for Attica, a review of some other earlier names of Attica might stand appropriately at, or near, the beginning.

σφοῖσιν ἴσοι μελέεσσι, τὸ καὶ τέλεοι καλέονται.

τοῖς τελείοις ἀριθμοῖς Pac: τοὺς τελείους ἀριθμοὺς Ppc, M Εὐφωρίων . . . Μοναψοποιᾷ codd., corr. Westerink σφίσιν οἶσι μελέσσι τῷ καὶ καλέονται τέλειοι codd., corr. Westerink, qui τὸ καὶ καλέουσι τελείους etiam proposuit

(b) Choeroboscus, de Orthogr., Bodl. MS Barocci 50 fol. 153ʳ, ap. Cramer, Anecd. Oxon. ii. p. 239.9

λείπω . . . ἐλλίπεες παρ' Εὐφορίωνι.

40 Philodemus, περὶ Εὐσεβείας, 192–3 (ll. 4956–4969) ed. Obbink

πρώτην τού]|||των τὴν ἐκ τῆς μ[ητρός]|, ἑτέραν δὲ τ[ὴν ἐκ]| τοῦ μηροῦ [Διός, τρί]|⁴⁹⁶⁰την δὲ τὴ[ν ὅτε δι]|α- σπασθεὶς ὑ[πὸ τῶν]| Τιτάνων Ῥέ[ας τὰ]| μέλη συν- θε[ίσης]| ἀνεβίω{ι}. κἀν̣ [τῆι]|⁴⁹⁶⁵Μοψοπία[ι] δ' Εὐ[φο- ρί]|ων [ὁ]μολογεῖ [τού]|τοις, [οἱ] δ' Ὀρ[φικοὶ]| καὶ παντά[πασιν]| ἐνδιατρε[ίβουσιν]| [59 F Bernabé].

4956–64 suppl. Bücheler, Gomperz, Philippson, Luppe 4965–6 suppl. Wilamowitz   4967–9 suppl. Schober, Henrichs: [ὁ] δ' Ὀρ[φεὺς ἐν ἅιδου] καὶ πάντα [χρόνον] ἐνδιατρε[ίβειν suppl. Gomperz, Wilamowitz

Huic carmini attrib. **85–86**, **100**, **101**, **136**, **162a**, **176– 177** Scheidweiler, qui G. Schultz atque Wilamowitz secu- tus Διόνυσον partem Μοψοπίας esse ratus est (pp. 27, 45–46); **182** Sitzler; **181** Powell.

Equal to its own members, and that is why they are
called "perfect".[71]

(b) Choeroboscus, *On Orthography*

leipō . . . ellipees ("deficient") in Euphorion.[72]

40 Philodemus, *On Piety*

The first of these (sc. births) is the one from his mother, the
second from Zeus' thigh, the third when he was torn apart
by the Titans, reassembled by Rhea, and brought back to
life. In the *Mopsopia* Euphorion agrees on these matters
(or, with these people[73]); the Orphics as a whole dwell on
(these myths).

---

[71] A perfect number is the sum of its positive divisors (Euphorion's "members"), not including the number itself. Hellenistic mathematicians knew the first four of these numbers ($6 = 1 + 2 + 3$; 28; 496; 8128). See Lightfoot 1998.

[72] Apparently complementing **39a**, this is the term for a number smaller than the sum of its parts.

[73] If so, authorities for the multiple births and deaths of Dionysus cited in the lost preceding column. Henrichs (1975, 35–38) argues that Philodemus' source probably also named Callimachus, who dealt with the dismemberment of Dionysus (fr. 643 Pf., cited together with **14**) and with Dionysus' third incarnation as Zagreus, son of Persephone and Zeus (fr. 43.117 Pf.).

271

EUPHORION

Ξένιος

Test.: Σ A *Il.* 5.39 c[1], ii. p. 8.74 Erbse

Ὀδίον] πρὸ τέλους ἡ ὀξεῖα, ἐπεὶ κύριόν ἐστιν. τὸ δὲ προσηγορικὸν ὅδιος ὡς "σκότιος" (cf. *Il.* 6.24)· βούλονται γὰρ τὰ τοιαῦτα τριβράχεα ἐπὶ κυρίων μὲν παροξύνειν, ἐπὶ δὲ προσηγορικῶν προπαροξύνειν ... ἔστι μέντοι γε διαπεφευγότα τινά, ὡς τὸ Ἄνιος καὶ Εὐφορίωνος "Ξένιος", καὶ ἐν τῇ συνηθείᾳ τὸ Κρόνιος.

41

(a) Σ Ap. Rhod. 2.353–356*b*, p. 155.21 Wendel

ἀκτή τε προβλής] ἄκρα κατὰ τὴν Ἡράκλειαν, ἣν Ἀχερούσιον καλοῦσιν οἱ ἐγχώριοι. Ἡρόδωρος [*FGrH* 31 F 31] δὲ καὶ Εὐφορίων ἐν τῷ Ξενίῳ ἐκείνῃ φασὶ τὸν Κέρβερον ἀνῆχθαι ὑπὸ τοῦ Ἡρακλέους καὶ ἐμέσαι χολήν, ἐξ ἧς φυῆναι τὸ καλούμενον ἀκόνιτον φάρμακον.

(b) "Aelius Promotus", περὶ τῶν ἰοβόλων θηρίων καὶ δηλητηρίων φαρμάκων, 53, p. 67.34 Ihm

τὸ ἀκόνιτον φύεται μὲν ἐν Ἀκόναις· λόφος δέ ἐστιν ἐν Ἡρακλείᾳ οὕτω καλούμενος, Ἀκόναι, ὡς ἱστορεῖ Θεόπομπος [*FGrH* 115 F 181*c*] καὶ Εὐφορίων ἐν τῷ Ξενίῳ.

POETIC FRAGMENTS

Xenios

Testimonium: Scholiast on Homer, *Iliad*

Hodíos] The acute accent is on the syllable before the
end, because it is a proper name. The common adjective
is *hódios* like *skótios*. For in the case of these trisyllabic
words, the general rule is that they are paroxytone with
proper names and proparoxytone with common names . . .
However, there are some exceptions, such as *Ánios* and
Euphorion's *Xénios*, and in common usage *Krónios*.

41

(a) Scholiast on Apollonius of Rhodes, *Argonautica*

"A jutting promontory"] A headland in the vicinity of
Heraclea, which the locals call Acherousion. Herodorus
and Euphorion in the *Xenios* say that it was there that Cer-
berus was fetched up by Heracles and vomited gall, from
which grew the drug known as aconite.

(b) "Aelius Promotus", *On Poisonous Animals and Nox-
ious Drugs*

Aconite grows in Aconai. There is a hill of this name in
Heraclea, as reported by Theopompus and Euphorion in
the *Xenios*.

(c) EtGud p. 69.13–18 de Stefani (cf. EtSym α 413 = EtMag 50.39, α 677; ps.-Zonaras, col. 108 Tittmann)

ἀκόνιτον· βοτάνη δηλητηριώδης· ὅτι ἐν τοῖς Ἀκοναίοις ὄρεσι τῆς Μαριανδυνίας φύεται. ἢ ὅτι ἀκαταπάλαιστον καὶ ἀήττητόν ἐστιν, ἀπὸ μεταφορᾶς τῶν ἀθλητῶν, ὧν οἱ νικηταί, ἀήττητοι ὄντες, οὐ κονιορτοῦνται· κονιοῦσθαι γὰρ τὸ παλαίειν . . . καὶ Εὐφορίων θηλυκῶς λέγει τὴν βοτάνην.

Huic carmini dubitanter attrib. **75–76** Powell

Πολυχάρης

42 EtGen AB, γ 9 (cf. EtMag 223.14)

Γαιζήται· οἱ Γαλάται. Εὐφορίων ἐν Πολυχάρει [ἢ Πολυχαρίη codd., corr. Meineke]· ὅθεν·

Γαιζῆται περὶ δείρεα χρυσοφορεῦντες

παρὰ τὴν γῆν ζητοῦντες. ἐκπεσόντες γὰρ τῆς ἑαυτῶν χώρας πολλὴν γῆν περιῆλθον ζητοῦντες ὅπη οἰκήσωσιν.

δειρὴν vel δειράδα Meineke: δειράσι conj. Scheidweiler

cf. Steph. Byz., γ 13 Billerbeck

Γάζα . . . λέγονται καὶ Γαζῖται παρὰ τοῖς ἐγχωρίοις . . . εἰσὶ καὶ διὰ τοῦ η ἔθνος Γαλατῶν χρυσοφοροῦν, ὡς Εὐφορίων.

[74] It remains slightly unclear what Euphorion said. **41a** indicates that he told the story, perhaps from a local historian, how ac-

(c) Etymologicum Gudianum

Aconite: a noxious plant, so-called because it grows in the Aconaean mountains of Mariandynia. Or because it is unconquerable and invincible, a metaphor from athletics, in which the victors, not being subject to defeat, are not tumbled in the dust; "rolling in the dust" is another expression for wrestling . . . Euphorion makes the plant feminine.[74]

Polychares

42 Etymologicum Genuinum

Gaizētai: the Galatians. Euphorion in the *Polychares*, whence:

> The Gaizetai, wearing gold around their necks.[75]

From "those who are searching (*zētountes*) for land (*gēn*)". For on being expelled from their own country, they wandered over a large area of land looking for somewhere to settle.

cf. Stephanus of Byzantium

Gaza . . . they (the inhabitants) are known locally as Gazitai . . . there is also a form spelt with an *ē*, which refers to a race of Galatians who wear gold, as in Euphorion.

onite originated from Cerberus' vomit (Dion. Per. 788–792 and Eustathius ad loc.; Σ Nic. *Al.* 13*b*; Pliny, *NH* 27.4), but **41b** that he also derived the name from the hill Aconae. (This implies that the other etymology in **41c**, which derives aconite from κονιοῦσθαι, "to be dusty", does not come from Euphorion.) The area in question is on the coast of Bithynia.

[75] Referring to the gold torques which the Gauls famously wore around their necks (Polyb. 2.31.5).

43 Choeroboscus, Εἰς τὸ ὀνοματικόν, i. p. 80.20 Gaisford

. . . θράνυξ θράνυκος (ἐπὶ τοῦ θρόνου παρὰ Κορίννῃ) [*PMG* 683]· θρῆνυξ θρήνυκος (ἐπὶ τοῦ αὐτοῦ, καὶ ἔστιν ἡ χρῆσις παρ' Εὐφορίωνι ἐν Πολυχάρει).

Ὑάκινθος

44 Σ Theocr. *Id.* 10.28*a*, p. 321.13 Wendel

τὴν γραπτὴν ὑάκινθόν φασιν ἀπὸ τοῦ αἵματος τοῦ Αἴαντος ἀναδοθῆναι· διά τοι τοῦτο ἔχειν ἐγγεγραμμένον αἲ αἴ, τὴν ἀρχὴν τοῦ ὀνόματος τοῦ Αἴαντος. εἰς ὃ Εὐφορίων ἀπιδὼν εἶπε·

> πορφυρέη ὑάκινθε, σὲ μὲν μία φῆμις ἀοιδῶν
> Ῥοιτείης ἀμάθοισι δεδουπότος Αἰακίδαο
> εἴαρος ἀντέλλειν τεὰ γράμματα κωκύουσαν.

1 φημί K: φάτις cett.: corr. Hemsterhuys   2 ῥοιτείην, ῥοιτείοις, ῥυτοίοις, ῥητίοις codd., corr. Brubach   3 γεγραμμένα codd., corr. Hermann

cf. Eustath. ad *Il.* 2.557, i. p. 439.33 van der Valk

. . . καὶ ὅτι Εὐφορίων λέγει τοῦ αἵματος τοῦ ῥυέντος ἐκ τῆς τοῦ Αἴαντος σφαγῆς ὑάκινθον ἐκφῦναι.

43 Choeroboscus, *On the substantive*

. . . *thrānyx thrānykos* (applied to a chair by Corinna), *thrēnyx thrēnykos* (applied to the same; the word is used by Euphorion in the *Polychares*).

Hyacinthus

44 Scholiast on Theocritus, *Idylls*

They say that the lettered hyacinth sprang from the blood of Ajax, and that for this reason the flower has the letters *ai ai* inscribed on it, the beginning of the name of Ajax. It was with regard to this that Euphorion said:

> Purple hyacinth, one story of the bards ⟨relates that⟩
> When the Aeacid fell on the Rhoeteian shore
> You sprang forth from his blood, inscribed with a
>   lament.[76]

cf. Eustathius on Homer, *Iliad*

. . . and (Porphyry reports) that Euphorion says that the hyacinth grew from the blood that flowed from Ajax's wound.

---

[76] Ajax killed himself on the shore of the Troad after considering himself dishonoured by the gift of Achilles' arms to Odysseus. "The Aeacid" refers to him, rather than (as usual) to Achilles, since Telamon and Peleus were sometimes both made sons of Aeacus. εἴαρος in the third line could mean "in the spring", when the hyacinth flowers, but also "from his blood" (the more recherché usage). The particle μέν in the first line implies that Euphorion offset the Ajax story against another or others: according to another tradition (also implied by Euphorion's title), the hyacinth sprang from the blood of Apollo's boyfriend Hyacinthus, accidentally killed by the god in a game of discus.

45 Σ Pindar, *Nem.* 7.39*a*, iii. p. 121.28 Drachmann

λευρὸν οἱ μὲν τὸ πλατύ· βέλτιον δὲ τὸ πλάγιον ἀκούειν, ἵνα νοήσωμεν οὐχὶ τὸ καθ᾽ ἑαυτὸ πλαγίως ἔχον, ἀλλὰ τὸ κατὰ τὴν πληγὴν πλαγίως ἐνεχθέν. οὕτω γὰρ καὶ ὁ Εὐφορίων τὴν πληγὴν ὑπεστήσατο·

πλευρά τε καὶ θώρηκα διήρικεν ἰνίου ἄχρις.

διήρεικεν codd., corr. Beck

46 EtGen AB = EtMag 247.52

δάνειον· παρὰ τὸ δάνος, ὃ σημαίνει τὸ δῶρον. Εὐφορίων·

τό ῥά οἱ δάνος ὤπασεν Ἕκτωρ.

Sic **45–46** conj. van Groningen:

πλευρά τε καὶ θώρηκα διήρικεν ἰνίου ἄχρις
⟨ἀργυρόηλον ἄορ⟩, τό ῥά οἱ δάνος ὤπασεν
Ἕκτωρ.

47 Ptolemy Hephaestion, ap. Photius, *Bibl.* 190, p. 146 B 31

εἶτα ὅτι τὸ παρ᾽ Εὐφορίωνι ἐν Ὑακίνθῳ ἀπορούμενον ·

Κωκυτὸς ⟨θ᾽ ὃς⟩ μοῦνος ἀφ᾽ ἕλκεα νίψεν Ἄδωνιν

---

77 The occiput is the lower part of the back of the head. This is an attempt to reconcile two traditions about the site of Ajax's wound. Soph. *Ajax* 833–834 and other authors have him pierce his

45 Scholiast on Pindar, *Nemean Odes*

Some say that that *leuros* means "flat". But it is better to take it in the sense "oblique", provided that we understand it to mean, not something oblique in itself, but something carried in an oblique stroke. For this is how Euphorion imagined the blow:

> It pierced through his side and breastplate as far as
>   the occipital bone.[77]

46 Etymologicum Genuinum

daneion (loan): from *danos*, which means "gift". Euphorion:

> Which Hector had given him as a gift.[78]

Van Groningen combined fragments **45–46** as follows:

> It pierced through his side and breastplate as far as
>   the occipital bone,
> The silver-studded sword, which Hector had given
>   him as a gift.

47 Ptolemy Hephaestion, ap. Photius, *Library*

Then (he says that) the sense of the controversial passage in Euphorion's *Hyacinthus*

> Cocytus ⟨who⟩ alone laved Adonis' wounds

side, whereas Quint. Smyrn. 5.483 and Σ D *Il*. 23.821 speak of the neck.

[78] The sword on which Ajax fell. This is the version of the myth familiar from Sophocles.

EUPHORION

τοιοῦτόν ἐστι· Κωκυτὸς ὄνομα, Χείρωνος ἐπὶ τῇ ἰατρικῇ
μαθητής, ἐθεράπευσε τὸν Ἄδωνιν ὑπὸ τοῦ συὸς τρω-
θέντα.

⟨θ' ὃς⟩ Hollis: ⟨τοι⟩ Scaliger

Huic carmini attrib. **185** Wilamowitz 1924, 263; **189**
Scheidweiler (cf. ad fr. eius 185); **74, 180** Powell

Φιλοκτήτης

48 Stobaeus, *Flor*. 4.17.16, iv. p. 403 Hense

Εὐφορίωνος Φιλοκτήτου·

τὸν δ' ἐκάλυψε θάλασσα λιλαιόμενον βιότοιο,
καὶ οἱ πήχεες ἄκρον ὑπερφαίνοντο ταθέντες
ἀχρεῖ' ἀσπαίροντος ἅλις Δολοπιονίδαο,
δυστήνου· ζωὴν δὲ μεθ' ὕδατος ἔκβαλε πᾶσαν
5 χεῖρας ὑπερπλάζων, ἅλμη δ' ἔκλυσσεν ὀδόντας.

3 ἀχρεῖ' ἀσπαίροντες vel ἀχρεῖα [ἅ χρεία] σπαίροντες codd.,
corr. Meineke   ἅλις] ἅδην Meineke   4 ἔμβαλε codd.,
corr. Valckenaer   post 4 lacunam statuit van Groningen, in
qua ⟨πόντος⟩ vel nomen simile supplendum videtur
5 ἐκάλυψεν codd., corr. Sitzler: ἐπέρησεν Elter   ὀδόντας]
θάνοντα Geel

Χιλιάδες

Test.: *Suda* ε 3801

Χιλιάδες· ἔχει δὲ ὑπόθεσιν εἰς τοὺς ἀποστερήσαντας
αὐτὸν χρήματα, ἃ παρέθετο, ὡς δίκην δοῖεν κἂν εἰς

280

is as follows: Cocytus was the name of a disciple of
Cheiron, to whom he taught medicine. He tended Adonis
when he was wounded by the boar. [79]

Philoctetes

48 Stobaeus

From Euphorion's *Philoctetes*:

> Clinging to life, the sea washed over him;
> His outstretched arms appeared above the surface,
> As Dolopion's son[80] gasped vainly for his fill of air,
> Poor wretch. And all his life he breathed forth with
>   the water,
> Tossing his hands on high, and the brine surged   [5]
>   round his teeth.

Chiliades

Testimonium: *Suda*, s.v. Euphorion [= Test. **1**, q.v.]

. . . the *Chiliades*, which are directed against people who
deprived him of money he had deposited with them, and

---

[79] This passage has been compared with Prop. 2.34.91–92,
where Gallus washes his wounds in the waters of the underworld:
this may be an echo of Gallus himself. Needless to say, Ptolemy's
interpretation is maverick.

[80] According to Hyginus, *Fab*. 102, a shepherd named
Iphimachus, who took care of Philoctetes when he was abandoned
by the Achaeans on Lemnos. The story of his drowning is other-
wise unknown; perhaps it happened when the returning Greeks
were shipwrecked off Euboea.

EUPHORION

μακράν· εἶτα συνάγει διὰ χιλίων ἐτῶν χρησμοὺς ἀπο-
τελεσθέντας· εἰσὶ δὲ βιβλία ε΄, ἐπιγράφεται δὲ ἡ
πέμπτη χιλιάς. περὶ χρησμῶν, ὡς διὰ χιλίων ἐτῶν ἀπο-
τελοῦνται.

περὶ χρησμῶν ... ἀποτελοῦνται om. vel in mg. codd. plerique

49 Steph. Byz., α 477 Billerbeck

Ἀσκανία . . . ἔστι καὶ Ἀσκάνιος ποταμός. Εὐφορίων
Χιλιάσι·

    καὶ Ψίλιν Ἀσκάνιόν τε <   > Ναναίθοιο

Ψίλις Μυσίας, Ναναιθος Ἰταλίας.

<καὶ εὖ νάοντα> Ναναιθον Salmasius, unde <κ. εὖ ν.> Νέαιθον
Meineke: <καὶ ὕδατα> Friedemann: <πρὸς ὕδατα> vel <ῥόον
προτὶ> Scheidweiler   <ῥόῳ πάρα> Ναναίθοιο | <γνωρί-
ζειν ἐτόπαζον> van Groningen

50 Steph. Byz., p. 240.13 Mein.

Δυμᾶνες, φυλὴ Δωριέων . . . Εὐφορίων Χιλιάσι·

    δαίμων <μωμή>σαιτο φιλοπλοκάμοισι Δυμαίναις

<οὐδέ κ᾽ ἐπελθὼν> | δαίμων <μωμή>σαιτο Schneider
    <ἀντιά>σαιτο Düntzer

whose premise is that they will eventually be punished, no matter how long in the future; then he assembles a collection of oracles that were fulfilled after [*or* in the course of] a thousand years. There are five books, and the fifth is entitled *chilias* ("thousand"). On oracles, how they are fulfilled after [*or* in the course of] a thousand years.

49 Stephanus of Byzantium

Ascania . . . There is also a river Ascanius. Euphorion in the *Chiliades*:

And Psilis and Ascanius ⟨ ⟩ of Nauaethus

Psilis is in Mysia, Nauaethus in Italy.[81]

50 Stephanus of Byzantium

Dymanes, a tribe of Dorians . . . Euphorion in the *Chiliades*:

⟨Nor⟩ would a god find fault with the Dymaenae, who delight in their tresses.[82]

[81] The Psilis and Ascanius are rivers of the Troad, less familiar than the Simois and Scamander. The Nauaethus or Neaethus is just north of Croton in southern Italy. It lent its name to a story that the Trojan women set fire to the ships of their Greek captors there (Σ, Tzetz. ad Lyc. 921). Virg. *Aen.* 5.635–718 locates the boat-burning in western Sicily, and makes the boats Trojan.

[82] One of the three Dorian tribes.

51 P. Oxy. 2220 fr. 10

```
          ] . . . . [
          ] Δωδῶ[
Ζηνὸς Χαονίοιο προμάντι]ες ηὐδάξ[αντο
          ].ισιπατε.[
5         ]αροπ.ομ[
          ]νει[
```

2 Δωδῶ[νι πέλειαι Hollis   3 Suppl. ex Steph. Byz. s.v.
Χαονία, p. 686.11 Mein. Εὐφορίων Χιλιάσι· Ζηνὸς, κτλ.

52 Athen. *Deipn.* 10.436 F

Ξέναρχος δ᾽ ὁ Ῥόδιος διὰ τὴν πολυποσίαν Μετρητὴς
ἐπεκαλεῖτο· μνημονεύει αὐτοῦ Εὐφορίων ὁ ἐποποιὸς ἐν
Χιλιάσι.

cf. Aelian, *VH* 12.26

ποτίστατοι γεγόνασιν ἄνθρωποι ὥσπερ φασί Ξενα-
γόρας ὁ Ῥόδιος, ὃν ἐκάλουν Ἀμφορέα . . .

53 P. Oxy. 2085

cf. **109**, fr. 1, col. ii, ll. 27–29

51 P. Oxy. 2220

] Dodo[na
The prophets of Chaonian Zeus spoke out.[83]

52 Athenaeus, *Deipnosophistae*

Xenarchus of Rhodes was known as "The liquid measure" because of his fondness for drinking. Euphorion the hexameter poet mentions him in the *Chiliades*.

cf. Aelian, *Historical Miscellany*

The most drink-loving men on record are Xenagoras of Rhodes, whom they called "Nine-gallons" . . .

53 P. Oxy. 2085

cf. **109**, fr. 1, col. ii, ll. 27–29.

---

[83] The Selloi were the (male) prophets at Dodona, though Hdt. 2.55.1 speaks of feminine *promanties*. Euphorion could mean either.

54 P. Oxy. 2528

cf. **111**, ll. 5–12

Huic carmini attrib. **187** Toup; **95** Heyne; **79**, **102**, **103** Meineke; fort. **10–11** (Ἀραί) Powell, van Groningen; cf. etiam Dindorf ap. **56**.

55–178 FRAGMENTA INCERTAE SEDIS

55 "Apuleius", *De Orthographia*, § 51, p. 12 ed. Osann

Azania est pars Arcadiae, ubi natum Iovem tradit Euphorion.

56 Σ Eur. *Phoen.* 682, i. p. 320.16 Schwartz

δεδόσθαι γὰρ τὰς Θήβας τῇ Περσεφόνῃ ὑπὸ Διὸς ἀνακαλυπτήρια, ὡς Εὐφορίων [ἅ νιν εὐηλίοισιν add. MT: φησὶν ἐν Χιλιάσιν Dindorf]·

> ἀλλ' οὔπω Θήβῃ πεπρωμένα κεῖτο τάλαντα,
> τὴν ῥά ποτε Κρονίδης δῶρον πόρε Περσεφονείῃ
> ἧ γαμέτῃ, ὅτε πρῶτον ὀπωπήσασθαι ἔμελλε,
> νυμφιδίου σπείροιο παρακλίνασα καλύπτρην.

1 τάλαντα] θέμεθλα Geel   3 ἧ γαμετῇ M: ὃν γαμέτην Mein.   ὀπωπήσεσθαι Schaefer, Cobet

54 P. Oxy. 2528

cf. **111**, ll. 5–12

55–178 FRAGMENTS OF
UNCERTAIN LOCATION

55 "Apuleius", *On Spelling*

Azania is a part of Arcadia, where Euphorion relates that Jupiter was born.[84]

56 Scholiast on Euripides, *Phoenissae*

For Zeus gave Thebes to Persephone as a bridal gift, on the occasion of her unveiling, as Euphorion says:

> But not yet were fate's balances fixed fast in Thebes,
> Which once the son of Cronos on Persephone
>   bestowed,
> His bride, when first she was about to see him,
> Moving aside the cover of her maiden snood.[85]

[84] For the vindication of this as a genuine citation of Euphorion, see Hollis 1992 *a* 110–112 and 1996, 165. It can be combined with **174**, just as in Call. *Hymn* 1 Zeus is born in Arcadia and handed over to a nymph called Nede.

[85] The custom referred to is that of presenting gifts to a bride when she first moves aside her veil and is seen by the bridegroom. Zeus was both father and husband of Persephone, who bore him Iacchus. With Meineke's emendation ("when first she was about to see her husband"), the allusion is to Persephone's union with Hades, when according to other sources she was presented with Sicily (e.g. Σ Pind. *Nem.* 1.17).

57 P. Oxy. 3830

fr. 2 col. ii

6   "γαίης [καὶ πόντοιο, ἵν' Ἰαπετός τε Κρόνος τε"

[*Il.* 8.479]

[desunt c. 2 versus]

fr. 3 col. ii

Οὐρ]ανοῦ καὶ Γῆς πα[ιδ-

]ηι ὅτι τε νέος ὤ[ν (?)

]ν· ὁ δὲ Ζεὺς μ[

].βαλὼν α.[

5   κερ]αυνοῖς καὶ ἀ[στραπαῖς

]ς ἐνεῖρξεν τεε[

] ἀρχὴν Κρόνωι.[

]τ.. διαφέρειν οφει[

την ἀ[π'] αὐτοῦ προση[γορευ-   ἡ ἱ-

10   στορία παρ'.Εὐφο.ρίων̣ι[

4 fort. ἐ]μβαλών Harder   6–7 τὴν τού]|[των ἀρχὴν
Κρόνωι π[αρέδωκεν Harder   8 πάν]τ̣ω̣ν dub. Harder
10 suppl. e PLitLond. 142

cf. Σ AD *Il.* 8.479 γαίης καὶ πόντοιο ἵν' Ἰαπετός τε
Κρόνος τε] Διὸς μεταστήσαντος τὸν πατέρα Κρόνον
τῆς βασιλείας καὶ τὴν τῶν θεῶν ἀρχὴν παραλα-
βόντος, Γίγαντες οἱ Γῆς παῖδες ἀγανακτήσαντες ἐν
Ταρτησῷ (πόλις δέ ἐστιν αὕτη παρὰ τὸν Ὠκεανόν)
μέγαν κατὰ Διὸς πόλεμον παρεσκεύαζον. Ζεὺς δὲ
συναντήσας αὐτοῖς καταγωνίζεται πάντας, καὶ μετα-

57 P. Oxy. 3830

fr. 2 col. ii

"of earth [and sea, where Iapetus and Cronos"
[c. 2 lines missing]

fr. 3 col. ii

Children of Heaven and Earth
and because being young
and Zeus
hurling
with thunderbolts and lightnings [5]
he confined them   [and he entrusted
the dominion to Cronos
to excel [all of them?] Ophi[
the (mountain?) named after him   The
story (is) in Euphorion.[86]

cf. Scholiast on Homer, *Iliad*, "Of the earth and sea, where
Iapetus and Cronos"] After Zeus displaced his father
Cronos from the kingship and took over the sovereignty of
the gods, the Giants, sons of Earth, grew angry in Tartesus
(a city beside the Ocean) and prepared a great war against
him. Meeting them in battle, Zeus overcame their entire

---

[86] Such "source" ascriptions cannot be relied upon to repro-
duce what the author in question actually said. The present story
(whether Euphorion or not) combines features of stories about
Giants and Titans, while the imprisonment of Ophion under a
mountain recalls Typho underneath Mount Etna.

στήσας αὐτοὺς εἰς Ἔρεβος τῷ πατρὶ Κρόνῳ τὴν
τούτων βασιλείαν μεταδίδωσιν. Ὀφίωνα δὲ τὸν δο-
κοῦντα πάντων ὑπερέχειν κατηγωνίσατο ὄρος ἐπιθείς,
ἀφ᾽ οὗ Ὀφιώνιον προσηγορεύθη.

58 Σ AD *Il.* 14.295

Ἥραν τρεφομένην παρὰ τοῖς γονεῦσιν εἷς τῶν Γιγάν-
των Εὐρυμέδων βιασάμενος ἔγκυον ἐποίησεν, ἡ δὲ
Προμηθέα ἐγέννησεν. Ζεὺς δὲ ὕστερον γήμας τὴν
ἀδελφὴν καὶ γνοὺς τὰ γενόμενα τὸν μὲν Εὐρυμέδοντα
κατεταρτάρωσεν, τὸν δὲ Προμηθέα προφάσει τοῦ πυ-
ρὸς δεσμοῖς ἀνήρτησεν. ἡ ἱστορία παρὰ Εὐφορίωνι.

cf. Σ T *Il.* 14.296*a*, iii. p. 636.1 Erbse, sine Euphorionis
nomine

59 Σ Nic. *Al.* 433*a*, p. 154 Geymonat

μήκωνος κεβληγόνου] τῆς ἐν τῇ κεφαλῇ τὸν γόνον
ἐχούσης . . . καὶ Εὐφορίων περὶ τῆς Ἀθηνᾶς·

κεβληγόνου Ἀτρυτώνης

cf. Ἐκλογαὶ διαφόρων λέξων, Bodl. MS Barocci 50 fol.
310ʳ, ap. Cramer, *Anecd. Oxon.* ii. p. 456.29

κεφάλη . . . Μακεδόνες δὲ κεβλήν, τὸ β̄ ἀντὶ τοῦ φ̄
λαμβάνοντες, ὡς ἐπὶ τῆς Βερενίκης, Φερενίκη γάρ
ἐστιν.

force, removed them to Erebus, and handed dominion over them to his father Cronos. As for Ophion, who towered over them all, he defeated him and penned him under a mountain, which came to be known as "Ophionion" after him.

58 Scholiast on Homer, *Iliad*

While Hera was still being brought up by her parents, one of the Giants, Eurymedon,[87] raped her and made her pregnant. She gave birth to Prometheus. Afterwards, when Zeus married his sister and found out what had happened, he consigned Eurymedon to Tartarus and used ⟨his theft of⟩ fire as a pretext to tied up Prometheus in chains. The story is in Euphorion.

59 Scholiast on Nicander, *Alexipharmaca*

"The *keblēgonos* poppy"] With the seeds in its head . . . Euphorion also uses the word of Athena:

The unwearied goddess, born from the head.

cf. *Selection of various glosses*

kephalē (head) . . . the Macedonian form is *keblē*, with a *b* instead of *f*, as also in the case of "Berenice" for "Pherenice".[88]

---

[87] King of the Giants, known from *Od.* 7.58–59.
[88] See also Call. fr. 657 and Pfeiffer ad loc.

EUPHORION

60 Commenta Bernensia in Lucan, *Phars*. 3.402

Pindarus [fr. 100 Snell] et ceteri dicunt Apollinis et Pene-
lopae filium [sc. Pana], alii Mercurii et eiusdem. Hunc
natum montanis nimfis a patre nutriendum traditum per-
hibent, unde hylicus deus factus. Euphorion Ulixis filium
manifestat.

cf. Σ ps.-Eur. *Rhes*. 36, ii. p. 328.18 Schwartz

τὸν ⟨Πᾶ⟩να οἱ μὲν Πηνελόπης φασὶ ⟨   ⟩ [Καλ-
λιστοῦς καὶ Διὸς παῖδας γενομένους ⟨   ⟩ ἀφ' ἧς
ὄρος Κυλλήνης del. Schwartz, praeeunte Münzel] ἄλλοι
δὲ Ἀπόλλωνος καὶ Πηνελόπης ⟨   ⟩ ὡς καὶ Εὐφο-
ρίων.

sic suppl. Schwartz: τὸν Πᾶνα οἱ μὲν Πηνελόπης φασὶ ⟨υἱὸν
καὶ πάντων τῶν μνηστήρων, ὅθεν καὶ Πᾶνα λέγεσθαι⟩, ἄλλοι
δὲ Ἀπόλλωνος καὶ Πηνελόπης, ⟨οἱ δὲ Ὀδυσσέως καὶ Πηνε-
λόπης⟩, ὡς καὶ Εὐφορίων.

61 Clem. Al. *Strom*. 4.5.24.1–2

αὐτίκα πρὸς τῶν ποιητῶν τυφλὸς ἐκ γενετῆς κηρύττεται
[sc. ὁ Πλοῦτος]·

   καί οἱ γείνατο κοῦρον, ὃς οὐκ ἴδεν ἠλέκτωρα,

φησὶν ὁ Χαλκιδεὺς Εὐφορίων.

εἶδεν ἠλέκτορα L, corr. Keydell, dein Wilamowitz 1924, 263 =
1962, 357 (cf. Choeroboscus, in Theodos. *Canon*., *GG* IV.1, p.
301.3 Hilgard): ἠλέκτορα εἶδεν Sylburg

60 Commentary on Lucan, *Pharsalia*

Pindar and others say that he [sc. Pan] was son of Apollo and Penelope, others that he was son of Mercury and the same mother, and that he was handed over by his father to the mountain nymphs to be nurtured, whence he became a god of the woodlands. Euphorion represents Pan as son of Ulysses.

cf. Scholiast on ps.-Euripides, *Rhesus*

Some say that Pan was son of Penelope ‹and all the suitors, whence he was named "Pan" ("All")›, others that he was son of Apollo and Penelope, ‹while others still say that he was son of Odysseus and Penelope›, which is Euphorion's version.[89]

61 Clement of Alexandria, *Stromateis*

Wealth is said by the poets to be blind from birth:

> And bore to him a son, who never saw the shining
> one[90]

as Euphorion of Chalcis says.

---

[89] In which case he was mortal (Σ Theocr. *Id*. 1.123*b* mentions the same lineage, but without naming Euphorion). Ancient authors sometimes distinguish two Pans; Plutarch of course knew of one who died (*Mor*. 419 C–D).

[90] i.e. the sun. The parents of Wealth were Demeter and Iasion (Hes. *Th*. 969–970), and he was born in Crete.

62 Σ Arat. *Phaen*. 34, p. 83.7 Martin

δοκεῖ δὲ πρὸς εὐτοκίαν συμβάλλεσθαι αὐτό [sc. δίκταμ-νον], ᾧ καὶ τὴν Εἰλείθυιαν στέφουσι· καί που ἐπ᾽ αὐτῆς Εὐφορίων·

στεψαμένη θαλεροῖσι συνήντετο δικτάμνοισι.

63 EtGen AB (cf. EtSym; EtMag 396.27)

εὐρυκόωσα· ἡ μέγα χάσμα ἔχουσα [hic desinit A]. Εὐφο-ρίων·

ὅσσους εὐρυκόωσα Τυφάονι κύσατο Κητώ.

παρὰ τὸ εὐρὺ καὶ τὸ κόον· ἡ μεγάλη καὶ πλατεῖα. κόον γὰρ λέγουσι τὸ μέγα οἱ Λάκωνες.

κύσσατο EtSym, EtMag

64 Σ T *Il*. 24.77*b*, v. p. 534.3 Erbse

Εὐφορίων·

ἀελλόποδος θ᾽ ἁρπυίας

αἰθαρύταο T, corr. Oder

65 Σ AD *Il*. 18.486

τό τε σθένος Ὠρίωνος] . . . Ὑριεὺς ὁ Ποσειδῶνος καὶ Ἀλκυόνης μιᾶς τῶν Ἄτλαντος θυγατρῶν ᾤκει μὲν ἐν Τανάγρᾳ τῆς Βοιωτίας, φιλοξενώτατος δὲ γενόμενος

62 Scholiast on Aratus, *Phaenomena*

It [sc. dittany] seems to contribute to the easing of labour-pains, and they crown Eileithyia with it. And Euphorion says of her:

> Crowned with fertile dittany[91] she met her.

63 Etymologicum Genuinum

eurykoōsa: having a large chasm. Euphorion:

> Those cavernous Keto brought to birth by Typho.[92]

From *eury* (wide) and *koon*: large and broad, for the Laconian word for "large" is *koon*.

64 Scholiast on Homer, *Iliad*

Euphorion:

> And of a storm-footed Harpy.

65 Scholiast on Homer, *Iliad*

"And the might of Orion"] Hyrieus, son of Poseidon and Alcyone, one of the daughters of Atlas, lived in Tanagra, in Boeotia. He was a most hospitable person, and once even

---

91 Ancient authors associate this plant with Crete, home and ancient cult-centre of the goddess of childbirth.

92 The offspring are presumably monsters of some sort. In Hesiod's *Theogony*, the offspring of Typho and Echidna are the hound of Geryon, Cerberus, and the Lernaean hydra. Euphorion has given Typho a different partner, unless he understood τῇ in 306 to refer to Typho's union, not with Echidna, but with Keto (whose offspring by Phorcys are the general subject of 270–336).

ὑπεδέξατο ποτὲ καὶ θεούς. Ζεὺς δὲ καὶ Ποσειδῶν καὶ
Ἑρμῆς ἐπιξενωθέντες αὐτῷ καὶ τὴν φιλοφροσύνην
ἀποδεξάμενοι παρήνεσαν αἰτεῖν ὅ τι ἂν βούλοιτο· ὁ δὲ
ἄτεκνος ὢν ᾐτήσατο παῖδα. λαβόντες οὖν οἱ θεοὶ τὴν
τοῦ ἱερουργηθέντος αὐτοῖς βοὸς βύρσαν, ἀπεσπέρμη-
ναν [κατούρησαν van Thiel] εἰς αὐτὴν καὶ ἐκέλευσαν
κρύψαι κατὰ γῆν καὶ μετὰ δέκα μῆνας ἀνελέσθαι. ὧν
διελθόντων ἐγένετο ὁ Οὐρίων, οὕτως ὀνομασθεὶς διὰ
τὸ οὐρῆσαι τὸ σπέρμα αὐτοῦ τοὺς θεοὺς [οὐρῆσαι
ὥσπερ τοὺς θεοὺς codd., corr. Scheidweiler], ἔπειτα κατ᾽
εὐφημισμὸν Ὠρίων. συγκυνηγετῶν δ᾽ οὗτος Ἀρτέμιδι
ἐπεχείρησεν αὐτὴν βιάσασθαι. ὀργισθεῖσα δ᾽ ἡ θεὸς
ἀνέδωκεν ἐκ τῆς γῆς σκορπίον, ὃς αὐτὸν πλήξας κατὰ
τὸν ἀστράγαλον ἀπέκτεινεν. Ζεὺς δὲ συμπαθήσας
κατηστέρισεν αὐτόν· διὸ τοῦ Σκορπίου ἀνατέλλοντος
Ὠρίων δύνει. ἡ ἱστορία παρὰ Εὐφορίωνι.

cf. Palaephatus, de incred. 51 (usque ad κατηστέρισεν
αὐτόν, nec porro).

66 Σ PQT Od. 5.121, i. p. 255.13 Dindorf

τούτου [sc. Ὠρίωνος] γὰρ ἐρασθεῖσα ἡ Ἡμέρα ἥρπα-
σεν ἀπὸ Ταναγρας εἰς Δῆλον, ἔνθα τὴν ἀμαλλοφόρον
Οὖπιν ἰδὼν ἠθέλησε βιάσασθαι. ἐφ᾽ ᾧ ὀργισθεῖσα ἡ
θεὸς ἀναιρεῖ αὐτόν, ὡς Εὐφορίων δηλοῖ.

---

93 Not to mention other authors: Hygin. Fab. 195; Ov. Fast.
5.493–536, Nonn. D. 13.96–103 (the birth); Aratus, Phaen. 636–

entertained deities. Zeus and Poseidon and Hermes were welcomed by him as guests, and after they had enjoyed his good cheer they encouraged him to ask for whatever he wanted. Being childless, he asked for a child. The gods therefore took the hide of the bull which had been sacrificed to them and ejaculated onto it, and they told him to hide it underground, then take it up again after ten months. After those ten months had passed, Ourion was born, his name derived from the gods "urinating" his seed, but later softened to "Orion". Once when he was out hunting with Artemis he tried to rape her. The goddess was angry and caused a scorpion to spring from the earth which bit him in the ankle and killed him. Zeus felt sympathy and translated him to the heavens. That is why, when Scorpio rises, Orion sets. The story is in Euphorion.[93]

66 Scholiast on Homer, *Odyssey*

For Day fell in love with him (sc. Orion) and snatched him from Tanagra to Delos, where he saw Oupis as she carried sheaves and wanted to force her to his will. The goddess was angry at this and slew him, as Euphorion relates.[94]

---

646 (the death). It is not clear whether Euphorion told all or part of the story.

[94] Is "the goddess" Day, acting out of jealousy (in *Od.* 5.121 Dawn abducts, but does not kill, Orion)? Is it Artemis (said to kill him in *Od.* 5.123–124 and often thereafter)? Or is it Oupis—and if so, is Oupis another name for Artemis (as in Call. *Hymn* 3.204–205) or is she an independent figure (one of the maidens who come from the Hyperboreans to Delos in Hdt. 4.35)? Not all of these possibilities can be reconciled with the previous fragment; Euphorion may have told the story more than once.

67 Σ Arat. *Phaen*. 324, p. 240.9 Martin

ὅτι δὲ ἔχει σφόδρα λαμπροὺς ἀστέρας, καὶ μάλιστα μὲν
τοὺς τὸ ζῶμα ἀποτελοῦντας, ἑτέρους δὲ τοὺς περὶ ⟨τοὺς⟩
ἱμάντας καὶ ⟨τοὺς τὸ⟩ ξίφος μιμουμένους, καὶ δύο λαμ-
προὺς τοὺς ἐπ' ἄκρων ποδῶν, φησὶ καὶ Εὐφορίων·

. . . οὐδὲ νεογνοὶ
παῖδες ἐδιζήσαντο πελώριον Ὠρίωνα

68 Σ AD *Il*. 24.602

Νιόβη θυγάτηρ μὲν ἦν Ταντάλου, γυνὴ δὲ Ἀμφίονος.
γαμηθεῖσα δὲ τῷ Ἀμφίονι παῖδας ἔσχεν δεκαδύο, ἓξ
μὲν θηλείας, ἓξ δὲ ἄρρενας. ἐπαρθεῖσά τε τῷ πλήθει
τῶν παίδων καὶ τῇ καλλονῇ ὠνείδιζεν τῇ Λητοῖ, ὅτι
δύο μόνους ἐγέννησεν, Ἀπόλλωνα καὶ Ἄρτεμιν, καὶ
ὅτι εὐτεκνοτέρα αὐτῆς ἐστιν. ἀγανακτήσασα δὲ ἡ θεὸς
ἔπεμψεν [ἀγανακτήσαντες δὲ οἱ θεοὶ ἔπεμψαν L] αὐ-
τοῖς τοὺς παῖδας αὐτῆς [ἔπεμψεν τοῖς παισὶν αὐτῆς
θάνατον QL: ἔπεμψεν ἰοὺς τοῖς παισὶν αὐτῆς A]· καὶ
Ἀπόλλων μὲν τοὺς ἄρσενας ἀναιρεῖ κυνηγετοῦντας ἐν
τῷ Κιθαιρῶνι, Ἄρτεμις δὲ τὰς θηλείας ἐπ' οἴκου
οὔσας. θρηνοῦσαν οὖν τὴν Νιόβην ἀφάτως τὸ τοιοῦτο
δυστύχημα Ζεὺς ἐλεήσας εἰς λίθον μετέβαλεν, ὃς καὶ
μέχρι νῦν ἐν Σιπύλῳ τῆς Φρυγίας ὁρᾶται παρὰ πάν-
των, πηγὰς δακρύων προϊέμενος. ἡ ἱστορία παρὰ
Εὐφορίωνι.

67 Scholiast on Aratus, *Phaenomena*

That it (sc. the constellation of Orion) has very bright stars, especially those that form the belt, and others around the straps and those that form the likeness of his sword, and two bright stars at the extremities of his feet, is stated also by Euphorion:

> . . . . not even infant
> Children seek (in vain) for the mighty Orion.

68 Scholiast on Homer, *Iliad*

Niobe was the daughter of Tantalus and wife of Amphion. From her marriage to Amphion she had twelve children, six girls and six boys. Priding herself on the number of her children and their beauty she taunted Leto with the fact that she (Leto) had only two, Apollo and Artemis, and that she (Niobe) was more blessed in offspring than the goddess. This angered Leto, who sent her children against Niobe's family: Apollo killed the males while they were out hunting on Cithaeron, Artemis the females while the latter were at home. Zeus felt pity for Niobe's indescribable grief at this calamity, and turned her into a stone, which even to this day is visible to all in Sipylus in Phrygia, weeping streams of tears. The story is in Euphorion.[95]

[95] In essentials, this is the standard version of the myth; it is not clear why Euphorion should be singled out.

EUPHORION

69 Σ Ap. Rhod. 1.181, p. 23.5 Wendel

οὗτος [sc. Τιτυός] δὲ ἐν Ἅιδου τετιμώρηται διὰ τὸ εἰς
Πυθῶνα στελλομένην κατασχεῖν τὴν Λητώ, ὡς καὶ
Ὅμηρος [Od. 11.576]· "Τιτυὸν Γαίης υἱόν". ὁ δὲ Εὐφο-
ρίων Ἀρτέμιδός φησιν αὐτὸν ἧφθαι καὶ διὰ τοῦτο
τιμωρεῖσθαι.

70 Σ Arat. Phaen. 519, p. 312.5 Martin

καμπή τ᾽ αἰθομένης] ἡ ἀπὸ τῆς κεφαλῆς πρώτη καμπή.
αἰθομένης δὲ τῆς ἐχούσης καυσώδη ἰόν. καυστικὸς γὰρ
αὐτῆς ὁ ἰός. Εὐφορίων·

> τῆς μὲν δὴ τῶν, ὅσσα φύει εὐδείελος αἶα,
> ἢ φύλλῳ <τινὸς> ἢ ποίῃ ὅτε χρίμψατο λύθρον,
> ὡς πυρὶ καρφόμενα ψαφαρῇ ἰνδάλλετο τέφρῃ.

2 Sic versum restituit Martin   φύλλον vel φῦλλον codd.:
φυτὸν Bekker, Lobeck: φύλλ᾽ Maass   ποίη codd., corr.
Martin   ὅτ(ε) (ἐ)χρίμψατο fere codd.: ὁτέῳ ἐγχρίμψατο
Lobeck: ὅτεῳ χριμψαίατο Meineke   3 καρφόμενον Est:
καρφώμενον cett.: corr. Bentley   ἰνδάλ(λ)εται codd., corr.
Bentley

71 *Berliner Klassikertexte*, V. i, ed. W. Schubart and U.
von Wilamowitz–Moellendorff (Berlin, 1907), p. 57, col. i

> αιπ[. . .
> ξανθὸς δ[. . .
> καί οἱ δειμαίνοντ[ι . . .

69 Scholiast on Apollonius of Rhodes, *Argonautica*

He (Tityos) is punished in Hades for having overpowered
Leto as she was on her way to Pytho, as when Homer men-
tions "Tityos son of Earth". Euphorion says that he laid
hands on Artemis, and that that is the reason for his pun-
ishment.

70 Scholiast on Aratus, *Phaenomena*

"The coil of the blazing" (sc. the constellation Hydra)] The
first coil from its head. "Blazing" because it had caustic
poison; for its poison had a fiery quality. Euphorion:

> Of all the things the sunny earth puts forth—
> Or leaf, or grass—whatever touched its gore,
> As if burned up it seemed like powdered ash.[96]

71 *Berliner Klassikertexte*

> Golden   [2]
> And in his fear

---

[96] The Lernaean hydra. Some authors report that Heracles
used its gall to poison his arrows.

ταρφέες ἀφλοισμῷ δι̣ [..

5   οἱ δ' ὄπιθεν λασίῃ ὑπὸ γαστέρι πεπ[τηῶτες]
 οὐραῖοι λιχμῶντο περὶ πλευρῇσι δρά̣[κοντες,]
ἐν καί οἱ βλεφάροις κυάνω ἠστράπτετο̣ν̣ [ὄσσε.
ἢ που θερμάστραις ἤ που Μελιγουνίδι τοῖαι
μαρμαρυγαί, αἵρησιν ὅτε ῥήσσοιτο σίδηρος,
10   ἠέρ' ἀναθρῴσκουσι (βοᾷ δ' εὐήλατος ἄκμων),
ἢ Αἴτνην ψολόεσσαν, ἐναύλιον Ἀστερόποιο.
ἵκετο μὴν Τίρυνθα παλιγκότῳ Εὐρυσθῆι
ζωὸς ὑπὲξ Ἀίδαο δυώδεκα λοῖσθος ἀέθλων·
καί μιν ἐνὶ τριόδοισι πολυκρίθοιο Μιδείης
15   ταρβαλέαι σὺν παισὶν ἐθηήσαντο γυναῖκες.

7 κυάνω van Groningen: κυάνῳ Schubart–Wilamowitz
[ὄσσε suppl. Schubart   11 cit. ap. Σ Nic. *Ther.* 288c, p.
132.5 Crugnola   Αἴτνῃ ψολοέσσῃ Sitzler

72 Eustath. ad Dion. Perieg. 558, *GGM* ii. p. 325ᵃ42
Müller

ᾄδεται δὲ Ἡρακλῆς εἰς αὐτὴν (sc. Ἐρύθειαν) πλεύσας
χαλκῷ λέβητι, ὅτε καὶ τὰς Γηρυονείους ἀπήλασε βοῦς

χαλκείῃ ἀκάτῳ βουπληθέος ἐξ Ἐρυθείης,

ὡς ὁ Εὐφορίων λέγεται ἱστορεῖν.

---

97 Cerberus.   98 Lipara, one of the Aeolian islands, just
north of Sicily (Call. *Hymn* 3.47–48). Euphorion's description is
also indebted to Callimachus' account of Hephaestus' smithy un-
der Etna (*Hymn* 4.144).

Thick (droplets?) with foam
And lurking under his[97] shaggy belly behind him   [5]
The serpents of his tail licked round his ribs,
And in their lids his eyes flashed out blue-black.
Such flashes from the furnaces, perhaps
In Meligounis,[98] when the hammer smites the iron,
Dart through the air (and the much-pounded anvil   [10]
    groans aloud)
Or sooty Etna, resting-place of Asteropus.[99]
To Tiryns, to Eurystheus in his spite,
He came alive from Hades: last of twelve ordeals.
And at the cross-roads of Midea,[100] rich in barley,
The frightened women watched him with their sons.   [15]

72 Eustathius on Dionysius the Periegete

Heracles is celebrated as having sailed to it [Erythea] in a
bronze cauldron, when he drove off the cattle of Geryon

In a light bronze vessel, from ox-rich Erythea

as Euphorion is said to relate.[101]

---

[99] Perhaps one of the Cyclopes. "Steropes" is listed among
their names elsewhere (Hes. *Th*. 140).

[100] City in Argolis; home of Heracles' mother (Theocr. *Id*.
13.20; Hunter ad loc.).

[101] Erythea is in the far west, later identified with Gadeira
(Cádiz). In order to get there, the Sun lent Heracles the vessel (in
Stesichorus, *PMG* 185, a golden goblet) in which he crossed the
ocean by night.

EUPHORION

73 Strab. 14.5.29 (= Apollodorus, *FGrH* 244 F 170)

λέγεσθαι γάρ φησι καὶ τῆς Μυσίας κώμην Ἀσκανίαν
περὶ λίμνην ὁμώνυμον, ἐξ ἧς καὶ τὸν Ἀσκάνιον ποταμὸν
ῥεῖν, οὗ μνημονεύει καὶ Εὐφορίων·

Μυσοῖο παρ᾽ ὕδασιν Ἀσκανίοιο.

cf. Strab. 12.4.8; Alex. Aetol. **9**

74

(a) Σ Theocr. *Id*. 13.7–9*a*, p. 259.9 Wendel

τὸν Ὕλαν Σωκράτης [*FGrH* 310 F 10] υἱὸν Ἡρακλέους
φησίν, Ἀπολλώνιος δὲ ὁ Ῥόδιος [1.1213, al.] Θειο-
δάμαντος, <Νί>καν<δρος [fr. 48 Gow–Scholfield] δὲ>
Κήυκος, Εὐφορίων [Εὐφορίδης K, corr. Callierges] δὲ
Πολυφήμου [Εὐφήμου K, corr. Hemsterhuys] τοῦ Πο-
σειδῶνος ἐρώμενον [ἐρωμένου K, corr. Brubach]· καὶ
ἄλλοι ἄλλων.

cf. Σ Ap. Rhod. 1.1207*b*, p. 109.22 Wendel

Σωκράτης δὲ ἐν τῷ πρὸς Εἰδόθεόν [F 15] φησι τὸν
Ὕλαν ἐρώμενον Πολυφήμου καὶ οὐχ Ἡρακλέους
γενέσθαι.

(b) ibid. 1.40–41, p. 10.13 Wendel

τὸν δὲ Πολύφημον Ἐλάτου παῖδα εἶπεν Ἀπολλώνιος,

73 Apollodorus, ap. Strabo

He (sc. Apollodorus) says that there is also in Mysia a village called Ascania bordering on a lake of the same name, from which flows the river Ascanius, which is mentioned by Euphorion:

> By the waters of the Mysian Ascanius.[102]

74

(a) Scholiast on Theocritus, *Idylls*

Socrates calls Hylas son of Heracles, Apollonius of Rhodes son of Theiodamas, Nicander son of Ceyx, and Euphorion boy-friend of Polyphemus son of Poseidon. Others have different versions.

cf. Scholiast on Apollonius of Rhodes, *Argonautica*

Socrates in his *Against Eidotheus* says that Hylas was the boy-friend of Polyphemus and not of Heracles.

(b) Scholiast on Apollonius of Rhodes, *Argonautica*

Apollonius says that Polyphemus was son of Elatus, Socra-

---

[102] For the river Ascanius, cf. **49**. Scheidweiler connected this fragment with the death of Hylas, and hence supposed that the context was Argonautic.

EUPHORION

Σωκράτης [Ἰσοκράτης codd., corr. Toup; F 18] δὲ καὶ
Εὐφορίων Ποσειδῶνος.

Ὑακίνθῳ attrib. Powell

75 Choeroboscus, in Theodos. *Canon.*, *GG* IV.1, p.
295.16–22 Hilgard

τὸ δὲ Βέβρυξ κατὰ τὰς πτώσεις τὰς μὴ ἐχούσας τὸ ξ
διφορεῖται κατὰ τὸν χρόνον· εὑρέθη γὰρ καὶ ἐκτεταμένον
ἔχον τὸ υ, οἷον "Βεβρύκων βασιλῆος ἀγήνορος" [Ap.
Rhod. 2.2], καὶ συνεσταλμένον, οἷον "οὐδ᾽ ἄρα Βέβρυκες
ἄνδρες ἀκήδησαν βασιλῆος" [Ap. Rhod. 2.98], καὶ παρ᾽
Εὐφορίωνι·

ἀπόπρο δὲ Βέβρυκα πύκτην

καὶ παρὰ Λυκόφρονι "εἰς Βεβρύκων ῥίψειαν ἐκβατηρίαν"
[*Al.* 516].

Ξενίῳ dubitanter attrib. Powell

76 Athen. *Deipn.* 6.263 D–E (Posidonius, fr. 60 Edel-
stein–Kidd = 147 Theiler = *FGrH* 87 F 8)

καὶ τούτῳ τῷ τρόπῳ Μαριανδυνοὶ μὲν Ἡρακλεώταις ὑπ-
ετάγησαν, διὰ τέλους ὑποσχόμενοι θητεύσειν παρέχου-
σιν αὐτοῖς τὰ δέοντα, προσδιαστειλάμενοι μηδενὸς αὐ-
τῶν ἔσεσθαι πρᾶσιν ἔξω τῆς Ἡρακλεωτῶν χώρας, ἀλλ᾽
ἐν αὐτῇ μόνον τῇ ἰδίᾳ χώρᾳ. τάχ᾽ οὖν διὰ τοῦτο καὶ

tes and Euphorion of Poseidon.[103]

75 Choeroboscus, scholia on Theodosius' *Canones*

"Bebryx", in the cases which do not have an *x*, varies according to quantity. For it was found both with a long $\bar{u}$, as in "the lordly king of the Bebrӯces", and also a short, as in "nor did the Bebrycian men neglect their king" and in Euphorion:

> From afar the Bebrycian boxer[104]

and in Lycophron: "May they cast into the landing-place of the Bebrycians."

76 Athenaeus, *Deipnosophistae*

And in this way the Mariandynoi put themselves in subjection to the Heracleotae, promising to serve them continuously provided that the Heracleotae supplied their wants, and further stipulating that none of them should be sold beyond the territory of the Heracleotae, but only in their own territory. Perhaps it is also for that reason that

---

[103] Socrates was a Hellenistic grammarian or antiquary from Argos. The manuscript reading in **74a** makes Euphorion's Hylas boyfriend of Euphemus, the Argonaut connected with Cyrene; but Hemsterhuys' emendation aligns Euphorion with Socrates as reported in the scholiast on Apollonius. If that is right, both authors share the peculiarity of making Poseidon (not Elatus) father of the Argonaut Polyphemus; for a Polyphemus of this parentage, one thinks more readily of the Cyclops.

[104] Doubtless Amycus, king of the Bebryces in Bithynia, who challenged the Argonauts and was killed by Polydeuces (Ap. Rhod. 2.1–97).

Εὐφορίων ὁ ἐποποιὸς τοὺς Μαριανδυνοὺς δωροφόρους κέκληκε·

δωροφόροι καλεοίαθ' ὑποφρίσσοντες ἄνακτας.

cf. Eustath. ad *Il*. 16.865, iii. p. 943.23 van der Valk, sine auctoris nomine

Ξενίῳ dubitanter attrib. Powell

77 EtGen AB = EtSym = EtMag 388.45

εὔαρχος· . . . φασὶ δὲ καὶ ποταμόν τινα παρὰ τὴν Σινώπην Εὔαρχον ὑπὸ τῶν Ἀργοναυτῶν προσαγορεύεσθαι, ἀφ' οὗ πρῶτον ἔπιον· Εὐφορίων·

ἠοῖ <δ'> Εὐάρχοιο φερεκλεὲς ἀμφὶ ῥέεθρον.

cf. Tzetzes ad Lyc. *Al*. 232, p. 107.3 Scheer

ἢ οἶ EtGen A: ἤ οἱ EtMag: οἶον EtGen B, corr. Kaibel φερεκλεος EtGen A: φερεκλέους EtGen B: φέρε κλέος EtMag, corr. Kaibel

78 Σ Pindar, *Ol*. 8.41*a*, i. p. 247.7 Drachmann

τὸν γὰρ Ποσειδῶνα καὶ Ἀπόλλωνα εἰς τὴν τοῦ τείχους κατασκευήν φησι τὸν Αἰακὸν προσλαβεῖν. καὶ τὸν λόγον ἀποδίδωσί, φησιν, ἵνα διὰ τούτου τοῦ μέρους <τοῦ> ὑπὸ Αἰακοῦ οἰκοδομηθέντος ἁλώσιμος γένηται ἡ Ἴλιος. παρ' οὐδενὶ δὲ πρεσβυτέρῳ Πινδάρου ἡ ἱστορία· ὁ δὲ Εὐφορίων φησίν·

Euphorion the hexameter poet called the Mariandynoi "tribute-bearers":

> Tribute-bearers may they be called, trembling in fear of their masters.[105]

77 Etymologicum Genuinum

Euarchus: . . . They say "Euarchus" was the name given by the Argonauts to a river, near Sinope,[106] from which they first drank. Euphorion:

> At dawn, around the celebrated river of Euarchus.

78 Scholiast on Pindar, *Olympian Odes*

For he (Pindar) says that Poseidon and Apollo co-opted Aeacus to help with the building of the wall. And he renders this account, he says, in order that Ilium should be vulnerable in the part Aeacus had built. The story is not found in anyone earlier than Pindar, but Euphorion says:

[105] The Mariandynoi lived in the eastern part of Bithynia, in the hinterland of Heraclea (**41**). Euphorion's epithet describes them in terms appropriate to the vassals of an overlord.

[106] For the Argonauts at Sinope, see Ap. Rhod. 2.946–961.

ἢ γὰρ δὴ Φοῖβός τε Ποσειδάων τ᾽ ἐκάλεσσαν
Αἰακόν, οὐκ ἀβοηθὶ περὶ κρήδεμνα δέμοντες.

1 δηίφοβός codd., corr. Gerhard   2 ἀβοήθητα περὶ
vel πρὸς codd.: ἀβοηθὶ πόλιος Lobeck: ἀβοήθητοι Boeckh:
ἀβοητὶ πατρός Meineke (cf. *Il.* 21.444): ἀβόητα περὶ
Mommsen

79 Servius ad Virg. *Aen.* 2.32

ut Euphorion dicit, Priamus ex Arisba filium vatem
suscepit. qui cum dixisset quadam die nasci puerum, per
quem Troia posset everti, pepererunt simul et Thymoetae
uxor et Hecuba, quae Priami legitima erat. sed Priamus
Thymoetae filium uxoremque iussit occidi.

Quinto libro Χιλιάδων attrib. Meineke

80 Σ, Tzetzes ad Lyc. *Al.* 265, p. 115[a]28, cf. [b]21 Scheer

Στησίχορος [*PMG* 224] δὲ καὶ Εὐφορίων τὸν ῞Εκτορά
φασιν εἶναι υἱὸν τοῦ Ἀπόλλωνος καὶ Ἀλέξανδρος ὁ
Αἰτωλῶν ποιητής [**12**].

cf. Σ AD *Il.* 3.314

Πορφύριος δὲ ἐν τοῖς παραλελειμμένοις [385 F. Smith]
φησὶν, ὅτι τὸν ῞Εκτορα Ἀπόλλωνος υἱὸν παραδίδωσιν
῎Ιβυκος [*PMG* 295], Ἀλέξανδρος, Εὐφορίων, Λυκό-
φρων [*Al.* 265].

Now Phoebus and Poseidon summoned Aeacus
Raising, not without his aid, the battlements all
   around.

79 Servius on Virgil, *Aeneid*

As Euphorion says, Priam had a son by Arisbe with prophetic powers. When he announced on a certain day that a child was being born who had the capacity to overthrow Troy, both Thymoetes' wife and Hecuba, Priam's legitimate spouse, gave birth simultaneously. But Priam ordered the son and wife of Thymoetes to be killed.[107]

80 Scholiast, Tzetzes on Lycophron, *Alexandra*

Stesichorus and Euphorion say that Hector was son of Apollo; so too Alexander the Aetolian poet.[108]

cf. Scholiast on Homer, *Iliad*

Porphyry in his *Omissions* says that Ibycus, Alexander, Euphorion, and Lycophron all made Hector the son of Apollo.

[107] The name of the seer was Aesacus, while the wife of Thymoetes was Cilla and her son Munippus (Lyc. *Al*. 224, 319, with Σ, Tzetzes ad loc.).

[108] Based on a misinterpretation, naïve or wilful, of *Il*. 24.258–259.

EUPHORION

81 EtMag 181.27, a 2215, ii. p. 357.16 L.–L.

Ἀχιλλεύς . . . ἢ διὰ τὸ μὴ θιγεῖν χείλεσι χιλῆς, ὅ ἐστι
τροφῆς· ὅλως γὰρ οὐ μετέσχε γάλακτος, ἀλλὰ μυελοῖς
ἐλάφων ἐτράφη ὑπὸ Χείρωνος. ὅτι ὑπὸ Μυρμιδόνων
ἐκλήθη, καθά φησιν Εὐφορίων·

ἐς Φθίην χιλοῖο κατήϊε πάμπαν ἄπαστος·
τοὔνεκα Μυρμιδόνες μιν Ἀχιλέα φημίξαντο.

cf. Σ h *Il.* 1.1 ap. Erbse, i. p. 6; Eustath. ad *Il.* 1.1, i. p.
24.30 van der Valk; Tzetzes, *Exegesis in Homeri Iliadem*
A.97–609, 121.85, p. 23.3 Lolos

1 χιλοῦ Eustathius   ἄπαστος EtMag: ἄπαυστος Tzetzes:
ἄγευστος Eustathius   2 Ἀχιλλέα Tzetzes

82 Σ AD Hom. *Il.* 2.212

Οἰνεῖ ἀμελήσαντι τῆς Ἀρτέμιδος θυσιῶν ἕνεκα ἡ θεὸς
ὀργισθεῖσα ἔπεμψε τῇ πόλει σῦν ἄγριον. ἐφ᾽ ὃν ἦλθεν
στρατεία τῶν ἀρίστων τῆς Ἑλλάδος, ἐπειδὴ ἐλυμαί-
νετο τῇ χώρᾳ ὥς φησιν αὐτὸς ὁ ποιητὴς ἐν τῇ Ι᾽ [533],
μεθ᾽ ὧν ἦν καὶ ὁ Θερσίτης, ὃς δειλωθεὶς κατέλειψεν
τὴν παραφυλακὴν ἐφ᾽ ἧς ἦν καὶ ἀπῆλθεν ἐπί τινα
τόπον ὑψηλὸν τὴν σωτηρίαν θηρώμενος. ὀνειδιζόμε-
νος δὲ ὑπὸ Μελεάγρου ἐδιώκετο καὶ κατὰ κρημνοῦ
πεσὼν τοιοῦτος ἐγένετο οἷον Ὅμηρος αὐτὸν παρίστη-
σιν. ἱστορεῖ Εὐφορίων.

81 Etymologicum Magnum

Achilles: . . . . or on account of *chīlē*, which means nourishment, never having passed his lips. For he never partook of milk, but was fed on the marrow of deer by Cheiron. His name was given him by the Myrmidons, as stated by Euphorion:

> To Phthia he returned,[109] of *chīlos* never having
> tasted
> And that is why the Myrmidons named him *A-chilles*.

82 Scholiast on Homer, *Iliad*

When Oeneus slighted Artemis by not giving her her due of sacrifice, the goddess grew angry and sent a wild boar against his city. An armed company of the best warriors of Greece set out against this boar, which was ravaging the countryside, as Homer himself records in *Iliad* 9. Among them was Thersites, who, in a fit of cowardice, abandoned the guard-post to which he had been assigned and withdrew to a high place in search of safety. Meleager was annoyed at this and set off in pursuit of him, and in the course of the pursuit Thersites fell from a cliff and became the way that Homer portrays him.[110] The story is in Euphorion.

---

109 After his upbringing by the centaur Cheiron.

110 i.e, deformed. See also Σ bT *Il.* 2.212*b*, where a very similar story is attributed to Pherecydes (*FGrH* 3 F 123).

EUPHORION

83 Σ b *Il.* 2.498c, i. p. 292.96 Erbse

Γραῖαν] ἀπὸ Γραίας τῆς Μεδεῶνος θυγατρός, Λευκίππου δὲ γυναικός· Ταναγραῖοι γὰρ οὐκ ἐστράτευσαν, ὡς Εὐφορίων·

> οἳ πλόον ἠρνήσαντο καὶ ὅρκους Αἰγιαλήων.

cf. Eustath. ad loc., i. p. 406.20 van der Valk

ὅρκον codd.: ὅρκιον vel ὅρμους Eustathius: corr. Meineke

84 Σ A *Il.* 2.496b, i. p. 291.63 Erbse (cf. Herodian, περὶ Ἰλιακῆς προσωδίας, *GG* III.2, p. 34.22 Lentz)

Αὐλίδα] ὡς ἀπὸ ὀξυτόνου εὐθείας ἡ ἀνάγνωσις, καὶ εἰ μέντοι παρὰ τῷ Εὐφορίωνι

> Αὐλίν τέ σφ' ἄγον

αἰτιατικὴ ἀπὸ εὐθείας βαρυνομένης γέγονεν· ἡ γὰρ εἰς ῑν κατάληξις ἀπὸ βαρυτόνων ἐστίν, ἡ δὲ εἰς δα καὶ ἀπὸ βαρυτόνων καὶ ὀξυτόνων.

τεσφάγον cod., corr. Dindorf: τέ σφ' ἄγαγον Meineke

85 Σ Ar. *Lys.* 645a, p. 34 Hangard

οἱ δὲ τὰ περὶ τὴν Ἰφιγένειαν ἐν Βραυρῶνί φασιν, οὐκ ἐν Αὐλίδι. Εὐφορίων·

> Ἀγχίαλον Βραυρῶνα, κενήριον Ἰφιγενείας.

314

83 Scholiast on Homer, *Iliad*

Graia] From Graia, daughter of Medeon, wife of Leucippus. For the Tanagraeans did not take part in the expedition, as Euphorion says:

> Who refused the voyage and the oaths of the men of
> Aigialeia.[111]

84 Scholiast on Homer, *Iliad*

Aulida] The reading derives from a nominative that is oxytone, even if in Euphorion

> They led her (or, them) to Aulis[112]

the accusative comes from a nominative with the accent thrown back. For the suffix *–in* comes from words that are not oxytone, whereas the suffix *–da* comes from both oxytones and non-oxytones.

85 Scholiast on Aristophanes, *Lysistrata*

Some set the Iphigenia story in Brauron, not in Aulis. Euphorion:

> Coastal Brauron, Iphigenia's empty tomb.[113]

---

111 A learned substitute for Homeric "Achaeans", Aigialeia being a former name for Achaea. For the oath sworn by all the suitors of Helen, see Stesichorus, *PMG* 190.

112 Possibly Iphigenia, and in any case probably dealing with the preliminaries of the Greek expedition against Troy.

113 In the myth familiar from Euripides, Iphigenia becomes priestess in Brauron when she leaves Tauris; but Euphorion apparently also located the sacrifice at Aulis there. His "empty tomb" contrasts with Eur. *IT* 1464.

cf. Σ 645*b*, p. 34 Hangard

δοκεῖ Ἀγαμέμνων σφαγιάσαι τὴν Ἰφιγένειαν ἐν
Βραυρῶνι, οὐκ ἐν Αὐλίδι, καὶ ἄρκτον ἀντ᾽ αὐτῆς, οὐκ
ἔλαφον δοθῆναι. ὅθεν μυστήριον ἄγουσιν αὐτῇ.

Μοψοπίᾳ attrib. Scheidweiler

86   EtParv ι 19 = EtGud p. 285.45 Sturz = EtMag 480.17
(cf. Ἐκλογαὶ διαφόρων λέξεων, Bodl. MS Barocci 50 fol.
306ᵛ, ap. Cramer, *Anecd. Oxon.* ii. p. 450.29)

Ἰφιγένεια· Εὐφορίων αὐτὴν ἐτυμολογεῖ, ἀγνοῶν αὐτὴν
Ἀγαμέμνονος, οἴεται δὲ αὐτὴν [ἀγνοῶν . . . αὐτὴν om.
EtParv, EtMag] Ἑλένης καὶ Θησέως ὑποβλῆτιν [-τὴν
EtParv, EtMag] δοθῆναι Κλυταιμνήστρᾳ·

. . . οὔνεκα δή μιν
   ἶφι βιησαμένῳ Ἑλένη ὑπεγείνατο Θησεῖ·

ἐξ Ἑλένης καὶ Θησέως.

1 δή μιν EtMag: δ᾽ ἡμῖν EtParv, EtGud, Ἐκλογαί   2 βιη-
σαμένῳ Ἐκλογαὶ: βιασαμένη vel βιησ- EtParv, EtGud,
EtMag

cf. Paus. 2.22.6–7

πλησίον δὲ τῶν Ἀνάκτων Εἰληθυίας ἐστὶν ἱερὸν ἀνά-
θημα Ἑλένης . . . ἔχειν μὲν γὰρ αὐτὴν λέγουσιν ἐν
γαστρί, τεκοῦσαν δὲ ἐν Ἄργει καὶ τῆς Εἰληθυίας

cf. Scholiast ibid.

It seems that Agamemnon sacrificed Iphigenia in Brauron, not Aulis, and the animal that was rendered up in her place was not a deer, but a bear. Hence the rites which they perform to her.

86 Etymologicum Parvum

Iphigenia: Euphorion offers an etymology of her name, ignoring the fact that she is Agamemnon's daughter, and supposing her to be the child of Helen and Theseus and given suppositiously to Clytaemnestra:

> . . . (so-called) because
> Helen bore her to Theseus, who subdued her by
>   main force.

Of Helen and Theseus.

cf. Pausanias

Near the Lords is a temple of Eilethyia, dedicated by Helen . . . for they say that she was with child, and gave birth in Argos, and that after she had dedicated the tem-

ἱδρυσαμένην τὸ ἱερὸν τὴν μὲν παῖδα ἣν ἔτεκε Κλυ-
ταιμνήστρᾳ δοῦναι—συνοικεῖν γὰρ ἤδη Κλυται-
μνήστραν Ἀγαμέμνονι—, αὐτὴν δὲ ὕστερον τούτων
Μενελάῳ γήμασθαι. καὶ ἐπὶ τῷδε Εὐφορίων Χαλκι-
δεὺς καὶ Πλευρώνιος Ἀλέξανδρος [11] ἔπη ποιήσαν-
τες, πρότερον δὲ ἔτι Στησίχορος ὁ Ἱμεραῖος [PMG
191], κατὰ ταὐτά φασιν Ἀργείοις Θησέως εἶναι θυγα-
τέρα Ἰφιγένειαν.

Μοψοπίᾳ attrib. Scheidweiler. Fragmenta sic coniunxit
Hollis 1992 b, 10:

Ἀγχίαλον Βραυρῶνα, κενήριον Ἰφιγενείας,
⟨   ⟩ οὕνεκα δή μιν
ἶφι βιησαμένῳ Ἑλένη ὑπεγείνατο Θησεῖ·

87 Σ, Tzetzes ad Lyc. Al. 658, p. 219.17 Scheer

Στησίχορός φησιν Ὀδυσσέα ἐπὶ τῆς ἀσπίδος φέρειν
δελφῖνος τύπον [PMG 225] καὶ Εὐφορίων δὲ τούτῳ
συμφθέγγεται.

88 Servius ad Virg. Aen. 3.17

Euphorio et Callimachus [fr. 697 Pf.] hoc dicunt etiam,
quod Aenum dicatur a socio Ulixis illic sepulto eo tempore
quo missus est ad frumenta portanda.

ple to Eilethyia, she gave to Clytaemnestra the child to
which she had give birth—for by this time Clytaemnestra
was married to Agamemnon—while later on she herself
married Menelaus. And on this matter, the hexameter po-
ets Euphorion of Chalcis and Alexander of Pleuron, and
still earlier Stesichorus of Himera, agree with the Argives
that Iphigenia was the daughter of Theseus.[114]

This and the previous fragment were thus combined by
A. S. Hollis:

> Coastal Brauron, Iphigenia's empty tomb
> . . . (Iphigenia, so-called) because
> Helen bore her to Theseus, who subdued her by
>   main force.

87 Scholiast, Tzetzes on Lycophron, *Alexandra*

Stesichorus says that Odysseus had the image of a dolphin
on his shield, and Euphorion agrees with him.[115]

88 Servius on Virgil, *Aeneid*

Euphorion and Callimachus also say that it (sc. the city
in Thrace) was called Ainos after a companion of Ulysses
buried there on the occasion when he was sent to fetch
provisions.[116]

---

[114] Also in agreement is Nicander fr. 58 (from the *Metamor-phoses*).   [115] Plutarch explains that the infant Telemachus
was once saved by dolphins (*Mor.* 985 B).

[116] For Odysseus' mission to fetch provisions from Thrace, see
Servius, on Virg. *Aen.* 2.81. Ainos recurs in **34**.3 and perhaps in
166.

EUPHORION

cf. Steph. Byz., α 135 Billerbeck

Αἶνος ... οἱ δὲ ἀπὸ τοῦ Αἴνου τοῦ Γουνέως ἀδελφοῦ.

Ἱππομέδοντι Μείζονι attrib. Bartoletti (ad PSI 1390, p. 43)

89 Clem. Al. *Strom.* 5.5.31.3–4

Ἀριστόκριτος δ᾿ ἐν τῇ πρώτῃ τῶν πρὸς Ἡρακλεόδωρον
ἀντιδοξουμένων μέμνηταί τινος ἐπιστολῆς οὕτως ἐχού-
σης· "Βασιλεὺς Σκυθῶν Ἀτοίας Βυζαντίων δήμῳ. μὴ
βλάπτετε προσόδους ἐμάς, ἵνα μὴ ἐμαὶ ἵπποι ὑμέτερον
ὕδωρ πίωσι." συμβολικῶς γὰρ ὁ βάρβαρος τὸν μέλλοντα
πόλεμον αὐτοῖς ἐπάγεσθαι παρεδήλωσεν. ὁμοίως καὶ
Εὐφορίων ὁ ποιητὴς τὸν Νέστορα παράγει λέγοντα·

οἳ δ᾿ οὔπω Σιμόεντος Ἀχαιίδας ἄρσαμεν ἵππους.

οἵ γ᾿ Heyse: εἰ δ᾿ Düntzer

90 P. Oxy. 2525

col. i

π]ερὶ Τροίηι πολέμι[ζ
πολλάκι οἱ κλισίηισι Π‚υλοιγενέεσσί τε ν‚ηυσίν
ἐννύχιοι πίλναντο ‚ νόσων ‚ἄ‚περ ἰητῆ‚ρος
]χ᾿ ὅτε μέγα δειμη[ν
]ν ἅλις δεδαηκότ[
]αις βοσκ[....].σας [
]νοωια.[....]το νηόν·

320

cf. Stephanus of Byzantium

Ainos . . . others derive the name from Ainos brother of Gouneus.

89 Clement of Alexander, *Stromateis*

Aristocritus, in the first book of his rebuttals of Heracleodorus, mentions a letter that went as follows: "Atoias, king of the Scythians, to the people of Byzantium. Do not damage my revenues, lest my horses drink your water." Thus in metaphorical terms the barbarian indicated the war that was about to be visited on them. In the same way, Euphorion the poet makes Nestor say:

> (We) who had not yet watered our Achaean horses in
>   the Simois.

90 P. Oxy. 2525

> . . . they(?) fought around Troy,
> Often to his huts and ships of Pylian manufacture
> At night-time they drew near, as to a healer of
>   disease.[117]
> . . . when greatly fear[ing
> . . . having learned sufficiently   [5]
> . . . flocks(?)
> . . . temple

---

[117] Nestor, of Pylos. Agamemnon pays him a night-time visit when the Greeks are at a low ebb in *Il.* 10.18 ff.

]τάφωι δ[.....]πριν
]ννίδα φ[.....]αντο
10   ].ον παρ[   ]
].[.].[   ]
] πολύλλιτε, σεῦ δέ τις, οἴω,
].υχατέουσα
]..[   ] Μιννήϊον Ὄλμου

1 πολέμι[ζον Lobel   2–3 Citata apud Σ T *Il.* 10.18*b*, iii. p.
7.25 Erbse: πρὸ ὀλίγου δὲ χωρισθεὶς ὡς ἂν εἰς ἰατροῦ νοσῶν
θέλει φοιτᾶν πάλιν, ὥς που καὶ Εὐφορίων φησίν· πολλάκι,
κτλ.   2 Πυληγενέεσι Σ T   3 πίτναντο Σ T, corr.
Heyne   4 e.g. δειμή[ναντες Ll.-J.–P.   6 βόσκ[εσκεν,
βοσκ[ῆισιν, βοσκ[οῖσιν, βοσκ[ήματα Ll.-J.–P.
8 ἀ]τάφωι West: κρο]τάφωι Ll.-J.–P.   δ[᾽ ἔπι Κύ]πριν
Lobel   9 Ἀργυ]ννίδα φ[ημίξ]αντο Lobel
13 εὐχατέουσα, σ]εῦ χατέουσα Ll.-J.–P.

col. ii
μ[
τ.ρ[
απ[
μο[
5   αιρα̣[
γαιη[
εγκ[
αρτ[
αξιο[

Φιλοκτήτῃ attrib. E. Livrea, ZPE 139 (2002), 35–39

... the Cy]prian(?)

... they named(?) [Argy]nnis(?)[118]   [9]

... oh, much-besought in prayer, someone, I think,   [12]
     your ...

... lacking(?)

... Minyeian, of Olmos[119]

[118] Lobel surmised a reference to the story of Argynnis (Phanocles, fr. 5 P.), with whom Agamemnon fell in love when he saw him swimming in the Cephisus. When Argynnis drowned, Agamemnon established a temple of Aphrodite in his memory. The geography makes sense, since the mouth of the Cephisus is very near Orchomenos (n. below).

[119] The eponymous founder of Orchomenos was son of Minyas and grandson of Olmos.

EUPHORION

91 Σ Ap. Rhod. 1.156–160a, p. 20.17 Wendel

ὅτι Νηλῆος παῖς Περικλύμενος, δῆλον . . . τοῦτον δὲ ὡς
ἔγγονον αὐτοῦ ὁ Ποσειδῶν (Νηλεὺς γὰρ Ποσειδῶνος) καὶ
τοῖς ἄλλοις ἐκόσμησεν καὶ ἐχαρίσατο αὐτῷ εἰς πάντα
μεταβάλλεσθαι, ὡς καὶ ὁ Εὐφορίων·

ὅς ῥά τε πᾶσιν ἔικτο, θαλάσσιος ἠύτε Πρωτεύς.

92 Eustath. ad *Od.* 1.107, i. p. 28.16 Stallbaum

ὁ δὲ τὰ περὶ Ἑλληνικῆς παιδιᾶς γράψας [i.e. Suetonius;
Suda τ 895], διαφορὰν καὶ αὐτὸς εἰδὼς κύβων καὶ πεσ-
σῶν, καὶ παλαιοτάτην εἰπὼν τὴν κυβευτικὴν παιδιάν,
παράγει Σοφοκλέους μὲν ἐκ Παλαμήδους . . . τὸ, ἐκεῖνος
ἐφεῦρε "πεσσοὺς κύβους τε τερπνὸν ἀργίας ἄκος" [fr. 479
Radt], καὶ Εὐφορίωνος τὸ

πεσσὰ ⟨τε⟩ Ναυπλιάδαο.

⟨τε⟩ Meineke

93 John Lydus, *De Mens.* 4.140

περὶ τοῦ δουρείου ἵππου ὁ Εὐφορίων φησὶν πλοῖον
γενέσθαι τοῖς Ἕλλησιν Ἵππον λεγόμενον· ἕτεροι δέ
φασιν πύλην γενέσθαι οὕτω προσαγορευομένην ἐν τῇ
Τροίᾳ, δι᾽ ἧς εἰσῆλθον οἱ Ἕλληνες.

Εὐφορίων lectio codicum, quam defendit Livrea 1980: Ἔφορος
Hecker: Εὐήμερος Lloyd-Jones 1979, 16 = 1990, 156.

---

120 Ap. Rhod. 1.156–160 tells us that Periclymenus had the
ability to shape-shift during battle.

91 Scholiast on Apollonius of Rhodes, *Argonautica*

The reference is obviously to Neleus' son Periclymenus . . .
Inasmuch as he was descended from him (Neleus being
the son of Poseidon), Poseidon bestowed on him various
endowments, including the boon of being able to turn
himself into any shape, as Euphorion says:

> Who changed himself to every form, like Proteus of
>   the sea.[120]

92 Eustathius on Homer, *Odyssey*

The author of the work on Greek games, who himself
knew the difference between dice and draughts, and calls
the game of dice very ancient, adduces from Sophocles'
Philoctetes a line to the effect that he (Palamedes) discov-
ered "draughts and dice, a pleasurable cure for boredom",
and Euphorion's

> Draughts of Nauplius' son.[121]

93 John Lydus, *On the Months*

Concerning the wooden horse, Euphorion says that the
Greeks had a ship called "Horse". Others say that there
was a gate of this name in Troy, through which the Greeks
entered the city.[122]

---

[121] Nauplius was father of Palamedes, to whom were ascribed
various inventions including board-games.

[122] A controversial fragment. It is true that the wooden horse
attracted the attention of the rationalisers (Palaephatus, *De
incred.* 16), but Euphorion is unlikely to have been among them.
Livrea 1980 suggested rather that he had used a well-attested
metaphor of the horse as a ship.

94 Servius ad Virg. *Aen.* 2.79

Autolycus quidam fur fuit, qui se varias formabat in species. hic habuit liberos Aesimum, unde natus est Sinon, et Anticliam, unde Ulixes: consobrini ergo sunt. nec inmerito Vergilius Sinoni dat et fallaciam et proditionis officium, ne multum discedat a fabula, quia secundum Euphorionem Ulixes haec fecit.

95 Servius ad Virg. *Aen.* 2.201

ut Euphorion dicit, post adventum Graecorum sacerdos Neptuni lapidibus occisus est, quia non sacrificiis eorum vetavit adventum. postea abscedentibus Graecis cum vellent sacrificare Neptuno, Laocoon Thymbraei Apollinis sacerdos sorte ductus est, ut solet fieri cum deest sacerdos certus. hic piaculum commiserat ante simulacrum numinis cum Antiopa sua uxore coeundo, et ob hoc inmissis draconibus cum suis filiis interemptus est.

Χιλιάσιν attrib. Heyne (cf. Meineke 1843, 153)

96 Servius ad Virg. *Aen.* 2.341

hunc autem Coroebum stultum inducit Euphorion, quem et Vergilius sequitur, dans ei "dolus an virtus" [*Aen.* 2.390].

---

123 It is unclear how much of this goes back to Euphorion himself, but clear that we are dealing with a variant on the Laocoon story in *Aeneid* 2.

124 In Virgil, Coroebus is a Trojan ally, engaged to Cassandra.

94 Servius on Virgil, *Aeneid*

Autolycus was a thief who was capable of forming himself
into various shapes. His children were Aesimus, father of
Sinon, and Anticleia, mother of Ulysses: thus these two
were cousins. So it is not undeservedly that Virgil endows
Sinon with deceitfulness, and gives him the role of trai-
tor, which is not a great departure from tradition, since
Euphorion's Ulysses did the same.

95 Servius on Virgil, *Aeneid*

As Euphorion reports, after the arrival of the Greeks, a
priest of Neptune was stoned to death because he had
not prevented their arrival by means of his sacrifices.
When, following the departure of the Greeks, they wanted
to sacrifice to Neptune, Laocoon the priest of Thymbraean
Apollo was chosen by lot, following the usual practice
when there is no regularly-appointed priest. But he com-
mitted an offence that needed expiation by having inter-
course with his wife Antiope in front of the god's image,
and it was on account of this that serpents were let loose
against him and he was killed together with his sons.[123]

96 Servius on Virgil, *Aeneid*

This Coroebus is depicted by Euphorion as a fool, and he is
followed by Virgil who gives him the words "Deceit or val-
our".[124]

He takes no heed of her warnings. On the night of Troy's fall, he
encourages the Trojans to don Greek weapons (whence the line
Servius quotes), but then gives himself away when he sees Cassan-
dra being dragged from the shrine of Athena and is killed by
Peneleos.

327

EUPHORION

97 Paus. 10.26.7–8

Ὅμηρος μέν γε ἐδήλωσεν ἐν Ἰλιάδι Μενελάου καὶ
Ὀδυσσέως ξενίαν παρὰ Ἀντήνορι [3.205–208] καὶ ὡς
Ἑλικάονι ἡ Λαοδίκη συνοικοίη τῷ Ἀντήνορος [3.123]·
Λέσχεως δὲ τετρωμένον τὸν Ἑλικάονα ἐν τῇ νυκτο-
μαχίᾳ γνωρισθῆναί τε ὑπὸ Ὀδυσσέως καὶ ἐξαχθῆναι
ζῶντα ἐκ τῆς μάχης φησίν. ἕποιτο ἂν οὖν τῇ Μενε-
λάου καὶ Ὀδυσσέως κηδεμονίᾳ περὶ οἶκον τὸν Ἀντή-
νορος μηδὲ ἐς τοῦ Ἑλικάονος τὴν γυναῖκα ἔργον
δυσμενὲς ὑπὸ Ἀγαμέμνονος καὶ Μενελάου γενέσθαι·
Εὐφορίων δὲ ἀνὴρ Χαλκιδεὺς σὺν οὐδενὶ εἰκότι τὰ ἐς
τὴν Λαοδίκην ἐποίησεν.

98 Tzetzes ad Lyc. Al. 495, p. 180.21 Scheer

παραγενομένων δὲ αὐτῶν εἰς Θρᾴκην καὶ ἐξελθόντων ἐν
κυνηγεσίῳ ὄφις τὸν Μούνιτον ἔτρωσε καὶ οὕτως ἐτελεύ-
τησεν, ὥς φησιν Εὐφορίων·

> ἤ οἱ Μούνιτον υἷα τέκε πλομένῳ ἐνὶ ὥρῳ.
> ἀλλά ἑ Σιθονίη τε καὶ ἐν κνημοῖσιν Ὀλύνθου
> ἀγρώσσονθ᾽ ἅμα πατρὶ πελώριος ἔκτανεν ὕδρος.

2 κνήμησιν codd., corr. Meineke

97 Pausanias

In the *Iliad* Homer mentioned the hospitality which
Menelaus and Odysseus received from Antenor, and how
Laodice was married to Antenor's son Helicaon. Lesche-
os[125] reports that Helicaon, wounded in the night-time
battle, was recognised by Odysseus and carried alive out of
the fighting. So it would seem to follow from the ties be-
tween Menelaus and Odysseus and the house of Antenor
that the wife of Helicaon is unlikely to have suffered any
hostile act from Agamemnon and Menelaus. What Eu-
phorion, a man of Chalcis, reports of Laodice has no de-
gree of probability.[126]

98 Tzetzes on Lycophron, *Alexandra*

When they [sc. Acamas and Munitus] came to Thrace and
went out hunting, Munitus was bitten by a snake and in this
way met his end, as Euphorion says:

> To him she bore a son, Munitus, as the months wore
>   on.[127]
> But in Sithonia, in the foothills of Olynthus,
> While hunting with his father, a huge water-snake
>   destroyed him.

[125] Usually known as Lesches, to whom was attributed the
Little Iliad.

[126] The implication being that Euphorion reported that
Laodice *did* suffer some such injury. In Lyc. *Al*. 316–318, she is
swallowed by the earth at the fall of Troy.

[127] The subject is Laodice, daughter of Priam, who fell in love
with the Athenian Acamas (see Parthenius, *Sufferings in Love*,
XVI and notes).

99 Σ, Tzetzes Lyc. *Al.* 374, p. 142.32 Scheer

τὸν δὲ Διρφωσσὸν ὁ Εὐφορίων Δίρφυν καλεῖ·

Δίρφυν ἀνὰ τρηχεῖαν ὑπ' Εὐβοίῃ κεκόνιστο.

100 Stobaeus, *Flor.* 4.24d.50, iv. p. 617 Hense

Εὐφορίωνος·

τέκνον, μὴ σύ γε μητρὸς ἀπ' ἀνθερεῶνας
   ἀμήσῃς,
ἠελίους ἥτις σε τριηκοσίους ἐφόρησα,
τέκνον, ὑπὸ ζώνῃ, φοβερὰς δ' ὠδῖνας ἀνέτλην,
εἰς φάος ἐρχομένου· λαρὸν δ' ἐπὶ χείλεσι πρώτῃ
5   μαστὸν ἐπισχομένη λευκῷ ‹σ'› ἔψισα γάλακτι.

cf. Arsenius, *Apophth.* 16.27b = ii. p. 665 Leutsch

1 versus ap. Σ T *Il.* 24.165a, p. 549.12 Erbse; EtGen AB, α 886, ii. p. 63.5 L.–L.; EtSym α 1041; EtMag 109.27, α 1420
2 cf. Cocondrius, περὶ τρόπων, iii. p. 234.24 Spengel ἠελίους τριακοσίους ἐφόρησα   5 ἔψησα Stob., corr. Meineke: ἔλοισα Apostolius

Μοψοπίᾳ attrib. Scheidweiler

101 Σ Soph. *OC* 681, p. 36.4 de Marco

ὅτι δὲ Ἐρινύων ἐστὶ τὸ στεφάνωμα δῆλον ἐν οἷς Εὐφορίων φησί·

99 Scholiast, Tzetzes on Lycophron, *Alexandra*

Euphorion calls Dirphossos "Dirphys":

> He perished hard by jagged Dirphys, at Euboea's
> foot.[128]

100 Stobaeus

Euphorion:

> Child, do not cut your mother's throat—
> I, who bore you through three hundred days,
> My child, beneath my girdle, and endured terrific
> pains,
> When you came to the light; and was the first to hold
> My sweet breast to your lips, and fed you on white   [5]
> milk.[129]

101 Scholiast on Sophocles, *Oedipus at Colonus*

That the crown (sc. of narcissus) belongs to the Erinyes is
clear from the verses in which Euphorion says:

---

[128] Subject unknown, but context perhaps the wreck of the
Greek fleet on the coast of Euboea, whither Nauplius lured them
in revenge for the death of his son, Palamedes. Dirphys is a moun-
tain in the centre of the island towards the east coast.

[129] The lines would obviously suit Clytaemnestra (cf. Aesch.
Choe. 896–898, 908; Eur. *El.* 1215).

πρόπρο δέ μιν δασπλῆτες ὀφειλομένην ⟨ἄγον⟩
   οἶμον
Εὐμενίδες μαργῆτα θυγατριδέαι Φόρκυνος
⟨   ⟩ ναρκίσσου ἐπιστεφέες πλοκαμῖδας.

1 ⟨ἄγον⟩ Meineke   2 ἀργῆτα θυγατριδαι L, corr.
Meineke   γήλοφον εἰς ἀργῆτα O. Müller, cf. Soph. OC
670 τὸν ἀργῆτα Κολωνόν; unde 3 ⟨Εὐμενίδες⟩ suppl. Hermann
3 ναρκίσσοι L: ⟨αὐσταλέας⟩ ναρκίσσου vel ν. ⟨καλύκεσσιν⟩
Meineke, qui postea κλήμασι ναρκίσσοιο περιστεφέες tempta-
vit   πλοκαμῖ L, corr. Triclinius

Μοψοπίᾳ attrib. Scheidweiler

102 Servius ad Virg. *Ecl.* 6.72

Gryneum nemus est in finibus Ioniis Apollini consecratum
. . . in quo aliquando Calchas et Mopsus dicuntur de
peritia divinandi inter se habuisse certamen; et cum de
pomorum arboris cuiusdam contenderent numero, stetit
gloria Mopso; cuius rei dolore Calchas interiit. hoc autem
Euphorionis continent carmina quae Gallus transtulit in
sermonem Latinum.

Quinto libro Χιλιάδων attrib. Meineke

103 Σ, Tzetzes ad Lyc. *Al.* 440, p. 162.9 Scheer

κατὰ τὸν αὐτὸν δὲ καιρὸν ὁ Ἀμφίλοχος ὁ Ἀμφιαράου

Insatiably they drove him forwards on his destined
    path,
The Furies and the maddened man, the
    granddaughters of Phorcys,
Their hair entwined with (garlands of?) narcissus.[130]

102 Servius on Virgil, *Eclogues*

The Grynean grove, in Ionian territory, is dedicated to
Apollo . . . It was in this grove that Calchas and Mopsus are
said once to have held a contest of skill in divination. They
contended over the number of fruits on a certain tree, and
the result was that the glory fell to Mopsus. Calchas died of
grief at this event. The subject is to be found in the poetry
of Euphorion, which Gallus adapted into the Latin lan-
guage.[131]

103 Scholiast, Tzetzes on Lycophron, *Alexandra*

At the same time the seers Amphilochus son of Amphi-

---

[130] Perhaps Orestes (so Meineke); alternatively Oedipus, with
O. Müller's emendation in the second line (though the Furies do
not pursue Oedipus in Sophocles' play). "Phorcys" is perhaps an
alternative for Phorcus, mentioned in ps.-Apoll. 1.2.6 as father of
the Phorcids and Gorgons; but this version of the Furies' lineage is
otherwise unknown.

[131] A famous but infuriating testimonium, which implies but
does not guarantee that Euphorion told the story of the contest.
He, or another teller, transferred it to Grynium from its earlier lo-
cation at Claros (Hes. fr. 278 M.–W.). See also Parthenius **10** and
n. ad loc.

EUPHORION

υἱὸς καὶ Μόψος οἱ μάντεις ἦλθον εἰς Κιλικίαν . . . μετὰ δὲ
ταῦτα ὁ Ἀμφίλοχος βουλόμενος χωρισθῆναι εἰς τὸ Ἄρ-
γος παρέθετο τῷ Μόψῳ τὴν βασιλείαν ἑαυτοῦ κελεύσας
φυλάξαι μεχρὶ ἐνιαυτοῦ ἑνός. πληρουμένου δὲ τοῦ ἐνι-
αυτοῦ ἦλθεν ὁ Ἀμφίλοχος καὶ οὐ παρεχώρει ὁ Μόψος, διὸ
περὶ τούτου πρὸς ἀλλήλους διαφερόμενοι ὑπ' ἀλλήλων
ἀνῃρέθησαν· οὓς θάψαντες οἱ ἐνοικοῦντες πύργον μεταξὺ
τῶν τάφων κατεσκεύασαν, ὅπως μηδὲ μετὰ θάνατον ἀλ-
λήλων κοινωνήσωσιν, ὡς καὶ ὁ Εὐφορίων·

> Πύραμον ἠχήεντα, πόλιν δ' ἐκτίσσατο Μαλλόν,
> ἧς πέρι δῆριν ἔθεντο κακοφράδες ἀλλήλοισι
> Μόψος ⟨τ'⟩ Ἀμφίλοχός τε, καὶ ἄκριτα
>   δηρινθέντες
> μουνὰξ ἀλλίστοιο πύλας ἔβαν Ἀιδωνῆος.

2 θέντες codd., corr. Meineke   3 ⟨τ'⟩ Spohn   ἄρκια
codd., corr. Meineke   4 ἀλήστοιο codd., corr. Meineke
Ἀϊδωνῆος codd., corr. Magnelli: Ἀϊδονῆος Meineke

Quinto libro Χιλιάδων attrib. Meineke

104 Σ, Tzetzes ad Lyc. Al. 420, p. 154.19 Scheer

Τυφρηστὸς καὶ πόλις καὶ ὄρος Τραχῖνος, ἀπὸ Τυφρη-
στοῦ βασιλέως υἱοῦ Σπερχειοῦ. ἢ τεφρηστός τις οὖσα,
ἀπὸ τῆς Ἡρακλέους τέφρας. λέγεται δὲ τὸ ὄρος [Lyc. Al.
902] ἀρσενικῶς, ἡ δὲ πόλις θηλυκῶς ὡς Εὐφορίων·

araus and Mopsus came to Cilicia . . . After this, Amphi-
lochus wanted to return to Argos, so he entrusted his king-
dom to Mopsus and told him to guard it for a year. After the
year was up, Amphilochus came back but Mopsus did not
make way for him, and so the two men fell out over this and
were eventually slain by each other. The inhabitants of
those regions buried them there and built a tower between
their graves lest they should have anything to do with one
another, even after death. So too Euphorion:

> Resonant Pyramus; and he founded the city of
> Mallus,[132]
> Concerning which, with ill will bent against each
> other,
> Mopsus and Amphilochus fought; and after
> unresolved strife,
> Singly they passed the gates of Hades the inexorable.

104 Scholiast, Tzetzes on Lycophron, *Alexandra*

Typhrestus is a city and a mountain of Trachis, named after
king Typhrestus, son of the Spercheius. Or because it is
"ashen", after the ashes of Heracles. The mountain is mas-
culine, the city feminine as in Euphorion:

---

132 The Pyramus is a river of Cilicia; it is presumably the object
of a verb meaning "he reached". Mallus is slightly to the west. We
cannot tell who Euphorion made its founder: in Strab. 14.5.16,
this role falls jointly to Mopsus and Amphilochus.

EUPHORION

βουκολέων Τρηχινίδα Τυμφρηστοῖο
αἰπῆς

β. Τρηχινίδ᾽ ὅπου Τυμφρήστιον αἶπος sive ὅπου Τυμφρηστι-
ὰς ἀκτή Meineke: β. Τρηχίν᾽ ἰδὲ Τυμφρηστοῦ ‹κλέτας› sive
‹πέδον› αἰπῆς Scheidweiler: β. Τρηχῖνα καὶ αἰπῆς Τυμ-
φρηστοῖο Sitzler: αἰπῆς βουκολέων κτλ. conj. van Groningen

105 Servius ad Virg. *Aen.* 6.618

hi (Phlegyae) namque secundum Euphorionem populi in-
sulani fuerunt, satis in deos impii et sacrilegi; unde iratus
Neptunus percussit tridenti eam partem insulae quam
Phlegyae tenebant, et omnes obruit.

106 Σ Ap. Rhod. 2.357–359*c*, p. 157.1 Wendel

τὸν δὲ Πέλοπα Παφλαγόνα τὸ γένος εἶπεν [sc.
Ἀπολλώνιος], ἄλλοι δὲ Λυδὸν αὐτὸν ἱστοροῦσιν· ὁ δὲ
Εὐφορίων ἀμφοτέραις ταῖς δόξαις συντίθεται.

107 Plut. *Mor.* 677 A

Εὐφορίωνα μὲν οὕτω πως περὶ Μελικέρτου λέγοντα·

κλαίοντες δέ τε κοῦρον ἐπ᾽ ἀγχιάλοις πιτύεσσι

---

133 See also Parthenius **40**. Meineke suggested that the herds-
man is Endymion, whose affair with Selene was set in the moun-
tains near Trachis by Nicander, frr. 6–7 G.–S.

134 Other authors know of the sacrilegious ways (HHom. Ap.
278–280) and destruction (Paus. 9.36.3) of this people. Nonn. *D.*
18.36–37 apparently names them in place of the impious Tel-

Pasturing his herds in Trachis, (country) of
    Tymphrestus
The lofty city.[133]

105 Servius on Virgil, *Aeneid*

They (the Phlegyae) according to Euphorion were island
people, impious towards the gods and sacrilegious to a de-
gree; with the result that Neptune grew angry with them
and struck the part of the island in which they lived with a
trident, and sank the lot of them.[134]

106 Scholiast on Apollonius of Rhodes, *Argonautica*

He (Apollonius) made Pelops a Paphlagonian by birth,
while others call him a Lydian. Euphorion adheres to both
opinions.[135]

107 Plutarch, *Table-Talk*

Euphorion for instance wrote about Melicertes along the
following lines:

Lamenting they deposited the youth on pines beside
    the shore,[136]

chines of Ceos (cf. Call. fr. 75.64–69 Pf.); Euphorion may well
have been the intermediary. See **191** B fr. 3.11, and n. 230.

[135] Perhaps in different poems, or perhaps mentioning both
variants in the same poem (cf. the two birthplaces of Zeus in Call.
Hymn 1?). For other variants, see Σ Pind. *Ol*. 1.37*a*, 9.15*a*.

[136] Melicertes, who died when his mother leapt with him into
the sea. The mourners could be Amphimachus and Donacinus,
who according to Tzetzes on Lyc. *Al*. 107 and 229 carried the
body to Corinth. Euphorion may mean that the pyre was made of
brands of pine.

κάτθεσαν, ὁκκόθε δὴ στεφάνωμ᾽ ἄθλοις
   φορέοντο·
οὐ γάρ πω τρηχεῖα λαβὴ καταμήσατο χειρῶν
Μήνης παῖδα χάρωνα παρ᾽ Ἀσωποῦ γενετείρῃ,
5   ἐξότε πυκνὰ σέλινα κατὰ κροτάφων ἐβάλοντο.

1–2 usque ad κάτθεσαν ap. Σ AP 9.357, cod. Par. suppl. Gr. 316
1 αἰλίσι codd., corr. Meineke: αἰγιαλοῦ Schneider: αὐαλέαις
Magnelli   αἰγιαλῖσι πίτυσσι H. Stephanus   2 ὀκ-
κότε codd., corr. Reiske   στεφάνων codd., corr. Bernar-
dakis: στεφάνους Reiske   φορέονται codd., corr. Koechly
ὧν τότε δὴ στεφάνωμ᾽ ἄθλοισι φέροντο Sitzler   3 κατ-
εμήσατο codd., corr. Meineke: κατενήρατο conj. Meineke
4 μίμης vel μήμης codd., corr. Duebner

cf. Σ Bern., Ambr., ad AP 9.357

. . . ἐπεὶ καὶ τὸν παῖδ᾽ ἐπέθηκαν πίτυος θαλλοῖς, ὡς
Εὐφορίων μαρτυρεῖ.

(De scholiis cf. Magnelli 2002, 152.)

Διονύσῳ attrib. Scheidweiler

108 PBerol. 13873, ed. W. Schubart, *Griechische literar-
ische Papyri* (Berlin, 1950), no. 7

col. i
]εριδροσος ἄνθεα τέρσαι
].α̣ν̣α̣λ̣ι̣ς καρφοίατο ποῖαι

Whence they derive a garland in the games.[137]
For not yet had the harsh grip of the hands
Mastered the moon's fierce child beside Asopus'
    mother,[138]
Since when they wore thick celery on their   [5]
    temples.[139]

cf. Scholia on Palatine Anthology 9.357

. . . since they laid the child on branches of pine, as Euphorion attests.

108 PBerol. 13873[140]

col. i

d]ewy . . . . to wither flowers
grass be parched

---

[137] The Isthmia.

[138] Heracles' hands. He killed the Nemean lion, son of the moon, by strangling it (so ps.-Apoll. 2.5.1). The mother of the Asopus is Kelossa, a mountain just west of Nemea whence the river takes its source.

[139] For the celery crown for victors at the Nemean games, see Call. fr. 54 Pf. / *SH* 266 (from the *Victoria Berenices*). Euphorion's claim, that celery displaced pine at the Isthmus under the influence of the Nemean games, agrees with Call. fr. 59.5–9 Pf.

[140] Ascribed to Euphorion on the grounds of the likely overlap of l. 48 with a line quoted as Euphorion's, and continuity of subject-matter in the next line. The alternative ascription, to Philitas, on the hypothesis that l. 9 alludes to Aeolus (**9**), and since line 46 and **10**.2 share the same *incipit*, is to be rejected. The subject of the poem is wholly unclear, but the rapid succession of mythographical details is wholly in Euphorion's manner.

]..ν οὐ θέμις ἀνδρὶ δạῆνạι
]τιμνηστη Περίβοια
].αο δ' ῦ̣δατα Γάλλου
].πευθέας Ὠρομέδον[το]ς
]ε̣ζ̣ην ταυρώπιδος Ἥρη[ς
]αραστρ̣ο̣φ̣..ωσι θαα̣.[.]..ν
]α̣ν̣αιολ̣ο̣ν ἐψεύσαντο
].ος μάλα παῦρα δαείη [
]ωνι̣δ̣.[.]η̣λητῆρ.ς
πα]λίγκοτ[ο]ν ἴσχετε φλοῖσ[βον]
]ε̣ελ̣μ̣..[.]ν ὀρκι..[.....].
]εφορη̣σα[.]ο κρωσ̣σ̣[
] ἀμαλδύνοντο θα..[
]$\overset{γ}{τ}$εω.εν̣α̣ φαρμαξα̣[
].η̣ τότε γίνεο γαῖα [
]υφολ̣μ̣..ε̣κτην̣α..[
πολ]υπώεος ἄγχι Πελίνν̣η[ς

3 τ]ῶ̣ν? 5 ἐσή]λ̣αο Carden 6 α̣πευθέας Carden ἐπ' εὐθέας Ὠρομέδον[το]ς | [νώτους Schubart 7].τ̣ην Ll.-J.–P. 8 π]αράστροφοι ὦσι Ll.-J.–P. θάα̣σ̣σ̣ο̣ν̣ Schubart: θαά̣σ̣σ̣ε̣ι̣ν̣ Livrea 9 π]αναίολον Schubart 10 κα]ὶ̣ ὃς Schubart 11 [κ]ηλητῆρες, [φ]ηλητῆρες Schubart: [δ]ηλητῆρες Carden 13 ἐ̣ελ̣μ̣έν̣[ο]ν Carden 14 ἐφορήσα[τ]ο κρωσ̣σ̣[όν Schubart: ἐφόρησ' ἀ[π]ὸ κρωσ̣σ̣[οῦ Carden 15 θαλ̣α̣[σσ vel θαμ̣ε̣[ι Carden: θαμε[ιαί Scheibner 16 φαρμάξα̣[ντο, -ά̣[σθαι Carden 18 ὅλμος "mortarium", cf. 22? ὑφόλ̣μ̣ι̣α̣ "fort. spatio longius" Ll.-J.–P. τ̣ε̣κτήν̣αι̣ο̣ Carden 19 πολ]υπώεος Schubart

it is not right for a man to know
wedded Periboea[141]
waters of the Gallus[142]   [5]
(not?) knowing Oromedon[143]
of ox-eyed Hera   [7]
deceived the shifty one(?)   [9]
even one who knows very little   [10]
restrain your jealous din   [12]
bore a pitcher(?)   [14]
were eradicated   [15]
drug[ged   [16]
be then earth   [17]
near to Pelinna, rich in flocks[144]   [19]

---

[141] From the reference to the Gallus in the next line, Livrea proposed that Periboea is the mother of Aura, heroine of Nonnus' last book (*D.* 48.246).

[142] River of Phrygia, which had the property of maddening those who drank from it (Call. fr. 411 Pf.).

[143] Alternatively Eurymedon, this name was given to a mountain (Theocr. *Id.* 7.46), apparently in Cos, and a giant (*Od.* 7.58) who tried to rape Hera (**58**); the Theocritus scholia ad loc. also give it as a name of Pan. Livrea suggests that these are virgin Nymphs.

[144] Town of northern Thessaly.

20   ].ὰρ πέζῃσιν Ἀχαιῶν
         ]ρησιος οιος ἀεῖραι
         ]ν ἐπικλείουσι θυείην
         ].σθε δὲ βασκαντῆρες
         ]ρυόεσσαν ἀμείψας
25   ]δρωμῶσι χίμαιραι
       μ]ηκάδες οὐ πατέουσιν
         ]γείτονας ὄρθριος ἔλθοις

20 γὰρ vel ἀ]τὰρ Schubart   21 Τιτα]ρήσιος Schubart
οἶος, οἷος?   23 χάσσ]ασθε Carden
24 δακ]ρυόεσσαν Schubart: ὀφ]ρυόεσσαν Maas
27 ἁλι]- vel κακο]γείτονας Maas

col. ii

       πυρ.[
       ουδ.[
30   μαψ[
       δικτ[
       καικ[
       τωιρ.[
       αεισα[
35   αψορρ.[
       ]επ.[
       κεκ[
       ενθα[
       δι..[
40   ωσ[
       [
       [

the shores of the Achaeans [20]
Tita]resian(?)[145] . . . to lift
they call a mortar
back(?)], ye enviers
having exchanged the jagged(?) . . .
goats (do not?) run [25]
the bleating ones do not tread[146]
you (might) come to the neighbours in early
      morning

col. ii

---

[145] If so, a reference to Mopsus (ps.-Hes. *Scut*. 181, Ap. Rhod.
1.65).
[146] i.e., in a high place.

[

[

45   [

ἤνυσα.[

Αἰγαιησ[

τῆς οὐδ̓ [αἴθυιαι οὐδὲ κρυεροὶ καύηκες

δύπται.[

50   αλλουχ[

.ρχεομ.[

ενθαντ[

ευτεπο.[

φαικοπ[

30 μάψ, μαψ[ιδ-   48 ap. EtGen ABJ = EtGud = EtSym = EtMag 493.48 = ps.-Zonaras, col. 1148.24 Tittmann; Tzetzes ad Lyc. *Al.* 741, p. 238.28 Scheer: καύηξ· ὁ λάρος, διὰ τὸ ἀδηφά- γον· καύη γὰρ ἡ τροφή· Εὐφορίων· τῆς [τῆς δ̓ EtGen B] . . . καύηκες. ἢ ἀπὸ τοῦ καῦ καῦ λέγειν.

109–110 P. Oxy. 2085, frr. 1, 3

109 (fr. 1)

col. i

— — — —

       ]μησαν

       ].βαλα κα

       ].κιδιο Κόμ-

βη c.5–10 Χα]λκίδα· φησὶν

5   ].ρβαντας

Than which neither [shearwaters nor chilly terns   [48]
Divers

109–110 P. Oxy. 2085, frr. 1, 3

109 (fr. 1)

col. i[147]

cym]bals(?)[148]   [2]

in Cha]lcis(?)   Com[be

Cha]lchis: he says

[that she was the mother of the C]orybants[149]   [5]

[147] Apparently from a commentary on Euphorion (not the *Chiliades*, to which a cross-reference is made in ii. 28). The reference to Combe in col. i. 3 recalls **191** B fr. 2.4; the Dionysian subject-matter in col. ii. 16–21 recalls Euphorion's *Dionysus*, while the reference to Ino in ii. 15–16 may also recall **191** B fr. 2 (see n. 222).

[148] Possibly the cymbals of the Corybants (see next note), or a learned etymology of her name.

[149] As stated in Σ *Il.* 14.291*a*; cf. Nonn. *D.* 13.148.

]ταυτην

].

— — — —

2 κύ]μβαλα Hunt: κό]μβαλα Ll.-J.–P.   3–4 Χα]λκιδι ὁ
Hunt (ὁ Ll.-J.–P.):]ακι διὸ Ll.-J.–P.   4–5 φησὶν | [δὲ αὐτὴν
γεννῆσαι τοὺς Κ]ύρβαντας Ll.-J.–P. (Κ]ύρβαντας iam Hunt)

col. ii

— — — —

8   ..].[..].[
     λυπτεοντα[
10   πρεσβυτιδ.[
      δωδεκιδ[..].[.].[
      τα ὡς μηδ.μι.ω..[
      ..]ωι.υβαστα ε...[
      θ]αλάσσης εφηστ.[
15   νον Ινειον τουν[
      ἀπ᾽ Ἰνοῦς   αὖθι.[

     —

     σι γυναιμανεα[
     νοωνεα κηλα[
     τὸν λόγον προ.[
20   ὁ δὲ βουλετα[

9 κα]|λυπτέον Ll.-J.–P.   10 πρεσβυτιδε[ς etc. Ll.-J.–P.
11 δωδεκίδ[ες, δώδεκ᾽ ἰδ[Hunt   12 μηδεμια ωη[Ll.-J.–P.
14–16 ἐφ᾽ ἧς τὸ [καλούμε]|ινον Ἴνειον, τοὔν[ομα ἐσχηκὸς]| ἀπ᾽
Ἰνοῦς Ll.-J.–P.   16–18 lemma hunc in modum: αὖθι ⌣̆
[–⌣–]σι γυναιμανέα[⌣⌣–⌣] |–⌣]νοων ἐὰ κῆλα Ll.-J.–P.
18 ἐκφα]νόων, ἐκκε]νόων Ll.-J.–P.   18–20 ἐπανάγει]| τὸν
λόγον πρὸς [τὸν Διόνυσον·] | ὁ δὲ βούλετα[ι Ll.-J.–P.

346

her

col. ii

of the sea, on which is [the so-called   [14]
Ineion, [which derives its name   [15]
from Ino(?).“Again . . .
woman-maddening . . .
his (their?) weapons . . . ” . . . [refers
the story to [Dionysus
and he wishe[s   [20]

```
     ...]ς μαινάδας επ[
     .]...αις καὶ ταυτα[
     ...].αρα παννυχιο.[
     ....]το γάλακτι     ν.[
25   ητε καὶ Ἴναχος     του.[
     Ἴν]αχος γνώριμος     [
     ___

     ...] Ὀρνέας ὅτι ποταμ[ός ἐστι τῆς
     Ἀρ]γείας ἐν ταῖς Χειλιά[σιν
     .]εν καὶ ὁ Χάρ[.]αδρος δε.[
     ___

30   ας ἐν τῶι περὶ ποταμῶ[ν Καλ-
     λίμαχος εἰρη( ) [fr. 457 Pf.]   Νῆριν δ[ὲ ποτα-
     ___

     μὸν μὲν οὐκ οἶδα λέγε[ιν
     δὲ ἐν ὧι οἱ Ἡρακλεῖδαι [ἐστρα-
     τοπέδευσαν κατὰ τὴν ε[ἰς Ἄρ-
35   γος στρατείαν. μήποτε δ[ὲ τῶι
     Α[ἰ]τωλῶι πεπίστευκεν [
```

23–25 alterum lemma hunc in modum: τοὶ] δ᾽ ἄρα παννύχιοι [λευκῶι λείβον]το γάλακτι | Νῆ[ρίς τ᾽ Ὀρνεί]η τε καὶ Ἴναχος ‹ἠδὲ Χάραδρος› Ll.-J.–P.   23 τοὶ] δ᾽ ἄρα παννύχιοι Hunt 24 Νῆ[ρις Hunt   25–26 τούτ[ων μὲν οὖν ὁ | Ἴν]αχος γνώριμος Ll.-J.–P.   27 ὁ δὲ] Ὀρνέας, περὶ δὲ | τῆς] Ὀρνέας Ll.-J.–P.   28–29 εἴρη|κ]εν Hunt: ἔφα[μ]εν Ll.-J.–P. 29–30 δὲ τ[ῆς Ἀργεί]ας Körte   31 εἴρη(κεν) Hunt (voluit scholiasta Καλλιμάχου /-ῶι εἴρηται?)   32 [ὅρος Di Benedetto: [χωρίον Ll.-J.–P.   33 κι^ω̈, id est ⟦κι⟧ωι pap.: Κίωι Hunt

maenads
and these
"And they all night long [made libations
of white] milk, Ne[ris . . .
and Inachus"   Of the[se was   [25]
   Inachus an acquaintance.
   . . . Orneas, that it is a river in
the Ar]golid [was stated by him, *or* by us]
in the *Chiliades*.[150] And the Charadrus [in the
   Argolid
is mentioned in Callimachus'   [30]
On Rivers.   As for the Neris, I know of
no river of this name, but [a mountain (*or* place)
in which the Heraclidae [en-
camped on their expedition a[gainst
Argos.[151] Perhaps he   [35]
relied on the Aetolian[152]

---

[150] For the river Orneas in the Argolid, see Strab. 8.6.24.
Lloyd-Jones and Parsons' reading need not imply that Euphorion
is speaking in his own person: the commentator could be referring
to a separate commentary which he wrote on the *Chiliades* (cf. Σ
Ar. *Pax* 1014a, referring to Σ Ar. *Ach*. 894).

[151] For Neris as the name of a mountain in the Argolid, see
Call. fr. 684 Pf.

[152] Alexander of Aetolia **16**.

110 (fr. 3)

— — — —

...].μ..[.].[
Λέλεγες. οὗτοι δ᾽ ἦσαν σύλλ[εκ-
τοί τινες καὶ μιγάδες ἐκ πολ[-
λῶν ἐθνῶν, ἐκαλεῖτο δ᾽ ἡ νῆ[-
5   σος Παρθενὶς ἀπὸ τῆς ἀρχῆς [
ἔχου[σα] τὴν προσηγορίαν τοῦ [
βασιλεύοντος τῶν Λελέγων [
τόν τε νῦν καλούμενον π[οτα-
μὸν Ἴμβρασον Παρθένιον [
10   ὠνόμασαν. Δόρυσσα δὲ κα[ὶ

—

Φυλλὶς παρώνυμον ὑπὸ τῶ[ν
ἔξωθεν ἀνθρώπων ε..[
δὲ διὰ τί Δόρυσσά τε κα[ὶ Φυλλὶς
ἐκλήθη ἐ.[...]......[
15   καρπῶν ἤγου[ν
ἤγο(υν) Ἀνθεμι[
ἡμεῖς ὑπ..[
λοντε..[
τον παρ.[
20   Ἑρμῆς η[

—

τῆμος ὅτ..[
ρον ἔδος .λ.[
φησιν πε..[

350

110 (fr. 3)

Leleges. These were a miscellaneous group [2]
gathered together from many
tribes. The island[153] was called
Parthenis from the beginning, [5]
deriving its name from the
ruler over the Leleges;
and as for the river now known
as the Imbrasus, they also named it
"Parthenius".[154] Doryssa an[d [10]
Phyllis are by-names employed
by outsiders.[155] I[f you were to enquire
why Doryssa an[d Phyllis
were names given to it [
of fruits, that is to sa[y [15]
that is to say Anthemi[s[156]
we . . . chang-]
ing [the name(?)
Parth[
to Hermes [20]
"at that time
seat"
says . . . . [to in-

153 The commentator is discussing the name-changes, or *me-tonomasiae*, of Samos; see also Aristotle fr. 570 Rose, Call. *Hymn* 4.49, Σ Ap. Rhod. 1.185–188*b* and 2.865–872*e*, Strab. 10.2.17 and 14.1.15, Steph. Byz. p. 553.14 Mein.

154 For this river and its name-change see Call. fr. 599 Pf.

155 For Doryssa (or Dryous(s)a), see also Hesych. δ 2238, 2431. For Phyllis, Hesych. φ 1001 and Σ Nic. *Al.* 149*c*.

156 Another of the names of Samos.

EUPHORION

μηναι βουλ. .[
25   ταύτην ο. .[
Εὐρωπε[
σιανοι τω[
]οι προσ[

12–14 ἐπε[δόθη· εἰ]|δὲ διὰ τί . . . | ἐκλήθη ἐρω[ταῖς Ll.-J.–P.
13 τε κα̣[ὶ Φυλλὶς Hunt, fort. spatio longius   15 ἤγου[ν
φύλλων Ll.-J.–P.   16 Ἀνθεμί[ς vel Ἀμθέμο[νσα Hunt:
ἀνθεμί[δων Ll.-J.–P.   17–18 τὸ ὄνομα μεταβα]λλόντες Ll.-
J.–P.   19 Παρθ[Ll.-J.–P.   21–22 fort. lemma, hunc in
modum: τῆμος ὅτ᾽ —‿‿—‿‿—‿‿ ρὸν ἕδος ἐλθ[ών vel ρον ἕδὸς
23–24 ση]|μῆναι Ll.-J.–P.   26 Εὐρώπε[ια Hunt
26–27 Ἀ]|σιανοί Hunt   27 Inter –νοι et τω vestigia
28 supra]οι vestigia

111 P. Oxy. 2528

].ο̣μ[   ]αρομ[
].α̣σημε[. . .] αἰγια-
λο]ῖο, Φθίης Ἑλλοπίη[ς
τ]ε καὶ αὐτῆς Κέκρο-
5   πο]ς αἴης. Ἑλλοπίης·
τῆ]ς Εὐβοίας, ἤτοι ἀ-
πὸ Ἕλλο]πο{υ}ς ἢ ὅτι ἐλέ-
γετ]ό τις Ἑλλοπία ἐν
τῆι] Εὐβοίαι ἀπὸ Ἕλλο-
10   πο]ς τοὔνομα λαβοῦσα,
πε]ρὶ ἧς ἐν ταῖς Χιλι-

352

dicate
her   [25]
Europe[ia[157] . . . . A-
sians

111 P. Oxy. 2528

"of the   [2]
shore,[158] | of Phthia, Ellopia,
and the very land of
Cecrops."[159] Ellopia: [5]
Euboea, either from
Ellops, or because there was
said to be a place called Ellopia
in Euboea, taking its
name from Ellops,[160]   [10]
concerning which we shall

[157] Possibly aunt of Ancaeus, king of the Leleges (Asius, fr. 7 West).

[158] Probably not the proper name Aigialos (*Il*. 2.575, and cf. "men of Aigialeia" in **83**), because not co-ordinated with the following names by a conjunction.

[159] Lobel remarked that Euboea, Phthia, and Attica again appear in proximity in Apollonius Rhodius' catalogue of Argonauts (1.77–104), but, against a similar context in Euphorion, van Groningen urged that the reference to the Argonauts beginning in 1. 13 sounds like a new topic. He suggested that the emphasis on Attica, land of Cecrops, might point to the *Mopsopia*.

[160] Ellops was son of either Ion (Strab. 10.1.3, Steph. Byz. p. 268.18 Mein.) or Tithonus (Eustath. on *Il*. 2.538, i. 431.13 van der Valk). Ellopia is associated with all (Philochorus, *FGrH* 328 F 225) or the northern part (Hdt. 8.23.2, Eustathius) of the island, and in Call. *Hymn* 4.20 the Euboeans are Ellopians.

ἀσι]ν διαλεξόμεθα.
] εἰς Ἀργὼ ἑτάρους
]νατ' Ἰήσων. περὶ
15 τοῦ] στόλου τῶν Ἀργο-
ναυτ]ῶν, [ὅ]τι οὐ τοὺς
αὐτοὺς ἀ]ναγράφουσ[ι]ν
]ευετον ̣ ̣

13–14 lemma videtur esse; si ita, in mg. sin. excucursisse veri-
simile est, e.g. καὶ γὰρ ὅτ']   14 ἐκρί]νατ' West: ἠνή]νατ'
Lobel   17 αὐτοὺς West

112 Σ AD *Il.* 13.21

Αἰγαὶ πόλις Ἀχαΐας ἐν Πελοποννήσῳ, ἔνθα τιμᾶται
μὲν ὁ Ποσειδῶν, ἄγεται δὲ καὶ Διονύσου ἑορτή. ἐν ᾗ
ἐπειδὰν ὁ χορὸς συστὰς τὰς τοῦ δαίμονος τελετὰς
ὀργιάζῃ, θαυμάσιον ἐπιτελεῖσθαι φασὶν ἔργον. ἄμ-
πελοι γὰρ ἃς καλοῦσιν ἐφημέρους, ἀνισχούσης μὲν
ἡμέρας καρπὸν βλαστάνουσιν, ὥστε δρέποντας αὐ-
τοὺς εἰς ἑσπέραν οἶνον ἄφθονον ἔχειν. ἡ ἱστορία παρὰ
Εὐφορίωνι.

113 Clem. Al. *Protr.* 2.39.9

πρόβατον, ὥς φησιν Εὐφορίων, σέβουσι Σάμιοι.

cf. Aelian, *NA* 12.40

τιμῶσι δὲ ἄρα Δελφοὶ μὲν λύκον, Σάμιοι δὲ πρόβατον

discourse in the *Chiliades*.[161]
"For once when] Jason
chose] his companions for the Argo".[162] This concerns
the] expedition of the Argo-   [15]
naut]s, because the [same names
are not always included

112 Scholiast on Homer, *Iliad*

Aegae, a city of Achaea in the Peloponnese. Poseidon is
honoured there, but a festival is also held for Dionysus in
which, when the chorus comes together to celebrate the
rites of the deity, a remarkable thing is said to come about.
For when day breaks, vines which they call "day's length"
put forth fruit, so that, come the evening, they gather the
fruit and have copious supplies of wine. The information is
in Euphorion.[163]

113 Clement of Alexandria, *Protrepticus*

The Samians, according to Euphorion, revere sheep.

cf. Aelian, *On the Nature of Animals*

The people of Delphi honour the wolf, the Samians the

---

[161] It is tempting to interpret this as a reference by Euphorion
himself to a projected work, but it could be a scholarly reference
to a planned commentary on another poem. Since Euphorion is
not named as author of the *Chiliades*, one infers that the present
commentary is on a Euphorion poem too.

[162] For Jason in Euphorion, see **152**.

[163] This legend is mentioned by other authors, but associated
with Aegae in Euboea (Sophocles, fr. 255 Radt; Σ T *Il.* 13.21*b*1) or
elsewhere.

. . . Σαμίοις δὲ . . . χρυσίον κλαπὲν πρόβατον ἀνεῦρε,
καὶ ἐντεῦθεν Μανδρόβουλος ὁ Σάμιος τῇ Ἥρᾳ πρό-
βατον ἀνάθημα ἀνῆψε.

114 Σ Nic. *Ther.* 406c, p. 172.2 Crugnola

κόραξ τ᾽ ὀμβρήρεα] ὅτι χειμῶνα δηλοῦσιν οἱ κόρακες . . .
καὶ Εὐφορίων ὁμοίως·

    ὑετόμαντις ὅτε κρώξειε κορώνη.

Ἡσιόδῳ dubitanter attrib. Nietzsche 1873, 236

115 Σ Nic. *Ther.* 35a, p. 48.16 Crugnola

θιβρὴν δὲ τὴν θερμὴν καὶ ὀξεῖαν διὰ τὰς ἐξ αὐτῆς
γινομένας φλεγμονάς· Καλλίμαχος [fr. 654 Pf.] "θιβρῆς
Κύπριδος ἁρμονίης." Εὐφορίων δὲ·

    θιβρήν τε Σεμίραμιν.

Ἀλεξάνδρῳ attrib. Scheidweiler

116 Pindar, *Hypothesis b Pythiorum*, ii. p. 3.5 Drach-
mann

Εὐρύλοχος ὁ Θεσσαλὸς καταπολεμήσας Κιρραίους ἀν-
εκτήσατο τὸν ἀγῶνα τοῦ θεοῦ . . . τὸν δὲ Εὐρύλοχον νέον
ἐκάλουν Ἀχιλλέα, ὡς Εὐφορίων ἱστορεῖ·

    ὁπλοτέρου τ᾽ Ἀχιλῆος ἀκούομεν Εὐρυλόχοιο,

sheep . . . A sheep once disclosed stolen money to the Samians, and it was for that reason that Mandroboulos of Samos dedicated a sheep to Hera.

114 Scholiast on Nicander, *Theriaca*

"And a rainy crow"] That crows indicate a storm . . . and Euphorion likewise:

> When the crow, the rain-prophet, should croak.[164]

115 Scholiast on Nicander, *Theriaca*

Thibrē means hot and sharp, on account of the fiery heat that emanates from it. Callimachus says "the coupling of the sultry Cyprian", and Euphorion:

> and sultry Semiramis.[165]

116 *Hypothesis b* to Pindar's *Pythian Odes*

Eurylochus the Thessalian overcame the men of Cirrha and thus acquired the sacred games[166] . . . They called Eurylochus a new Achilles, as Euphorion records:

> A new Achilles was Eurylochus, we hear,

[164] For the crow as a weather-sign, see Aratus, *Phaen*. 949–953 and Kidd ad loc.

[165] For Semiramis, see **26** col. i. 9. In fact Hesych. *θ* 579 indicates that the adjective has many other meanings, but Euphorion appears to have followed or stayed close to Nicander, *Ther*. 35.

[166] In the First Sacred War (early 6th c. BC).

EUPHORION

Δελφίδες ᾧ ὕπο καλὸν Ἰήϊον ἀντιβόησαν
⟨Κρῖσαν⟩ πορθήσαντι, Λυκωρέος οἰκία Φοίβου.

2 ᾧ ἔπι Meineke   ἀντηγώνισαν vel sim. codd, corr. Drach-
mann: ἀντεβόησαν iam Boeckh   3 ⟨Κρῖσαν⟩ Boeckh

cf. *Hypothesis d Pythiorum*, ii. p. 5.6–8 Drachmann

καὶ ὅτι Εὐρύλοχος ὁ Θεσσαλὸς τοὺς Κιρραίους ἐπόρ-
θησε, μαρτυρεῖ καὶ Εὐφορίων·

ὁπλοτέρου τ' Ἀχιλῆος ἀκούομεν Εὐρυλόχοιο.

Ἀλεξάνδρῳ attrib. Scheidweiler

117 Herodian, περὶ μον. λεξ., *GG* III.2, p. 915.16 Lentz

Τὰ (sc. εἰς ω̄ν) περισπώμενα, εἰ λέγοιτο ἐν πλείοσι συλ-
λαβαῖς, διὰ τοῦ ō λέγεται . . . Εὐφορίων·

κακώτερε Καλλικόωντος.

Ἀραῖς attrib. Scheidweiler

358

To whom the Delphian maids gave back the fair cry
of Iëion
When he sacked Crisa, home of Lycorean[167]
Phoebus.

cf. *Hypothesis d* to Pindar's *Pythian Odes*

That Eurylochus the Thessalian ravaged the people of Cirrha is also attested by Euphorion:

A new Achilles was Eurylochus, we hear.

117 Herodian, *On unique word-formation*

Words that end (in *-ōn*) with a circumflex accent, if pronounced over more than one syllable, have an *o* . . . Euphorion:

(Thou) more base than Callicoon.[168]

---

[167] The epithet, which is also used in Call. *Hymn* 2.19, derives from Lycoreia, a city high on Parnassus. As the fragment stands, this phrase is in apposition to Crisa, despite the arrogant behaviour that led Eurylochus to punish it (Strab. 9.3.4). The fuller context of the fragment might have made things clearer, or there may be a corruption.

[168] Callicoon (or Cillicon) betrayed his city (Ar. *Pax* 363 and scholia ad loc.; Call. fr. 607 Pf.). This could derive from a curse poem; in **26** and perhaps also **25** (*Thrax*), optative imprecations are directed against a second-person offender.

118 Johannes Diaconus, comm. ad Hermogen. περὶ μεθ-
όδου δεινότητος, f. 462 (Rabe, *RhM* 63 (1908), 141)

πολλῶν γὰρ Εὐρυβάτων καὶ πανούργων γενομένων ἄλ-
λοις ἄλλα ἐπράττετο, ὡς μέμνηται καὶ Εὐφορίων·

ἠδ' ὅσσα προτέροισιν ἀείδεται Εὐρυβάτοισιν.

cf. Pausanias, Ἀττικῶν ὀνομάτων συναγωγή, ε 83.19;
Eustath. ad *Od*. 19.247, ii. 202.14 Stallbaum

ὅσα Johannes Diaconus: ὅσσα Pausanias, Eustathius

Ἀραῖς attrib. Scheidweiler

119 Tertullian, *de Anima* 46.6, p. 63.25 Waszink

Seleuco regnum Asiae Laodice mater nondum eum enixa
praevidit; Euphorion promulgavit.

120 Σ bT Hom. *Il*. 19.263*a*, iv. p. 624.1 Erbse

ἀπροτίμαστος] ἀνέπαφος· μάσσασθαι γὰρ τὸ ἐφάψα-
σθαι. καὶ Εὐφορίων·

Μοῦσαι ποιήσαντο καὶ ἀπροτίμαστος Ὅμηρος,

οὗ δυσχερὲς ἐφικέσθαι τῆς δυνάμεως.

cf. Σ ibid. 263*b*, p. 624.8 Erbse; Eustath. ad loc., iv. p.
326.8 van der Valk

118 John the Deacon, commentary on Hermogenes' *On the Means of Attaining Forcefulness*

For there were many people called Eurybatus, all of them villains in one way or another, as Euphorion also mentions:

> And all that is sung of the Eurybati of former days.[169]

119 Tertullian, *On the Soul*

Seleucus' mother Laodice foresaw that he would rule over Asia even before she had given birth to him; Euphorion broadcast the fact.[170]

120 Scholiast on Homer, *Iliad*

aprotimastos] "Untouched": "touch" means the same thing as "lay hands on". Also in Euphorion:

> The Muses made it, and unattainable Homer

that is, difficult to reach his calibre.

---

[169] Eurybatus or Eurybates was a by-word for duplicitous behaviour (Plato, *Prot.* 327 D; Dem. *Cor.* 24, Aesch. *Ctes.* 137), but so many stories were told about him (some of which are reported by John) that several characters were created out of the original.

[170] Justin, *Epit.* 15.4.3–4, reports that Laodice dreamed she had been made pregnant by Apollo, and received as a pledge from him a ring which she was to give to the offspring of their union; Appian, *Syr.* 284–285, adds that he would rule where this ring fell (it fell into the Euphrates). It is not clear whether Euphorion dealt with this in poetry (Meineke thought of the *Chiliades*) or prose.

121 EtGen AB, α 1308, ii. p. 262.1 L.–L.

ἀστέμβακτον· ἀκίνητον ἢ βέβαιον ἢ τετιμημένον· Εὐφο-
ρίων, οἷον·

πάντη δὲ σέθεν κλέος ἀστέμβακτον.

εἴρηται κατὰ ἀπόφασιν τοῦ στεμβάξαι, ὅ ἐστιν ὑβρίσαι.
οὕτως ἐν ὑπομνήματι ἀνεπιγράφῳ εἰς τὸν Κεχηνότα Διό-
νυσον Εὐφορίωνος.

cf. Tzetzes ad Lyc. *Al.* 1117, p. 332.24 Scheer

122 EtGen AB, α 1339, ii. p. 277.3 L.–L. = EtSym α 1510
= EtMag 162.5, α 2009 = ps.-Zonaras, col. 336 Tittmann

ἀτάρμυκτον· τὸ ἄφοβον· κυρίως δὲ τὸ μὴ μῦον· Εὐφο-
ρίων·

†ὅτι ἀτάρμυκτον τρέπεν ὄμμα.

ὅτι EtGen, EtMag: om. Sym, ps.-Zon.   τρέπεν EtGen:
πρέπεν *vl* ap. EtSym, EtMag, ps.-Zon.

123 Hermogenes, Περὶ ἰδεῶν 2.5, p. 341.18 Rabe

καὶ ὁ Εὐφορίων·

ἀτρέα δῆμον Ἀθηνῶν

ἀντὶ τοῦ ἄτρεστον καὶ ἄφοβον. ὅλως τε πολὺς ὁ κίνδυνος
ἐν ταῖς τοιαύταις δριμύτησιν ἐκπεσεῖν εἰς ψυχρότητα.

cf. Joannes Rhet., *Rhet. Gr.* vi. p. 409.12 Walz; Joseph

121 Etymologicum Genuinum

astembakton: unmoved, firm, or honoured. Euphorion, as in:

Your fame remains in all directions firmly founded.

It derives from the negation of *stembaxai*, which means to insult. Thus in the untitled commentary on the *Gaping Dionysus* of Euphorion.

122 Etymologicum Genuinum

atarmykton: fearless. Properly speaking, that which does not blink. Euphorion:

An unflinching eye . . . .

123 Hermogenes, *On Types of Style*

And Euphorion:

un-terrified (*a-trea*) people of Athens

instead of "fearless" and "unafraid". But in general, in using striking turns of phrase, there is considerable danger of falling into frigidity.

Rhacendyta, *Rhet. Gr.* iii. p. 502.2 Walz, sine auctoris nomine uterque

cf. Tzetzes, Scholia in Hermogen. (Cramer, *Anecd. Oxon.* iv, p. 130.17)

> εἴτε τὸν Εὐφορίωνα μιμούμενος ἢ ἄλλον
> τὴν Ἱπποδάμειαν αὐτὴν ὁμοίως καὶ Ἀτρέα
> οὐ θήσεις ὡς ὀνόματα, ὡς δὲ δριμείας λέξεις,
> ἀτρέα δῆμον ἄτρεστον ὡς Εὐφορίων λέγων
> 5 καὶ χεῖρ' ἱπποδάμεια⟨ν⟩ τὴν ἡνιόχων χεῖρα.

unde etiam χεῖρ' ἱπποδαμείαν Euphorioni tribuit Meineke

124 EtGen AB, λ 101 = EtMag 564.45 (cf. Tzetzes on Lyc. *Al.* 107, p. 56.1 Scheer)

λιβδοῦμεν . . . Εὐφορίων δὲ βύνην τὴν θάλασσαν λέγει, οἷον·

> πολύτροφα δάκρυα βύνης

τοὺς ἅλας βουλόμενος εἰπεῖν.

cf. EtGen AB, β 292, ii. p. 515.7 L.–L. = EtMag 217.4, β 363; Tzetzes on Lyc. *Al.* 107, p. 55.30 Scheer

Βύνη [Lyc. *Al.* 107]· ἡ Λευκοθέα, ἡ Ἰνώ, οἷον [Call. incert. auct. fr. 745 Pf.]·

> Βύνης καταδέκτριαι αὐδηέσσης.

καταλέκτριαι codd., corr. Pfeiffer

cf. Tzetzes' scholia on Hermogenes

> Next, whether you're imitating Euphorion or
>   someone else,
> Don't use the names "Hippodameia" and "Atreus"
> As common nouns, as far-fetched turns of phrase,
> Calling a fearless people "un-terrified" (*a-trea*), like
>   Euphorion,
> And a charioteer's hand a "horse-taming" (*hippo-*   [5]
>   *dameia*) one.

124 Etymologicum Genuinum

libdoumen: . . . Euphorion calls the sea *bȳnē*, as in:

> Copious tears of the sea

when he means "brine".

cf. Etymologicum Genuinum

Bȳnē: Leukothea, or Ino, as in:

> welcomers of Byne, goddess with a human voice.

EUPHORION

125 EtGen AB = EtSym = EtMag 389.25

εὐβύριον· τὸ εὔοικον. Εὐφορίων·

    ἄστυ κατ᾽ εὐβύριον.

εἴρηται ὅτι κατὰ τὴν βαυριάν, ἢ κατὰ Μεσσαπίους ση-
μαίνει τὴν οἰκίαν· Κλέων ὁ ἐλεγειοποιός [*SH* 340]·

    τοῦτο μὲν οὖν ῥέξαντες, ἀολλέες ἠγερέθοντο
    βαυριόθεν βριαροὶ Γοργοφόνοι νέποδες.

κατ᾽ ἔλλειψιν οὖν τοῦ ᾱ, τὸ βαύριον, βύριον· καὶ ἐν
συνθέσει, εὐβύριον.

126 EtGen B (cf. EtGen A, EtMag 401.38, ps.-Zonaras,
col. 905 Tittmann)

εὔωροι· ἀπαραφύλακτοι, ἀμελεῖς. Εὐφορίων·

    οὐδέ τοι εὔωροι θυέων.

παρὰ τὸ εὐωρεῖν, ὅ ἐστι φυλάσσειν, κατὰ ἀντίφρασιν, οἱ
ἀφύλακτοι. ἢ παρὰ τὸ εὖ καὶ τὴν ὥραν, τὴν φροντίδα,
κατὰ ἀντίφρασιν ὁ μὴ φροντίζων. ἐξ οὗ καὶ εὐωρία, ἡ
ὀλιγωρία καὶ ἡ ῥαθυμία κατὰ ἀντίφρασιν.

Εὐφορίων ... θυέων, κατὰ ἀντίφρασιν[1] ... μὴ φροντίζων, καὶ
ἡ ῥαθυμία usque ad finem om. EtGen A

366

125 Etymologicum Genuinum

eubyrion: well-furnished with houses. Euphorion:

> In a town well-off for homesteads.

It derives from *bauria*, which signifies "house" in the dialect of the Messapians, as in the elegiac poet Cleon:

> This done, all came together from their homes,
> The mighty offspring of the Gorgon-slayer.[171]

By ellipsis of *ā*, *baurion* yields *byrion*, and, compounded, *eubyrion*.

126 Etymologicum Genuinum

euōroi: careless, heedless. Euphorion:

> Not even those unmindful of the sacrifices.

From *euōrein*, which means "guard", by contraries; that is, those not on their guard. Or from *eu* and *ōran*, "thought", by contraries one who pays no heed. Whence also *euōria*, negligence or laxity by contraries.

---

[171] Perhaps the Persians, who were descended from the Gorgon-slayer Perseus.

127 Athen. *Deipn.* 11.475 F

καὶ Εὐφορίων·

ἠὲ πόθεν ποταμῶν κελέβῃ ἀποήφυσας ὕδωρ;

ποθεν A, corr. Meineke: ἠὲ (πόθεν;) ποταμῶν van Groningen

128 Σ Nic. *Ther.* 20*b*, p. 43.18 Crugnola

κυνηλατέοντος δὲ ἀντὶ τοῦ κυνηγετοῦντος, ὡς Εὐφορίων·

            ⟨κυνηλατέοντος⟩

αὐτῷ σὺν τελαμῶνι νεοσμήκτῳ τε μαχαίρῃ.

⟨κυνηλατέοντος⟩ suppl. I. G. Schneider

129 Σ Nic. *Al.* 147*b*, p. 77 Geymonat

ἡ μολόθουρος] βοτάνη ἐστίν, ἀειθαλὴς· διὸ καὶ Εὐφορίων φησί·

πτῶκες ἀειχλώροισιν ἰαύεσκον μολοθούροις.

ἀει χλωροῖσιν codd., corr. Meineke

De Διονύσῳ cogitavit Magnelli 2002, 155, coll. Call. *Hec.* fr. 84 + Stat. *Theb.* 12.619.

127 Athenaeus, *Deipnosophistae*

And Euphorion:

> You have drawn river-water in a cup—how can that
>   be?

128 Scholiast on Nicander, *Theriaca*

"Follow the hounds" instead of "hunt", as in Euphorion:

> ⟨of one who followed hounds⟩
> With leathern belt and knife newly wiped clean.

129 Scholiast on Nicander, *Alexipharmaca*

"The *molothouros*" (asphodel?)] It is a plant, an ever-
green. Hence Euphorion says:

> Hares used to sleep in evergreen asphodel.

130 Herodian, περὶ μον. λέξ., *GG* III.2, p. 951.20 Lentz

ὁ μέντοι Εὐφορίων παρὰ τὸ εἰς ῦς παραγωγὸν ποιήσας
ἐπίρρημα οὐκ ἔδωκε πρὸ τέλους τὸ ῦ, ἀλλὰ τὸ ῆ,

πάντα δέ οἱ νεκυηδὸν ἐλευκαίνοντο πρόσωπα.

νέκυνα ἐλεύκαινον τὰ cod., corr. Cramer

Ἡσιόδῳ attrib. Nietzsche 1873, 236

131 Galen, comm. ad Hippocr. *Epid.* vi, *CMG* V.10.2.2,
pp. 50–51 Wenkebach

διὸ καὶ τῶν γραμματικῶν [sic Wenkebach, e Scor. arab. 805
(H): προγνωστικῶν Marc. Venet. gr. 283 (U)] οἱ πλεῖστοι
ἐπὶ τῶν κατὰ τοὺς ὄμβρους σταγόνων εἰρῆσθαί φασι τὰς
πέμφιγας. < . . . > [lacunam statuit Wenkebach; nam H prae-
bet: "Und die Grammatiker erwähnen, daß die eine der Be-
deutungen, welche dieses Wort anzeigt, "der Hauch" ist, und
Kallimachos und Euphorion haben mit diesem Worte den
Hauch bennant."] ὁ μὲν <γὰρ> Καλλίμαχος ὧδε [fr. 43.41
Pf.] . . . ὁ δὲ Εὐφορίων οὕτως·

ἠπεδαναὶ πέμφιγες ἐπιτρύζουσι θανόντα.

εἶπε δ' ἄνθη (corr. Bentley: ἠπεδανὸν Hermann) πέμφιγγες
ἐπιτρύζουσι (ἐπικλύζουσι Bentley) θανόντα (θανόντων Elter)
U: <ἀμφὶ γὰρ αὐτόν> | ἠπεδαναὶ, κτλ. suppl. Magnelli: "und
Euphorion, indem er sagt: 'Sanfte Hauche umsäuseln den Toten'"
H   εἶτ' ἄνθη πέμφιγες ἐπικλύζουσι θάλοντα Schneide-
win

130 Herodian, *On unique word-formation*

Euphorion, in forming an adverb from a noun in *–us*, made the stem vowel not *u*, but *ē*:

His face was all cadaverously pale.[172]

131 Galen, commentary on Hippocrates, *Epidemics*

Greek version: Therefore most of the grammarians report that *pemphigas* is used of droplets of rain ‹ . . . ›. For Callimachus says [fr. 43.41 Pf.] . . . and Euphorion:

Fine droplets purl around the dead man.

Arabic version: The grammarians mention that one of the meanings of this word is "breeze", and Callimachus and Euphorion both used this word to denote a breeze. Callimachus . . . and Euphorion, when he says:

Gentle breezes whisper around the dead man.[173]

---

[172] *Or* "her face". It could refer to a face covered by chalk (cf. Nonn. *D*. 6. 169–170, 29.274) or pale in terror (Nietzsche's interpretation, of the murderers of Hesiod when they discovered the innocence of their victim).

[173] The Arabic version is perhaps more plausible. Two other possibilities: "frail ghosts gibber around the dead man" (cf. Lyc. *Al*. 1106); or, with Elter's conjecture, "frail ghosts of the dead gibber around (him)".

EUPHORION

132 Σ Nic. *Ther.* 180c, p. 97.17 Crugnola

τὸ ποιφύζειν πολλαχῶς λέγεται, καί ποτε μὲν ἐπὶ τοῦ
ἐκφοβεῖν . . . ποτὲ δὲ ἐπὶ τοῦ πνεῖν, ὡς Εὐφορίων·

Ζεφύρου μέγα ποιφύξαντος.

133 Apollonius Sophistes, *Lex. Hom.*, p. 133.19 Bekker

πόποι ἐπιφώνημα σχετλιαστικόν. τινὲς δὲ ἔδοξαν σημαί-
νειν ὦ θεοί· ὁ γοῦν Εὐφορίων φησὶν·

ἐν δὲ πόποις ἔσσαντο.

τινὲς δὲ τούτῳ βοηθοῦντες φασὶ συναλοιφὴν εἶναι, ἐν δὲ
ἐπόποις, ἀντὶ τοῦ ἐπόπταις.

ἔσσαντο codd.: θέσσαντο Meineke, cf. Hesych. θ 408

134 Σ Nic. *Ther.* 860a, p. 300.4 Crugnola

οὐ μόνον ἀπαλέξειν ἐστὶν ἀγαθὴ ἡ ῥάμνος εἰς φάρμακα,
ἀλλὰ καὶ εἰς φαντάσματα, ὅθεν καὶ πρὸ τῶν θυρῶν ἐν
τοῖς ἐναγίσμασι κρεμῶσιν αὐτήν. ἔστι δὲ λευκὴ καὶ
μέλαινα. μέμνηται δὲ τῆς βοτάνης καὶ Εὐφορίων·

ἀλεξίκακον φύε ῥάμνον.

132 Scholiast on Nicander, *Theriaca*

Poiphyzein has various meanings, sometimes "to terrify"
. . . and sometimes "to blow", as in Euphorion:

> Of the Zephyr's strong blasts.

133 Apollonius the Sophist, *Homeric Lexicon*

Popoi is an interjection expressive of anger. Some[174] think
that it means "ye gods". At all events, Euphorion says:

> They took their place among the gods.

Some who are of his school of thought say that, through co-
alescence of letters, *epopois* stands for *epoptais* (initiates).

134 Scholiast on Nicander, *Theriaca*

The *rhamnos* (a type of prickly shrub) is not only good as a
defence against drugs, but also against ghosts, and for that
reason they hang it before doorways when offerings are
made to the dead. It is black and white. Euphorion also
mentions the plant:

> Grow the protecting thorn-bush.[175]

---

[174] The Dryopians, according to other sources that note this
gloss (Plut. *Mor.* 22 D et al.).

[175] The subject is perhaps the earth or another deity.

135 Harpocration, *Lex*. i. p. 296.11 Dindorf

ὑποκυδής ἐστιν ὁ δίυγρος, ὡς ἐκ τῆς γ΄ Κτησίου φανερόν ἐστιν. Εὐφορίων·

οἷόν θ᾽ εἱαμενῆς ὑποκυδέος

τ᾽ (corr. Meineke) εἱαμενῆς ὑποκυδέες (corr. Salmasius, Ruhnken) codd.

136 Σ Ap. Rhod. 4.55, p. 263.24 Wendel

φοιταλέην] ἐμμανῆ, μανιωδῶς πορευομένην· φοῖτος γὰρ ἡ μανία λέγεται. καὶ Εὐφορίων·

φοιταλέος διὰ πᾶσαν ἄδην ἐπάτησε κοθόρνῳ.

φοιταλέῳ ... κοθόρνῳ vel φοιταλέοις ... κοθόρνοις Meineke
δ᾽ ἀνά P   ἄλην Valckenaer

Μοψοπίᾳ attrib. Scheidweiler

137 Σ Nic. *Ther*. 288c, p. 132.4 Crugnola

Εὐφορίων· "ἢ Αἴτνην ψολόεσσαν . . ." [**71**.11] καὶ ἔτι·

λιγνύν τε ψολόεσσαν ἀϊδνήεντά τε καπνόν

138 Photius, *Lexicon, Initium*, p. 77.7 Reitzenstein

ἀλκυών· . . . ἐπὶ δὲ τοῦ ἀλκυὼν ὁ μὲν ποιητὴς [*Il*. 9.563] συστέλλει τὸ ῡ, ὁ δὲ Εὐφορίων ἐκτείνει.

135 Harpocration, *Lexicon*

Hypokȳdes means "moist", as is clear from the third book of Ctesias. Euphorion:

> As of a marshy meadow.

136 Scholiast on Apollonius of Rhodes, *Argonautica*

phoitaleēn] Distracted, roaming about wildly: for madness is called *phoitos*. Euphorion:

> Booted, s/he roamed distraught through all that land,
>   unceasing.[176]

137 Scholiast on Nicander, *Theriaca*

Euphorion: "Or sooty Etna . . . " and again:

> A sooty conflagration and a nigrous smoke

138 Photius, Beginning of the *Lexicon*

Halcyon: in the word "halcyon", Homer employs a short *u*, while Euphorion lengthens it.

---

[176] The word for "boot", *cothornus*, suggests that this is either a woman or a effeminate male.

139 Hesych. α 3141

ἄλλιξ· χιτὼν χειριδωτός, παρὰ Εὐφορίωνι.

140 Σ Ap. Rhod. 1.1117–1119a, p. 99.7 Wendel

. . . καὶ Εὐφορίων δὲ ἐκ τούτου [sc. Ap. Rhod. 1.1117–
1125] κινηθεὶς τὸ ξόανον τῆς μητρὸς τῶν θεῶν φησιν
ἀμπέλινον εἶναι, διὰ τὸ τὴν ἄμπελον ἴσως ἱερὰν εἶναι
τῆς Ῥέας.

141 Photius, *Lexicon, Initium*, p. 96.23 Reitzenstein

ἀμύξ, ἀντὶ τοῦ μόλις· Εὐφορίων.

142 Hesych. α 5328

ἄνταρ· ἀετός, ὑπὸ Τυρρηνῶν. Εὐφορίων δὲ δίασμα.

143 EtGen AB, β 85, ii. p. 422.4 L.–L. = EtMag 194.22,
β 108

βέθρον· βέρεθρον καὶ κατὰ συγκοπὴν βέθρον· Κρα-
τῖνος [= Crates fr. pseud. 71 Bonanno] καὶ Εὐφορίων.

144 Choeroboscus, in Theodos. *Canon.*, *GG* IV.1, p.
234.1–3, cf. 29–30 Hilgard

Σεσημείωται παρ᾽ Εὐφορίωνι ἅπαξ εὑρεθὲν τὸ βό-
τρυα, καὶ παρὰ Διονυσίῳ, οὐκ ἐν τῇ Περιηγήσει ἀλλ᾽
ἐν ἑτέρῳ αὐτοῦ ποιήματι, τὸ δρύα.

139 Hesychius

allix: a sleeved chiton, in Euphorion.[177]

140 Scholiast on Apollonius of Rhodes, *Argonautica*

. . . And hence Euphorion says that the statue of the Mother of the Gods is made of vine-wood, on the probable grounds that the vine is sacred to Rhea.[178]

141 Photius, Beginning of the *Lexicon*

amyx, instead of "barely": Euphorion.

142 Hesychius

antar: eagle, in the dialect of the Tyrrhenians. Euphorion uses it to mean the warp thread.[179]

143 Etymologicum Genuinum

bethron: *berethron* (gulf) and through syncope *bethron*: Cratinus and Euphorion.

144 Choeroboscus, scholia on Theodosius' *Canones*

The forms *botrya* (accusative) found once in Euphorion, and *drya* in Dionysius—not in the *Periegesis*, but in one of his other poems—are noted as exceptions.

---

[177] Apparently a Thessalian garment (EtGen AB, *a* 515, etc.). Callimachus used the word of the man from Aphidnae (*Hecale* fr. 42.5 Hollis).   [178] The context may be Argonautic, as in Apollonius: the Argonauts on Arctonnesus construct an image of the Idaean Mother from a vine-stock.

[179] For δίασμα, cf. Call. fr. 520 Pf.

145 Scholia Vaticana in Dionysii Thracis Artem Grammaticam, *GG* I.3, p. 233.22–23 Hilgard

Εὐφορίων ὁ ποιητὴς . . . εἶπεν . . . τὴν ἐλαίαν
γλαυκῶπιν.

cf. **188**.

146 Scholia Vaticana in Dionysii Thracis Artem Grammaticam, *GG* I.3, p. 233.22–23 Hilgard

Εὐφορίων ὁ ποιητὴς περὶ τοῦ ἀρότρου εἶπεν ἐνο-
σίχθονι.

ἐρυσίχθονι W. Schulze, sed cf. Nonn. *D*. 2.67   ἀρότρῳ add.
Schol. Londinensia

147 Strab. 8.5.3

Εὐφορίων δὲ καὶ τὸν ἧλον λέγει ἦλ.

ἧλον Strab.: ἥλιον *Chrest*. 8.28 (*GGM* ii. p. 584 Müller)
ἦλ Strab.: ἦλι *Chrest*.

cf. Eustath. ad *Il*. 5.416, ii. 114.10 van der Valk (cf. eund.
ad *Il*. 14.265–266, iii. 637.4)

. . . τοῦ Γεωγράφου ἱστοροῦντος καινήν τινα ἀποκοπὴν
τοῦ ἧλος ἦλ, οἷον "δαιμόνιος ἦλ" . . .

145 Vatican Scholia on Dionysius Thrax's *Ars Grammatica*

Euphorion the poet . . . called . . . the olive "grey-eyed".

146 ibid.

Euphorion the poet, writing about the plough, called it "earth-shaker".[180]

147 Strabo

For *hēlos* Euphorion uses the form *hēl*.

cf. Eustathius on Homer, *Iliad*

. . . the Geographer reporting a new apocopated form of *hēlos*, viz. *hēl*, as in "numinous *hēl*".[181]

---

[180] This and the last fragment are mischievous re-assignments of Homeric epithets.

[181] *Hēlos* usually means "nail", but the quotation (which may or may not be by Euphorion) cannot mean that. Servius, on Virg. *Aen*. 1.642, links ἥλιος with an Assyrian word *(h)el*. Euphorion may have had this in mind, and there is a good chance that the quotation does.

EUPHORION

148 Helladius, ap. Photius, *Bibl.* 279, p. 532 в 21 (cf. Test. **3**).

καὶ τὸν τὰ χρυσᾶ μῆλα τῶν Ἑσπερίδων φρουροῦντα
ὄφιν κηπουρὸν ὠνόμασε.

149 Σ A *Il.* 9.206a¹, ii. p. 442.24 Erbse

Εὐφορίων κρεῖον τὸ κρέας ἐξεδέξατο, Ὅμηρος δὲ τὸ
κρεοδόχον ἀγγεῖον.

cf. EtGen ABJ = EtGud p. 344.13 Sturz = EtMag 536.56

κρεῖον· . . . ἰστέον δὲ ὅτι ἡ μὲν κοινὴ δόξα ἔχει, ὅτι τὸ
κρεῖον κρεοδόχον ἀγγεῖον σημαίνει· ὁ δὲ Εὐφορίων τὸ
κρέας λέγει αὐτὸ εἶναι, ὡς καὶ Ὅμηρος [*Il.* 9.206].

Eustath. ad *Il.* 9.206–208, ii. p. 701.11 van der Valk

Εὐφορίων δὲ κρεῖον αὐτὸ τὸ κρέας νοεῖ, ὥς φησιν
Ἀπίων καὶ Ἡρόδωρος [Ἡρωδιανός conj. van Gronin-
gen], διὰ τὸ τὸν ποιητὴν κατωτέρω μηδαμοῦ μεμνῆ-
σθαι κρεῶν ἐφθῶν ἐν ἀγγείῳ, ἀλλὰ μόνων ὀπτῶν.

150 Ἐπιμερισμοὶ κατὰ στοιχεῖον γραφικά, Bodl. MS
Barocci 50 fol. 245ʳ, ap. Cramer, *Anecd. Oxon.* ii. p. 378.1
(cf. EtGud p. 280.21 Sturz; EtMag 472.43)

ἴος . . . μνιὸς ὁ ἁπαλὸς παρ᾽ Εὐφορίωνι.

148 Helladius, ap. Photius, *Library*

He also called the snake that watched over the golden apples of the Hesperides "gardener" (i.e., keeper of the garden).

149 Scholiast on Homer, *Iliad*

Euphorion understood *kreion* in the sense "flesh", whereas Homer used it to mean a vessel that contains meat.

cf. Etymologicum Genuinum

kreion: . . . the common view is that *kreion* means a vessel that contains meat, but Euphorion says it means the meat itself, as does Homer.

Eustathius on Homer, *Iliad*

By *kreion* Euphorion understands the meat itself, according to Apion and Herodorus, because hereafter the poet never mentions flesh boiled in a vessel, but only roast meat.[182]

150 *Alphabetical Analyses of Words*

ios . . . mnios means "tender" in Euphorion.

[182] Powell raised the possibility that Euphorion put forward this interpretation in a prose work.

EUPHORION

151 Helladius, ap. Photius, *Bibl.* 279, p. 531 A 2

τὸ γὰρ ζητεῖν Δωριεῖς λέγουσι μῶ, καὶ μῶται τὸ
τρίτον πρόσωπον παρ᾽ Ἐπιχάρμῳ [fr. 117 Kaibel], καὶ
μῶνται παρὰ Εὐφορίωνι.

152 ibid. p. 532 B 17 (cf. Test. **3**)

ὅτι παρὰ Εὐφορίωνι . . . κακοζήλους ἐστὶν εὑρεῖν
λέξεις. καὶ γὰρ τὸν Ἰάσονα ναυαγὸν εἶπεν, ὅπερ οὐ
νεναυαγηκότα μᾶλλον, τὸν δὲ ναῦν ἄγοντα δηλοῖ.

153 Harpocration, *Lex.* i. p. 249 Dindorf (cf. Photius,
Lex. p. 424 Porson; *Suda* π 1342)

πεφοριῶσθαι· Λυσίας ἐν τῇ πρὸς Πολυκράτην κατ᾽
Ἐμπέδου ἐπιστολῇ, εἰ γνήσιος, φησὶν "ἢ τὸν ὀφθαλ-
μὸν τὸν ἕτερον γλαυκότερον εἶναι ἢ πεφοριῶσθαι" ἐπὶ
τοῦ ἀποκεκλειμένου, ὥσπερ Εὐφορίων κέχρηται τῷ
ὀνόματι· εἰσὶ γάρ τινες ὀφθαλμοὶ κατακεχαλασμένα
ἔχοντες τὰ βλέφαρα καὶ οἰονεὶ μύοντες. ἐὰν δὲ γράφη-
ται "πεφορινῶσθαι", εἴη ἂν πεπαχύνθαι, ἀπὸ τῆς φο-
ρίνης.

154 Σ T *Il.* 23.197*b*, v. p. 400.82 Erbse

φλεγεθοίατο] Εὐφορίων κακῶς τῷ ῥήματι ἑνικῶς χρῆ-
ται.

151 Helladius, ap. Photius, *Library*

For the Dorian word for "seek" is *mō*; the third person is *mōtai*, as found in Epicharmus, and *mōntai* in Euphorion.

152 ibid.

In Euphorion . . . one can find affected vocabulary. For example, he calls Jason *nauagos*, not in the sense of "someone who has suffered shipwreck", but in that of "one who leads / is captain of a ship".[183]

153 Harpocration, *Lexicon*

Pephoriōsthai: Lysias in the letter in reply to Polycrates against Empedus, if it is genuine, says "either one of his eyes was greyish in colour, or it had a hooded lid", of a closed eye. Euphorion uses the word in the same way. For some eyes have lids which droop and are virtually shut. If it were spelt *pephorinōsthai*, it would mean "to have become congealed", from *phorīnē* (fat).[184]

154 Scholiast on Homer, *Iliad*

phlegethoiato (they might be burned)] Euphorion incorrectly uses the verb form as a singular.[185]

---

183 In fact these two derivations presuppppose different scansions: *nauāgos* and *nauăgos*.

184 Its other meaning is "skin", but the gloss suggests that "fat" is the right meaning here.

185 A common misapprehension from the Hellenistic period onwards (see e.g. Call. fr. 497 and Pfeiffer ad loc.).

EUPHORION

155 Σ D *Il.* 16.235 (Par. Graec. 2679, ap. Cramer, *Anecd. Paris.* iii. 21, cf. iv. p. 223 Erbse)

χαμαιεῦναι δὲ οἱ ἐπὶ τοῦ ἐδάφους κοιμώμενοι λέγονται παρὰ Εὐφορίωνι.

⟨χαμαικοίται⟩ vel ⟨χαμαιλεχέες⟩ λέγονται van Groningen.

156 Steph. Byz., α 84 Billerbeck

Ἀθύρας, ἐπίνειον καὶ ποταμὸς περὶ τὸ Βυζάντιον. ἔστι δὲ καὶ κόλπος Ἀθύρας. κλίνεται δὲ ἰσοσυλλάβως, ὡς Εὐφορίων·

ὕδατα δινήεντος ἀμευσάμενος Ἀθύραο.

157 Steph. Byz., α 201 Billerbeck

Ἀλήσιον, ⟨πόλις⟩ [suppl. Berkel] τῆς Ἤλιδος . . . ἔστι καὶ Ἀλήσιον πεδίον τῆς Ἠπείρου, ὡς πηγνύμενον ἐκεῖ πολλοῦ ἁλός. ὁ δὲ Εὐφορίων

οὐ γὰρ Ἀλήσιοί ἐστε

φησίν.

158 Steph. Byz., β 116 Billerbeck

Βοιωτία . . . γενέσθαι δέ φασι Βοιωτὸν Ἰτώνου τοῦ Ἀμφικτύονος . . . Νικοκράτης [*FGrH* 376 F 5] δέ φησιν ὅτι Ποσειδῶνος καὶ Ἄρνης ἦν παῖς. Εὐφορίων·

384

155 Scholiast on Homer, *Iliad*

Those who sleep on the ground are called *chamaieunai* by Euphorion.[186]

156 Stephanus of Byzantium

Athyras, a port and river near Byzantium. There is also a gulf named Athyras. In declension its stem has the same number of syllables, as in Euphorion:

Passing by the waters of the eddying Athyras.

157 Stephanus of Byzantium

Alesion, ‹a city› in Elis . . . there is also a Halesian plain in Epirus, since a lot of salt (*halos*) solidified there. Euphorion says:

For you are not Halesians.[187]

158 Stephanus of Byzantium

Boeotia . . . they say that Boeotus was son of Itonus son of Amphictyon . . . Nicocrates says that he was son of Poseidon and Arne. Euphorion:

[186] *chamaieunai* is already Homeric epithet for the priests of Zeus at Dodona known as the Selloi. It is not clear why Euphorion need be adduced, unless perhaps another word has fallen out explaining that he called them by a different title.

[187] Of the two places named (H)alesion, the town in Elis had already been mentioned by Nestor in *Il.* 11.757. Scheidweiler suggested that this fragment likewise belonged to Nestor's reminiscences, while van Groningen conjectured a reference to the divine favour enjoyed by the Elean town.

ὄφρα κε μαντεύοιτο μεθ᾽ υἱάσι Βοιωτοῖο,
τόν ῥα Ποσειδάωνι δαμασσαμένῳ τέκεν Ἄρνη,
Βοιωτὸν δ᾽ ὀνόμηνε. τὸ γὰρ καλέσαντο νομῆες,
ὅττι ῥα πατρῴῃσι βοῶν ἀπεθήκατο κόπροις.

2–4 ap. EtGen AB, β 169, ii. p. 460.13 L.–L.; EtGud p. 277.4 de
Stefani; EtMag 203.10, β 203.　　3–4 ap. EtSym β 142; Eustath.
ad *Il*. 2.507, i. p. 414.6 van der Valk.　　3 ap. EtGen AB, β 190, ii.
p. 470.3 L.–L.

2 δαμασσαμένη codd., corr. Meineke　　　τέκε μήτηρ Ety-
mologica　　3 καλέουσι βοτῆρες Etymologica

159　EtGen AB, γ 77 (cf. EtMag 228.20)

Γεράνεια· ὄρος Μεγάρων. Εὐφορίων·

　δεξιτερὴν ὑπερέσχε καὶ ὀχθηρῆς Γερανείης.

εἴρηται ὅτι Μεγαρεὺς ὁ Διὸς καὶ μιᾶς τῶν καλουμένων
†θηΐδων [Θηβαΐδων A: Νηΐδων vel Νηρηΐδων vel Νυσηΐδων Sylburg: Σιθνίδων Berkel, cf. Paus. 1.40.1] νυμφῶν,
τοῦ κατακλυσμοῦ γενομένου, πρὸς φωνὴν γεράνων νηχό-
μενος, προσέφυγε τῇ ἄκρᾳ τοῦ ὄρους. ἀπὸ δὲ τῶν γε-
ράνων Γεράνειαν ἐκάλεσαν τὸν τόπον.

δεξιτερὴν ὑπερέσχε om. EtMag　　　"Supple, si libet,
δράξατο vel sim." Scheidweiler

So that he should prophesy among Boeotus' sons,
Whom Arne, overmastered by Poseidon, bore
And named Boeotus; thus the herdsmen called him
Because she bore him in the steadings of her father's
    herds.[188]

159 Etymologicum Genuinum

Geraneia: a mountain in Megara. Euphorion:

He stretched his right hand (and) over hilly Geraneia
  . . . [189]

It is so called because when, in the time of the flood,
Megareus the son of Zeus and one of the Sithnid(?)
nymphs, swam in the direction from which cranes could be
heard, he found refuge on the peak of this mountain. So
from the cranes they called the place Geraneia.

---

[188] The subject of the first line could be Tiresias. Stephanus
goes on to cite Eur. fr. 489 Kannicht (*Melanippe* fr. 12 Jouan–van
Looy), which offers the same etymology of Boeotus' name.

[189] The construction would permit Geraneia as the object of a
second verb. The context could be one of protection or of menace.

160 Steph. Byz., p. 241.17 Mein.

Δύμη . . . τὸ θηλυκὸν Δυμαία. Εὐφορίων·

  ἤ τις ἔχεις κληῖδας ἐπιζεφύροιο Δυμαίης,

διὰ τὸ πρὸς δύσιν ἐπιζέφυρον.

ἐπιζεφύρου Δυμαίης Meineke (cf. AP 7.445.2 Δῦμαῖοι).

161 Steph. Byz., p. 244.5 Mein.

Δυρράχιον . . . λέγεται δὲ καὶ ἡ χώρα τῆς Ἰλλυρίας Δυρραχία. Εὐφορίων·

  ἄστεα Δυρραχίης τε καὶ ἔθνεα Ταυλαντίνων.

cf. Steph. Byz., p. 607.14 Mein.

Ταυλάντιοι, Ἰλλυρικὸν ἔθνος. Εὐφορίων δὲ μετὰ τοῦ ν̄ Ταυλαντίνους αὐτούς φησι.

Διονύσῳ attrib. Scheidweiler

162(a–b) EtGen AB ζ 66 = EtSym (amplius EtMag 414.19, cf. Magnelli 2002, 141)

ζωστήρ· τόπος τῆς Ἀττικῆς· καὶ Ζώστριος Ἀπόλλων. Εὐφορίων·

  οὗτος μὲν Ζωστὴρ, Φοίβου πέδον

καὶ

160 Stephanus of Byzantium

Dyme . . . the feminine is Dymaia. Euphorion:

> Who hold the keys of the westerly Dymaean (city)[190]

so called because it lies towards the sunset.

161 Stephanus of Byzantium

Dyrrhachium . . . the land of Illyria is also called Dyrrhachia. Euphorion:

> Cities of Dyrrhachia, and tribes of the Taulantini.[191]

cf. Stephanus of Byzantium

Taulantii, a tribe of Illyria. Euphorion calls them Taulantini, with an *n*.

162(a–b) Etymologicum Genuinum

Zōstēr: a place in Attica.[192] And "Zostrian Apollo". Euphorion:

> This is Zoster, sacred ground of Phoebus

and

---

[190] Dyme is a city in Achaea, and the subject of the verb is apparently its patron-goddess, Athena (Paus. 7.17.9).

[191] Dyrrhachia is the territory of the Illyrian city of Dyrrhachium / Epidamnus, and the Taulanti(n)i were a tribe in the area (Strab. 7.7.8).

[192] A cape, south of Hymettus.

ἠδ᾽ ἐπαπειλήσας Ζωστηρίῳ Ἀπόλλωνι.

φασὶ γὰρ τὴν Λητὼ ὠδίνουσαν ἐκεῖσε τὴν ζώνην λῦσαι.

ἠδ᾽ EtGen AB: ἠδ᾽ EtMag, Tzetzes ad Lyc. Al. 1278, p. 361.15 Scheer.

162(a) Μοψοπίᾳ attrib. Scheidweiler

163 Julius Pollux, *Onom.* 4.95

τάχα δὲ καὶ Ὀρχομενὸς παρὰ τὴν τῶν Χαρίτων ὄρχησιν, ὡς Εὐφορίων·

Ὀρχομενὸν Χαρίτεσσιν ἀφαρέσιν ὀρχηθέντα.

Ὀρχούμενον, -νῶν codd., corr. Pierson   Χαρίτων A
φάρεσιν, ἀφαίρεσιν codd.: corr. Pierson.

Ἡσιόδῳ attrib. Bergk 1846, 31 [= 1886, 221]; Nietzsche 1873, 236.

164 Σ AD *Il.* 2.157

Ζεὺς Κρόνου καὶ Ῥέας γενόμενος ἐν Κρήτῃ δὲ ἐπικληθεὶς Αἰγίοχος διὰ τὸ αὐτόθι τραφῆναι ὑπὸ αἰγὸς, ἢ ὥς τινές φασιν διὰ τὸ αἶγα ἀνελόντα τὴν μὲν δορὰν ἀμφιάσασθαι, τοῖς δὲ κέρασιν εἰς τόξον χρήσασθαι. ὅθεν καὶ Αἰγιδόκον τόπον τινὰ ἐν Κρήτῃ καλεῖσθαι. ἱστορεῖ Εὐφορίων.

And having threatened Apollo of the Girdle.

For they say that, when Leto was suffering birth-pangs, this was the place where she undid her girdle.

163 Pollux, *Onomastikon*

Moreover Orchomenos may derive from the dance (*orchē-sis*) of the Graces, as in Euphorion:

Orchomenos, danced-upon by unrobed Graces.

164 Scholiast on Homer, *Iliad*

Zeus, son of Cronos and Rhea, had the epithet *Aigiochos* in Crete, because he was nurtured there by a goat, or, as some people say, because, having killed a goat, he put on the hide as a garment, and used the horns for a bow. A place in Crete is named Aigidokos after this. The story is in Euphorion.

165 Steph. Byz., α 113 Billerbeck

Αἶγυς, πόλις Λακωνικῆς, ὡς Εὐφορίων.

166 P. Oxy. 2527

```
        ]εσβηνιν . . νμε . ν . εξ[
            ] . [ . ] . . ρεσβήνωσ . [
          ]ηνομενουννευ[
          ]τοναινονοιδε . [
5      Ἀρ]ιστοτέλης ἐν τῆι αι . [
```
— — — — —

2 πρεσβήν Ll.-J.–P. (cf. Ἐρωτικὰ Παθήματα XIII.3 and n. 33)?
. [: littera supra σ addita   3–4 ὁ μὲν οὖν Εὐ[φορίων . . .]
τὸν Αἶνον οἶδε Lobel   5 ἐν τῆι Αἰγ[ίων vel Αἰγ[ινητῶν
πολιτείαι Lobel

167 Steph. Byz., α 229 Billerbeck

Ἄλπωνος, πόλις καὶ ὄρος ἐν Μακεδονίᾳ, ὡς Εὐφορίων.

de Ἀλμωπία agi suspicatus est Günther

168 Choeroboscus, in Theodos. *Canon.*, *GG* IV.1, p. 142.16 Hilgard

Ἀφίας Ἀφίαντος παρ' Εὐφορίωνι.

Ἀπφίας Osann: Ἀφείδας, Ἀφίδας Meineke

165 Stephanus of Byzantium

Aigys, a city of Laconia, as in Euphorion.

166 P. Oxy. 2527

Eu[phorion   [3]
] knows Ainos[193]
Ar]istotle in the Ai[nian (*or* Aeg[inetan) Constitution   [5]

167 Stephanus of Byzantium

Alponos, a city and mountain in Macedonia, as in Euphorion.

168 Choeroboscus, scholia on Theodosius' *Canones*

Aphias–Aphiantos in Euphorion.

[193] For Ainos, see **34**.3, **88**.

169 Σ Dion. Perieg. 64, *GGM* ii. p. 434[b]4 Müller

αὗται δὲ πρότερον Κρόνου ἐλέγοντο στῆλαι, διὰ τὸ
μέχρι τῶν τῇδε ὁρίζεσθαι δῆθεν τὴν ἀρχὴν αὐτοῦ·
δεύτερον δὲ ἐλέχθησαν Βριάρεω, ὥς φησιν Εὐφορίων·
τρίτον δὲ Ἡρακλέους.

cf. Σ Pindar, *Nem.* 3.40, iii. p. 48.10 Drachmann

αἱ δὲ Ἡράκλειαι στῆλαι καὶ Βριάρεω λέγονται εἶναι,
καθά φησι ‹   ›·

στῆλαί τ' Αἰγαίωνος ἁλὸς †μεδέοντι Γίγαντος.

‹Εὐφορίων› Drachmann   τ'] τὴν codd., corr. Boeckh   μεδέ-
οντος ἄνακτος dub. Kinkel

170 Steph. Byz., p. 222.14 Mein.

Δαφνοῦς, Φωκικὴ πόλις, ἀρσενικῶς λεγομένη. ὁ
πολίτης Δαφνούντιος ἢ Δαφνούσιος, καὶ θηλυκῶς
Δαφνουσίς. Δάφνουσαν δὲ αὐτήν φησιν Εὐφορίων.

Δαφνοῦσ‹σ›αν Lloyd-Jones 1979, 17 = 1990, 157

171 "Apuleius", *De Orthographia*, § 28, p. 9 Osann

Eridanus . . . est item Italiae qui et Padus, item Hiberiae,
auctoribus Aeschylo [fr. 73a Radt], Pausania [1.4.1], Eu-
phorione minore.

---

[194] See Parthenius **34**.   [195] ps.-Apuleius has a poor rep-
utation (see Lightfoot 1999, 212–214), but, following Hollis' vin-

169 Scholiast on Dionysius the Periegete

These pillars were initially called the pillars of Cronos, because the boundary of his kingdom lay in these regions; next they were said to belong to Briareus, as Euphorion says; and thirdly they became known as the pillars of Heracles.

cf. Scholiast on Pindar, *Nemean Odes*

The pillars of Heracles are also known as the pillars of Briareus, according to < Euphorion?? >:

> And the pillars of Aegaeon, the Giant, lord of the
> sea.[194]

170 Stephanus of Byzantium

Daphnous, a city of Phocis. The name is masculine. The inhabitant is *Daphnountios* or *Daphnousios*, the feminine *Daphnousis*. Euphorion calls it *Daphnousa*.

171 "Apuleius", *On Spelling*

The river Eridanus . . . is located both in Italy, where it is also known as the Po, and in Iberia, according to Aeschylus, Pausanias, and Euphorion the younger.[195]

dication of **55**, I have included this among the genuine fragments. The datum about Aeschylus is drawn from Pliny, *NH* 37.32, who also reports that Aeschylus identified the Eridanus with the Rhone. Pausanias 1.4.1 does not use the word "Iberia", but makes the Eridanus run through a country that borders on the Atlantic. We cannot tell what Euphorion said, except that he presumably opposed the common identification of the river with the Po. "Euphorion the younger" presumably distinguishes the Hellenistic poet from the son of Aeschylus.

EUPHORION

172 Steph. Byz., p. 466.16 Mein.

Μωριεῖς, ἔθνος Ἰνδικόν, ἐν ξυλίνοις οἰκοῦντες οἴκοις, ὡς Εὐφορίων.

cf. Hesych. μ 2067

Ἀλεξάνδρῳ attrib. Scheidweiler

173 Steph. Byz., p. 468.9 Mein.

Νάξος . . . Εὐφορίων δὲ παρὰ τὸ νάξαι, ὅ φασι θῦσαί τινες.

θῦσαι codd., Eustath. ad Dion. Perieg. 525 (*GGM* ii. p. 319ᵃ23 Müller), *Suda* ν 27: βῦσαι Salmasius, cf. Hesych. ν 63 νάξαι· σάξαι. βῦσαι.

174 Steph. Byz., p. 471.13 Mein.

Νέδη, πόλις Ἀρκαδίας, ἀπὸ νύμφης Νέδης. Εὐφορίων δὲ Νεδέην αὐτήν φησι. τὸ κτητικὸν Νεδεήσιος.

πόλις codd.: ποταμός Meineke (cf. Call. *Hymn* 1.33–38) καὶ αὐτήν φησι. τὸ κτ. codd.: φησί. καὶ ὁ αὐτὸς τὸ κτ. Meineke

175 Eustath. ad *Od.* 15.376, ii. p. 103.25 Stallbaum

ἰστέον δὲ ὅτι ἐς τοσοῦτον ἠξιώθη λόγου τοῖς παλαιοῖς ὁ εὐνοϊκὸς οὗτος δοῦλος Εὔμαιος, ὥστε καὶ μητέρα

172 Stephanus of Byzantium

Morieis, an Indian tribe who live in wooden houses, as Euphorion says.[196]

173 Stephanus of Byzantium

Naxos . . . Euphorion derives it from *naxai*, which some say means "sacrifice" [*or*, "stuff"].

174 Stephanus of Byzantium

Nede, a city of Arcadia, from the nymph Nede. Euphorion calls her *Nedeē*. The possessive is *Nedeēsios*.

175 Eustathius on Homer, *Odyssey*

This loyal-hearted slave, Eumaeus, was of such account to the ancients that they even discovered a mother for

[196] If the name is connected with the Maurya dynasty (322–185 BC), Hesychius is more exact in glossing Morieis as "the kings of India".

αὐτοῦ ἐξευρίσκουσι. Δημόκριτος μὲν Πενίαν [68 Β 24 D.–Κ.], Εὐφορίων δὲ Πάνθειαν, Φιλόξενος δὲ ὁ Σιδώνιος Δανάην.

176 Σ ad Dion. Perieg. 420, *GGM* ii. p. 447[b]19 Müller (cf. EtGen AB = EtSym = EtMag 708.51 Σαρωνίς)

καὶ ταύτην τὴν Κορινθίαν (sc. θάλασσαν) Σαρωνίδα καλοῦσιν, ὡς μὲν Εὐφορίων φησὶν, ἐπειδὴ Σάρων τις κυνηγὸς ἐπιδιώκων ‹σὺν› ἐκεῖθεν κατεκρημνίσθη εἰς θάλασσαν, καὶ διὰ τοῦτο Σαρωνικὸν κληθῆναι τὸ πέλαγος.

‹σὺν› Hudson, nec non Meineke in EtMag (cf. Eustath. in Dion. Perieg. 420, *GGM* ii. p. 295[a]1 Müller)

Μοψοπίᾳ attrib. Scheidweiler

177 Steph. Byz., p. 635.5 Mein.

Τρικόρυνθον, οὐδετέρως Δίδυμος καὶ Διόδωρος, Διονύσιος ἀρσενικῶς, Εὐφορίων θηλυκῶς. ἔστι δὲ δῆμος τῆς Αἰαντίδος φυλῆς.

Μοψοπίᾳ attrib. Scheidweiler

him. Democritus calls her Penia, Euphorion Pantheia, and Philoxenus the Sidonian Danae.

176 Scholiast on Dionysius the Periegete

And they call this sea off Corinth Saronic, as Euphorion says, because a certain hunter called Saron was chasing a boar and plunged from there into the sea, whence it became known as Saronic.[197]

177 Stephanus of Byzantium

Tricorynthus: Didymus and Diodorus make it neuter, Dionysius masculine, Euphorion feminine. It is a deme of the tribe of Ajax.[198]

[197] The story of the hunter also appears in Σ Eur. *Hipp*. 1200, but there he chases a deer. Parthenius **24** gives an alternative etymology.

[198] The Attic deme of Tricorynthus is just north of Marathon. Strabo 8.6.19 reports that, Eurystheus having died fighting against Iolaus and the sons of Heracles, his head was cut off by Iolaus and buried there. This story may or may not have been told by Euphorion himself.

178 P. Oxy. 2220 fr. 5

— — — — —

].[.].[
].ριστονιθ[
]αίοιο κέρητ[ος
]οιο λίπον ῥ[
5   ]ς Ἀμφιαρήου·
]΄.ος ὕδασινιπ[
]σαντο βο[
]οναριω[.].[

— — — — —

2 ἀμφ]ήριστον Ἰθ[ώμην Lobel   3 Ἡρ]αίοιο Livrea
κέρητ[ος de cornu fluminis cog. Lobel   4 Λάμ]οιο Livrea
ῥ[οῦν Lobel, unde οἶο vel τ]οῖο Ll.-J.–P.   6 ὕδασι νιπ[τ-
vel ὕδασιν ἱπ[π- Lobel: Γοργ]όνος ὕδασιν ἱπ[που Livrea
7 Βο[ιωτοί Lobel   8 Ἀρίων Lobel

de Euphorionis Κλήτορι cogitavit Lobel

179–192 DUBIE TRIBUTA

Γέρανος

179 Athen. *Deipn.* 3.82 A

διάφορα δὲ μῆλα γίνεται ἐν Σιδοῦντι. κώμη δ᾽ ἐστὶν αὕτη
Κορίνθου, ὡς Εὐφορίων ἢ Ἀρχύτας [fr. 2 P.] ἐν Γεράνῳ
φησίν·

---

199 The placement of this fragment is uncertain, since it is un-
clear whether all the fragments of P. Oxy. 2220 come from a single

178 P. Oxy. 2220 fr. 5[199]

dis]puted Ith[ome[200]   [2]
] . . . . horn
] they left the s[tream
] . . . of Amphiaraus   [5]
] in the waters of the hor[se? (*or*, was[h?)
] . . . Bo[eotian
] . . . Ario[n[201]

179–192 DUBIOUSLY ATTRIBUTED

Crane

179 Athenaeus, *Deipnosophistae*

Different kinds of apples grow in Sidous. This is a village belonging to Corinth, as either Euphorion or Archytas says in the *Crane*:[202]

---

poem or not. Lobel suggested it comes from the *Cletor* (**36**); Barigazzi assigned all the fragments to the *Dionysus*, though at least one (**51**) seems to derive from the *Chiliades*. Livrea 1995, 56–57, developed the idea that the context is Dionysus' "triumphal march" through Thessaly and Boeotia, and suggested a link with **15**, where he restores a reference to the Pheres of Thessaly (see n. 17).   [200] Given the other indications of place, perhaps an allusion to the Thessalian town, rather than the Messenian mountain?   [201] Arion was the horse of Adrastus. He and the seer Amphiaraus may have been mentioned in connection with the Boeotian village of Harma (Strab. 9.2.11), but the connection with what precedes is unclear.   [202] Apparently Archytas of Amphissa, who must have lived in or after the time of Eratosthenes, since he is known to have read the *Hermes* (Archytas fr. 3 P.). We can only guess at the subject of the *Crane*: perhaps the dance of this name performed by the Athenians on Delos, or a pygmy-woman who was transformed into a crane (Ant. Lib. 16)?

ὥριον οἷά τε μῆλον, ὅ τ᾽ ἀργιλώδεσιν ὄχθαις
πορφύρεον ἐλαχείῃ ἐνιτρέφεται Σιδόεντι.

2 πορφυρόειν Meineke   Ἐφυρείῃ Kaibel

180 EtGen AB, α 1131, ii. p. 176.9 L.–L. = EtMag
135.27, α 1726

Ἀργανθώνειον . . . τινὲς δ᾽ Ἀργανθώνην αὐτό φασιν.
Εὐφορίων καὶ Φιλί‹τ›ας [Φιλίας AB, EtMag: Φιλήτας Vb,
suprascr. γρ. Φιλίας: Φιλέας Toup] [**25**] Ἀργανθώνιον
λέγουσι διὰ τοῦ ῑ, οἷον·

χθιζόν μοι κνώσσοντι παρ᾽ Ἀργανθώνιον αἶπος.

Ὑακίνθῳ attrib. Powell

181 Anonymus I, Isagoga ad Arat., 5. περὶ κύκλων, p.
95.9 Maass

οἱ δὲ ποιηταὶ Ὠκεανὸν αὐτὸν (sc. τὸν ὁρίζοντα) καλοῦσιν.
ὁ γοῦν Εὐφορίων [Παριανὸς conj. Hiller, Maass, cf. infra]
φησίν·

Ὠκεανός, τῷ πᾶσα περίρρυτος ἐνδέδεται χθών.

cf. Achilles, Isagoga Excerpta, 22. περὶ κύκλων καὶ ὅτι
ιαʹ, p. 51.30 Maass

ὅθεν καὶ Νεοπτόλεμος ὁ Παριανὸς [fr. 2 P.] ἐν τῇ Τρι-
χθονίᾳ [Ἐριχθονίδι vel Ἐριχθονιάδι conj. Meineke]
φησὶν "τῷ πᾶσα περίρρυτος ἐνδέδεται χθών."

Ripe as an apple which on the marley slopes
Ripens in little Sidous to a ruddy glow.

180 Etymologicum Genuinum

Arganthoneion . . . some call it *Arganthōnē*. Euphorion
and Philitas say *Arganthōnion*, with an *i*, as in:

> To me as yesterday I slept beside the Arganthonian
>   height.[203]

181 Anonymus I, *Introduction* to Aratus, *On circles*

The poets call it (sc. the horizon) "Ocean". Euphorion [*or*,
the Parian?] says:

> Ocean, by which the sea-girt earth is all
>   encompassed.

cf. Achilles, *Introduction–Excerpts*: *On circles, and that
there are eleven of them*

Whence Neoptolemus of Paros in the *Trichthonia*(?) says:
"by which the sea-girt earth is all encompassed."

---

[203] Scholarly consensus gives this fragment to Euphorion,
though the citation is not unambiguous. Apparently the first line
of a narration (a dream-narrative?), and possibly in the context
of the Hylas story, which took place near this mountain on the
Propontis, north of Cius (Ap. Rhod. 1.1178; Prop. 1.20.33).

Σ A *Il.* 18.490, Σ D *Il.* 18.491, Σ Genev. *Il.* 20.7, cf. Por-
phyry, *Quaestiones Homericae ad Iliadem pertinentes*, p.
239.11 Schrader

φησὶν γάρ <   > "Ὠκεανὸς, ᾧ", κτλ.

<ὁ Παριανός> in A suppl. Meineke, Maass

Probus in Virg. *Georg.* 1.244–246, p. 364.8 Hagen

. . . formam referunt oceani, quem recte ζωστῆρα τοῦ
κόσμου dixerunt, et Cyrillus, cum ait: Ὠκεανός, ᾧ, κτλ.

Graeca ex ed. princ. dedit Keil: lacuna in codicibus

Versum cum duobus aliis ap. Strab. 2.3.5 sine auctoris
nomine citatis coniunxit Meineke:

    οὐ γάρ μιν δεσμὸς περιβάλλεται ἠπείροιο,
    ἀλλ᾽ ἐς ἀπειρεσίην κέχυται· τό μιν οὔτι μιαίνει.

Μοψοπίᾳ attrib. Powell

182 Herodian, περὶ μον. λεξ., *GG* III.2, p. 915.16 Lentz

Τὰ [sc. εἰς ω̄ν] περισπώμενα, εἰ λέγοιτο ἐν πλείοσι
συλλαβαῖς, διὰ τοῦ ō λέγεται . . . Εὐφορίων· "κακώτερε
Καλλικόωντος" [**117**], Ἱπποθόων,

    Εὔμολπος Δόλιχός τε καὶ Ἱπποθόων μεγάθυμος.

Euphorioni attrib. Meineke; Μοψοπίᾳ attrib. Sitzler ob
colorem nominum Atticum

Scholiast on Homer, *Iliad*

For < the Parian? > says: "Ocean, by which . . . "

Probus on Virgil, *Georgics*

. . . they compare with the shape of the ocean, which they have rightly called "girdle of the cosmos", and Cyril, when he says: "Ocean, by which . . ."

Meineke combined this line with two others cited anonymously by Strabo, 2.3.5:

> No bonds of continent encompass him;
> To infinity he stretches, and by nothing is defiled.

182 Herodian, *On unique word-formation*

Words that end in –*ōn* with a circumflex accent, if pronounced over more than one syllable, have an *o* . . . Euphorion: "(Thou) more base than Callicoon", Hippothoon,

> Eumolpus, Dolichus, and great-spirited
> Hippothoon.[204]

[204] Eumolpus and Dolichus were nobles and early priests of Eleusis (HHom. Dem. 154–155, 475). Hippothoon was eponymous hero of an Attic tribe, and may have had some Eleusinian connection too.

EUPHORION

183 P. Oxy. 2442, fr. 29, 1–8 (Σ Pind. *Pa.* VIII)

].[.].ἐκπεσόντος χρησμοῦ Ἐργίνωι στρατευομ(έν)ωι
ἐπὶ Θήβας ἑτέρου[· | λέγει] γ(ὰρ)· "ἀλλ' οὕτως τῶι
Ἐργίνωι ἔπεμψας χρησμοὺς τῶι ἐπὶ τὰς Θήβας [| ἑλ-
κ]υσαμένωι τὸ ξίφος", ἀν(τὶ) στρατεύσαντι· τὸ γ(ὰρ)
ἑλκόμ(εν)ον ἀν(τὶ) ἑλκ[υσ]άμ(εν)ον [εἴρηται. | καὶ τὸν
Κλύμ(εν)]ον ἀναιρεθῆ(ναί) [φ(ησιν) Εὐφορί]ων [suppl.
Fowler 1993] μ(ὲν) ὑπὸ Περιήρους, Ἑλλάνι(κος) δ[ὲ . . .
| . . . . ὑπ]ό τινος Καδ[μείων] κ[(ατ') Ὀ]γχηστὸν (?)
μαχόμ(εν)ον, Ἐπιμενίδη[ς] | δ' ἐν ε̄' Γε[νεαλογ]ιῶν ὑπὸ
Γλαύκου ἐρίσαντα τῶι ζεύγει τ·[| δύο δὲ πόλ]εμοι
ἐγένο(ντο), ὁ μ(ὲν) Κλυμένου ἀναιρεθέντο(ς), | ὁ δὲ τοὺς
ἐπὶ] δασμὸ(ν) π[(αρ)ό]ντ(ας) Ἡρακλέο(υς) ἀκρωτηρι-
ά[σαντος.

184 EtGen AB = EtMag 665.45

Περσεύς·

> τῶ μιν καὶ Περσῆα μετεκλήϊσσαν Ἀχαιοὶ
> οὕνεκεν ἄστεα πέρσεν ἀπειρεσίων ἀνθρώπων.

Ὦρος [om. EtGen B.]

1 τὸν μὲν EtMag: om. EtGen: corr. Hemsterhuys
2 πέρθεν EtMag: πέρθαι EtGen, corr. Meineke

---

205 The papyrus contains a scholium on Pindar, *Paean* VIII S.–
M. (B2 Rutherford), indicating that Pindar told the story of
Erginus (ps.-Apoll. 2.4.11, Paus. 9.37.2–4), father of the architects
of the archaic temple in Delphi. The essential is that Clymenus,

183 P. Oxy. 2442[205]

Another oracle was given to Erginus as he was making an expedition against Thebes. For he says, "But thus you sent oracles to Erginus, who had drawn the sword against Thebes", instead of "who had marched against"; "drawing" is used instead of "having drawn". Euphorion(?) says that Clymenus was killed by Perieres; Hellanicus, that he was killed by one of the Cadmeians as he was fighting in the vicinity of Onchestus(?); Epimenides, in book 60 of the *Genealogies*, that he was killed by Glaucus as he was competing in the chariot race . . . There were two wars, one when Clymenus was killed, the other when Heracles mutilated those who had come to fetch the tribute.[206]

184 Etymologicum Genuinum

Perseus:

> The Achaeans therefore named him Perseus [*lit.* "destroyer"],
> Because he razed the towns of countless men.[207]

king of the Minyans, was killed by a Theban or Thebans and charged his son Erginus to avenge him, which led to war between Erginus and Thebes. The scholiast gives three different versions of Clymenus' killing; according to ps.-Apoll., Perieres was charioteer of Menoeceus (father of Jocasta and Creon).

[206] As Fowler notes, Heracles mutilated Erginus' envoys, who were travelling to Thebes to collect the tribute for Clymenus' death, just after his killing of the lion of Cithaeron—an exploit which may have been mentioned by Euphorion in **19a** 17 (see n. ad loc.). [207] Meineke suggested the lines were Euphorion's. But the subject-matter overlaps with **19a** 43–44: either Euphorion repeated himself or these lines (which are again simpler in style than usual) are another's.

185 EtGen AB, α 790, ii. p. 26.8 L.–L.

ἀνὰ δρυμά·

σεῦ γὰρ † δι<***>
Εἰρήνη πολύβοια, καὶ ἀνδράσιν ἤπιος αἰών
πιλναμένης, καὶ θῆρες ἀνὰ δρυμὰ πρηΰνονται.

1 δία <δήμῳ> Bergk–Hiller: δῖα <θεάων> Powell: διὰ <βουλήν>
van Groningen   2 εἰρήνη, Πολύβοια, Wilamowitz 1924,
263 = 1962, 356, cf. Paus. 3.19.4

Ὑακίνθῳ attrib. Wilamowitz loc. cit.

186 Didymi de Demosthene commenta, in *Berliner Klassikertexte*, I., ed. H. Diels–W. Schubart (Berlin, 1904), col. 14, 3–18

λέγεται τοίνυν ὀργὰς κοινότερον μὲν ἅπαν χωρίον δεν-
δρῶδες οἷον ἄλσος . . . τὰς δ᾽ ὀργάδας ἄλματά τε καὶ
ἄλση προσηγόρευον ἀπὸ τῆς εἰς τὸ μῆκος ἄλσεως·

ἔνθα Τρώιον ἄλμα καὶ ἤρια Μουνίπποιο.

μυνειτοιο pap.: Μουνίπποιο Wilamowitz: Μουνίτοιο Ll.-J.–P.

187 Plut. *Mor.* 557 C–D

ἆρ᾽ οὖν οὐκ ἀτοπώτερος τούτων ὁ Ἀπόλλων, εἰ Φενεάτας
ἀπόλλυσι τοὺς νῦν, ἐμφράξας τὸ βάραθρον καὶ κατα-
κλύσας τὴν χώραν ἅπασαν αὐτῶν, ὅτι πρὸ χιλίων ἐτῶν,
ὥς φασιν, ὁ Ἡρακλῆς ἀνασπάσας τὸν τρίποδα τὸν μαν-

185 Etymologicum Genuinum

"In the thickets":

> Peace who multiplies oxen, and a gentle life for men
> When you prevail, and in the thickets beasts grow
>   tame.[208]

186 Didymus' commentary on Demosthenes

The more general meaning of *orgas* is any wooded place, such as a grove . . . they called such places "groves" (*almata* and *alsē*) from their "springing" (*halsis*) to a height:

> There is the grove of Troos and the tomb of
>   Munippus.[209]

187 Plutarch, *The Divine Vengeance*

Is not Apollo more absurd than this, if he brings ruin on the Pheneates of the present day by blocking up their channel and flooding their entire territory, because a thousand years ago (so they say) Heracles tore up the mantic

---

[208] The epithet of Peace recurs in **26** col. ii. 4, though that does not clinch the case for common authorship.

[209] The fragment was assigned to Euphorion by Wilamowitz, who restored a reference to Munippus the son of Cilla (cf. **79** and n. 107); the alternative restoration by Ll.-J.–P., to Munitus son of Laodice, might connect with **98**. But in either case the reference is glancing, not a narrative account. A grove of Ilus and the tomb of Cilla and Munippus are mentioned in Lyc. *Al.* 319–322 as the place where Laodice was swallowed by the earth (**97** and n. 126).

EUPHORION

τικὸν εἰς Φενεὸν ἀπήνεγκε, Συβαρίταις δὲ φράζων ἀπό-
λυσιν τῶν κακῶν, ὅταν τρισὶν ὀλέθροις ἱλάσωνται τὸ
μήνιμα τῆς Λευκαδίας Ἥρας; καὶ μὴν οὐ πολὺς χρόνος
ἀφ' οὗ Λοκροὶ πέμποντες εἰς Τροίαν πέπαυνται τὰς
παρθένους,

> αἳ καὶ ἀναμπέχονοι γυμνοῖς ποσὶν ἠύτε δοῦλαι
> ἠοῖαι σαίρεσκον Ἀθηναίης περὶ βωμόν,
> νόσφι κρηδέμνοιο, καὶ εἰ βαθὺ γῆρας ἱκάνοι,

διὰ τὴν Αἴαντος ἀκολασίαν.

Χιλιάσιν attrib. Toup

188 EtGen B s.v. τευμήσατο

παρεσκευάσατο, ἐτεχνήσατο·

> Κεκροπίης τευμήσατ' ἐπίσκυρος Εὐρύκλεια

ἐπίσκυρος δέ ἐστιν οἷον ἐπικυρῶτις, ἡγεμών. εἴρηται δὲ
τὸ τευμήσατο ὅτι τὸν Τευμησὸν τὸ ὄρος ὑπὸ τοῦ Διὸς
κατασκευασθέντα εἰς ἀπόκρυψιν τῆς Εὐρώπης, καὶ ἀπὸ
τούτου κληθῆναι Τευμησόν, ἀπὸ τοῦ κατεσκευάσθαι [cf.
Antim. fr. 3 Matthews].

tripod and carried it off to Pheneus; or, again, if he pro-
claims to the people of Sybaris relief from their troubles
after they have appeased the wrath of Leucadian Hera by
being destroyed three times over? Indeed, it is not such a
long time since the Locrians stopped sending maidens to
Troy

> Who, without cloaks, bare-foot, like slaves at dawn
> Swept all around the altar of Athena
> Unveiled, even to burdensome old age.

on account of Ajax's licentiousness.[210]

188 Etymologicum Genuinum

teumēsato: contrived, devised:

> The far-famed commander of the Cecropian land[211]
>   devised

episkūros means one who ratifies, a governor. *teumēsato*:
the etymology is that the mountain Teumesos, which was
fashioned by Zeus for the concealment of Europa, was
called Teumesos because it had been "fashioned".

---

[210] The story of the punishment of the Pheneates with its
thousand-year deferral would fit the *Chiliades*. That of the
Locrian women, who for a thousand years were sent from Locris
to Troy as a penalty for Oilean Ajax's rape of Cassandra, was told in
the first book of Callimachus' *Aitia* (fr. 35 Pf.). That poem of
course was elegiac, but these lines could be by an imitator.

[211] Probably meaning Athena.

411

EUPHORION

Fragmentum Euphorioni attrib., cum **145** sic coniunxit Hollis 1993:

> . . . γλαυκῶπιν ἐλαίην
> Κεκροπίης τευμήσατ᾽ ἐπίσκυρος Εὐρύκλεια

189 Plut. *Mor.* 682 B–C

τί δ᾽, ὦ πρὸς τοῦ Διός, ἐρεῖς περὶ τῶν ἑαυτοὺς κατα-
βασκαίνειν λεγομένων; καὶ γὰρ τοῦτ᾽ ἀκήκοας· εἰ δὲ μή,
πάντως ταῦτ᾽ ἀνέγνωκας·

> καλαὶ μέν ποτ᾽ ἔσαν, καλαὶ φόβαι Εὐτελίδαο·
> ἀλλ᾽ αὐτὸν βάσκαινεν ἰδὼν ὀλοφώιος ἀνὴρ
> δίνῃ ἐνὶ ποταμοῦ· τὸν δ᾽ αὐτίκα νοῦσος ἀεικής

ὁ γὰρ Εὐτελίδας λέγεται, καλὸς ἑαυτῷ φανεὶς καὶ παθών
τι πρὸς τὴν ὄψιν, ἐκ τούτου νοσῆσαι καὶ τὴν εὐεξίαν μετὰ
τῆς ὥρας ἀποβαλεῖν.

2 αὐτὸν codd., corr. Xylander   ἀποφώλιος Magnelli
3 διηέντι ποταμῷ codd., corr. Meineke: δίνῃ ἐν ποταμοῦ
Amyot, Stephanus: ἐν δίνῃ ποταμοῦ Turnebus: διηῆντι ποταμῷ
Meineke 1823: διῆντ᾽ ἐν ποταμῷ Powell   4 <ἔλλαβε>
Meineke

Ὑακίνθῳ attrib. Scheidweiler

The fragment was attributed to Euphorion, and combined with the previous one, by A. S. Hollis:

> The far-famed commander of the Cecropian land devised
> The grey-eyed olive.

189 Plutarch, *Table-Talk*

What, in heaven's name, will you say about those who are said to bewitch themselves? You must surely have heard of that; and if not, you must certainly have read the following lines:

> Fair, ah fair, were once the tresses of Eutelidas;
> But in a river's eddies that disastrous man
> Glimpsed, and bewitched, himself; forthwith an ugly
> plague . . .

For Eutelidas, according to the story, thought himself beautiful, and being smitten by his own image fell ill as a result so that he lost his health as well as his good looks.[212]

---

[212] This fragment, cited anonymously, was attributed to Euphorion by Valckenaer, and conjecturally assigned by Scheidweiler to the *Hyacinthus* on the grounds of its subject-matter. The language is, however, much less recherché than most Euphorion.

190 Julian, *Or.* 4. 149b (cf. Eustath. ad *Il.* 1.200, i. p. 132.27 van der Valk)

καὶ τοῦτο δὲ αὐτὸ Πρόνοιαν Ἀθηνᾶν λέγοντες οὐ καινοτομοῦμεν, εἴπερ ὀρθῶς ἀκούομεν·

ἵκετο δ᾽ ἐς Πυθῶνα καὶ ἐς Γλαυκῶπα Προνοίην.

Cum **4** coniungi posse monuit Meineke 1843, 401–2

191 P. Oxy. 2526

A fr. 1

— — — — —

    . .]ισιν υπ.[
    αὐτώρηστ.[
    δαιμονιον[
    Βοιωτωνε[
5   τοῖσιν ὅ γεκ[
    ἄνδιχα δεκ[
    ξυνὰ πέλει[
    .]ιτα τιτυσκ.[
    .].ῖα δ᾽ ἐσαντ[
10 .]υ[

— — — — —

1 το]ῖσιν ὑπο[vel –ε Lobel   5 ἐκ [τρίποδος, τριπόδων Ll.-J.–P.   8 ε]ῖτα Lobel: σ]ῖτα, λ]ιτὰ Ll.-J.–P.   τιτυσκο[, τιτυσκε[9 ῷια, τ]οῖα Ll.-J.–P

190 Julian, *Oration* 4 (*Hymn to King Helios*)

And when I use the very phrase "Athena Pronoia" (Athena Forethought) I am introducing no innovation, if I have rightly comprehended the line:

He came to Python and to grey-eyed Pronoia.[213]

191 P. Oxy. 2526 (= *SH* 433–452)[214]

A fr. 1

Speaking spontaneously	[2]
Miraculous	
Boeotian	
To them what, from [the tripod(?)	[5]
Asunder	
In common	
. . . brandish	
S]uch were(?)	

[213] A common confusion for Pronaia, epithet of Athena at Delphi.

[214] The case for Euphorion's authorship of these fragments is based on the equation of B fr. 3.11, where the Phlegyae are mentioned, with **105**. If **109–110** come from a commentary on the *Chiliades*, the two fragments are connected by the mention of Combe (**109** col. i. 3–4 / **191** B fr. 2.4). Compare also the vocabulary in B fr. 2.2 with **2**.4 and **19a** 36, B fr. 2.8 with **26** col. i. 23, B fr. 2.11 with **19a** 40, B fr. 3.5 with **70**.3; the "envoi" of B fr. 3.12–14 with **26** col. ii. 24–26 and **90** col. i. 12–13. The consecutive spondeiazones at B frr. 2.2–3 and 3.10–11, and the lengthening at B fr. 2.4, are also characteristic of Euphorion, though none of this amounts to proof.

415

A fr. 3

```
            — — — — —
            ]σα[
            ].απ[
            ]ος· οδε[
            ]φραδιω[
  5         ].ησεβ.[
            ].τεπι.[
            ]γαῖαν φ.[
            ]κεσοδο[
            ]θος ἐϋ[
  10   Λυκ]ώρειαν[
         μ]ελιηγ[ενέ—
            ]αι ἡγη[
            ].ατιζε[
            — — — — —
```

10 Λυκ]ώρειαν F. J. Williams: ἀκρ-, πρυμν-, ὑπ-, Ἀνεμ]ώρειαν
Lobel   11 suppl. Lobel (cf. Ap. Rhod. 4.1641)
13 φατιζε[Ll.-J.–P.

A fr. 7a

```
            — — — — —
            ]οτεροις ὑδ[
            ].οσσαμενη[
            ].εν στύξαι τ.[
            ]ουνόμον ἱ[
```

A fr. 3

Lyc]oreia[215]   [10]
ash-born[216]   [11]
dishonour (*or*, say?)   [13]

A fr. 7a

former men . . . call(?)   [1]
b]laming   [2]
to hate   [3]

[215] See **116**.3 and n. 167.
[216] An apparent reference to the men of Hesiod's Bronze Age (*Op*. 145).

5   ].[

— — — — —

1 πρ]οτέροις   2 ὁ]νοσσαμένη Lobel

A fr. 10

— — — — —

        ].α.[
      ].ιδεδ[..].[
     ]ων θέον ωμ[
     ]ραι δὲ θαλάσση[
5   ]ωι ἐνὶ Ῥήνῃ
-υ]γλαγέος κυτίσο[ιο
   ]έδρακε παπτ[
   ]αλεγουσα
   ']σ.[.]..ι ὕδωρ
10   ].αιησιν[
     ]..[.]ενν[
     ].ινα[
     ]ησεξ·
    ].γείην
15   ]μηλοισ[
    ].ντ[ ].[

— — — — —

6 ἐϋ] vel πολυ]γλαγέος Lobel   7 παπτ[αίνουσα vel sim.
Lobel   14]υγείην, fort.]τείην Ll.-J.–P.

418

A fr. 10

they were running   [3]
the sea
in Rhene[217]   [5]
marsh-grass, bountiful in milk
regarded, glanc[ing around
not heeding
water

[217] Rhenea, the small island adjoining Delos.

A fr. 12

– – – – –

```
        ]νι.[
      ]έην.[
     ]ενδεμ[
    ]σεασθ' ὑπο[
5   ]ῆισιν ἀνασ[
   ]μήριγγες ε.[
   '].σοιο· κελα[
   ]ωνησεϋ[
   ].ιῆισι[
```

– – – – –

6 μήριγγες (Hesych. μ 1255), σ]μήριγγες (Hesych. σ 1244–1245), βαθυ-, ἐϋσ]μήριγγες etc.   7 κελα[ιν- Ll.-J.–P.

A fr. 15

– – – – –

```
     ]..[        ]
     ].η.[      ].[
   ]ατο κυανοχαίτηι·
   ] Μυρμιδόνεσσιν
5  ]νισε Πηλεΐωνος
     ] εἴσατο κούρηι
     ]νίηθεν ἑταῖροι
   ]εσσεύοντο·
     ] ἔργα τε Χρύσης
```

A fr. 12

prickles (*or*, tresses) [6]

A fr. 15

with sable locks[218] [3]
for the Myrmidons
of the son of Peleus [5]
established for the maiden[219]
from Haemon]ia(?)[220] . . . . companions
sped
the works of Chryse[221]

[218] Poseidon; or the epithet of a missing noun.
[219] Or, the Maiden, i.e. Persephone?
[220] Ancient name of Thessaly, home of the Myrmidons (l. 4),
or perhaps in the context of Jason and the Argonauts.
[221] Numerous possibilities, for example the deity of the north-
east Aegean whose snake wounded Philoctetes, thus suggesting a
connection with Euphorion's poem of that name.

EUPHORION

10   ]ς·

— — — —

7 Αἰμο]νίηθεν Lobel

B fr. 2

```
            ] ᾿Αονίο[ι]ο περαίης
            ] κροκάλαις ὕπο κυμανθεῖσα
            ]σανήλυθε Ληλάντοιο·
            ].ο πόλ[ι]ν ἀλιτειχέα Κόμβης·
5       μέ]λαν περιτέτροφε φῦκος
            ]ς, νοτερὴ δ᾿ ἀνεκήκιεν ἅλμη
                ]ς βρεκτῶν τε κομάων·
        π]ολυνείκεος αἰθύσσῃσιν
        θα]λασσογενῆ Διο[ν]ύσου·
10      ]αταριγηλὰ βεβή[
            ].ατηισ[ι
                ].κρα[
                ]άν[
```

— — — —

1 in mg. dextr. Βοι[ωτίου manus altera   3 in mg. dextr.
Λήλαντον· (ἔστι) δ(ὲ) ὄρος κ(αὶ) πόλ(ις) manus altera
8 in mg. dextr. ¹προ[, ²γυ[manus altera   10 βεβή[λοις
Ll.-J.–P.   11 supra τηισ[addidit ·δες[ ] manus altera, unde
δε]κάτηισ[ι varia cum lectione vel glossa δεκάδεσσι [cf. **19a** 40]
Lobel

B fr. 2[222]

the opposite shore of the Aonian . . .[223]
tossed by the waves by the pebbly shore
went up from(?) the Lelantine plain
the city of Combe,[224] walled by the sea
black seaweed clotted all around   [5]
and the damp brine came oozing out
    and from the soaked hair
of the strife-ridden[225] . . . sets in rapid motion
sea-born . . . of Dionysus
to make the profane shudder(?)   [10]
in compa]nies of ten

[222] The fragment seems to refer to a corpse, drowned in the strait between Boeotia and Euboea and washed up near Chalcis. The subject would be female (Ino, step-mother of Dionysus?) if the feminine participle in line 2 agreed with it; but it may agree with, say, a word for "brine".

[223] Ambiguous: the coast of Boeotia (Aonia) opposite Euboea, or *vice versa*.

[224] Chalcis, birthplace of Euphorion; Steph. Byz. p. 683.11 Mein. reports that she was equated with the town's eponym.

[225] Possibly an attempt to conjure an epithet out of the proper name Polynices, parallel to the word-games in **123**.

B fr. 3

— — — —

].ε..[

] εὐθυδίκοισι πο[

]ν· τοῖοι μιν ἐκαρτυ[ν

]Ἀρισταίοιο θεοφροσ[ύνη]ς ἀλεγο[

5   ]ε διψαλέωι Κυνὶ κάρφεται ἡμερὶς [ὕ]λη[

]ων καὶ γούνατ' ἀναρδέα σειραίνονται,

]α φράζονται καματώδεος ἀστέρα Μαίρη[ς

].αι· δὴ γάρ.[.]το [σί]νεται ἠδ' ὀνίνησιν·

εὖ φρασθ]εὶς ὀνίη[σιν, ἐσίνα]το δ' εὖτε λάθηισι.

10   ]ναμφότερα̣[   ]ιος ἱλήκοιτε

] Φλεγύηισι σὺν ἀνδράσιν εὐνηθε[ῖ]σα·

].οι καὶ ἔπειτα φίλε μνησαίμεθ' ἀο̣ιδέ,

] παρπεπιθόντες, ὅ σοι χαριτήσιον εἴη

] μειλιχίης, ἧς ἂν πέρι .μ[.].αφαιη.

3 e.g. ἐκαρτύ[ναντο Lobel   4 e.g. ἀλέγο[ντες Lobel
5 ὁππότ]ε van Groningen   6 αἰζη]ῶν vel ἠθέ]ων Lobel
7 αὐτίκ]α, τηνίκ]α Lobel   8 σ[ε] τὸ Lobel   9 init.
suppl. Ll.-J.–P.   fin. suppl. Lobel   12 τῶν ἤ]τοι
Lobel: τῆς δ' ἤ]τοι van Groningen: σοῦ δ' ἤ]τοι Ll.-J.–P.
13 Φοῖβον] Ll.-J.–P.   14 ἧς ἂν πέρι [[.]] μ[υρ]ία φαίην
dub. Lobel

---

226 Ap. Rhod. 2.516–527 and Call. fr. 75.33–37 Pf. relate how
Aristaeus founded a line of priests on Ceos who sacrificed at the
rising of Sirius, the Dog-Star, and propitiated its ill-effects.

B fr. 3

for those who keep straight justice [2]
such people gave him succour
heeding the divinatory skills of Aristaeus[226]
[when] the cultivated tree is parched by the [5]
    thirsty Dog-Star
and the limbs [of young men], deprived of water,
    are parched dry,[227]
they observe the star of wearisome Maira[228]
for that brings [you] both harm and benefit:
benefit when clear to view, harm when obscured.[229]
both . . . be propitious [10]
laid to rest with the Phlegyaean men;[230]
May we remember hereafter, dear singer,[231]
Prevailing upon . . . , as a gift to repay you
for your kindness, about which . . . . could tell

---

[227] Recalling the description of the effects of the Dog-Star in Hesiod, *Op.* 587–588.

[228] "They" could be the priests or the Ceans in general. Maira is also the name of the Dog-Star in Call. fr. 75.35 Pf.

[229] Illuminated by Heraclides Ponticus fr. 141 Wehrli: the Ceans drew conclusions about the weather of the coming year from the visibility or otherwise of the Dog Star at its rising.

[230] See **105** and n. 134 for the impiety and punishment of the Phlegyae. If this myth carries back into line 10 (which is not certain), Ll.-J.–P. suggest that the subject of "be propitious" could be the punishing deities (named by Nonnus as Zeus and Apollo), and that "both" could refer to these gods, or to the two women spared for their piety when the rest of their countrymen were punished.

[231] Perhaps the poet hails his source (cf. Call. fr. 75.53–77 Pf.); or perhaps the Muses address the poet.

192 P. Lugd. Bat. 25.1 (ed. R. W. Daniel, in F. A. J. Hoogendijk and P. van Minnen, *Papyri, Ostraca, Parchments and Waxed Tablets in the Leiden Papyrological Institute (P. L. Bat. 25)* (Leiden et al., 1991), 1–2)

— — — — — — — —

```
      ]..ιθα[..]...[...]..
      ] ιρους Ἱππ[ομ]έδοντ[.].
              ]..[.].ραστειν
              ]...[.]δωμεν
  5           ].εριτασ...
          ]...σον ἑκὸν ῥως
      ].... βόσκει
          ]..μεναι ἀνέβαινον
          ]..πλει ἁμαξῶν
 10       ].σιν ἅμα πάντες
          ].ουντες
      ]...ς ὅτι μικρας
              ].εσθουσιν
              ]...ανγα
 15           ]...ζ.
              ]....[
```

— — — —

2 ἑτα]ίρους(?) Ἱππ[ομ]έδοντ[ο]ς, Ἱππ[ομ]έδοντ[ι] ed.
3]φι[λ]εραστεῖν? ed.   4 ἀε[ί]δωμεν? Ed.
8 [cantantes "'Ὑμὴ]ν 'Ὑμέναι'" ἀνέβαινον ed.
12 μικρᾶς vel μικράς

192 P. Lugd. Bat. 25.1

compa]nions of(?) Hippomedon[232]   [2]
strength(?)   [6]
feeds
[singing "Hyme]n Hymenaie" they came up
of chariots
all together   [10]
small   [12]

---

[232] See **32–34**? The name, the metrical lengthening in 10 and perhaps 12, and the monosyllabic *hapax* in 6 (cf. **5**, **6**.2, **19a** 17, **147**), all suggest Euphorion as possible author of this fragment.

FRAGMENTA PROSAE
ORATIONIS

193–203 FRAGMENTA
CERTIS LIBRIS TRIBUTA

Ἱστορικὰ ὑπομνήματα

193 Aelian, *NA* 17.28

Εὐφορίων δὲ ἐν τοῖς Ὑπομνήμασι λέγει τὴν Σάμον ἐν
τοῖς παλαιτάτοις χρόνοις ἐρήμην γενέσθαι· φανῆναι
γὰρ ἐν αὐτῇ θηρία μεγέθει μὲν μέγιστα, ἄγρια δέ, καὶ
προσπελάσαι τῳ δεινά, καλεῖσθαί γε μὴν νηάδας.
ἅπερ οὖν καὶ μόνῃ τῇ βοῇ ῥηγνύναι τὴν γῆν. παροι-
μίαν οὖν ἐν τῇ Σάμῳ διαρρεῖν τὴν λέγουσαν "μεῖζον
βοᾷ τῶν νηάδων." ὀστᾶ δὲ ἔτι καὶ νῦν αὐτῶν δείκνυ-
σθαι μεγάλα ὁ αὐτός φησι.

194 Athen. *Deipn.* 4.154 c

Εὐφορίων δ' ὁ Χαλκιδεὺς ἐν ἱστορικοῖς ὑπομνήμασιν
οὕτω γράφει· "παρὰ δὲ τοῖς Ῥωμαίοις προτίθεσθαι
πέντε μνᾶς τοῖς ὑπομένειν βουλομένοις τὴν κεφαλὴν
ἀποκοπῆναι πελέκει, ὥστε τοὺς κληρονόμους κομίσα-
σθαι τὸ ἆθλον· καὶ πολλάκις ἀπογραφομένους πλεί-

PROSE FRAGMENTS

193–203 FRAGMENTS OF
KNOWN LOCATION

Historical Commentaries
193 Aelian, *On the Nature of Animals*

In his *Commentaries*, Euphorion says that in the remotest past Samos was uninhabited. For there had appeared in it wild beasts that were enormous in bulk and of such savagery that it was dangerous for anyone to approach them. They were called *nēades*, and were able to create fissures in the earth through their cries alone. As a result there is in Samos a proverb that runs: "He shouts louder than the *nēades*." The same writer reports that even now their bones can be seen, and they are very large.[1]

194 Athenaeus, *Deipnosophistae*

In his *Historical Commentaries*, Euphorion of Chalcis writes as follows: "Among the Romans, five minae are offered to anyone willing to have his head cut off with an axe, provided that the heirs get the prize. Often several people

---

[1] This report was perhaps drawn from Aristotle (fr. 611.30 Rose). It aims to explain the gashes in the earth caused by mining in Samos by means of the remains of prehistoric animals.

ους δικαιολογεῖσθαι καθ᾿ ὃ δικαιότατός ἐστιν ἕκαστος
αὐτῶν ἀποτυμπανισθῆναι."

195 Athen. *Deipn.* 15.700 D

Εὐφορίων δ᾿ ἐν Ἱστορικοῖς Ὑπομνήμασιν Διονύσιόν
φησι τὸν νεώτερον Σικελίας τύραννον Ταραντίνοις εἰς
τὸ πρυτανεῖον ἀναθεῖναι λυχνεῖον δυνάμενον καίειν
τοσούτους λύχνους ὅσος ὁ τῶν ἡμερῶν ἐστιν ἀριθμὸς
εἰς τὸν ἐνιαυτόν.

Λέξις Ἱπποκράτους

Test.: Erotian, *Vocum Hippocraticarum Collectio*, 32, p.
5.14 Nachmanson

τῶν δὲ γραμματικῶν οὐκ ἔστιν ὅστις ἐλλόγιμος φα-
νεὶς παρῆλθε τὸν ἄνδρα. καὶ γὰρ ὁ ἀναδεξάμενος
αὐτὸν Εὐφορίων πᾶσαν ἐσπούδασε λέξιν ἐξηγήσα-
σθαι διὰ βιβλίων ϛ´, περὶ ὧν γεγράφασιν Ἀριστο-
κλῆς καὶ Ἀριστέας οἱ Ῥόδιοι.

196 Erotian, ibid. β 8, p. 28.10 Nachmanson

βλιχῶδες· οἱ δὲ γλισχρῶδες. Ἐπικλῆς μέν φησι τὸ
λελιπασμένον μετὰ γλοιώδους ὑγρασίας ἀκαθάρτου,
Εὐφορίων δὲ τὸ ἐκπεπιεσμένον καὶ κατάξηρον.

197 Erotian, ibid. fr. 29, p. 107.11 Nachmanson

γογγρῶναι· οἱ μὲν τὰ ἐν τῷ τραχήλῳ γινόμενα παρα-

sign themselves down and then altercate over which of
them is most worthy of going to the block."

195 Athenaeus, *Deipnosophistae*

In his *Historical Commentaries*, Euphorion says that Dio-
nysius the younger, tyrant of Sicily, dedicated a lamp-stand
in the town-hall of the Tarentines that was capable of hold-
ing as many burning lamps as there are days in the year.[2]

Hippocratic Lexicon

Testimonium: Erotian, *Hippocratic Glossary*

Among grammarians, there is not a single one of any dis-
tinction who failed to engage with him [sc. Hippocrates].
For Euphorion, the man who took him up, went to some
pains to explain every word in need of glossing in six books,
concerning which the Rhodians Aristocles and Aristeas
have written.

196 Erotian, ibid.

blīchōdes: some say it means glutinous. Epicles defines it
as a fatty deposit with an impure, oily liquid, Euphorion as
something pressed-out and dry.

197 Erotian, ibid.

gongrōnai: some define them as oblong swellings that oc-

---

[2] Dionysius II (reigned 367–357 and 347–344). The town hall
was home of the public hearth, symbolic centre of the community;
it was presumably here that the famous lamp-stand was dedicated.

431

μήκη ἐπάρματα, οἱ δὲ τὰς βρογχοκήλας, ἄλλοι δὲ τὰς
γαγγραίνας. ὁ δὲ Εὐφορίων τὰς χοιράδας οἴεται κα-
λεῖσθαι. εἴρηται γάρ, φησί, παρὰ τὸν γόγγρον, ὅς
ἐστιν ἰχθὺς περιφερὴς καὶ ἐπιμήκης. Θεόφραστος δὲ
ἐν τοῖς Φυτικοῖς γόγγρους φησὶν εἶναι τὰς ὀζώδεις
ἐκφύσεις τῆς ἐλαίας. ἔστι δὲ ἰχθὺς θαλάττιος, ὡς
εἰρήκαμεν, ὁ γόγγρος.

Περὶ Ἀλευαδῶν

198 Clem. Al. *Strom.* 1.21.117.9

Εὐφορίων δὲ ἐν τῷ περὶ Ἀλευαδῶν κατὰ Γύγην αὐτὸν
τίθησι γεγονέναι, ὃς βασιλεύειν ἤρξατο ἀπὸ τῆς
ὀκτωκαιδεκάτης Ὀλυμπιάδος [708–704], ὃν καί φησι
πρῶτον ὠνομάσθαι τύραννον.

199 Σ Theocr. *Id.* 16.34/35a, p. 327.8 Wendel

τὰ δὲ περὶ Ἀλεύαν τὸν Σίμου πάντα ἀνείλεκται Εὐ-
φορίων.

Σιμίου codd., corr. Meineke

200 Quintilian, *Inst. Or.* 11.2.14

est autem magna inter auctores dissensio . . . Pharsali fue-
rit haec domus, ut ipse quodam loco significare Simonides
videtur utque Apollodorus et Eratosthenes et Eupho-

---

3 Euphorion here seems to have followed Theopompus
(*FGrH* 115 F 205), whose is the lowest known ancient dating of

cur on the neck, others as tumours in the throat, others again as gangrene. Euphorion thinks that the word designates scrofulous swellings in the glands of the neck; for it derives, according to him, from the *gongros*, which is a long, round fish. Theophrastus in his work on plants says that *gongrous* are the knotted excrescences of the olive tree. As I have already said, the *gongros* is a sea fish.

On the Aleuadae

198 Clement of Alexandria, *Stromateis*

In his work on the Aleuadae, Euphorion places him (sc. Homer) at around the time of Gyges, whose reign commenced in the eighteenth Olympiad, and who he says was the first to be given the name of tyrant.[3]

199 Scholiast on Theocritus, *Idylls*

All the material on Aleuas son of Simus has been assembled by Euphorion.[4]

200 Quintilian, *The Orator's Education*

There is a great difference of opinion among the various authors . . . as to whether the house was at Pharsalus, as Simonides himself seems to indicate somewhere or other, and as Apollodorus, Eratosthenes, Euphorion, and Eu-

Homer: he derived a *terminus post quem* by identifying the Cimmerians of *Od.* 11.14–19 with those who invaded Asia Minor during the reign of Gyges. Euphorion uses, or coincides, with Theopompus again in **41b**. Presumably he mentioned Gyges, king of the Lydians, in connection with the early history of the Aleuadae, dynasts of Thessaly.

[4] Simus was an erstwhile ally of Philip II of Macedon.

rion et Larissaeus Eurypylus tradiderunt, an Crannone, ut
Apollas Callimachusque.

Apollas Cal(l)imachus *codd.*, *corr. Schneidewin*

Περὶ Ἰσθμίων

201

(a) Athen. *Deipn.* 4.182 E–F

Εὐφορίων δὲ ὁ ἐποποιὸς ἐν τῷ περὶ Ἰσθμίων, "οἱ νῦν",
φησίν, "καλούμενοι ναβλισταὶ καὶ πανδουρισταὶ καὶ
σαμβυκισταὶ καινῷ μὲν οὐδενὶ χρῶνται ὀργάνῳ. τὸν
γὰρ βάρωμον καὶ βάρβιτον, ὧν Σαπφὼ [fr. 176] καὶ
Ἀνακρέων [PMG 472] μνημονεύουσι, καὶ τὴν μάγαδιν
καὶ τὰ τρίγωνα καὶ τὰς σαμβύκας ἀρχαῖα εἶναι. ἐν
γοῦν Μιτυλήνῃ μίαν τῶν Μουσῶν πεποιῆσθαι ὑπὸ
Λεσβοθέμιδος ἔχουσαν σαμβύκην."

(b) op. cit. 14.635 A

Εὐφορίων δὲ ἐν τῷ περὶ Ἰσθμίων παλαιὸν μέν φησι τὸ
ὄργανον εἶναι τὴν μάγαδιν, μετασκευασθῆναι δ' ὀψέ
ποτε καὶ σαμβύκην μετονομασθῆναι. πλεῖστον δ' εἶ-
ναι τοῦτο τὸ ὄργανον ἐν Μιτυλήνῃ, ὡς καὶ μίαν τῶν
Μουσῶν ἔχουσαν αὐτὸ ὑπὸ Λεσβοθέμιδος ποιηθῆναι
ἀρχαίου ἀγαλματοποιοῦ.

rypylus of Larissa have reported, or at Crannon, according to Apollas and Callimachus.[5]

On the Isthmian Games

201

(a) Athenaeus, *Deipnosophistae*

Euphorion the hexameter poet says in his work on the Isthmian games that the modern instrumentalists called *nablas*-players and *pandoura*-players and *sambūkē*-players are not playing a new instrument. For he says that the *barōmos* and *barbitos*, which Sappho and Anacreon mention, and the *magadis* and *trigōna* and the *sambūkai*, are ancient; and in fact that in Mitylene one of the Muses was portrayed by Lesbothemis as holding a *sambūkē*.

(b) op. cit.

Euphorion in his work on the Isthmian games says that the *magadis* is an ancient instrument, but that at a later date it was modified and renamed the *sambūkē*. This instrument was very popular in Mitylene, to such an extent that Lesbothemis, an ancient sculptor, portrayed one of the Muses holding it.

[5] The house whose dining-hall famously collapsed while Simonides was dining with his patrons, sparing only the poet himself (Cic. *de Or.* 2.352–353). As Meineke saw, the relationship between the Scopadae and the Aleuadae suggest a context in the work on the latter.

EUPHORION

(c) op. cit. 14.635 F

Εὐφορίων τε ἐν τῷ περὶ Ἰσθμίων τὰ πολύχορδά φησι τῶν ὀργάνων ὀνόμασι μόνον παρηλλάχθαι, παμπάλαιον δ' αὐτῶν εἶναι τὴν χρῆσιν.

202 op. cit. 14.633 F

περὶ σαμβύκης ἔφη ὁ Μασσούριος ὀξύφθογγον εἶναι μουσικὸν ὄργανον τὴν σαμβύκην διειλέχθαι τε περὶ αὐτοῦ Εὐφορίωνα τὸν ἐποποιὸν ἐν τῷ περὶ Ἰσθμίων, χρῆσθαι φήσας αὐτῷ Πάρθους καὶ Τρωγλοδύτας τετραχόρδῳ ὄντι· ἱστορεῖν δὲ τοῦτο Πυθαγόραν ἐν τῷ περὶ τῆς Ἐρυθρᾶς Θαλάσσης.

Περὶ Μελοποιῶν

203 op. cit. 4.184 A

Εὐφορίων δ' ὁ ἐποποιὸς ἐν τῷ περὶ μελοποιῶν τὴν μὲν μονοκάλαμον σύριγγα Ἑρμῆν εὑρεῖν, τινὰς δ' ἱστορεῖν Σεύθην καὶ Ῥωνάκην τοὺς Μαιδούς, τὴν δὲ πολυκάλαμον Σιληνόν, Μαρσύαν δὲ τὴν κηρόδετον.

τοὺς μήδους A, corr. Schweighäuser

436

(c) op. cit.

Euphorion in his work on the Isthmian games says that stringed instruments have only changed their names, but that their mode of use is very ancient.

202 op. cit.

Concerning the *sambūkē*, Massurius said that it was a musical instrument with a high pitch, and that Euphorion the hexameter poet discussed it in his work on the Isthmian games; he said, too, that the Parthians and Troglodytes used it and that it had four strings. This last detail, he said, was reported by Pythagoras in his work on the Red Sea.

On Lyric Poets

203 op. cit.

Euphorion the hexameter poet in his work on lyric poets reports that it was Hermes who discovered the pan-pipe with a single reed, though others attribute it to Seuthes and Rhonaces, who were Maidi;[6] Silenus, the version with multiple reeds; and Marsyas, the version bound together with wax.

---

[6] A people of Thrace, though these two figures are unknown.

204–207 FRAGMENTA
INCERTAE SEDIS

204 op. cit. 2.44 F–2.45 A

Εὐφορίων δὲ ὁ Χαλκιδεὺς οὕτω που γράφει· "Λασύρτας ‹ὁ› Λασιώνιος οὐδὲν προσεδεῖτο ποτοῦ καθάπερ οἱ ἄλλοι, οὖρον δὲ προίετο καθάπερ πάντες ἄνθρωποι. καὶ πολλοὶ διὰ φιλοτιμίαν ἐπεχείρησαν παρατηρῆσαι καὶ ἀπέστησαν πρὸ τοῦ εὑρεῖν τὸ πραττόμενον. θέρους γὰρ ὥρᾳ καὶ τριακονθήμερον προσεδρεύοντες καὶ οὐδενὸς μὲν ὁρῶντες ἀπεχόμενον ἁλμυροῦ, τὴν κύστιν δ' αὑτοῦ ἔχοντα [αὐτὸν εὖ ἔχοντα Cramer: εὔλυτον ἔχοντα Wilamowitz: αὑτοῦ ‹οὖρον› ἔχοντα van Groningen] συνεπείσθησαν ἀληθεύειν. ἐχρῆτο δὲ καὶ τῷ ποτῷ, ἀλλ' οὐδὲν ἧττον οὐ προσεδεῖτο τούτου."

205 Helladius, ap. Photius, *Bibl.* 279, p. 533 A 29

ὅτι ὁ Εὐφορίων, φησίν, ἱστορεῖ τινα ἐνύπνια μηδέποτε ἑωρακέναι.

206 Σ Aesch. *Pers.* 660 sqq., p. 190 Dähnhardt

βαλλὴν βαρβαρικῶς ὁ βασιλεὺς λέγεται. Εὐφορίων δέ φησι Θουρίων εἶναι τὴν διάλεκτον.

Φρυγίων Meineke, cf. Sext. Empir. *Adv. Math.* 1.313, Hesych. β 154: Τυρίων Huschk

204–207 FRAGMENTS OF
UNCERTAIN LOCATION

204 op. cit.

Euphorion of Chalcis writes as follows: Lasyrtas of Lasion had no need of drink like other people, although he produced urine like all mankind. Many were spurred on to keep watch over him, but always went away before they were able to discover him performing the action in question. They would sit beside him in summer for thirty days at a time, during which they could see that he abstained from no salty foods, and that his bladder was in perfect working order(?); so they became convinced that he was speaking the truth. Indeed, he did drink; but nonetheless he was not positively in need of it.

205 Helladius, ap. Photius, *Library*

He mentions Euphorion as reporting that a certain individual had never had a dream.

206 Scholiast on Aeschylus, *Persae*

Ballēn is a non-Greek word for "king". Euphorion says that it is a dialect-word from (?)Thurii.

EUPHORION

207 Diog. Laert. 3.37

Εὐφορίων δὲ καὶ Παναίτιος [fr. 130 van Straaten] εἰρήκασι πολλάκις ἐστραμμένην εὑρῆσθαι τὴν ἀρχὴν τῆς Πολιτείας [sc. τοῦ Πλάτωνος].

208–210 SPURIA

208 Σ Ap. Rhod. 2.351–352a, p. 155.10 Wendel

τὴν δὲ Μαριανδυνῶν ⟨γῆν⟩ σὺν Γνησιόχῳ τῷ Μεγαρεῖ Βοιωτοὶ κατέσχον, ὡς Εὐφορίων ἱστορεῖ.

Εὐφορίων lectio codicum, quam defendit Meineke 1843, 151 (de Mariandynis cf. **76**): Ἔφορος M. Marx, *Eph. Cum.* 1815, 6 [*FGrH* 70 F 44 b, cf. F 44 a]

209 Tzetzes ad Lyc. *Al.* 911, p. 294.10 Scheer

Φιλοκτήτης δὲ ἐξώσθη εἰς Ἰταλίαν πρὸς Καμπανοὺς καὶ πολεμήσας αὐτοὺς πλησίον Κρότωνος καὶ †θορυκίνου Κρίμισσαν κατοικεῖ καὶ παυθεὶς τῆς ἄλης Ἀλαίου Ἀπόλλωνος ἱερὸν κτίζει, †οῦ καὶ τὸ τόξον αὐτῷ ἀνέθετο, ὥς φησιν Εὐφορίων.

Εὐφορίων Par. gr. 2723; Ὠρίων codd. alterius generis

PROSE FRAGMENTS

207 Diogenes Laertius

Euphorion and Panaetius have reported that the beginning of [Plato's] *Republic* was discovered with the words in numerous different arrangements.[7]

208–210 SPURIOUS CITATIONS

208 Scholiast on Apollonius of Rhodes, *Argonautica*

The Boeotians occupied the land of the Mariandynoi with the aid of Gnesiochus of Megara, as Euphorion reports.

209 Tzetzes on Lycophron, *Alexandra*

Philoctetes was driven out in the direction of Italy, where he came to the country of the Campanians; and after doing battle with them near Croton and . . . he founded a settlement at Crimissa. And being now at the end of his wanderings he founded a temple of Alaios Apollo, where he also dedicated his bow to the god, as Euphorion says.[8]

---

[7] The story illustrates the care Plato is supposed to have taken over the rhythm of his prose.

[8] Also mentioned by Lyc. *Al.* 920. Meineke conjectured that he might also have mentioned Philoctetes' foundation of the temple of Eilenian Athena (EtMag 298.27).

de auctore, cf. EtGen B, α 405, i. p. 259.11 L.–L.

Ἀλαῖος· ‹ὁ Ἀπόλλων·› Φιλοκτήτης γὰρ παραγενάμε-
νος εἰς Ἰταλίαν ἀπὸ τοῦ συμβεβηκότος ἱδρύσατο
Ἀπόλλωνος Ἀλαίου ἱερόν, ἐν ᾧ καὶ τὸ τόξον ἀπέθετο.
οὕτως Ὧρος.

Ὧρ B; cf. EtSym. 472, ubi οὕτως Ὧρος; EtMag 58.6, ubi οὕτως
Ὠρίων Va

de grammatico Oro haec omnia defluxisse ostendit Gian-
giulio 1993.

210 Varro, *De Re Rust.* 1.1.9

de reliquis, quorum quae fuerit patria non accepi, sunt . . .
Euphiton, Euphorion, Eubulus . . .

cf. Etymologicum Genuinum

Alaios: Apollo. On arrival in Italy, Philoctetes established a temple of Apollo named *Alaios* after what had happened to him, in which he dedicated his bow. Thus Oros.

210 Varro, *Agricultural Topics*

Among the rest, whose place of origin has not come down to me, there are . . . Euphiton, Euphorion, Eubulus . . . [9]

[9] Varro is listing writers on agricultural topics, but since "Euphorion" occurs in the list of those whose place of origin he does not know, it seems unlikely that he has in mind the well-known poet of Chalcis.

COMPARATIVE NUMERATION

I. CONVERSION OF OTHER EDITIONS TO THIS EDITION

Table to be read as follows: fr. 1 Meineke = fr. 3 Lightfoot; fr. 2 Scheidweiler = fr. 4 + 190 Lightfoot, etc.

	Meineke	Scheidweiler	Powell	van Groningen	de Cuenca	Supplementum Hellenisticum
1	3	3	3	1	3	
2	4	4 + 190	4 + 190	2	4 + 190	
3	5	5	5	3	5	
4	6	9	6	4 + 190	6	
5	8	6	7	5	9	
6	10	8	8	6	8	
7	12	7	9	9	7	
8	179	10	10	7	10	
9	13	12	11	8	11	
10	15c	179	12	10	12	
11	18	13	179	11	179	
12	17	14	13	12	13	

	Meineke	Scheidweiler	Powell	van Groningen	de Cuenca	Supplementum Hellenisticum
13	16	15a–b–c	14	13	14	
14	15a	16	15a–b–c	14	15a–b–c	
15	14	17	16	15a–b–c	16	
16	19a 40–41 + 184	18	17	16	17	
17	32	19a 40–41	18	17	18	
18	33	21	19a 40–41	18	19a 40–41	
19	27	20	20	19a–b, 51, 178	19a 44	
20	cf. 24.4(P) ff.	22	21	21	107	
21	cf. 26 i. 12 ff.	27	22	121	161	
22	30 + 31	cf. 24.4(?) ff.	23b	22	19a + b, 51, 178	
23	194	cf. 26 i. 12 ff.	27	23	20	
24	35 + 195	28	28	24–26	21	
25	193	29	29	27	22	
26	196	31	cf. 24.4(P) ff.	28	ante 23 (Test.)	
27	37 + 38a–b	30	cf. 26 i. 12 ff.	29	23	
28	41a–b–c	32	30	30	163	
29	198	33	31	31	130	
30	199	35	32	32	114	
31	200	36	33	33	27	

32	201a–b–c + 202	37	35	34	28
33	203	40	36	35	29
34	42	38a–b	37	36	30
35	43	41a–b–c	38a–b + 182	37	31
36	44	42	40	39a	cf. 24.4(?) ff.
37	47	43	41a–b–c	39b	cf. 26 i. 12 ff.
38	45	44	42	38a–b	24, 25, 26
39	48	45	43	40	32
40	209	46	44	41c	33
41	49	47	45	41a	34
42	50	48	46	42	88
43	51.3	209	47	43	35
44	52	49	48	44	194
45	119	50	209	45	195
46	100	51.3	49	46	193
47	107	52	50	47	204
48	56	193	51.3	48	36
49	158	194	52	209	196
50	103	195	70	49	197
51	100	196	71	50	37
52	101	197	72	51.3	38a–b
53	116	198	187	52	40
54	70	199	78	54	39a

	Meineke	Scheidweiler	Powell	van Groningen	de Cuenca	Supplementum Hellenisticum
55	98	200	79	53	39b	
56	81	201a–b–c	80	70	41a–b–c + Test.	
57	22	202	81	71	75	
58	78	203	98	72	76	
59	90.2–3	70	83	78	198	
60	71.11 + 137	169	84	79	199	
61	86	72	92	80	200	
62	120	71	88	81	201a–b–c	
63	128	187	90.2–3	98	202	
64	129	78	91	83	203	
65	114	79	157	84	42	
66	163	80	89	92	43	
67	19a 44	81	87	88	44	
68	160	98	93	90	47	
69	36	83	94	91	45	
70	156	84	95	157	46	
71	161	92	96	89	180	
72	127	88	97	87	74a–b	
73	76	90.2–3	99	93	48	
74	61	91	73	94	209	

75	89	157	180	95	49
76	131	89	74a–b	96	50
77	91	87	75	97	51.3
78	136	93	76	99	52
79	62	94	77	73	187
80	83	95	116	180	70
81	85	96	115	74a–b	71
82	72	97	117	75	169
83	99	99	118	76	72
84	104	148	107	77	78
85	180	73	161	116	79
86	77	180	19a 44	115	186
87	63	74a–b	163	117	98
88	108 col. ii. 48	75	130	118	97
89	162	76	114	107	80
90	46	208	86	161	81
91	124	77	85	163	83
92	159	116	100	130	84
93	125	115	136	114	92
94	73	172	101	86	90
95	123	11	162	85	91
96	132	117	158	100	157
97	134	118	102	136	89

	Meineke	Scheidweiler	Powell	van Groningen	de Cuenca	Supplementum Hellenisticum
98	115	107	103	101	87	
99	133	161	58	162	93	
100	157	19a 44	112	158	94	
101	135	23	65	102	95	
102	126	163	68	103	96	
103	122	130	66	58	99	
104	75	114	67	112	148, 152	
105	147	86	69	65	73	
106	121	85	82	66	77	
107	92	100	56	67	116	
108	65	136	59	68	115	
109	66 + 151	101	60	69	172	
110	205	162	61	82	117	
111	152 + 148	177	62	56	118	
112	139	176	63	59	86	
113	142	158	64	60	85	
114	170	102	104	61	100	
115	167	103	105	62	136	
116	165	164	106	63	101	
117	173	58	113	64	162	

118	177	112	120	104	177
119	174	68	156	105	176
120	93	65	159	106	158
121	204	66	160	113	102
122	20	67	181	120	103
123	113	69	121	156	164
124	207	82	122	159	58
125	80	140	123	160	112
126	87	56	cf. 123	122	68
127	206	59	124	123	65
128	155	60	125	124	66
129	84	61	126	125	67
130	164	62	108 col. ii. 48	126	69
131	82	63	127	108	82
132	112	64	128	127	140
133	149	104	129	128	56
134	58	105	131	129	59
135	68	106	132	131	60
136	143	175	133	132	61
137	150	113	134	133	62
138	15b	120	135	134	63
139	176	165	137	135	64

	Meineke	Scheidweiler	Powell	van Groningen	de Cuenca	Supplementum Hellenisticum
140	145 + 146	156	1	137	104	
141	168	167	2	111	105	
142	175	159	41c	109–110	106	
143	153	170	138	138	175	
144	74b	160	139	139	113	
145	69	173	140	140	120	
146	140	174	141	141	156	
147	208	181	142	142	165	
148	106	119	143	143	167	
149	74a	204	144	144	159	
150	79	205	145	145	170	
151	94	206	39b	146	160	
152	95	207	146	147	173	
153	96	138	147	152, 148	174	
154	88	139	148	149	181	
155	105	141	149	150	138	
156	117	142	150	151	139	
157	130	121	151	153	141	
158	181	122	152	154	142	
159	59	123	153	155	121	

	Meineke	Scheidweiler	Powell	van Groningen	de Cuenca	Supplementum Hellenisticum
182		154		203	154	
183		155		119	155	
184		137		204	137	
185		189		205	149	
186		210		206	119	
187				207	205	
188				179	206	
189				181	207	
190				189		
191				184		
192				187		
193				191		
194				162b		
195				185		
fr. dub. 1	187				189	
fr. dub. 2	189				210	
fr. dub. 3	—				55, 171	
fr. dub. 4	171				109–110, 191, 111	
fr. dub. 5	—					

II. CONVERSION OF THIS EDITION TO OTHER EDITIONS

This edition	Epigrammata 1 / Epigrammata 2	Epigrammata 1 / Epigrammata 2	Epigrammata 1 / Epigrammata 2	Epigrammata 1 140 / Epigrammata 2 141	Epigrammata 1 / Epigrammata 2
1	1	1	1	1	1
2	2	2.1	2	2.1	2.1
3	3	3	3	3	3
4	4	5	4	4	4
5	—	7	5	5	7
6	5	6	6	6	6
7	pp. 41–42	4	8	7	5
8	6	8	9	8	8
9	—	95	7	9	9
10	7	9	10	10	10
11	9	11	11		
12	15	12	12	12	12
13	14	13	13	13	13
14	138	13	14	14	14
15a	10	13	15	14	14
15b	13	14	15	14	14
15c	12	15	15		
16	11	16	16	15	15
17			17	16	16
18			18	17	17
19a	cf. 16 + 67	cf. 17 + 100	19e	cf. 18 + 86	22 A, cf. 18 + 19 418

	Meineke	Scheidweiler	Powell	van Groningen	de Cuenca	Supplementum Hellenisticum
19b	—	—	—	19b	22 F	421
20	122	19	19	cf. 21	23	
21	—	18	20	20	24	
22	57	20	21	22	25	
23	168	101, cf. p. 31	22	23	27	
24	—	—	cf. 26	24a	38 A + 36	413
25	—	—	—	24b	38 B	414
26	—	—	cf. 27	24c	38 C + 37	415
27	19	21	23	25	31	
28	—	24	24	26	32	
29	—	25	25	27	33	
30	22	27	28	28	34	
31	22b	26	29	29	35	
32	17	28	30	30	39	
33	18	29	31	31	40	
34	—	—	—	32	41	416
35	24	30	32	33	43	
36	69	31	33	34	48	
37	27	32	34	35	51	
38a	27b	34a	35a	38a	52	

	27b	34b	35b	38b		
38b	—	—	—	36	52	417
39a	169	164	151	37	54	
39b	—	33	36	39	55	
40	28	35	37	41	53	
41a	28	35	37	cf. 41	56	
41b	28	35	142	40	56	
41c	34	36	38	42	56	
42	35	37	39	43	65	
43	36	38	40	44	66	
44	38	39	41	45	67	
45	90	40	42	46	69	
46	37	41	43	47	70	
47	39	42	44	48	68	
48	41	44	46	50	73	
49	42	45	47	51	75	
50	cf. 43	cf. 46	cf. 48	cf. 52	76	
51	44	47	49	53	cf. 77	427
52	—	—	—	55	78	
53	—	—	—	54	—	
54			—	—	—	
55	166	cf. 186			fr. dub. 3	430 ii. 27–29
56	48	126	107	111	133	432.5–12

	Meineke	Scheidweiler	Powell	van Groningen	de Cuenca	Supplementum Hellenisticum
57					—	
58	134	117	99	103	124	
59	159	127	108	112	134	
60	164	128	109	113	135	
61	74	129	110	114	136	
62	79	130	111	115	137	
63	87	131	112	116	138	
64	163	132	113	117	139	
65	108	120	101	105	127	
66	109	121	103	106	128	
67	—	122	104	107	129	
68	135	119	102	108	126	
69	145	123	105	109	130	
70	54	59	50	56	80	
71	cf. 60a	62	51	57	81	
72	82	61	52	58	83	
73	94	85	74	79	105	
74a	149	87	76	cf. 81	72	
74b	144	87	76	81	72	
75	104	88	77	82	57	

76	73	89	78	83	58
77	86	91	79	84	106
78	58	64	54	59	84
79	150	65	55	60	85
80	125	66	56	61	89
81	56	67	57	62	90
82	131	124	106	110	131
83	80	69	59	64	91
84	129	70	60	65	92
85	81	106	91	95	113
86	61	105	90	94	112
87	126	77	67	72	98
88	154	72	62	67	42
89	75	76	66	71	97
90	cf. 59	cf. 73	cf. 63	68	94
91	77	74	64	69	95
92	107	71	61	66	93
93	120	78	68	73	99
94	151	79	69	74	100
95	152	80	70	75	101
96	153	81	71	76	102
97	cf. pp. 97–98	82	72	77	88

428

	Meineke	Scheidweiler	Powell	van Groningen	de Cuenca	Supplementum Hellenisticum
98	55	68	58	63	87	
99	83	83	73	78	103	
100	51	107	92	96	114	
101	52	109	94	98	116	
102	46	114	97	101	121	
103	50	115	98	102	122	
104	84	133	114	118	140	
105	155	134	115	119	141	
106	148	135	116	120	142	
107	47	98	84	89	20	
108	—	—	—	131	—	429
109–110	—	—	—	142	cf. fr. dub. 4	430 + 431
111	—	—	—	cf. 54 + 141	cf. fr. dub. 4	432
112	132	118	100	104	125	
113	123	137	117	121	144	
114	65	104	89	93	30	
115	98	93	81	86	108	
116	53	92	80	85	107	
117	156	96	82	87	110	
118	—	97	83	88	111	

119	45	148	174	183	186
120	62	138	118	122	145
121	106	157	123	21	159
122	103	158	124	126	160
123	95	159	125	127	161
124	91	163	127	128	165
125	93	166	128	129	167
126	102	167	129	130	168
127	72	170	131	132	171
128	63	172	132	133	172
129	64	174	133	134	174
130	157	103	88	92	29
131	76	176	134	135	176
132	96	178	135	136	178
133	99	179	136	137	179
134	97	180	137	138	180
135	101	181	138	139	181
136	78	108	93	97	115
137	60b	184	139	140	184
138	—	153	143	143	155
139	112	154	144	144	156
140	146	125	145	145	132

	Meineke	Scheidweiler	Powell	van Groningen	de Cuenca	Supplementum Hellenisticum
141	—	155	146	146	157	
142	113	156	147	147	158	
143	136	161	148	148	163	
144	161	162	149	149	164	
145	140b	165	150	150	166	
146	140a	165	152	151	166	
147	105	168	153a–b	152	169	
148	111b	84	154	153	104	
149	133	171	155	154	185	
150	137	173	156	155	173	
151	109b	175	157	156	175	
152	111a	84	158	153	104	
153	143	177	159	157	177	
154	162	182	160	158	182	
155	128	183	161	159	183	
156	70	140	119	123	146	
157	100	75	65	70	96	
158	49	113	96	100	120	
159	92	142	120	124	149	
160	68	144	121	125	151	

	Meineke	Scheidweiler	Powell	van Groningen	de Cuenca	Supplementum Hellenisticum
182	cf. 156	cf. 96	35c	cf. 87	cf. 52, 110	
183	—		—	—	—	
184	16		176	191	—	
185	—		cf. 177	195	—	
186				—	86	453
187	dub. 1	63	53	192	79	
188				—	—	
189	dub. 2	185	175	190	fr. dub. 1	
190	pp. 401–402	2.2	2.2	4	2.2	
191	—			193	fr. dub. 4	433–452
192	—	—		—	—	
193	25	48		172	46	
194	23	49		173	44	
195	24b	50		174	45	
196	26	51		175	49	
197	—	52		176	50	
198	29	53		177	59	
199	30	54		178	60	
200	31	55		179	61	
201a–b–c	32	56		180	62	

202	32b	57	—	181	63
203	33	58	—	182	64
204	121	149	—	184	47
205	110	150	—	185	187
206	127	151	—	186	188
207	124	152	—	187	189
208	147	90	cf. 177	—	—
209	40	43	45	49	74
210	—	cf. 186	cf. 177	—	fr. dub. 2

PARTHENIUS OF NICAEA

INTRODUCTION

As with Euphorion, our main biographical source for Parthenius is the *Suda* entry. It does not give a date of birth, though it does tell us that he was captured by Cinna "when the Romans defeated Mithridates". The third Mithridatic War lasted from 74–63 BC, but we do not know for certain whether Parthenius was captured at the beginning of the war or at the end; nor can we be sure of the identity of the Cinna who captured him. It could have been the neoteric poet himself, whose epyllion *Zmyrna* (celebrated in Catullus 95) seems to have been influenced by Parthenius. Or it could have been his father, particularly if Parthenius was captured earlier, rather than later, in the war. At any rate, Parthenius was one of numerous first-century Bithynian men of culture (doctors, poets, grammarians) who left their homeland for Rome, and he was not the only one to have been brought there as a prisoner of the Mithridatic Wars.

The tradition about his servile status seems also to be known to Erycius (Test. **2**), who portrays him with a slave's collar round his neck. But, like other distinguished prisoners of the war, Parthenius was freed "on account of his *paideia*". Witnesses to his subsequent career are short on detail, but tantalising. The obvious inference is that he went to Rome, in whose vicinity his tombstone was apparently discovered (Test. **4**); but it is also possible that he spent time in north Italy, where the Cinnas had their estates,[1] and/or Naples, Virgil's home for many years. Wherever they met, Macrobius reports that Parthenius was Virgil's teacher (*grammaticus*) in Greek (Test. **9a**),[2] and there are scattered indications of Parthenius' influence on Virgil's poetry (Test. **9b–c**; cf. also **25**). Two testimonia concern Roman emperors known for their unorthodox literary tastes and their favour for Parthenius: Tiberius had his portrait included with those of other litterati in public libraries, and Hadrian (apparently) renovated his grave (Test. **3–4**).[3] Several times he is bracketed together with other Hellenistic literary celebrities, whose recherché subject-matter and minuteness of detail he is said to share: Euphorion (Test. **3**, **6**), Rhianus (Test. **3**), Callimachus (Test. **5**, **6**), Lycophron (Test. **7**).

Given his celebrity, the yield of fragments and citations is disappointingly meagre. The longest continuous fragment is only six lines long, and the largest part of the fragments are single words quoted in grammarians and Stephanus of Byzantium. However, the indications are interesting. First, to judge from the *Suda* (cf. also Test. **7**), his fame rested largely on his elegies (otherwise, of the "various metres" that the *Suda* credits him with, there are traces only of hexameters). In fact, evidence for elegy largely dries up after the third century, and non-hexametric poetry from then on mostly takes the form of

---

[1] Dyer 1996.

[2] On the meaning of *grammaticus* here, Francese 1999.

[3] It is highly unlikely that he lived into the reign of Tiberius, as the *Suda* says, but he may well have lived into Tiberius' maturity.

epigram.[4] In that respect, Parthenius seems a throw-back
to the century that produced Philitas, Callimachus, and
Eratosthenes. Second, he not only revived elegy, but wrote
an elegiac lament / encomium of his wife in three books:
the length and the female honorand hint at a genealogy
that goes back to the early Hellenistic poets (and to their
image of Mimnermus' *Nanno*), while the occasion seems
to point particularly to Antimachus' four-book *Lyde* writ-
ten, as Hermesianax tells us (**3**.41–46), when his wife died.
Should we infer that Parthenius renewed, or somehow
took a stance, in the Hellenistic literary-critical controver-
sies over that poem? A papyrus fragment of the *Arete*
equipped with scholia (**2–5**) indicates that the poem con-
tained geographical and mythological allusions, glosses,
and other linguistic oddities in the high Hellenistic man-
ner: interesting, but not yet enough to advance the rela-
tionship to Antimachus.

Apart from the *Arete*, there are other funerary laments
(**6**, **17**, and perhaps **8–9**?) and poems for contemporaries
(**13**, **26**), possibly hymns (**7**, **10–12**?, **19–22**?), epyllia
(**15–16**?, **23**?), a work on metamorphoses that seems like-
lier to be poetry than prose (**24a–b**); maybe even a mime
(**18**), which, if that is right, would be another reversion to
the poetic interests of the third century. It is often sug-
gested that Parthenius mediated the Hellenistic poets,
especially Euphorion, to the neoterics, and **10** provides

[4] For an exception, see the sixty-line elegiac poem by a local
poet of (approximately) late 2nd Halicarnassus, which seems to
stand in the high Hellenistic tradition of catalogue elegy (so G. B.
d'Alessio, in Isager and Pedersen 2004, 44; see General Introduc-
tion and n. 4).

the link in a chain that leads straight from Euphorion to Gallus and Virgil.[5] Yet there is no trace of curse poetry, nor of wilful obscurity. One fragment in which Parthenius offered an alternative etymology for the stock Homeric epithet *Argeiphontes* is a *jeu d'esprit* in rather Euphorionic vein (**38**; compare Euphorion **123**, **152**). But on the few occasions when we can study any continuous pieces of Parthenius' verse (**28**, **33**) the effect is different. The myth of Byblis' doomed love for her brother certainly offered scope for Chalcidian lugubriousness or neoteric melodrama, but Parthenius' treatment (**33**), despite a couple of well-chosen glosses from Callimachus and Euphorionic fifth-foot spondees, is gentle and rather understated.

When Hellenistic poetry was taken over by the neoterics, so too were some of its controversies and mannerisms (cf. Catullus 95), and one of the most frustrating questions about Parthenius was whether he was involved in them, or in mediating them. Test. **2** makes Parthenius criticise Homer, and Test. **5** aligns Parthenius and Callimachus against mindless Homeric pastichists. It is impossible to believe that either poet drew the lines so crudely, though entirely possible that Parthenius, like Callimachus, advertised his delicacy and refinement of taste.

In partial compensation for the loss of Parthenius' poetry is the survival of a prose compendium of myths on erotic themes which he addressed to Cornelius Gallus, purportedly so that Gallus could versify them. It is not certain how seriously we should take this dedication. It may simply be an advertising ploy for Parthenius' little work of

[5] See e.g. Rostagni 1932–1933; Clausen 1964; Crowther 1976, 1980; Lyne 1978; Horsfall 1991; Francese 2001.

mythography—though one that rests on an understood connection between Gallus and erotic subject-matter. Some of the stories might translate well into neoteric epyllion. Elegiac exempla are another obvious destination—although many of Parthenius' myths seem too obscure and too out-of-the-way. In many cases at least the story-patterns, if not the characters, are familiar; there is also a very Hellenistic taste for local myth, aetiology, and the registration of variants. Most of the stories in the manuscript are annotated with the names of earlier poets and prose writers in whom the story occurs. It is still controversial whether these annotations are by Parthenius himself (for Parthenius sometimes gives quite different indications in the course of the stories), and, as we can see from the fragments of Euphorion's *Thrax* that overlap with stories XIII and XXVI, the annotations by no means guarantee that the "source" told the story at length, or even in the same way as Parthenius.[6] Whatever their origin, they give some insight into the curious world of Hellenistic myth-history which has been largely lost to us. We also see something of the reciprocal relations of Hellenistic poetry and prose: local histories furnish the subject-matter for poets, are epitomated into handbooks—and perhaps, eventually, retransformed into verse.

EDITIONS

Both *Sufferings in Love* and poetic fragments:

A. Meineke, *Analecta Alexandrina* (Berlin, 1843) (repr. Hildesheim, 1964), 255–338.

---

[6] Cameron 2004, 106–116.

E. Martini, *Mythographi Graeci* ii/1 suppl.: *Parthenii Nicaeni quae supersunt* (Leipzig, 1902).

S. Gaselee, *The Love Romances of Parthenius and other Fragments* (London and New York, 1916).

E. Calderón Dorda, *Partenio de Nicea—Sufrimientos de Amor y Fragmentos* (Madrid, 1988).

J. L. Lightfoot, *Parthenius of Nicaea. The Poetical Fragments and the Erotika pathemata* (Oxford, 1999).

Poetic fragments only:

T. Bergk, *Anthologia Lyrica* (Leipzig, ²1868), 169–170.

E. Diehl, *Anthologia Lyrica Graeca*, vol. ii. 6 (Leipzig, ²1942), 94–101.

H. Lloyd-Jones and P. J. Parsons, *Supplementum Hellenisticum* (Berlin, 1983), 289–315.

For a full list of the editions of the *Sufferings in Love*, see J. L. Lightfoot, *Parthenius of Nicaea* (Oxford, 1999), 306, to which add:

F. J. Cuartero Iborra, *Partenio, Dissorts d'amor. Text rev. i trad.* (Barcelona, 1988).

K. Brodersen, *Liebesleiden in der Antike. Die "Erotika Pathemata" des Parthenios* (Darmstadt, 2000).

G. Schilardi and G. Cerri, *Partenio di Nicea, Amori infelici. Alle radici del romanzo* (Lecce, 1993).

G. Spatafora, *Partenio de Nicea, Erotikà Pathémata. Introduzione, testo critico, traduzione e commento* (Athens, 1995).

M. Biraud, D. Voisin, A. Zucker, with contributions by E. Delbey, *Passions d'amour / Parthénios de Nicée* (Grenoble, 2008).

473

Translations of the *Sufferings in Love*:

J. Stern, *Parthenius, Erotika Pathemata* (New York, 1992).
G. Paduano, *Partenio, Pene d'amore* (Pisa, 1992).

CRITICISM

H. Bernsdorff, "*P.Oxy.* 4711 and the Poetry of Parthenius", *JHS* 127 (2007), 1–18.

W. Clausen, "Callimachus and Latin poetry", *GRBS* 5 (1964), 181–196.

N. B. Crowther, "Parthenius and Roman poetry", *Mnemosyne* 29 (1976), 65–71.

————"Parthenius, Laevius and Cicero. Hexameter poetry and Euphorionic myth", *LCM* 5 (1980), 181–183.

R. R. Dyer, "Where did Parthenius teach Vergil?", *Vergilius* 42 (1996), 14–24.

C. Francese, "Parthenius « grammaticus »", *Mnemosyne* 52 (1999), 63–71.

————*Parthenius of Nicaea and Roman poetry* (Bern, 2001).

N. Horsfall, "Virgil, Parthenius and the Art of Mythological Reference", *Vergilius* 37 (1991), 31–36.

H. Lloyd-Jones, *Supplementum Supplementi Hellenistici* (Berlin and New York, 2005), 71–78.

R. O. A. M. Lyne, "The neoteric poets", *CQ* 28 (1978), 167–187.

R. Mayer G'Schrey, "Parthenius Nicaeensis quale in fabularum amatoriarum breviario dicendi genus secutus sit" (Diss. Heidelberg, 1898).

A. Rostagni, "Partenio di Nicea, Elvio Cinna ed i 'poeti novi'", *AAT* 68,2 (1932–1933), 497–545.

K. Spanoudakis, "Adesp. Pap. Eleg. SH 964: Parthenius?",
APF 50 (2004), 37–41.

M. van Rossum-Steenbeek, *Greek Readers' Digests?
Studies on a selection of subliterary papyri* (Leiden,
1998), 172–175.

A. Zucker (ed.), *Littérature et érotisme dans les Passions
d'amour de Parthénios de Nicée: actes du colloque de
Nice, 31 mai 2006* (Grenoble, 2008).

TESTIMONIA

1 *Suda* π 664

Παρθένιος, Ἡρακλείδου καὶ Εὐδώρας, Ἕρμιππος δὲ
[Hermippus Berytius, *FHG* iii. 51–2, *RE* viii (1913), 853]
Τήθας φησί· Νικαεὺς ἢ Μυρλεανός, ἐλεγειοποιὸς καὶ
μέτρων διαφόρων ποιητής. οὗτος ἐλήφθη ὑπὸ Κίννα
λάφυρον, ὅτε Μιθριδάτην Ῥωμαῖοι κατεπολέμησαν·
εἶτα ἠφείθη διὰ τὴν παίδευσιν καὶ ἐβίω μέχρι Τιβε-
ρίου τοῦ Καίσαρος. ἔγραψε δὲ ἐλεγείας, Ἀφροδίτην,
Ἀρήτης ἐπικήδειον, τῆς γαμετῆς Ἀρήτης ἐγκώμιον, ἐν
τρισὶ βιβλίοις· καὶ ἄλλα πολλά. περὶ μεταμορφώσεως
ἔγραψε.

δὲ ἐλεγείας AVMac: δὲ ἐλεγεῖα εἰς GMpc: δι᾽ ἐλεγείας Schneider
<περὶ μεταμορφώσεως ἔγραψε add. M in marg.: οὗτος ἔγραψε
καὶ περὶ μεταμορφώσεως post 665 add. A.: om. GV.>

2 *Garland* 2274–2281 = *AP* 7.377 (Erycius)

Ἐρυκίου εἰς Παρθένιον τὸν Φωκαέα τὸν εἰς τὸν Ὅμηρον
παροινήσαντα [J]·

    εἰ καὶ ὑπὸ χθονὶ κεῖται, ὅμως ἔτι καὶ κατὰ
        πίσσαν
      τοῦ μιαρογλώσσου χεύατε Παρθενίου,

TESTIMONIA

1 *Suda*

Parthenius, son of Heraclides and Eudora, though Hermippus calls her Tetha. From Nicaea or Myrlea, an elegist and poet in various metres. He was among the spoils taken by Cinna, when the Romans defeated Mithridates. Then he was freed on account of his education, and lived until the time of Tiberius Caesar. He wrote elegies: *Aphrodite*; an epicedium for Arete, an encomium for his wife Arete, in three books; and many more. He wrote about metamorphosis.

2 Palatine Anthology 7.377 (Erycius)

Erycius; on Parthenius of Phocis, who reviled Homer.

Although he lies below the earth, pour pitch
Upon the filthy-tongued Parthenius,

οὕνεκα Πιερίδεσσιν ἐνήμεσε μυρία κεῖνα
φλέγματα καὶ μυσαρῶν ἀπλυσίην ἐλέγων·
5   ἤλασε καὶ μανίης ἐπὶ δὴ τόσον ὥστ' ἀγορεῦσαι
πηλὸν Ὀδυσσείην καὶ πάτον Ἰλιάδα.
τοιγὰρ ὑπὸ ζοφίαισιν Ἐρινύσιν ἀμμέσον ἧπται
Κωκυτοῦ κλοιῷ λαιμὸν ἀπαγχόμενος.

3 Suetonius, *Tib.* 70.2

Fecit (sc. Tiberius) poemata Graeca imitatus Euphorio-
nem et Rhianum et Parthenium, quibus poetis admodum
delectatus scripta omnium et imagines publicis bibliothe-
cis inter veteres et praecipuos auctores dedicavit; et ob
hoc plerique eruditorum certatim ad eum multa de his
ediderunt.

4 Anonymi (Hadriani?) epigramma, *IG* 14.1089 (Kaibel,
Ep.Gr. 1089; Peek, *Gr.Vers.* I 2050, Page *FGE* 568–571)

[............ ἀ]ριδείκετον [ἀν]δρὸ[ς] ἀοι[δοῦ,
  [γαῖ]α τὸν Ἀ[σ]κανίη [γ]είνατο Πα[ρθέ]νιο[ν,
ἀε[ὶ τ]ιμ[ήε]σ‹σ›ι τετιμένον ἡγεμόνεσ‹σ›ι,
  [λυγρὰ] δ' ἐ[π]' Ἀ[ρήτῃ] μ[υ]ράμενον
    [φθ]ιμέν[ῃ,
5 [......]ροῖσιν [ἐ]πὶ φθιμένῃ ἐλέγοισιν,
  [ου   ἄ]μμορον εὐεπίης.
[καὶ] τὸ μὲν οἴχετ' ἄ[ισ]τον ὑπ[ὸ π]λη[σ]μῆσιν
  [ἀ]ναύρου,
  [.....]..γραπτὴν [σ]υραμένοιο λίθον·

478

Because upon the Pierian maids he spewed that
    endless
Bile and dirt of his polluted elegies.
His madness went so far as to denote   [5]
The *Odyssey* "mud", the *Iliad* "ordure".
So by the dusky Furies he is bound amid
Cocytus, choked on a slave's collar round his neck.

3 Suetonius, *Tiberius*

He composed Greek verse in imitation of Euphorion and
Rhianus and Parthenius. He took great delight in these po-
ets, collected all their writings, and consecrated their stat-
ues among the ancient classic authors in the public librar-
ies; and for this reason many learned men vied with each
other to publish long commentaries on their works.

4 *IG* 14.1089

famed . . . of a minstrel
. . . Parthenius, a son of the Ascanian land,
One ever honoured by statesmen of honour.
He uttered sorrowful laments for dead Arete
. . . in elegies upon her death   [5]
. . . not] lacking in poetic eloquence.
That one[1] an overflowing stream washed clean away,
. . . sweeping before it the engraved stone.

[1] I.e, the former epitaph.

[τὴ]ν δ᾽ ἄρ᾽ ὕπερ[θ]ε νέην α[ὐτὸς] πάλι [θ]ήκατο
[τ]ύμ[β]ο[υ
10   Ἀ[δ]ριανὸς Μουσ[ῶν...........
.... δ᾽ ἐν ὀψιγόνοισι{ν} π[ολυ]κλέα........
[ἀστὸν] Ἀπαμ[ε]ίης [κ]αὶ [θ]άλος
Εὐφρ[οσ]ύν[ης.

1 π]ρὶν ἔ[θεντ᾽ ἀ]ριδείκετον Peek   ἀοι[δοῦ Peek: ἀοι[δήν
Gruyter   2 γαῖ]α, τὸν Kaibel, Peek: σῆμ]α, τὸν Page
3 ἀε[ὶ τ]ιμ[ήε]σ<σ>ι Kaibel   4 [λυγρὰ] δ᾽ ἔ[π]᾽ vel μυρί]᾽
ἐ[π]᾽ Kaibel   [φθ]ιμέν[ῃ Kaibel   5 Ἀρήτῃ λυγ]ροῖ-
σιν Page: μυράμενον λυγ]ροῖσιν Kaibel   6 ἀνέρα παν-
τ]οίη[ς ἔ]μμορον Kaibel: [ου   ἄ]μμορον Gruyter
7 καὶ] Kaibel   ἄ[ισ]τον Ll.-J.-P.: ἄ[φαν]τον Wilamowitz:
ἄ[ω]τον Gruyter   Ἀναύρου Kaibel   8 init. π]ε[τρο-
φ]υᾶ Kaibel   9 τὴ]ν Kaibel: νῦ]ν Page   α[ὐτὸς] vel
[δελτὸν] Kaibel   10 Μουσ[ῶν δῶρον ἀφ᾽ ἀγνο-
τάτων] Kaibel: Μούσ[αις ἄρμενα τευξάμενος] Peek
11 κλῇ]ζε δ᾽ ἐν ὀψιγόνοισι π[ολυ]κλέα τ[όν ποτ᾽ ἐόντα Peek
12 [ἀστὸν] Kaibel: [κόσμον] Peek [κ]αὶ [θ]άλος Εὐφρ[οσ]ύν[ης
Kaibel

5 AP 11.130 (Pollianus)

τοὺς κυκλι<κ>οὺς τούτους, τοὺς "αὐτὰρ ἔπειτα"
λέγοντας
μισῶ, λωποδύτας ἀλλοτρίων ἐπέων.
καὶ διὰ τοῦτ᾽ ἐλέγοις προσέχω πλέον· οὐδὲν ἔχω
γὰρ
Παρθενίου κλέπτειν ἢ πάλι Καλλιμάχου.

But this new one was reinstated on the tomb
By Hadrian himself, the Mus[es' friend,   [10]
. . . renowned among men to come
. . . citizen of Apamea, scion of Euphrosyne.

5 Palatine Anthology 11.130 (Pollianus)

Those cyclic poets, those who say, "But thereafter"—
How I detest them, thieves of others' words.
And so I set more store by elegies, for I can steal
Nothing from Parthenius, nor Callimachus.

5   "θηρὶ μὲν οὐατόεντι" γενοίμην, εἴ ποτε γράψω,
   "εἴκελος", "ἐκ ποταμῶν χλωρὰ χελιδόνια".
   οἱ δ' οὕτως τὸν Ὅμηρον ἀναιδῶς λωποδυτοῦσιν,
   ὥστε γράφειν ἤδη "μῆνιν ἄειδε θεά".

6 Lucian, *De Hist. Conscrib.* 56–57

. . . λέγω δέ, εἰ παραθέοις μὲν τὰ μικρὰ καὶ ἧττον
ἀναγκαῖα, λέγοις δὲ ἱκανῶς τὰ μεγάλα . . . οἷον ὁρᾷς
τι καὶ Ὅμηρος ὡς μεγαλόφρων ποιεῖ· καίτοι ποιητὴς
ὢν παραθεῖ τὸν Τάνταλον καὶ τὸν Ἰξίονα καὶ Τιτυὸν
καὶ τοὺς ἄλλους [*Od.* 11.576–600]. εἰ δὲ Παρθένιος ἢ
Εὐφορίων [Test. **9**] ἢ Καλλίμαχος [Test. 78 Pf.] ἔλεγεν,
πόσοις ἂν οἴει ἔπεσι τὸ ὕδωρ ἄχρι πρὸς τὸ χεῖλος τοῦ
Ταντάλου ἤγαγεν; εἶτα πόσοις ἂν Ἰξίονα ἐκύλισεν;

7 Artemidorus, *Oneirocr.* 4.63

. . . εἰσὶ γὰρ καὶ παρὰ Λυκόφρονι ἐν τῇ Ἀλεξάνδρᾳ
καὶ παρὰ Ἡρακλείδῃ τῷ Ποντικῷ ἐν ταῖς Λέσχαις καὶ
παρὰ Παρθενίῳ ἐν ⟨ταῖς⟩ ἐλεγείαις καὶ παρ' ἄλλοις
πολλοῖς ἱστορίαι ξέναι καὶ ἄτριπτοι.

8 Galen, *De Sent. Med.* ap. K. Kalbfleisch, *Hermes* 77
(1942), 377

Ait Galienus, quia mihi accidit prout dicitur quod accidit
Bertheni versificatori, quod dicitur quod versus sui perve-
nerunt in vita sua ad aliquos, et cum transiret per terram

"Like a long-eared beast" may I become, if I   [5]
Should ever write "Pale celandine from the rivers".
But they loot Homer so bare-facedly
As even to write "Sing, goddess, of the wrath".

6 Lucian, *On Writing History*

I mean, if you skim over the small and less important de-
tails, and you give adequate coverage to the larger matters
. . . as you see the great-minded Homer doing: he, although
a poet, skims over Tantalus and Ixion and Tityos and the
rest. But if Parthenius or Euphorion or Callimachus were
speaking, can you imagine how many lines it would take to
get the cup as far as the lips of Tantalus, and how many
more to set Ixion a-spin?

7 Artemidorus, *On the interpretation of dreams*

In Lycophron's *Alexandra* and Heraclides Ponticus' *Con-
versations* and Parthenius' elegies and in many other writ-
ers there are strange and out-of-the-way stories.

8 Galen, *On the opinions of doctors*

Galen said that something similar to what happened to the
poet Parthenius also happened to him—the story about
how, his poems having reached a certain readership within
his own lifetime, he was travelling through the land of the

illorum, invenit duos grammaticantes in loco scolarum altercantes de sententia illorum versuum, unus quorum exponebat versus secundum quod Berthenis versificator intellexit cum eos composuit, alter vero exponebat contrario modo. Berthenis autem incepit reprobare expositionem illius qui exponebat non secundum quod ipse voluit, dicens ipsum errare et sententiam illorum versuum contrariam sententie sue expositionis. qui cum noluisset recipere dictum eius, respondit eidem: "ego audivi Berthenem versificatorem exponere ipsos versus secundum sentenciam quam modo narro." et cum ille noluisset recipere verba sua secundum quod ipse dixit, ait, "timeo quod ymaginatio mea sit infecta sive destructa, cum indigeam inducere istos familiares meos in testimonium secundum quod sim Berthenis."

9

(a) Macrobius, *Sat.* 5.17.18

Versus est Parthenii, quo grammatico in Graecis Vergilius usus est.

(b) Aulus Gellius, *NA* 13.27.1 (cf. **36**)

Partheni poetae versus est: Γλαύκῳ καὶ Νηρῆι καὶ εἰναλίῳ Μελικέρτῃ. eum versum Vergilius aemulatus est itaque fecit duobus vocabulis venuste inmutatis parem: "Glauco et Panopeae et Inoo Melicertae" [*Georg.* 1.437].

people concerned, when he found two grammarians in a school debating the meaning of his verses, one of whom was expounding them according to Parthenius' own understanding when he had composed them, and the other in a contrary sense. Parthenius began to criticise the exposition of the one who proposed a sense different from the one he himself intended, saying he was wrong and that the sense of those verses was contrary to the sense of his exposition. When the man refused to accept his teaching, he said to him, "I have heard the poet Parthenius himself expound those very verses in the sense which I am proposing now." And when the man still refused to take the words in the sense in which he himself enunciated them, he said, "I am afraid that the idea of me must be fading or forgotten, because I lack the power to convince my own friends that I am Parthenius."

9

(a) Macrobius, *Saturnalia*

There is a verse of Parthenius, who was Virgil's teacher of Greek.

(b) Aulus Gellius, *Attic Nights*

There is a verse of Parthenius the poet: "To Glaucus and Nereus and sea-dwelling Melicertes." This verse was imitated by Virgil who, with a charming two-word change, made its match: "To Glaucus and Panopea and Melicertes, Ino's son."

(c) Aulus Gellius, *NA* 9.9.3

Quando ex poematis Graecis vertendae imitandaeque sunt insignes sententiae, non semper aiunt enitendum ut omnia omnino verba in eum in quem dicta sunt modum vertamus. perdunt enim gratiam pleraque, si quasi invita et recusantia violentius transferantur. scite ergo et considerate Vergilius, cum aut Homeri aut Hesiodi aut Apollonii aut Parthenii aut Callimachi aut Theocriti aut quorundam alios locos effingeret, partim reliquit, alia expressit.

(c) Aulus Gellius, *Attic Nights*

When noteworthy expressions are to be translated and imitated from Greek poems, they say that one should not always strive to render all the words in exactly the same way in which they were composed. Many lose their charm if they are rendered too harshly, as if they were unwilling and resisting. And so Virgil acted with deliberate tact when he reproduced passages from Homer or Hesiod or Apollonius or Parthenius or Callimachus or Theocritus or whoever else it might be, in adapting some passages and leaving others unattempted.

FRAGMENTA POETICA

1–26 FRAGMENTA CERTIS
CARMINIBUS TRIBUTA

1–14 Elegiaca

Ἀρήτη

Cf. Test. 1 ἔγραψε δὲ ἐλεγείας . . . Ἀρήτης ἐπικήδειον, τῆς γαμετῆς Ἀρήτης ἐγκώμιον, ἐν τρισὶ βιβλίοις.

1 Σ Pindar, *Isth.* 2.68, iii. p. 222.16 Drachmann

καὶ Παρθένιος ἐν τῇ Ἀρήτῃ τὸ ἄννειμαι ἀντὶ τοῦ ἀνάγνωθι.

ἄννειμε codd., corr. P. A. Hansen: ἄννεμε Valckenaer: ἄννειμε . . . ἀνέγνω Toup

2–5 P.Genev. inv. 97

2

Fol. 1   Recto

> ου μεν[..]..[
> κεῖνον οτις.[
> κήδεα μοιμ[

488

POETIC FRAGMENTS

1–26 FRAGMENTS OF KNOWN LOCATION

1–14 Elegiac Fragments

Arete

Cf. Test. **1** He wrote in elegiacs . . . a funerary lament for Arete, an encomium of his wife Arete, in three books.

1 Scholiast on Pindar, *Isthmian Odes*

. . . and Parthenius in the *Arete* uses *anneimai* ("read thou") instead of *anagnōthi*.

2–5 P.Genev. inv. 97

2 First folio, front
　Him
　Cares for me　　　　　　　　　　　　　　[2]

τρύομαι· εχ[
νείσομαι· εφ[
αὐτίκα· καὶ φα[
καί νύ μοι ἀργυ[
πρηῢς απη.[
μηδ' ογεκο[
τουτάκι μη[
ἀλλά μιν αμ.[
ἇ φίλος εἰρη[
στέλλεοκα[
σήμερον α[
Ἰρις τοικ[
...]πριν.[

- - - -

7 ἀργυ[ρ-, ἀρφυ[φ-: ἀργύ[φεος Livrea   8 πρηῢς ἀπ'
ἠώ[ιης . . . ἁλός Pfeiffer: πρηῢς ἀπ' ἠώ[ης πνευσάμενος
Ζέφυρος Livrea   13 στέλλεο vel στέλλε, ὃ
16 Κύ]πριν Pfeiffer

Scholia in marg. sinistr.

1 (ad l. 2)   ἀκτῆς
2–7 (ad ll. 4–6)   ²τὴν Νίκ(αι)|³αν εν.. |⁴ἀπώλετο |
                     ⁵ .. Ἀρήτη |⁶ ..κ ἑτάρᾳ|⁷ξε
8–10 (ad l. 8)   vestigia
11–14 (ad l. 15)   ¹¹τὸν Ζέφ(υρον)· ἐκεί|¹²νῳ γ(ὰρ)
                     ἐγα|¹³μήθη ἡ Ἰρις |¹⁴vestigia

4–5 ἀπώλετο ἡ Ἀρήτη (Ll.-J.–P.) vel ἀπώλετο γ(ὰρ) ἡ Ἀρήτη
(Pfeiffer)

I am wracked;
I shall go; [5]
Forthwith; and
And for me a silver (?)
Gentle from (?)
Nor let him (?)
At that time [10]
But him
Ah, dear
Set out
Today
Iris [15]
Cy]pris(?)[1]

Scholia in left margin

1 (on l. 2)	of the shore
2–7 (on ll. 4–6)	Nicaea . . . died
	Arete . . . and threw into confusion
11–14 (on l. 15)	Zephyrus. For Iris was married to him.[2]

[1] If there is a reference here to Aphrodite, both Iris and Zephyrus (n. below) sometimes act as escorts to her (*Il.* 5.353, HHom. 6.3), and Zephyrus conveys Berenice's lock of hair to Arsinoe Aphrodite in Call. fr. 110.52–56 Pf.

[2] According to Alc. fr. 327 Voigt and later sources, Iris and Zephyrus were parents of Eros. The implication of the note is that Parthenius referred to Zephyrus in an indirect way, perhaps by an ornamental epithet.

3

Fol. 1   Verso

```
].ο.[..].δε
].
]σεμενεῖσθαι
]φόρος
```
5
```
με]τανάσται
]πόλιν
]ημένος ἄζῃ
]ῆς
]ασα
```
10
```
]λύκον
]ηγίνησε
]ους
].ε.ολοισθον
].γονας
```
15
```
]..[.]..έχουσα
          ]..
```

– – – –

5 suppl. Lobel   7 βεβολ]ήμενος ἄζῃ Pfeiffer
14 γονάς, λ]αγόνας, στ]αγόνας   15 ἧτ]ορ Pfeiffer

Scholia in marg. sup.

1   ..λ..ο
2   .σεθηκετο

ε]ἰσέθηκε τὸ Ll.-J.–P.

3

First folio, back

. . . me to go there (?)	[3]
colonists	[5]
city	[6]
stricken with dry sorrow	[7]
Lycus[3]	[10]
led	[11]
(?) holding	[15]

[3] Perhaps a reference to the Bithynian river which (like the Cales mentioned in the scholia) flows into the Black Sea near Heraclea.

Scholia in marg. dextr.

3–4 (ad l. 2)	³α̣ρ̣.[..].....εν |⁴χει..ν̣.........
5 (ad l. 5)	Ἀθηναῖοι
6–10 (ad ll. 7–9)	⁶ξηρασίαι, |⁷ λύπῃ διὰ|⁸ τὴν ἀπου|⁹σίαν τῆς |¹⁰ Ἀρήτης
11–20 (ad ll. 11–15)	¹¹πίσυρον ὡς ἀπὸ |¹² εὐθείας τοῦ πί|¹³συρος.....|¹⁴...... πί-συρες |¹⁵ ὡς ἀπὸ εὐθείας|¹⁶ τοῦ πίσυρ .|¹⁷λα μεταπλα|¹⁸σμός (ἐστιν) ὡς |¹⁹χρυσάρματοι |²⁰ ἐρυσάρματες
21–2 (ad ll. 12–13)	vestigia
23–25 (ad l. 16)	²³Κ̣άλ(ης) ποταμ(ὸς) Μυγδονί|²⁴ας περὶ Βιθυνίαν |²⁵ vestigia

3–4 ἄρκ[τος] (Nicole)   διὰ τὸ ἐν \| χειμῶνι Pfeiffer
17 ἀ⟨λ⟩\|λά   23 Κ̣άλ(πης) Livrea

4

Fol. 2   Verso

          – – –
1   εσβλεπ[
          μα̣λ̣κ[
          καιρο[
          α.c..οc[
          – –

Vestigia scholiorum

Scholia in right margin

3–4 (on l. 2)	the bear . . . in winter (?)
5 (on l. 5)	Athenians[4]
6–10 (on ll. 7–9)	Dryness, grief over the absence of Arete
11–20 (on ll. 11–15)	*pisyron* (four), as if from the nominative *pisyros* . . . *pisyres* as if from the nominative *pisyr*. Metaplasm is as in *chrȳs-armatoi—erysarmates*.
23–25 (on l. 16)	Cales is a river in Mygdonia, in the territory of Bithynia.

4

Second folio, back

Regard	[1]
Chilly	[2]
Time	[3]

[4] In connection with ll. 3–4, a reference to the Athenian colonists on Arctonnesus ("Bear-Island"), another name for Cyzicus on the Propontis?

5

Fol. 2   Recto

] . . . . δηρον
] . ος
] ις
] . . . .
5   ] . . ε
] . .
] . . ν
] . . .
]
10   ]

– – –

1 σίδηρον Ll.-J.–P.

Scholia in marg. sup.

1   ]αις ἐχθροι . [

Scholia in marg. dextr.

2–8 (ad ll. 2–4)   ²[   ]αλαι ³[   ] . και ⁴[   ] . . τε
                ⁵[   ] . . ργα ⁶[ ] . . Σαρμα|⁷τίδες
                γὰρ αἱ |⁸κατοικοῦσαι
9–10 (ad l. 6)   ⁹καὶ Ὅμ(ηρος) πλω|¹⁰τῆι ἐνὶ νήσωι
11 (ad l. 7)   ¹¹ὑψηλά
12 (ad l. 8)   ¹²]πρωτεια

5

Second folio, front; scholia in right margin

2–8 (on ll. 2–4)	. . . For the women who live there are called Sarmatides[5]
9–10 (on l. 6)	And Homer says "on a floating isle"[6]
11 (on l. 7)	High

[5] The Sauromatians were a nomadic tribe who bordered on the Scythians beyond the Don. Herodotus tells how they were descended from the union of Scythians with Amazon women, and how their women still adhere to some of the customs of their ancestors (Hdt. 4.110–117).

[6] The island of Aeolus (*Od.* 10.3).

PARTHENIUS

13–14 (ad l. 9)   vestigia
15 (ad l. 10)   ¹⁵] ομο`

Εἰς Ἀρχελαΐδα ἐπικήδειον

6 Hephaestio, p. 4.4 Consbruch

καὶ Παρθένιος δὲ ἐπικήδειον εἰς Ἀρχελαΐδα γράφων
ἐλεγειακὸν τὸν τελευταῖον μόνον στίχον ἀντὶ ἐλεγείου
ἰαμβικὸν ἐποίησεν, ἐν ᾧ τὸ ὄνομα ἐρεῖν ἔμελλεν·

   ἀμυσχρὸν οὔνομ᾿ †ἔσσετ᾿ Ἀρχελαΐδος

cf. Choeroboscus, in Hephaestionem, p. 192.21 Cons-
bruch

ὁμοίως καὶ Παρθένιος εἰς Ἀρχελαΐδα γράφων καὶ μὴ
θέλων ἐν ἐλεγείοις ποιεῖσθαι ἐν μέσῳ λέξεως κοινήν
[sc. συλλαβήν], ἀντὶ ἐλεγείου ἴαμβον ἐποίησεν οὕτως·
"ἀμυσχρόν—Ἀρχελαΐδος".

ἔρχετ᾿, sscr. εὔχετ᾿, Hephaest. cod. D: ἔσετ᾿ Choerob. cod. K:
ἐστὶν Choerob. cod. U: ἔσκεν Livrea

Ἀφροδίτη

Cf. Test. **1** ἔγραψε δι᾿ ἐλεγείας Ἀφροδίτην . . .

7 Steph. Byz., α 150 Billerbeck

Ἀκαμάντιον, πόλις τῆς μεγάλης Φρυγίας, Ἀκάμαντος
κτίσμα τοῦ Θησέως, ᾧ συμμαχήσαντι πρὸς τοὺς Σο-
λύμους τὸν τόπον δέδωκε ‹Πείσανδρος› [suppl. Biller-

Funerary Lament for Archelais

6 Hephaestio

And Parthenius in his elegiac funerary lament for Archelais made just the last line, which contained the proper name, iambic instead of elegiac:

> Without taint shall the name of Archelais be.

cf. Choeroboscus, scholia on Hephaestion

In the same way, when Parthenius wrote his poem to Archelais and did not want to create an internally corrupted syllable in a word in elegiacs, he wrote an iambic instead of an elegiac verse, thus: "Without taint", etc.

Aphrodite

Cf. Test. **1** He wrote in elegiacs an *Aphrodite* . . .

7 Stephanus of Byzantium

Acamantium, a city of Greater Phrygia, the foundation of Acamas son of Theseus, who received the territory from Pisander when fighting against the Solymi. The ethnic ad-

beck]. τὸ ἐθνικὸν Ἀκαμάντιος ὡς Βυζάντιος, τὸ δὲ κτητικὸν τοῦ Ἀκάμαντος διὰ τῆς ει διφθόγγου. λέγεται καὶ Ἀκαμαντὶς ὡς Βυζαντίς. Παρθένιος δ᾽ ἐν Ἀφροδίτῃ Ἀκαμαντίδα αὐτήν φησι.

Βίας sive εἰς Βίαντα

8 Choeroboscus, in Theodos. *Canon.*, *GG* IV.1, p. 252.21 Hilgard

εἰ δέ τις εἴποι, καὶ πῶς τὸ ἵλαος συνεσταλμένον ἔχον τὸ ᾱ, οἷον ὡς παρὰ Παρθενίῳ Ἵλαος ὦ Ὑμέναιε [**37**], γίνεται παρὰ τοῖς Ἀθηναίοις διὰ τοῦ ε καὶ ω, οἷον ἵλεως, λέγομεν ὅτι τὸ ἵλαος μᾶλλον ἐκτείνει τὸ ᾱ, σπάνιον γὰρ τὸ <ᾱ> ἐν συστολῇ ἐστιν εὑρισκόμενον, καὶ τούτου χάριν ἐγένετο παρὰ τοῖς Ἀθηναίοις ἵλεως· ὅτι γὰρ ἐκτείνει τὸ ᾱ, ἐδήλωσε Παρθένιος ἐν τῷ εἰς Βίαντα εἰπών·

ἵλαος ταύτην δέχνυσο πυρκαϊήν

καὶ ἐν τῷ Εὐφορίωνος Δημοσθένει ὁμοίως ἐκτεταμένον εὑρίσκεται, οἷον Δαίμονος ἱλάοιο [**13**].

δὲ χρυσο, δὲ χρύσω, δὲ χρυσοῦ codd., corr. Bekker

9 Σ Τ *Il.* 9.446*a*, ii. p. 493.96 Erbse

γῆρας ἀποξύσας] . . . Ἀττικὴ [Ἰακὴ conj. Meineke] δὲ ἡ ἔκτασις. Παρθένιος γοῦν ἐν Βίαντι συνέστειλεν·

ὅστις ἐπ᾽ ἀνθρώπους ἔξυσεν αἰγανέας

jective is *Akamantios* like *Byzantios*, the possessive adjective of Acamas (sc. *Akamanteios*) has the *ei* diphthong. There is also a form *Akamantis* like *Byzantis*. Parthenius in the *Aphrodite* calls her *Akamantis*.[7]

Bias or *To Bias*

8 Choeroboscus on Theodosius, *Canones*

If one should ask, "How is it that *hīlaos*, which has a short *a*, as in Parthenius' *Hīlăos ō Hymenaie*, is used by the Athenians with *e* and *ō*, as in *hīleōs*?", we say it is rather the case that *hīlaos* lengthens the *a*, since shortened *a* is rare, and it is for this reason that it became *hīleōs* among the Athenians. That it does lengthen the *a* is demonstrated by Parthenius in his poem *To Bias*, when he says:

Graciously receive this pyre.

It is also found in Euphorion's *Demosthenes* likewise lengthened, as in *Daimonos hīlāoio*.

9 Scholiast on Homer, *Iliad*

"Having scraped off old age"] The lengthening is Attic. Parthenius in the *Bias* shortened it:

Who planed hunting-spears for use against humans.[8]

---

[7] The Athenian hero Acamas and the place-names Acamas and Acamantis are also associated with Cyprus. Parthenius' epithet may mean "she of Acamantium" or "she of Acamas", with reference to the promontory of that name, or perhaps even a cult established in memory of the hero.

[8] A curse on the first man to turn hunting-spears against humans, a token of the loss of Golden Age innocence.

Δῆλος

10 Steph. Byz., γ 112 Billerbeck

Γρῦνοι, πολίχνιον Μυριναίων, οὗ καὶ "ἱερὸν Ἀπόλλωνος καὶ μαντεῖον ἀρχαῖον καὶ ναὸς πολυτελὴς λευκοῦ λίθου" [Strab. 13.3.5] ἐν ᾧ τιμᾶται. Ἑκαταῖος δὲ τὴν πόλιν Γρύνειαν καλεῖ [FGrH 1 F 225]. τὸ ἐθνικὸν Γρυνεύς, καὶ Γρυνῇς τὸ θηλυκόν λέγεται καὶ

Γρύνειος Ἀπόλλων

ὡς Παρθένιος Δήλῳ, καὶ Γρυνήιος καὶ Γρυνικός τὸ κτη-τικόν, καὶ οὐδετέρως τὰ Γρύνεια.

11 Steph. Byz., p. 705.14 Mein.

Ὤγενος, ἀρχαῖος θεὸς, ὅθεν ὠγενίδαι καὶ ὠγένιοι ἀρ-χαῖοι. Παρθένιος ὁ Φωκαεὺς [Νικαεὺς Meineke] Δήλῳ·

σὺν τῇ ἐγὼ Τηθύν τε καὶ ὠγενίης Στυγὸς ὕδωρ

Τηθα vel -θά codd., corr. Salmasius (-θύς Passow)

12 Steph. Byz., β 61 Billerbeck

Βεληδόνιοι· ἔθνος παρ' Ὠκεανῷ. Παρθένιος ἐν Δήλῳ·

οὐδ' ἀποτηλίστων ἄκρα Βεληδονίων.

ἀπὸ τηλίτων τῶν πόρρω vel ἀτιλίτων πόρρω codd., corr. Bergk: ἀποτηλίτων Salmasius [recte -λιτῶν]: ἀπὸ τηλίστων Gavel: ἐπὶ τηλίστων Meineke: ἀπὸ ληιστῶν Blumenthal

Delos

10 Stephanus of Byzantium

Grynoi, a little town belonging to Myrina, where there is also "a temple of Apollo, an ancient oracle, and a costly temple of white stone" (so Strabo) in which the god is honoured. Hecataeus calls the city *Grȳneia*. The ethnic adjective is *Grȳneus*, the feminine *Grȳnēïs*. Also attested are

Grynean Apollo

(*Grȳneios Apollōn*) as Parthenius in his *Delos*;[9] and *Grȳnēïos* and *Grȳnikos* the possessive, and *Grȳneia* in the neuter.

11 Stephanus of Byzantium

Ogenus, an ancient god, whence *ōgenidae* and *ōgenioi*, "ancient". Parthenius of Nicaea in the *Delos*:

With whom / which,[10] I (name?) Tethys and ancient Styx's water.

12 Stephanus of Byzantium

Beledonii, a race beside the Ocean. Parthenius in the *Delos*:

Nor the heights of the distant Beledonii.[11]

[9] Also mentioned in Virg. *Ecl.* 6.72, where Gallus is told to sing of its foundation myth. Servius' note ad loc. suggests a link with Euphorion **102**.   [10] Probably earth. Tethys is a metonym for the sea. Together with the Styx, these would make up the three elements in the divine oath at *Il.* 14.271–273.

[11] Unknown; perhaps a people of the far north?

Κριναγόρας

13 EtGen AB, α 1225, ii. p. 223.6 L.-L. = EtMag 148.32, α 1854

Ἅρπυς· ὁ Ἔρως· ἡ χρῆσις παρὰ τῷ Παρθενίῳ ἐν Κριναγόρα·

ἀμφοτέροις ἐπιβὰς Ἅρπυς ἐληΐσατο.

εἴρηται δὲ παρὰ τὸ ἁρπάζειν τὰς φρένας· οὕτως Διονύσιος ὁ τοῦ Φιλοξένου.

ἐληΐσαν τὸ B

Λευκαδίαι

14 Steph. Byz., p. 324.19 Mein.

Ἰβηρίαι δύο . . . λέγεται δὲ καὶ Ἰβηρίτης. Παρθένιος ἐν Λευκαδίαις·

⟨–∪⟩ Ἰβηρίτῃ †πλεύσειεν αἰγιαλῷ

πλεύσει ἐν Meineke: πλεύσῃ ἐν Bekker

15–26 Incerta Elegiaca an Hexametrica

Ἀνθίππη

15 Steph. Byz., p. 381.16 Mein.

Κρανίδες· συνοικία πρὸς τῷ Πόντῳ. Παρθένιος ἐν Ἀνθίππῃ.

Crinagoras

13 Etymologicum Genuinum

Harpys: Eros. The usage occurs in Parthenius' *Crinagoras*:[12]

> With both feet trampling him, the Snatcher took his
>   spoil.

The name derives from the fact that it snatches away the
wits: so Dionysius the son of Philoxenus.[13]

Leucadiae

14 Stephanus of Byzantium

Two Iberias . . . There is also a form *Ibērītēs*. Parthenius in
the *Leucadiae*:

> (???) on (?) the Iberian shore.

15–26 Elegiac or Hexametric

Anthippe

15 Stephanus of Byzantium

Cranides, a little village on the Black Sea. Parthenius in the
Anthippe.[14]

---

[12] A notable of Mytilene, contemporary with Parthenius; his
part in various embassies to Julius Caesar and Augustus is known
from local inscriptions; author of fifty-one surviving epigrams in
the *Garland* of Philip.

[13] Grammarian of the 1st c. BC.

[14] For the likely subject of this poem see *Sufferings in Love*,
XXXII.

16 Steph. Byz., p. 409.15 Mein.

Λάμπεια· ὄρος Ἀρκαδίας· Παρθένιος Ἀνθίππῃ.

Λάμεια editio Aldina

εἰς Αὐξίθεμιν ἐπικήδειον

17 Steph. Byz., γ 26 Billerbeck

Γαλλήσιον· ὄρος Ἐφέσου· Παρθένιος ἐν ἐπικηδείῳ τῷ εἰς Αὐξίθεμιν.

ὄρος] πόλις codd., corr. Meineke

Εἰδωλοφανής

18 Apollonius Dyscolus, de Pronom., GG I.1, p. 92.20 Schneider

αἱ πληθυντικαὶ {καὶ} κοινολεκτοῦνται κατ᾽ εὐθεῖαν πρός τε Ἰώνων καὶ Ἀττικῶν, ἡμεῖς, ὑμεῖς, σφεῖς. ἔστι πιστώσασθαι καὶ τὸ ἀδιαίρετον τῆς εὐθείας παρ᾽ Ἴωσιν ἐκ τῶν περὶ Δημόκριτον, Φερεκύδην, Ἑκαταῖον [68 B 29a, 7 B 11 D.–K.; FGrH 1 F 360]. τὸ γὰρ ἐν Εἰδωλοφανεῖ·

ὑμέες Αἰόλιον περιχεύετε

παρὰ Παρθενίῳ ὑπὸ ποιητικῆς ἀδείας παραληφθὲν οὐ καταψεύσεται διαλέκτου πιστουμένης ἐλλογίμοις συγγραφεῦσιν.

Ἡρακλῆς

19 Steph. Byz., p. 339.14 Mein.

Ἴσσα· πόλις ἐν Λέσβῳ, κληθεῖσα Ἱμέρα, εἶτα Πε-

16 Stephanus of Byzantium

Lampea, a mountain in Arcadia. Parthenius in the *Anthippe*.

Funerary Lament for Auxithemis

17 Stephanus of Byzantium

Gallesium, a mountain in the territory of Ephesus. Parthenius in the funerary lament for Auxithemis.

Eidolophanes ("Dream Vision")

18 Apollonius Dyscolus, *On Pronouns*

The plurals used in common speech in the nominative by the Ionians and Athenians are *hēmeis*, *hymeis*, *spheis*. The unresolved form of the nominative in Ionic can be confirmed from writers such as Democritus, Pherecydes and Hecataeus. The form used in Parthenius' *Eidolophanes*

You pour Aeolian (sulphur) all around[15]

by poetic licence will not give the lie to the dialectal form attested in reputable authors.

Heracles

19 Stephanus of Byzantium

Issa, a city in Lesbos, called Himera, then Pelasgia and Issa

[15] By way of purification after a disturbing vision?

λασγία καὶ Ἴσσα ἀπὸ τῆς Ἴσσης τῆς Μάκαρος . . .
ἔστι καὶ θηλυκὸν Ἰσσὰς ἐπὶ τῆς Λέσβου παρὰ Παρ-
θενίῳ ἐν Ἡρακλεῖ.

Ἰσσάς, Ἰσάς, Ἰσσεύς codd.: Ἰσσηίς Salmasius

20 Steph. Byz., p. 486.13 Mein.

Οἰνώνη· νῆσος τῶν Αἰακιδῶν. οἱ οἰκήτορες Οἰνωναῖοι,
ὡς Παρθένιος Ἡρακλεῖ.

Αἰακίδων] Κυκλάδων conj. Meineke

21 EtGen AB, α 1408, ii. p. 312.6 L.-L. = EtMag 170.47,
α 2092

αὐρόσχας· ἡ ἄμπελος· μέμνηται Παρθένιος ἐν Ἡρακλεῖ·

αὐρόσχαδα βότρυν Ἰκαριωνίης.

Ἐρατοσθένης δὲ ἐν Ἐπιθαλαμίῳ [frr. 28, 37 P.] τὸ κατὰ
βότρυν κλῆμα. εἴρηται δὲ ἐπαιωρημένη τις οὖσα ὄσχη·
ὄσχη γὰρ τὸ κλῆμα καὶ ὄσχος εἴρηται.

αὐρόσχαλα EtGen AB, EtMag cod. R, corr. Callierges
Ἰκαριωνείης seq. e.g. <κούρης> Bergk: < > Ἰκαριώνη casu vel
recto vel obliquo Bergk, Maass, Meineke: Ἰκαριωνίνης Haupt.
Totam sententiam sic emendavit Hiller: αὐρόσχας· ἡ ἄμπελος.
μέμνηται Παρθένιος ἐν Ἡρακλεῖ. "αὐρόσχαλα βότρυν Ἰκα-
ριωνίης" Ἐρατοσθένης <ἐν Ἡριγόνῃ· > δὲ ἐν Ἐπιθαλαμίῳ
κτλ.

after Issa daughter of Macar . . . There is also a feminine *Issas*, used of Lesbos by Parthenius in the *Heracles*.

20 Stephanus of Byzantium

Oenone, an island connected with the Aeacidae.[16] The inhabitants are *Oenōnaioi*, as Parthenius has it in the *Heracles*.

21 Etymologicum Genuinum

auroschas: the vine. Parthenius mentions it in the *Heracles*:

> The vine-branch, bunch of grapes of the Icarian
> maid[17]

Eratosthenes in his *Epithalamium* uses the word for the twig attached to the bunch of grapes. It is also used of an elevated (or "overhanging") vine-branch or *oschē*: *oschē* and *oschos* are other names for the vine-branch.

---

[16] i.e. Aegina.

[17] The "Icarian maid" is Erigone, daughter of Icarius. Eratosthenes' *Erigone* told how Dionysus introduced Icarius to the vine, how he was murdered by drunken peasants (cf. the next fragment?), how Erigone killed herself in grief, and how the Attic festival of the Aiora was founded in her memory. The sense of the original is unclear: perhaps Erigone was said to hate the fruit that killed her father; or perhaps there is an allusion to the story that Dionysus took the form of a bunch of grapes to seduce her (Ov. *Met*. 6.125).

22 EtMag 374.50

ἐρίσχηλος· ὁ λοίδορος, ἀπὸ τοῦ ἐρίζειν διὰ τῶν χείλεων, ἐρίλεσχός τις ὤν, παρὰ τὴν ἔριν καὶ τὴν λέσχην, ὁ ἐξ ἔριδος λεσχαίνων. Παρθένιος ἐν Ἡρακλεῖ·

  ἐρισχήλοις κορυνήταις

cf. EtGen AB ἐρίσχηλος· ὁ λοίδορος, ἀπὸ τοῦ ἐρίζειν διὰ τῶν χείλεων, ἐρίλεσχός τις ὤν, παρὰ τὴν ἔριν καὶ τὴν λέσχην, ὁ ἐξ ἔριδος λεσχαίνων. καὶ ἐρισχηλεῖν τὸ εἰς ἔριν προκαλεῖσθαι.

Ἴφικλος

23 Steph. Byz., α 380 Billerbeck

Ἀράφεια· νῆσος Καρίας. Παρθένιος ἐν Ἰφίκλῳ·

  καὶ εἰναλίην Ἀράφειαν

εἰναλίαν vl

Μεταμορφώσεις

Test.: *Suda* ν 261

Νέστωρ, Λαρανδεύς, ἐποποιός, πατὴρ Πεισάνδρου τοῦ ποιητοῦ . . . Μεταμορφώσεις, ὥσπερ καὶ Παρθένιος ὁ Νικαεύς, καὶ ἄλλα. Ibid. π 664: περὶ μεταμορφώσεως ἔγραψε add. M in marg.: οὗτος ἔγραψε καὶ περὶ μεταμορφώσεως post 665 add. A: om. GV.

22 Etymologicum Magnum

erischēlos: one who is abusive, from "quarrelling" (*erizein*) through the "lips" (*cheilea*); or a quarrelsome person (*erileschos*), from "strife" (*eris*) and "chatter" (*leschē*), a person who banters aggressively. Parthenius in the *Heracles*:

> For abusive club-men.

cf. Etymologicum Genuinum

erischēlos: one who is abusive . . . aggressively. And to quarrel (*erischēlein*) is to provoke to strife.

Iphiclus

23 Stephanus of Byzantium

Araphea: an island off Caria. Parthenius in the *Iphiclus*:[18]

> And sea-girt Araphea.

Metamorphoses

Testimonium: *Suda*

Nestor of Laranda, a hexameter poet, father of the poet Peisander . . . *Metamorphoses*, like Parthenius of Nicaea, and other things.   Cf. Test. **1**: He wrote about metamorphosis.[19]

---

[18] Of various mythological figures of this name, the best known was the son of Phylacus, owner of a herd of cattle which the seer Melampus tried to steal (*Od*. 11.287–297). But there may be a reference to the Argonautic Iphiclus, who ran so fast that he could speed over the surface of the sea.

[19] The *Suda* does not say explicitly that the work was in verse, though otherwise mentions only poetic titles by Parthenius. If it was verse, it is a possible home for **33** (Byblis).

24

(a) Σ Dion. Perieg. 420, *GGM* ii. p. 447[b]15 Müller

περὶ δὲ τὰ Ἴσθμια νῶτα ἤτοι τὰ στενὰ δύο θάλασσαι
ἠχοῦσιν, ἥ τε Κορινθία καὶ ἡ Σαρωνική· ἥτις Κοριν-
θία ἐξεναντίας τῆς Ἐφύρης πόλεως πρὸς τὴν δύσιν
κατὰ τοῦ Ἀδριατικοῦ ἐστι πελάγους, ἥ τε Σαρωνικὴ
συρομένη ἐστὶ πρὸς ἀνατολάς. καὶ ταύτην {τὴν Κοριν-
θίαν deleverunt editores *SH*} Σαρωνίδα καλοῦσιν, ὡς
μὲν Εὐφορίων φησίν [**176**], ἐπειδὴ Σάρων τις κυνηγὸς
ἐπιδιώκων ⟨σὺν⟩ ἐκεῖθεν κατεκρημνίσθη εἰς θάλασ-
σαν, καὶ διὰ τοῦτο Σαρωνικὸν κληθῆναι τὸ πέλαγος·
ὡς δὲ Παρθένιος ἐν ταῖς Μεταμορφώσεσι λέγει, ἐπει-
δὴ Μίνως λαβὼν τὰ Μέγαρα διὰ τῆς Νίσου θυγατρὸς
ἐρασθείσης αὐτοῦ καὶ ἀποτεμούσης τῆς κεφαλῆς τοῦ
πατρὸς τὸν μόρσιμον πλόκαμον καὶ οὕτως αὐτὸν προ-
δούσης, ἐννοηθεὶς ὡς ἡ ⟨τὸν⟩ πατέρα προδοῦσα οὐ-
δενὸς ἄν ποτε ῥᾷστα φείσαιτο, προσδήσας αὐτὴν
⟨πηδαλίῳ νεὼς ἀφῆκεν⟩ ἐπισύρεσθαι τῇ θαλάσσῃ.
ὅθεν Σαρωνικὸς οὗτος ὁ πόντος ἐκλήθη. † ὅτι εἰς ὄρ-
νεον ἡ κόρη μετεβλήθη.   ⟨ ⟩ ex Eustathio suppleta,
vid. (**b**).

(**b**) Eustath. ad Dion. Perieg. 420, *GGM* ii. p. 295[a]7
Müller

οἱ δὲ ἄλλως τὴν τοῦ Σαρωνικοῦ πελάγους κλῆσιν
αἰτιολογοῦντές φασιν ὅτι Μίνως λαβὼν τὰ Μέγαρα

24

(a) Scholiast on Dionysius the Periegete

Two seas resound around the Isthmian straits or narrows, the Corinthian and the Saronic. The Corinthian is opposite the city of Ephyra towards the west and the Adriatic mere, the Saronic surges towards the east. They call this latter Saronic, as Euphorion says, because a certain hunter called Saron was chasing a boar and plunged from there into the sea, whence it became known as Saronic. As Parthenius says in the *Metamorphoses*, when Minos captured Megara with the help of Nisus' daughter, who had fallen in love with him and cut off the fateful lock from her father's head and thus betrayed him, he reckoned that one who had betrayed her father would not readily stop at anything, so he bound her to the ship's rudder and left her to be dragged (*sȳresthai*) along in the sea. Whence this sea is called Saronic.[20]

(b) Eustathius on Dionysius the Periegete

Those who offer a different aetiology for the Saronic sea say that Minos, who had captured Megara when Scylla, the

---

[20] In his etymology of the Saronic Gulf Parthenius differs from Euphorion **176** and other authors who derive it from the personal name or toponym Saron, but he seems to have influenced Roman poets whose versions use the verb *trahere* ("drag").

διὰ Σκύλλης τῆς Νίσου θυγατρὸς ἐρασθείσης αὐτοῦ
καὶ ἀποτεμούσης τὴν τοῦ πατρὸς κεφαλὴν [sic], ἐνε-
νοήσατο ὅτι ἡ τὸν πατέρα προδοῦσα οὐδενὸς ἂν ῥᾳδί-
ως φείδοιτο, καὶ διὰ τοῦτο προσδήσας πηδαλίῳ νηὸς
τὴν προδότιν καὶ πατροφόντιν ἀφῆκε σύρεσθαι διὰ
θαλάσσης. καὶ αὐτὴ μὲν εἰς ὄρνεον μετεβλήθη, ὥς
φησι Παρθένιος ὁ τὰς Μεταμορφώσεις γράψαι λεγό-
μενος, ὁ δὲ κόλπος παραγραμματισθεὶς ἔσχε τὴν
κλῆσιν ἀπὸ τοῦ σύρεσθαι. ἀπὸ δὲ τῆς τοιαύτης Σκύλ-
λης καὶ Σκύλλαιον ἔτι νῦν καλεῖται τόπος ἐν Ἑρμιόνῃ
τῇ κατὰ Πελοπόννησον, ἔνθα ἡ γυνὴ ἐξεκυμάνθη μετὰ
τὸ καταποντισθῆναι.

Moretum?

25 Schol. Verg. in cod. Ambros. T 21 sup. (saec. xv), fol.
33ʳ, ap. A. Mai, *Virgilii Maronis Interpretes Veteres* (Mi-
lan, 1818), 37

Parthenius Moretum scripsit in Graeco, quem Vergilius
imitatus est.

Προπεμπτικόν

26 Steph. Byz., p. 401.18 Mein.

Κώρυκος· πόλις Κιλικίας. Παρθένιος Προπεμπτικῷ.
παρ' ᾗ τὸ Κωρύκιον ἄντρον νυμφῶν, ἀξιάγαστον
θαῦμα. ᾧ ὁμώνυμον ἐν Παρνασσῷ.

daughter of Nisus, fell in love with him and cut off her fa-
ther's head (*sic*), realised that one who had betrayed her
father would readily stop at nothing, and so he bound the
traitress and patricide to the ship's rudder and left her to
be dragged through the sea. She herself was transformed
into a bird, according to Parthenius in the *Metamorphoses*
he is said to have written, while the gulf changed its spell-
ing and received its new name from her being dragged.
From this same Scylla a place in Hermione in the Pelopon-
nese is still called Scyllaeum, where the woman was cast
ashore by the waves after being drowned.

Moretum?

25 Scholiast on Virgil, codex Ambrosianus T 21 sup.

Parthenius wrote a *Moretum* in Greek, which Virgil imi-
tated.[21]

Propemptikon

26 Stephanus of Byzantium

Corycus, a city of Cilicia. Parthenius in the *Propemptikon*.
In it is the Corycian cave of the nymphs, a remarkable
wonder. It has a namesake on Parnassus.

---

[21] The *Moretum* is a short poem in the *Appendix Vergiliana*
describing how a ploughman prepares for himself a vegetarian
meal of cheese and herbs; the ascription to Virgil need not be an-
cient. We hear of another poem of the same name by Sueius, con-
temporary of Cicero.

27–53 FRAGMENTA INCERTAE SEDIS

27–32 Elegiaca

27 P.Lit.Lond. 64 (Add. MS 34473)

(a)

```
    –∪∪ ] ος γλυκερῶν οὐκ ἀπελ[–∪∪–
    –∪∪ ] εἴνεκα χαῖρε καὶ οφρας [–∪∪––
         ]χη τοίας φυςεπιδεμνι[
         ]τοιω Τίμανδρ' ἐπιδακρυ[
  5      ]ν οἰκείης τῆλε καταφθι[
         ]ιεν ὀθνείη πεπυρωμένα λ[
         ] ᾿Αχιλλείων θῆκεν ἐπὶ σκοπέ[λων
         ]θιην· εἰ δή με φίλος μαλαπυ[
         ]ς ἀλγεινοὶ παιδὸς εχ [ι [
  10     ] ομενου γὰρ εγωγετ [
         ] σοι οὔτ' αλλοιςοιδε [
         ]ταφιλος προτέρου[
         ] οπαρευτελιου [
         ]ελεωςειη [
  15     ]υτοιας [
         ] [ο [
```

– – – –

1 δύστη]νος Ll.-J.–P.   ἀπέλ[αυσε (-σα Ll.-J.–P.) γάμων
Crönert: τέκνων Cazzaniga   3 δέμνι' [ἄγει Ll.-J.–P.
4 πολλά] τοι, ὦ Τίμανδρ', ἐπὶ δάκρυ[α λεῖβον ἀφ' οὗ σε Mette
5 ἔκλυο]ν οἰκείης τῆλε καταφθί[μενον Pfeiffer

27–53 FRAGMENTS OF UNCERTAIN LOCATION

27–32 *Elegiac Fragments*

27 P.Lit.Lond. 64

(a)

. . . derived no profit from sweet marriage (?)
. . . and so farewell, and
. . . born from such a woman, to a bed (?)
. . . Timander, tears
. . . perished far from your native soil   [5]
. . . in a foreign (land) your cremated (remains)
. . . laid them on the Achillean rocks[22]
. . . if indeed dear . . . me
. . . painful . . . of the boy
. . . for I   [10]
. . . (neither) for you nor (for?) others (?)
. . . dear . . . of the former (?)
. . . from Eutelias (?)

---

[22] Several places were associated with Achilles. The mention of "rocks" possibly points to Achilles' grave-mound on the promontory of Sigeum in the Troad.

---

6 χώρη]ι ἐν ὀθνείης‹ι› Cazzaniga, Mette   πεπυρωμένα
λ[είψανα Cazzaniga, Pfeiffer   9 ἔχωσι Milne
10 τρυ]χομένου Mette   11 οὔτ]ε σοι οὔτ᾽ ἄλλοις Pfeiffer
12 ταῦ]τα φίλος Pfeiffer   13 οὐ]χ ὁ παρ᾽ Εὐτελίου Ll.-J.–P.
14 εὐτ]ελέως Pfeiffer

(b)

–◡◡–◡◡–◡◡–]λεγοι ου σύ γε φωτός

–◡◡–◡◡––◡].τεροιο νέκυν

]ηρειφθημενος

].ην σε κεύθει

5   ]κουρα.. δροίτης

]κιοντες

]υρόμεθα

]πουλὺ πνέουσαν

].…ερσης

10   ]..επτου

]πι μάχλωι

]ν

]ους

– – – –

3 κατ]ηρείφθη Ll.-J.–P.: φθιμενος Livrea   5 κουράδα
Mette, κεφαλῇ περι]κουράδι Ll.-J.–P.   6 κίοντες, μαλ]κί-
οντες Ll.-J.-P.   7 ὀδ]υρόμεθα, μ]υρόμεθα, σ]υρόμεθα
9]αρ ἐέρσης Ll.-J.–P.   10]α λεπτοῦ Milne   11 ἐ]πὶ,
ἔλλο]πι, κόλλο]πι etc. Ll.-J.–P.

Scholia in mg. dextr.

ad l. 3   κατ[: κάτ[ω Pfeiffer

ad l. 4   εἰς.. [: εἰς δρ[οίτην Milne

ad l. 5   σοροῦ (vel σορός) σ…: cf. EtMag 288.3
           δροίτη . . . Παρθένιος δὲ τὴν σορόν, καὶ
           Αἰσχύλος.

ad l. 9   …ερση.[

(b)

> . . . you . . . of a man
> . . . corpse
> . . . fell in ruins (?)
> . . . covers you
> . . . cropping(?) . . . of a bier   [5]
> . . . cold (?)
> . . . we mourn (?)
> . . . breathing deeply   [8]
> . . . wanton   [11]

Scholia in the right margin

3	below
4	to a bier
5	(of) a coffin

28 Steph. Byz., ap. Eustath. ad *Il.* 2.712, i. p. 327.37 van der Valk

κώμη Κιλικίας ἐστὶ Γλαφύραι καλουμένη, ἀπέχουσα Ταρσοῦ τριάκοντα σταδίους πρὸς δύσιν [hactenus etiam Stephani codd., p. 209.5 Mein.], ἐν ᾗ πηγὴ ἀπὸ ῥωγάδος καταρρέουσα καὶ συνιοῦσα τῷ εἰς Ταρσὸν εἰσβάλλοντι ποταμῷ. περὶ ἧς Παρθένιος γράφων ἄλλα τε λέγει καὶ ὅτι·

> παρθένος ἡ Κιλίκων εἶχεν ἀνακτορίην,
> ἀγχίγαμος δ᾽ ἔπελεν, καθαρῷ δ᾽ ἐπεμαίνετο
> Κύδνῳ,
> Κύπριδος ἐξ ἀδύτων πυρσὸν ἀναψαμένη,
> εἰσόκε μιν Κύπρις πηγὴν θέτο, μῖξε δ᾽ ἔρωτι
> 5   Κύδνου καὶ νύμφης ὑδατόεντα γάμον.

1–2 Versus restituit Hermann, *Zeitschr. f. d. Alterthumswiss.* 1836, 351: παρθένος Κιλίκων ἀνακτορίην ἔχουσα ἀγχίγαμος πέλε καθαρῷ δ᾽ κτλ. cod.   3 ἀναψαμένη ex -νης corr. cod.

29 EtGen AB, α 1543, ii. p. 370.6 L.-L. = EtMag 117.33, α 1514

Ἀῶος· ποταμὸς τῆς Κύπρου· Ἀῶος γὰρ ὁ Ἄδωνις ὠνομάζετο, καὶ ἀπ᾽ αὐτοῦ οἱ Κύπριοι βασιλεῖς. Ζωΐλος δὲ ὁ Κεδρασεὺς [*FGrH* 758 F 7] καὶ αὐτὸν ἀπὸ τῆς ἑαυτοῦ μητρὸς κληθῆναι· τὴν γὰρ Θείαντος θυγατέρα [μητέρα codd., corr. Haupt] οὐ Σμύρναν ἀλλ᾽ Ἀῶαν καλεῖσθαι. Φιλέας δὲ [fr. 12 Gisinger] πρῶτον βασιλεῦσαι Ἀῶον, Ἠοῦς ὄντα καὶ Κεφάλου, ἀφ᾽ οὗ καὶ ὄρος τι ὠνομάσθη

28 Stephanus of Byzantium, quoted by Eustathius

There is a village in Cilicia called Glaphyrai, about thirty stades to the west of Tarsus, in which a stream flows from a crevice in a rock and converges with the river which flows into Tarsus. Among the other things that Parthenius writes about this stream is the following:

> A maiden, ruling over the Cilicians.[23]
> To wedlock near, she raved with love for Cydnus,
> Lighting a torch for him from Cypris' shrine;
> Till, rendering her a spring, Cypris conjoined
> Of river and of nymph an aqueous match. [5]

29 Etymologicum Genuinum

Aous: a river in Cyprus. For Adonis was called Aous, and after him the Cyprian kings. Zoilus of Cedrasa says that he in turn was called after his mother; for the daughter of Theias was called, not Smyrna, but Aoa. Phileas says that the first ruler was Aous, son of the Dawn and Cephalus, after whom a mountain was called Aoum. From this moun-

[23] Comaetho: for the maiden's name see Nonnus, *D.* 2.143–144, 40.141–143.

Ἀώϊον· ἐξ οὗ δύο ποταμῶν φερομένων Σε<τ>ράχου καὶ
Ἀπλιέως [Α: Πλιέως Β, EtMag], τὸν ἕνα τούτων ὁ Παρ-
θένιος Ἀῶον κέκληκεν ἢ διὰ τὸ πρὸς τὴν ἠῶ τετραμμένην
ἔχειν τὴν ῥύσιν, καθώς φησιν ὁ Παρθένιος·

<−∪∪> Κωρυκίων σεύμενος ἐξ ὀρέων

ἀνατολικῶν ὄντων· δύναται δὲ οὕτως καλεῖσθαι καθ' ὃ ἡ
Κιλικία Ἀφᾶ πάλαι ὠνομάζετο.

30 EtGen AB = EtMag 288.58

δρύψελλον· τὸ λέμμα, ὁ φλοιός. Παρθένιος, οἷον·

οὐδὲ πόροι ῥίζης δρύψελα Ποντιάδος

παρὰ τὸ δρύψαι ὅ ἐστι λεπίσαι· δρύπελλον γὰρ ὁ ἀπο-
δρυπτόμενος φλοιός· καταχρηστικῶς δὲ καὶ φύλλον· δρύ-
ψελλον ἐπὶ τοῦ σελίνου ὁ Παρθένιος [**31**].

δρύψελλα Α, EtMag cod. D

31 v. ad **30**

δρύψελλον ἐπὶ τοῦ σελίνου ὁ Παρθένιος.

32 *AP* 11.130 (Pollianus) (cf. Test. **5**)

    . . . καὶ διὰ τοῦτ' ἐλέγοις προσέχω πλέον· οὐδὲν
        ἔχω γὰρ
    Παρθενίου κλέπτειν ἢ πάλι Καλλιμάχου.

tain flow two rivers, the Setrachus and the Aplieus, one of which Parthenius called Aous, perhaps because the direction of its flow is eastwards, as Parthenius says:

Rushing from the Corycian mountains,

which are in the east. But it could also be called this because Cilicia was once named Aoa.[24]

30–31 Etymologicum Genuinum

drypsellon: peel, bark. Parthenius:

Nor furnish scrapings of the Pontic root.

It comes from *drypsai*, which means to peel off a husk. *Drypellon* is the peeled-off bark, and is also misapplied to the leaf. Parthenius applies *drypsellon* to celery.

32 Palatine Anthology 11.130 (Pollianus)

And so I set more store by elegies, for I can steal Nothing from Parthenius, nor Callimachus.

[24] In other words, Parthenius called the river Setrachus or Satrachus "Aous" because it flowed underground from "eastern" or "Aoan" Cilicia. He was probably talking about Adonis, with whom the Satrachus is connected in Cat. 95.5 and Nonn. *D.* 13.458–460.

5 "θηρὶ μὲν οὐατόεντι" γενοίμην, εἴ ποτε γράψω,
   "εἴκελος", "ἐκ ποταμῶν χλωρὰ χελιδόνια" . . .

5–6 = Call. fr. 1.31 Pf.; unde "ἐκ . . . χελιδόνια" Parthenii esse
conicias   χελιδόνεα codd.: corr. H. Stephanus

33–34 Hexametrica

33 Parthenius, Ἐρωτικὰ Παθήματα XI. 3 (ubi de con-
textu agitur)

. . . λέγεται δὲ καὶ παρ' ἡμῖν οὕτως·

   ἡ δ' ὅτε δή <ῥ'> ὀλοοῖο κασιγνήτου νόον ἔγνω,
   κλαῖεν ἀ<η>δονίδων θαμινώτερον, αἵτ' ἐνὶ
        βήσσῃς
   Σιθονίῳ κούρῳ πέρι μυρίον αἰάζουσιν.
   καί ῥα κατὰ στυφελοῖο σαρωνίδος αὐτίκα μίτρην
5 ἁψαμένη δειρὴν ἐνεθήκατο. ταὶ δ' ἐπ' ἐκείνῃ
   βεύδεα παρθενικαὶ Μιλησίδες ἐρρήξαντο.

34 Σ Dion. Perieg. 456, *GGM* ii. p. 448ᵇ25 Müller

. . . Γάδειρα, καὶ ἐνταῦθα εἰσιν αἱ στῆλαι τοῦ Ἡρακλέος.
αἱ δὲ τοῦ Διονύσου ἑῷαι. ὁ δὲ Παρθένιος Βριάρεω τὰς
στήλας φησὶν εἶναι·

   μάρτυρα δ' †ἄμμιν τὴν ἐπὶ Γάδειρα λίπε †θυμόν
   ἀρχαίου Βριαρῆος ἀπ' οὔνομα τὸ πρὶν ἀρ<ά>ξας.

1 μάρτυρα δ' αἰνικτὴν ἐπὶ Γαδείρᾳ λίπε μῦθον Ll.-J.–P.: μάρ-
τυρα δ' ἄμμιν ἑῆς ἐπὶ Γαδείρῃ λίπεν οἵμου Hollis
2 Βριάρεω codd., corr. Meineke   ἀρ<ά>ξας Hermann

"Like a long-eared beast" may I become, if I
Should ever write "Pale celandine from the rivers".[25]   [5]

33–34 Hexameter Fragments

33 Parthenius, *Sufferings in Love*, "About Byblis"

Here is my own version of the story:

> And once she knew her cruel brother's mind,
> Her cries came thicker than the nightingales'
> In woods, who ever mourn the Thracian lad.
> Her girdle to a rugged oak she tied,
> And laid her neck within. And over her
> Milesian maidens rent their lovely robes.[26]   [5]

34 Scholiast on Dionysius the Periegete

. . . Cádiz, and that is where the pillars of Heracles are.
Dionysus' are in the east. Parthenius says the pillars belong
to Briareus:

> To bear us witness, at Cádiz he left a record (?),
> Erasing the old name of ancient Briareus.[27]

[25] Apparently from a celebrated passage of Parthenius, since it
can be paralleled with a quotation from the *Aitia* prologue.

[26] For notes, see on the *Sufferings in Love*.

[27] One of the hundred-handers or hekatogcheirs who sup-
ported Zeus against the Titans in Hesiod's *Theogony*. For his con-
nection with the Pillars of Heracles, see Aristotle fr. 678 Rose,
Plut. *Mor.* 420 A, and Euphorion **169**.

35–53 *Incerta Elegiaca an Hexametrica*

35 EtGen B = EtMag 375.33

Ἐρκύνιος δρυμός· ὁ τῆς Ἰταλίας ἐνδοτάτω· Ἀπολλώνιος
ἐν δ΄ Ἀργοναυτικῶν, "Σκοπελίοιο (sic) καθ᾽ Ἐρκυνίου
ἰάχησε" [4.640]. καὶ Παρθένιος·

ἀλλ᾽ ὅτ᾽ ἀφ᾽ ἑσπερίης Ἐρκυνίδος ὥρετο γαίης

διὰ τὸ εὑρεῖν ἐν αὐτῷ χοῖρον ὑπὸ κυνὸς ἐσθιόμενον· ὅθεν
τὸν μὲν δρυμὸν ερκον φασί, τὸν δὲ κύνα κυνον, καὶ ἐν
συνθέσει ἔρκυννος καὶ ἐρκύνιος.

36 Aulus Gellius, *NA* 13.27.1

Partheni poetae versus est:

Γλαύκῳ καὶ Νηρῆι καὶ εἰναλίῳ Μελικέρτῃ.

eum versum Vergilius aemulatus est itaque fecit duobus
vocabulis venuste immutatis parem: "Glauco et Panopeae
et Inoo Melicertae" [*Georg.* 1.437].

35–53 Elegiac or Hexametric

35 Etymologicum Genuinum

The Ercynian forest: the one in the heart of Italy.[28]
Apollonius in the fourth book of the *Argonautica*: "It re-
sounded across the Hercynian rock", and Parthenius:

> But when he rose up from the west's Hercynian
>   land.[29]

It is thus named because a pig was found in it being eaten
by a dog, whence they called the forest an *erkos* and the
dog *kynos*, and putting these together you get *erkynos* and
erkynios.

36 Aulus Gellius, *Attic Nights*

There is a verse of Parthenius the poet:

> To Glaucus and Nereus and sea-dwelling
>   Melicertes.[30]

This verse was imitated by Virgil who, with a charming
two-word change, made its match: "To Glaucus and Pano-
pea and Melicertes, Ino's son."

---

[28] Locations of the Hercynian wood or mountain-range vary,
but it was broadly central European and not usually set in Italy.

[29] Possibly referring to Heracles' route back from the far west
(see the previous fragment).

[30] Probably from the *Propemptikon*, in which the sea-deities
were invoked to ensure a safe voyage.

cf. Macrobius, *Sat.* 5.17.18

Versus est Parthenii, quo grammatico in Graecis Vergilius usus est: Γλαύκῳ καὶ Νηρῆι καὶ Ἰνώῳ Μελικέρτῃ. Hic ait: "Glauco et Panopeae et Inoo Melicertae".

AP 6.164.1 (Lucili? Lucillii?): Γλαύκῳ καὶ Νηρῆι καὶ Ἰνοῖ καὶ Μελικέρτῃ.

Νηρεῖ fere codd. omnes, corr. J. J. Scaliger

37 Choeroboscus, in Theodos. *Canon.*, *GG* IV.1, p. 252.21 Hilgard

. . . τὸ ἵλαος συνεσταλμένον ἔχον τὸ ᾱ, οἷον ὡς παρὰ Παρθενίῳ·

ἵλαος ὦ Ὑμέναιε

Cf. **8**.

38 EtGud p. 185.19 de Stefani

ἀργειφόντης· ὁ Ἑρμῆς παρ' Ὁμήρῳ καὶ παρὰ πολλοῖς. παρὰ δὲ Σοφοκλεῖ [fr. 1024 Radt] καὶ ἐπὶ τοῦ Ἀπόλλωνος, καὶ παρὰ Παρθενίῳ καὶ ἐπὶ τοῦ Τηλέφου.

cf. Macrobius, *Saturnalia*

There is a verse of Parthenius, who was Virgil's teacher of Greek: "To Glaucus and Nereus and Melicertes, Ino's son." Virgil says: "To Glaucus and Panopea and Melicertes, Ino's son."

AP 6.164.1 (Lucilius? Lucillus?): To Glaucus and Nereus and Ino and Melicertes.

37 Choeroboscus on Theodosius, *Canones*

Hīlaos with a short *a*, as in Parthenius:

Be gracious, o Hymenaeus.

38 Etymologicum Gudianum

Argeiphontēs: Hermes in Homer and in many other writers. It is used by Sophocles of Apollo, and by Parthenius of Telephus.[31]

[31] Apparently through learned re-etymology (the conventional interpretation is Argus-slayer), but it is not clear exactly how Parthenius proposed to understand it.

39 Apollonius Dyscolus, *de Adv.*, *GG* I.1, p. 127.5
Schneider

ὤμοι . . . τὸ πλῆρες τῆς φωνῆς ἀκούουσιν ὦ ἐμοί, ὡς ἔχει
καὶ παρὰ Παρθενίῳ·

ὦ ἐμὲ τὴν τὰ περισσά

<καὶ οὐκ ἔτι τλητὰ παθοῦσαν> vel <καὶ ἄλγεα δεινὰ πα-
θοῦσαν> suppl. Meineke

40 Steph. Byz., p. 643.22 Mein.

Τυφρηστός, πόλις τῆς Τραχῖνος ὀνομασθεῖσα ἀπὸ τῆς
τέφρας Ἡρακλέους ἢ ἀπὸ Τυφρηστοῦ υἱοῦ Σπερχειοῦ. τὸ
ἐθνικὸν Τυφρήστιος. καὶ τὸ οὐδέτερον Παρθένιος·

Τυφρήστιον αἶπος.

41 EtGen AB (cf. EtMag 260.28)

δείκελον· λέγεται δὲ καὶ δείκηλον· σημαίνει δὲ ἄγαλμα ἢ
ὁμοίωμα, οἷον "Δείκηλα προΐαλλεν ἐπιζάφελον κοτέ-
ουσα" [Ap. Rhod. 4.1672]. ζάφελος δέ ἐστι μεγαλόκοτος.
ὥσπερ γὰρ παρὰ τὸ πέμπω γίνεται πέμπελος, σημαίνει
δὲ τὸν πολλῶν ἐνιαυτῶν ὄντα, καὶ ἀπὸ τοῦ ἄγω ἄγγελος,
τὸν αὐτὸν τρόπον καὶ ἀπὸ τοῦ δείκω το<ῦ> δεικνύω γίνε-
ται δείκελος καὶ κατ' ἐπέκτασιν τοῦ ε εἰς τὸ η δείκηλον.
εὕρηται δὲ καὶ δείκελον παρὰ Παρθενίῳ [Β: εὕρηται γὰρ
διὰ τοῦ η ὡς παρὰ Π. οἷον Α]·

δείκελον Ἰφιγόνης.

Ἰφιγένης codd., corr. Meineke.

39 Apollonius Dyscolus, *On Adverbs*

"Alas": . . . the full version of the expression is "alas for me", as in Parthenius:

> Alas for me, whom the greatest . . .

40 Stephanus of Byzantium

Typhrestus, a city of Trachis called after the ashes of Heracles or after Typhrestus the son of Spercheius. The ethnic adjective is *Typhrēstios*, and the neuter is in Parthenius:

> The Typhrestian height.[32]

41 Etymologicum Genuinum

deikelon ("image"): it is also spelt *deikēlon*. It indicates a statue or a likeness, as in, "She spurred on images, raging furiously (*epizaphelon*)." *zaphelos* means very angry. Just as *pempelos* comes from *pempō*, and indicates someone of advanced years, and from *agō* angelos, in the same way from *deikō*, or *deiknuō*, comes *deikelos* and by extension of *e* to *ē deikēlon. Deikelon* is also found in Parthenius:

> The image of Iphigone.[33]

---

[32] Possibly in connection with the cremation of Heracles.

[33] Variant form of the name of Iphigenia, and a possible reference to the famous statue of Artemis which Iphigenia and Orestes brought back with them from Tauris (Eur. *IT* 1441–1453).

42 Steph. Byz., β 128 Billerbeck

. . . ἀπὸ γὰρ τῆς εἰς ος εὐθείας ἡ διὰ τοῦ ιτης
παραγωγὴ πλεονάζει μιᾷ συλλαβῇ, ὡς τόπος τοπίτης,
Κανωπίτης ὁ Ἄδωνις παρὰ Παρθενίῳ.

43 Steph. Byz., γ 47 Billerbeck

Γενέα, κώμη Κορίνθου, ὁ οἰκήτωρ Γενεάτης. ἀφ' οὗ
παροιμία "εὐδαίμων ὁ Κόρινθος, ἐγὼ δ' εἴην Γενεά-
της." τινὲς τὰς ἀπὸ ταύτης καλοῦσι Γενειάδας, ὡς
Παρθένιος. τινὲς δὲ Τενέα γράφουσι.

Τενειάδες Meineke

Cf. Append. Prov. 2.88: εὐορκότερος Τενεάτου [Τελ-
cod.] ἢ Γενεάτου.

44 Steph. Byz., p. 266.13 Mein.

⟨Ἐλεφαντίνη, πόλις Αἰγύπτου·⟩ Παρθένιος δὲ Ἐλε-
φαντίδα αὐτήν φησιν.

45 Steph. Byz., p. 273.3 Mein.

Ἐπίδαμνος, πόλις Ἰλλυρίας . . . τὸ ἐθνικὸν Ἐπι-
δάμνιος. εὕρηται παρὰ Παρθενίῳ καὶ διὰ διφθόγγου.

42 Stephanus of Byzantium

For from the nominative in *-os* the suffix *-ītēs* lengthens the word by one syllable, as *topos topītēs*, and *Kanōpītēs* ("he of Canopus") the title of Adonis in Parthenius.

43 Stephanus of Byzantium

Genea, a village of Corinth, the inhabitant *Geneatēs*. Hence the proverb, "Blessed is Corinth; but I would be a Genean." Some call its women *Geneiades*, as Parthenius. Some spell it *Tenea*.

cf. Appendix of Proverbs: Truer to an oath than a Tenean or Genean.

44 Stephanus of Byzantium

Elephantine, a city in Egypt. Parthenius calls it *Elephantis*.

45 Stephanus of Byzantium

Epidamnus, a city in Illyria . . . the ethnic adjective is *Epidamnios*. It is also used by Parthenius with a diphthong (*Epidamneios*).

46 Steph. Byz., p. 424.19 Mein.

Μαγνησία, πόλις παρὰ τῷ Μαιάνδρῳ καὶ χώρα . . . ὁ πολίτης Μάγνης . . . τὸ θηλυκὸν [ἐθνικὸν codd., corr. Salmasius] Μάγνησσα παρὰ Καλλιμάχῳ [fr. 708 Pf.] καὶ Μάγνησις παρὰ Παρθενίῳ καὶ Μαγνῆτις παρὰ Σοφοκλεῖ [fr. 1066 Radt].

Μαγνησίς vel Μαγνησ⟨σ⟩ίς Meineke

47 Steph. Byz., p. 463.14 Mein.

Μύρκινος, τόπος καὶ πόλις κτισθεῖσα παρὰ τῷ Στρυμόνι ποταμῷ. τὸ ἐθνικὸν Μυρκίνιος καὶ Μυρκινία. Παρθένιος δὲ Μυρκιννίαν αὐτήν φησιν.

Μυρκινίαν coni. Meineke: Μυρκιννί⟨δ⟩α coni. Ll.-J.–P.

48 Steph. Byz., p. 465.5 Mein.

Μυτιλήνη, πόλις ἐν Λέσβῳ μεγίστη . . . οἱ δὲ ἀπὸ Μύτωνος τοῦ Ποσειδῶνος καὶ Μυτιλήνης. ὅθεν Μυτωνίδα καλεῖ τὴν Λέσβον Καλλίμαχος ἐν τῷ τετάρτῳ [fr. 111 Pf.], Παρθένιος δὲ Μυτωνίδας τὰς Λεσβικάς [Λεσβίας Meineke: Λεσβίδας Martini] φησι.

Μυτωνίδας Xylander: -ίδου codd.

46 Stephanus of Byzantium

Magnesia, a city on the Maeander, and the territory . . . The inhabitant is a *Magnēs* . . . The feminine *Magnēssa* in Callimachus and *Magnē(s)sis* in Parthenius and *Magnētis* in Sophocles.

47 Stephanus of Byzantium

Myrcinus, a terrain and city founded on the banks of the river Strymon. The ethnic adjective is *Myrkinios* and *Myrkinia*. Parthenius calls a woman of Myrcinus *Myrkinnia*.

48 Stephanus of Byzantium

Mytilene, the largest city in Lesbos . . . Some derive the name from Myton son of Poseidon and Mytilene. Whence Callimachus calls Lesbos *Mytōnis* in the fourth book, and Parthenius calls the women of Lesbos *Mytōnides*.

49 EtGen AB = EtMag 288.3 (cf. ps. Zonaras, col. 571 Tittmann)

δροίτη· ἡ πύελος. ὁ δὲ Αἰτωλός φησι τὴν σκάφην ἐν ᾗ τιθηνεῖται τὰ βρέφη [Alex. Aet. **15**]. Παρθένιος δὲ τὴν σορόν [cf. **27b** 5], καὶ Αἰσχύλος [Choe. 999]. κτλ.

50 Choeroboscus, *de Orthogr.*, Bodl. MS Barocci 50 fol. 167ᵛ, ap. Cramer, *Anecd. Oxon.* ii. p. 266.10

Ταύχειρα· εῖ, ἐπειδὴ εὕρηται καὶ χωρὶς τοῦ ῑ παρὰ Παρθενίῳ· ἐκεῖνος γὰρ εἶπεν Ταυχέριος τὸ ἐθνικόν.

Ταυχείριος cod.

cf. Cyrilli Lex. (Bodl. MS Auct. T 2.11 fol. 283ʳ, ap. Cramer, *Anecd. Paris.* iv. p. 191.31)

Τα<ύ>χειρα· πόλις Λιβύης. <ὁ πολίτης Ταυχείριος καὶ Ταυχέριος suppl. Martini e Steph. Byz. p. 609.1 Mein.> Ταυχερίων [Ταυχειρίων codd., corr. Martini] γοῦν ὁ Παρθένιος.

Ἡρακλεῖ attrib. Livrea

51 EtGen AB

ἠλαίνω· δηλοῖ τὸ μωραίνω· καὶ ἠλαίνουσα παρὰ Παρθενίῳ.

cf. EtMag 425.7.

49 Etymologicum Genuinum

droitē: a coffin. The Aetolian says it is the cradle in which babies are nursed. Parthenius uses it of a coffin, and so does Aeschylus.

50 Choeroboscus, *On Orthography*

Taucheira (Tūkra): *ei*, since it is also found without the *i* in Parthenius: he used the ethnic form *Taucherios*.

cf. Cyril, *Lexicon*

Taucheira: a city in Libya. The inhabitant is *Taucheirios* and *Taucherios*. *Taucheriōn* (genitive plural) in Parthenius.

51 Etymologicum Genuinum

ēlainō ("wander", "be distracted") means "to be mad". "Distracted" occurs in Parthenius.

52 Steph. Byz., p. 472.4 Mein.

Νέμαυσος, πόλις Γαλλίας, ἀπὸ Νεμαύσου Ἡρακλεί-
δου, ὡς Παρθένιος.

πόλις Ἰταλίας codd., corr. Xylander. "Nisi haec ad Parthenium
Phocaeensem spectant" Meineke.

53 EtGen AB (cf. ps. Zonaras, col. 1435 Tittmann)

Οἰταῖον· ἔστι δὲ ὄρος· καὶ Οἰταῖον ἀπὸ Οἴτης παρὰ
Παρθενίῳ.

54–57 DUBIE TRIBUTA

54 P.Ryl. III 486 (1st c. AD)

De Parthenio auctore cogitavit A. Colonna, *SIFC* 22
(1947), 238; de Euphorione B. Snell, *Gnomon* 15 (1939),
542.

```
                    – – – –
              ]..[.].o̲ν̲ε̲λ̲[.]..[
         –∪∪–]ευση.ε γένοισθε δὲ τυ.[ ∪∪– –
           τ]αχινὸς καταδυννεομενο.[
           ] Λάανδρον ἰδ‹ε›ῖν μόνον ηνδα[
5          ]ντι...πάλιν Ἔ[σ]περε λαθρ[
           ]νδρε καὶ αστ[....] ιππευ[
           ]ει νὺξ οὐρανὸς ἠελιο[
           ]...ο̲υ̲ς οπλει.[.].αι ε.περ[
```

52 Stephanus of Byzantium

Nemausus (Nîmes), a city of Gaul, from Nemausus the Heraclid. So Parthenius.

53 Etymologicum Genuinum

Oetaeum: this is a mountain. *Oitaios* from *Oitē* is used by Parthenius.[34]

54–57 DUBIOUSLY ATTRIBUTED

54 P.Ryl. III 486

. . . may you become sightless (?)	[2]
. . . swiftly set	
. . . only to see Laandros[35] pleased	
. . . again, Hesperus, secretly	[5]
. . . Laa]nder, and the stars like mounted riders(?)[36]	
. . . night, heaven, sun, (earth?)	[7]

[34] Possibly of Heracles' funeral pyre; or connected with the rising of the Evening Star (cf. Cat. 62.7).

[35] A dialectal variant of the name of Leander, lover of Hero. For their story, see Virg. *Georg.* 3.258–263; Ovid, *Heroides* 18–19; Antipater of Thessalonica, *HE* 129–134 = *AP* 7.666; Musaeus' *Hero and Leander*. The emphasis on starlight—natural light—in this fragment perhaps suggests that the lamp with its artificial light, prominent in Musaeus' version, also played a part here.

[36] For this image, see Eur. fr. 929 Kannicht; Tib. 1.9.62; Ov. *Am.* 1.6.65.

−∪∪−] Λάανδρε τέτηκε γάρ [−∪∪−−

10   ]εθων τ[η]λεσκόπος ερπε[

2 ν]εύσητε Roberts: λ]εύσητε Snell: ἱππ]εύσητε Ll.-J.-P.
τυφ[λοί, etc.   3 καταδυν{ε}όμενον Roberts: καταδυν{ε}ο-
μένοι[ο Ll.-J.-P.: καταδύνεο †μενον Snell   4 ἤνδα[νε
θυμῶι Roberts: ἤνδα[νεν Ἡροῖ Snell   5 ἀ]ντιάαις Roberts
λάθρ[α, λάθρ[ιος vel sim.   6 Λάα]νδρε Roberts
    ἀστ[έρες] Snell   ἱππευ[τῆρες Snell: ἱππευ[όντων Page
7 σοὶ γὰρ ὑπηρετέ]ει Keydell   ἠέλιο[ς γῆ Snell
8 ὁπλίζεαι Roberts: ὁπλ{ε}ίζ[ε]ται Ll.-J.-P.   9 τέτηκε γὰρ
ἀ[μφί σε νύμφη Snell   10 φα]έθων Roberts: φλεγ]έθων
Ll.-J.-P.   Φα]έθων ... ἔρπ᾽ ἐ[πὶ πόντον Snell

55 *PSI* 1389 (4th–5th c. AD)

De Parthenio auctore cogitavit dubitanter H. Lloyd-
Jones, *Gnomon* 31 (1959), 111.

(a)

    ]και χρόνος οἶδε διώκειν
    ]αμειβόμενον δ᾽ ἐνὶ καιρῶι
    ]ραίνεται ὡς νέον ἄνθος
    ] αμείβετο δάκρυ χέουσα
5   ].ο Κύπριδος ὄλβον
    ]υ γὰρ ἔγωγε
    ]πασσας

− − − − −

... Laandros, for ... was melting [9]
... (Pha]ethon?) the far-sighted [10]

55 *PSI* 1389

(a)

   ... and Time knows how to pursue
   ... changing in due order
   ... withers like a new flower
   ... replied, shedding a tear
   ... the riches of the Cyprian [5]
   ... for I

(b)

αὐτὰρ ὅτε κλύε μῦθον ἀπηνέα δ.[
αὖτις δ' ἔλπετό μιν ξυνὸν π.[
ἠὲ παραιφασίησ' ἠὲ κρα[
ἔνθεν δ' αὖ πλώεσκε[
5   ἔστι δέ τις μέσση.[
νῆσος ἀφικ[
τηνα[

_ _ _ _ _

(a) 1 ὄν] καί Ll.-J.–P.   3 μα]ραίνεται Vitelli
4]σ, προ]σαμείβετο Ll.-J.–P.   5 ἀ]πό, ὑ]πό Ll.-J.–P.
7 ὀ]πάσσας Bartoletti   **(b)** 2 πο[τὶ λέκτρον ἄγεσθαι
Merkelbach   3 κρα[τερῆς ὑπ' ἀνάγκης Merkelbach
5 μέσση π[Bartoletti: μεσσηγ[ύς Ll.-J.–P.

56 EtGen AB, α 1123, ii. 172.11 L.-L. (cf. EtMag 135.32,
α 1727)

Ἀργαφίης· οἶον·

   νιψάμεναι κρήνης ἔδραμον Ἀργαφίης

τινὲς δὲ διὰ τοῦ ε̄, ἀπὸ Γεργάφου τοῦ Ποσειδῶνος· τὸ δὲ
ἐντελὲς ἐν τῷ Ἑρμῇ· "κρήνης Γαργαφίης". ὁ †Παρμένιος
[Παρθένιος Sylburg: Παρμενίων Meineke: Παρμενίσκος
Bergk, _Zeitschr. f. d. Altertumswiss._ 1841, 867] ἄνευ τοῦ γ̄. ἡ
ἔλλειψις ἀπὸ ἱστορίας. οὕτως Ἡρωδιανὸς ἐν τοῖς Περὶ
παθῶν [GG III.2, p. 187.24 Lentz].

νιψόμεναι C. A. Lobeck, _Pathologiae Graeci sermonis elementa_, i.
(Königsberg, 1853), 93.

(b)

But when he heard the thankless word
Again he hoped to . . . a common
Either by persuasion or by mighty (constraint?)
Then again he went sailing
There is a certain . . . in the middle   [5]
An island . . . arriving

56 Etymologicum Genuinum

Argaphiēs: as in

Having washed in the stream of Argaphia, they ran
. . . [37]

Some spell it with an *e*, from Gergaphus the son of Posei-
don. It is found in its complete form in the *Hermes*: "Of the
spring of Gargaphia". Parmenius (?) has it without the *g*.
The omission is by convention: so, Herodian in *On Cases*.

[37] The Graces are the subject: see Alciphron, *Epist.* 1.11.3.

57 Steph. Byz., p. 508.18 Mein. (= Callimachus fr. 802 Pf., incerti auctoris)

Παρρασία· πόλις Ἀρκαδίας ... ὁ πολίτης Παρράσιος καὶ Παρρασιεύς καὶ Παρρασίς·

δέξονται Φολόης οὔρεα Παρρασίδος,

καὶ Παρρασική.

Φιλορρόης vel -λορόης codd., corr. Salmasius

Parthenio tributa sunt etiam *SH* 964.1–20 (Spanoudakis 2004); POxy 4711 (a primo editore, W. B. Henry; sed cf. contra Bernsdorff 2007).

58 SPURIUM

58 "Apuleius", *De Orthographia*, in Bibliothecae Valli-cellianae cod. R. 26, fo. 208ᵛ

Pasiphae nec hya nec diphthongum habet. Daphne dice-batur Spartanis [-nus cod.]: quod certissima daret oracula. fuit et Cretensis regina, Minotauri partu famosa, quo in-terfecto, Theseus abduxit Ariadnem uxorem sibi et filio Hippolyto Phaedram; cui, Serapione [-ni cod.] Rhodio tra-dente et Philocoro, vim intulit eius forma captus, uxore necata. at Phaedra indignata filium patri incusavit, quod se attentasset [appellasset cod., corr. Meineke]; qui diras in filium iactavit. quae ratae fuerunt, a suis enim equis in ra-

57 Stephanus of Byzantium

Parrhasia: a city of Arcadia . . . The inhabitant is *Parrhasios*
and *Parrhasieus* and *Parrhasis*:

> The mountains of Parrhasian Pholoe will receive

and *Parrhasikē*.

58 SPURIOUS

58 "Apuleius", *On Spelling*

Pasiphae has neither upsilon nor diphthong. The Spartans
called her Daphne, because she gave most reliable ora-
cles. She was also a queen of Crete, famous for giving
birth to the Minotaur, after whose killing Theseus abduc-
ted Ariadne as his wife together with Phaedra for his son
Hippolytus. According to Serapion of Rhodes and Philo-
chorus, he was captivated by Phaedra's beauty and used
force against her, having killed his own wife. Phaedra was
outraged and accused the son to the father of having made
an attempt on her. He hurled curses upon his son. They
were fulfilled when his horses went mad and tore him, in-

biem versis innocens discerptus est. sic illa de se et sorore ultionem sumpsit. Lupus Anilius idem scribit in Helene tragaedia, Parthenius aliter.

nocent as he was, to pieces. Thus she took revenge for her-self and her sister. Lupus Anilius says the same in his *Helen* tragedy. It is otherwise in Parthenius.[38]

[38] "Apuleius" is known only from two 16th c. scholars, and may be an invention. This bizarre version of the story of Theseus and Hippolytus seems to have been conflated with the Tereus myth (see Euphorion **25** n. 36). The citation of Parthenius' name in this extract is wholly unreliable.

ΠΑΡΘΕΝΙΟΥ ΠΕΡΙ ΕΡΩΤΙΚΩΝ ΠΑΘΗΜΑΤΩΝ

ταῦτα ἐν τῷδε τῷ συγγράμματι περιέχεται

SUFFERINGS IN LOVE

This work contains the following stories:

Παρθένιος Κορνηλίῳ Γάλλῳ χαίρειν.

(1) Μάλιστα σοὶ δοκῶν ἁρμόττειν, Κορνήλιε Γάλλε, τὴν ἄθροισιν τῶν ἐρωτικῶν παθημάτων, ἀναλεξάμενος ὡς ὅτι μάλιστα ἐν βραχυτάτοις ἀπέσταλκα. τὰ γὰρ παρά τισι τῶν ποιητῶν κείμενα τούτων, μὴ αὐτοτελῶς λελεγμένα[1], κατανοήσεις ἐκ τῶνδε τὰ πλεῖστα· (2) αὐτῷ τέ σοι παρέσται εἰς ἔπη καὶ ἐλεγείας ἀνάγειν τὰ μάλιστα ἐξ αὐτῶν ἁρμόδια. ⟨μηδὲ⟩[2] διὰ τὸ μὴ παρεῖναι τὸ περιττὸν αὐτοῖς, ὃ δὴ σὺ μετέρχῃ, χεῖρον περὶ αὐτῶν ἐννοηθῇς[3]· οἱονεὶ γὰρ ὑπομνηματίων τρόπον αὐτὰ συνελεξάμεθα, καὶ σοὶ νυνὶ τὴν χρῆσιν ὁμοίαν, ὡς ἔοικε, παρέξεται.

1 κείμενα τούτων μὴ αὐτοτελῶς λελεγμένων P, corr. Lehrs: κείμενα, ⟨ὑπὸ δὲ⟩ τούτων μὴ αὐτοτέλως λελεγμένα Hutchinson   2 ⟨μηδὲ⟩ Lehrs   3 ἐνενοήθης P, corr. Lehrs

Α´ Περὶ Λύρκου

Ἡ ἱστορία παρὰ Νικαινέτῳ ἐν τῷ Λύρκῳ καὶ Ἀπολλωνίῳ Ῥοδίῳ Καύνῳ

(1) Ἁρπασθείσης Ἰοῦς τῆς Ἀργείας ὑπὸ λῃστῶν, ὁ πατὴρ αὐτῆς Ἴναχος μαστῆράς τε καὶ ἐρευνητὰς ἄλλους[1] καθῆκεν, ἐν δὲ αὐτοῖς[2] Λύρκον τὸν Φορωνέως, ὃς μάλα πολλὴν γῆν ἐπιδραμὼν καὶ πολλὴν θάλασ-

1 ⟨πολλοὺς μὲν⟩ ἄλλους Meineke   2 ἐν δὲ αὐτοῖς ⟨καὶ⟩ Meineke, Zangoiannes

Parthenius to Cornelius Gallus, greetings.

Thinking, Cornelius Gallus, that the collection of sufferings in love was very appropriate to you, I have selected them and send them in as brief a form as possible. For those among them which occur in certain poets where they are not narrated in their own right, you will find out for the most part from what follows. (2) You, too, will be able to render the most suitable of them into hexameters and elegiacs. Think none the worse of them because they lack that quality of refined elaboration which you pursue. For I have collected them after the fashion of a little notebook, and they will, I trust, serve you in the same way.

I. LYRCUS

The story occurs in Nicaenetus in his Lyrcus, *and in Apollonius Rhodius'* Caunus[1]

When Io of Argos was stolen by pirates, her father Inachus dispatched various people to search and track her down, among them Lyrcus, son of Phoroneus. He traversed vast areas of land, crossed huge tracts of sea, but finally, when

[1] See also XI, which cites Apollonius' *Foundation of Caunus* and quotes an unnamed poem by Nicaenetus.

σαν περαιωθεὶς τέλος, ὡς οὐχ εὕρισκεν, ἀπεῖπε τῷ
καμάτῳ. καὶ εἰς μὲν Ἄργος, δεδοικὼς τὸν Ἴναχον, οὐ
μάλα τι κατῄει· ἀφικόμενος δὲ εἰς Καῦνον πρὸς Αἰγι-
αλὸν³ γαμεῖ αὐτοῦ τὴν θυγατέρα Εἰλεβίην. (2) ἔφα-
σαν⁴ γὰρ τὴν κόρην ἰδοῦσαν τὸν Λύρκον εἰς ἔρωτα
ἐλθεῖν καὶ πολλὰ τοῦ πατρὸς δεηθῆναι κατασχεῖν
αὐτόν. ὁ δὲ τῆς τε βασιλείας μοῖραν οὐκ ἐλαχίστην
ἀποδασάμενος καὶ τῶν λοιπῶν ὑπαργμάτων γαμβρὸν
εἶχεν. χρόνου δὲ πολλοῦ προϊόντος, ὡς τῷ Λύρκῳ
παῖδες οὐκ ἐγίνοντο, ἦλθεν εἰς Διδυμέως, χρησόμενος
περὶ γονῆς τέκνων· καὶ αὐτῷ θεσπίζει ὁ θεὸς παῖδας
φύσειν, ᾗ ἂν ἐκ τοῦ ναοῦ χωρισθεὶς πρώτῃ συγ-
γένηται. (3) ὁ δὲ μάλα γεγηθὼς ἠπείγετο πρὸς τὴν
γυναῖκα, πειθόμενος κατὰ νοῦν ἂν αὐτῷ χωρήσειν τὸ
μαντεῖον. ἐπεὶ δὲ πλέων ἀφίκετο ἐς Βύβαστον πρὸς
Στάφυλον τὸν Διονύσου, μάλα φιλοφρόνως ἐκεῖνος
αὐτὸν ὑποδεχόμενος εἰς πολὺν οἶνον προετρέψατο· καὶ
ἐπειδὴ πολλῇ μέθῃ παρεῖτο, συγκατέκλινεν αὐτῷ
Ἡμιθέαν τὴν θυγατέρα. (4) ταῦτα δὲ ἐποίει προπε-
πυσμένος τὸ τοῦ χρηστηρίου καὶ βουλόμενος ἐκ ταύ-
της αὐτῷ παῖδας γενέσθαι. δι' ἔριδος μέντοι ἐγένοντο
Ῥοιώ τε καὶ Ἡμιθέα αἱ τοῦ Σταφύλου· τίς αὐτῶν
μιχθείη τῷ ξένῳ· τοσοῦτος ἀμφοτέρας κατέσχε πόθος.
(5) Λύρκος δὲ ἐπιγνοὺς τῇ ὑστεραίᾳ οἷα ἐδεδράκει καὶ
τὴν Ἡμιθέαν ὁρῶν συγκατακεκλιμένην, ἐδυσφόρει τε
καὶ πολλὰ κατεμέμφετο τὸν Στάφυλον, ὡς ἀπατεῶνα

---

³ αἰβίαλον, βι in rasura P; corr. Heyne   ⁴ φασὶ Rohde

he could not find her, he gave up out of weariness. To Argos he certainly would not return, for fear of Inachus; so he went instead to Caunus[2] and called upon Aegialus, whose daughter Heilebie he married: (2) they said that on seeing Lyrcus the girl fell in love and pleaded with her father to have him. He portioned off not the smallest share of his kingdom and other possessions, and made Lyrcus his son-in-law. A long time elapsed, but Lyrcus had no issue; so he went to Didyma to consult the oracle about begetting children. The god told him that he would father children on the first woman he had intercourse with when he left the temple. (3) In great delight he began to hurry back to his wife, convinced that the oracle would turn out as he wished. But when his voyage brought him to Bybastus,[3] he was most cordially entertained there by Staphylus, Dionysus' son, who encouraged him in some heavy drinking; and once the quantities of alcohol had softened him up, Staphylus put him to bed with his daughter Hemithea. (4) He did this because he had advance knowledge of the oracle and wanted Lyrcus to father children on his daughter. There had been some squabbling between Rhoeo and Hemithea, the daughters of Staphylus, as to which of them should sleep with the stranger, so overcome were they both with desire. (5) On the next day Lyrcus realised what he had done when he saw Hemithea lying next to him. He took it badly and blamed Staphylus bitterly for deceiv-

[2] It is not clear why a connection is being claimed between Argos and Caunus, in Caria, though other myths connect the quest for Io with the foundation of cities in Asia Minor.

[3] In the Carian Chersonese, *en route* between Didyma and Lyrcus' home.

γενόμενον αὐτοῦ. ὕστερον δὲ μηδὲν ἔχων ὅ τι ποιῇ,
περιελόμενος τὴν ζώνην δίδωσι τῇ κόρῃ κελεύων ἡβή-
σαντι τῷ παιδὶ φυλάττειν, ὅπως ἔχῃ γνώρισμα, ὁπότ᾽
ἂν ἀφίκοιτο πρὸς τὸν πατέρα αὐτοῦ εἰς Καῦνον, καὶ
ἐξέπλευσεν. (6) Αἰγιαλὸς δὲ ὡς ᾔσθετο τά τε κατὰ τὸ
χρηστήριον καὶ τὴν Ἡμιθέαν, ἤλαυνε[5] τῆς γῆς αὐτόν.
ἔνθα δὴ μάχη συνεχὴς ἦν τοῖς τε τῷ Λύρκῳ προσ-
θεμένοις[6] καὶ τοῖς τὰ Αἰγιαλοῦ φρονοῦσιν· μάλιστα δὲ
συνεργὸς ἐγίνετο Εἰλεβίῃ· οὐ γὰρ ἀπεῖπε τὸν Λύρκον.
μετὰ δὲ ταῦτα ἀνδρωθεὶς ὁ ἐξ Ἡμιθέας καὶ Λύρκου
(Βασίλος αὐτῷ ὄνομα) ἦλθεν εἰς τὴν Καυνίαν· καὶ
αὐτὸν γνωρίσας ὁ Λύρκος ἤδη γηραιὸς ὢν ἡγεμόνα
καθίστησι τῶν σφετέρων λαῶν.

---

5 ἤλαυνε ⟨ἐκ⟩ Hirschig   6 τοῖς τε τὸν Λύρκον προσιε-
μένοις P, corr. Hercher

Β΄ Περὶ Πολυμήλης

Ἱστορεῖ Φιλίτας Ἑρμῇ

(1) Ὀδυσσεὺς ⟨δὲ⟩[1] ἀλώμενος περὶ Σικελίαν καὶ τὴν
Τυρρηνῶν καὶ τὴν Σικελῶν θάλασσαν ἀφίκετο πρὸς
Αἴολον καὶ Μελιγουνίδα νῆσον· ὃς αὐτὸν κατὰ κλέος
σοφίας τεθηπὼς ἐν πολλῇ φροντίδι εἶχεν. τά ⟨τε⟩[2]
περὶ Τροίης ἅλωσιν καὶ ὃν τρόπον αὐτοῖς ἐσκεδάσθη-

---

1 ⟨δὲ⟩ Meineke   2 ⟨τε⟩ Legrand

ing him; but afterwards, since there was nothing he could do, he took off his belt and gave it to the girl, telling her to save it for their son when he grew up, so that the boy should have a token when he came looking for his father in Caunus. And so he sailed away. (6) When Aegialus learned about the oracle and Hemithea, he tried to banish Lyrcus from his country, and from then on there was constant fighting between the supporters of Lyrcus and those on Aegialus' side. But Heilebie was Lyrcus' staunchest ally, for she would not repudiate her husband. Afterwards, when the son of Hemithea and Lyrcus had grown up (he was called Basilus), he arrived in Caunus, where he was recognised by the now aging Lyrcus, who made him leader of his own people.[4]

II. POLYMELA

Philitas tells the story in his Hermes

(1) While Odysseus was roaming around Sicily and the Etruscan and Sicilian seas, he came to Aeolus on the island of Meligounis. Admiring him on account of his famous wisdom, Aeolus treated Odysseus with the highest consideration; he plied him with questions about the capture of

---

[4] In many respects the story is a copy of the myth of Aegeus, who consulted the Delphic oracle about his childlessness, was tricked by Pittheus on his return, and fathered Theseus on Pittheus' daughter. The civil strife between Lyrcus, on his return, and his father-in-law may also recall the strife between Aegeus and his nephews, the Pallantidae. The main difference is that when Theseus comes to find his father, he faces hostility from his step-mother (Medea), and Lyrcus does not.

σαν αἱ νῆες κομιζομένοις ἀπὸ τῆς Ἰλίου διεπυνθάνετο,
ξενίζων τε αὐτὸν πολὺν χρόνον διῆγεν. (2) τῷ δ' ἄρα
καὶ αὐτῷ ἦν ἡ μονὴ ἡδομένῳ[3]· Πολυμήλη γὰρ τῶν
Αἰολίδων τις ἐρασθεῖσα αὐτοῦ κρύφα συνῆν. ὡς δὲ
τοὺς ἀνέμους ἐγκεκλεισμένους παραλαβὼν ἀπέπλευ-
σεν, ἡ κόρη φωρᾶταί τινα τῶν Τρωϊκῶν λαφύρων
ἔχουσα καὶ τούτοις[4] μετὰ πολλῶν δακρύων ἀλινδου-
μένη. (3) ἔνθα ⟨δὴ⟩[5] ὁ Αἴολος τὸν μὲν Ὀδυσσέα
καίπερ οὐ παρόντα ἐκάκισεν· τὴν δὲ Πολυμήλην ἐν νῷ
ἔσχε τίσασθαι. ἔτυχε δὲ αὐτῆς ἠρασμένος ὁ ἀδελφὸς
Διώρης, ὃς αὐτὴν παραιτεῖταί τε καὶ πείθει τὸν πα-
τέρα αὐτῷ συνοικίσαι.

3 ἡδομένη P, corr. Leopardus   4 κἀν τούτοις Kayser
5 ⟨δὴ⟩ Hercher

Γ´ Περὶ Εὐίππης

Ἱστορεῖ Σοφοκλῆς Εὐρυάλῳ

(1) Οὐ μόνον δὲ Ὀδυσσεὺς περὶ Αἴολον ἐξήμαρτεν,
ἀλλὰ καὶ μετὰ τὴν ἄλην, ὡς τοὺς μνηστῆρας ἐφό-
νευσεν, εἰς Ἤπειρον ἐλθὼν χρηστηρίων τινῶν ἕνεκα,
τὴν Τυρίμμα θυγατέρα ἔφθειρεν Εὐίππην, ὃς αὐτὸν
οἰκείως τε ὑπεδέξατο καὶ μετὰ πάσης προθυμίας ἐξέ-
νιζεν. παῖς δὲ αὐτῷ γίνεται ἐκ ταύτης Εὐρύαλος. (2)
τοῦτον ἡ μήτηρ, ἐπεὶ εἰς ἥβην ἦλθεν, ἀποπέμπεται εἰς

Troy and the way their ships had been scattered on the return from Ilium, and acted as his host for a long time. (2) In fact the stay was not without its pleasures for Odysseus too. Polymela, one of Aeolus' daughters, had fallen in love with him and was conducting a secret liaison with him. When Odysseus sailed away, taking the winds enclosed in a bag, the girl was discovered clinging to some of the spoils from Troy, and rolling about on them in floods of tears. (3) Then Aeolus cursed Odysseus, even in his absence, and had a good mind to punish Polymela. But it so happened that her brother Diores was in love with her; he asked for her punishment to be remitted and persuaded their father to make her his wife.[5]

III. EUIPPE

Sophocles tells the story in his Euryalus

(1) Aeolus was not the only one Odysseus wronged. Even after his wanderings, after he had killed the suitors, he went to Epirus because of some oracles[6] and there seduced Euippe the daughter of Tyrimmas, who had welcomed him kindly and entertained him with all possible goodwill. She bore him a son, Euryalus. (2) Once the boy had reached early manhood, his mother sent him to Ithaca

[5] Based on *Od.* 10.1–27, especially the brother-sister incest of 7. Possible influences include an early form of the story of Dido and Aeneas, and Euripides' *Aeolus*, which dealt with another Aeolid couple, Canace and her brother Macareus. But unlike either of these stories, Parthenius' has a happy ending.

[6] Deliberately obscure: perhaps referring to Teiresias' message in *Od.* 11.121–125, or perhaps to a consultation at Dodona of which there are only hints in the *Odyssey*.

Ἰθάκην συμβόλαιά τινα δοῦσα ἐν δέλτῳ κατεσφρα-
γισμένα. τοῦ δὲ Ὀδυσσέως κατὰ τύχην τότε μὴ παρ-
όντος, Πηνελόπη καταμαθοῦσα ταῦτα, καὶ ἄλλως δὲ
προπεπυσμένη τὸν τῆς Εὐίππης ἔρωτα, πείθει τὸν
Ὀδυσσέα παραγενόμενον, πρὶν ἢ γνῶναί τι τούτων ὡς
ἔχει, κατακτεῖναι τὸν Εὐρύαλον ὡς ἐπιβουλεύοντα
αὐτῷ. (3) καὶ Ὀδυσσεὺς μὲν διὰ τὸ μὴ ἐγκρατὴς φῦναι
μηδὲ ἄλλως ἐπιεικής, αὐτόχειρ τοῦ παιδὸς ἐγένετο.
καὶ οὐ μετὰ πολὺν χρόνον ἢ τόδε ἀπεργάσασθαι[1]
πρὸς τῆς αὐτὸς αὐτοῦ γενεᾶς τρωθεὶς ἀκάνθῃ θαλασ-
σίας τρυγόνος ἐτελεύτησεν.

1 ἀπεργάσθαι P, corr. Gale

Δ΄ Περὶ Οἰνώνης

Ἱστορεῖ Νίκανδρος ἐν τῷ Περὶ Ποιητῶν καὶ Κεφάλων
ὁ Γεργίθιος ἐν Τρωϊκοῖς

(1) Ἀλέξανδρος ⟨δὲ⟩[1] ὁ Πριάμου βουκολῶν κατὰ τὴν
Ἴδην ἠράσθη τῆς Κεβρῆνος θυγατρὸς Οἰνώνης. λέγε-
ται δὲ ταύτην ἔκ του θεῶν κατεχομένην θεσπίζειν περὶ
τῶν μελλόντων καὶ ἄλλως δὲ ἐπὶ συνέσει φρενῶν ἐπὶ
μέγα διαβεβοῆσθαι. (2) ὁ οὖν Ἀλέξανδρος αὐτὴν
ἀγαγόμενος παρὰ τοῦ πατρὸς εἰς τὴν Ἴδην, ὅπου
αὐτῷ οἱ σταθμοὶ ἦσαν, εἶχε γυναῖκα· καὶ αὐτῇ φιλο-
φρονούμενος ⟨ ⟩[2] μηδαμὰ προλείψειν ἐν περισσοτέρᾳ

1 ⟨δὲ⟩ Meineke   2 ⟨ὑπέσχετο⟩ Legrand, exempli gratia

with some tokens sealed up in a wax tablet. By chance
Odysseus was not there at the time; but Penelope found
out what was going on—indeed, she had earlier knowl-
edge of Odysseus' affair with Euippe—and she persuaded
Odysseus, on his return, to kill Euryalus as a conspirator
before he knew the truth of the matter. (3) And so, through
lack of self-control, and because in other ways he was not a
reasonable man, Odysseus became the murderer of his
own son. Not long afterwards he was wounded by the
prickle of a sting-ray, and died at the hands of his own flesh
and blood.[7]

IV. OENONE

The story is told by Nicander in his On Poets *and by Ceph-
alon of Gergitha*[8] *in his* Troica

(1) When Priam's son Alexander was a shepherd on Mount
Ida he fell in love with Oenone, the daughter of Cebren.
She is supposed to have been inspired by one of the gods to
prophesy about the future, and to be very celebrated, be-
sides, for her keen intelligence. (2) And so Alexander took
her from her father's house to Ida, where his steadings
were, and made her his wife; he ⟨promised⟩ her lovingly
that he would never leave her and that he would hold her

---

[7] The *Telegony* told how Telegonus, Odysseus' son by Circe,
unwittingly slew his father with a spear tipped with the barb of a
sting-ray. This was one attempt to clarify Teiresias' prediction that
death would come to Odysseus "from the sea" (*Od.* 11.134).

[8] i.e. Hegesianax of Alexandria Troas, who composed a Troy
romance in the person of the fictitious Cephalon. "Cephalon" is
also cited in the manchette of XXXIV for the story of Oenone's son
Corythus.

τε τιμῇ ἄξειν. (3) ἡ δὲ συνιέναι μὲν ἔφασκεν εἰς τὸ
παρὸν ὡς δὴ πάνυ αὐτῆς ἐρῴη· χρόνον μέντοι τινὰ
γενήσεσθαι ἐν ᾧ ἀπαλλάξας αὐτὴν εἰς τὴν Εὐρώπην
περαιωθήσεται, κἀκεῖ πτοηθεὶς ἐπὶ γυναικὶ ξένῃ πόλε-
μον ἐπάξεται τοῖς οἰκείοις. (4) ἐξηγεῖτο δὲ ὡς δεῖ
αὐτὸν ἐν τῷ πολέμῳ τρωθῆναι καὶ ὅτι οὐδεὶς αὐτὸν
οἷός τε ἔσται ὑγιῆ ποιῆσαι ἢ αὐτή. ἑκάστοτε δὲ
ἐπιλεγομένης αὐτῆς ‹ταῦτα›[3] ἐκεῖνος οὐκ εἴα μεμνῆ-
σθαι. χρόνου δὲ προϊόντος, ἐπειδὴ Ἑλένην ἔγημεν, ἡ
μὲν Οἰνώνη, μεμφομένη τῶν πραχθέντων τὸν Ἀλέξαν-
δρον, εἰς Κεβρῆνα, ὅθενπερ ἦν γένος, ἀπεχώρησεν· ὁ
δέ, παρήκοντος ἤδη τοῦ πολέμου, διατοξευόμενος Φι-
λοκτήτῃ τιτρώσκεται. (5) ἐν νῷ δὲ λαβὼν τὸ τῆς
Οἰνώνης ἔπος, ὅτε ἔφατο αὐτὸν πρὸς αὐτῆς μόνης οἷόν
τε εἶναι ἰαθῆναι, κήρυκα πέμπει δεησόμενον ὅπως
ἐπειχθεῖσα ἀκέσηταί τε αὐτὸν καὶ τῶν παροιχομένων
λήθην ποιήσηται, ἅτε δὴ κατὰ θεῶν βούλησίν [τε]
ἀφικόμενων[4]. (6) ἡ δὲ αὐθαδέστερον ἀπεκρίνατο ὡς
χρὴ παρ᾽ Ἑλένην αὐτὸν ἰέναι κἀκείνης δεῖσθαι· αὐτὴ
δὲ μάλιστα ἠπείγετο ἔνθα διεπέπυστο[5] κεῖσθαι αὐτόν.
τοῦ δὲ κήρυκος τὰ λεχθέντα παρὰ τῆς Οἰνώνης θᾶττον
ἀπαγγείλαντος, ἀθυμήσας ὁ Ἀλέξανδρος ἐξέπνευσεν·
(7) Οἰνώνη δέ, ἐπεὶ νέκυν ἤδη κατὰ γῆς κείμενον
ἐλθοῦσα εἶδεν[6], ἀνῴμωξέ τε καὶ πολλὰ κατολοφυρα-
μένη διεχρήσατο ἑαυτήν.

3 ‹ταῦτα› Zangoiannes   4 [τε] ἀφικόμενων Meineke: τε
ἀφικόμενον P   5 ἔνθα δὴ ἐπέπυστο P, corr. Schultze
6 ἴδεν P, corr. Passow

in ever-increasing honour. (3) She used to reply that she knew very well that he was totally devoted to her for the time being, but that there would come a time when he would abandon her and cross over to Europe, and there, infatuated with a foreign woman, would bring war upon his own people. (4) She went on to explain that it was fated for him to be wounded in the war and that nobody would be able to heal him save her, herself. But whenever she mentioned this he would not allow her to continue. Time went by, and Paris married Helen; Oenone resented him for what had happened[9] and went back to Cebren and her family home. But then, once the war came on, Paris was wounded by a bow-shot from Philoctetes. (5) He remembered Oenone's words, when she had said that he could be healed only by her, and he sent a herald to beg her to come quickly and cure him, to forget about the past since it had all happened through the will of the gods. (6) She responded, haughtily, that he would have to go to Helen and make the request of her. Nevertheless, she made all haste to the place where she had found out that he was lying. But the herald reported back Oenone's words too soon, and Alexander lost all heart and died. (7) When Oenone arrived and saw him now dead and lying on the ground, she wailed aloud and in deep distress put an end to her own life.

[9] It may be that Parthenius' source motivated Oenone's resentment through Paris' murder of their son (see XXXIV).

PARTHENIUS

Ε´ Περὶ Λευκίππου

Ἱστορεῖ Ἑρμησιάναξ Λεοντίῳ

(1) Λεύκιππος δέ, Ξανθίου παῖς, γένος τῶν ἀπὸ Βελλεροφόντου, διαφέρων ἰσχύϊ μάλιστα τῶν καθ᾽ ἑαυτόν, ἤσκει τὰ πολεμικά· διὸ πολὺς ἦν λόγος περὶ αὐτοῦ παρά τε Λυκίοις καὶ τοῖς προσεχέσι τούτοις, ἅτε δὴ ἀγομένοις καὶ πᾶν ὁτιοῦν δυσχερὲς πάσχουσιν. (2) οὗτος κατὰ μῆνιν Ἀφροδίτης εἰς ἔρωτα ἀφικόμενος τῆς ἀδελφῆς τέως μὲν ἐκαρτέρει, οἰόμενος ῥᾷστα ἀπαλλάξασθαι[1] τῆς νόσου. ἐπεὶ μέντοι χρόνου διαγενομένου οὐδὲ ἐπ᾽ ὀλίγον ἐλώφα τὸ πάθος, ἀνακοινοῦται τῇ μητρὶ καὶ πολλὰ καθικέτευε μὴ περιδεῖν αὐτὸν ἀπολλύμενον· εἰ γὰρ αὐτῷ μὴ συνεργήσειεν, ἀποσφάξειν αὐτὸν ἠπείλει. τῆς δὲ παραχρῆμα τὴν ἐπιθυμίαν φαμένης τελευτ⟨ήσ⟩ειν[2], ῥᾴων ἤδη γέγονεν. (3) ἀνακαλεσαμένη δὲ τὴν κόρην συγκατακλίνει τἀδελφῷ· κἀκ τούτου συνῆσαν οὐ μάλα τινὰ δεδοικότες, ἕως τις ἐξαγγέλλει τῷ κατεγγυημένῳ τὴν κόρην μνηστῆρι. ὁ δὲ τόν τε αὐτοῦ πατέρα παραλαβὼν καί τινας τῶν προσηκόντων πρόσεισι τῷ Ξανθίῳ καὶ τὴν πρᾶξιν καταμηνύει, μὴ δηλῶν τοὔνομα τοῦ Λευκίππου. (4) Ξάνθιος δὲ δυσφορῶν ἐπὶ τοῖς προσηγγελμένοις πολλὴν σπουδὴν ἐτίθετο φωρᾶσαι τὸν φθορέα καὶ διεκελεύσατο τῷ μηνυτῇ, ὁπότε ἴδοι συνόντας, αὑτῷ δηλῶσαι. τοῦ δὲ ἑτοίμως ὑπακούσαντος καὶ αὐτίκα τὸν πρεσβύτην ἐπαγομένου τῷ θαλάμῳ, ἡ

V. LEUCIPPUS

Hermesianax tells the story in the Leontium

(1) Leucippus, the son of Xanthius and a descendant of Bellerophon, excelled his contemporaries in strength and practised the arts of war. There was much talk of him among the Lycians and their neighbours, who were being plundered by him and suffering every sort of unpleasantness. (2) Through the wrath of Aphrodite this man fell in love with his own sister. For some time he held out against it, thinking that he would easily be cured of his sickness; but when time passed and the condition had not eased at all, he told his mother and pleaded with her not to look on while he died of love: he threatened that unless she helped him, he would kill himself. Without hesitation his mother promised to accomplish his desire, and this immediately made him easier. (3) She sent for the girl and put her to bed with her brother, and after this they carried on their affair without fear of anyone until someone went and told the suitor who was betrothed to the girl. Taking his father and some of his male kinsmen he approached Xanthius and told him of the affair, except that he did not reveal the name of Leucippus. (4) Xanthius was distressed by what he was told and made it his main business to hunt out the seducer: he told the informer to let him know when he found the two of them together. The other readily agreed, and brought the old man straightaway to the bedchamber. At

---

1 ἀπαλλάξεσθαι Cornarius   2 τελεύτειν P, corr. Martini

παῖς, αἰφνιδίου ψόφου γενηθέντος, ἵετο διὰ θυρῶν,
οἰομένη λήσεσθαι τὸν ἐπιόντα· καὶ αὐτὴν ὁ πατὴρ
ὑπολαβὼν εἶναι τὸν φθορέα πατάξας μαχαίρᾳ κατα-
βάλλει. (5) τῆς δὲ περιωδύνου γενομένης καὶ ἀνα-
κραγούσης, ὁ Λεύκιππος ἐπαμύνων αὐτῇ καὶ διὰ τὸ
ἐκπεπλῆχθαι μὴ προϊδόμενος ὅστις ἦν, κατακτείνει
τὸν πατέρα. δι' ἣν αἰτίαν ἀπολιπὼν τὴν οἰκείαν[3] Θετ-
ταλοῖς [ἐπὶ τοῖς συμβεβηκόσιν][4] εἰς Κρήτην ἡγήσα-
το, κἀκεῖθεν ἐξελαθεὶς ὑπὸ τῶν προσοίκων εἰς τὴν
Ἐφεσίαν ἀφίκετο, ἔνθα χωρίον ᾤκησε τὸ Κρητιναῖον
ἐπικληθέν. (6) τοῦ δὲ Λευκίππου τούτου λέγεται τὴν
Μανδρολύτου θυγατέρα Λευκοφρύην ἐρασθεῖσαν
προδοῦναι τὴν πόλιν τοῖς πολεμίοις, ὧν ἐτύγχανεν
ἡγούμενος ὁ Λεύκιππος, ἑλομένων αὐτὸν κατὰ θεο-
πρόπιον τῶν δεκατευθέντων ἐκ Φερῶν ὑπ' Ἀδμήτου.

[3] οἰκείαν Rohde, Wilamowitz: οἰκίαν P   [4] [ἐπὶ τοῖς συμ-
βεβηκόσιν] Hutchinson: [ἐπὶ] τοῖς συμβεβηκόσιν Rohde: post
ἀπολιπών transp. Legrand

ϛ′ Περὶ Παλλήνης

Ἱστορεῖ Θεαγένης[1] καὶ Ἡγήσιππος ἐν Παλληνιακοῖς

(1) Λέγεται ⟨δὲ⟩[2] καὶ Σίθωνα, τὸν Ὀδομάντων βασι-
λέα, γεννῆσαι θυγατέρα Παλλήνην καλήν τε καὶ[3] ἐπί-

[1] ΔΙΟΓΕΝΗΣ P, corr. Gale   [2] ⟨δὲ⟩ Meineke
[3] δὲ καὶ P, corr. Heyne

the sudden noise the girl darted through the door, thinking that she would escape whoever was coming in; but her father thought she was the seducer, stabbed her with a dagger, and struck her down. (5) In agony she cried out, and Leucippus came to her rescue; yet, in the chaos, he did not look to see who was there, and killed his father. He had to leave his homeland after this, and put himself at the head of a band of Thessalians who were on their way to Crete; but, driven thence by the neighbouring peoples, he went to Ephesian territory where he founded the place called Cretinaeum. (6) It was this Leucippus for love of whom Leucophrye, the daughter of Mandrolytus, is supposed to have betrayed her city to the enemy under Leucippus' command; the tithed force sent out from Pherae by Admetus had chosen him for their leader on the advice of an oracle.[10]

VI. PALLENE

The story is told by Theagenes and in Hegesippus' Palleniaca

(1) It is also said that Sithon, king of the Odomanti, had a lovely and charming daughter Pallene, whose fame spread

---

[10] Leucippus is also known from the foundation inscription of Magnesia on the Maeander, which tells how the Delphic oracle appointed him leader of a party of Thessalian exiles who were seeking to return home from Crete. Parthenius seems to refer to different versions of this tradition in §§5 and 6. The inscription does not mention the story of his sister (which, however, has much in common with accounts of other colonisation-figures driven to leave home because of some polluting crime).

χαριν, καὶ διὰ τοῦτο ἐπὶ πλεῖστον χωρῆσαι κλέος
αὐτῆς φοιτᾶν τε μνηστῆρας οὐ μόνον ἀπ' αὐτῆς Θρᾴ-
κης ἀλλὰ καὶ ἔτι πρόσωθέν τινας, ἀπό τε Ἰλλυρίδος
<καὶ>⁴ τῶν ἐπὶ Τανάϊδος ποταμοῦ κατῳκημένων. (2)
τὸν δὲ Σίθωνα πρῶτον μὲν κελεύειν τοὺς ἀφικνου-
μένους μνηστῆρας πρὸς μάχην ἰέναι < > τὴν κόρην
ἔχοντα, εἰ δὲ ἥττων φανείη, τεθνάναι, τούτῳ τε τῷ
τρόπῳ πάνυ συχνοὺς ἀνῃρήκει. (3) μετὰ δέ, ὡς αὐτόν
τε ἡ πλείων ἰσχὺς ἐπιλελοίπει, ἔγνωστό τε αὐτῷ τὴν
κόρην ἁρμόσασθαι, δύο μνηστῆρας ἀφιγμένους, Δρύ-
αντά τε καὶ Κλεῖτον, ἐκέλευεν, ἄθλου προκειμένου τῆς
κόρης, ἀλλήλοις διαμάχεσθαι· καὶ τὸν μὲν τεθνάναι,
τὸν δὲ περιγενόμενον τήν τε βασιλείαν καὶ τὴν παῖδα
ἔχειν. (4) τῆς δὲ ἀφωρισμένης ἡμέρας παρούσης, ἡ
Παλλήνη (ἔτυχε γὰρ ἐρῶσα τοῦ Κλείτου) πάνυ ὀρρώ-
δει περὶ αὐτοῦ· καὶ σημῆναι μὲν οὐκ ἐτόλμα τινὶ τῶν
ἀμφ' αὐτήν⁵, δάκρυα δὲ πολλὰ ἐχεῖτο τῶν παρειῶν
αὐτῆς, ἕως ὅτε <ὁ>⁶ τροφεὺς αὐτῆς πρεσβύτης, ἀνα-
πυνθανόμενος καὶ ἐπιγνοὺς τὸ πάθος, τῇ μὲν θαρρεῖν
παρεκελεύσατο ὡς, ᾗ βούλεται, ταύτῃ τοῦ πράγματος
χωρήσοντος· αὐτὸς δὲ κρύφα ὑπέρχεται τὸν ἡνίοχον
τοῦ Δρύαντος καὶ αὐτῷ χρυσὸν πολὺν ὁμολογήσας
πείθει διὰ τῶν ἁρματηγῶν⁷ τροχῶν μὴ διεῖναι τὰς
περόνας. (5) ἔνθα δή, ὡς ἐς μάχην ἐξῄεσαν καὶ ἤλαυ-
νεν ὁ Δρύας ἐπὶ τὸν Κλεῖτον, [καὶ]⁸ οἱ τροχοὶ περιερ-
ρύησαν αὐτῷ τῶν ἁρμάτων καὶ οὕτως πεσόντα αὐτὸν
ἐπιδραμὼν ὁ Κλεῖτος ἀναιρεῖ. (6) αἰσθόμενος δὲ ὁ
Σίθων τόν τε ἔρωτα καὶ τὴν ἐπιβουλὴν τῆς θυγατρός,

far and wide, and for whose sake suitors came not only
from Thrace itself, but also from further afield, from Illyria
and from among the people settled on the banks of the
Tanais. (2) First Sithon had the incoming suitors fight
(him) < > taking the girl, while the one who showed himself
the weaker was to die; and in this way he killed off a great
many. (3) Later, when the greater part of his strength had
left him and he resolved to get the girl married, he ordered
two new arrivals, Dryas and Cleitus, to fight with each
other with the girl as prize. One was to die, the survivor to
have the girl and the kingdom. (4) When the appointed day
dawned, Pallene (who, so it turned out, had fallen in love
with Cleitus) was very much afraid for him. She had not
the heart to confess this to any of her attendants; but her
cheeks so ran with tears that eventually her old tutor real-
ised and diagnosed her condition. He told her to keep her
spirits up, that things would go just as she wanted. Secretly
he approached Dryas' charioteer, promising him a great
deal of money if he would not insert the linch-pins in the
chariot-wheels. (5) So when they went out to battle and
Dryas charged at Cleitus, the wheels fell away from under
the car, and Cleitus rushed up to him as he lay there and
dispatched him. (6) But Sithon realised both his daugh-
ter's passion and her stratagem. He heaped up an enor-

---

4 ⟨καὶ⟩ Cornarius   5 αὐτήν Holford-Strevens: αὐτόν P
6 ⟨ὁ⟩ Martini   7 ἁρματηίων Meineke
8 [καὶ] Meineke

μάλα μεγάλην πυρὰν νήσας καὶ ἐπιθεὶς τὸν Δρύαντα
οἷός τε ἦν ἐπισφάζειν⁹ καὶ τὴν Παλλήνην. φαντάσμα-
τος δὲ θείου γενομένου καὶ ἐξαπιναίως ὕδατος ἐξ
οὐρανοῦ πολλοῦ καταρραγέντος, μετέγνω τε καὶ γά-
μοις ἀρεσάμενος τὸν παρόντα Θρᾳκῶν ὅμιλον ἐφίησι
τῷ Κλείτῳ τὴν κόρην ἄγεσθαι.

Ζ΄ Περὶ Ἱππαρίνου

Ἱστορεῖ Φανίας ὁ Ἐρέσιος

(1) Ἐν δὲ τῇ Ἰταλῇ Ἡρακλείᾳ παιδὸς διαφόρου τὴν
ὄψιν (Ἱππαρῖνος [ἦν]¹ αὐτῷ ὄνομα) τῶν πάνυ δοκίμων
Ἀντιλέων ἠράσθη· ὃς πολλὰ μηχανώμενος οὐδαμῇ
δυνατὸς ἦν αὐτὸν ἁρμόσασθαι, περὶ δὲ γυμνάσια
διατρίβοντι πολλὰ τῷ παιδὶ προσρυεὶς ἔφη τοσοῦτον
αὐτοῦ πόθον ἔχειν ὥστε πάντα πόνον ἂν τλῆναι² καὶ ὅ
τι ἂν κελεύοι³, μηδενὸς αὐτὸν ἁμαρτήσεσθαι. (2) ὁ δὲ
ἄρα κατειρωνευόμενος προσέταξεν αὐτῷ ἀπό τινος
ἐρυμνοῦ χωρίου, ὃ μάλιστα ἐφρουρεῖτο ὑπὸ τοῦ⁴ τῶν
Ἡρακλεωτῶν τυράννου, τὸν κώδωνα κατακομίσαι,
πειθόμενος μὴ ἄν ποτε τελέσειν αὐτὸν τόνδε τὸν
ἄθλον. (3) Ἀντιλέων δὲ κρύφα τὸ φρούριον ὑπελθὼν
καὶ λοχήσας τὸν φύλακα τοῦ κώδωνος κατακαίνει· καὶ
ἐπειδὴ ἀφίκετο πρὸς τὸ μειράκιον ἐπιτελέσας τὴν

---

⁹ οιστεοσιν ἐπισφάξειν P¹ (ᾤετο συνεπισφάξειν P²), corr.
Martini   ¹ [ἦν] Meineke   ² ἀνατλῆναι P, corr.
Meineke   ³ κελεύῃ Meineke   ⁴ του P, corr. Gale

mous pyre and set Dryas on top. He was going to slay
Pallene on it, too, only a divine visitation stopped him: sud-
denly a huge shower of rain burst forth from the heavens,
and Sithon relented. He treated the assembled Thracian
crowd to a wedding-feast, and let Cleitus have the girl.[11]

VII. HIPPARINUS

The story occurs in Phanias of Eresus

(1) In Heraclea in Italy there was a beautiful boy called
Hipparinus who came from a very good family. His lover,
Antileon, tried everything but was wholly unable to win
him round. He would often dash up to the boy, who was a
regular at the gymnasia, declaring that he wanted him so
much that he would endure any hardship, that whatever
the boy told him to do, he would fail in nothing. (2) Now
the boy asked him ironically to fetch the bugle from a cer-
tain rocky place that was kept under special guard by the
Heraclean tyrant,[12] convinced that Antileon would never
manage this feat. (3) But Antileon secretly approached the
fort, lay in wait for the man who was guarding the bugle,
and killed him. And when he came back to the boy, the

[11] A rewritten version of the myth of Oenomaus, Pelops, and
Hippodameia, the difference being that Sithon eventually agrees
to his daughter's marriage; the pursuit of the suitor by the father is
replaced by a head-to-head between two suitors.

[12] A gloss in the right margin at this point names the tyrant as
Archelaus.

ὑπόσχεσιν, ἐν πολλῇ αὐτῷ εὐνοίᾳ ἐγένετο, καὶ ἐκ
τοῦδε μάλιστα ἀλλήλους ἐφίλουν. (4) ἐπεὶ δὲ ὁ τύ-
ραννος τῆς ὥρας ἐγλίχετο τοῦ παιδὸς καὶ οἷός τε ἦν
αὐτὸν βίᾳ ἄγεσθαι[5], δυσανασχετήσας ὁ Ἀντιλέων
ἐκείνῳ μὲν παρεκελεύσατο μὴ ἀντιλέγοντα[6] κινδυνεύ-
ειν· αὐτὸς δὲ οἴκοθεν ἐξιόντα τὸν τύραννον προσδρα-
μὼν ἀνεῖλεν. (5) καὶ τοῦτο δράσας δρόμῳ ἵετο καὶ
διέφυγεν ἄν, εἰ μὴ προβάτοις συνδεδεμένοις ἀμφι-
πεσὼν ἐχειρώθη. διὸ τῆς πόλεως εἰς τἀρχαῖον ἀπο-
καταστάσης, ἀμφοτέροις παρὰ τοῖς Ἡρακλεώταις
ἐτέθησαν εἰκόνες χαλκαῖ, καὶ νόμος ἐγράφη, μηδένα
ἐλαύνειν τοῦ λοιποῦ πρόβατα συνδεδεμένα.

5 βίᾳ <προσ>άγεσθαι Hercher: βιάζεσθαι Cobet
6 ἀντιλέγειν P, corr. Scaliger

Η΄ Περὶ Ἡρίππης

Ἱστορεῖ Ἀριστόδημος ὁ Νυσαεὺς ἐν α΄ Ἱστοριῶν περὶ
τούτων[1], πλὴν ὅτι τὰ ὀνόματα ὑπαλλάττει ἀντὶ Ἡρίπ-
πης καλῶν Εὐθυμίαν[2], τὸν δὲ βάρβαρον Καυάραν

(1) Ὅτε δὲ οἱ Γαλάται κατέδραμον τὴν Ἰωνίαν καὶ τὰς
πόλεις ἐπόρθουν, ἐν Μιλήτῳ Θεσμοφορίων ὄντων καὶ
συνηθροισμένων <τῶν>[3] γυναικῶν ἐν τῷ ἱερῷ, ὃ βρα-

1 Ἱστοριῶν Περὶ Τόπων Calderon Dorda   2 ΓΥΘΤΜΙΑΝ
P, corr. Dindorf   3 <τῶν> Schneider

misson accomplished, the boy became very fond of him and from that time onwards they loved each other dearly. (4) When the tyrant began to lust after the young man's beauty and was on the point of using force to abduct him, Antileon was outraged. He told the boy not to incur risks by a refusal; but he himself, when the tyrant was leaving his house one day, rushed up and assassinated him.[13] (5) This done, he fled and would have escaped had he not fallen in with a flock of sheep all tied together and been captured. So once the city had returned to its original constitution the Heracleotes erected bronze statues to both men, and a law was enacted that no-one in the future was to drive bound sheep.

VIII. HERIPPE

The story is told by Aristodemus of Nysa in the first book of his Histories, *except that he changes the names and calls the woman Euthymia instead of Herippe, and the barbarian Cauaras*[14]

(1) It was the time when the Gauls had invaded Ionia and were sacking its cities.[15] The Thesmophoria were being celebrated in Miletus, and the women were gathered in

[13] A simplified copy of the Athenian tyrannicide legend surrounding Harmodius and Aristogeiton (Thuc. 6.54–58). Heraclea was founded in 433–432, though variant versions locate the story in nearby Metapontum.

[14] The name suggests a connection with Massilia (Marseilles) and the surrounding territory. Gallus himself came from Forum Julii (Fréjus) not far to the east.

[15] In and after 278/7; Miletus was sacked in about 277.

χὺ τῆς πόλεως ἀπέχει, ἀποσπασθέν τι μέρος τοῦ βαρβαρικοῦ διῆλθεν εἰς τὴν Μιλησίαν καὶ ἐξαπιναίως ἐπιδραμὸν ἀνεῖλε τὰς γυναῖκας. (2) ἔνθα δὴ τὰς μὲν ἐρρύσαντο πολὺ ἀργύριόν τε καὶ χρυσίον ἀντιδόντες· τινὲς δὲ, τῶν βαρβάρων αὐταῖς οἰκειωθέντων, ἀπήχθησαν, ἐν δὲ αὐταῖς καὶ Ἡρίππη, γυνὴ ἡ Ξάνθου, ἀνδρὸς ἐν Μιλήτῳ πάνυ δοκίμου γένους τε τοῦ πρώτου, παιδίον ἀπολιποῦσα διετές. (3) ταύτης πολὺν πόθον ἔχων ὁ Ξάνθος ἐξηργυρίσατο μέρος τῶν ὑπαργμάτων καὶ κατασκευασάμενος χρυσοῦς ⟨δισ⟩χιλίους[4] τὸ μὲν πρῶτον εἰς Ἰταλίαν ἐπεραιώθη, ἐντεῦθεν δὲ ὑπὸ ἰδιοξένων τινῶν κομιζόμενος εἰς Μασσαλίαν ἀφικνεῖται, κἀκεῖθεν εἰς τὴν Κελτικήν. (4) καὶ προσελθὼν τῇ οἰκίᾳ, ἔνθα αὐτοῦ συνῆν ἡ γυνὴ ἀνδρὶ τῶν μάλιστα παρὰ Κελτοῖς δοξαζομένων, ὑποδοχῆς ἐδεῖτο τυχεῖν. τῶν δὲ διὰ φιλοξενίαν ἑτοίμως αὐτὸν ὑποδεξαμένων, εἰσελθὼν ὁρᾷ τὴν γυναῖκα, καὶ αὐτὸν ἐκείνη τὼ χεῖρε ἀμφιβαλοῦσα μάλα φιλοφρόνως προσηγάγετο. (5) παραχρῆμα δὲ τοῦ Κελτοῦ παραγενομένου, διεξῆλθεν αὐτῷ τήν τε ἄλην τἀνδρὸς ἡ Ἡρίππη καὶ ὡς αὐτῆς ἕνεκα [καὶ][5] ἥκοι λύτρα καταθησόμενος. ὁ δὲ ἠγάσθη τῆς ψυχῆς τὸν Ξάνθον καὶ αὐτίκα συνουσίαν ποιησάμενος τῶν μάλιστα προσηκόντων ἐξένιζεν αὐτόν. παρατείνοντος δὲ τοῦ πότου, τὴν γυναῖκα συγκατακλίνει αὐτῷ καὶ δι᾽ ἑρμηνέως ἐπυνθάνετο πηλίκην οὐσίαν εἴη κεκτημένος τὴν σύμπασαν. τοῦ δὲ εἰς ἀριθμὸν χιλίων χρυσῶν φήσαντος, ὁ βάρβαρος εἰς τέσσαρα μέρη κατανέμειν αὐτὸν ἐκέλευε καὶ τὰ μὲν

the temple which lay at a short distance from the city, when a detachment of the barbarian army entered Milesian territory and made a sudden raid in which they carried off the women. (2) Some of them were ransomed for large sums of gold and silver, but others became the wives of the barbarians and were taken away. Among them was Herippe, the wife of Xanthus, a highly-respected man in Miletus from one of its foremost families, leaving behind a little child of two years old. (3) Xanthus, who missed her greatly, turning part of his possessions into cash and assembling two thousand pieces of gold, first crossed to Italy, then was conveyed by some private friends into Massiliote territory, and thence reached the country of the Celts. (4) He approached the house where his wife was living with one of the most distinguished Celtic chieftains, and asked to receive a welcome. They did accord him a ready and hospitable welcome, and when he went in he saw his wife, who threw her arms around him and drew him towards her with great affection. (5) The Celt appeared directly. Herippe told him about her husband's journey and how he had come for her sake, in order to pay a ransom. The Celt admired Xanthus' spirit, and immediately ordered a banquet for his closest friends, at which he entertained Xanthus. As the drinks were circulating, he placed his wife beside him and inquired through interpreters how much money he had in all; when he replied that he had a thousand gold pieces in total the barbarian told him to divide them into

---

4 ⟨δισ⟩χιλίους Passow   5 [καὶ] Bast

τρία ὑπεξαιρεῖσθαι αὐτῷ, γυναικί, παιδίῳ, τὸ δὲ τέ-
ταρτον ἀπολείπειν ἄποινα τῆς γυναικός. (6) ὡς δὲ ἐς
κοῖτόν ποτε ἀπετράποντο⁶, πολλὰ κατεμέμφετο τὸν
Ξάνθον ἡ γυνὴ διὰ τὸ μὴ ἔχοντα τοσοῦτο χρυσίον
ὑποσχέσθαι τῷ βαρβάρῳ κινδυνεύσειν τε αὐτόν, εἰ μὴ
ἐμπεδώσειε τὴν ἐπαγγελίαν. (7) τοῦ δὲ φήσαντος ἐν
ταῖς κρηπῖσι τῶν παίδων καὶ ἄλλους τινὰς χιλίους
χρυσοῦς κεκρύφθαι διὰ τὸ μὴ ἐλπίζειν ἐπιεικῆ τινα
βάρβαρον καταλήψεσθαι, δεήσειν δὲ πολλῶν λύτρων,
ἡ γυνὴ τῇ ὑστεραίᾳ τῷ Κελτῷ καταμηνύει τὸ πλῆθος
τοῦ χρυσοῦ καὶ παρεκελεύετο κτεῖναι τὸν Ξάνθον,
φάσκουσα πολὺ μᾶλλον αἱρεῖσθαι αὐτὸν τῆς τε πα-
τρίδος καὶ τοῦ παιδίου· τὸν μὲν γὰρ Ξάνθον παν-
τάπασιν ἀποστυγεῖν. (8) τῷ δὲ ἄρα οὐ πρὸς ἡδονῆς ἦν
τὰ λεχθέντα, ἐν νῷ δὲ εἶχεν αὐτὴν τίσασθαι. ἐπειδὴ
δὲ ὁ Ξάνθος ἐσπούδαζεν ἀπιέναι, μάλα φιλοφρόνως
προύπεμπεν ὁ Κελτὸς ἐπαγόμενος καὶ τὴν Ἡρίππην.
ὡς δὲ ἐπὶ τοὺς ὅρους τῆς Κελτῶν χώρας ἀφίκοντο⁷,
θυσίαν ὁ βάρβαρος ἔφη τελέσαι βούλεσθαι πρὶν
αὐτοὺς ἀπ᾽ ἀλλήλων χωρισθῆναι. (9) καὶ κομισθέντος
ἱερείου, τὴν Ἡρίππην ἐκέλευσεν ἀντιλαβέσθαι· τῆς δὲ
κατασχούσης, ὡς καὶ ἄλλοτε σύνηθες αὐτῇ, ἐπανα-
τεινάμενος τὸ ξίφος καθικνεῖται καὶ τὴν κεφαλὴν
αὐτῆς ἀφαιρεῖ, τῷ τε Ξάνθῳ παρεκελεύετο μὴ δυσφο-
ρεῖν, ἐξαγγείλας τὴν ἐπιβουλὴν αὐτῆς, ἐπέτρεπέ τε τὸ
χρυσίον ἅπαν κομίζειν αὐτῷ.

⁶ ἀπετράπετο P, corr. Hercher   ⁷ ἀφίκετο P, corr. Hirschig

four pieces and reserve three parts for himself, his wife, and his child, and leave the fourth as ransom for his wife. (6) When at length they went to bed, his wife heaped reproaches on Xanthus for offering the barbarian a great quantity of money that he did not have: he would be running a risk, she said, if he did not make good his promise. (7) Xanthus replied that in the soles of his servants' boots another thousand pieces of gold had been concealed, because he had not expected to meet with so reasonable a barbarian; rather, that he had expected to need a large ransom. Next day the woman told the Celt how much gold her husband had, and tried to persuade him to kill Xanthus: she much preferred him, she said, to her native country and her child, and as for Xanthus, she utterly detested him. (8) But what she said did not please the Celt, and he formed a plan to punish her. When Xanthus was in a hurry to be gone, the Celt escorted him with a great show of kindness, taking Herippe along as well. And when they reached the boundaries of the Celtic country, the barbarian said he wanted to make a sacrifice before they separated. (9) The victim brought in, he bade Herippe take hold of it, and she did, as she had often done in the past. Then, stretching up his sword, he brought it down and beheaded her.[16] He tried to persuade Xanthus not to take it badly: he told him about her plot and permitted him to take all the gold back with him.

---

[16] Celts were notorious for decapitating their enemies: see Edelstein–Kidd on Posidonius, fr. 274 (Strab. 4.4.5).

PARTHENIUS

Θ΄ Περὶ Πολυκρίτης

Ἡ ἱστορία αὕτη ἐλήφθη ἐκ τῆς α΄ Ἀνδρίσκου Ναξιακῶν· γράφει περὶ αὐτῆς καὶ Θεόφραστος ἐν τῷ δ΄ ⟨τῶν⟩[1] Πρὸς τοὺς καιρούς

(1) Καθ᾿ ὃν δὲ χρόνον ἐπὶ Ναξίους Μιλήσιοι διέβησαν[2] σὺν ἐπικούροις καὶ τεῖχος πρὸ τῆς πόλεως ἐνοικοδομησάμενοι τήν τε χώραν ἔτεμνον καὶ καθείρξαντες τοὺς Ναξίους ἐφρούρουν, τότε παρθένος ἀπολειφθεῖσα κατά τινα δαίμονα ἐν Δηλίῳ ἱερῷ, ὃ πλησίον τῆς πόλεως κεῖται (Πολυκρίτη ὄνομα αὐτῇ) τὸν τῶν Ἐρυθραίων ἡγεμόνα Διόγνητον εἷλεν, ὃς οἰκείαν δύναμιν ἔχων συνεμάχει τοῖς Μιλησίοις. (2) πολλῷ δὲ ἐνεχόμενος πόθῳ διεπέμπετο πρὸς αὐτήν· οὐ γὰρ δή γε θεμιτὸν ἦν ἱκέτιν οὖσαν ἐν τῷ ἱερῷ βιάζεσθαι. ἡ δὲ ἕως μέν τινος οὐ προσίετο τοὺς παραγινομένους· ἐπεὶ μέντοι πολὺς ἐνέκειτο, οὐκ ἔφη πεισθήσεσθαι αὐτῷ, εἰ μὴ ὀμόσειεν ὑπηρετήσειν αὐτῇ ὅ τι ἂν βουληθῇ. (3) ὁ δὲ Διόγνητος, οὐδὲν ὑποτοπήσας τοιόνδε, μάλα προθύμως ὤμοσεν Ἄρτεμιν χαριεῖσθαι αὐτῇ ὅ τι ἂν προαιρῆται. κατομοσαμένου δὲ ἐκείνου καὶ[3] λαβομένη τῆς χειρὸς αὐτοῦ ἡ Πολυκρίτη μιμνήσκεται περὶ προδοσίας τοῦ χωρίου καὶ πολλὰ καθικετεύει[4] αὐτήν τε οἰκτείρειν καὶ τὰς συμφορὰς τῆς πόλεως. (4) ὁ ⟨δὲ⟩[5]

1 ⟨τῶν⟩ Heyne   2 συνέβησαν P, corr. Russell
3 [καὶ] Bast   4 καθικετεύειν P, corr. Legrand
5 ⟨δὲ⟩ Meineke

576

IX. POLYCRITE

This story is taken from the first book of Andriscus'
Naxiaca. *Theophrastus also writes about it in the fourth
book of his work* Responses to Political Crises

(1) It was the time when the Milesians and their allies were
making an attack on the Naxians: they had built a wall be-
fore the city, and were ravaging the countryside and keep-
ing guard over the blockaded Naxians. By some chance a
maiden called Polycrite had been left behind in the Delian
shrine which lay near the city, and she completely capti-
vated the Erythraean leader Diognetus, who had come to
fight on the Milesian side with a force of his own. (2) Over-
whelmed with desire he kept sending messages to her: it
was contrary to religion to use force against her, since she
was a suppliant in the temple. Up to a certain point she did
not admit his emissaries; but when he really laid it on thick,
she told him she would not do his will unless he swore to do
whatever she wished. (3) Diognetus had no suspicion of
what was coming, and he very readily took his oath by Arte-
mis that he would please her in whatever thing she chose.
So when he had sworn, she grasped his hand and made
mention of the betrayal of the stronghold;[17] she besought
him to pity her as well as the plight of her city. (4) Hearing

---

[17] What stronghold (cf. also §5)? Parthenius seems to have
combined two stories, in one of which the Naxians attack the
Milesians during a festival, in the other of which Diognetus is
bound by a lover's oath to hand over a piece of fortified ground
(see Plutarch, *Mor.* 254 F).

Διόγνητος ἀκούσας τοῦ λόγου ἐκτός τε ἐγένετο αὑτοῦ
καὶ σπασάμενος τὴν μάχαιραν ὥρμησε διεργάσα-
σθαι τὴν κόρην. ἐν νῷ μέντοι λαβὼν τὸ εὔγνωμον
αὐτῆς καὶ ἅμα ὑπ᾽ ἔρωτος κρατούμενος (ἔδει γὰρ, ὡς
ἔοικε, [καὶ][6] Ναξίοις μεταβολὴν γενέσθαι τῶν παρόν-
των κακῶν) τότε μὲν οὐδὲν ἀπεκρίνατο, βουλευόμενος
τί ποιητέον εἴη· τῇ δ᾽ ὑστεραίᾳ καθωμολογήσατο
προδώσειν. (5) καὶ ἐν ᾧ δὴ[7] τοῖς Μιλησίοις ἑορτὴ μετὰ
τρίτην ἡμέραν Θαργήλια ἐπῄει, ἐν ᾗ πολύν τε ἄκρα-
τον εἰσφοροῦνται καὶ τὰ πλείστου ἄξια κατανα-
λίσκουσιν, τότε παρεσκευάζετο προδιδόναι τὸ χωρίον.
καὶ εὐθέως διὰ τῆς Πολυκρίτης ἐνθέμενος εἰς ἄρτον
μολυβδίνην ἐπιστολὴν ⟨ἐπιστέλλει⟩[8] τοῖς ἀδελφοῖς
αὐτῆς (ἐτύγχανον δὲ ἄρα τῆς πόλεως ἡγεμόνες οὗτοι),
ὅπως εἰς ἐκείνην τὴν νύκτα παρασκευασάμενοι ἥκω-
σιν· σημεῖον δὲ αὐτοῖς ἀνασχήσειν αὐτὸς ἔφη λαμ-
πτῆρα. (6) καὶ ἡ Πολυκρίτη δὲ τῷ κομίζοντι τὸν ἄρτον
φράζειν ἐκέλευε τοῖς ἀδελφοῖς μὴ ἐνδοιασθ⟨ῆν⟩αι[9], ὡς
τῆς πράξεως ἐπὶ τέλος ἀχθησομένης, εἰ μὴ ἐκεῖνοι
ἐνδοιασθεῖεν. τοῦ δὲ ἀγγέλου ταχέως εἰς τὴν πόλιν
ἐλθόντος, Πολυκλῆς, ὁ τῆς Πολυκρίτης ἀδελφός, ἐν
πολλῇ φροντίδι ἐγίνετο εἴτε πεισθείη τοῖς ἐπεσταλ-
μένοις εἴτε μή. (7) τέλος δέ, ὡς ἐδόκει πᾶσι πείθεσθαι
καὶ νὺξ ἐπῆλθεν ἐν ᾗ προσετέτακτο πᾶσι παραγίνε-

6 [καὶ] Hercher   7 καὶ ἐν τῷ δὴ P, corr. Lightfoot
8 ⟨ἐπιστέλλει⟩ vel ⟨σημαίνει⟩ Legrand   9 ἐνδοιᾶσθαι P,
corr. Passow

this, Diognetus was beside himself; drawing his sword he made as if to kill the girl. But then, reflecting on her good nature and, at the same time, overmastered with love—it seems it was fated for the Naxians' present troubles to come to an end—he made no reply for the time being, debating what could be done. The next day he promised to undertake the betrayal. (5) A couple of days later there was a Milesian festival, the Thargelia,[18] in which they consume a great deal of unmixed wine and there is much expenditure of the costliest things. That was when he prepared to betray the stronghold. Encouraged by Polycrite, he inserted a lead tablet in a loaf of bread and sent it to her brothers (who happened to be the commanders of the city), instructing them to make preparations and come that night: he himself undertook to hold up a light for them, as a sign. (6) Polycrite instructed the bearer of the loaf to tell her brothers to be in no doubt, since the plan would succeed provided they did not hesitate. The messenger soon reached the city, and Polycles, Polycrite's brother, was in two minds whether he should obey the instructions or not. (7) At long last all agreed that they should act; and when the night came on which it had been arranged that all

[18] An Attic and Ionic festival of Artemis and Apollo; note also the setting in the Delian shrine (§1). It was traditional at this festival for a community to expel a *pharmakos* or scapegoat; in a similar way, Polycrite, who dies at the end of the story, can be seen as a victim (her name means "chosen from many") to ensure the safety of her city.

σθαι, πολλὰ κατευξάμενοι τοῖς θεοῖς, δεχομένων αὐ-
τοὺς τῶν ἀμφὶ Διόγνητον, ἐσπίπτουσιν εἰς τὸ τεῖχος
τῶν Μιλησίων, οἱ μέν τινες κατὰ τὴν[10] ἀνεῳγμένην
πυλίδα, οἱ δὲ καὶ τὸ τεῖχος ὑπερελθόντες, ἀθρόοι τε
ἐντὸς γενόμενοι κατέκαινον τοὺς Μιλησίους. (8) ἔνθα
δὴ κατ' ἄγνοιαν ἀποθνήσκει καὶ Διόγνητος. τῇ δ' ἐπι-
ούσῃ οἱ Νάξιοι πάντες πολὺν πόθον εἶχον ἱλάσα-
σθαι[11] τὴν κόρην· καὶ οἱ μέν τινες[12] αὐτὴν μίτραις
ἀνέδουν, οἱ δὲ ζώναις, αἷς βαρηθεῖσα ἡ παῖς διὰ
πλῆθος τῶν ἐπιρριπτουμένων ἀπεπνίγη. καὶ αὐτὴν
δημοσίᾳ θάπτουσιν ἐν τῷ πεδίῳ[13], πάντα[14] ἑκατὸν
ἐναγίσαντες αὐτῇ. φασὶ δέ τινες καὶ Διόγνητον ἐν τῷ
αὐτῷ καῆναι ἐν ᾧ καὶ ἡ παῖς, σπουδασάντων Ναξίων.

[10] κατά τιν' Zangoiannes   [11] βιάσασθαι P, corr. Meineke,
Rossbach   [12] τισιν P, corr. Hercher   [13] an ἐν τῷ
προαστείῳ?   [14] πάντα P: πρόβατα Rohde

Ι´ Περὶ Λευκώνης

ΟΤ

(1) Ἐν δὲ Θεσσαλίᾳ Κυάνιππος, υἱὸς Φάρακος, μάλα
καλῆς παιδὸς εἰς ἐπιθυμίαν Λευκώνης ἐλθών, παρὰ
τῶν πατέρων αἰτησάμενος αὐτὴν ἠγάγετο γυναῖκα. ἦν
δὲ φιλοκύνηγος· μεθ' ἡμέραν μὲν ἐπί τε λέοντας καὶ
κάπρους ἐφέρετο, νύκτωρ δὲ κατῄει πάνυ κεκμηκὼς
πρὸς τὴν κόρην, ὥστε μηδὲ διὰ λόγων ἔσθ' ὅτε γινό-
μενος[1] αὐτῇ εἰς βαθὺν ὕπνον καταφέρεσθαι. (2) ἡ δ'

should assemble, they prayed long and hard to the gods, met up with Diognetus' forces and fell upon the Milesians' wall, some through the open gate, others scaling the wall, until finally, when all were inside, they set about killing the Milesians. (8) Diognetus was one of the casualties, a victim of misrecognition. Next day the Naxians very much wanted to congratulate the girl. Some bound her with head-dresses, others with girdles, and with the combined weight of the things thrown on her the girl was suffocated.[19] They gave her a public burial in the plain, and sacrificed a hundred of everything to her. Some say that Diognetus was cremated on the same pyre as the girl, because the Naxians wished it.

X. LEUCONE

(1) In Thessaly Cyanippus, son of Pharax, fell in love with a very beautiful girl Leucone. He asked permission from her parents and married her. Now, he was very fond of hunting and used to spend the day in pursuit of lions and boars, coming home at night to the girl in such a state of exhaustion that he sometimes did not even speak to her and simply fell into a deep sleep. (2) She was annoyed and dis-

---

[19] On the one hand, this recalls garlanding as a gesture of congratulation (Hollis on Call. *Hec*. fr. 69.15); on the other, the suffocation (Tarpeia was buried beneath a pile of shields) or stoning (XXI.3) of maidens who *betray* their cities—the reflex of Polycrite.

---

[1] γινόμενον P[1]

ἄρα ὑπό τε ἀνίας καὶ ἀλγηδόνων συνεχομένη ἐν πολ-
λῇ ἀμηχανίᾳ ἦν, σπουδήν τε ἐποιεῖτο κατοπτεῦσαι
τὸν Κυάνιππον ὅ τι ποιῶν ἥδοιτο τῇ κατ' ὄρος διαίτῃ.
αὐτίκα δὲ εἰς γόνυ ζωσαμένη κρύφα τῶν θεραπαι-
νίδων εἰς τὴν ὕλην καταδύνει. (3) αἱ δὲ τοῦ Κυανίππου
κύνες ἐδίωκον μὲν ἔλαφον· οὖσαι δὲ οὐ πάνυ κτίλοι
ἅτε δὴ ἐκ πολλοῦ ⟨τοῦ θηρᾶν⟩[2] ἠγριωμέναι, ὡς
ὠσφρήσαντο τῆς κόρης, ἐπηνέχθησαν αὐτῇ καὶ μηδε-
νὸς παρόντος πᾶσαν διεσπάραξαν. καὶ ἡ μὲν διὰ
πόθον ἀνδρὸς κουριδίου ταύτῃ τέλος ἔσχεν· (4) Κυά-
νιππος δέ, ὡς ἐπελθὼν κατελάβετο λελωβημένην τὴν
Λευκώνην, μεγάλῳ τε ἄχει ἐπληρώθη καὶ ἀνακαλε-
σάμενος τοὺς ἀμφ' αὑτόν, ἐκείνην μὲν πυρὰν νήσας
ἐπέθετο[3]· αὐτὸς δὲ πρῶτον μὲν τὰς κύνας ἐπικατ-
έσφαξε τῇ πυρᾷ, ἔπειτα δὲ πολλὰ ἀποδυρόμενος τὴν
παῖδα διεχρήσατο ἑαυτόν.

[2] ⟨τοῦ θηρᾶν⟩ Zangoiannes   [3] ἐνέθετο P, corr. Hirschig

IA΄ Περὶ Βυβλίδος

Ἱστορεῖ Ἀριστόκριτος περὶ Μιλήτου καὶ Ἀπολλώνιος
ὁ Ῥόδιος Καύνου κτίσει

(1) Περὶ δὲ Καύνου καὶ Βυβλίδος, τῶν Μιλήτου παί-
δων, διαφόρως ἱστορεῖται. Νικαίνετος μὲν γάρ φησι
τὸν Καῦνον ἐρασθέντα τῆς ἀδελφῆς, ὡς οὐκ ἔληγε τοῦ
πάθους, ἀπολιπεῖν τὴν οἰκίαν καὶ ὁδεύσαντα πόρρω
τῆς οἰκείας χώρας πόλιν τε κτίσαι καὶ τοὺς ἀπεσκε-

tressed and did not know what to do, and made it her special concern to spy on Cyanippus and find out what it was that he was doing to make him take so much pleasure in his sojourns in the mountains. So she hitched her dress up as far as her knees and, in secret from her maids, entered the woods. (3) Cyanippus' bitches were chasing a stag. But they were pretty wild, maddened after a long day's hunting, and when they scented the girl they attacked her and tore her quite to pieces. No-one else was present. And in this way, out of desire for her husband, the girl met her end. (4) When Cyanippus came up and found the mangled body of Leucone, he was full of grief. He summoned his attendants, heaped up a pyre and placed her on it. He then slew the bitches on top of the pyre, and finally, mourning deeply for the girl, he killed himself.[20]

XI. BYBLIS

Aristocritus tells the story in his On Miletus, *and Apollonius of Rhodes in the* Foundation of Caunus

(1) Various stories are told about Caunus and Byblis, the children of Miletus. Nicaenetus says that Caunus fell in love with his sister, and that when the passion did not abate he left his home and travelled far from his native land,

---

[20] The story is closely related to the Athenian myth of Cephalus and Procris, save that (i) Procris is not torn apart by dogs, but shot by her husband's javelin; (ii) Cephalus does not kill himself over his wife's body.

δασμένους τότε Ἴωνας ἐνοικίσαι. (2) λέγει δὲ ἔπεσι
τοῖσδε:

αὐτὰρ ὅ γε προτέρωσε κιὼν Οἰκούσιον ἄστυ
κτίσσατο, Τραγασίην δὲ Κελαινέος[1] ἤγετο
παῖδα[2]
ἥ οἱ Καῦνον ἔτικτεν ἀεὶ φιλέοντα θέμιστας·
γείνατο δὲ ῥαδαλῆς ἐναλίγκιον ἀρκεύθοισι
5   Βυβλίδα. τῆς ἤτοι ἀέκων ἠράσσατο Καῦνος[3]
⟨   ⟩
βῆ δὲ †φερένδιος[4] φεύγων ὀφιώδεα †Κύπρον[5],
καὶ †κάπρος[6] ὑλιγενὲς[7] καὶ †κάρια[8] ἱρὰ λοετρά[9]
⟨   ⟩
ἔνθ᾽ ἤτοι πτολίεθρον ἐδείματο πρῶτος Ἰώνων.
αὐτὴ δὲ γνωτὴ[10] ὀλολυγόνος οἶτον ἔχουσα
10   Βυβλὶς ἀποπρὸ πυλῶν Καύνου ὠδύρατο νόστον.

[1] Καλαινέες P, corr. Passow, Ellis   [2] εἴχετο παιδί P, corr.
Hecker   [3] post versum lacunam statuit Meineke
[4] βῆ δ᾽ ἄφαρ ἔνδιος Kayser   [5] †Κύπρον: nomen urbis vel
montis latere suspiceris   [6] Κάπρον θ᾽ Martini: Κράγος I.
Vossius   [7] ὑλιγενὲς P: ἠλιτενές Meineke: ὑψιτενῆ Hecker
(de monte uterque)   [8] Καρῶν Heyne   de his versibus
alii alia temptaverunt; cf. quae disserui, 1999, 440–1
[9] post versum lacunam statuit Meineke   [10] αὐτοκασιγνήτη
Legrand: αὐτοκασιγνήτη ⟨δ᾽⟩ Knaack

21 The subject is Miletus, who left Crete after a dispute with
Minos and founded Oecous, a small settlement near Miletus. This

founding a city and settling there the scattered Ionians. (2)
He says in the following hexameters:

> But faring further on, the town of Oecous
> He founded,[21] took to wife Celaeneus' daughter
> Tragasia, who bore him justice-loving Caunus.
> But like the slender poplars was her girl—
> Byblis, whom Caunus loved against his will.　　　　　[5]
>
> 〈 　〉
>
> He left, †all in the mid-day heat[22], the snaky
> 　　†Cyprus[23] fled,
> And †Caprus, home of wooded hills,[24] and †Caria's
> 　　sacred streams
>
> 〈 　〉
>
> The first Ionian, there he built his city.[25]
> But Byblis shared the nightingale's sad fate:
> Without the gates she mourned for Caunus gone.　　　[10]

version attributes the foundation of Miletus itself to Miletus' son
Celadon (Σ Dion. Per. 825).

[22] Adopting Kayser's emendation; others have tried to find a
place-name here.

[23] Corruption has obscured Caunus' route, whether inland
and up the Maeander valley, or, perhaps more probably, into Lycia
and then doubling back to Caunus. In either case, "Cyprus" can-
not be right. Other suggestions have included Cydna (Ellis), a
Lycian city at the foot of Mount Cragos, and Cadmus (Martini), a
mountain near Laodicea ad Lycum.

[24] The Caprus is a tributary of the upper Maeander. On the
route that takes Caunus across Lycia, Vossius' Cragos has the
support of Byblis' wanderings in Ov. *Met.* 9.646.

[25] This can hardly refer to the foundation of Caunus by its
eponym, who was no Ionian. In the original poem, did this line
refer to Neleus, (re-)founder of Miletus?

(3) οἱ δὲ πλείους τὴν Βυβλίδα φασὶν ἐρασθεῖσαν τοῦ Καύνου λόγους αὐτῷ προσφέρειν καὶ δεῖσθαι μὴ περιιδεῖν αὐτὴν εἰς πᾶν κακὸν προελθοῦσαν. ἀποστυγήσαντα δὲ οὕτως τὸν Καῦνον περαιωθῆναι εἰς τὴν τότε ὑπὸ Λελέγων κατεχομένην γῆν, ἔνθα κρήνη Ἐχενηΐς, πόλιν τε κτίσαι τὴν ἀπ' αὐτοῦ κληθεῖσαν Καῦνον. τὴν δὲ ἄρα, ὑπὸ τοῦ πάθους μὴ ἀνιεμένην, πρὸς δὲ καὶ δοκοῦσαν αἰτίαν γεγονέναι Καύνῳ τῆς ἀπαλλαγῆς, ἀναψαμένην ἀπό τινος δρυὸς τὴν μίτραν ἐνθεῖναι τὸν τράχηλον. (4) λέγεται δὲ καὶ παρ' ἡμῖν οὕτως:

ἡ δ' ὅτε δή <ῥ'>[11] ὀλοοῖο κασιγνήτου νόον ἔγνω,
κλαῖεν ἀ<η>δονίδων[12] θαμινώτερον[13], αἵ τ' ἐνὶ
  βήσσῃς
Σιθονίῳ κούρῳ πέρι μυρίον αἰάζουσιν.
καί ῥα κατὰ στυφελοῖο σαρωνίδος αὐτίκα μίτρην
ἁψαμένη δειρὴν ἐνεθήκατο·[14] ταὶ δ' ἐπ' ἐκείνῃ
βεύδεα παρθενικαὶ Μιλησίδες ἐρρήξαντο.

φασὶ δέ τινες καὶ ἀπὸ τῶν δακρύων κρήνην ῥυῆναι ἀίδιον[15] τὴν καλουμένην Βυβλίδα.

5

11 <ῥ'> Legrand   12 κλαῖεν ἀΔ·ονίδων P, Δ· super ἀ, corr.
D. Heinsius: ἔκλαι' ἀδονίδων vel κλαῖεν ἄρ' ἀδονίδων Meineke
13 ἀδινώτερον Bast, Ruhnken: θαλερώτερον Barber
14 post ἐνεθήκατο aliqua excidisse coniecit Rohde
15 ἀίδιον Zangoiannes: ἰδίαι P

(3) Most, however, say that Byblis fell in love with Caunus and made overtures to him, begging him not to look on while she went through every sort of misery. But Caunus felt only loathing, and crossed over into the land at that time possessed by the Leleges,[26] where there is a stream called Echeneis; and there he founded a city named Caunus after him. But as for her, her passion did not abate; and in addition, when she considered that she was the reason for Caunus' departure, she fastened her girdle to an oak tree and put her neck in it. (4) Here is my own version of the story:

> And once she knew her cruel brother's mind,
> Her cries came thicker than the nightingales'
> In woods, who ever mourn the Thracian lad.[27]
> Her girdle to a rugged oak she tied,
> And laid her neck within. And over her   [5]
> Milesian maidens rent their lovely robes.

Some also say that from her tears flowed the everlasting stream called Byblis.[28]

[26] Classical sources refer to the Leleges as the aboriginal population of south-western Anatolia.

[27] For the story, see Euphorion **25**.13–15 and n. 36. The mourning of the nightingale figures already in *Od*. 19.518–523 and Aesch. *Ag*. 1142–1145.

[28] Parthenius and other authors make it clear that Byblis' spring is located in Miletus. But in other authors she leaves home and goes wandering (Ov. *Met*. 9.640–651; Conon, *FGrH* 26 F 2), and the spring is located at the end of her wanderings.

IB´ Περὶ Κάλκου

OΥ

(1) Λέγεται δὲ καὶ Κίρκης, πρὸς ἣν Ὀδυσσεὺς ἦλθε, Δαύνιόν τινα Κάλχον ἐρασθέντα τήν τε βασιλείαν ἐπιτρέπειν τὴν Δαυνίων αὐτῇ καὶ ἄλλα πολλὰ μει- λίγματα παρέχεσθαι. τὴν δὲ ὑποκαιομένην Ὀδυσ- σέως (τότε γὰρ ἐτύγχανε παρών) ἀποστυγεῖν τε αὐτὸν καὶ κωλύειν ἐπιβαίνειν τῆς νήσου[1]. (2) ἐπεὶ μέντοι οὐκ ἀνίει φοιτῶν καὶ διὰ στόμα ἔχων τὴν Κίρκην, μάλα ἀχθεσθεῖσα ὑπέρχεται αὐτὸν καὶ αὐτίκα εἰσκαλεσα- μένη τράπεζαν αὐτῷ παντοδαπῆς θοίνης πλήσασα παρατίθησιν· ἦν δ᾽ ἄρα φαρμάκων ἀνάπλεω τὰ ἐδέσματα, φαγών τε ὁ Κάλχος εὐθέως παραπλὴξ γίνεται[2] καὶ αὐτὸν ἤλασεν ἐς συφεούς. (3) ἐπεὶ μέντοι μετὰ χρόνον Δαύνιος στρατὸς ἐπῄει τῇ νήσῳ ζήτησιν ποιούμενος τοῦ Κάλχου, μεθίησιν αὐτόν, πρότερον ὁρκίοις καταδησαμένη μὴ ἀφίξεσθαί ποτε εἰς τὴν νῆσον, μήτε μνηστείας μήτε ἄλλου του χάριν.

---

[1] νήσου] εὐνῆς Naber   [2] γίνεται Hercher: ἴεται P

XII. CALCHUS

(1) The story is also related that a certain Daunian Calchus fell in love with Circe, whom Odysseus visited; he made over to her his Daunian kingdom[29] and lavished on her many other delights. But she was smouldering with love for Odysseus, who was staying with her at the time, and, feeling only loathing for Calchus, she forbade him even to set foot on her island. (2) However, when he did not stop visiting her and constantly having her name on his lips, she grew quite sick of him and went on the offensive. She invited him in, filled a table full of all sorts of sweetmeats, and placed them before him. But the food was drugged and when Calchus ate it he immediately became deranged, whereupon she drove him to the pigsties. (3) After a time, however, when an army of Daunians invaded the island to make a search for Calchus, she let him go, first, however, binding him with oaths that he would never again set foot on the island, whether to pay court to her or for any other reason.

[29] The Italian Calchus seems to be a duplicate of his Colophonian namesake, brought over when the Colophonians colonised Siris in Lucania. Daunia is in northern Apulia; it had close links with Lucania, but is at a curious remove from Circe's traditional post-Homeric location on the opposite side of Italy, at Capo Circeo north of Naples.

PARTHENIUS

ΙΓ΄ Περὶ Ἁρπαλύκης

Ἱστορεῖ Εὐφορίων Θρᾳκὶ καὶ Δεκτάδας[1]

(1) Κλύμενος δὲ ὁ Τελέως ἐν Ἄργει γήμας Ἐπικάστην γεννᾷ παῖδας, ἄρρενας μὲν Ἴδαν καὶ Θήραγρον, θυγατέρα δὲ Ἁρπαλύκην, πολύ τι τῶν ἡλίκων θηλειῶν κάλλει διαφέρουσαν. ταύτης εἰς ἔρωτα ἐλθὼν χρόνον μέν τινα ἐκαρτέρει καὶ περιῆν τοῦ παθήματος· ὡς δὲ πολὺ μᾶλλον αὐτὸν ὑπέρρει τὸ νόσημα, τότε διὰ τῆς τροφοῦ κατεργασάμενος τὴν κόρην λαθραίως αὐτῇ συνῆλθεν. (2) ἐπεὶ μέντοι γάμου καιρὸς ἦν καὶ παρῆν Ἀλάστωρ, εἷς τῶν Νηλειδῶν, ἀξόμενος αὐτήν, ᾧ καθωμολόγητο, παραχρῆμα μὲν ἐνεχείρισε, πάνυ λαμπροὺς γάμους δαίσας. (3) μεταγνοὺς δὲ οὐ πολὺ ὕστερον διὰ τὸ ἔκφρων εἶναι μεταθεῖ[2] τὸν Ἀλάστορα καὶ περὶ μέσην ὁδὸν αὐτῶν ἤδη ὄντων ἀφαιρεῖται τὴν κόρην, ἀγ‹αγ›όμενός[3] τε εἰς Ἄργος ἀναφανδὸν αὐτῇ ἐμίσγετο. ἡ δὲ δεινὰ καὶ ἔκνομα πρὸς τοῦ πατρὸς ἀξιοῦσα πεπονθέναι τὸν νεώτερον ἀδελφὸν κατακόπτει· καί τινος ἑορτῆς καὶ θυσίας παρ᾽ Ἀργείοις τελουμένης, ἐν ᾗ δημοσίᾳ πάντες εὐωχοῦνται, [καὶ][4]

[1] Δωσιάδας Dittrich, Rohde: Διευχίδας Gale: Ἀρητάδας Cobet: Ἀθανάδας Bast: Δεινίας Hecker   [2] καταθεῖ P, corr. Schneider   [3] ἀγ‹αγ›όμενος Hercher   [4] [καὶ] Heyne

XIII. HARPALYCE

The story is told by Euphorion in his Thrax,[30] *and by Dectadas*

(1) In Argos,[31] Clymenus the son of Teleus married Epicasta and had children: sons called Idas and Theragrus, and a daughter, Harpalyce,[32] who far outstripped her female age-mates in loveliness. He fell in love with her but held out against it for some time, trying to master his passion. But when the disease became too much for him, he got access to the girl by means of her nurse and secretly slept with her. (2) However, when it was time for her to marry and Alastor the Neleid, her fiancé, came to take her away, he initially handed her over, holding a splendid wedding. (3) But shortly afterwards he had a change of heart— he was, after all, out of his mind—and went chasing after Alastor. He found them still mid-journey, seized the girl, and took her back to Argos where he lived openly with her as his wife. She considered that she had suffered outrageous injustice from her father, so she cut up her younger brother and, on the occasion of a certain festival and sacrifice among the Argives which involves a public feast, she

---

[30] See Euphorion **24**, and notes ad loc.

[31] Parthenius' setting is unique. Clymenus is king of Arcadia in Hyginus, *Fab*. 206, 242; Euphorion's setting is unclear.

[32] Another Harpalyce, a Thracian hunting-maiden, is known from Virg. *Aen*. 1.316–317. Cross-contamination of the two stories is possible. Harpalyce's brothers' names in Parthenius have associations with hunting (Theragrus means "wild-animal-catcher"; Idas is a hunter in other myths), as has Harpalyce herself ("wolf-catcher").

τότε σκευάσασα τὰ κρέα τοῦ παιδὸς παρατίθησι †τῷ
πατρί. (4) καὶ ταῦτα δράσασα αὐτὴ μὲν εὐξαμένη
θεοῖς ἐξ ἀνθρώπων ἀπαλλαγῆναι, μεταβάλλει τὴν
ὄψιν εἰς χαλκίδα⁵ ὄρνιν· Κλύμενος δέ, ὡς ἔννοιαν
ἔλαβε τῶν συμφορῶν, διαχρῆται ἑαυτόν.

⁵ καλχίδα P, corr. Gale

ΙΔ΄ Περὶ Ἀνθέως

Ἱστορεῖ Ἀριστοτέλης καὶ οἱ τὰ Μιλησιακά

(1) Ἐκ δὲ Ἀσσησοῦ¹ παῖς Ἀνθεὺς ἐκ βασιλείου γέ-
νους ὡμήρευσε παρὰ Φοβίῳ, ἑνὶ τῶν Νειλειδῶν, τότε
κρατοῦντι Μιλησίων. τούτου Κλεόβοια, ἥν τινες Φι-
λαίχμην ἐκάλεσαν, τοῦ Φοβίου γυνή, ἐρασθεῖσα πολ-
λὰ ἐμηχανᾶτο εἰς τὸ προσαγαγέσθαι τὸν παῖδα. (2)
ὡς δὲ ἐκεῖνος ἀπεωθεῖτο, ποτὲ μὲν φάσκων ὀρρωδεῖν
μὴ κατάδηλος γένοιτο, ποτὲ δὲ Δία Ξένιον καὶ κοινὴν
τράπεζαν προϊσχόμενος², ἡ Κλεόβοια κακῶς φερομέ-
νη ἐν νῷ εἶχε τίσασθαι αὐτόν, ἀνηλεῆ τε καὶ ὑπέραυ-
χον ἀποκαλουμένη. (3) ἔνθα δὴ χρόνου προϊόντος, τοῦ
μὲν ἔρωτος ἀπηλλάχθαι προσεποιήθη· πέρδικα δὲ
τιθασὸν εἰς βαθὺ φρέαρ κατασοβήσασα ἐδεῖτο τοῦ

¹ Ἀσσησοῦ Lightfoot: Ἁλικαρνασσοῦ P
² προσισχόμενος P, corr. Legrand

prepared the child's flesh and put it before her father.[33] (4) This done, she prayed to the gods to be removed from humankind, and was transformed into the chalcis-bird.[34] When Clymenus took stock of his calamity, he committed suicide.

XIV. ANTHEUS

The story is told by Aristotle and the Milesian writers

(1) From Assesus a boy from the royal house, Antheus, was a hostage at the court of Phobius, a Neleid, the then ruler of Miletus. Phobius' wife Cleoboea—or, as some call her, Philaechme—fell in love with Antheus and did everything she could to win him over. (2) But he assiduously declined her, at one time pleading dread of discovery, at another appealing to Zeus as god of hospitality and the common table at which they ate; Cleoboea took this badly and got it into her head to punish him, calling him merciless and arrogant. (3) Time passed, and she pretended to be cured of her love. Then she shooed a tame partridge down a deep

---

[33] The Argive Heraea, at which there was a public feast of beef. So, too, Atreus used the occasion of a festival to serve up his own children to Thyestes (Aesch. *Ag.* 1592–1593). Hyginus and Σ T *Il.* 14.291*a* make clear, as Parthenius does not, that the slain child was also the product of the incestuous union, and the *Iliad* scholiast adds that the child's name was Presbon.

[34] For which *Il.* 14.291 gives the alternative name *kymindis*. According to Euphorion (**24**.13), the bird was Athena's handmaid; it may well have been a species of owl. In the light of the Tereus story (Euphorion **25**.13–15 and n. 36), it is surprising that no source reports a transformation for Clymenus.

Ἀνθέως ὅπως κατελθὼν ἀνέλοιτο αὐτόν. (4) τοῦ δὲ
ἑτοίμως ὑπακούσαντος διὰ τὸ μηδὲν ὑφορᾶσθαι, ἡ
Κλεόβοια ἐπισείει στιβαρὸν αὐτῷ πέτρον. καὶ ὁ μὲν
παραχρῆμα ἐτεθνήκει· ἡ δὲ ἄρα ἐννοηθεῖσα ὡς δεινὸν
ἔργον δεδράκοι, καὶ ἄλλως δὲ καιομένη σφοδρῷ ἔρωτι
τοῦ παιδός, ἀναρτᾷ ἑαυτήν. (5) Φοβίος μέντοι, διὰ
ταύτην τὴν αἰτίαν ὡς ἐναγής, παρεχώρησε Φρυγίῳ
τῆς ἀρχῆς. ἔφασαν δέ τινες οὐ πέρδικα, σκεῦος δὲ
χρυσοῦν εἰς τὸ φρέαρ βεβλῆσθαι· ὡς καὶ Ἀλέξανδρος
ὁ Αἰτωλὸς μέμνηται ἐν τοῖσδε ἐν Ἀπόλλωνι·

παῖς Ἱπποκλῆος Φοβίος Νηληϊάδαο
ἔσται ἰθαιγενέων γνήσιος ἐκ πατέρων.
τῷ δ' ἄλοχος μνηστὴ δόμον ἵξεται³, ἧς ἔτι
    νύμφης
ἠλάκατ' ἐν θαλάμοις καλὸν ἐλισσομένης⁴,
5   Ἀσσησοῦ βασιλῆος ἐλεύσεται ἔκγονος Ἀνθεύς,
ὅρκι' ὁμηρείης πίστ' ἐπιβωσόμενος⁵,
πρωθήβης, ἔαρος θαλερώτερος· οὐδὲ Μελίσσῳ
Πειρήνης⁶ τοιόνδ' ἀλφεσίβοιον ὕδωρ
θηλήσει⁷ †μέγαν⁸ υἱόν· ἀφ' οὗ μέγα χάρμα
    Κορίνθῳ
10 ἔσται καὶ βριαροῖς ἄλγεα Βακχιάδαις·

---

3 ἥξεται P, corr. Bast   4 ἐλισσομένη P, corr. Gale
5 ἐπιβωσάμενος P, corr. Meineke   6 πετρήνης P, corr.
Valesius   7 θελήσει P, corr. Teucher   8 μέγαν P:
τέρεν' Haupt: καλὸν Hartung

well and asked Antheus to go down and fetch it. (4) Having no suspicions at all, he readily consented; whereupon Cleoboea hurled down on top of him a huge boulder. He was killed straightaway. She, on the other hand, began to realise that she had committed a dreadful crime and besides was still on fire with love for the boy, and so she hanged herself. (5) For this reason Phobius considered himself under a curse and handed his kingdom over to Phrygius.[35] Some said that it was not a partridge but a gold vessel that was thrown into the well, as Alexander of Aetolia mentions in the following verses from his *Apollo*:

> Phobius, the Neleid Hippocles' child,
> Shall be the lawful son of true-born stock.
> His house shall get a wedded wife; while yet the
>   bride
> The spindle in her chambers finely twirls,
> Antheus shall come, son of Assesus' king,   [5]
> His plea based on a hostage's sure oaths,
> In bloom of youth, fresher than spring (no son
> So tender shall Peirene's fruitful flood
> Rear for Melissus, whence shall come great joy
> To Corinth, to cruel Bacchiads a woe[36]);   [10]

[35] Also known from Callimachus' story of Phrygius and Pieria (fr. 80–83 Pf.).

[36] Melissus' son, Actaeon, was loved by the Bacchiad Archias. Archias tried to abduct him, and Actaeon was killed in the ensuing struggle. Melissus got his revenge by killing himself at the Isthmia and calling down Poseidon's anger on those responsible. As a result Archias had to go into exile, and founded Syracuse. Alexander will probably have got the story from a writer of Sicilian history, or a Peripatetic work on the fall of tyrants.

Ἀνθεὺς Ἑρμείῃ ταχινῷ φίλος, ᾧ ἔπι[9] νύμφη
  μαινὰς ἄφαρ σχήσει τὸν λιθόλευστον ἔρων·
καί ἑ καθαψαμένη γούνων ἀτέλεστα κομίσσαι[10]
  πείσει· ὁ δὲ Ζῆνα Ξείνιον αἰδόμενος
15 σπονδάς τ᾽ ἐν Φοβίου καὶ ἅλα ξυνεῶνα
      τραπέζης[11],
  κρήναις καὶ ποταμοῖς νίψετ᾽ ἀεικὲς ἔπος.
ἡ δ᾽ ὅταν ἀρνῆται μέλεον γάμον ἀγλαὸς Ἀνθεύς,
  δὴ τότε οἱ τεύξει μητιόεντα δόλον,
μύθοις ἐξαπαφοῦσα· λόγος δέ οἱ ἔσσεται οὗτος·
20   "Γαυλός μοι χρύσεος φρείατος ἐκ μυχάτου
†νῦν ὄγ᾽[12] ἀνελκόμενος διὰ μὲν κακὸν[13] ἤρικεν
      οὖσον,
  αὐτὸς δ᾽ ἐς Νύμφας ᾤχετ᾽ ἐφυδριάδας.
πρός σε θεῶν, ἀλλ᾽ εἴ μοι, ἐπεὶ καὶ πᾶσιν ἀκούω
  ῥηϊδίην οἶμον τοῦδ᾽ ἔμεναι στομίου,
25 ἰθύσας ἀνέλοιο, τότ᾽ ἂν μέγα[14] φίλτατος εἴης."
  ὧδε μὲν ἡ Φοβίου Νηλιάδαο[15] δάμαρ
φθέγξεθ᾽[16]· ὁ δ᾽ οὐ φρασθεὶς ἀπὸ μὲν Λελεγήϊον
      εἷμα,
  μητρὸς ἑῆς ἔργον, θήσεται Ἑλλαμενῆς,
αὐτὸς δὲ σπεύδων κοῖλον καταβήσεται ἄγκος
30 φρείατος· ἡ δ᾽ ἐπί οἱ λιρὰ νοεῦσα γυνὴ
  ἀμφοτέραις χείρεσσι μυλακρίδα λᾶαν ἐνήσει.
καὶ τόθ᾽ ὁ μὲν ξείνων πολλὸν ἀποτμότατος

---

9 ἔνι P, corr. Heyne   10 ἀθέμιστα τελέσσαι Heyne
11 θαλάσσης P, corr. Brunck: θαλείης Bergk

Antheus, beloved of swift-foot Hermes, him
The maddened bride will love to stony death.
Clutching his knees, to commit wrong she'll try
To win him; but the god of guests he'll heed,
Phobius' truce, their common table-salt,   [15]
And cleanse the shameful word in springs and
    brooks.
So glorious Antheus spurns that wretched bed;
But cunning plots against him shall she work,
Seizing on stories, telling thus her tale:
"My golden pail, from down within the well,   [20]
Just now, being hauled back up, snapped through its
    rope,
And down it went to meet the water-nymphs.
In God's name, please go down—I hear the way
Down to this pit is open wide for all—
And fetch it up: go on; for love of me."   [25]
And in this way, the Neleid Phobius' wife
Will speak. And, nothing guessed, his Lelegan[37]
    cloak—
Ellamene's work, his mother—he'll put off,
And down into the cavern's hollow mouth
Will hurry. Then, with shameless thoughts, she'll hurl   [30]
A mill-stone down upon him, with both hands.
And then the most ill-starred of hosts will heap

[37] See n. 26.

---

12 νῦν ὅτ' Meineke: νεῖον Pierson: νῦν ὅδ' Hartung
13 δια μὲν καλὸν P, corr. Villoison   14 τοι . . . μέτα P, corr.
Pierson   15 Νειλιάδαο P, corr. Passow   16 φθέγξατ' P,
corr. Brunck

ἠρίον ὀγκώσει[17] τὸ μεμορμένον· ἡ δ' ὑπὸ δειρὴν
ἁψαμένη †σὺν τῷ[18] βήσεται εἰς Ἀίδην.

17 ὀκχήσει Bergk: οἰκήσει Brunck   18 σχοῖνον, σχοίνῳ
Hercher

ΙΕ΄ Περὶ Δάφνης

Ἡ ἱστορία παρὰ Διοδώρῳ τῷ Ἐλαΐτῃ ἐν ἐλεγείαις καὶ
Φυλάρχῳ ἐν ιε΄

(1) Περὶ δὲ τῆς Ἀμύκλα θυγατρὸς τάδε λέγεται
Δάφνης. αὕτη τὸ μὲν ἅπαν εἰς πόλιν οὐ κατήει, οὐδ'
ἀνεμίσγετο ταῖς λοιπαῖς παρθένοις· παρασκευασα-
μένη δὲ πολλοὺς κύνας[1] ἐθήρευεν καὶ ἐν τῇ Λακωνικῇ
καὶ ἔστιν ὅτε[2] ἐπιφοιτῶσα εἰς τὰ λοιπὰ τῆς Πελοπον-
νήσου ὄρη· δι' ἣν αἰτίαν μάλα καταθύμιος ἦν Ἀρτέ-
μιδι καὶ αὐτὴν εὔστοχα βάλλειν ἐποίει. (2) ταύτης
περὶ τὴν Ἠλιδίαν[3] ἀλωμένης Λεύκιππος[4], Οἰνομάου
παῖς, εἰς ἐπιθυμίαν ἦλθε καὶ τὸ μὲν ἄλλως πως αὐτῆς
πειρᾶσθαι ἀπέγνω· ἀμφιεσάμενος δὲ γυναικείαις ἀμ-
πεχόναις καὶ ὁμοιωθεὶς κόρῃ συνεθήρα αὐτῇ. ἔτυχε δέ
πως αὐτῇ κατὰ νοῦν γενόμενος, οὐ μεθίει τε αὐτὸν

1 πολλοὺς κύνας Zangoiannes: πυκνὰς P, υ in rasura: πολλὰς
κύνας F. Williams   2 ἔστιν ὅτε ante ἐπιφοιτῶσα transp.
Zangoiannes: ἐθήρευεν ἔστιν ὅτε P   3 Ἠλιδίαν Meineke:
ἡλικίαν P   4 Λεύκιππος Cornarius, Frobenius: εὔιππος P

The fated tomb of Antheus; she, meanwhile,
Will follow him to Hades in a noose.

XV. DAPHNE

The story is told by Diodorus of Elaea in his elegies and in the fifteenth book of Phylarchus[38]

(1) This is what is said about Amyclas' daughter Daphne. She would not go down to the city at all, nor would she mix with the other girls, but gathering together a pack of dogs, she would go hunting in the Laconian countryside, sometimes straying further into the other mountains of the Peloponnese.[39] For this reason she was very dear to Artemis, who taught her to shoot straight. (2) Now while she was wandering through the Elian landscape she attracted the love of Leucippus, son of Oenomaus. He despaired of making any other sort of attempt on her, but donned women's garments and went hunting with her in the guise of a girl.[40] Somehow or other he came to please her, and

---

[38] Parthenius' is the earliest extant account of the Daphne story, and the reference to Phylarchus (3rd c. BC) the earliest testimonium.   [39] The Laconian setting was already found in Phylarchus, but many later sources (including Pausanias 8.20.2–4, the only other reference to Leucippus) locate Daphne in Arcadia, and Ovid makes her Thessalian. Both Parthenius and Pausanias connect Leucippus with Elis (north-western Peloponnese), implying a conflation of two different Peloponnesian locations.

[40] Cross-dressing is associated with a character called Leucippus or Leucippe in other stories (Hyg. *Fab.* 190; Ant. Lib. 17), and also recalls the myth of Callisto, in which Zeus assumed the likeness of Artemis in order to seduce her.

ἀμφιπεσοῦσά τε καὶ ἐξηρτημένη πᾶσαν ὥραν. (3)
Ἀπόλλων δὲ καὶ αὐτὸς τῆς παιδὸς πόθῳ καιόμενος
ὀργῇ τε καὶ φθόνῳ εἴχετο τοῦ Λευκίππου συνόντος καὶ
ἐπὶ νοῦν αὐτῇ βάλλει σὺν ταῖς λοιπαῖς παρθένοις ἐπὶ
κρήνην ἐλθούσαις λούεσθαι. ἔνθα δή, ὡς ἀφίκοντο
ἀπεδιδύσκοντο καὶ ἑώρων τὸν Λεύκιππον μὴ βουλό-
μενον, περιέρρηξαν αὐτόν· μαθοῦσαι δὲ τὴν ἀπάτην
καὶ ὡς ἐπεβούλευεν αὐταῖς, πᾶσαι μεθίεσαν εἰς αὐτὸν
τὰς αἰχμάς. (4) καὶ ὁ μὲν δὴ κατὰ θεῶν βούλησιν
ἀφανὴς γίνεται· Ἀπόλλωνα δὲ Δάφνη ἐπ᾽ αὐτὴν ἰόντα
προϊδομένη μάλα ἐρρωμένως ἔφευγεν. ὡς δὲ συνεδι-
ώκετο, παρὰ Διὸς αἰτεῖται ἐξ ἀνθρώπων ἀπαλλαγῆναι·
καὶ αὐτήν φασι γενέσθαι τὸ δένδρον τὸ ἐπικληθὲν ἀπ᾽
ἐκείνης δάφνην.

ιϛ΄ Περὶ Λαοδίκης

Ἱστορεῖ Ἡγήσιππος Παλληνιακῶν[1] α΄

(1) Ἐλέχθη δὲ καὶ περὶ Λαοδίκης ὅδε λόγος, ὡς ἄρα
παραγενομένων ἐπὶ Ἑλένης ἀπαίτησιν Διομήδους καὶ
Ἀκάμαντος, πολλὴν ἐπιθυμίαν ἔχειν μιγῆναι παν-
τάπασι νέῳ ὄντι Ἀκάμαντι. καὶ μέχρι μέν τινος ὑπ᾽
αἰδοῦς κατέχεσθαι· ὕστερον δὲ νικωμένην ὑπὸ τοῦ
πάθους ἀνακοινώσασθαι Περσέως γυναικί (Φιλοβίη
αὐτῇ ὄνομα) παρακαλεῖν τε αὐτὴν ὅσον οὐκ ἤδη

---

[1] Παλληνιακῶν Hecker: ΜΙΛΗΣΙΑΚΩΝ P

she would never let go of him, embracing and clinging to him at all times. (3) But Apollo himself was in love with the girl, and was possessed with rage and jealousy when he saw Leucippus associating with her; so he put it into her mind to go bathing in a stream along with the other maidens. When they got there they all stripped off, and, seeing Leucippus' reluctance, tore the clothes from his back. And, his treachery and duplicity laid bare, they all cast their javelins at him. (4) The gods willed it that he disappeared. Daphne, meanwhile, saw Apollo coming after her, and turned and fled with great alacrity. When she was almost on the point of being overtaken, she asked Zeus to be translated from the mortal world. And they say she became the tree named after her, the laurel.[41]

XVI. LAODICE

The story is told in the first book of Hegesippus' Palleniaca[42]

(1) This story is also told about Laodice. When Diomedes and Acamas came to Troy to demand the restoration of Helen,[43] she had a great wish to have intercourse with Acamas, who was then a very young man. Up to a point she controlled herself for shame, but later, when she was over-

---

[41] The perfunctory reference to Apollo at the end suggests how the Leucippus and Apollo stories could perfectly well coexist on their own.

[42] It is also referred to by Euphorion **98**.

[43] In *Il.* 3.205–224, this embassy is conducted by Odysseus and Menelaus. Laodice is mentioned in 3.122–124 as daughter-in-law of Antenor, who hosted the ambassadors.

διοιχομένη ἀρήγειν αὐτῇ. (2) κατοικτείρουσα δὲ τὴν
συμφορὰν τῆς κόρης δεῖται τοῦ Περσέως ὅπως συνερ-
γὸς αὐτῇ γένηται, ἐκέλευέ τε ξενίαν καὶ φιλότητα
τίθεσθαι πρὸς τὸν Ἀκάμαντα. Περσεὺς δὲ τὸ μὲν καὶ
τῇ γυναικὶ βουλόμενος ἁρμόδιος εἶναι, τὸ δὲ καὶ τὴν
Λαοδίκην οἰκτείρων, πάσῃ μηχανῇ [ἐπεὶ]² τὸν Ἀκά-
μαντα εἰς Δάρδανον ἀφικέσθαι πείθει· καθίστατο γὰρ
ὕπαρχος τοῦ χωρίου. (3) ἦλθε ‹δὲ›³ καὶ Λαοδίκη ὡς εἰς
ἑορτήν τινα σὺν ἄλλαις τῶν Τρωάδων ἔτι παρθένος
οὖσα. ἔνθα δὴ παντοδαπὴν θοίνην ἑτοιμασάμενος
συγκατακλίνει [καὶ]⁴ τὴν Λαοδίκην αὐτῷ, φάμενος
μίαν εἶναι τῶν τοῦ βασιλέως παλλακίδων. (4) καὶ
Λαοδίκη μὲν οὕτως ἐξέπλησε τὴν ἐπιθυμίαν· χρόνου
δὲ προϊόντος γίνεται τῷ Ἀκάμαντι υἱὸς Μούνιτος, ὃν
ὑπ᾽ Αἴθρᾳ τραφέντα μετὰ Τροίας ἅλωσιν διεκόμισεν
ἐπ᾽ οἴκου· καὶ αὐτὸν θηρεύοντα ἐν Ὀλύνθῳ τῆς Θρᾴ-
κης ὄφις ἀνεῖλεν.

² [ἐπεὶ] Martini   ³ ‹δὲ› Legrand   ⁴ [καὶ] Hercher

IZ′ Περὶ τῆς Περιάνδρου μητρός

ΟΥ

(1) Λέγεται δὲ καὶ Περίανδρον τὸν Κορίνθιον τὴν μὲν
ἀρχὴν ἐπιεικῆ τε καὶ πρᾶον εἶναι· ὕστερον δὲ φονι-
κώτερον γενέσθαι δι᾽ αἰτίαν τήνδε. ἡ μήτηρ αὐτοῦ
κομιδῇ νέου πολλῷ ‹πόθῳ›¹ κατείχετο· καὶ τέως

come by passion, she communicated it to the wife of Perseus (whose name was Philobia), and appealed to her to come to her aid, as to one already all but dead. (2) Pitying the girl's plight the woman asked for Perseus' help, and told him to prepare hospitality and a banquet for Acamas. Perseus wanted to be accommodating to his wife, and at the same time he pitied Laodice, so he used all means of persuasion to get Acamas to come to Dardanum,[44] where he was governor. (3) Laodice also came as if to a festival, accompanied by some other Trojan maidens. She was still a virgin. Preparing a lavish feast he made Laodice recline beside him, saying she was one of the royal concubines. (4) And that is how Laodice achieved her desire. When time went on, a son, Munitus, was born to Acamas; he was brought up by Aethra and after the fall of Troy Acamas took him home. But while he was hunting in Olynthus, in Thrace, a snake killed him.[45]

XVII. PERIANDER'S MOTHER

(1) It is also said that Periander of Corinth was, initially, reasonable and mild of disposition, but that he later became more blood-thirsty for the following reason. His mother was smitten with a violent passion for him when he

[44] Probably the city called Dardania in *Il.* 20.216–218, where it is said to be older than Troy, and located in the foothills of Ida.

[45] Euphorion **98** also locates the death in Olynthus; for Olynthus himself, see Conon, *FGrH* 26 F 4.

---

[1] ⟨πόθῳ⟩ Gale

⟨μὲν⟩[2] ἀνεπίμπλατο τῆς ἐπιθυμίας περιπλεκομένη τῷ
παιδί· (2) προϊόντος δὲ τοῦ χρόνου τὸ πάθος ἐπὶ μεῖζον
ηὔξετο καὶ κατέχειν τὴν νόσον οὐκ ἔτι οἵα τε ἦν, ἕως
ἀποτολμήσασα προσφέρει λόγους τῷ παιδί, ὡς αὐτοῦ
γυνή τις ἐρῴη τῶν πάνυ καλῶν, παρεκάλει τε αὐτὸν
μὴ περιορᾶν αὐτὴν περαιτέρω καταξαινομένην. (3) ὁ
δὲ τὸ μὲν πρῶτον οὐκ ἔφη φθερεῖν ἐζευγμένην γυναῖ-
κα ὑπό τε νόμων καὶ ἐθῶν· λιπαρῶς δὲ προσκειμένης
τῆς μητρὸς συγκατατίθεται. καὶ ἐπειδὴ νὺξ ἐπῆλθεν,
εἰς ἣν ἐτέτακτο τῷ παιδί, προεδήλωσεν αὐτῷ μήτε
λύχνα[3] φαίνειν ἐν τῷ θαλάμῳ, μήτε ἀνάγκην αὐτῇ
ἐπάγειν πρὸς τὸ διαλεχθῆναί τι· ἐπιπροσθέσθαι[4] γὰρ
αὐτὴν ⟨τοῦτο⟩[5] ὑπ' αἰδοῦς. (4) καθομολογησαμένου δὲ
τοῦ Περιάνδρου πάντα ποιήσειν κατὰ τὴν ὑφήγησιν
τῆς μητρός, ὡς ὅτι κράτιστα αὐτὴν ἀσκήσασα εἰσέρ-
χεται παρὰ τὸν παῖδα καὶ πρὶν ἢ ὑποφαίνειν[6] ἕω,
λαθραίως ἔξεισιν. τῇ δ' ὑστεραίᾳ ἀναπυνθανομένης
αὐτῆς εἰ κατὰ νοῦν αὐτῷ γένοιτο καὶ εἰ αὖτις λέγοι[7]
αὐτὴν παρ' αὐτὸν ἀφικέσθαι, ὁ Περίανδρος σπουδά-
ζειν τε ἔφη καὶ ἡσθῆναι οὐ μετρίως. (5) ὡς δὲ ⟨ἐκ⟩[8]
τούτου οὐκ ἀνίει φοιτῶσα πρὸς τὸν παῖδα καί τις ἔρως
ἐπήει τὸν Περίανδρον, ἤδη σπουδὴν ἐτίθετο γνωρίσαι
τὴν ἄνθρωπον ἥτις ἦν. καὶ ἕως μέν τινος ἐδεῖτο τῆς
μητρὸς ἐξικετεῦσαι ἐκείνην, ὅπως τε εἰς λόγους αὐτῷ
ἀφίκοιτο καί, ἐπειδὴ εἰς πολὺν πόθον ἐπαγ⟨άγ⟩οιτο[9]

---

[2] ⟨μὲν⟩ Meineke   [3] λύχνα Gale: νύκτα P
[4] ἐπιπροσθεῖσθαι P, corr. Lightfoot   [5] ⟨τοῦτο⟩ Rohde

was still a very young man, and for a while satisfied her desires by embracing the boy. (2) But as time went on the passion got worse and she was no longer able to contain her malady, so that she finally summoned up the courage to broach the subject with her son, telling him that a certain woman, a very beautiful one, was in love with him, and exhorting him not to look on while this woman was further tortured. (3) At first he refused to corrupt a woman married according to all due laws and ordinances. But when his mother continued to press him, he consented. When the agreed-on night arrived, she pre-instructed her son that he must not show any light in the chamber and must place the woman under no constraint to speak, saying that she made this additional stipulation from modesty. (4) When Periander agreed to do everything as his mother told him, she decked herself out as well as she could and went in to her son, leaving again secretly before the first glimmerings of dawn. Next day, she asked if everything had gone according to his taste, and whether she should tell the woman to come again, to which Periander replied that he was very keen, indeed that he had derived no little pleasure. (5) After this she never stopped coming to her son and Periander even began to fall slightly in love. He began to consider it a matter of some urgency to find out who the woman was. For a while he begged his mother to ask the woman to speak to him, and, since she had brought him into a state of great desire, at some point to reveal her-

---

⁶ περιφαίνειν P, corr. Meineke   ⁷ λέγει P, corr. Heyne
⁸ ⟨ἐκ⟩ Koen   ⁹ ἐπαγ⟨άγ⟩οιτο Meineke

αὐτόν, δήλη ποτὲ γένοιτο[10]. νυνὶ δὲ παντάπασι πρᾶγ-
μα ἄγνωμον πάσχειν διὰ τὸ μὴ ἐφίεσθαι αὐτῷ καθο-
ρᾶν τὴν ἐκ πολλοῦ χρόνου συνοῦσαν αὐτῷ. (6) ἐπεὶ δὲ
ἡ μήτηρ ἀπεῖργεν αἰτιωμένη τὴν αἰσχύνην τῆς γυναι-
κός, κελεύει τινὰ τῶν ἀμφ' αὐτὸν οἰκετῶν λύχνα κατα-
κρύψαι. τῆς δὲ κατὰ τὸ σύνηθες ἀφικομένης καὶ μελ-
λούσης κατακλίνεσθαι, ἀναδραμὼν ὁ Περίανδρος
ἀναιρεῖ τὸ φῶς καὶ κατιδὼν τὴν μητέρα ὥρμησεν ἐπὶ
τὸ διεργάσασθαι αὐτήν. (7) κατασχεθεὶς δὲ ὑπό τινος
δαιμονίου φαντάσματος ἀπετράπετο, κἀκ τούτου
παραπλὴξ ἦν νοῦ τε καὶ φρενῶν κατέσκηψέ τε εἰς
ὠμότητα καὶ πολλοὺς ἀπέσφαξε τῶν πολιτῶν. ἡ δὲ
μήτηρ πολλὰ κατολοφυραμένη τὸν ἑαυτῆς δαίμονα
ἀνεῖλεν ἑαυτήν.

[10] ποτὲ γένοιτο Martini: τότε γεγένηται P

ΙΗ´ Περὶ Νεαίρας

Ἱστορεῖ Θεόφραστος ἐν α´ τῶν Πρὸς τοὺς καιρούς

(1) Ὑψικρέων δὲ Μιλήσιος καὶ Προμέδων Νάξιος
μάλιστα φίλω ἤστην. ἀφικομένου οὖν ποτε Προ-
μέδοντος εἰς Μίλητον, θατέρου λέγεται τὴν γυναῖκα
Νέαιραν ἐρασθῆναι αὐτοῦ. καὶ παρόντος μὲν τοῦ
Ὑψικρέοντος μὴ τολμᾶν αὐτὴν διαλέγεσθαι τῷ ξένῳ·
μετὰ δὲ χρόνον, ὡς ὁ μὲν Ὑψικρέων ἐτύγχανεν ἀπο-
δημῶν, ὁ δὲ αὖτις ἀφίκετο, νύκτωρ αὐτοῦ κοιμωμένου

self: as it was, he was suffering an altogether senseless situation because he was not allowed to see the woman who had been his lover for so long. (6) But when his mother forbade it, urging the woman's modesty, he told one of his servants to conceal a light. So, when she came in as usual and was about to lie down, Periander ran up and picked up the lamp; and when he saw his mother he rushed upon her as if to kill her. (7) But he desisted, checked by a divine apparition; and ever after this he was stricken in mind and soul, plunging into savagery and murdering many of the citizens. Meanwhile his mother, greatly bewailing her own fate, put an end to her own life.[46]

XVIII. NEAERA

The story is told in the first book of Theophrastus' Responses to Political Crises[47]

(1) Hypsicreon of Miletus and Promedon of Naxos were the greatest of friends. When once Promedon came to Miletus it is said that the other man's wife fell in love with him. While Hypsicreon was around, she dared not speak to the guest; but after a time, when Hypsicreon happened to have gone abroad and the other was again staying with her,

[46] The incest-motif is also applied to Nero (Tac. *Ann.* 14.2).

[47] The fourth book of this work is cited for the Polycrite story (IX), the sequel to the events here.

ἐπεισέρχεται ἡ Νέαιρα. (2) καὶ πρῶτον[1] μὲν οἷα τε ἦν
πείθειν αὐτόν· ἐπειδὴ δὲ ἐκεῖνος οὐκ ἐνεδίδου[2], Δία τε
Ἑταιρήιον καὶ Ξένιον αἰδούμενος, προσέταξεν ἡ Νέ-
αιρα ταῖς θεραπαίναις ἀποκλεῖσαι τὸν θάλαμον· καὶ
οὕτως πολλὰ ἐπαγωγὰ ποιούσης, ἠναγκάσθη μιγῆναι
αὐτῇ. (3) τῇ μέντοι ὑστεραίᾳ δεινὸν ἡγησάμενος εἶναι
τὸ πραχθέν, ᾤχετο πλέων ἐπὶ τῆς Νάξου. ἔνθα ⟨δὴ⟩[3]
καὶ ἡ Νέαιρα δείσασα τὸν Ὑψικρέοντα διέπλευσεν εἰς
τὴν Νάξον. καὶ ἐπειδὴ αὐτὴν ἐξῄτει ὁ Ὑψικρέων,
ἱκέτις[4] προσκαθίζετο ἐπὶ τῆς ἑστίας τῆς ἐν τῷ πρυ-
τανείῳ. (4) οἱ δὲ Νάξιοι λιπαροῦντι τῷ Ὑψικρέοντι
ἐκδώσειν μὲν οὐκ ἔφασαν· ἐκέλευον μέντοι πείσαντα
αὐτὴν ἄγεσθαι. δόξας δὲ ὁ Ὑψικρέων ἀσεβεῖσθαι
πείθει Μιλησίους πολεμεῖν τοῖς Ναξίοις.

[1] πρώτα P, corr. Legrand   [2] ἐνεδίδου Heyne: ἐδίδου P
[3] ⟨δὴ⟩ Hercher   [4] ἱκέτης P, corr. Legrand

ΙΘ´ Περὶ Παγκρατοῦς

Ἱστορεῖ Ἀνδρίσκος ἐν Ναξιακῶν β´

(1) Σκέλλις δὲ καὶ Ἀγασσαμενὸς[1] ⟨οἱ⟩ Ἑκήτορος ἐκ
Θρᾴκης[2] ὁρμήσαντες ἀπὸ νήσου τῆς πρότερον μὲν
Στρογγύλης, ὕστερον δὲ Νάξου κληθείσης, ἐληΐζοντο
μὲν τήν τε Πελοπόννησον καὶ τὰς πέριξ νήσους.
προσσχόντες δὲ Θεσσαλίᾳ πολλάς τε ἄλλας γυναῖκας
κατέσυραν, ἐν δὲ καὶ τὴν Ἀλωέως γυναῖκα Ἰφιμέδην

Neaera sallied forth against him by night when he was in bed. (2) First she tried to persuade him; but when he would not give in, through reverence for Zeus in his capacity as patron of friendship and hospitality, she had the maidservants bar the door. And in this way, what with Neaera employing many forms of seduction, he was forced to have intercourse with her. (3) On the next day, however, thinking that he had done a dreadful thing, he went sailing back to Naxos. Neaera sailed to Naxos too, in fear of Hypsicreon; and when Hypsicreon asked for her back, she stationed herself as suppliant on the hearth in the prytaneum. (4) Though Hypsicreon was insistent, the Naxians refused to surrender her, yet urged that he might take her if he could persuade her. Hypsicreon thought this treatment outrageous, and persuaded the Milesians to declare war on the Naxians.

XIX. PANCRATO

Andriscus tells the story in the second book of his Naxiaca

(1) Scellis and Agassamenus, sons of Hecetor from Thrace, set out from the island formerly called Strongyle, later Naxos, and plundered the Peloponnese and surrounding islands. Putting in at Thessaly they carried off a great number of women, among them Iphimede the wife of Aloeus

---

1 Ἀγασσαμενὸς Knaack: κασσαμενος P   2 ⟨οἱ⟩ Ἑκή-
τορος ἐκ Θράκης Knaack: κήτορος οἱ Θράικης P

καὶ θυγατέρα αὐτῆς Παγκρατώ· ἧς ἀμφότεροι εἰς
ἔρωτα ἀφικόμενοι ἀλλήλους κατέκτειναν.

Κ΄ Περὶ Λειροῦς[1]

(1) Λέγεται δὲ καὶ Οἰνοπίωνος καὶ νύμφης Ἑλίκης
Λειρὼ κόρην γενέσθαι. ταύτης δὲ Ὠρίωνα τὸν Ὑριέως
ἐρασθέντα παρὰ τοῦ πατρὸς αἰτεῖσθαι[2] τὴν κόρην, καὶ
διὰ ταύτην τήν τε νῆσον ἐξημερῶσαι τότε θηρίων
ἀνάπλεων οὖσαν, λείαν τε πολλὴν περιελαύνοντα τῶν
προσχώρων ἔδνα διδόναι. (2) τοῦ μέντοι Οἰνοπίωνος
ἑκάστοτε ὑπερτιθεμένου τὸν γάμον διὰ τὸ ἀποστυγεῖν
αὐτῷ γαμβρὸν τοιοῦτον γενέσθαι, ὑπὸ μέθης ἔκφρονα
γενόμενον τὸν Ὠρίωνα κατᾶξαι τὸν θάλαμον, [καὶ][3]
ἔνθα ἡ παῖς ἐκοιμᾶτο, καὶ βιαζόμενον ἐκκαῆναι τοὺς
ὀφθαλμοὺς ὑπὸ τοῦ Οἰνοπίωνος.

---

[1] Λειροῦς Lightfoot: Αἱροῦς P   [2] παρὰ τοῦ πατρὸς αἰτεῖ-
σθαι Legrand: παρ' αὐτοῦ παραιτεῖσθαι P   [3] [καὶ] Heyne

ΚΑ΄ Περὶ Πεισιδίκης

(1) Λέγεται δὲ καὶ ὅτε Ἀχιλλεὺς πλέων τὰς προσεχεῖς
τῇ ἠπείρῳ νήσους ἐπόρθει, προσσχεῖν αὐτὸν Λέσβῳ.
ἔνθα δὴ καθ' ἑκάστην τῶν πόλεων αὐτὸν ἐπιόντα
κεραΐζειν. (2) ὡς δὲ οἱ Μήθυμναν οἰκοῦντες μάλα

---

[48] A much fuller version in Diod. Sic. 5.50–51, who adds
a Dionysiac dimension (recalling Homer's story of Lycurgus,

and her daughter Pancrato. Both fell in love with this girl, and killed each other.[48]

XX. LEIRO

(1) It is also said that Leiro was the daughter of Oenopion and the nymph Helice. Orion, son of Hyrieus, fell in love with this girl and asked her father's permission to marry her, and for her sake he cleaned out the island which at that time was infested with wild animals. He also rounded up a great deal of booty from the neighbouring peoples and gave it to her as a bridal gift. (2) However, Oenopion kept putting off the marriage because he was revolted at the thought that such a man should become his son-in-law. One day when Orion was blind drunk he broke in the doors of the chamber where the girl slept, and as he tried to rape her had his eyes burnt out by Oenopion.[49]

XXI. PISIDICE

(1) It is also said that when Achilles was sailing round and sacking the islands adjoining the mainland he put in at Lesbos.[50] There he went round each of the cities plundering them. (2) When the inhabitants of Methymna fiercely

Il. 6.130–140): the women were abducted while celebrating a Bacchic rite.   [49] Apparently a combination of two versions of the story: (i) Orion clears the island as a favour to his friend (Arat. *Phaen.* 636–640); (ii) Orion drunkenly rapes Oenopion's daughter (Hes. fr. 148a M.–W.).

[50] For Achilles' sack of Lesbos, see *Il.* 9.129, 664, and compare the story of the maiden of Pedasus in Σ AD, bT *Il.* 6.35*a*.

κρατερῶς ἀντεῖχον καὶ ἐν πολλῇ ἀμηχανίᾳ ἦν διὰ τὸ
μὴ δύνασθαι ἑλεῖν τὴν πόλιν, Πεισιδίκην τινὰ Μη-
θυμναίαν, τοῦ βασιλέως θυγατέρα, θεασαμένην ἀπὸ
τοῦ τείχους τὸν Ἀχιλλέα ἐρασθῆναι αὐτοῦ· καὶ οὕτως
τὴν τροφὸν διαπεμψαμένην ὑπισχνεῖσθαι ἐγχειρίσειν
αὐτῷ τὴν πόλιν, εἴγε μέλλοι αὐτὴν γυναῖκα ἕξειν. (3) ὁ
δὲ τὸ μὲν παραυτίκα καθωμολογήσατο· ἐπεὶ μέντοι
ἐγκρατὴς ⟨τῆς⟩[1] πόλεως ἐγένετο, νεμεσήσας ἐπὶ τῷ
δρασθέντι προὐτρέψατο τοὺς στρατιώτας καταλεῦσαι
τὴν κόρην. μέμνηται τοῦ πάθους τοῦδε καὶ ὁ τὴν
Λέσβου κτίσιν ποιήσας ἐν τοῖσδε·

ἔνθα δὲ Πηλείδης κατὰ μὲν κτάνε Λάμπετον[2]
     ἥρω,
ἐκ δ' Ἱκετάονα πέφνεν, ἰθαγενέος Λεπετύμνου
υἱέα Μηθύμνης τε, καὶ ἀλκηέστατον ἄλλων
αὐτοκασίγνητον Ἑλικάονος ἔνδοθι πάτρης
5   †τηλίκον Ὑψίπυλον[3]· θαλερὴ[4] δέ μιν ἄασε
     Κύπρις.
ἡ γὰρ ἐπ' Αἰακίδῃ κούρης φρένας ἐπτοίησεν
Πεισιδίκης[5], ὅτε τόν γε μετὰ προμάχοισιν
     Ἀχαιῶν
χάρμῃ ἀγαλλόμενον θηέσκετο[6], πολλὰ δ' ἐς
     ὑγρὴν
ἠέρα χεῖρας ἔτεινεν ἐελδομένη φιλότητος.

εἶτα μικρὸν ὑποβάς·

1 ⟨τῆς⟩ Schneider   2 λάμπεδον P, corr. Gale
3 Τήλεμον Ὑψιπύλου Hermann

resisted, and Achilles was quite baffled because he was unable to take the city, a certain Methymnaean maiden called Pisidice, the king's daughter, saw Achilles from the walls and fell in love with him. Using her nurse as an intermediary, she promised to hand over the city to him if he would make her his wife. (3) For the time being he agreed. But when he got control of the city, he was outraged at what she had done and urged his soldiers to stone the girl. The poet of the *Foundation of Lesbos*[51] also mentions this calamity in the following lines:

Then Peleus' son slew Lampetus the brave;
Slew Hiketaon (of true-born Lepetymnus[52]
Son, and of Methymna), and bravest of all
Within the country, Helicaon's brother,
Hypsipylus, so tall.[53] Fair Cypris, though, wrought   [5]
    harm.
By whom Pisidice was set astir,
Watching the son of Aeacus exult
Among the Achaean champions: oft she stretched
Her arms to the damp air, wanting his love.

(4) And then a little later on:

[51] Possibly Apollonius of Rhodes, whose Medea can be seen as a more complex version of Pisidice.   [52] Eponym of a mountain in the north of Lesbos.   [53] These lines, describing Achilles' military successes, read oddly before an account of his involvement with a traitress. In any case, the brothers should be penned up within the besieged city. Hence Kayser proposed to transpose 1–4 (to "Helicaon") to the end of the fragment.

---

[4] lacunam inter Ὑψιπύλον et θαλερὴ statuit Knaack
[5] κούρῃ ... Πεισιδίκῃ P, corr. Heyne   [6] θνέσκετο P, corr. Gale

10 δέκτο μὲν αὐτίκα λαὸν Ἀχαιϊκὸν ἔνδοθι πάτρης
  παρθενική, κληῖδας ὑποχλίσσασα πυλάων·
  ἔτλη δ᾽ οἷσιν ἰδέσθαι ἐν ὀφθαλμοῖσι τοκῆας
  χαλκῷ ἐληλαμένους, καὶ δούλια δεσμὰ γυναικῶν
  ἑλκομένων ἐπὶ νῆας, ὑποσχεσίης Ἀχιλῆος
15 ὄφρα νυὸς γλαυκῆς Θέτιδος πέλοι, ὄφρα οἱ εἶεν[7]
  πενθεροὶ Αἰακίδαι, Φθίῃ δ᾽ ἔνι[8] δώματα ναίοι
  ἀνδρὸς ἀριστῆος πινυτὴ δάμαρ—οὐδ᾽ ὅγ᾽ ἔμελλεν
  τὰ ῥέξειν—ὀλοῷ δ᾽ ἐπαγάσσατο πατρίδος οἴτῳ.
  ἔνθ᾽ ἥγ᾽ αἰνότατον γάμον εἴσιδε Πηλείδαο
20 Ἀργείων ὑπὸ χερσὶ δυσάμμορος, οἵ μιν ἔπεφνον
  πανσυδίῃ θαμινῇσιν ἀράσσοντες λιθάδεσσιν.

[7] εἶεν Legrand: ἦεν P [8] ἐν P, corr. Meineke

ΚΒ′ Περὶ Νανίδος

Ἡ ἱστορία παρὰ Λικυμνίῳ τῷ Χίῳ μελοποιῷ καὶ
Ἑρμησιάνακτι

(1) Ἔφασαν δέ τινες καὶ τὴν Σαρδίων ἀκρόπολιν ὑπὸ
Κύρου τοῦ Περσῶν βασιλέως ἁλῶναι προδούσης τῆς
Κροίσου θυγατρὸς Νανίδος. ἐπειδὴ γὰρ ἐπολιόρκει
Σάρδεις Κῦρος καὶ οὐδὲν αὐτῷ εἰς ἅλωσιν τῆς πόλεως
προὔβαινεν, ἐν πολλῷ τε δέει ἦν μὴ ἀθροισθὲν τὸ
συμμαχικὸν αὖτις[1] τῷ Κροίσῳ διαλύσειεν[2] αὐτῷ τὴν

1 αὖτις Cobet: αὐτῆς P 2 διαλύσειν P, corr. Legrand

614

Directly the Achaean host within   [10]
Her country she received, its gates unlocked;
With her own eyes she could endure to see
Her parents riven with bronze, the women's chains,
Dragged at Achilles' bidding to the ships:
All to be grey-eyed Thetis' daughter, all   [15]
For Aeacid kinsmen, and a Phthian home
As a great hero's prudent wife——though he'd
Refuse——and at her country's bloody fall
She laughed. Poor wretch, the bitterest match with
    him
The Argives' hands accorded her: they slew   [20]
Her there and then, dashing her with great stones.[54]

XXII. NANIS

The story occurs in Licymnius of Chios, the lyric poet, and Hermesianax

(1) Some have also related that the acropolis of Sardis was captured by Cyrus the king of Persia because Nanis, Croesus' daughter,[55] betrayed it to him. For when Cyrus was besieging Sardis and nothing was going right for him in the matter of the city's capture, he was much afraid lest the allied force of Croesus should reassemble and overthrow

---

[54] See n. 19.

[55] Nanis is a late, romantic creation, otherwise unknown except for an entry in a Roman chronicle. Croesus has unnamed daughters in Bacchylides 3.34–35.

στρατιάν, (2) τότε τὴν παρθένον ταύτην ἔχει³ λόγος περὶ προδοσίας συνθεμένην τῷ Κύρῳ, εἰ κατὰ νόμους Περσῶν ἕξει γυναῖκα αὐτήν, κατὰ τὴν ἄκραν, μηδενὸς φυλάσσοντος δι᾽ ὀχυρότητα τοῦ χωρίου, εἰσδέχεσθαι τοὺς πολεμίους, συνεργῶν αὐτῇ καὶ ἄλλων τινῶν γενομένων. τὸν μέντοι Κῦρον μὴ ἐμπεδῶσαι αὐτῇ τὴν ὑπόσχεσιν.

³ ἔχει Legrand: εἶχε P

ΚΓ´ Περὶ Χιλωνίδος¹

(1) Κλεώνυμος ⟨δὲ⟩² ὁ Λακεδαιμόνιος βασιλείου γένους ὢν καὶ πολλὰ κατορθωσάμενος Λακεδαιμονίοις ἔγημε Χιλωνίδα προσήκουσαν αὐτῷ κατὰ γένος. ταύτῃ σφοδρῶς ἐπιτεταμένου τοῦ Κλεωνύμου καὶ τὸν ἔρωτα οὐκ ἠρέμα φέροντος, τοῦ μὲν κατηλόγει, πᾶσα δὲ ἐνέκειτο Ἀκροτάτῳ³, τῷ τοῦ βασιλέως υἱεῖ. (2) καὶ γὰρ ὁ μειρακίσκος αὐτῆς ἀναφανδὸν ὑπεκαίετο, ὥστε πάντας ἀνὰ στόμα ἔχειν τὴν ὁμιλίαν αὐτῶν⁴. δι᾽ ἣν αἰτίαν δυσανασχετήσας ὁ Κλεώνυμος, καὶ ἄλλως δὲ οὐκ ἀρεσκόμενος τοῖς Λακεδαιμονίοις ἔθεσιν⁵, ἐπεραιώθη πρὸς Πύρρον εἰς Ἤπειρον καὶ αὐτὸν ἀναπείθει πειρᾶσθαι τῆς Πελοποννήσου, ὡς, εἴ γε ἐντόνως ἅψαιντο τοῦ πολέμου, ῥᾳδίως ἐκπολιορκήσοντες

1 ΧΕΙΛΩΝΙΔΟΣ, ΕΙ in rasura P   2 ⟨δὲ⟩ Meineke
3 ἀποκροτάτῳ P, corr. Cornarius   4 αὐτῷ P, corr. Gale
5 ἔθεσιν Gale: ἤθεσιν P

his own army. (2) It was then, so the story goes, that the girl treated with Cyrus about treachery; that, on condition he would marry her according to Persian custom, she and a few other helpers would let the enemy in through the citadel where, on account of the place's strength, there was no-one watching. But Cyrus did not keep his promise.

XXIII. CHILONIS

(1) Cleonymus of Sparta, a man of royal lineage who had done much for the Spartans, married Chilonis who was a kinswoman.[56] Cleonymus was violently enamoured of her and did not bear his love lightly; but she took no notice of him and lavished all her affections on Acrotatus, the king's son. (2) The young man was flagrantly infatuated with her, and their affair was on everyone's lips. Cleonymus was aggrieved by this, but besides that he was also displeased with Spartan ways for other reasons.[57] So he crossed over to Pyrrhus in Epirus and induced him to make an attempt on the Peloponnese,[58] pleading that they would easily take the cities there by storm if they prosecuted the war enthu-

---

[56] He was son of Cleomenes II (d. 309/8); she was daughter of the Eurypontid Leotychidas.

[57] He had been passed over for the kingship in favour of his nephew Areus.

[58] This can be dated to 273–272 BC.

τὰς ἐν αὐτῇ πόλεις. ἔφη δὲ καὶ αὐτῷ τι ἤδη προδι-
ειργάσθαι, ὥστε καὶ στάσιν ἐγγενέσθαι τισὶ τῶν
πόλεων[6] < >[7]

6 τῶν πόλεων Heyne: τῶν πολεμίων P
7 lacunam indicavit Oder

ΚΔ΄ Περὶ Ἱππαρίνου

(1) Ἱππαρῖνος δὲ Συρακοσίων τύραννος εἰς ἐπιθυμίαν
ἀφίκετο πάνυ καλοῦ παιδός (Ἀχαιὸς αὐτῷ ὄνομα).
τοῦτον ἐξαλλάγμασι πολλοῖς ὑπαγόμενος πείθει τὴν
οἰκίαν ἀπολιπόντα σὺν αὐτῷ μένειν. χρόνου δὲ προϊ-
όντος, ὡς πολεμίων τις ἔφοδος προσηγγέλη πρός τι
τῶν ὑπ᾽ ἐκείνου κατεχομένων χωρίων καὶ ἔδει κατὰ
τάχος βοηθεῖν, ἐξορμῶν ὁ Ἱππαρῖνος παρεκελεύσατο
τῷ παιδί, εἴ τις ἐντὸς τῆς αὐλῆς βιάζοιτο, κατακαίνειν
αὐτὸν τῇ σπάθῃ ἣν ἐτύγχανεν αὐτῷ κεχαρισμένος. (2)
καὶ ἐπειδὴ συμβαλὼν τοῖς πολεμίοις κατὰ κράτος
αὐτοὺς εἷλεν, ἐπὶ πολὺν οἶνον ἐτράπετο καὶ συνου-
σίαν. ἐκκαιόμενος δὲ ὑπὸ μέθης καὶ πόθου τοῦ παιδὸς
ἀφίππευσεν εἰς τὰς Συρακούσας καὶ παραγενόμενος
ἐπὶ τὴν οἰκίαν ἔνθα τῷ παιδὶ παρεκελεύσατο μένειν, ὃς
μὲν ἦν οὐκ ἐδήλου, Θετταλίζων[1] δὲ τῇ φωνῇ τὸν Ἱππα-
ρῖνον ἔφησεν ἀπεκτονηκέναι. ὁ δὲ παῖς διαγανακτή-

---

59 Plutarch's *Life of Pyrrhus* helps to fill out the material lost in
the lacuna. Acrotatus valiantly attacks the rear of the troops led by
Pyrrhus' son, so that the Spartan women envy Chilonis her lover

siastically enough. He added that he had already made some preparations by bringing about party strife in some of the cities. ⟨ ⟩ [59]

XXIV. HIPPARINUS

(1) Hipparinus the tyrant of Syracuse[60] fell in love with a very beautiful boy called Achaeus. He used many inducements and diversions to persuade him to leave home and stay with him. Time went by, and word came of an enemy attack on one of the territories occupied by him: immediate action was needed. Hipparinus, on his way out, instructed the boy that if anyone should offer him violence inside the palace, then he was to kill him with the short sword he had given him. (2) Then, coming to blows with the enemy, he defeated them soundly, and afterwards turned to wine and carousing. Inflamed with drink and desire for the boy, he spurred his horse away to Syracuse; when he reached the house where he had told the boy to stay, he concealed his identity but adopted a Thessalian accent,[61] and declared he had killed Hipparinus. The boy

and bid him make her pregnant with sons for Sparta. *SIG*[3] 430 apparently indicates that he did so.

[60] Hipparinus the younger, son of Dionysius I, tyrant of Syracuse in the mid-4th c. A tradition reaching back to the 4th c. makes the sons of Dionysius I all heavy drinkers (cf. esp. Theopompus, *FGrH* 115 F 185–188).

[61] Unclear; does a Thessalian accent suggest thuggishness (*Suda θ* 291)? Or should the sense be "with drunken, slurred speech" and the participle be emended accordingly?

---

[1] ψελλίζων Meineke: βατταρίζων Russell

σας σκότους ὄντος παίει καιρίαν τὸν Ἱππαρῖνον· ὁ δὲ τρεῖς ἡμέρας ἐπιβιοὺς καὶ τοῦ φόνου τὸν Ἀχαιὸν ἀπολύσας ἐτελεύτησεν.

ΚΕ´ Περὶ Φαύλλου

Ἱστορεῖ Φύλαρχος

(1) Φάϋλλος δὲ τύραννος ἠράσθη τῆς Ἀρίστωνος γυναικός, ὃς Οἰταίων προστάτης ἦν. οὗτος διαπεμπόμενος πρὸς αὐτὴν χρυσόν τε πολὺν καὶ ἄργυρον ἐπηγγέλλετο δώσειν, εἴ τε τινὸς ἄλλου δέοιτο, φράζειν ἐκέλευεν, ὡς οὐχ ἁμαρτησομένην. (2) τὴν δ᾽ ἄρα πολὺς εἶχε πόθος ὅρμου τοῦ τότε κειμένου ἐν τῷ τῆς Προνοίας Ἀθηνᾶς ἱερῷ, ὃν εἶχε λόγος Ἐριφύλης γεγονέναι, ἠξίου τε ταύτης τῆς δωρεᾶς τυχεῖν. Φάϋλλος δὲ τά τε ἄλλα κατασύρων ἐκ Δελφῶν ἀναθήματα ἀναιρεῖται καὶ τὸν ὅρμον. (3) ἐπεὶ δὲ διεκομίσθη εἰς οἶκον τὸν Ἀρίστωνος, χρόνον μέν τινα ἐφόρει αὐτὸν ἡ γυνὴ μάλα περίπυστος οὖσα[1]. μετὰ δὲ ταῦτα παραπλήσιον αὐτῇ πάθος συνέβη τῶν περὶ τὴν Ἐριφύλην γενομένων· ὁ γὰρ νεώτερος τῶν υἱῶν αὐτῆς μανεὶς τὴν οἰκίαν ὑφῆψε καὶ τήν τε μητέρα καὶ τὰ πολλὰ τῶν κτημάτων κατέφλεξεν.

[1] περίπυστον ὄντα Heyne

was outraged and, it being dark, delivered Hipparinus a fatal wound. He lived on for three days after that, and died after absolving Achaeus of the murder.

XXV. PHAYLLUS

Phylarchus tells the story

(1) Phayllus the tyrant fell in love with the wife of the Oetaean champion, Ariston.[62] He kept sending messages to her, promising to give her a great deal of gold and silver, and told her that if there was anything else she wanted, she was just to say, and should not fail to get it. (2) As it was, her greatest desire was for a necklace which at that time lay in the temple of Athena Pronoia; the story was that it had once belonged to Eriphyle, and this was the gift she saw fit to demand. When Phayllus plundered the other dedications from Delphi,[63] he also lifted the necklace. (3) It was conveyed to the house of Ariston; the woman wore it for a while, becoming quite notorious. But afterwards she suffered a very similar calamity to that of Eriphyle: her younger son went mad and set fire to the house, burning his mother and the greater part of their possessions.[64]

[62] "Tyrant" here means military leader. Plutarch, *Mor.* 553 D makes Ariston a commander of mercenaries.

[63] During the Third Sacred War (356–346), when the Phocian generals plundered the sacred treasures in order to finance mercenaries in their struggle against the Thebans.

[64] But in the story of Eriphyle, Alcmaeon had a real grievance against his mother (bribed with the necklace of Harmonia, she had forced her husband Amphiaraus to go to his death in the expedition against Thebes) and he only went mad after the matricide, pursued by his mother's Furies.

PARTHENIUS

Κ϶´ Περὶ Ἀπριάτης

Ἱστορεῖ Εὐφορίων Θρᾳκί

(1) Ἐν ⟨δὲ⟩[1] Λέσβῳ παιδὸς Ἀπριάτης Τράμβηλος ὁ Τελαμῶνος ἐρασθεὶς πολλὰ ἐποιεῖτο εἰς τὸ προσαγαγέσθαι τὴν κόρην. ὡς δὲ ἐκείνη οὐ πάνυ ἐνεδίδου, ἐνενοεῖτο δόλῳ καὶ ἀπάτῃ περιγενέσθαι αὐτῆς. (2) πορευομένην οὖν ποτε σὺν θεραπαινιδίοις ἐπί τι τῶν πατρῴων χωρίων, ὃ πλησίον τῆς θαλάσσης ἔκειτο, λοχήσας εἷλεν. ὡς δὲ ἐκείνη πολὺ μᾶλλον ἀπεμάχετο περὶ τῆς παρθενίας, ὀργισθεὶς Τράμβηλος ἔρριψεν αὐτὴν εἰς τὴν θάλασσαν· ἐτύγχανε δὲ ἀγχιβαθὴς οὖσα. καὶ ἡ μὲν ἄρα οὕτως ἀπολώλει. τινὲς μέντοι ἔφασαν διωκομένην ἑαυτὴν ῥῖψαι. (3) Τράμβηλον δὲ οὐ πολὺ μετέπειτα τίσις ἐλάμβανεν ἐκ θεῶν. ἐπειδὴ γὰρ Ἀχιλλεὺς ἐκ τῆς Λέσβου πολλὴν λείαν ἀποτεμόμενος ἤγαγεν, οὗτος, ἐπαγομένων αὐτὸν τῶν ἐγχωρίων βοηθόν, συνίσταται αὐτῷ. (4) ἔνθα δὴ πληγεὶς εἰς τὰ στέρνα παραχρῆμα πίπτει. ἀγάμενος δὲ τῆς ἀλκῆς αὐτὸν Ἀχιλλεὺς ἔτι ἔμπνουν ἀνέκρινεν ὅστις τε ἦν καὶ ὁπόθεν. ἐπεὶ δὲ ἔγνω παῖδα Τελαμῶνος ὄντα, πολλὰ κατοδυρόμενος ἐπὶ τῆς ἠιόνος μέγα χῶμα ἔχωσε· τοῦτο ἔτι νῦν ἡρῷον[2] Τραμβήλου καλεῖται.

---

[1] ⟨δὲ⟩ Meineke   [2] ἠρίον Meineke

XXVI. APRIATE

Euphorion tells the story in the Thrax[65]

(1) In Lesbos Trambelus, son of Telamon, fell in love with a girl called Apriate and did much to win her over. But when she showed no signs at all of giving in, he took it into his head to overcome her by deceit and trickery. (2) So, one day when she was strolling with her maidservants on one of her father's estates, which lay near the sea, he ambushed and captured her. But when she fought back all the harder to defend her virginity, Trambelus grew angry and threw her into the sea, which happened to be deep inshore. And that was how she died. Others, however, said she threw herself in because she was being chased. (3) Not long after, the gods sent retribution on Trambelus.[66] For when Achilles came with a great deal of booty which he had driven off from Lesbos, the natives called in Trambelus to help them, and he confronted him. (4) In the fight he was wounded in the chest and immediately fell. But Achilles admired his prowess and asked him, while still breathing, who he was and whose son. When he found he was the son of Telamon, he was full of grief and built a large tumulus on the coast. Even to this day it is called Trambelus' shrine.

[65] See Euphorion **26** col. i. 12–21, and nn. ad loc. Given that in Euphorion, too, the girl jumps, we do not know Parthenius' source for the version according to which she was pushed.

[66] A marginal note here adduces "Aristocritus in his *On Miletus*". Callimachus' pupil Istros and the Alexander historian Aristobulus (*FGrH* 334 F 57; 139 F 6) also know of the Milesian Trambelus who fell victim to Achilles.

PARTHENIUS

ΚΖ΄ Περὶ Ἀλκινόης

Ἱστορεῖ Μοιρὼ ἐν ταῖς Ἀραῖς

(1) Ἔχει δὲ λόγος καὶ Ἀλκινόην, τὴν Πολύβου μὲν τοῦ Κορινθίου θυγατέρα, γυναῖκα δὲ Ἀμφιλόχου τοῦ Δρύαντος, κατὰ μῆνιν Ἀθηνᾶς ἐπιμανῆναι ξένῳ Σαμίῳ (Ξάνθος αὐτῷ ὄνομα). ἐπὶ μισθῷ γὰρ αὐτὴν ἀγαγομένην χερνῆτιν γυναῖκα Νικάνδρην καὶ ἐργασαμένην ἐνιαυτόν, ὕστερον ἐκ τῶν οἰκείων ἐλάσαι μὴ ἐντελῆ τὸν μισθὸν ἀποδοῦσαν· τὴν δὲ ἀράσασθαι πολλὰ Ἀθηνᾷ τίσασθαι αὐτὴν ἀντ᾽ ἀδίκου στερήσεως. (2) ὅθεν εἰς τοσοῦτον [τε]¹ ἐλθεῖν, ὥστε ἀπολιπεῖν οἶκόν τε καὶ παῖδας ἤδη γεγονότας συνεκπλεῦσαί τε τῷ Ξάνθῳ. γενομένην δὲ κατὰ μέσον πόρον ἔννοιαν λαβεῖν τῶν εἰργασμένων, καὶ αὐτίκα πολλά τε δάκρυα προΐεσθαι καὶ ἀνακαλεῖν, ὁτὲ μὲν ἄνδρα κουρίδιον, ὁτὲ δὲ τοὺς παῖδας, τέλος δέ, πολλὰ τοῦ Ξάνθου παρηγοροῦντος καὶ φαμένου γυναῖκα ἕξειν, μὴ πειθομένην ῥῖψαι ἑαυτὴν εἰς θάλασσαν.

¹ [τε] Peerlkamp

XXVII. ALCINOE

Moero tells the story in her Curses[67]

(1) There is also a story that Alcinoe, daughter of Polybus of Corinth and wife of Amphilochus son of Dryas, went mad with love for a stranger from Samos called Xanthus, and all through the wrath of Athena. She had taken on a labouring woman called Nicandra for hire, and after she had worked for a year had driven her from her home without paying her wages in full. The woman prayed earnestly to Athena to requite her for this unjust deprivation. (2) And so Alcinoe reached such a pitch that she left home and the children already born to her, and sailed away with Xanthus. But once in mid-ocean she began to reflect on what she had done, and at that started to weep copiously and call now on her husband, now on her children. Finally, though Xanthus offered plenty of consolation and declared he would make her his wife, she was unconvinced and threw herself into the sea.[68]

[67] The *Arai* are the first known example of Hellenistic curse poetry. A story about the unjust withholding of wages would be at home there: compare Euphorion's *Chiliades*, composed because of the withholding of a deposit, and *Curses or the Cup-Thief*, on the occasion of a theft.

[68] Should we compare and contrast Alcyone, loyal wife of Ceyx, who throws herself into the sea when Ceyx dies in a shipwreck (Hyg. *Fab.* 65)?

ΚΗ´ Περὶ Κλείτης

Ἱστορεῖ Εὐφορίων Ἀπολλοδώρῳ, τὰ ἑξῆς Ἀπολλώνιος
Ἀργοναυτικῶν α´

(1) Διαφόρως δὲ ἱστορεῖται περὶ Κυζίκου τοῦ Αἰνέως[1].
οἱ μὲν γὰρ αὐτὸν ἔφασαν ἁρμοσάμενον Λάρισαν τὴν
Πιάσου, ᾗ ὁ πατὴρ ἐμίγη πρὸ γάμου, μαχόμενον
ἀποθανεῖν· τινὲς δὲ προσφάτως γήμαντα Κλείτην
συμβαλεῖν δι᾽ ἄγνοιαν τοῖς μετὰ Ἰάσονος ἐπὶ τῆς
Ἀργοῦς πλέουσι, καὶ οὕτως πεσόντα πᾶσι μεγάλως
ἀλγεινὸν πόθον ἐμβαλεῖν, ἐξόχως δὲ τῇ Κλείτῃ. (2)
ἰδοῦσα γὰρ αὐτὸν ἐρριμμένον περιέσχετο[2] καὶ πολλὰ
κατωδύρατο, νύκτωρ δὲ λαθοῦσα τὰς θεραπαινίδας
ἀπό τινος δένδρου ἀνήρτησεν ⟨ἑαυτήν⟩[3].

[1] Αἰνέως, Αἴνου Martini: αἰνέου P   [2] περιέσχετο Light-
foot: περιεσχέθη P   [3] ⟨ἑαυτήν⟩ Goens, an potius ⟨αὑτήν⟩?

ΚΘ´ Περὶ Δάφνιδος

Ἱστορεῖ Τίμαιος Σικελικοῖς

(1) Ἐν Σικελίᾳ δὲ Δάφνις Ἑρμοῦ παῖς ἐγένετο, σύ-
ριγγί τ᾽[1] ἐπιδέξιος[2] χρήσασθαι καὶ τὴν ἰδέαν ἐκπρε-
πής. οὗτος εἰς μὲν τὸν πολὺν ὅμιλον ἀνδρῶν οὐ κατῄει,
βουκολῶν δὲ κατὰ τὴν Αἴτνην χείματός τε καὶ θέρους
ἠγραύλει. τούτου λέγουσιν Ἐχεναΐδα νύμφην ἐρα-

[1] τ᾽ Lightfoot: δή τε P   [2] ἐπιδέξιος Lightfoot: δεξιῶς P

XXVIII. CLEITE

Euphorion tells the story in the Apollodorus, *and there-after Apollonius of Rhodes in the first book of the* Argonautica[69]

(1) The story of Cyzicus, son of Aeneus, is variously related. Some said he was engaged to Piasus' daughter Larisa, whom her father seduced before her marriage, and died fighting. Others say that he had recently married Cleite and clashed, in ignorance of their identity, with the followers of Jason who were sailing on the Argo. The manner of his death caused great and bitter grief to all, but especially to Cleite. (2) For when she saw him lying prostrate, she embraced him and lamented long; then at night she eluded her chamber-maids and hanged herself from a tree.

XXIX. DAPHNIS

Timaeus tells the story in the Sicelica

(1) In Sicily was born a son of Hermes, Daphnis, who was skilled at playing the pan-pipes and exceedingly good-looking. He shunned the great crowd of humanity, but spent his life in the open air both summer and winter as a shepherd on Etna. They say that a nymph, Echenais,[70] fell

[69] Euphorion **6**, **9**; Ap. Rhod. 1.1012–1077. Parthenius' first version seems to correspond to Euphorion (who implies in **9** that the couple were engaged, in **6** that they were married). His second is like that of Apollonius, but with extra details concerning the lamentation and suicide.

[70] cf. Nais in [Theoc.] *Id.* 8.93, Ov. *AA* 1.732.

σθεῖσαν παρακελεύσασθαι αὐτῷ γυναικὶ μὴ πλησι-
άζειν· μὴ πειθομένου γὰρ αὐτοῦ, συμβήσεσθαι[3] τὰς
ὄψεις ἀποβαλεῖν. (2) ὁ δὲ χρόνον μέν τινα καρτερῶς
ἀντεῖχεν, καίπερ οὐκ ὀλίγων ἐπιμαινομένων αὐτῷ·
ὕστερον δὲ μία τῶν κατὰ τὴν Σικελίαν βασιλίδων
οἴνῳ πολλῷ δηλησαμένη αὐτὸν ἤγαγεν εἰς ἐπιθυμίαν
αὐτῇ[4] μιγῆναι. καὶ οὗτος ἐκ τοῦδε ὁμοίως Θαμύρᾳ τῷ
Θρᾳκὶ δι᾽ ἀφροσύνην ἐπεπήρωτο.

[3] συμβήσεται P, corr. Legrand   [4] αὐτῇ Heyne: αὐτῷ P

Λ΄ Περὶ Κελτίνης

ΟΥ

(1) Λέγεται δὲ καὶ Ἡρακλέα, ὅτε ἀπ᾽ Ἐρυθείας τὰς
Γηρυόνου βοῦς ἤγαγεν, ἀλώμενον διὰ τῆς Κελτῶν
χώρας ἀφικέσθαι παρὰ Βρεταννόν. τῷ δὲ ἄρα ὑπάρ-
χειν θυγατέρα, Κελτίνην ὄνομα. ταύτην δὲ ἐρασθεῖ-
σαν τοῦ Ἡρακλέους κατακρύψαι τὰς βοῦς μὴ θέλειν
τε ἀποδοῦναι εἰ μὴ πρότερον αὐτῇ μιχθῆναι[1]. (2) τὸν
δὲ Ἡρακλέα τὸ μέν τι καὶ τὰς βοῦς ἐπειγόμενον
ἀνασώσασθαι, πολὺ μᾶλλον μέντοι τὸ κάλλος ἐκπλα-
γέντα τῆς κόρης συγγενέσθαι αὐτῇ. καὶ αὐτοῖς χρό-
νου περιήκοντος γενέσθαι παῖδα Κελτόν, ἀφ᾽ οὗ δὴ
Κελτοὶ προσηγορεύθησαν.

[1] μιγείη Hercher

628

in love with him, and told him to have no commerce with women; if he did, she said, he would lose his eyesight. (2) For a time he held out resolutely, even though not a few women were mad with love for him. Later, one of the princesses in Sicily deceived him by plying him with wine and made him want to have intercourse with her. And as a result of this, he too, like Thamyras the Thracian,[71] was blinded through his own folly.

XXX. CELTINE

(1) It is also said of Heracles that when he was bringing the cattle of Geryon from Erythea, his wanderings through the land of the Celts brought him to the court of Bretannus. This king had a daughter called Celtine. She fell in love with Heracles and hid his cattle, refusing to surrender them unless he first had intercourse with her. (2) Heracles was in a hurry to get his cattle back, but he was even more struck by the girl's beauty, and so he did have intercourse with her. When the time came round, a child was born to them, Celtus, from whom the Celts take their name.[72]

---

[71] *Il.* 2.595–600; Conon, *FGrH* 26 F 7; hero of a Sophoclean tragedy. Both he and Daphnis were born to nymphs and grew up as musicians. Thamyras challenged the Muses to a singing contest, lost, and was blinded.

[72] Classical authors variously make the Celts descendants of Polyphemus and Galatea or of Heracles and native royalty; others make them autochthonous. Parthenius' story is a variant on that of Heracles and Echidna (Hdt. 4.8–10). That Bretannus lives in the land of the Celts presumably reflects the idea that Celtic migration into Britain had not yet taken place, but it remains surprising that Celtus is descended from Bretannus and not *vice versa*.

ΛΑ΄ Περὶ Θυμοίτου[1]

Ἱστορεῖ Φύλαρχος

(1) Λέγεται δὲ καὶ Θυμοίτην ἁρμόσασθαι μὲν Τροιζῆνος τἀδελφοῦ θυγατέρα Εὐῶπιν· αἰσθανόμενον[2] δὲ συνοῦσαν αὐτὴν διὰ σφοδρὸν ἔρωτα τἀδελφῷ δηλῶσαι τῷ Τροιζῆνι. τὴν δὲ διά τε δέος[3] καὶ αἰσχύνην ἀναρτῆσαι αὐτήν, πολλὰ πρότερον λυπηρὰ καταρασαμένην τῷ αἰτίῳ τῆς συμφορᾶς. (2) ἔνθα δὴ τὸν Θυμοίτην μετ᾽ οὐ πολὺν χρόνον ἐπιτυχεῖν γυναικὶ μάλα καλῇ τὴν ὄψιν ὑπὸ τῶν κυμάτων ἐκβεβλημένῃ, καὶ αὐτῆς εἰς ἐπιθυμίαν ἐλθόντα συνεῖναι. ὡς δὲ ἤδη ἐνεδίδου τὸ σῶμα διὰ μῆκος χρόνου, χῶσαι αὐτῇ μέγαν τάφον καὶ οὐδ᾽ ὡς[4] ἀνιέμενον τοῦ πάθους ἐπικατασφάξαι αὐτόν.

[1] Θυμοίτου Maass: ΔΙΜΟΙΤΟΥ P (et in seqq.) [2] αἰσθανόμενος P, corr. Heyne [3] διὰ τὸ δέος P, corr. Rohde [4] οὐδ᾽ ὡς Jacobs: οὕτως μὴ P

ΛΒ΄ Περὶ Ἀνθίππης

ΟΥ

(1) Παρὰ δὲ Χάοσι μειρακίσκος τις τῶν πάνυ δοκίμων Ἀνθίππης ἠράσθη. ταύτην[1] ὑπελθὼν πάσῃ μηχανῇ πείθει αὐτῷ συμμιγῆναι. ἡ δὲ ἄρα καὶ αὐτὴ οὐκ ἐκτὸς ἦν τοῦ πρὸς τὸν παῖδα πόθου, καὶ ἐκ τοῦδε λαν-

XXXI. THYMOETES

Phylarchus relates the story

(1) It is also said that Thymoetes married Euopis, the daughter of his brother Troezen.[73] But when he realised that she was passionately involved with her brother, he revealed the business to Troezen. She hanged herself through fear and shame, first, however, calling down many horrid imprecations on the author of her misfortune. (2) Not long afterwards, Thymoetes encountered a very beautiful woman who had been cast ashore by the waves, fell in love, and had intercourse with her. But when the body at last began to decompose, owing to the length of time it had been exposed, he heaped up a great mound for the woman; and when his passion did not abate even thus, he slew himself over the tomb.

XXXII. ANTHIPPE

(1) Among the Chaonians there was a very well-born lad who fell in love with Anthippe. He approached her secretly and used every means to persuade her to sleep with him. She herself was not unaffected by desire for the lad, and af-

---

[73] Thymoetes, Maass' correction of Dimoetes, is presumably eponym of the Attic deme of Thymoetadae or Thymaetadae, near the Piraeus and appropriately near the coast. But why this story should be associated with him is unknown.

---

[1] ταύτηι P, puncto super ι addito, corr. Abresch

θάνοντες τοὺς αὑτῶν γονεῖς ἐξεπίμπλασαν τὴν ἐπιθυμίαν. (2) ἑορτῆς δέ ποτε τοῖς Χάοσι δημοτελοῦς ἀγομένης καὶ πάντων εὐωχουμένων, ἀποσκεδασθέντες εἴς τινα δρυμὸν κατειλήθησαν. ἔτυχεν δὲ ἄρα ὁ τοῦ βασιλέως υἱὸς Κίχυρος πάρδαλιν διώκων· ἧς συνελαθείσης εἰς ἐκεῖνον τὸν δρυμόν, ἀφίησιν ἐπ' αὐτὴν τὸν ἄκοντα. καὶ τῆς μὲν ἁμαρτάνει, τυγχάνει δὲ τῆς παιδός. (3) ὑπολαβὼν δὲ τὸ θηρίον καταβεβληκέναι ἐγγυτέρω τὸν ἵππον προσελαύνει· καὶ καταμαθὼν τὸ μειράκιον ἐπὶ τοῦ τραύματος τῆς παιδὸς ἔχον τὼ χεῖρε, ἐκτός τε φρενῶν ἐγένετο καὶ περιδινηθεὶς ἀπολισθάνει τοῦ ἵππου εἰς χωρίον ἀπόκρημνον καὶ πετρῶδες. ἔνθα δὴ ὁ μὲν ἐτεθνήκει· οἱ δὲ Χάονες, τιμῶντες τὸν βασιλέα, κατὰ τὸν αὐτὸν τόπον τείχη περιεβάλοντο καὶ τὴν πόλιν ἐκάλεσαν Κίχυρον. (4) φασὶ δέ τινες τὸν δρυμὸν ἐκεῖνον[2] εἶναι τῆς Ἐχίονος θυγατρὸς Ἠπείρου, ἣν μεταναστᾶσαν ἐκ Βοιωτίας βαδίζειν μεθ' Ἁρμονίας καὶ Κάδμου φερομένην τὰ Πενθέως λείψανα, ἀποθανοῦσαν δὲ περὶ τὸν δρυμὸν τόνδε ταφῆναι· διὸ καὶ τὴν γῆν Ἤπειρον ἀπὸ ταύτης ὀνομασθῆναι.

---

2 ἐκεῖνον ‹τάφον› Rohde, ‹ἱερὸν› Castiglioni

ter this they gave their parents the slip and satisfied their desires. (2) On one occasion, when a public festival was being celebrated among the Chaonians and everyone was feasting, they slipped away and squeezed into a thicket. Now Cichyrus the king's son happened to be hunting a leopard which had taken cover in that thicket, and he let fly his javelin at it. He missed the animal, but hit the girl. (3) Supposing he had hit the beast, he rode his horse closer; but finding the lad clasping his hands over the girl's wound, he went out of his mind, span round, and slipped from his horse into a sheer and rocky place. That was where he died; and the Chaonians, to honour their king, built walls round that very spot and named the city Cichyrus.[74] (4) Some say the thicket belonged to Epirus the daughter of Echion, who had migrated from Boeotia and arrived here along with Harmonia and Cadmus, bearing the remnants of Pentheus. They say she died and was buried somehere near this thicket, and that the country is for that reason called Epirus after her.[75]

[74] Also called Ephyra. Cichyrus' father Mermerus is killed by a lioness in the same place (*Naupactia* fr. 9 West).

[75] Very possibly the subject of Parthenius' *Anthippe* poem (**15–16**), and similar in outline to Ovid's story of Pyramus and Thisbe (*Met.* 4.55–166). Note especially how the thicket near Epirus' tomb in Parthenius matches the mulberry bush near Ninus' in Ovid.

ΛΓ΄ Περὶ Ἀσσάονος

Ἱστορεῖ Ξάνθος Λυδιακοῖς καὶ Νεάνθης[1] β΄ καὶ Σιμίας ὁ Ῥόδιος

(1) Διαφόρως δὲ [καὶ][2] τοῖς πολλοῖς ἱστορεῖται καὶ τὰ Νιόβης. οὐ γὰρ Ταντάλου φασὶν αὐτὴν γενέσθαι ἀλλ᾽ Ἀσσάονος μὲν θυγατέρα, Φιλόττου δὲ γυναῖκα, εἰς ἔριν δὲ ἀφικομένην Λητοῖ περὶ καλλιτεκνίας ὑποσχεῖν τίσιν τοιάνδε· (2) τὸν μὲν Φίλοττον ἐν κυνηγίᾳ διαφθαρῆναι, τὸν δὲ Ἀσσάονα τῆς θυγατρὸς πόθῳ σχόμενον αὐτὴν αὑτῷ γήμασθαι ⟨βούλεσθαι⟩[3]. μὴ ἐνδιδούσης δὲ τῆς Νιόβης τοὺς παῖδας αὐτῆς εἰς εὐωχίαν καλέσαντα καταπρῆσαι. (3) καὶ τὴν μὲν διὰ ταύτην τὴν συμφορὰν ἀπὸ πέτρας ὑψηλοτάτης αὐτὴν ῥῖψαι· ἔννοιαν δὲ λαβόντα τῶν σφετέρων ἁμαρτημάτων διαχρήσασθαι τὸν Ἀσσάονα ἑαυτόν.

[1] ΝΕΑΝΘΟΣ P, corr. Heyne   [2] [καὶ] Meineke
[3] γήμασθαι ⟨βούλεσθαι⟩ Zangoiannes

ΛΔ΄ Περὶ Κορύθου

Ἱστορεῖ Ἑλλάνικος Τρωϊκῶν ⟨β΄⟩[1] καὶ Κεφάλων ὁ Γεργίθιος

(1) Ἐκ δὲ Οἰνώνης καὶ Ἀλεξάνδρου παῖς ἐγένετο Κόρυθος. οὗτος ἐπίκουρος ἀφικόμενος εἰς Ἴλιον Ἑλέ-

[1] Τρωϊκῶν ⟨β΄⟩ Heyne: Τρωϊκοῖς Meursius

XXXIII. ASSAON

The story is told by Xanthus in his Lydiaca, *in the second book of Neanthes, and by Simmias of Rhodes*

(1) The story of Niobe is also related differently from the majority version. For they say she was not Tantalus' daughter, but daughter of Assaon and wife of Philottus, and that when she entered into contention with Leto about the fineness of her offspring, she was punished in the following way. (2) Philottus perished in a hunting-accident, and Assaon, smitten with desire for his daughter, wanted to marry her himself. When Niobe would not give in, he called her children to a banquet and burnt them all to death. (3) As a result of this disaster Niobe threw herself off a high rock;[76] as for Assaon, when he reflected on his crimes, he took his own life.

XXXIV. CORYTHUS

The story is told by Hellanicus in the second book of the Troica *and by Cephalon of Gergitha*[77]

(1) Oenone and Alexander had a son, Corythus, who came to Ilium as a Trojan ally, and there fell in love with Helen.

[76] A rationalisation of the more familiar form of the story, in which Niobe was turned into a rock? Since Xanthus was presumably concerned with the aetiology of the rock-face with a likeness to a woman in his native Lydia, it would seem likelier that his version had petrification rather than the leap from a rock.

[77] See on IV, the sequel to this story.

νης ἠράσθη, καὶ αὐτὸν ἐκείνη μάλα φιλοφρόνως ὑπ-
εδέχετο· ἦν δὲ τὴν ἰδέαν κράτιστος. φωράσας δὲ αὐτὸν
ὁ πατὴρ ἀνεῖλεν. (2) Νίκανδρος μέντοι τὸν Κόρυθον
οὐκ Οἰνώνης, ἀλλὰ Ἑλένης καὶ Ἀλεξάνδρου φησὶ
γενέσθαι, λέγων ἐν τούτοις·

ἠρία τ᾽ εἰν Ἀΐδαο κατοιχομένου Κορύθοιο,
ὅν τε καὶ² ἁρπακτοῖσιν ὑποδμηθεῖσ᾽ ὑμεναίοις
Τυνδαρὶς αἶν᾽ ἀχέουσα κακὸν³ γόνον ἤρατο
βούτεω.

² ὃν τέκεν Hecker   ³ κακοῦ Schneider: καλὸν Meineke

ΛΕ΄ Περὶ Εὐλιμένης

(1) Ἐν δὲ Κρήτῃ ἠράσθη Λύκαστος τῆς Κύδωνος
θυγατρὸς Εὐλιμένης, ἣν ὁ πατὴρ Ἀπτέρῳ καθωμολό-
γητο πρωτεύοντι τότε Κρητῶν. ταύτῃ κρύφα συνὼν
ἐλελήθει. (2) ὡς δὲ τῶν Κρητικῶν τινες πόλεων ἐπι-
συνέστησαν Κύδωνι καὶ πολὺ περιῆσαν, πέμπει τοὺς
πευσομένους εἰς θεοῦ, ὅ τι ἂν ποιῶν κρατήσειεν τῶν
πολεμίων. καὶ αὐτῷ θεσπίζεται τοῖς ἐγχωρίοις ἥρωσι
σφαγιάσαι παρθένον. (3) ἀκούσας δὲ τοῦ χρηστηρίου
Κύδων διεκλήρου τὰς παρθένους πάσας, καὶ κατὰ
δαίμονα ἡ θυγάτηρ λαγχάνει¹. Λύκαστος δὲ δείσας

¹ λαγχάνει Heyne: τυγχάνει P

She received him very kindly; he was extremely good looking. But finding him out, his father killed him. (2) Nicander, however, says that Corythus was son, not of Oenone, but of Helen and Alexander, in the following lines:[78]

> And the tomb of Corythus, dead and gone to Hades;
> Whom the Tyndarid, subdued to a forced marriage,
> Conceived in pain, the herdsman's wicked[79] brood.

XXXV. EULIMENE

(1) In Crete Lycastus fell in love with Eulimene the daughter of Cydon, whom her father had already betrothed to Apterus, at that time the foremost man in Crete.[80] He secretly became her lover. (2) When some of the Cretan cities joined in revolt against Cydon and got by far the upper hand, he sent ambassadors to the god to ask what he must do in order to defeat his enemies. The divine response was that he must sacrifice a maiden to the native heroes. (3) When he heard this oracle, Cydon subjected all the maidens to a ballot, which by chance fell on his own daughter. Fearing for her Lycastus revealed the seduction

[78] Sometimes attributed to the *On Poets*, on the strength of IV; but not if that was a prose work.

[79] If the reading is right, wicked because he was a traitor to his country (Lyc. *Al.* 57–60), or tainted by the scandalous nature of his parents' union?

[80] All the males are eponyms of towns in Crete: Lycastus s. of Cnossus, Cydonia on the n.w. coast, and Aptera some 15 km away from Cydonia. A very similar story is set in Ithome at the time of the Messenian wars (Paus. 4.9.3–10).

περὶ αὐτῆς μηνύει τὴν φθορὰν καὶ ὡς ἐκ πολλοῦ χρόνου συνείη αὐτῇ· ὁ δὲ πολὺς ὅμιλος πολὺ μᾶλλον ἐδικαίου αὐτὴν τεθνάναι. (4) ἐπειδὴ δὲ ἐσφαγιάσθη, ὁ Κύδων τὸν ἱερέα κελεύει αὐτῆς διατεμεῖν τὸ ἐπομφάλιον, καὶ οὕτως εὑρέθη ἔγκυος. Ἄπτερος δὲ δόξας ὑπὸ Λυκάστου δεινὰ πεπονθέναι λοχήσας αὐτὸν ἀνεῖλε· καὶ διὰ ταύτην τὴν αἰτίαν ἔφυγε πρὸς Ξάνθον εἰς Τέρμερα.

ΛϚ´ Περὶ Ἀργανθώνης

Ἱστορεῖ Ἀσκληπιάδης ὁ Μυρλεανὸς Βιθυνιακῶν α´[1]

(1) Λέγεται δὲ καὶ Ῥῆσον, πρὶν ἐς Τροίαν ἐπίκουρον ἐλθεῖν, ἐπὶ πολλὴν γῆν ἰέναι προσαγόμενόν τε καὶ δασμὸν ἐπιτιθέντα. ἔνθα δὴ καὶ εἰς Κίον ἀφικέσθαι κατὰ κλέος γυναικὸς καλῆς (Ἀργανθώνη αὐτῇ ὄνομα). (2) αὕτη τὴν μὲν κατ᾽ οἶκον δίαιταν καὶ μονὴν ἀπέστυγεν· ἀθροισαμένη δὲ κύνας πολλοὺς[2] ἐθήρευεν οὐ μάλα τινὰ προσιεμένη. ἐλθὼν οὖν ὁ Ῥῆσος εἰς τόνδε τὸν χῶρον βίᾳ μὲν αὐτὴν οὐκ ἦγεν· ἔφη δὲ θέλειν αὐτῇ συγκυνηγεῖν· καὶ αὐτὸς γὰρ ὁμοίως ἐκείνῃ τὴν πρὸς ἀνθρώπους ὁμιλίαν ἐχθαίρειν. ἡ δὲ ταῦτα λέξαντος ἐκείνου κατήνεσε, πειθομένη αὐτὸν ἀληθῆ

---

[1] fontis indiculum a fabula superiore huc traiecit Sakolowski
[2] πολλὰς Hirschig

and the fact that he had been her lover for a long time. But at this the assembled crowd were all the more for condemning her to death. (4) After her sacrifice, Cydon told the priest to cut through her belly: she was thus found to be pregnant. Considering that he had been treated outrageously by Lycastus, Apterus ambushed and killed him, and for this reason had to take refuge with Xanthus at Termera.[81]

XXXVI. ARGANTHONE

The story occurs in the first book of Asclepiades of Myrlea's Bithyniaca

(1) It is also said that Rhesus, before going to Troy as an ally, travelled through many lands winning over allies and imposing tribute. Among them he visited Cius, having heard reports of a lovely woman called Arganthone.[82] (2) She loathed inactivity and staying at home and preferred to assemble packs of hounds and go hunting, admitting none to her company. So when Rhesus came to this country he did not take her by force; he said he wanted to go hunting with her, for he detested human company as much as she. She approved his sentiments, believing him

[81] Termera is on the same peninsula as Halicarnassus, jutting out from Caria. Xanthus is unknown, as are Apterus' connections with him.

[82] Eponym of Mount Arganthoneion, at the foot of which is Cius, on the Propontis. There was also a stream Arganthone (*SH* 725), raising the possibility of a variant story in which she was metamorphosed into water.

λέγειν. (3) χρόνου δ᾽ <οὐ>³ πολλοῦ διαγενομένου, εἰς
πολὺν ἔρωτα παραγίνεται τοῦ Ῥήσου. καὶ τὸ μὲν
πρῶτον ἡσυχάζει⁴ αἰδοῖ κατεχομένη⁵· ἐπειδὴ δὲ σφο-
δρότερον ἐγίνετο τὸ πάθος, ἀπετόλμησεν εἰς λόγους
ἐλθεῖν αὐτῷ καὶ οὕτως ἐθέλων <ἐθέλουσαν>⁶ αὐτὴν
ἐκεῖνος ἠγάγετο γυναῖκα. (4) ὕστερον δὲ πολέμου
γενομένου τοῖς Τρωσί, μετήεσαν αὐτὸν οἱ βασιλεῖς
ἐπίκουρον. ἡ δὲ Ἀργανθώνη, εἴτε καὶ δι᾽ ἔρωτα ὃς
πολὺς ὑπῆν αὐτῇ, εἴτε καὶ ἄλλως καταμαντευομένη τὸ
μέλλον, βαδίζειν αὐτὸν οὐκ εἴα. Ῥῆσος δὲ μαλακι-
ζόμενος τῇ ἐπιμονῇ⁷ οὐκ ἠνέσχετο, ἀλλὰ ἦλθεν εἰς
Τροίαν καὶ μαχόμενος ἐπὶ ποταμῷ τῷ νῦν ἀπ᾽ ἐκείνου
Ῥήσῳ καλουμένῳ, πληγεὶς ὑπὸ Διομήδους ἀποθνή-
σκει. (5) ἡ δέ, ὡς ᾔσθετο τεθνηκότος αὐτοῦ, αὖτις
ἀπεχώρησεν εἰς τὸν τόπον ἔνθα ἐμίγη πρῶτον αὐτῷ·
καὶ περὶ αὐτὸν ἀλωμένη θαμὰ ἐβόα τοὔνομα τοῦ
Ῥήσου. τέλος δὲ σῖτα καὶ ποτὰ μὴ⁸ προσιεμένη διὰ
λύπην ἐξ ἀνθρώπων ἀπηλλάγη.

ΠΑΡΘΕΝΙΟΥ ΝΙΚΑΕΩΣ
ΠΕΡΙ ΕΡΩΤΙΚΩΝ ΠΑΘΗΜΑΤΩΝ

3 δ᾽ <οὐ> Jacobs: δὲ P   4 ἡσυχάζειν P, corr. Heyne
5 κατεχόμενον P, corr. Heyne   6 <ἐθέλουσαν> Passow
7 τῇ ἐπιμονῇ Rohde: ἐπιμονῇ P   8 σῖτα καὶ ποτὰ μὴ
Rohde: εἶτα καὶ ποταμῷ P

to speak the truth. (3) Before very long she came to feel a deep love for Rhesus. At first she kept silent, restrained by modesty; but when her passion became more violent she summoned the courage to speak with him, and in this way the willing man took a willing bride. (4) Later, when the Trojan war began, the princes summoned him as an ally. Whether it was great love or some other instinct which led her to foresee the future, Arganthone refused to let him go. Rhesus could not bear becoming weak and effeminate by staying at home, so he went to Troy where he fought on the banks of the river now called Rhesus after him, and was killed by a blow from Diomedes.[83] (5) When she learned of his death, Arganthone returned to the spot of their first union, where she wandered around repeatedly crying out Rhesus' name.[84] And finally, abstaining from food or drink, she passed away from mankind through grief.

PARTHENIUS OF NICAEA
ON SUFFERINGS IN LOVE

[83] This differs from the versions of Rhesus' death in *Il*. 10, Pindar fr. 262 Snell, and ps.-Euripides' *Rhesus*. But there was also a version (known to Virg. *Aen*. 1.472–473) according to which Rhesus would be invincible if he drank the water of the Scamander. Perhaps this version told of a struggle between Rhesus and Diomedes on the banks of the river, in which Rhesus was killed before he could drink the water.

[84] Recalling the ritual cries for Hylas, likewise at the stream under Mount Arganthone (Ap. Rhod. 1.1178, 1354; Strab. 12.4.3; Ant. Lib. 26).

COMPARATIVE NUMERATION

I. Conversion of Other Editions to This Edition

Table to be read as follows: fr. 1 Diehl = fr. 6 Lightfoot; fr. 2 Meineke = fr. 17 Lightfoot, etc.

	Meineke	Martini, Gaselee	Diehl	Calderón Dorda
1	1	1	6	1
2	17	6	8	2 + 3
3	6	7	9	4 + 5
4	7	8	10	6
5	8	9	11	7
6	9	10	12	8
7	11	11	13	9
8	12	12	14	10
9	10	13	18	11
10	13	14	21	12
11	14	15	22	13
12	15	16	23	14
13	16	17	—	27
14	18	18	28	15
15	23	19	29	16
16	24	20	30	17
17	24	21	32	18
18	26	22	35	19

19	21	23	33	20
20	22	24	36	21
21	19	26	34	22
22	20	28	37	23
23	35	29	38	24a–b
24	28	29	39	26
25	34	30	40	28
26	29	31	41	29
27	29	32		29
28	56	35		30
29	30 + 31	33		31
30	32	36		32
31	41	34		35
32	33	37		33
33	36	38		36
34	37	39		34
35	38	40		37
36	39	41		38
37	42	42		39
38	43	43		40
39	44	44		41
40	45	45		42
41	46	46		43
42	47	47		44
43	48	48		45
44	52	49		46
45	40	50		47
46	49	51		48
47	58	52		49
48	50	58		50
49				51
50				52

51	53
52	Test. **2**
53	Test. **2**
54	58

II. CONVERSION OF THIS EDITION TO OTHER EDITIONS

Lightfoot	*SH*	Meineke	Martini, Gaselee	Diehl	Calderón Dorda
1	606	1	1	—	1
2	609(a) + 610	—	—	—	2
3	609(b) + 611	—	—	—	2
4	612(a) + 613	—	—	—	3
5	612(b) + 614	—	—	—	3
6	615	3	2	1	4
7	616 + 617	4	3	—	5
8	618	5	4	2	6
9	619	6	5	3	7
10	620	9	6	4	8
11	621	7	7	5	9
12	622	8	8	6	10
13	624	10	9	7	11
14	625	11	10	8	12
15	627	12	11	—	14
16	628	13	12	—	15
17	629	2	13	—	16
18	630	14	14	9	17
19	631	21	15	—	18
20	632	22	16	—	19
21	633	19	17	10	20
22	634	20	18	11	21

23	635	15	19	12	22
24	636 + 637	16–17	20	—	23
25	638	inter frr. 17–18	inter frr. 20–21	—	—
26	639	18	21	—	24
27	626	—	—	—	13
28	640	24	22	14	25
29	641	26 + 27	23 + 24	15	26 + 27
30	642	29	25	16	28
31	643	29	26	—	29
32	644	30	27	17	30
33	646	32	29	19	32
34	648	25	31	21	34
35	645	23	28	18	31
36	647	33	30	20	33
37	649	34	32	22	35
38	650	35	33	23	36
39	651	36	34	24	37
40	652	45	35	25	38
41	653	31	36	26	39
42	654	37	37	—	40
43	655	38	38	—	41
44	656	39	39	—	42
45	657	40	40	—	43
46	658	41	41	—	44
47	659	42	42	—	45
48	660	43	43	—	46
49	661	46	44	—	47
50	662	48	45	—	48
51	663	—	46	—	49
52	664	44	47	—	50
53	666	—	—	—	51

54	951	—	—	—	—
55	955 + 956	—	—	—	—
56	—	28	—	—	—
57	—	49	—	—	—
58	665	47	48	—	54

INDEX

INDEX

INDEX

Diognetus of Erythrae 577, 579, 581

Diomedes 601, 641

Dionysius I (tyrant of Sicily) 171n, 205, 619n

Dionysius II (tyrant of Sicily) 431

Dionysius (author of *Ktiseis*) 83, 131

of Heraclea (philosopher) 13, 15, 109

ὁ Φιλοξένου (grammarian) 505

Dionysus 51, 169, 345n, 347, 401n, 423, 525, 610n; *see also* Aegae (Peloponnese); Erigone; Hyes; Pheres; Phlius; Staphylus; Zagreus

Apatenor 235

"Gaping" 192, 239, 241, 363

Diores 557

Dioscuri 185, 259

Dirphys 331

Dodona 133n, 217, 235n, 285, 557n; *see also* Helloi

Doliche 215

Dolichus 405

dolphins 251, 319

Doric (dialect) 51n

Doryssa 351

Dracanon 215

Dryas 567, 569

Dryopes 217, 373n

Dymaean 389

Dyrrhachia 389

Echenais (nymph) 627

Echeneis (stream) 587

Echinades 254n, 255

Edessa *See* Aegae

editions xiii–xiv, 17, 101, 110–15

Eile(i)thyia 295, 317, 319

elegy 35n

and Alexander of Aetolia 102, 103

and Callimachus 23, 25, 35, 411, 481

and Euphorion 192, 213

and Gallus 213, 551

and Hermesianax 148, 157, 175

and Parthenius 469–70, 477, 479, 481, 483, 489, 499, 523

and Philitas 2, 3, 4, 9, 23, 25, 35, 149

canons 23, 25

development of Hellenistic x

from Halicarnassus xii, 470n

pre-Hellenistic xi

Elephantine 533

Eleusis 51, 75n, 165, 261n, 405n

Ellopia 353

encomium 193, 470, 477, 489

Ephesus 102, 125, 155, 171n, 507, 565; *see also* Zenodotus

epicedium x, 193, 241, 477

Epidamnus 389, 533

Epimenides 31n, 407

Epirus 243n, 385, 557, 617, 633

epyllion 102, 135n, 148, 193, 197, 198, 468, 470, 472

Eratosthenes 61, 111, 193, 205, 239, 401n, 433, 470, 509

Erechtheus 233n

Erginus 406n, 407